Between the Lion & the Wolf

Blake Goulette

Brightest Stars Publishing Co.

ISBN-13: 978-1-7346505-2-5

Cover image and book design by Blake Goulette

Printed and bound in USA

Published by Brightest Stars Publishing Co.
520 Gooseberry Dr
Holly Springs, North Carolina 27540
USA

Visit **www.blakegoulette.com**

For Pamela and Thomas—
Zhi uskathin tinirme shiro niras yamas

CONTENTS

PART I.

vii

PART I.

Chapter I

Into the West Again

INSECURITIES AND UNCERTAINTIES PLAYED THEMSELVES out over and over again in Kalas' dreams, accompanied by vivid scenes of all his recent losses thrust toward the forefront of his memory. It had been two—no, this was the third: *three* nights since the amethyst *eru* Loradan had hurled them across time and space, ejected them from the Vault of Stars, and dropped them within an empty, secluded room at Mbirin's Place. Yëlisha, friend and owner and proprietor of the establishment, had shared in their losses: the emerald *eru* Sharuyan (whom Kalas and the others knew as Falthwën) had been a mythic, grandfatherly figure to her, too, and news of his *unmaking* had been no easier for the innkeeper to bear.

He woke with a start, heart pounding and lungs heaving, and tried to remember the particulars of his most recent dream. He couldn't, and decided maybe that was a good thing. His unsubtle cry woke Zhalera. She sat upright in her bed, nestled against the wall across from his, and rubbed the sleep from her eyes. She stood and crossed the narrow distance between them, said nothing as she sat beside him, and placed a hand on his shoulder. She waited with him until he drifted back to sleep. As his heavy eyes closed, he imagined new ways to postpone their return trip home: the small, insignificant and unremarkable town of Lohwàlar in the desert far to the West.

How can I explain everything to Tsharak? to Vàyana? he wondered in silence. *Going home means acknowledging all these things really happened…*

"I'm not ready," he mumbled aloud as Zhalera eased him into his pillow and the lightless, unconscious solitude only sleep could afford.

He hoped no dreams would come: if they did, he hoped he wouldn't remember them.

When morning came, Kalas found himself alone in the room. Yëlisha had offered them the same space they'd used when they'd first traveled to Ïsriba, and he and the others had accepted. Their hostess had squeezed in a fifth bed for Abarandal, the most recent addition to their company. Nashmur chose the room next door. Nïmrïk chose one of the barstools downstairs.

"It's what everyone expects," he'd explained: "If people suddenly see me in the company of foreigners—from the West, no less!—it'll raise suspicion. I assume we don't want that? It'll be all right: I've managed for hundreds of Sevens—a few more days is nothing, really!"

Nashmur said he'd have to remain out of sight lest Ësfàyami's soldiers recognize him, chain him, and haul him back to Ïsriba, assuming they didn't simply cut him down where he stood. Yëlisha offered him a few unclaimed pieces of clothing for a simple disguise.

"Better than nothing, *shâuyahal,*" he said, "but it'll be best—safest—if I keep to my room whenever possible. I don't mean to sound ungrateful, but the people who'll be looking for me? Until recently, *I* was one of them! If nothing else, the queen's—*regent!*—The queen-*regent's* soldiers are highly skilled. I guess that means you and I will be seeing a lot of each other over the next…however long we're here for!"

As Kalas stepped out of the room's familiarity, its safety, he thought he sensed the fading vestiges of Falthwën's…spell? charm? protective magic around its doorway.

Become the light…I know *you to be!* the cleric—his friend and mentor—had said.

I don't know what that means! Kalas admitted to himself.

From the balcony, Kalas heard muffled voices coming from the great room below. Again, friends were voicing their concern for him:

"How many more days do you think we'll be here?" said Rül as he gnawed on a cold turkey leg left over from the night before. "I mean, everything here is great, but…well, it's just not *home*. We've been away from Lohwàlar for just about two months, right? When do you think he'll be ready to go?"

"I wonder if my parents are still searching for me," Pava nodded as she pushed at the food on her plate.

"I'm sure they are: I mean, I'm sure they haven't given up hope. You told us they'd hear about the…*Ilosar,* was it? That they'd assume you'd followed him?" Zhalera reminded her.

"No, you're right," the *úrukilmukrit* girl admitted. "I guess I'm feeling a little homesick, too. I've never been away from the *Áthradho*—the Gateway—for this long."

"I get it," Zhalera continued, "and he has to understand that we can't stay here forever. I miss Lohwàlar, too: even though everything—every*one*—I've ever loved from there is gone."

"Everyone?" said Kalas, leaning over the balcony railing.

"Almost everyone," she confessed.

Kalas joined his companions at the bar, where Yëlisha had already set a place for him. Abarandal smiled and sang something Kalas interpreted as "hello" or "good morning" as he took his seat. Unable to speak with words, Abarandal seemed most comfortable in Kalas' presence: it seemed he alone could understand the message wrapped within her songs.

He thought he wasn't hungry, but a few whiffs of seasoned boiled potatoes, cured ham folded into a sheath of eggs and topped with aged cheese, and fresh, crusty bread changed his mind.

"Hi, Kalas," the others said with sidelong glances, as though embarrassed by what they'd been discussing without his presence.

"We'll leave today," he said as he paused devouring his breakfast and downed a glass of water. "Zhalera's right—you're all right, really: we can't stay here forever, and it's time I stopped hiding."

"I'm looking forward to it," whispered Nashmur from beneath an oversized pointed hat with a wide brim. "Never been west of the Gateway, but the stories you've told have me interested!"

"Really?" scoffed Zhalera. "What could someone from Âivambar find interesting in a bowl of dust like Lohwàlar?"

"I have no idea! That's what makes it interesting!"

"I haven't been to the West since Kësharan was a kingdom," muttered Nïmrïk from a nearby table.

"I imagine a lot has changed since then," Kalas said. "That would have been when the River—the *Rumilswàr*—flowed strong and deep through town, when its sands were soils that held the earth in place rather than letting it blow across the sky. That's what Tsharak said, I think."

"So *that's* why it's called 'Lohwàlar'!" said Nashmur. "You've all described it as a desert: I wondered how it got its name. See? *Interesting!*"

"Pava, we'll need to get you home, too," Kalas continued. "You've been—"

"But...*do* we?" interrupted Rül, his meaning plain.

"Rül! Just because we're passing through my home doesn't mean I have to stay there," Pava clarified. "Not necessarily, anyway..."

"Oh!" said the farm boy, not even pretending to hide his grin.

"I mean, if you'll continue to abide my presence, *Ilosar*," she added.

Kalas winced at the appellation. Pava's people considered him something of a mythic hero, but he chafed at the idea.

"Of course we will. Even if you weren't a part of our strange little family now, I'm pretty sure Rül would march me straight back to Ïsriba if I said otherwise!"

He smiled—one of his few real smiles since Falthwën's death. Rül suggested the capital was too far to march to, that he'd tie him to the back of a horse instead. Everyone laughed—even Abarandal trilled a phrase that intimated laughter—and, for an instant, the world and its waiting problems were infinitely distant.

2.

"Master Kalas," said Yëlisha as she wrapped bundles of foodstuffs and other supplies for their trip. "I know you have things you must tend to, and I know your friends are anxious to get underway as well. That said, my great-great-grandmother's offer to Falthwën I now extend to you and your clan: anytime you're in Thosha, consider this place your home.

"You don't need me to tell you to be safe, but I'm going to all the same: *Be safe!* Take care of one another, as I know you will. Be discerning—yes, my grandmother got the same advice from Sharuyan, too. He and Loradan were good...*people:* they might have been stars, but they were good people. Not all *erume* are good, though. There's a fine line between good and evil sometimes, and it's my understanding that some *erume* straddle that line rather indiscriminately."

"I'll be careful—*we'll* be careful," Kalas promised as he helped tie down another bale atop the coach's imperial. "We *have* to be: there's a lot more going on than I ever thought possible. I still have no idea what I'm doing, but I have to start somewhere."

· · ·

When they finished loading all the supplies, after the horses had been brushed out and rubbed down again, they retreated into the tavern's great room. Yëlisha had closed the place down for the day, ensuring they'd have the necessary privacy to finalize their plans. None of them had discussed much in the open, opting instead to whisper their designs in awkward, coded fragments over the last few days just in case the queen-regent's spies had ears in Thosha; now, with the room to themselves, they could speak freely as they enjoyed their last meal in town beneath Yëlisha's roof.

"I know it would be a lot faster if we…Falthwën called it *kal-swàra*: I know we'd get to where we're going in almost no time if we—that is, if I could take us through the *kalthesh*, that realm of light the *erume—and* the *ekume*—inhabit. After all that's happened, I don't think…I'll confess I'm not ready to give that another try. Not yet. Maybe someday. I'm sorry…" Kalas explained.

"We understand," said Zhalera, responding on everyone's behalf.

"Anyway, once we're over the hills west of Thosha, we'll be traveling downhill most of the way, so the horses should have an easier time of things," Rül noted as he traced a finger over an ancient map Yëlisha found in one of her store rooms. "It's nearly winter: the days are shorter, so we'll have to stop more frequently. There might even be days when we have to stay put.

"Looks like it'd be a couple of weeks—in good weather—before we reach the Wastes. Maybe less. I hope the colder temperatures keep the poison out of the air…Guess we'll see. A day or two later, we'll reach the *Áthradholarme*…"

"I'm sure my parents will like you just fine!" Pava assured the farm boy with a placating stroke along his arm: she'd discerned something in his tone; Kalas and Zhalera shared a smirk as the red in Rül's cheeks deepened.

Be nice! they thought at one another.

"Uh, yeah, I…Right! I hope so!" he admitted as he wiped his brow.

"Oh, one thing: I don't think I mentioned it, but my father is the chief elder of the *úrukilmukritme* under the Áthradho. That's not a big deal though, right?"

Rül's cheeks paled in an instant.

"You're telling us we kidnapped your people's ruler's daughter, but it's 'not a big deal'?!" said Kalas, no longer smirking.

"No, she's right," interrupted Zhalera before Pava could respond: "What could we have done differently? Would we have treated her some other way?"

"Uh…*maybe?*" squeaked Rül.

"Our cart was broken—each of us was banged up to some degree, too! Knowing she was a…a *princess* or whatever wouldn't have made a difference."

"I'm not a princess," Pava insisted. Rül's face still possessed all the color of lambswool.

"All right," said Kalas as he ran his eyes across the map.

Looks like something my grandfather might have kept buried in his study!

"We'll have to rely on you, Pava, for introductions. On our way east, you said in passing that you saw some horses coming down through the Áthradho about a month or so before we arrived. Shosafin said Commander Valderïk's men 'interacted' with the *úrukilmukritme*. From what I gathered, it wasn't a pleasant encounter. Any of that sound familiar to you?"

Pava nodded. "A neighboring settlement thought they were *ilrâigme-edhume*—eaters of men. That's the story, anyway: the *úrukilmukritme* attacked from above, but they were no match for the riders. Most dwellers managed to retreat to the safety of their caves.

Most: not all.

"No, there's nothing to be sorry for," she insisted as Nashmur offered an apology on Valderïk's behalf. "It was just a bad situation: everyone could have handled things better…

"Thinking about it now, though, I'll bet our town wasn't the first *Áthradholar* Marugan visited. Wouldn't surprise me if he's the one who suggested *ilrâigme* were coming. It had been a long time since we'd had to deal with them. Yes, it *had* to be Marugan: we wouldn't have assumed they were eaters otherwise!"

"Well, we want your people—your father in particular!—to understand we're not looking for trouble!" Kalas said.

"They'll understand," Pava promised.

"After we cross the Gateway, we'll reach the steppes. I've never been west of the steppes!" said Nashmur, excited. "What are they like?"

"Windy!" said Zhalera, her mouth a thin line. "Dry and windy. The sooner we get past the steppes, the better."

"It's not quite a desert—not like the Wastes and not like Lohwàlar," added Rül. "There's some grassy places for the horses and not much else. Some wells. And Zhalera's right: there's too much wind!"

"After that, it's plains, forests, and *then* desert," concluded Kalas. "The weather should be warmer there; still, it'll probably be cold. Lohwàlar is about a day's journey from the edge of the forest.

"It's good to have a plan, but it's important to understand that some—most? all?—of this could change along the way. I don't know what we're looking at, time-wise. We don't know what Ilnëshras' servants are up to…And we don't know how the five remaining members of the *Kathin Sâash*—the Great Swath—fared against the *ekume*. In short, we don't know what we're facing…"

"Sifuran—the blue one, right? He said they'd been *betrayed*. Peradan thought it was me, but, like Heshradan pointed out, I'd never been there before," said Nïmrïk. "What if Sifuran was right, though? What if someone *did* betray them?"

Kalas considered Nïmrïk's suggestion. He thought about what Yëlisha had told him earlier, too.

"Someone must have," he agreed. "But there are unnumbered *erume,* and I have no idea if all of them have access to the Vault, or if it's just a few. For all we know, it could have been any *eru*. Which means we'll have to be careful—*discerning,* as Yëlisha reminded me not too long ago! I don't suppose we'll meet too many of them along the way, but it makes sense to keep our guard up."

Abandon your naïveté, Shosafin had warned him.

"Are you sure you won't spend just one more night?" Yëlisha asked all of them as they rolled up her map and finished the last of the meal she'd prepared for them. She spared Nashmur a glance—

Convince him! she implored the former commander.

—then regarded Kalas with her curiously gold-colored eyes.

"*Shâu,* if I agree to stay another night, I'll stay two, then three, and we'd be that much closer to winter. I'd probably decide we could start out in the spring, instead…No, as much as I'd love to stay, we need to leave now."

"I know, I know," she sighed as she wrapped her arms across her buxom chest. "Very well. I'll have someone bring your coach."

In a short while, standing outside the door to Mbirin's Place, Kalas, Zhalera, and Abarandal piled into the cab while Rül helped Pava into the plush box seat.

"Your boys became good friends with Dalafar and Gilfën here," said Yëlisha as she trotted up behind Runner and Dancer while holding Gilfën's reins, Kalas presumed. "Commander, Nïmrïk: the coach won't hold the five of you—not comfortably! These are two of my best horses. Consider them my contribution toward fulfillment of this prophecy!"

"Yëlisha! This is too much!" insisted Kalas even though he knew she'd hear none of it.

"You sound like Sharuyan—that is, Falthwën," she grinned. In more solemn tones, she continued, "This rising darkness must be stopped. If putting you up for the night, providing a couple of horses can help you in any way, then permit me this small gesture!

"Sharuyan—yes, *of course* I knew Falthwën was the emerald *eru!* He rescued my ancestors from a great evil not of their making. Nïmrïk, you, better than anyone alive, know what I'm talking about! I wish you would have shared your secret with me! Had Sharuyan and Loradan—*and* you, you old wolf!—not intervened, it's no exaggeration to say that I wouldn't be here today."

Kalas said nothing, but he smiled, and Yëlisha beamed at the sight.

"Thank you," he said at last.

"Nïmrïk, I think you'd take to Dalafar best," she said as she handed him the reins.

The former *elu* accepted and gave the blue roan a smile as he ran his hands along its withers. The horse shivered, flicked his tail, then pawed the ground with a snort. Placing his boot in the stirrup, he heaved himself into the saddle; once situated, he leaned forward, massaged the horse's neck beneath its mane and whispered something only Dalafar seemed to hear or understand.

"He knows I'm…not like the others," Nïmrïk said, bemused. "Yet he doesn't seem to mind…"

"Commander, I think you and Gilfën will get along just fine," said Yëlisha as she led the strawberry roan toward Nashmur.

"Please, it's just Nashmur now, Miss Yëlisha," he insisted.

As he reached for the reins, she held his hand for a moment—just a moment—and stayed him with an entrancing gaze. She reached her free hand around his neck, pulled him close, and, her voice just above a whisper, said, "It's just Yëlisha." Standing on tiptoe, she pressed her full lips against his, held him a moment longer, then let go.

Nashmur seemed unable to speak. With a wink, Yëlisha traced the line of his jaw, twirling the hairs of his beard around her fingers before patting him on the cheek. Gilfën whinnied: the noise almost sounded like laughter.

"I'll say it again: *be safe,* all of you! This had better not be the last time we cross paths! I'm tempted to shutter Mbirin's Place and come with you—I've thought about it over the last few days!—but I believe my gifts are best used here.

"Before I start repeating myself, I'll say good-bye. For now. Kalas, Abarandal—all of you: regarding this prophecy, I can't imagine how heavy your burden must be! Still, I *can* see what I think Sharuyan saw in you. You'll succeed! You *have* to! And someday, when the world's a quieter place, come back to me!"

After one last glance at Nashmur and with tears welling in her eyes, she brushed away one of her roguish pumpkin-colored curls, turned toward her gilded sign with its deep red letters, and walked inside, the graceful curves of her rounded hips bouncing with every step.

3.

The two suns had parted company in the clear blue autumn sky by the time Rül snapped his reins and began the long and arduous journey toward Lohwàlar via the *Áthradho dohàyi Ilvurkanzhime*— what Pava's people called the Gateway under the Wastes-that-Devour. Thosha's tidy grid of avenues and boulevards soon decayed into random-looking side streets and rutted dirt roads as they pulled farther from town and approached its more rural outskirts. When they'd arrived here nearly a month ago, Kalas remembered seeing teams of farm hands harvesting crops from the fields they passed; now, their work complete, these same fields lay empty. On a slight hill in the distance, lazy smoke curled from a stone chimney. Zhalera watched its haphazard ascent and shivered, pulled a woolen blanket from under her seat, and wrapped herself in its fuzzy warmth.

"Abarandal, do you want one?" she asked as she grabbed another blanket and handed it to her. She examined it for a moment and whispered a few phrases of her song before setting it down at her side.

"There's something about your voice," Zhalera observed, her expression shrewd. "I keep thinking I've heard it before, but that's impossible, right?"

The *eru* smiled and offered a few additional bars of melody that Zhalera still didn't understand.

"Maybe it's just because it sounds so pretty," she suggested. Abarandal blushed.

After ascending the mountain switchbacks into the forest that bordered Thosha's pastoral environs, the suns had almost set: Miryan's last rays mixed with Tàfayan's and lined the outstretched clouds with a mix of pinks and oranges. Most trees had surrendered their various shades of green for vibrant reds and yellows. A number of leaves had already fallen to the earth, but those that hadn't still suggested warmth as they passed by. The coach's suspension soaked up the uneven pavement over the old stone bridge that spanned the *Óronas Lohwà*—the Hidden River, situated far below.

This is where Shosafin parted company with us, Kalas noted.

"Something on your mind?" Zhalera asked him as she watched his thoughts reconfigure his expression.

"Shosafin said he was looking for Marugan when he went off on his own. We saw Marugan in Ïsriba, but we didn't see Shosafin. I just wonder what happened to him…"

"I'm sure he's all right," she insisted. "Ësfàyami didn't know where he was, and I think Marugan would have told her something if he'd seen him. Like you said: we'll find each other. Someday."

"Marugan *might* have told her, but it's clear he doesn't tell her everything. Still, you're probably right: I have to think he would have been gloating otherwise…"

Changing topics, he said, "Did you know there's some kind of cave down there? Under a waterfall? I thought about trying to see for myself, but the water moves fast, and I'm sure it's even deeper than it looks…"

Abarandal listened as they spoke, observed as they exchanged ideas with words. With a sigh, she muttered a few frustrated notes and stared through one of the cab's windows.

"I know it's not ideal. I'm sorry," Kalas apologized, unsure how to respond to the despondency in her voice. She acknowledged him with a half-smile.

"Hey, can you *write?* What if we got you something to write on—like a slate or something? Kalas, do we have anything like that with us?" Zhalera wondered.

Abarandal's face brightened and her smile broadened as she latched onto Zhalera's idea. She sang, her excited melodies up-tempo and staccato.

"It's almost time to stop for the night: I'm sure we've got something packed away!" said Kalas, letting the *erudas* energy infect him as well.

"I can't believe we didn't think to try it sooner!" Zhalera added as she shook her head and laughed at herself.

"Rül!" Kalas called out to his friend. "Whenever you find a place!"

Having discovered an open space within the forest, the farm boy steered his team as far from the highway as he could. Nashmur and Nïmrïk helped set up camp, and after establishing a fire, Kalas searched his belongings for a scrap of paper and something Abarandal could use to write.

"There's nothing other than this old book and this…whatever *this* thing is," he frowned as he held up both the ancient volume and the *not-paper* from his grandfather Wodram's study. "I have an idea, though! Be right back!"

Kalas disappeared beyond the fringe of the shadowed glade and returned a moment later, a large, dry stick in hand. He placed its tip inside the fire and waited.

"We'll wait a few minutes for that to blacken," he nodded, "then Abarandal can try writing with it on one of those big flagstones. Before that, however, let's get supper started! Yëlisha packed us all kinds of goodies: be a shame to let any go to waste!"

After a meal of smoke-cured meat, pickled vegetables, and some kind of sweet, pastry-like confection, Kalas removed the stick from the fire, gestured for Abarandal to follow him, and swept away the dirt from the flattest stone he could find. Curious, Zhalera and Pava followed them.

"All right, maybe try writing your name? Here, this is my name," Kalas suggested as he scratched his name onto the rock—

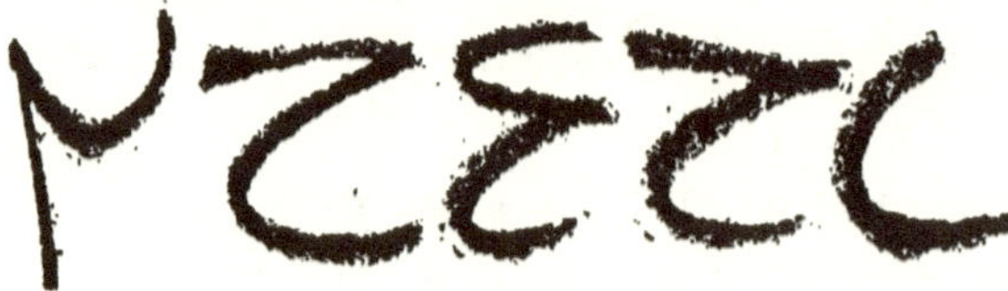

—then handed her the stick. Abarandal pointed it at the ground, scribbled some shapes and made a few strokes: she frowned when the others regarded her with confused looks.

"I know, I know," soothed Kalas when she attempted to explain.

Her harried song had an insistent quality Pava and Zhalera immediately grasped. "It almost looks like music," he said. "I think. I don't know. I can't read music…"

"That's what it looks like to me, too," Pava concurred.

Zhalera studied the marks Abarandal had made and closed her eyes for a moment. She took a deep breath, held it for a moment, and…*sang*. The *eru* dropped the stick, clapped, and grabbed Zhalera's arms in her excitement. She pointed to the notes she'd scrawled, pointed at her chest, and echoed the motif before she pointed to herself again.

"That's your name? That's what your name sounds like?" asked Zhalera. Abarandal nodded.

"Right!" said Kalas. "That's what she sang beneath the Vault! Zhalera! Why have I never heard you sing before?!"

"It's beautiful," agreed Pava.

Zhalera blushed. "Kalas, I don't know if you remember, but Mother used to sing to me all the time. She taught *me* how to sing, how to read music…"

"Is that why you wondered what it sounded like in the Empty Sea? Why you said you were jealous under the Vault?"

She nodded, offered him a wry frown. "When she passed away, I just felt like…I just didn't have the heart for it anymore! Kalas, I've missed the sound of her voice for so long! When you said you heard *music*…I didn't say anything then because I didn't want to think about it. I didn't want to be reminded. And then, in the dungeons…all that singing just reminded me of her too much. I told you before—and I meant it!—that I believe she and Father are together again at last. I would never take that away from either of them, but still…"

Kalas had no words. Abarandal took hold of Zhalera's shoulder, leaned forward until their foreheads touched, and hummed something neither Kalas nor Pava could hear. Light from the fire sparkled in the single tear that fell from Zhalera's cheek. The *eru* leaned back and offered the reluctant singer another brief phrase.

"What did she say?" Pava whispered when no one else spoke.

"I don't know exactly—not in words, at least. An *emotion*, I think."

Abarandal smiled with a gentle nod.

"She hopes you'll sing again," translated Kalas. "That's what she meant. Pava's right: you really do have a beautiful voice."

"I'll try to remember that," Zhalera said, wiping at her eyes.

4.

A couple of days later, when they exited the dwindling remnants of the forest onto the blasted heaths—the southern boundary of the Wastes—the season's chill had indeed minimized its nastiness, just as Rül had hoped. On occasion, an errant gust of wind would push a weak cloud of sulfurous, blighted air across their path; however, after a few tentative sniffs, neither Runner nor Dancer exhibited much of a reaction. Dalafar and Gilfën seemed similarly unconcerned as they proceeded toward the Áthradho.

Hours passed as the party traveled the King's Highway—again more of a wide, hard-packed squiggle than a genuine thoroughfare—without incident. At midday, when the suns touched, Abarandal looked up, as if she could see *through* the coach's roof as the *chimes* of the Song's music pealed in Kalas' thoughts. He thought the *eru shimmered* as the notes' vibrations diminished, and he remembered how Falthwën looked like he'd been wreathed in emerald after a similar incident on his second Seven.

Do all erume *have a* color? he wondered. *Why—how—does Abarandal seem to have* all *the colors and* none at all *at the same time?!*

• • •

After a few uneventful hours, a sound like thunder seemed to percolate up through the fabric of the earth and rock their coach with hot waves as the horses started. Rül stopped without warning, but Kalas was already out the door before the wheels ceased turning.

"What was that?!" shouted Nashmur as he did his best to soothe Gilfën.

"*Ildurgul Taruín,*" said Pava, looking to the north.

"The Death-bringing Mountain," Kalas agreed with a nod. He shielded his eyes from the suns with one hand and pointed across the yellow-tinted sky. "That's the volcano Falthwën told you about."

"And now İsriba's whole way of life will change?" he scoffed. Kalas laughed.

"That's not what he meant," corrected Pava. "We've felt tremors like that before, back at the Gateway. Some weaker, some stronger. Those quakes are bad enough—even *under* the earth!—but if Falthwën's right, it's the smoke and ash that does lasting damage. Kalas, do you see something? I see you pointing, but all I see is murk."

"I'm just wondering how far across the Wastes it is to the mountain: I can't see through this dust and ash, either."

"You don't actually want to *go there,* do you?" said Rül with hesitation in his voice.

"No! Of course not! It's just surprising to me that something so far away could make a wreck of things as far from here as the Áthradho."

"You're young, lad, and I hope you never have to learn the hard way: damage and distance aren't always in direct proportion to one another," grumbled Nimrïk. "This volcano though: consider it a lesson." Dalafar whinnied, pawed the ground and snorted as the *egu* clucked his tongue and worked the reins.

"I think Yëlisha's horse has the right idea," said Rül with a sidelong glance at the pewter-colored steed. "Let me check the coach real quick, make sure nothing's broken; then, let's get out of here!"

"We should reach the Gateway just after suns-down, I think," said Pava. "It's hard to gauge coming from this direction. And it feels like the wind might be shifting…"

They traversed the rest of the Ilvurkanzhime as the suns separated. Zhalera happened to glimpse a few carrion birds picking at what she knew to be the skeletal remains of a *Lohwàlarrin* named Dzhamïs and his horse. According to Shosafin, they'd perished on the initial journey to Ïsriba. The corpses had been in rough shape when they'd discovered them nearly a month ago; now, it looked like scavengers had strewn most of their bones across the area. Dzhamïs' skull was missing. So was one of his horse's forelegs. A bird, somehow wary of Zhalera's stare, paused long enough to caw its annoyance before it resumed pecking at the dead animal's ribcage. Another, satisfied for the moment, beat the air with its vast black wings and disappeared in the sudden swirl of red dust.

"If we turn right here, we'll end up outside of Deridzhas again," Rül hollered from his seat.

Zhalera shuddered and exclaimed "Do *not* turn right!" Abarandal cocked her head.

"We ran into some…unpleasantness up there not too long ago," Kalas explained. "It used to be a mining town, but from the things we saw, it hasn't been anything but a people-slaughterhouse for ages. *Ilrâigme-edhume,* Falthwën called them. Pava's people call them that, too. Zhalera and I had the bad fortune to stumble across one of their…farms, I guess. Yes, it was *worse* than it sounds, and *everything* about that place is awful. Just *awful.*"

The *eru* recoiled in disgust as Kalas described what they'd uncovered within one of Deridzhas' cellars. She sang—just a little— and the young man laughed. Not with joy, but with bitterness as unanswered questions bubbled up from the dark places where he'd tried to hide them, tried to ignore them for as long as he could.

"That's just it! I still have *no idea* how to put a stop to things like that! To be honest, I'm not sure Falthwën—*any* of the Great Swath, for that matter!—has any real idea what happens next. I know, I know: it's not like you're blaming me for what the world looks like today. And I know the other *erume* weren't, either, but everyone's right: there *is* a darkness coming—no, the darkness is *already here,* and like Yëlisha said, it must be stopped. There's so much I don't know: you have no idea how hopeful I am that Tsharak uncovered something while we've been away…"

Abarandal nodded, and in her pained expression Kalas knew she hadn't intended her brief melody as an indictment. She reached for his cheek with a trembling hand. He leaned forward and let her delicate fingers brush his face with a subtle electricity that hummed across his mere skin and penetrated the substance of his flesh. In her touch he understood she'd intended her music to encourage him, to bear him aloft as he continued his desperate search for his place within the phrases of the ancient prophecy.

"You'll figure it out," added Zhalera, placing a hand of her own atop his shaking knee. "Like you said: we *all* will! Maybe…maybe Abarandal's purpose here is to teach you how to use The Song? Maybe *she* can help you in ways not even Falthwën—nor the rest of the *Kathin Sâash*—could? Falthwën—even Loradan—said their memories weren't complete: 'inaccessible,' right? Maybe Abarandal's *are* 'accessible,' and maybe, the more she sings, the more she'll be able to tell you that the other *erume* couldn't!"

"That's…a lot of 'maybes,'" Kalas said with a slow smile.

5.

The last threads of Miryan's fading light painted hot pink lines in the finger-like clouds caressing the horizon when Rül brought the coach to a stop just inside the Áthradho. What began as a subtle decline soon became a steep drop into a narrow gorge that cut through the earth. Desert varnish glinted in the suns' dying rays, which also bounced around within a handful of crystalline constructs built across the upper reaches of the canyon. The *úruk-ilmukritme* called these constructs *iltithme-kal*—light-collectors; through them, they harvested the suns' energy during the day, though when night arrived (as it soon would), they mostly relied on fire, much like any other civilization. In front of them, a pair of massive blocks of dressed stone jutted from the sides of the road.

From his seat within the cabin, Kalas heard Pava whisper to Rül: "Is something wrong?"

"Uh…no…?"

"Then why'd you stop?! We're *here!*" Though she tried to exercise patience, Kalas caught the eagerness that colored her voice.

"I know!" Rül said, with perhaps more insistence than required. He calmed himself and continued, "I know. I guess I'm thinking about the last time we were here…"

"But *I'm* with you now! And like I've explained: it was a misunderstanding! We were lied to. When Kalas…when he *shined*, we realized we'd made a terrible mistake! If anything, I'll bet the cave-dwellers will treat you like kings and queens!"

"You think so?" said Rül, relaxing—*just* a little.

She rescued an arm from the heavy furs heating her lap and reached up and rubbed his back. "I know so!"

Like the iris of some inescapable celestial eye, the firmament turned ultramarine as night widened like a pupil high above. They'd descended beneath the rim of Gateway's almost sheer cliffs which now obscured the sky's paler shades. Other than the ringing echo of the horses' hooves on the packed ground, the chasm was silent.

No voices. No evening drums.

Nothing.

"Are you *sure?*" Rül wondered again, his voice a hoarse whisper that seemed like profanity against the weighted quiet. Kalas assumed Pava nodded.

"I don't get it," she confessed. "People should be here!"

Nïmrïk pulled Dalafar alongside the coach box, sniffed the air and muttered, "People *are* here. Watching us. Waiting for something…"

With a huff, Pava raised her hands to her mouth and shouted, *"Úrukilmukritme! Im alu nir—Pava! Ëzhe vendaralu!"*

A gust of icy wind loped across the open space between the walls, played with a lock of Pava's black-and-blonde hair and whipped away into the silent dark.

Nïmrïk grunted and nodded at the same time Rül began to say something: he stopped himself when pricks of yellow-orange light flared along the hidden paths cut into the cliffs just above them. Bobbing up and down and following a snake-like course, the lights converged on the coach. Kalas heard Nashmur's sword rattle in its sheath as he placed a hand on its hilt.

"Pava?!" said a man's surprised voice from behind a wavering torch. "Can it be?! No! *How?!* We saw what happened when the *Ilosar* filled the Kathin Iltith! We thought you—is it *really* you?! But where's—?"

"It's really me, Dese!" affirmed the cave-dweller-girl as she leapt from her seat. "Rül, everyone: it's all right! We're among friends!"

Rül's sigh seemed loud enough to rock the coach despite its excellent suspension. Kalas stifled a laugh as he helped Zhalera and Abarandal onto the ground. Nïmrïk and Nashmur dismounted and, along with everyone else, stood behind Pava as she made her introductions.

"Friends, this is Dese, Mother's younger brother. Dese, these are my friends. This is Rül."

"The *Ilosar?* The Shining One?" he wondered with an approving nod.

"No, *âu!* Just a farm boy!" he insisted. "Kalas here's your *Ilosar!*"

Pava's uncle—a lithe, rangy-looking figure bound in a close-fitting costume much like hers—raised his torch and stepped toward the young man. He examined him for a moment, arched an eyebrow, and said, "I thought he'd be taller…"

Kalas felt Zhalera bristle at his elbow. He laughed aloud this time.

"Dese, what's going on?" said Pava, indicating the odd circumstances and uneasy atmosphere surrounding the Gateway. "Where's Father? Mother?"

"I was going to ask you the same thing!"

"You—what? Why? I don't understand!"

"When you disappeared—*how* you disappeared!—we knew we'd been wrong about that *ilímbâ*—that pretender. Most of us spent the next few days rebuilding the Great Collector—"

"Sorry about that," said Kalas as he looked down, jabbed his toe at a loose rock. "Hey, what do you mean, *others* who went—?"

"—others searched the Áthradho for you. *And* for you…*Kalas,* is it? How fitting! Anyway, we looked everywhere for a couple of days, but other than broken crystals, we couldn't find any sign of you.

"We had enough people grinding lenses throughout our settlements, and we'd redirected enough lesser collectors to move the suns-light where we needed it, so we moved our search into the Wastes. We found some wagon tracks coming down from one of the old ghost towns: some of us turned north to check things out—"

Zhalera gasped. Dese paused, nodded, and continued, "—the rest of us kept going east. I was a part of that group. The winds coming down off the Taruún must have erased your tracks—the same winds that made the air too hard to breathe. We had to turn back. We figured maybe the party to the north would've found you. We figured wrong, obviously. When we got back to the Gateway, that northbound party still hadn't returned. We waited another day and still saw no sign of anyone.

"We searched everywhere for the next couple of weeks. We were getting ready to head out again when my cousin Kode came running down the road! Stumbling, really: his clothes were all torn and there was blood everywhere. It took us a minute to understand he'd been attacked by *ilrâigme-edhume*, that eaters had captured almost all of his group and carried them off somewhere! We called for a healer, but Kode had already lost too much blood. Before he died, he warned us that the eaters were following him, that they'd be here soon.

"He was right: not an hour later, eaters fell upon us! We fought them off, but not without a few casualties. Pava, I'm sorry: your father, Rive, was part of Kode's party! Tsana begged him not to go, but you know your father: he wouldn't listen to her. Toward the end of the attack, Tsana chased down the last *ilrâig*, hurled her *tëvët* through his back, then ripped it out and ran it through his skull. I've never seen my sister so angry! So *violent!* After that, she chased down the next to last—that ancient bloodlust, I think. No one's seen her since…"

Rül placed a callused hand on Pava's immobile shoulder, let it rest there for a while as she waited for Dese's words to make sense.

Shock, thought Kalas.

"Deridzhas," said Zhalera, interrupting the uncomfortable moment. "They'll take them to Deridzhas."

"Deridzhas?" said one of the other cavefolk, surprised.

"That town to the north, into the Wastes," she nodded. "They keep…uh…"

"You said *everywhere,*" Pava reminded her uncle.

"We searched for our missing people—for your parents, Pava!—

every day," Dese insisted, his voice *weak*. "But that far north? That's…Pava! The eaters!"

Their cave-dweller friend allowed a solitary shudder to traverse the length of her body before she spoke. When she did, there was jagged metal in her words.

"You *coward*," she smoldered. More in observation than in judgment. Turning toward Rül and the others, she said, "I have no right to ask you this, but—"

"We'll leave right now," said Rül as he jumped back into his seat. Kalas looked to Zhalera, who nodded; to Abarandal, whose song communicated an unlikely blend of uncertainty and faith. He held Pava with his gaze just long enough to offer her a nod of his own.

"This'll be interesting!" said Nashmur as he twisted his foot into his stirrup and climbed into his saddle.

"Dese," said Pava, her tone flat. "You're coming with us."

"I…I can't! I know I should—I'm sorry! But—"

"Here, you can ride my horse," growled Nïmrïk as he walked uphill toward the Wastes.

"I—that's generous, but how—?"

"He'll manage," Pava seethed through gritted teeth. "So will you. Now: *get on that horse* and *help rescue our people!*"

CHAPTER II

Under the Mines at Deridzhas

"WHY DIDN'T YOU CLOSE THE UPPER GATE WHEN Kode told you the eaters were coming?" Pava demanded to know as she and the others began their impromptu rescue mission.

Dese said nothing: he just stared at the back of Dalafar's neck as they trotted toward Deridzhas. Rül had taken a few minutes to hang a pair of lanterns from the coach, and in their shifting light Kalas saw the anger she tried so hard to hide stretched across her face.

"Kode was so out of it, we weren't sure he even knew what he was talking about!" admitted Hwanzho, the other cave-dweller who'd ridden with them on his donkey. "It's been ages—Sevens, even!—since we last closed the upper gate. And it takes a long time, too: the *ilrâigme* would have reached us long before we could've closed it; still, we marshaled our best pikemen, just in case. They put up a good fight. Not good enough, though. I'm sorry, *Shëmîuín*..."

"Hey! Pava told us she *wasn't* a princess!" Zhalera grumbled with a self-satisfied smirk. "I knew it!"

"You'd just better hope everyone's still alive, Hwanzho! You, too, Dese!"

"We might have some time," said Kalas as he poked his head through the window. "They keep, uh, *people* underground—like livestock in a pen or something. It sounds bad, I know—and it is!—but my point is that I don't think they'll kill your people right away. I, uh, I don't know for sure: I'm just guessing."

"No, I think you're right," added Zhalera. "Still, we can't waste any time, otherwise there's no guarantee your—"

"They get it, I'm sure," Kalas interrupted. He made hacking motions at his arms and shook his head: *Let's hope we don't have to worry about such details!*

"Right! Sorry!" she whispered.

"*Sàme*, we need to stop for a while," said Rül after a few hours of hard driving. "It's been a long day for these two. For me, too, if I'm honest. Let's give the horses—and ourselves!—just a couple hours to rest. We'll pick it up again before the suns rise. I promise!"

"I'll keep watch," said Kalas. He exited the coach and drew Shosafin's sword.

"I'll keep you company," huffed an enormous black wolf-like creature.

"*Gili erume!* An *egu?!*" shouted Dese as he scrambled for his *tëvët*.

"No! It's Nïmrïk!" Kalas explained as he stepped in front of the beast. The "wolf" stretched its forelegs and lowered all but its haunches toward the ground in its best approximation of a bow.

"*Lushà rist, úrukilmukrit,*" said Nïmrïk.

"Pava, you've found yourself the strangest company," said Dese with an uneasy glance at the *egu*.

The night's chill, while present, bore almost no comparison to the gelid air settling into Thosha's valley; still, Rül pulled a selection of furs and hides from storage and passed them around.

"Yëlisha wasn't fooling around when she loaded this thing!" he said as he handed a blanket to Pava. "Wouldn't surprise me if there's stuff in here I don't find until we're back in Lohwàlar!"

It seemed the coverings alone wouldn't provide enough warmth to fend off the coldest winds, so Kalas scoured the ground for any available fuel, scooped out a shallow pit, and built a small fire. Dese cantilevered plate-like rocks around its rim, creating a chimney of sorts. He fashioned low vents along the bottom in such a way that the flames' glow would be hard to see unless one were almost on top of them. Aware, at last, of Kalas' impressed stare, he mumbled, "I just, uh, well…this should keep any unwanted guests from noticing us from afar. The rocks should help hold in the heat, too."

After everyone else had huddled up, Kalas and Nïmrïk shared a brief word, then separated toward opposite ends of the makeshift camp.

Per Rül's plan, Nashmur rustled Kalas' shoulder and woke him from a fitful sleep, having traded places with him a few hours ago. The young man shivered in spite of his furs, removed himself from their relative warmth, and resuscitated the remnants of his fire. Neither sun had risen, though a few rosy blotches dappled the sky's farthest reaches. Tàfayan—Nalënahwu, the Premier Sun—would climb above the horizon within the hour. It didn't take long for everyone to eat a quick breakfast and pack everything up: the first sun was still behind the plateau when they resumed their trip toward Deridzhas.

After two more days and nights without incident, they came to the place where Kalas had dropped them out of the sky not too long ago. Rül steered his team toward the same thin copse from before and pointed out the stump from the tree he'd felled for his axle.

"The *ilrâigme-edhume* usually just have small knives for weapons. Not even knives, really: just sharpened bits of metal," said Hwanzho as he walked the perimeter implied by the trees. The changing season and its accompanying winds had torn most of the leaves from their branches, but what few remained provided at least a hint of cover.

"You've encountered them recently?!" said Pava, surprised.

"No, I meant…I mean historically speaking! Anyway, I think we can defend this place if necessary. Our *tëvëtme* and your swords—and the *Ilosardas* powers—should have a much better reach than anything the eaters might be carrying: all we have to do is keep the trees between us."

"It'll be midday soon," Kalas noted. He ignored Hwanzho's *Ilosar* comment as he scanned the surrounding rocks and hills for any signs of movement. "What do the rest of you think? Lunch, then head out? If I remember correctly, Deridzhas is a little more than a league from here."

"Sounds good to me," said Zhalera as she strapped her sword across her back. Falthwën had instructed her to keep it covered when they first left Lohwàlar; now, however, that admonition seemed moot. When fighting against the *ekume*—"dark stars," or, as Rül's grandfather called them, *ilnàfëlme*—within the Vault beneath Ïsriba, her sword had been the only human-wielded weapon to have any effect on the shifting shapes of living shadow. Zhalera had learned one of her ancestors forged it with the help of the *eru* Valaran, another departed member of the Great Swath: maybe that's why it seemed to possess supernatural powers? abilities? some otherwise indescribable attribute that allowed it to cleave the immaterial substance from which the *ekume* proceeded.

"The sooner the better," Pava added as she hefted her *tëvët*—the crystal-tipped pike weapon the cavefolk preferred.

"I'm coming, too!" insisted Rül as he rooted around for his axe.

"Uh, shouldn't someone stay and, well, guard the horses? the coach?" suggested Dese. Pava spat her disgust and glared at him through slitted eyes.

"No, he's right," Kalas admitted. "Actually…Nashmur, will you stay with the horses? We can't let anything happen to them."

"You don't want me to come with you?"

"It's not that: It's, well…*you,* I trust…And I think it'd be best if Nïmrïk came with us. If there *is* a poison surrounding Deridzhas, and if it's anything like what we uncovered in our own Empty Sea, he's probably best suited to handle it."

"Ah, then of course!" Nashmur nodded.

Kalas and the others turned toward Deridzhas. As they headed out, Abarandal sang a troubled melody. Kalas stopped. He walked over to her, put a hand on her shoulder and tried to explain: "I don't know what we're facing in Deridzhas. I'll be honest with you: the only thing I know for sure is that it will *not* be safe! Nashmur will protect you while we're gone. If all goes well, we should be back here tonight. Tomorrow morning at the latest.

She added to her song, her notes suggesting worry in such a way that the others felt it, too, even if they didn't understand her thoughts the same way Kalas did.

"I know, *eruín,* I know, but if I can't do what's right because I'm afraid, then how can I be expected to…do whatever it is the prophecy expects from me when the time comes? What if *this* event is part of that? Have faith! We'll return as soon as we're able—*with* Pava's people!"

If any of them are still alive…

2.

As soon as they reached the sickly forest with its thin, spidery trees and bruise-colored fungal blooms, the air turned sour. Zhalera, having anticipated such an occurrence, had preemptively wrapped a length of cloth across her face. Pava pulled a previously hidden gusset from beneath her shirt over her mouth and nose. Kalas and Rül tore strips of cloth from their sleeves for the same purpose. No one had intercepted them as they crossed the wide, barren fields between their tiny staging area and the cracked and crumbling remains of an old stone wall.

Nïmrïk paused on the opposite side of the wall, sniffed, and looked around.

"Someone's been through here. Not too long ago, I'd say. Maybe a day or two? Looks like…yes, I'd say they were headed toward Deridzhas. See this slight dip? how these twigs and grasses are bent and broken? Whoever made this impression was running. If we look around a little more, we'll probably find other tracks."

"We don't have time to look around! We're almost there, right? Let's keep moving!" Pava insisted. Nïmrïk dropped his head in a passable approximation of a shrug and followed after her.

"Keep her safe: Zhalera and I will scout our flanks. Shout—growl, roar, whatever!—if you need us!"

Nïmrïk nodded and padded after Pava—and Rül, who stayed close by her side.

"All right, Zhalera: Pava's not thinking clearly. She's rushing blindly into something none of us understands. Not fully. Can't say I blame her: I'd probably do—no, I *tried to do* the same thing not so long ago. Your sword cuts through *ekume*—let's hope, if necessary, it cuts through *ilrâigme* just as easily!"

Zhalera removed her sword from its sheath and held it tight. Suns-light rippled across its surface, drawing honeyed threads of light from within its…steel? Kalas realized he had no idea from what substance her ancestors had made it: based on its properties, it had to be more than an alloy of mere charcoal and iron.

Kalas nodded at her weapon and asked, "Does it have a name?"

"A name? What?"

"Your sword! Loradan called her weapon *Hàfilrifar.* I just wondered if Gandhan or your grandfathers had given that sword a name."

"We're surrounded by cannibals, and *that's* what you're thinking about?!" she reminded him with a reluctant chuckle. "No, I don't think anyone named it. If they did, Father never told me what it was. After everything that happened under the Vault, though, I started thinking of it as *Valarandal.*"

It might have been just a trick of the suns-light as it filtered through the sparse and pitted leaves overhead, but the veins of fire within Zhalera's blade seemed to swell with intensity.

Kalas offered her a broad smile. "That sounds like the perfect name! All right, take Valarandal and cover Pava's right flank. I'll take Shosafin's sword and cover the left. Whistle, shout, make some kind of noise if you run into trouble!"

Zhalera nodded, grunted, and disappeared behind a yellowed tree. Kalas watched her until she was out of sight, then picked his way across the diseased forest and collapsed stonework that bordered Deridzhas.

Maneuvering through the thorny underbrush, Kalas worked his way close enough to the town's outskirts to see a small collection of low, domed structures surrounding an immense mound of earth and scaffolding. When they'd last explored Deridzhas, they hadn't traveled this far beyond the "town hall," as he'd thought of it then. At first, Kalas wondered if this larger construct might have been another town hall-like building; then, remembering what Falthwën had told them about the town's history, he wondered if perhaps it had something to do with its fabled mines. The sensation of fatigue and weakness, of *wrongness,* seemed stronger here. He waited, scanned the area again, and—

Wait, what's that? It's blood! Lots of it! he observed as he focused on a series of dark red striations woven between the domes. He worked his fingers over the hilt of his sword, testing his grip before he stepped beyond his concealment and into the open, bloodied avenue. With heightened senses, he moved toward the trail and the curious building.

A shallow ditch, maybe a few feet deep and twice as wide, surrounded the town hall. When Kalas reached the front of this structure, he discovered it boasted an empty ring at least twelve feet deep and four or five feet wide. The town hall's doorway had been uncovered, its door ripped away by wind or time or, perhaps, both. This building's door appeared to be made from some kind of bluish metal. In places, it still gleamed in the suns-light, but most of it had rusted. Fashioned from two halves, one remained hanging from a single corroded hinge; the other, torn from its frame and leaning against the wall of the ring, looked like something had ripped four wide gashes across its surface. Whatever the cause, it had taken place years before: a small, almost naked sapling struggled up through one of the gaps.

The blood trail vanished within the shadows of the curious construct. Kalas descended a broad set of stairs into the ring-like hole, stepped inside the building, and waited a minute for his eyes to adjust. When they did, he realized his suspicions about Deridzhas' mines had been correct.

Illuminated by a strange sort of half-light that filtered in through the open door and patchy holes in the ceiling, Kalas saw the huge, single room was empty apart from a smattering of fallen rocks and beams and other debris. Following the blood with his eyes, he noted this space had a regular path cut through the accumulated dust, and at its center gaped a black maw that appeared to stretch deep within the earth. The path of blood ended at its lip. Kalas braced himself, leaned over the edge, and nearly vomited from the reek that wafted up from its unknown depths.

Not again, he thought. He tried to *send* a thought to Nïmrïk and the others as he raced toward daylight and up the stairs carved into the ring.

His eyes hadn't adjusted to the full light of the suns, but he maintained enough situational awareness to sense at least a couple of dark, upright blobs rush upon him as something *foul* choked his lungs. He blinked, planted his feet, and raised his sword just in time to block a strike from what rang like a metal bar. Summoning skills he'd acquired through Shosafin's instruction, he pivoted, reversed his grip, and drove his weapon through his attacker's abdomen. He wrenched it free and prepared for the next blow: his would-be assailant never screamed as he dropped his bludgeon and collapsed in a fetid pile.

"Think you can *take?!* From *her?!*" raved a voice with a disconcerting clarity in its enunciation. "Can't! *Won't!*"

His eyes adjusted, Kalas found himself face to face with what had to be an emaciated *ilrâig-edhume*—an eater-of-men. The man's—the *creature's* face was aflame with mania, his sallow skin pocked with blisters, some of which had ruptured and oozed putrescent, greenish filth. His eyes, wide and white with naught but tight black circles of pupil, sized him up as he tasted the air with his wicked-looking tongue and licked his cracked and bleeding lips. He, too, held a long chunk of rusted metal—part of some old machine, from the look. With a crazed shout, he raised it overhead and rushed upon Kalas.

Nïmrïk! he shouted. Tried to, at least: as he parried the eater's blow, he wasn't sure if he'd spoken the *egudas* name aloud or only within his thoughts. With a quick jab, he punched his aggressor in the face with the gilded pommel of his sword. Sheets of syrupy black blood and clots of whitish pus spurted from the sudden wound as the man staggered back. He wiped at the injury with one hand and studied it for a moment before he licked away the fluids with a grin.

"Nïmrïk! Zhalera!" Kalas roared, unashamed at the obvious horror in his voice. He flipped his sword and aimed its glittering point toward his attacker.

"No, no, no!" the *ilrâig* cackled. "She is safe with us!"

"'*She*'? What are you talking about?!"

Rather than answer Kalas with words—incoherent as they might have been, the gaunt figure raised his weapon and charged him again. Kalas stepped aside and made a quick thrust, but the man anticipated his move: he adjusted his trajectory and blocked Kalas' strike. Before the eater could recover, Kalas leaned into him, shoved him away and made his own adjustments.

"We don't have to do this!" Kalas insisted. "I just want to know: Did you *take* some people not too long ago? Some *úrukilmukritme* from the Áthradho? I just want to know if they're still alive!"

The eater risked a glance toward the bottomless shaft within the odd building, smoothed back a greasy shock of bleached, wiry hair, and laughed as he regarded the young man again.

"She was *hungry!*" he insisted as he approached with measured steps. Instead of brutish lunges, he made a few feints this time and pirouetted out of the way as he repelled Kalas' counter attacks. The taint in the atmosphere, coupled with his lack of sleep, sapped Kalas' strength as the fight dragged on.

I have to be careful!

As the eater lunged again, Kalas, having expected a subtler advance, stumbled over an abandoned fragment of mining apparatus. The eater failed to correct for Kalas' fall: instead of bringing his club down on the young man's head, he buried it in the dirt, carried off balance by his unchecked momentum. Seizing the opportunity, Kalas sliced at the *ilrâigdas* leg and separated it from his adversary's body. He heard what sounded like footsteps fast approaching from the south—the center of town.

The eater screamed—and *laughed* again—as he fell sideways. Kalas stood, and with a reluctant sigh, drove Shosafin's sword through the still-gibbering figure's heart.

"I'm sorry," he muttered.

The footsteps sounded closer now. Panting, he removed his weapon from the dead eater's chest, wiped it on the rags that had been its clothes, and readied for the next attack.

3.

"Kalas! Are you all right?!" demanded Zhalera as she and the others rushed into view.

"We heard you shout!" said Rül, out of breath and with blood on his axe. Pava's *tëvët* bore similar crimson streaks. "We were, uh, a little busy, but we got here as soon as we could!"

"Looks like you handled yourself well enough," said Nïmrïk, catching sight of the deceased *ilrâigme*.

Rül helped Kalas to his feet and confessed, "We shouldn't have just marched right in here like we did. I'm sorry: with time running out…Anyway, a couple eaters caught us off-guard. They were hauling one of Pava's people—what was left of her!—toward one of those domed buildings. Pava ended one with her *tëvët*, but it got stuck. His friend attacked her, but I got him with my axe."

"Sufa—the woman those *nëshras ilrâigme* murdered—she deserved better! Kalas, you said they wouldn't have started killing them yet! You were wrong!"

Zhalera started to defend him, but Kalas raised a hand and, with as much calm as he could manage, said, "I'm sorry, Pava."

"It's not your fault," she said, after a moment, as she wiped away a spate of unwelcome tears.

"Zhalera wanted to tell you about…*this*, but I hoped you wouldn't have to see it. From our last visit here, it seemed like the eaters were feeding on people one limb at a time, keeping them locked in cellars, underground and out of the sun until…

"Maybe Zhalera had the right idea. I guess it doesn't really mat-

37

ter now. And maybe there's some good news. *Maybe.* Before these two attacked me, I found a trail—of blood, I'm sorry—leading into that strange building right there. There's a huge pit—a mine shaft, I'm guessing, and I wouldn't be surprised if that's where they're keeping most of your people. I was on my way to find you when, well, I got a little busy, too.

"We need to see what's down there. I don't know about the rest of you, but I feel weak. Sluggish. Like my legs don't wanna listen to me. Something tells me that feeling's only gonna get worse. Rül's right: time *is* running out, and no matter how sick this place makes us, *now* is our only chance to rescue anyone. Let's go!"

Out of the suns, everyone allowed his eyes to adapt before investigating the opening at the center of the chamber. Rül gagged and spewed a portion of his lunch through the aperture. Nïmrïk sniffed the noxious air rising from the hole: other than a curt twist of his muzzle, he seemed no worse for the experience.

"Tell you what," he said as he faced the others. "Let me see what's at the bottom of this thing. These vapors don't affect me the same way they do you. And I can see in the dark!" As if to underscore his point, his eyes emitted a faint yellow glow that brightened as he bared his teeth in his best wolfish smile.

"I'll return when I have some information—good or bad."

"*Âu* Nïmrïk!" said Pava as she jogged to his side. "Please, take this. If you see any *úrukilmukritme,* show this ring to them: they might recognize it and know you're there to help."

Beneath the Vault of Stars, Falthwën had bequeathed her an ugly, jeweled ring. According to Pava, in her people's ancient past, an *eru* wearing that ring had built—and taught them how to use— the *iltithme-kal* to collect the suns' light and direct it underground: without its light collectors, *nimúrukilmukrit* civilization would perish. Now, Pava looped it through a length of cord and tied it around

Nïmrïk's shaggy neck.

"Thank you!" she said as she finished her knot and stepped back. With a gruff nod and a flick of his ears, the *egu* loped onto the rickety stairway descending into the shaft and vanished.

Long minutes—half an hour, perhaps—elapsed with no sign of Nïmrïk. Kalas and Rül had dragged the fallen *ilrâigme* bodies inside one of the other domed outbuildings and scattered the bloodied sand to prevent others from taking an interest in their deeds. Despite having grown up on a farm, where manual labor and exertion were rote facets of daily life, Deridzhas' poisoned air had begun to leech Rül's strength, too. Still pale from throwing up, when they were back inside the structure with the mine shaft, he admitted, "I see what you mean about this place. Feels like my arms and legs are covered with mud! How much longer do you think Nïmrïk'll be down there?"

"No idea," said Kalas. "When I looked over that ledge, I couldn't see anything. I don't have Nïmrïk's eyes, though—I didn't even see the stairs at first. Zhalera, do you remember Falthwën telling us the last time he was here—many Sevens ago—the *Deridzhasrinme* were planning on digging deeper than ever before? I'm starting to think this shaft might be what he was telling us about. This building is different from all the others. Bigger, anyway, and maybe I'm wrong, but I'd guess it's newer, too.

"One of the eaters said something about…someone? some*thing?* I don't know. He said, 'She's safe with us!' and 'She was *hungry.*' I have no idea what he was talking about, but even as crazy as he was, he sounded *worshipful,* I guess. Creepy!"

A sudden gust of ash and smoke jetted from the mouth at the center of the room. Yellow-orange light from some unknown source cast irregular flashes along its cylindrical column. The structure groaned as the earth rumbled and shed additional parts of its walls and ceiling in a rain of hot dust. A pair of knotted hands reached up from the shaft as one of the eaters collapsed onto the ground.

"Awake! *Awake!*" she raved. Kalas raised his sword, but the *ilrâig* paid him no mind as she stood and bolted from the enclosure. A few more eaters followed in her stead, every one of their faces rigid with horror. None seemed to notice them as they fled in abject terror.

More flashes. More quakes.

One last eater, a leg recently ripped from his hips, dragged himself into the room and clawed his way across the floor toward the door. He screamed a string of incoherent syllables before blood loss overcame him.

"Nïmrïk's down there!" Kalas shouted and raced toward the pit. The amber light, weak and inconsistent, afforded him enough illumination to see the wood-and-metal staircase the *ilrâigme* used. "Hey, I see the stairs! It's not as far down as I thought!"

"Kalas! What are you—where are you going?!" demanded Zhalera.

"Nïmrïk's down there! And more than that, I have a hunch your people are down there, too, Pava!"

She was hungry.

"This is foolishness!" Zhalera grumbled as she trotted over to him. "Well? We're wasting time! If we're gonna do this, let's do it!"

Before Kalas could insist she remain behind, she cleared the first level and was halfway to the second. With a gruff sigh, he chased after her, Rül and Pava right behind. More *ilrâigme-edhume* passed them on their way out of the mine, each as curiously disinterested in them as the last.

"Whatever's down there must be…I mean, if it's bad enough to scare away these eaters?!" mused Rül, his axe glinting in the shifting light.

• • •

After nine levels, the stairs dumped them at the slanted bottom of a natural cavern. Abandoned mining apparatus piled at the center had already begun to rust: frayed cordage and frozen chains hung useless from defunct pulley systems while parts of shattered barrels and exploded crates lie strewn across the rest of the floor.

"I thought it'd be deeper," Rül admitted as he looked up at the circle of light almost one hundred feet above.

At one end of the cavern, a small aperture cut from the rock seemed to be the source of the light and smoke. Zhalera followed a narrow cart track through the opening before Kalas and the others could reach her.

"This more like it?" she deadpanned as the rest caught up.

At one time, the track probably served a purpose; now, however, it simply stopped in mid-air, its rails sheared away. Bright, yellow-white light streamed upward from a broader shaft perhaps thirty to forty feet across. From Kalas' perspective, it seemed at least as deep as the Empty Sea. Ringed with a parapet no wider than five feet at most, four sets of slick-looking stairs carved into the stone spiraled toward its bottom. Another gush of acrid wind and another blast of light—greenish-yellow this time—rose up from below.

As did another series of screams.

"This place," Kalas muttered as he coughed. He pictured his father, Tàran, for one brief instant, then shook his head clear. "We've gotta get down there. Find Pava's people. Find Nimrïk. And then get far away from Deridzhas as fast as possible!"

4.

Despite their increasing fatigue and the malignant effect of whatever it was that gnawed at their strength, within roughly thirty minutes they reached the cratered ground at the bottom of the stairs. Fragments of the old track littered the floor. Surrounded by broken tools and tangled rigging, the light—and *heat*, Kalas realized—emanated from the largest of three lesser passages.

A series of shuttered buildings lined the rest of the chamber. Unlike almost everything else about the place, these looked like they'd been used recently. Reddish-brown streaks reminiscent of dried blood trailed up to and away from the structures' interiors. Someone coughed.

"That wasn't one of us…was it?" Rül wondered.

"No, it wasn't! We're not alone down here!" Pava answered him.

Something inside one of the sheds railed against its rickety door. Kalas—*everyone*—jumped.

It banged again. Louder, this time.

"Pava?! Pava, is that you?!"

"Mother?!" Pava exclaimed as she tore at the clumsy bindings securing the door. When they opened, a frail-looking woman who bore a remarkable resemblance to her daughter toppled onto the cave-dweller girl. Pava caught her—Rül caught them both as their shared momentum upset her balance.

"Mother! What are you doing down here?! Where's Father?! Where are the others?!"

"Pava, is it really you? No, of course it is! I—Who are these people?! Not *úrukilmukritme!*"

"They're friends, Mother! They…We were on our way home when Dese told us what happened to Father. To you!"

"A monster!" Tsana remembered. "A monster shoved me in here! A giant wolf-creature! An *egu*, I think! Had to be! Said it was for my protection, that he'd come back for me. Said he had to find the others first. You don't think he's going to…? *Ilrâigme-edhume* are bad enough, but—?"

"No, Nimrïk's not…he's nothing like the eaters—or other *egume*, for that matter," Pava explained. "Mother, this is Kalas—an *ilosar!* I think he's *the Ilosar!* This is his…friend Zhalera, and this… this is Rül. Nïmrïk you've met: because he can see in the dark, he volunteered to come look for you. He'd been gone a while, then eaters came climbing out of this pit when the smoke and fire started. Have you seen Father? Any others?"

"No, daughter, I have not. When the eaters attacked the Gateway, I…the *yash aódru*—the red mist…I got a little carried away. I killed four—five? I lost count—before I realized I'd chased them all the way to this wretched place. I saw eaters drag a group of our people into the building above this mine shaft. I followed them down, but after the *aódru* burned itself out of my blood, I felt *sick.* I crawled into one of those passages and rested. It was supposed to be for just a few minutes, but I think it's been days now!"

Rül offered the dehydrated woman a swig from his waterskin. She gulped it down, wiped her mouth and handed it back. She tried to stand; with Pava's help, at last, she managed, flipped her waist-length braided hair behind her shoulders and offered a grateful—if peaked—smile.

Kalas listened to Tsana's story with one ear while he explored the cavern. Garbage and debris lined the smaller tunnels, and without light, it seemed unwise to explore them.

"Seems like this is the only way to go," he said as he examined the third and largest passage. A wave of heat rolled over him, drawing beads of sweat from his already exhausted frame. "Pava, why don't you stay here, with Tsana: let us keep going?"

"But—!"

"He's right," agreed Rül with a light hand on her shoulder. "Actually, see if you can help your mother reach the surface. Maybe getting away from whatever's down here will help her—help you *both* feel better?"

"That's a good idea, Rül," nodded Kalas. "If you're able, get her back to the others. Get her more water and something to eat. Send

Nashmur—and tell him to keep his sword unsheathed!"

Though loath to leave her friends—her people, whom she presumed were somewhere amid the fires below, she knew Rül was right: her expression revealed as much.

"I'll send Nashmur right away!" she promised. Tsana wobbled for a moment, then rediscovered her legs and walked with her daughter toward one of the spiral stairways. Rül watched them go, his concern unmistakable.

"They'll be fine! Pava's quite the little warrior," Zhalera assured him.

"Yeah, I know," he told himself.

Light flickered in random patterns, syncopated with a smattering of rumbles emanating from somewhere even deeper underground. Each tremor exposed additional weaknesses in the surrounding rock as cracks chipped away portions of the reddish-brown tunnel walls, each fissure wider than the last. With every step, the blood trail broadened. Some of it had become footprints heading down into the earth.

If this is all from one person, there's no way he's still alive, Kalas frowned.

The stench of *wrongness* intensified with every step. Rül coughed again: he showed Kalas and Zhalera his bloody palm before he wiped it against the rocks.

The next quake split the ground underfoot: without warning, the three of them toppled into new darkness. When the dust settled, between coughing fits, Kalas asked: "Everyone all right?!"

"I'm all right!" Zhalera assured him. Rül, too.

"That *smell* though!" the farm boy added. Kalas nodded, felt it rankle in his nostrils and wondered why it seemed familiar.

"Doesn't seem like we fell too far: the tunnel's maybe ten feet above us. Any way to climb back up?" he wondered.

A bright punch of light washed over the collapsed passage, and as its greenish after-image subsided, Kalas gasped.

"Zhalera?!"

"I saw it too!" she exclaimed.

"Saw what?" said Rül, confused.

"This place is like…We discovered something back home, back in the Empty Sea. It had the same stink, the same…meaty fibers we just saw. Being near it made my father sick: being inside it made us sick, too.

"Zhalera, this has to be another *artifact!* Looks upside down or sideways compared to the one back home. Remember what Falthwën said? Do you think being so close to this thing for so long is what…*ruined* the *Deridzhasrinme?*"

"I don't know, but we've gotta get out of here! We've gotta find Pava's people—if they're still alive!—and get away from this place! Look, we can use these rocks as a ladder. Let me test it first…"

Zhalera clambered up the slide as quickly as she could. Rül followed. Kalas lingered a moment, hoping for another glimpse at the bizarre construct's interior features. In the darkness, he traced a hand along its invisible contours. In the afterglow of another burst of light, he saw what looked like row upon row of human-sized cylindrical pods. Most were cracked or ruptured in some fashion and looked like they'd been abandoned for Sevens.

"Kalas! Let's go!" hollered Zhalera.

"Coming!" he coughed as he made his way toward the others.

Falthwën said the thing Father and I discovered wasn't unique. I wonder: how many more of these things are there?! Where did they come from?! How did they end up like this?!

Before he cleared the hole's perimeter, he thought he glimpsed pale blue radiance coming from behind him. He whirled around and saw nothing but darkness.

This thing's messing with my mind…

...

"Voices!" Zhalera hissed as after a few more minutes of walking. She flattened out on her belly as they reached an opening that emptied into another large room about nine or ten feet above the ground. Peering over the edge, they saw Nïmrïk surrounded by *ilrâigme-edhume*. From appearances, the *egu* had been wounded. When an eater would draw his attention, another would slash at his backside. He growled with every fresh injury, snapped and snarled as he fought against his assailants: more than a few of them had reached a bitter end between his blood-stained teeth and poisoned claws.

"Wolf demon!" one of the eaters shouted. Others repeated the taunt. "Your black god has no power here! No! Down here, *she* reigns forever! *She* reigns *forever!*"

'She'? mouthed Zhalera. Kalas shrugged.

"We've gotta get to Nïmrïk," he whispered. "He might be an *egu*, but he's cut off from The Song: he's gonna need our help!"

"What do we do?" hissed Rül. "There's, what, ten, twelve of them? We're just three kids!"

"Three kids with swords! And an axe!" Zhalera reminded him with a grim look. She twisted Valarandal in the room's yellow-orange light, where fiery filaments glittered across its surface.

Nïmrïk turned toward his latest antagonist, wrapped his jaws around the eater's knobby ankle and held on tight. The others swarmed around him, raised their jagged metal implements and prepared to strike.

"*Now!*" Kalas roared as he leapt onto one of the eater's backs. His target crumpled underneath the force of his attack: crushed flat, it didn't move again. Zhalera jumped and landed with a fluid roll: she planted her feet and thrust her sword at an upward angle, catching one of the *ilrâigme* beneath the rib cage. Abandoning any semblance of grace, Rül dropped upon a pair of eaters with his arms outstretched, caught one under each of his shoulders and dragged both to the ground. He righted himself, palmed their heads, and cracked them together with enough force to shatter bone.

"Kalas!" shouted Nïmrïk, having chewed through his foe's lower leg. "What are you—*Behind you!*"

The young man sensed someone approaching from his left side. He ducked, spun, and sliced in one motion, rolling to his right at the end of his stroke. The *ilrâig* dropped his weapon as his steaming innards piled up on the ground. The madman clutched at his intestines, laughing as he doubled over and died in a puddle of his own filth.

Why do they always laugh?! Kalas wondered with a shiver.

Between the four of them, the remaining eaters-of-men stood little chance. When the last of them gurgled his final breath, dark blood bubbling on his chin and dripping onto the dirt, Nïmrïk explained: "I got through the first room without incident. About halfway down the second room, one of them saw me, raised an alarm. Sometimes four legs are better than two: navigating that staircase is not one of them! I reached the bottom and found one of the cave-dwellers. I locked her in one of those shed buildings—she was *not* happy about that!

"That's when some kind of tremor hit. It didn't seem all that impressive, but all of a sudden, hordes of eaters came running from that passageway. It had been dark up to that point, but now there was light—I still don't know from what. I hid in one of those empty passages while they ran past. They kept saying something about how *she* would be upset if their sacrifice escaped. No idea what they were talking about—*'she?'*—but 'sacrifice' and 'escape' made me think *cave-dwellers.* Some, I hoped, might still be alive. I thought all the eaters had fled—must be something down here that confuses my sense of smell: when I reached this room, I discovered I was wrong.

"I held them off for a while. I don't know why these guys stayed behind while their friends couldn't seem to get out of here fast enough. Doesn't really matter: they recognized me for who—no, for *what* I am, and decided I'd make an even better sacrifice. Said because I walked right in here it must be an omen. If you hadn't shown up when you did…Hey, where's Pava?! The eaters—?"

"No, no! That cave-dweller you saved was her mother, Tsana! They're on their way back to the others. I told Pava to stay with Hwanzho and send Nashmur," said Kalas, breathless. "That'll be at least an hour or two: this air is toxic, and it'll take Pava and her mother some time to reach the surface. Once they're clear of the town, they'll feel better.

"One of them said something like, 'she reigns forever,'" Rül said.

"On the surface, one of them said something about a *she*, too," Kalas added as he remembered the eater's rapturous expression.

"What—who's this *she* they're talking about?" finished Zhalera.

"I have no idea," Nimrïk admitted. He took a step, yelped as one of his injuries protested. "Oh, that's not good…"

"You're hurt!" said Kalas.

"I've suffered worse," Nimrïk grunted.

What was that part of The Song Falthwën sang for Shosafin? the young man tried to remember.

The *egu* rested a moment. He stood and took a few steps, but his gait had lost its easy lope.

"There's only two ways to go now: out, or deeper in…" he said as he half limped, half dragged himself toward an elaborate exit carved into the opposite wall. Rül and Zhalera followed, exchanging uneasy glances as Nimrïk tried to camouflage his pain.

Kalas closed his eyes and held a picture of his *egu* friend in his mind. He remembered how he seemed to *ooze* across the dungeons beneath İsriba not so long ago, a living portrait of grace and strength.

He needs to be like that again, he sang without words. *He needs to be…better.*

With his eyes still closed, with phrases from The Song still gliding through his mouth and gathering strength, he heard Zhalera gasp as Nïmrïk collapsed.

"Nïmrïk!" Rül shouted.

5.

Is that too much? What if it's not enough? What if I'm killing *him? What if—No! I can't think like that! I have to* focus! *But he's not* edhu; *I don't know anything about* egume!

Fronds of white light unfurled from some of Nïmrïk's severest wounds. The wolf writhed and twisted as brilliance cascaded across his damaged form. When the light blinked out, he exhaled and remained still. A loud crack echoed up from some place beneath them as the ground split and canted. The others stumbled and strove for balance until the aftershocks ended. The light flickered, weakened, then stabilized with just a fraction of its former intensity.

"Kalas! What's going on?! Nïmrïk needs—you're *on fire!* Are you—what are you doing to him?!" Zhalera said, tugging at his outstretched arm.

The young man concluded his silent recitation with an inaudible prayer. He opened his eyes and *descended* to the floor, having lost contact with it somehow. The room's reddish light abated: Zhalera must have been right about him being *on fire.*

When his feet touched the ground, he stumbled. Zhalera helped him up and wiped away a rivulet of fresh blood trickling from his nose. Kalas coughed, expelled a stringy gray wad of something not unlike phlegm, and suddenly, the worst of the mine's polluted atmosphere seemed to dissipate, taking with it its deleterious effects.

"Did the air in here get better?" Rül asked as he spat into the

49

shadows. "Seems…*lighter*, I guess."

"It does, doesn't it?" Zhalera agreed with an awed look at Kalas. Still weary, he offered her a half-grin, arched his eyebrows, and approached Nïmrïk, who remained where he'd fallen.

"Nïmrïk! Nïmrïk! Time, uh…*dzhâra afilo im nir!* Time to wake up!" he insisted with a gentle tug on the wolf-beast's shoulder.

"I'm awake, lad! I'm awake! *Ahwume á erume!* What happened?!"

"How are your injuries? How do you feel?"

"Better," he said, after a brief moment. He stood, stretched his limbs and wagged his tail, and walked a few tight circles.

"*Much* better!" he added. With a shrewd, perceptive look, discernible despite his lupine shape, he continued, "You did that…"

"I…yeah, I just—you're all right though?"

"I am. I'm…I don't know, exactly, but I *heard* you. Sounded a little like Sharuyan's arrangement, but…*different.* And the air in here seems *brighter,* if that's the right word. The cave-dweller girl calls you *Ilosar.* Now I understand why."

"This isn't just an ordinary doorway," Rül stated as he examined the friezes and reliefs adorning the wall into which it had been cut. Most had suffered damage from the recent tremors: slabs of decorative granite leaned against one another in ragged piles. The embellishment continued into the tunnel; now, it, too, had cracked, and through those cracks, Kalas glimpsed hints of familiar light, harsh and blue, that pulsed in time to a slow beat.

Another artifact? Or is it the same one from before? Just how big is this thing?!

Several cages lined the far end of the passageway. Most of their doors had been ripped from their hinges by the quake, but the cells' occupants seemed too tired to attempt an escape. Most had slept through the incident—too spent to care about what might happen next. A few, however, staggered toward Kalas and the others.

"*Arelaru!* Help us! Please!"

"Of course!" said Rül as he gripped the door, braced himself, and, with a grunt, tore it from its twisted frame. "Pava's people, right?"

Hearing Pava's name, one of the figures stood, though the act required considerable effort. He turned toward Rül's voice, and that's when they realized his eyes had been gouged away.

"Pava?! You know my daughter?!"

"Rive?" Rül ventured.

"You do! Oh! *Zhi Ilun dàbras nir!* Is she safe? We've been searching for her for weeks now, and—"

"She's safe! She and Tsana went to get—"

"Tsana?! What about my bride?! Is she—?"

"No, mister! She'll be all right! Pava got her out of here—just a little while ago! They went to get help! But you...you don't look so good, sir! What happened?"

"I need to get my people out of here! We were twelve when we set out; now, we're only five. Please, you don't understand! *She* is waiting just beyond this hall! *She* will destroy us all!"

She was hungry.

"Rül, Zhalera: please get everyone to the surface. Nïmrïk and I will be right behind you: right after we find out who this '*she*' is."

"You can't! You don't understand!" Rive repeated, his eyeless face exuding horror. "She's unlike anything you've ever known! Just—all of us need to leave! We need to leave *right now!*"

"Rül, please!" Kalas insisted. "Get them away from—

this artifact

—here! Hopefully Nashmur will be topside by the time you reach the surface!"

"Kalas, are you sure? No, never mind: *of course* you are!" Zhalera sighed. "All right then. Rül! Let's get the rest of these cages open and get these people out of here! C'mon, Mister Rive! Your family's waiting for you! Here, take my hand—"

"*Ëmîu!* There's an *egu* with them!"

Rive cocked his head as though listening for something. With an impatient shake, he said, "*Egu* or no, if these friends of my daughter are offering their aid, I suggest we accept! I don't know how or why, but the *evil* in the air feels weaker now: it's the perfect time to escape! Stay here with *her* if you like! I'm in no condition to force you—*any* of you!—to do anything! Anyone who wants to *live*, however: come with me!"

Zhalera and Rül began their exodus from beneath the mines. One of the *úrukilmukritme* collapsed before they reached the prior chamber. Kalas looked back when he heard him hit the ground. He didn't think the motionless figure would ever get up again.

Nïmrïk led Kalas down a steep, narrow slope. After about a hundred feet, the path turned one hundred eighty degrees, and the subterranean switchback opened into a vaguely circular, vault-like space. Lights flashed from high above while others coruscated in rectilinear shapes across a dome-like ceiling. Banks of semitransparent glass—mostly shattered—buzzed with inconstant yellow light, and Kalas assumed they'd been the source of the brilliance flooding the labyrinthine network of mines and caverns before the quakes destroyed them. Rings of those cylindrical pods—most broken—hung from thick rods descending from the ceiling like metal stalactites. Pools of dark green slime glistened from ruptured hoses entering and exiting heads of that fleshy, meaty substance. Diffuse threads of violet-tinted energy sparked with hollow-sounding cracks amid the fibers of one such conglomeration: tiny lightning bolts arced across the air, triggering haphazard spasms as the bundles contracted.

This is *another artifact!* Kalas decided.

When another, brighter surge of light flared at the far end of the *craft* (as Falthwën might have described it), Nïmrïk stopped, growled, and puffed out the fur along his back as he bared his reddened teeth. Kalas squinted and stared in the direction the *egu* faced, but the brief spate of illumination died in a cataract of amber sparks; was mourned with a series of rapid beeps.

"You see something," Kalas accused with a hiss. He coughed when his lungs caught the taint of something foul and acrid.

"I think we've discovered the *'she'* the *ilrâigme-edhume* were raving about: before the lights went out, I saw something impossible! Something I believed departed from history since the day the Creator cracked the world. If they discovered her *here,* in a place with all these sights and sounds…"

"I don't know what you're talking about, but I'm starting to think Rive had the right idea! Whatever *she* is, they think she's as powerful as Ilnëshras—I'm guessing that's what they meant when they said *your* 'black god'?"

Nïmrïk turned toward Kalas with his eyes aglow. "Ilnëshras!" he spat. "He's…No, I made my own choices. No, lad, he's no 'god,' no matter how many souls he deludes…

"*She* is most likely *powerful,* but not after the manner of the *elume.* Not according to The Song. And I don't think this *gròma—* this dragon—is anything the eaters think she is. She's enormous, sure—takes up nearly half the room!—but most *gròmame* were peaceful—unless, of course, they felt threatened."

A deafening blare, emanating from unseen sources and surrounding them with invisible waves, pierced the relative silence of the chamber; a new wash of brilliant, yellow-white light stabbed at their eyes. Kalas blinked and looked away, but not fast enough: his world became a multicolored blur. Before he could ask Nïmrïk what was happening, the vault suffered another violent shake, the most destructive they'd experienced. Panes of material crashed all around them as lights fired at random and ear-splitting, artificial beeps grated in their minds. Another rumble, deep and resonant, pounded against the insides of their skulls. It took Kalas a moment to realize *she* was its source as her breath, hot and stinking of sulfur, rolled over them.

As if divining his thoughts, the *egu* snarled, "I'm sorry lad, but unless I miss my guess, I'd say *she* feels *threatened!*"

CHAPTER III

From Within the Cave-Dwellers' Cities

KALAS BLINKED AND WILLED HIS VISION TO RETURN AS he steadied himself against the shifting stones on the chamber's floor. Through the blear in his eyes, he saw the far side of the room shear away from its greater wall. He raised his arms to protect himself when—

No, that's not a wall! That's her!

The creature arched its sinuous neck and roared as something stopped her with a brusque twist. She belched a gout of green flame from her cavernous mouth: in its glinting light, Kalas caught the outline of what looked like a giant collar cast from the same bluish metal scattered throughout the mines.

They trapped *her?!*

The unbroken artifact panels pulsed again, triggering a wave of weak, colorless light. The creature swayed its vast head and tried to free a foreleg from beneath the stone. Her movements brought new debris cascading from the ceiling. Her energy nearly spent, she roared again—sighed, really—and let her horned head collapse onto the ground. Bony spirals at least as tall as a full-grown man protruded from her wearied crown. Beneath her horns, sharp-looking spikes webbed with translucent, membranous skin protected her ears. When the wave of dust settled, twin curls of thick, white smoke still wafted from her flaring nostrils.

"She's their prisoner!" Kalas exclaimed. "But the way they *worship* her?! I don't get it!"

"I can't answer that, lad, but we have to get out of here! All her thrashing about is bringing this place down!"

"We can't just leave her like that!" Kalas insisted as he took a tentative step toward the hulking shape. One huge, yellow-green eye, half-lidded, followed him as he walked toward her. She struggled as he approached, guttering a pained and pitiable whine when she realized she was too weak to move.

"It's all right, *Shâu,* I'm not here to hurt you!"

He was close enough to touch her coarse, leathery skin. He reached out, but before he made contact, Nïmrïk implored him, "Please, lad! Whatever you're doing, make it quick!"

As if to punctuate the *egudas* desire for haste, the whole room shifted as a sizable portion of the ceiling high above wrenched free: it flipped over and might have crushed the dragon—and Kalas— had one end not slammed into a notch-like section of a wall, where it held fast. One of the cylinders popped from its moorings, hit the ground at an angle, and rolled a few feet. Though distracted, Kalas thought it sounded almost hollow.

"There's a pin, I think, holding this collar on! If I could just…"

Kalas ran his hand along her hide: she tensed at first, and he could feel impossibly strong cords of muscle contract beneath her thick skin. She relaxed when he made no hostile maneuvers.

"Lady, if it's all right with you, I'm going to climb over your arm and try to remove that collar. I don't know if you can understand me, but I mean you no harm. I want to *undo* what those…those *others* did to you…"

The creature offered no reaction. Kalas waited a moment longer. Just in case.

"Here we go," he muttered.

He reached for one of the horny protrusions that lined her

foreleg and tried to haul himself up, tried to use another spur as a foothold. He struggled for a while before Nïmrïk trotted over, stood on his hind legs and pushed Kalas within reach.

"Thanks!"

"Just hurry!"

Lady, as Kalas dubbed her, recoiled at his presence. He held on tight, doing his best to maintain some semblance of external calm while his internal fears mounted. He spoke in soothing tones and petted her with soft, reassuring strokes. She settled, and he hummed a portion of the Song's melodies for her.

Please: relax! Sleep, if you're able! he suggested. In his peripheral vision, he saw her half-opened eye close fully, its slitted pupil disappear beneath immense folds of skin.

Seizing the opportunity, Kalas almost danced across her "arm" and onto her shoulder. When he reached her collar, he discovered it wasn't merely pinned as he'd suspected; rather, someone had driven spikes into the flesh around her neck. Over the Sevens, she'd managed to work a few of them loose; now, only three remained.

With his knife—the knife Zhalera had made him for his second Seven—he pried apart the pins securing the collar's two halves. He tried loosening the spikes, but his knife provided too little leverage. He sheathed it and worked the tip of Shosafin's sword beneath one. Rocking it back and forth, he succeeded in breaking it free, but it was too heavy for him to lift away by himself.

"Nïmrïk! I need your help!"

The *egu* leapt across Lady's knobbed skin. Together, they pulled at the spike until it fell to the ground. Kalas tried to ignore the bizarre sight of wolf-Nïmrïk's paws as he shook away their flesh to reveal human-like hands and fingers, which he used to work on the next spike, then the next.

When all three spikes had been undone, both halves of the collar fell away. They hit the ground with clanks that even the unsubtle cracks and groans all around them failed to drown out. The creature woke and swung its freed head from side to side. The motion launched Nïmrïk into space, but he managed to tuck and roll when he hit the ground. Kalas held on to one of her voluted horns until she calmed down.

"These wounds look infected, Lady! I don't know how long they've been this way! I don't—I'm going to try something. I don't know if it will hurt—it might, but please, trust me!"

Kalas closed his eyes and let the Song consume every shred of his being as he willed its power to manifest as health within the maimed creature's injuries. He continued to hold on as she roared again: from pain or confusion or something else, he couldn't tell. He sensed the infection lessening: when the Song had burned it all away, he spat away the sudden nasty taste in his mouth, opened his eyes, and studied the wounds within her neck.

The holes were still there, and the impression of her collar remained, but the reddish-white putrescence that had seeped from her punctures and lacerations had disappeared. She wrenched both forelegs free from the surrounding stone, flared the frill-like protuberances at the sides of her massive head, and snorted yellow-green fire as she stood. She took a few heavy steps into the remains of the cavern and flexed vast, fibrous wings that sprouted from the back of her shoulders. To Kalas, they appeared atrophied from disuse: he wondered if they ever could have supported her weight. She whipped around with surprising speed, given her size, and Kalas tumbled from her neck, hit the ground with a hard smack that produced a buzz of dazzling sparks inside his thoughts. He tried to pick himself up, to get clear of Lady as she tested her sudden freedom, but his eyes told him untruths about the floor's location. He tried again and managed to gain his feet for a moment. He would have fallen but Nïmrïk was there: he caught him and held him steady until the immediate wave of confusion passed.

"Good work, lad! Now, perhaps we can be on our way?"

"Yeah, I think you're right!" he agreed. "But, uh, what *is* our way? Looks like too much of this place caved in: the door is gone! And my head is *pounding!*"

Part of the cylinder that had separated from its anchor exploded with a sharp crack and a guttering hiss as it split in two. Rancid, brownish-green gas leached from its exposed interior as something inside pushed one half out of the way: when it stood and stared sightlessly at the room with pale white eyes, it sniffed the tainted air and wiped gobs of yellowed slime from its face.

"Did an eater just…*hatch* from that metal egg?!" Kalas exclaimed, coughing as its virulent fumes assaulted his senses.

Before Nïmrïk could answer, Lady thundered past them, crushed the pod's former occupant beneath her taloned foot, and vomited fire against the rock until it melted into slag. With claws as long as Kalas was tall, she slashed at the tunnel until it was large enough for her to squeeze through, liquefying portions where necessary with additional jets of flame. In a matter of minutes, she'd reached the larger central shaft. Kalas and Nïmrïk followed. She beat her useless wings against the air; when they failed to carry her aloft, she thrust a clawed foot into one side of the shaft, then the other, until she managed to pick her way to the top.

"Look out!" Kalas shouted: he thought he saw movement near the upper reaches of the chamber.

Zhalera! Rül! The úrukilmukritme!

"C'mon, Nïmrïk! Let's go!" Kalas shouted as he raced toward one set of spiral stairs.

Before they were a quarter of the way up, another shake—high above them, this time—rocked the mine, and even from their underground vantage point, they saw suns-light filtering through the roiling clouds of dust.

"I'd say she escaped," Nïmrïk observed.

"She breathed *fire!*" Kalas said, as though Nïmrïk hadn't witnessed the same things.

"She did. Guess I forgot to mention they could do that," he shrugged. "Anyway, let's get up there, make sure the others are all right."

2.

"Nïmrïk, I don't think—" Kalas began: before he could finish, he threw up what little remained within his stomach, then dry heaved a time or two before the *egu* turned around and assessed his condition. Even in his wolf-form his expression betrayed his concern.

"This place, that fall: not a good combination, lad. Here, climb onto my back and hold on: I'll carry you the rest of the way."

Kalas had climbed nearly one third the distance to the lesser chamber when the pain in his head erupted in a wave of vertigo. With a careful nod, he hoisted himself up and draped his arms around Nïmrïk's neck, where he found the cord Pava had tied there. He looped his hands through it and hoped it would hold.

"Don't you do it!" the *egu* insisted as Kalas' eyes fluttered closed. He opened them, surprised.

"How did you—?"

"Stay awake!" Nïmrïk interrupted. "We'll be at the surface in just a little while. We still need to get everyone back to the Gateway, and with the creature gone, there's no telling how the *ilrâigme* will react! Your friends will need you. They'll need your sword! So stay with me! You're sleepy, I know, but I need you—*they* need you to fight it!"

"They—what? Where are we?"

"Just hang on, lad! Stay awake!"

• • •

Despite Nïmrïk's warnings, Kalas realized he must have dozed off: when he opened his eyes, it was under the waning light of the setting suns. Someone had propped him up against a wall. He blinked and tried to remember why his head was so *mad* at him when he noticed the wolf standing guard. Sensing the boy's gaze, he stood and turned toward him, looked him over, and asked, "How's the head?"

"Hurts!" Kalas admitted as he squinted. "What happened? How'd we get…where are we?"

"What's the last thing you remember?"

"Someone's mother and father…Pava! Pava's parents—and her people! They disappeared…no, the eaters-of-men captured them, dragged them away…Why is it so hard to remember?!"

"Take your time, lad! We seem to be safe for now. Well, maybe not *safe,* but unseen. That'll have to do. When you're ready, what else do you remember?"

"We found them, right? Pava and her mother got—Deridzhas! We're in Deridzhas! The mine! You went down first, there was an explosion…*ilrâigme*…Did you get hurt?"

"I did," he admitted. "I'm…*better* now…"

"You are? Good! I…" Kalas frowned, wincing as the skin across his skull stretched taut. "There were lights, I think. Sounds. Something *huge! Gròma,* you called it—*her!* called *her!* A creature from a long, long time ago, right?"

Nïmrïk nodded.

"We were on our way up. Lady—the creature, she climbed out…Did she have wings? Anyway, I…then I woke up right here."

The wolf observed him for a moment, studied his movements and mannerisms and, with a sigh, suggested, "I think you'll be all right. Would be best for a healer to examine you, figure it out for sure. Rül…Zhalera—"

"They were still inside when Lady clawed her way to the top! Are they all right?! Pava's people!"

"I think so, lad! Easy now! Looked like 'Lady' missed the stairs, and I didn't see anything on our way up."

"How long have I been asleep?"

"Only a little while, I think. We escaped the mine about fifteen minutes ago."

"We need to keep moving," Kalas insisted as he righted himself. He laughed at Nïmrïk's worried expression.

"When your face looks like that, it's hard to think of you as a wolf-demon."

The *egu* paused. Frowned and looked at the ground.

"No, no! I meant—I'm sorry! I just…I told you before that it'd be hard to look at you without seeing Dzharëth, without remembering what he did to my father. But for a while now—today, especially!—I realized I don't think of you as just an *egu*. I think of you as…Nïmrïk."

"I'm grateful, lad," he said. Though his countenance remained clouded, it brightened ever so slightly.

"I mean it, Nïmrïk. Truly. Thank you for all your help—and not just today."

For a moment, Nïmrïk said nothing; then, after ensuring the boy was strong enough to move, he led him through the dead town toward Deridzhas' broken wall.

"Kalas! Nïmrïk!" Zhalera shouted when she saw them stagger into view. "When I saw that…that *shape* ripping up the walls, I thought the worst! What *was* that thing?!"

"*Gròma,*" Kalas answered with a nod toward the *egu*. "Maybe the last of them, according to Nïmrïk. I'd never heard of them before! Looked like the *ilrâigme*—someone, anyway—chained her to the wall. Nïmrïk and I freed her: the—"

"You *freed her?!*" thundered Rive as he felt his way toward the sound of Kalas' voice. "What malign spirit possessed you to do such a thing?!"

"With respect, she had spikes driven into her neck! Maybe the eaters were feeding *people* to her, but that's not her fault! She's probably been there for Sevens. Dozens of Sevens! And you were down there: you felt the *wrongness* of everything in that place, yes?"

Rive hung his head and sighed with a reluctant nod.

"As fearsome as they look, I've never known the dragons to prefer human flesh, but if that's the only thing they put in front of her, what choice would she have?" added Nïmrïk. "Tell me, how are your people faring?"

"As strange as it'll sound for a cave-dweller to admit, it's refreshing to be free of that noisome place! After a couple of days, I was sure it would be our tomb. The eaters have plagued us for longer than I can remember, but it's been quite some time since they ventured as far as the Áthradho in search of…well, *food.*"

"I wonder why the *ilrâigme* only recently started attacking your settlements," Zhalera mused. "I mean, from the look of things, they'd been…worshiping her for Sevens. Wouldn't she need to eat between then and now?"

"Our people have been disappearing for a while now. At first, just a few, but in recent years…? We never dared to imagine it could be eaters. Even now, the idea seems…unlikely."

"That eater, the one that hatched from that thing that fell from the ceiling! What was that?!" Kalas interjected as he remembered the strange scene.

"The one that *what?!*" Zhalera gasped.

"*Gròmame* could go for long years without feeding," Nïmrïk supplied. "It didn't seem like we'd encountered too many eaters: perhaps most had already been fed to her? Or perhaps they're conducting 'harvests' of their own in other lands?

"As for the *ilrâig* that hatched from that pod, I can't say. I don't *remember* ever seeing anything like that…though it's possible I *have* and I've just forgotten…"

"Well, wherever they are—wherever they *came from!*—she's free of them now!" said Kalas with triumph in his voice. He touched the back of his head, felt a thin film of sticky blood and winced. "I wonder where she'll go. I wonder, Nïmrïk: could she really be the last of her kind? Or are there others like her? Do you think she'll find them, if they exist?"

The *egu* laughed and shook his head. "You're asking questions I can't answer, lad! I thought they were *all* gone from the face of the earth…I hadn't considered any might have survived *under* the earth! Perhaps there are still dragons in the world. Perhaps we'll never know."

After shambling across the barrens for a slow half-mile, Gilfën rumbled into view. Nashmur reined him in, dismounted, and handed waterskins to the *úrukilmukritme,* who blessed him in the name of the Creator. Abarandal had ridden with him, and Kalas grinned at the sense of wonder writ within her wide eyes and gleaming white smile.

"Pava and her mother are fine!" the former commander promised as he answered a slew of fast-paced questions. "Dese is looking after them. Hwanzho, too. We haven't seen anything out of the ordinary: the *ilrâigme-edhume* must be otherwise engaged.

"Kalas, I didn't want to leave Abarandal alone. Not that I don't trust the cave-dwellers, but, well, after the Vault, it just seemed prudent to keep her close."

"No, I agree," Kalas nodded, winced, and squinted as hammer-like pressure assaulted him from within his skull. His eyelids suddenly felt heavy. "Let's get everyone back to camp, rest up for a while, then head back to the Gateway."

He turned toward Zhalera to ask her something, to say something, maybe, but before he could speak, he stumbled, grabbed her shoulder for support, and almost pulled her to the ground before she braced herself.

"Kalas?!"

"I...I think I need to lie down..." he admitted.

From her place atop the roan, Abarandal sang for a moment. She tried to hide her frustration with her inability to communicate with anyone save Kalas as she alighted from the saddle. She seemed to float toward the earth as she glided over to him, gently cupped his chin, and repeated her melody.

"No, I can walk: you ride," he insisted.

Abarandal furrowed her brow. Before she could sing again, Zhalera chuckled as she worked out her own interpretation.

"He can be pretty stubborn," she agreed as she motioned for Rül and Nashmur to help lift him into the saddle. Once Kalas had been secured, and after the cave-dwellers had emptied all the waterskins and eaten a little something, they hurried toward their small camp, where Pava and the others would be waiting for them.

3.

When Rive and the others approached the camp, Pava rushed toward her father, wrapped her arms around his neck, and would not let him go. Tsana gasped at the sight of him and placed a reassuring hand on his shoulder. After a while, Pava held him at arm's length, pressed her palm against his face, and with her fingers traced the still-raw gouges where his eyes had been.

"Your eyes! *Ude,* what did they do to you?!"

Rive reached up and clasped his fingers over hers, letting tears flow from his sightless sockets as he reveled in her and Tsana's

65

touch.

"Some kind of ceremony, I think. I didn't know they had ceremonies, but it appears the *ilrâigme-edhume* discovered…what did you call it, *egu*? 'Gròma'? A dragon—some huge beast from the world's past. The eaters have never had much to say, but I got the idea they revered this monstrosity as a deity of some kind. I must have said or done something they didn't like, because they dragged me in front of her, made me watch as they slaughtered and butchered Kisa and fed pieces of her to the creature. They plucked out my eyes so it would be the last thing I'd ever see.

"I begged them to spare Kisa, to…do whatever to me instead, but they'd already made their choice. The way that thing gobbled up her arms and legs, I thought she was just hungry for flesh and blood, but your friend Nïmrïk says she—that *gròmame* were originally plant-eaters. We'll have to hope he's right, since…Kalas, was it? Since Kalas unbound her!"

"*Ude*—Father, Kalas is the *Ilosar* who brought light to the Great Collector! If he released this creature, he must have had his reasons."

"The *Ilosar*, you say?!" Rive exclaimed and took a step back, tried to look around out of habit.

"I'm sorry I cracked your *Kathin Iltith*," said Kalas from Gilfën's back.

"No! It is we who should be sorry! We—"

"Pava's explained things, *Âu!* If someone with Marugan's abilities told me people were coming to eat *my* flesh, I'd defend myself, too!"

"Marugan?"

"Gozhira," Pava explained.

When Rive heard that name, he spat, scowled, and shook his head.

"Then I'll be bold enough to make a request, *Ilosar*. Did Pava tell you what's been happening to our *iltithme?* We've tried everything we know, but nothing helps. A few months ago, you did something; now, the *Kathin Iltith* and its nearest collectors shine brighter than they have in Sevens! The light within the rest of our cities, however, is getting dimmer..."

"The Ildurgul Taruún is...waking up, a friend told me not too long ago. It's because of that mountain that the atmosphere surrounding the Áthradho is interfering with your collectors. Pava thinks I'm the 'Shining One' your legends describe, but I'll tell you the truth: I don't know if that's me. That doesn't mean I won't try, *Ëmîu...*"

"That reminds me," said Nïmrïk as he padded over to Pava, sat down and pawed at her leg. "This ring tied around my neck belongs to you."

"Oh! Of course! Thank you!"

Even seated, wolf-Nïmrïk's head was about even with Pava's. She stooped, undid her knots, and retrieved her prize. With a smile, she reached behind one of his ears, gave it a scratch, and kissed his fuzzy cheek before she turned toward her parents.

"Thank you for protecting my mother," she said.

Nïmrïk blinked, his golden eyes moist in a peculiarly human way.

"This ring!" she said as she held it up for Tsana to see before the first sun completed its descent beneath the horizon. "An *eru* gave it to me! It's the ring from our history! The ring another *eru* wore when he first made our collectors!"

"It certainly looks like it," Tsana agreed as Pava handed it to her. "Tell me, *shadathahal,* how do we *use* this ring? What instructions did this *eru* give you?"

Pava's cheeks flared beneath the sun's final rays. She looked at Kalas and the others and, in a low voice, said "He's...he's *gone* now. He didn't have time to explain what it does, how someone like me might use it. He just said it holds *magic* from each member of something called the *Great Swath*—a bunch of *erume* who…I don't know, exactly, but from what we saw, I think they've been watching over the world for some time now."

"From the time the world was cracked," added Nïmrïk.

"'The world…was *cracked*'?" Tsana said with a confused look as she handed the ring back to Pava.

"It's part of the same prophecy that foretells the advent of the *Ilosar!* We learned a little of it while I was away. The *erume* said there was more—enough to fill a book!"

"What else does this prophecy say?" said Rive, his interest piqued.

"If the *erume* are right, I've got a big choice coming up," said Kalas, his eyes somewhat glassy. Too bad none of them told me what it was!"

When you're confronted with a choice…I know you'll make the right one!

"I'm sorry, I'm just…tired all of a sudden…"

"Here, let me help you," offered Nashmur as Kalas almost tumbled from the saddle. When his feet were on the ground, Zhalera looped one of his arms over her shoulders and ushered him toward one of the tents Hwanzho and Dese had set up. The two *úruk-ilmukritme* had started several small fires as well. The hot air rolling off their flames soothed away some of the ache attacking the back of his skull. Once she had him situated, Zhalera sat down beside him: with a wet cloth, she wiped away some of the grime from his forehead.

"Sleep, Kalas. I'll be right here when you awake."

"Zhalera, what am I doing?" he mumbled. "It's one thing to put on a brave face when I'm surrounded by you and Rül and the others, but here, in the midst of all these cave-dwellers who think I'm someone I'm not…I don't know what to *do*. I don't know who

I'm supposed to *be*. Falthwën talked to me—to us, really, about *privilege;* Nïmrïk said something about the Creator's *purpose* for us…He said *things hold together* when *ilhadzhalasme* exercise their privilege in accordance with the Creator's will. The last few days… longer, maybe…I just feel like I'm *falling apart*…"

Zhalera lay down beside him as he stared at the animal hide ceiling. She propped herself up on one elbow, tucked that lemony-silver shock of hair behind her ear, then traced lazy circles across his chest as it rose and fell with its slow, measured rhythm.

"Maybe Pava's right," she countered after a while. "Maybe you *are* their *Ilosar.* And maybe she's wrong. Maybe you aren't. I don't know who you'll become, Kalas, but can anyone know the precise line of his life with absolute certainty? Even *erume* and *egume* admit they don't know the mind of the Creator! I *do* know who you are *today,* and I'll be honest with you: I don't care whether you're the dwellers' 'Shining One' or not. No, I don't mean that in a callous way: I just mean that I think *you* will have to decide who you are— *what* you are.

"This is also my way of apologizing. On our way out here—to Ïsriba, I mean—I said maybe swords weren't your thing, that maybe you should stick with The Song. I still believe you should learn as much as you can about The Song—if that's not why Abarandal's with us now, then why else?!—but I was wrong about you and swords. I was…The way you went on and on about that silly little knife I made for you! I'm afraid anything else I make won't be as good. I'm afraid it won't measure up to the standard raised by my ancestors…and exceeded by my father."

"You're wrong, Âsrufin," Kalas whispered before sleep took him. "You're right about a lot of things—took me long enough to realize it! But this? You couldn't be more mistaken about this! Maybe you—no, you *do* know me. Well, I know *you,* too. And I…I…"

Whatever else Kalas might have said dissolved into insensate monosyllables as he ceased struggling against the weight in his eyes and allowed them to close.

"Sleep, *ilmazhasahal*," Zhalera whispered. She leaned over, placed her mouth atop his forehead and let her kiss linger. "Sleep."

4.

Kalas woke as his head bobbed up and down on something soft. He opened his eyes and stared up into Zhalera's as she cradled him in her arms.

"*Lushà vam*, Kalas!" she beamed as she smoothed away his hair. "Sleep well?"

"Yeah, I—where are we? How long have I been asleep?"

"We're still a couple days out from the Gateway. After you fell asleep at the camp, you pretty much stayed that way until now! I was worried. A little. How are you feeling?"

He sat up, removed his head from the folded blanket atop her lap and reached toward his injury. Nowhere near as painful as he remembered, it still felt tender, and he winced. They were in the coach, pressed in by a handful of people rescued from the mines.

"Better," he assured her. Abarandal, across from them, posed a similar question through her music. "When that creature—Lady— threw me, I guess I hit pretty hard. By the time we reach the Áthradho, I think I'll be fine. Assuming we're done running into *gròmame* and *ilrâigme-edhume*, that is!"

The cave-dwellers surrounding him said nothing, simply considered him with what appeared to be a mix of awe and uncertainty. Not sure what to say, but feeling like he should at least say *something*, he added, "Uh, how are all of you doing? I'm sorry the eaters-of-men…your friend, Kisa, and the others, and…You're safe now, yeah? Should be home in a couple days. Uh, Zhalera, how are Rive and Tsana?"

"Nashmur let Rive ride Gilfën: Tsana's riding Dalafar—Dese agreed to give up 'his' mount easily enough, but I could tell he wasn't thrilled with having to walk. Nïmrïk helped 'convince' him! Wouldn't surprise me if he's planning a little mischief—sorry, I mean *skylarking*—on Dese's behalf! On my right is Tshise; next to Abarandal are Dara, on the right, and Rofe."

"*Ilosar. Ágazhëthu,*" one of the cave-dwellers—Tshise—whispered. "Thank you for bringing light back to the Gateway!"

"Please, save your thanks," he muttered, embarrassed. "I haven't done anything yet except break your Great Collector…"

"It's true, the *Kathin Iltith* broke when you…disappeared, but when our people had repaired it, the light it reflected underground was brighter than it's been in Sevens!" she explained.

"It was?"

She nodded. So did the others.

"Rive said so," Zhalera affirmed. "Don't you remember?"

"I…well, you're welcome," he offered without much conviction.

"In the mine, the same thing happened," Zhalera nodded. "Remember Rül said something about the air getting better? Must've been the same effect."

"Yeah…maybe," Kalas shrugged.

Hours passed, stretching into evening and into morning. Kalas' head continued to improve: so did the condition of the *úruk-ilmukritme,* absent Deridzhas' life-sapping atmosphere. The cave-dwellers devoured most of the provisions Yëlisha had packed: Rive promised to resupply their stores upon reaching the Áthradho. As their water supply dwindled, they made use of solar stills to collect whatever condensate they could coax from the selfish air.

Late that afternoon, they reached the imposing slabs of the upper gate. Open when Kalas and the others had first seen them, now they were meshed together, blocking the party's entry into the

Áthradholarme. Rül stopped the coach and Kalas exited as Nashmur, Gilfën's reins in hand, bade the roan stop. Nïmrïk, Dalafar's reins between his teeth, instructed his horse to do the same.

"Better late than never!" Pava smirked. Like fluid, she seemed to flow from the coach's box seat toward the sands with a combination of acrobatic and gymnastic grace as she approached her father.

"Gate's closed, *Ude,*" she informed him. "Like it *should have been* before Kode died!"

The ruler of the cave-dwellers frowned and turned his head toward the sound of Pava's voice. "Such spitefulness is unbecoming, *shadathahal.* Dese has admitted his mistake. Had I been here at the time, I might have hesitated, too."

"Maybe," Pava gritted in a small voice.

"Where is everyone?" Kalas asked. "I mean, how do we get inside? That gate looks like it's impossible to move!"

"That's the idea!" Rive smiled. "Here, watch! *Úrukilmukritme! Zhi Áthradho di ëmîuyëhazh kafem!*"

The last reverberations of his bellowed command dissolved into the subtle winds whipping at the impassable stone construct.

Nothing happened.

Kalas almost asked Pava's father if he'd misunderstood something, but before he could open his mouth the blinded chief whispered, "Just watch!"

Less than a minute later, a shock like a thunderclap rattled both walls of the cliff as something within gave way. Soon, each half of the gate began its slow recession into "pockets" hewn from the surrounding rock.

"Why leave the gates open at all?" Kalas asked as he watched them move. He realized they'd be waiting outside for quite some time before the gateway opened wide enough to admit them.

"Not too many people pass through the Áthradho," Rive explained. "Sometimes months come and go without us seeing a soul!

When someone does pass through, we usually stay out of the way. Usually. Again, I'm sorry for what our people did when—"

"Like I told you, I understand! Pava explained things to us! Please, accept our forgiveness!"

"Right, of course. Thank you! Anyway, it's simpler for us to allow travelers to spend as little time as necessary within the Gateway. As rare as such sights might be, imagine the hassle of having to open and close the gate every time?! Long ago, our ancestors made an agreement with Ïsriba's king. Part of that was allowing him to use this canyon as part of his Highway. We're a private people: only rarely do we permit *ilròumbume*—outsiders—access to our cities. But you're not outsiders! Not anymore! Not after what you've done for us!"

"Sir, please!" said Kalas as a feeling of unworthiness gnawed at him. Pava's father laughed. Tsana, however, offered him a sympathetic smile.

After almost half an hour, the gate opened wide enough for Rül to drive the coach through it and into the Áthradho. Beneath them, Kalas noticed gleaming lengths of polished steel that hadn't been there before—or maybe they'd always been there, simply covered by the sand. As they crossed the threshold, he caught subtle shifts in the lengthening shadows along the cliffs above.

Not unlike the first time we traveled through this place...

The gates, at least ten feet thick through the middle, reversed direction once everyone was through.

"How does the gate work?" he asked.

"You'll understand if we keep at least a few of our secrets, *hish?*" Rive smiled.

"Nashmur, if you'll steer Gilfën this way?" said Tsana from behind her husband. She gestured toward a small outcropping almost invisible against the layers of sand- and mudstones folded into the canyon's walls. It proved too narrow for the coach to pass through, so Pava told Rül where he could leave it once everyone had disembarked. No more than ten or fifteen minutes later, the pair returned, both astride Runner's naked back with Rül holding both horses' reins.

"We don't have horses in the Áthradho, but I think these four will fit through our corridors," Pava said, including Dalafar and Gilfën.

"Now then," said Rive as he turned toward Tsana. "Let's introduce these *ilròumbume* to the wonders beneath the Gateway!"

Tsana nodded, slipped away from the group, and disappeared behind a wall of rock. After a moment—and a loud click, the cliff face under the overhang sank into the ground with almost no noise. Nothing but a faint whirring sound and a whispered hum within the earth gave any indication that something was subtly *rearranging* a network of camouflaged elements embedded in the rock. In seconds, when all the moving pieces were in place, an opening at least a few hands taller than Runner (the largest of the four horses) appeared, revealing a stepped slope stretching into wavy, orange-red luminescence.

"How did—? No, never mind. Secrets, right?" marveled Kalas. Rive laughed.

"Secrets indeed! Come now, all of you! And welcome!"

"Uh, Pava?" Rül ventured. "Are *all* your passageways like this?"

"No, most aren't quite this big, but—"

"That's what I was afraid of. I'm not sure this is the best place for the horses. They might fit through *here,* but the slope is pretty steep, and it looks slick. I don't know about Yëlisha's boys, but Runner and Dancer have never been confined like this. I don't know how they'll react. It might be better if I find someplace out here for them. On the way up, near the bottom of the Highway here, we spent the day in a shallow cave. I could take them there, stay with them…"

Pava looked wounded. She placed a hand on his arm and asked,

"You don't want to see my city?"

"Of course I do! I just…I can't bring the horses down there, and I'm not comfortable leaving them alone. They're Mother's horses. And Yëlisha's. Not mine, but in my care."

"Uh, *I'll* stay with them. And your coach. Rodo here can help them get acquainted with things," offered Hwanzho as he patted his donkey's cheek.

"You'd be willing to do that?"

"Yes! I mean, of course! Like most of us, I'm embarrassed by how we treated you, and I, uh, I'd like to make up for it somehow. I see the way the *shëmiuín* looks at you! And, uh, you really would be missing out! I'd be happy to tend to your horses!"

"Ágazhëthu! Thank you!" said Rül as a bright smile broke across his previously sullen face.

"I…I'll go with Hwanzho," said Dese as he stared at the ground. "If that's all right, I mean. Least I can do…"

"No! Uh, I mean: you will? Dese, that's, uh, that's really not necessary…"

"Yes, it is…"

"I can handle things! Stay with Pava and—"

"The faster both of us take care of things, the faster we can get back here."

"Well…all right. Fine. C'mon, then," sighed Hwanzho as he turned away from Dese's sagging shoulders.

Rül grinned at Pava, then walked with the *úrukilmukritme* and the horses as he described their personalities. When they'd finished their conversation, Rül handed Hwanzho the leads and returned to the others. Pava's smile was as wide as his as she grabbed his hand and led him into the descending tunnel. The others followed. As the "door" closed behind them, Kalas found it hard to breathe in the moments before his eyes adjusted to the weak light.

"Are you all right?" Zhalera whispered as she squeezed his hand.

"I…yeah, I will be. I guess after being down in that mine, these closed-in spaces…I'll get over it. I think. I hope!"

"It opens up in just a little bit. You'll see!" Pava promised.

5.

The path underground wasn't as long as Kalas had expected. Once everyone was inside, Tshise worked a hidden lever and closed the door. After a couple of twists not unlike the spirals beneath Deridzhas, the cave-dwellers ushered everyone into a small but pleasant room, furnished with nothing more than a few low benches chiseled from its walls and an alcove hewn from another. Each seat had a plush-looking, overstuffed cushion that seemed just right in the space's warm (but not too warm) atmosphere. Occasional glimmers from a bed of embers burning within a shallow fireplace flickered within the facets of a series of crystals mounted along the walls. In addition to the inconstant firelight, suns-light glowed from within each gem, powered by the fading rays of the Premier Sun. At the opposite end of the chamber, another, larger door opened into another tunnel. Strings thick with beads of stone, bone, and wood obscured whatever lay beyond.

"This is nice!" said Rül, with more enthusiasm than necessary. Pava giggled. "No, it is!" he insisted.

"No, I'm laughing because this is just a guard post! We haven't reached the actual cities yet! Or the *gardens!* This place used to be for storage, I'm told, but that was a long time ago. Here, look at this!"

Pava directed Rül toward a nondescript portion of the wall. Kalas followed with his eyes, but all he saw were rocks. At first. Looking closer, he realized lines he'd initially considered cleavage fractures were in fact the borders of a large panel. With a touch, the young girl pushed inward until something within the wall clicked.

The panel ascended to reveal a highly polished surface reflecting the Highway outside and above them. Rül and the other "outsiders" observed politely for a moment until they saw Hwanzho in its face, glancing over his shoulder with every other step as he picked his way up the road.

"What is that? How is that possible?" Kalas exclaimed. "Magic, right? Has to be! How did you capture *seranà* within the rock like this?!"

Behind him, Dara laughed. So did most other cave-dwellers. With a smile, she explained, "Not magic, friend! *Mirrors!* The same way we reflect light from the *iltithme*. Light carries pictures—we need it to see anything: that's why we can't see in perfect darkness. With the right equipment, we can move these pictures around, through channels spanning the whole Áthradho, and display them where we like!"

"We have *barafi-isadme* back home," Zhalera added, "but those are mostly polished steel. I've never seen mirrors made to work like this!"

"Not *looking*-glasses: *seeing*-glasses!" Pava explained.

"It's amazing!" Rül marveled.

"If you think *this* is amazing, just wait!" she grinned. She pressed the lower edge of the panel, releasing a catch of some kind, and it slid back into place. "The end of the next tunnel isn't that far from here! C'mon!"

Despite both suns having descended below the horizon, the vast cavern into which Pava led the others seemed about as bright as late afternoon or maybe early twilight. Vast crystalline plates suspended from the ceiling or mounted at various points along the walls glowed with residual daylight, squeezing every last photon from the rays of the receding suns. Half-silvered mirrors split incoming beams into multiple streams and directed them wherever the cave-dwellers intended.

Thick limestone columns in an irregular array supported the unimaginable weight of the world above the Gateway. Rippling with miniature formations, Kalas thought some of the more delicate specimens resembled cascading waterfalls—like those within the Rumilswàr at the bottom of the Empty Sea, or maybe the one he'd spied beneath the Hidden River—frozen in time and space. Sparse droplets of groundwater collected along the rounded points of other stalactites and dripped into collection systems that piped it somewhere still further underground.

The cave-dwellers had built numerous avenues, each lined with an eclectic mix of structures and open spaces. As Pava had described, many buildings seemed stacked on top of one another, each level connected to those above and below by cantilevered stairs constructed from dressed stone slabs. Though the light captured and magnified by the *iltithme* provided enough illumination to see, most buildings had fires flickering within them. Traveling deeper into the city, their hosts led them through park-like spaces filled with healthy-looking plants and an impressive collection of flowers.

"Are these your gardens?" Rül asked, awed, as they passed.

"Not exactly! Our actual gardens take up rooms nearly as large as this entire district! They're more like subterranean forests in some respects, with a blend of young and mature trees scattered among other, smaller species," said Tsana with a grin.

She's proud of this place. Just like her daughter, Kalas thought. *And why wouldn't she be? This place is amazing!*

"Do the *iltithme* put light beneath these plants?" he said as he pointed to a pale, blue-green glow seeping from underneath some leaves nearly as tall as himself.

"Oh, no: that's bioluminescence from a few different strains of fungi. If you look closely, you'll see what looks like several mushrooms clustered around one another. The brightest of these 'lights' are all part of the same parent mass far below us. Up here, while pleasing to the eye, they're not really bright enough for more than gauging your steps: down there, it's much brighter."

"So the light…comes from these 'mushrooms'?"

"Indeed!"

Amazing!

"I don't think I've ever seen anything like it!" Zhalera admitted.

"It's beautiful!" gushed Rül.

They passed what seemed to be a sculpture formed from growths of rough cut gems, each easily the size of a full-grown man. Faceted in some places, untouched in others, the multicolored jewels splayed weak refractions along the cavern floor. Kalas noticed a series of marks etched around the conglomeration's circumference: some periodic, some less obviously so.

"What do you think that is?" he asked Zhalera.

"A timekeeping device," answered Rofe. "Only works when the suns are above the sky: in a few minutes, it won't look like anything but a pile of shiny rocks."

"A pile of shiny rocks?!" said Nashmur as he walked its perimeter. "You could sell just one of these pieces in Ïsriba for almost any price you'd care to name!"

"We used to. Long ago," interrupted Tsana with annoyance in her voice. "*Ilròumbume* always…complicate things," she snarled. "Simpler to keep to ourselves as much as possible."

Nashmur nodded and uttered something apologetic as he resumed his place in line. As they passed the curious item, Kalas paused and listened for a few seconds.

Chimes? he wondered. *Is that what Pava hears? Is that—*

"Kalas, can I borrow your knife?" Pava asked, interrupting his thoughts as she pulled a few torches from a small crate that smelled of naphtha.

"Hmm? Yeah, of course," he said as he handed it to her.

With a few well-struck blows, she showered her torches with sparks until they ignited with a puff of displaced air. She handed out the torches before returning Kalas' knife.

"Any chance I could get you to make me one of these?" she wondered with an expectant grin in Zhalera's direction. The apprentice blacksmith offered her a noncommittal shrug.

"I, uh…maybe someday," she deflected.

6.

Pava, Tsana, and the other *úrukilmukritme* led Kalas and company through their city, each structure more elaborate, more ornate than the last, until they reached a façade boasting such opulence it bordered on gaudy. Mosaics spanned its exterior from top to bottom. Tiles cast or cut from a multitude of different materials—including highly polished gems, sparkling crystal, and dyed bone—had been arranged in "stories," Kalas guessed, each distinct yet still integrated into an overarching tale: none truly *ended* so much as *transitioned* to the next. One of the larger mosaics featured a figure wreathed in light and projecting beams of the same toward the *Kathin Iltith*—the Great Collector: from shapes arrayed around this collector, light split into multiple streams and fed lesser collectors. Surrounding all of this was a patchwork of darker tiles interrupted here and there with pairs of greenish-yellow stones. As he considered the work as a whole, Kalas couldn't ignore a sense of *patient malice* stemming from the darkness. He shivered despite the fact that the temperature within the dwellers' city had remained constant and comfortable.

"What's wrong?" Zhalera whispered.

"This mosaic," Kalas admitted. "I see their *Ilosar*, I think, but I also see…something else…*waiting* for him. It's a little unnerving!"

"This…is *home!*" said Pava with a sweeping gesture. Bas-reliefs carved above high openings punctuated the mosaics. Steady light shone through each glassless window. "C'mon inside!" she insisted as Tsana opened an old wooden door and beckoned everyone to follow. She led them through a small room lined with slits at varying heights—

I'll bet a tëvët could fit through those ports, Kalas assumed.

—and into a larger anteroom furnished with padded stone benches and lit with rows of what he believed to be torches at first. Closer inspection revealed several shallow vessels sporting thick, fibrous wicks; each vessel had a narrow pipe running from one to the next. He traced the network with his eyes, but the last conduit disappeared within a wall.

"*Ëmîu!* Your eyes!" someone gasped as they exited the anteroom into a much larger, more formal space. A figure—a servant, perhaps an elderly relative, Kalas guessed—stepped into view. "Rive, what happened?!"

"Eaters!" he said as she took his arm from Tsana and led him toward a high-backed chair at the far end of the room. She maneuvered him around an immense stone table and helped him sit as he outlined his recent adventures.

"But she's safe!" he beamed, scanning the room for his daughter. "I'm here, *Ude!*"

He swiveled toward the sound of her voice and nodded. Smiled.

"And," Pava continued, "we've returned with the *Ilosar!*"

"Oh?" said the woman, her skepticism bare.

"Yes! Not like that other *pretender!* Kalas is the Shining One who made the Great Collector shine!"

"Oh!" said the woman, her tone improved.

"Hi, *Shâu…?*"

"Sina! Call me Sina!" she insisted with a low bow. "I've heard— by now, *everyone* has heard—how you brought light back to our cities! Thank you!"

"I…yeah," Kalas mumbled. "You're welcome."

"What will you do next? The Great Collector shines more brightly than it has in Sevens! Brighter than it's been since I was a child! These last few weeks have been the best in a long time!"

"They have?" Kalas said, puzzled.

"Hey, remember when you…did that thing to Nïmrïk? Remember how the air got better? What if whatever you did the last time we were here did something like that?" suggested Rül.

"Yeah!" agreed Zhalera. "I told you! Falthwën said stuff from the Ildurgul Taruún was scattering light before it reached the collectors, right? If you somehow cleared the air…?"

"I don't know," Kalas countered. "The Áthradho is leagues away from the Death-bringing Mountain. Anything I might have done here wouldn't have done anything that far north…Would it? No, unlikely."

"Suns-light doesn't come from out of the Ilvurkanzhime!" Zhalera reminded him. "If you 'fixed' the air around—and *above*—the Gateway, that would have probably been enough!"

"Oh? Maybe. That makes sense, I guess," he allowed.

"Sina, my dear: please prepare rooms for the *ilròumbume;* Pava: show them where they can get cleaned up while I—no, not I…"

Tsana rubbed Rive's sagging shoulders as the consequence of his infirmity exerted itself. "We'll work through this," she promised. "Pava: return here in an hour. Dara, Tshise, Rofe: I'll summon someone to escort you to your homes. I'm sure your families are desperate to know you're safe!"

She smiled. For a moment. Then she remembered the casualties inflicted by the *ilrâigme.* "And I'll need to share some unwanted news with other families…"

"No, Tsana," Rive insisted: "I'll need your arm, but I want them to hear such news from me. As their *ëmîu,* I am responsible: it *must* come from me."

Neither Dara, Tshise, nor Rofe would accept an escort: "I know where I live!" each insisted. "Be well," they said as they departed for their homes. Rive, guided by his bride, followed after them into torchlit darkness on his unhappy errand.

When Pava's parents returned, Kalas and the others had finished cleaning up. Pava had them seated around a smaller stone table within a smaller room with heaping plates in front of them. Too hungry to ask about the strange shapes and colors of their meal, each dug in.

"Spicy!" noted Rül between mouthfuls.

"Is it too hot?" Pava asked. "I know it's hotter than what you're used to…"

"No! It's good!" he insisted as he stuffed another forkful into his mouth and ignored the tears welling in his eyes.

"I'm glad you like it!" she smiled. "The seasoning helps tame some of the hyrax' gamey flavor."

"Well, whatever you put in here, it's tasty!"

As Tsana and Rive entered the dining area, everyone fell silent. Rive's eyeless face expressed his people's shared sorrow despite his disfigurement. Tsana's looked equally downcast. Pava helped her father to his seat and placed a fork in his hand. His bride sat beside him.

"I'm sorry, Father," Pava began. "If I hadn't been above the Collector when…Maybe none of this would have happened. Maybe you'd still have your eyes. And maybe Kisa and the others—"

"Daughter-of-mine, enough!" Rive insisted. He ran a shaking hand across his wearied brow. "Enough. We've all made mistakes. We'd all stopped believing we'd ever *really* have to deal with the *ilrâigme-edhume* again! If blame must fall on someone, let it fall on me: as the prince of our people, I should have kept us prepared… And I should have been more discerning when it came to Gozhira.

We—”

“Who?” Kalas interrupted.

“Marugan,” Pava explained. “That’s what he called himself when he pretended to be an *eru*.”

“We should have recognized him for what he was. For what he *wasn’t*…We didn’t, and while I’d gladly pay with my sight for my failures, it crushes me to know that others have paid a much dearer price for their elders’ mistakes. For *my* mistakes.”

Without eyes, Rive seemed to focus on some distant, indiscernible point for a long moment before he concluded with a sigh: “Ah, *shadathahal*, it is good to have you back!”

“I…yeah, about that…”

“Oh?”

“I thought…I believe I can help the *Ilosar*. Part of our prophecy speaks of someone *bringing light*, but I think we’ve been considering things from too narrow a perspective.”

“What are you saying, child?” said Tsana as she tensed.

“When I was with the *Kel Erume*—the Seven Stars, they said there’s another prophecy that was only for the *erume*. They didn’t explain it, but…but I think Kalas-Ilosar is destined to bring the light to more than just us cave-dwellers!”

“You—? Do other peoples have *iltithme?*”

“No! Well, I don’t know, but that’s not what I mean! I can’t explain it. Not really. I just…I’ve told you about the sounds—the *music*—I hear inside the crystals sometimes. While I was away, I learned there’s something called *The Song*. I—Kalas can hear it all the time, but all of us within the Vault heard it, too, when the *erume* were drawing Abarandal. Maybe I’m wrong, but I think what I hear through the crystals is part of The Song, and I…I *have* to go with him. With all of them.”

She glanced at Rül when she finished speaking, and so did the others, just in time to catch the rising glow atop his cheeks.

Everyone at the table ceased to move, waiting for Rive's response. Tsana, too, regarded her husband with cool consideration. This time, no one could read his expression as he contemplated things in motionless silence.

"Then you must go," he sighed at last, and the tension in the room seemed to migrate from everyone else and condense within Tsana's eyes. Kalas winced as they slammed shut and her face tightened with a sharp frown.

"What right do I have to demand that *my* child remain within the safety of the Áthradho when I've just returned from consoling those who've lost *their* children at my behest?! I'll own having been a fool, but I will not be a hypocrite! Go, beloved daughter, and return to us—to your people—when your task is complete."

"Thank you, *Ude!* Thank you! I will!"

She knelt and embraced her father, who wrapped his arms around her slight frame and squeezed. Tsana, beside them, had been looking down. She glanced up, briefly, and in her eyes Kalas glimpsed red tendrils stretching from their corners toward her darkening irises before she caught his stare and looked away.

What did Dese call it? The 'ancient bloodlust'? What did Tsana herself say? 'Yash àódru'? 'Red mist'?

He glanced at Zhalera, who hadn't seemed to notice. At Abarandal, Nashmur, and Rül. Only Nïmrïk had taken note: with his ears tucked flat against his skull, he shook his wolfish head and looked away.

After several deep breaths, Pava's mother collected herself and wiped a spate of tears from her eyes, her sclera white and her irises the same subtle violet as her daughter's. She said nothing as she placed a trembling hand on Pava's shoulder. After a moment, she opened her mouth, but before any words came out, Sina burst into the room.

"*Ëmîu! Shëmîume!* Dese and Hwanzho are gone!"

"Gone? I thought they were tending Master Rül's horses?"

"They were! They were supposed to be! I thought I'd take them something to eat, thank them for helping return our prince and princesses, but when I arrived at the cave, they weren't there! And… there was *blood* all over the sand! A *lot* of blood!"

Chapter IV

To Lohwàlar, Resurrected

"Not Hwanzho's blood: we saw him through your mirror-things," said Nashmur, picturing recent events in his mind: "He was headed *up* through the Gateway—*east*, not west, where the horses were resting, and he didn't seem to be hurt..."

"He was alone, too," remembered Zhalera. "Maybe something happened to Dese? Maybe Hwanzho was looking for help?"

"Master Kalas, do you think—is there any chance the *eaters* might have followed you through the gate?" Sina suggested, her fair features surrendering what little color they possessed.

"I don't know, I was—"

"No, we would have known it. The horses would have—*The horses!*" said Rül with fear in his voice. "Were—are they...?"

"The horses were fine!" Sina assured him. "Looked that way, at least! Your coach, however: it looked like someone was looking for something!"

"I didn't smell anything," added Nïmrïk. *"Ilrâigme* have a distinct...fragrance."

"We saw him headed east hours ago. If he *was* looking for help, He would have found it by now," Nashmur posited. "I know the *Áthradholarme* are vast, but still..."

"His house was one of Gozhira's most ardent supporters," admitted Rive. "Hwanzho himself was always a quiet boy. A quiet man, too. Kalas, when you *shined* beneath the Great Collector, most *úrukilmukritme* recognized you for who—for *what* you are: we realized we'd been too quick to place our faith in this pretender. As Pava has told you, we realized our folly too late: not everyone, however, abandoned the hope they'd placed in Gozhira. Marugan, as you know him. Normally, we dwellers prefer to keep our internecine complexities to ourselves; however, I think it's important you understand a little of our recent history.

"House Murase only recently emerged as the governing entity beneath the Gateway, starting with my great-grandfather. I won't bore you with the details, but Hwanzho's ancestors governed us for Sevens, and House Kado had nothing but contempt for ours. Sometime during my father's tenure, House Kado got...quieter. I believed it was because they'd accepted the people's will at last; now, I wonder if perhaps they continued to harbor their old hatreds, only in silence."

"But he's always been so trustworthy!" Pava exclaimed. "He was always like an older cousin to me! And when we came to look for you, forgive me for saying so, but I had to shame Dese into coming: Hwanzho volunteered!"

"Lass, maybe it's not my place," began Nïmrïk, "but Hwanzho wouldn't be the first to play a long game. I've...seen such things before. Confidence schemes lasting hundreds of Sevens. If his house has aligned itself with Marugan, it's not outside the realm of possibility they'd struck some kind of bargain with him."

"Why not kill us above the Gateway?" said Tsana. "He had Pava and me all to himself for nearly a day!"

"Dese was there, too," Pava interjected.

"I'm only speculating. I'd like to be wrong, but I've been around for a long, long time. You're right: he could have easily claimed *ilrâigme-edhume* slaughtered the three of you before the rest of us returned, though he wouldn't have had much time. Maybe he thought we'd return before he'd be able to make it look good? Maybe he thought—correctly, I'd wager—that you'd put up a fight and possibly overpower him? Especially if you're prone to episodes of the red mist, Madam Tsana."

"You—?"

"Dese said as much, and I watched your eyes when your daughter spoke her intentions to go with us rather than remain here. No, I'm in no position to judge! You know what I am. *Why* I am. *Your* curse is undeserved…"

Abarandal, who'd remained silent until now, whispered a tune to Kalas, who nodded.

"You're probably right," he agreed. "It *does* look like Hwanzho attacked Dese, ransacked our things—for what, I don't know— then…what? Just…*disappeared?* He was headed east, toward the Wastes, right? What could be waiting for him outside the Áthradho?"

"If you don't mind, uh, *Ëmîu* Rive, I'd like to check on the horses. Our coach. Make sure they're all right," stammered Rül as he stood.

"I'll come with you!" said Pava as she retrieved her *tëvët*.

"So will I," growled Nïmrïk.

"Yes, of course," he nodded.

The trio grabbed a couple of torches and disappeared. The room remained silent for a while until Rive, lips pursed, wondered aloud: "I hadn't considered that the prophesied *Shining One* should 'bring light' to those *beyond* the Gateway as well…"

"You and me both," mumbled Kalas.

"Tell me, young man: your friend Rül. Does he have designs on my daughter?"

It took Kalas a moment to come up with a response.

"Uh, I mean, they get along really well," he suggested, unsure of how to answer the cave-dweller's question. "I think…I mean, they saved each other's life at least a few times…"

Zhalera! Help me out here!

"They've become close," she admitted as she risked a glance at Kalas.

"Yes: even without eyes, I gathered as much," he nodded.

"Pava knows full well her responsibilities," said Tsana, and even Nashmur squirmed at the uncomfortable rigidity in her tone.

"I followed a set of hurried-looking footprints headed for the upper gate," Nïmrïk began when he and the others returned. "That's where they disappeared, though the gate itself was covered with Hwanzho's scent. He must have escaped by scaling the walls."

Still manifesting his lupine *otherform*, Nïmrïk mumbled something to Pava, who led him toward a door and pointed down a hallway. He nodded and padded out of the room.

"I'll bet he was on his way to see Marugan!" Rül suggested. "Sina, you were right about the horses: looks like he might have been afraid of them, too! But Kalas, he *did* take something: Falthwën's staff! What if he uses it to do magic against us?!"

"It doesn't work that way," Nïmrïk corrected him as he reentered the chamber in his human form. Both Tsana and Sina gasped, alarmed at the intruder's presence, until Pava explained things.

"It's been…well, hundreds of Sevens—millennia, maybe, since I've taken my *otherform*. These last few days—no, weeks!—have been…peculiar, to say the least!"

"Does it…does it *hurt* when you change?" Kalas dared to ask.

The *egu* nodded. "Every time. *Edhu-i-rudzhún* or *rudzhún-i-edhu*. Doesn't matter which 'direction.'"

"Why would you…y'know…?"

"As painful as every change is, sometimes the strengths inherent in one form or another make it worthwhile. That's not the worst of it, though: despite the wolf's improved abilities, I still have hazy memories of the lion and his glory…"

"The lion?" said Sina, curious.

"*Fàrokelu. Zhàfàrok.* The exalted form the *elume* possess: the *elume* who rightly rejected Ilnëshras' unholy pride. With the *lion*, there is no *hurt*…"

"Like in the book! My grandfather's book!" said Kalas. "Nïmrïk, I'm sorry—"

"No! That's not—no, I know my sins. I don't—please: do *not* be sorry for *me!*"

"Uh, all right, yeah, I'm s—ah, never mind…" Kalas stammered.

"As I was saying," Nïmrïk continued, "In hands other than Sharuyan's—or someone blessed with his permission, his staff is nothing but a pretty stick. If Hwanzho stole it hoping to conjure *seranà* from it, he'll understand soon enough he murdered his kinsman for nothing."

"Hwanzho knows his way around the Wastes that skirt the Gateway. He has at least a couple hours' head start," acknowledged Pava. "We're all tired. We all need rest. I don't see any benefit in hunting him down tonight while the moon is thin. C'mon, everyone: I'll show you to your quarters."

"Pava, please! Such a task shouldn't fall to you! *Shëmîu,* allow me to—" Sina began. The cave-dweller girl cut her off.

"I'm not—Sina, don't call me that!"

"Just a minute," Kalas said. The others, who'd begun trickling from the room, stopped and turned toward him. He looked at his hands, flexed his fingers a time or two, and tried to remember the parts of the Song he'd used under Deridzhas. Holding it within his mind, he approached Rive. Extending both hands, he looked up at Tsana, who seemed unsure of his intentions but kept her silence. Gently, he pointed his palms at the *ëmîudas* eyeless sockets and the ragged red streaks stretching out across his face. He looked to

Abarandal, who followed him; to Zhalera, who followed *her;* and closed his eyes as he began his song.

Almost immediately, he knew something wasn't right. The notes were tortured. Reluctant. Hard to *see.* He persisted even as he felt his knees buckle: other hands caught him before he fell. He screamed—so did Rive.

"What are you doing *to him?!"* Tsana demanded.

She must have tried to stop him, because Zhalera warned her not to interfere. Hot, bloody bubbles trickled from Kalas' nostrils: the trickle became a stream, became a flood, and he stumbled despite the arms supporting him.

"You're *hurting* him! You're—!" Tsana roared. Kalas wondered if red threads wove themselves across her eyes.

"No, my bride!" Rive said as he reached for his own face. "It's all right! He was…it's better now! Before, there was *heat* in my blood. I didn't say anything because others among our people were suffering so much more, but now, that heat is gone!"

"Kalas!" Zhalera shouted as she held onto him. "What happened?"

With animated notes, Abarandal voiced her own concern from his other side.

"The Song! I can't *see* it! Something's happened!" he coughed.

"That fall, lad, in the mines, when the dragon tossed you through the air," suggested Nïmrïk as he shook his head. Interpreting Kalas' horrified expression, he continued, "When you've had some *real* rest—more than a few days bouncing around in the back of that coach—you'll *see* again. Even with your injury you saw well enough to burn away Rive's infection: take comfort in that!"

"But I can still *hear* it…"

"Hearing and *seeing* are two very different things! *I* can *hear* The Song: I can't *see* it. *You* will again, though—right now, give your material substance time to recover."

"Here, let me help you," said Nashmur as he approached the shaking young man. Together, he and Nïmrïk lifted him and, following Pava's lead, carried him toward his quarters.

"Rül, young man," Rive began before the farm boy could leave: "A word, please."

2.

Kalas woke when numerous shafts of warm, silvery light struck him in the face as the Premier Sun ascended above the horizon, its rays reflected from the *úrukilmukritmedas* glasses arrayed about the room. His head was pounding—an all-too-frequent sensation of late, though the ache was nowhere near as severe as it had been the night before. Nïmrïk and Abarandal were awake and smiling politely (yet awkwardly) at one another, waiting for the others to join them.

Do eru *or* egu *ever sleep? Do they* need *to?* he wondered.

Zhalera stirred, squinted, and rubbed her eyes as she sat up and scanned the room—a palatial apartment furnished with soft pillows and supple, vegetable-tanned hides. She cocked her head when she noticed Rül wasn't with them.

"Hey, Pava," she said, rousing the young girl with a nudge. "What did your father say to Rül last night? He's not here. Did he ever come back?"

Pava stared at her for a few moments and tried to overcome the haze of lingering sleep before she admitted, "I don't know...I figured Sina or someone would bring him down whenever Father finished...whatever it was he had to say to him. You haven't seen him, either?" She sat up as well, a puzzled expression on her face. "Anyway, let's figure out what's going on. And get something to eat. Maybe not in that order."

. . .

Rive, Rül, and Sina were waiting for them in the dining hall where they'd last seen the *ëmïu* and the farm boy. Sina had set places for everyone around the table: Rül and Pava's father had almost finished their breakfast as the others filed in and took their seats.

"There you are! I—uh, we were wondering what happened to you!" said Pava as she sat down next to Rül. "Have you two been talking all this time? What about?"

"Not *all* this time, *shadathahal*," Rive replied, turning his head toward the sound of her voice. Kalas' head still ached, but he risked a smile when he noticed the crimson feathers of infection that had outlined the *ëmïudas* eye sockets were now a healthy-looking shade of…pale. Healthy for a cave-dweller, at least. "We had much to discuss…Come now, enjoy your breakfast. Rül and I will visit the horses and—"

"Hey, where's *Shude?* Did Mother have something going on this morning?"

"Sina, would you accompany us?" Rive ignored his daughter's question.

"Of course," she curtseyed.

"You're welcome to remain within the *Áthradholarme* for as long as you like, of course, though I have reason to believe you'd prefer to set out for Lohwàlar without delay."

"Thank you, *Ëmïu* Rive," Kalas said between mouthfuls of stewed root vegetables. "If we can spend the day underground and leave when the suns have set, we—I would be really grateful!"

"Of course! Rül, Sina, if you please?"

Rül, who hadn't said anything since Kalas and the others had entered the lavish room with its polished table and padded cushions, avoided making eye contact with anyone. Especially Pava. As the three of them prepared to leave, he tried to steal a glance at the girl, but she'd been looking at *him* the whole time. When their eyes met, he looked away as the tan in his cheeks burned red, accentuated in the reflectors' light.

"Rül?" Pava wondered. "What's going on? Are you all right?"

"I, uh…Fine! Fine! Just…the horses, y'know? I'll…I'd better catch up to the *Ëm*—uh, your…I'll be back in a little while!"

His eyes darted between Rive and Pava as he stammered. He flashed her a smile overloaded with teeth as he disappeared around a corner.

"Father, *what* did you say to him?!" she grumbled under her breath.

After searching for Tsana (and not finding her), Pava spent the morning showing everyone around her city, explaining the history behind some of its caves and other constructs. She led them up a series of wide stairs whose flights crisscrossed one another and told them to look through the narrow portals cut into the wall.

"It's the Highway!" said Nashmur, who moved between them to double-check his assumption.

"At night, we usually have no reason to be up here, but sometimes—when liar-pretenders tell us *ilrâigme-edhume* are near, for example—we'll have people keep an eye on the Gateway from here and other, similar vantage points."

"I saw something like this—from the other side," Kalas nodded, "when we were here last."

"What a view! And you say there are other places like this? Why, I'll bet you know what's happening throughout the entire Gateway!" Nashmur marveled.

"We do. Usually. I don't mind admitting to you that some places like this are lined with mirrors positioned in such a way that a single torch looks like hundreds. Makes our numbers look more impressive, too."

Pava next brought them through a high, vaulted cavern filled with strange, tree-like vegetation neither Kalas nor most of the others had ever seen. Woody stems or trunks covered with vari-colored bark-like material stretched dozens of feet into the air; along the way, forking branches bearing jagged green-and-yellow leaves radiated from their centers. Complex networks of reflectors bathed the cultivated forest with suns-light filtered through various crystals. A faint mist heavy with the fragrance of petrichor hovered just above a carpet of diverse and delicate ferns and grasses.

"These trees! Are they trees?! These…whatever they are: they're amazing!" Zhalera raved.

"Thank you!" Pava grinned. "These gardens are some of Mother's favorite places. I'd hoped we might run into her down here, but it could take hours—maybe days—to search just one of them completely…

"I'll bet Father's back from the horses by now. And maybe Mother's back from…wherever she's been hiding. I'll show you another passage on the way up: it has a waterfall that's—"

"A waterfall?! Underground?!" Kalas exclaimed.

"How else do you think we'd get enough water down here to keep these trees healthy? Some of the *iltithme* are placed in such a way that they make a column of rainbows all around it. It's really something! Abarandal, when you first appeared to us, your dress: the first thing I thought of was those rainbows! C'mon!"

When they returned to their quarters, Rül was sitting on a pillow, staring at a wall. Or maybe through it. He held a long, elaborate *tëvët* with strange runes carved along its polished black shaft. Suns-light glittered along its knapped crystal head and cast iridescent shapes across the floor. He seemed not to notice them as Pava called his name and sat down beside him.

"Rül!" she repeated. "Where did you get that?! Rül? Everything all right?"

The farm boy hesitated for a long while before he spoke: when he did, he ignored her question.

"Horses are fine. Brushed 'em down and packed up the coach. Couple of people—Tshise and Rofe—brought us some stuff for the trip. Everything looks good: we're ready to leave whenever."

"Father's *tëvët!*" Pava repeated, wrapping her fingers around Rül's as they gripped the ornate weapon. The red in her suns-burned face had long since given way to a subtle tan; when she recognized what the farm boy was holding, that color had drained away; now, some of it returned.

"I'll bet *that's* why Mother's nowhere to be found," she said, as though everyone would understand her meaning. Kalas looked at Zhalera, who shrugged when she caught his eye.

"You must have made quite an impression," Pava almost whispered to Rül. She let go of his hand, and with both of hers, she turned his head and held it until he blinked a few times and, at last, seemed to return to his present circumstances. With a slow smile, she leaned forward, closed her eyes, and kissed him. Startled, Rül just sat there for a moment—for *just* a moment, his widened eyes betraying his difficulty parsing the situation before he closed them and responded in kind.

"About time!" Zhalera muttered with a sly smile. Kalas laughed.

Just before suns-down, when everyone and everything was ready, Kalas and his companions prepared to resume their trek for Lohwàlar. Rive, Sina on his elbow, offered them his benediction as other *úrukilmukritme* gathered along the elevated paths on either side of the Gateway and touched the backs of their hands to their foreheads. Pava looked from ridge to ridge, hoping to glimpse her mother. She tried not to let Tsana's absence bother her, but Kalas could tell she was disappointed. He wondered if her mother kept her distance because of the unknown substance of Rül's and Rive's late night conversation. As curious as he was, he said nothing. Neither did anyone else.

Descending the Áthradho in twilit silence, a shape—a woman's figure, from the silhouette—interrupted the flat planes of the cliffs high above them. The first breaths of the steppes' winds whipped her flowing braid around as she watched the travelers. Kalas poked his head through the window and pointed Pava toward the ledge.

"I know, I just wish she'd been able to see things through Father's eyes…"

She laughed at the unintended irony and shook her head.

"Maybe someday," she sighed. "Traditions have always been important to her. Sometimes *too* important, I think. Doesn't change anything, but still…"

He nodded as he returned to his seat.

'Doesn't change anything'? What's she talking about? he wondered.

3.

The winds whipping over the steppes were just as ferocious as Kalas remembered; now, they blew even colder as winter stretched across the plains. After weeks of travel through frozen grasslands, sparse with flora struggling against the cold, he caught himself counting down the days until they'd reach Lohwàlar. A strange suspension of sadness and excitement roiled within Kalas' thoughts, each clamoring for consideration. The closer they got to those old, familiar dunes, the greater the conflict.

One morning, Zhalera squealed with delight when she discovered a light rime of frost clinging to tufts of grass; when she touched it, however, it melted from the heat in her fingers.

"I can't believe we didn't see any snow!" she lamented one afternoon, just before they reached the elaborate, seven-walled cistern where they'd recovered Shosafin, where Falthwën, with Kalas' "assistance," had healed the old soldier from what should have been a mortal wound. "I thought for sure we'd see some in Thosha!"

"Seems like it's been a dry winter," Nashmur concurred. "Can't say that bothers me! There's enough danger traveling all this way even when the ground is clear!"

"Easy for you to say! You've seen snow before, right? You probably see it every year!" she countered.

"Uh, we're here," said Rül as he reined in his team. Kalas left Zhalera and Abarandal—one buried beneath a mound of skins and blankets, the other unconcerned with the temperature—and exited the cabin. Rül planted the heel of Rive's *tëvët* in the dirt and vaulted from his seat. He seemed to hover for a slow moment before his booted feet touched the ground. "This thing's pretty handy," he muttered. Pava smiled, and Kalas noticed something in her eyes he hadn't noticed before. Something *expectant,* perhaps. He shrugged and approached one of the arches. Along the way, a strange sensation raised the hairs at the back of his neck as an ethereal chill played icy fingers down his spine. He shivered.

This has nothing to do with the weather, he thought.

Nïmrïk, beside him, saw the tremor ripple through his body and nodded.

"That's new to you, is it?" he wondered. "That…I don't know… *presence?*"

"Yeah, someone's been through here—no, not some*one.* Some*thing.*"

"Eaters?! Brigands?!" suggested Rül as he dropped what he was doing and raised his weapon.

"No, I don't think so," Kalas allowed. "Maybe it's nothing but my head. That bump under the mines."

"It's more than that," Nïmrïk growled.

"I…I know," Kalas confessed.

• • •

Near the bottom of the stairs leading toward a fathomless pool of water so clear it seemed invisible, Kalas stopped and almost dropped his empty water skins. He'd seen—and ignored—the flaking remains of Shosafin's bloody footprints on the way down; however, on the last step, where the wounded soldier had spilled an unhealthy amount of blood, someone had carved a series of arcane…symbols? shapes? words? onto the gleaming surface of the wall. Kalas couldn't decipher their meaning, nor could he shake the impression that he'd seen something similar not too long ago.

"Nïmrïk, look!" he pointed.

"I see, lad. I see."

"Can you read it? Or understand it? Are they even words?"

"This writing holds the shapes the *elume* use. I can't read it, I'm sorry. I *used to* recognize these designs. I don't anymore. Probably a consequence of my iniquity. Doesn't matter: without The Song, I couldn't understand it anyway…"

"I wonder what it means! Maybe it sounds crazy, but I'm pretty sure I've seen something like this before! The shapes, at least…"

Nïmrïk cracked a thin film of ice that had formed atop the water's surface; as he filled his skins, Kalas studied the characters, committed each design to memory, and tried to remember why it seemed so familiar. With a heavy sigh and a shrug to match, he filled his own skins and followed the *egu* out of darkness and into the light.

"That the last of 'em?" Rül asked, eyeing Kalas' and Nïmrïk's waterskins as he harnessed Dancer and Runner to the coach.

"Yeah, this is it. I don't know about you, but I'm ready to get moving again: these winds are cold!" said Kalas.

As the young man stowed his and Nïmrïk's skins, that strange feeling tickled the nape of his neck again. He tried to shut it out, but the impression would not be ignored. He turned to say something when a shadow—wingèd, vast, and nimble—zoomed overhead, mere yards above him. It passed, and he discovered he was sweating: drops of liquid dread collected on his brow and beneath his arms before the slashing wind could drink his fear away. Paralyzed for a moment, he struggled to scream. When the paralysis passed, all he managed was a hoarse gurgle.

"Kalas? You all right?" said Nashmur as he finished securing his gear. "Couldn't make out what you were saying…"

"That…that *thing!*" he wheezed at last as he pointed toward the empty, yellow-gray sky.

"Thing?" the former commander repeated. "Kalas, I don't… there's nothing there…How's your head?"

"Better! No, I'm fine! I just—" he stopped himself, looked around again and lowered his arm as he tried to remember the particulars of what he'd just experienced. Whatever tightness he'd felt inside his head had disappeared; still, since he'd tried to help Rive, he'd hesitated to exercise his *privilege,* as Falthwën had described it: his unique relationship with the Song through which all creation found expression. Now, he turned his frightened thoughts toward its omnipresent melodies, and in their strident major chords, he heard—he *felt* the echo of the passing entity. He cried out—uninhibited, this time—and Nashmur rushed to his side.

"Kalas!" said Zhalera as she hopped down from the coach. Abarandal followed her.

"None of you saw that? *Felt* that?!" he asked, incredulous.

"Saw what?" said Zhalera as she looked around.

"No, not down here: *up there!*" he corrected her as he gestured at the sky again. "It was *huge!* And *fast!* And when it was gone, I was…I was *afraid…*"

Abarandal placed a hand on his cheek and sang to him. He nodded, excited.

"Exactly! *Fear,* but not because of something evil! Because of something *good!*"

"You're…afraid of…something *good?*" repeated Rül, head cocked.

"Yes! No! I mean, not *good* the way we use the word: I mean… ugh, I can't explain it! Just being near it made me see my flaws, my every imperfection. It suggested…I don't know, a *reckoning,* maybe. I was *afraid* because in that moment, I knew I'd never measure up. Maybe that doesn't make sense. Maybe it's—"

Abarandal shook her head. She was about to sing again when Nïmrïk interjected, "It makes perfect sense, lad."

As he wheeled Dalafar toward Kalas' direction, suns-light glinted from the residue of tears streaking his face. Abarandal withdrew her hand from Kalas and approached the weeping *egu.* She sang to him, and Nïmrïk's dour expression brightened at the sound.

"Thank you, lass—whatever you just said!"

"She said it's not on *us* to 'measure up,'" Kalas translated. "How is that—? I don't understand what she means!"

"Neither do I, lad, but that feeling? that sense of *righteous* dread? That can only come from the presence of an *elu.*"

"An *elu?! Here?!*" shouted Pava with wild glances in all directions.

"*Edhume* have always felt the way you've just described when in the presence of *elume.* I never understood why until…" Nïmrïk mumbled his last few words as his thoughts retreated toward his darker memories. Returning to the present, he continued: "Unless I miss my guess, I'd say an *elu* wrote those symbols on the wall down there. I'd say the same *elu* has been watching this place since then, too."

"But why?" Pava demanded. "Why here? Why now? Wait— *what* symbols?"

"Near the bottom step, someone carved words or something into the wall," Kalas explained. "Why here? Why now? No idea!

I—Hey, wait a minute!"

He hopped onto the step leading into the coach's cabin, reached for one of the bars surrounding the imperial, and rummaged through his pack until he found the old book. He sat down and thumbed through its pages until—

"Here!" he shouted, jabbing at the exposed pages. "*This* is where I'd seen those symbols before! Look! I recognize this, this, and this: they were cut into that wall. I still have no idea what it means!"

"May I see that?" Nïmrïk held out his hands.

"Yeah, sure! Do you see what I'm talking about? These symbols look the same, don't they?"

"They do, lad," he confirmed. "Where did you ever find this?!"

As Nïmrïk turned each page with careful reverence, he ran his eyes over every symbol, every word, hoping, it seemed, to draw out its meaning through prolonged exposure.

"My father had it. Got it from his father. Before that, I have no idea."

Nïmrïk stopped on the woodcut Falthwën had explained to them in Wodram's study: a single *zhàfàrok* surrounded by seven streams of *eruseranà*—star magic—and standing against a horde of *zhàrudzhme.* He stopped and ran his trembling fingers across the image.

"*Nanësra,*" he said, his hand resting just beneath the lone *fàrokelu.*

"You can read it?!" said Kalas, surprised. "How?! I thought—"

"No, lad, I cannot! *Nanësra* is the name of the *elu* pictured here. I remember this battle. I was *there.* I was one of these *rudzhegume* she's fighting."

Cold wind scrambled over the steppes, but no one seemed to notice. Nïmrïk sighed, closed the book and handed it back to Kalas.

"You were there...?" Nashmur repeated, prompting him to go on.

"I was."

"Well?" said Zhalera. "What happened? This Nanësra versus a pack of demon-wolves: did—"

"Stars, too," Nïmrïk added. "The Great Swath in all its glory. This streak? I'm pretty sure it represents Sharuyan. Were it not for the *Kel Erume*, Nanësra might have been undone…"

A sound like thunder cracked the sky as the shadow returned. The gusts whipping through the steppes died down, and above them, a beast wearing the form of a daunting lioness beat the air with gleaming, silvery wings. White light shone from her eyes as she threshed the wind; immune to physics, she remained aloft. With a noise like the rush of many waters, she opened her mouth and spoke. None seemed to understand her words, though everyone (except Abarandal) staggered beneath the weight of her indisputable supremacy. Nïmrïk fell to his knees and wept openly as she adopted the language of *edhunàm* and repeated: "That I was *not undone* must grate against your spirit even now, Kadhëmba!"

"Nanësra?!" whispered Nïmrïk, barely audible. "Nanësra! *Zhi Ilun tsaváras nir!* Forgive me! *Aswanthalu!*"

The *zhàfàrok* said nothing.

Abarandal stepped from Nïmrïk's side and stood between him and Nanësra. She raised her hands in a show of peace and sang a brief cantata for the *elu*.

"I know who you are, child—I know *what* you are—but *this?* You expect me to believe something so preposterous?!"

Nanësra descended until her padded hind feet touched the ground. She stood upright for a moment before folding her expansive wings, which shimmered out of sight; a moment later, she became a bloom of light, and as its brilliance receded, she stood as a human, draped in shining garb and clad in armor. Constructed from simple patterns, her clothing exuded excellence; her greaves, gauntlets, and mail sparkled in the suns-light: so too did the jeweled pommel of a long sword strapped to her side. Silver sheets of undulating fire tumbled from her crown across her sculpted features and seemed to leap atop her lithe, well-muscled shoulders. Her smoldering eyes, framed by high cheekbones, surrendered enough of their ethereal radiance to reveal dazzling, deep green irises; her lips, full and glistening, held a tight, disapproving line as she continued speaking.

"You're…new to this world, child, so perhaps you're unaccustomed to deceit. To malice. That…*man* you're protecting is responsible for uncounted evils!"

"She—we know! Nïmrïk told us all about it! We know he's an *egu*, that long ago, he joined Ilnëshras in his rebellion! He's been helping us! Saved our lives more than once!" Kalas blurted.

"You *don't* know! You—you think that undoes Kadhëmba's prior deeds?" Nanësra retorted as she appraised the young man.

"No, I…" he began, faltering when the *elu* drew her sword. Subtle white flames danced along its length as she held it at her side. "Look, *Shâu* Nanësra—that's you, right?—I don't know how all this works, but all of us would have been captured or killed—or worse!—if Nïmrïk hadn't intervened! He saved us from *ilrâigme-edhume* under Deridzhas! He carried me to safety when I was injured by a *gròma!* He took an arrow cursed with *nimnàfël seranà*. Heshradan—*zhi heresheru*—he believes him!"

"That a star would believe the lies of a dog like this is not surprising. Step aside, and I'll *unmake* him: never again will his *rilâ*—his immaterial essence—trouble your world."

"No!" Kalas insisted. The others joined him, steadfast in their protective regard for the *egu*. He played countless thoughts across his mind's eye as he searched for the words that might dissuade Nanësra from her single-minded task.

"The symbols! *You* carved those symbols, didn't you? What do they mean?"

She paused. "You can't read them?"

"They're shapes only the *elume* use. According to Nïmrïk. *Kadhëmba*, you called him. He can't use The Song, so no, he couldn't read them. You hear The Song though, right? You can even understand Abarandal when she sings!"

"Of course," she muttered as her eyes flicked from the kneeling *egu* to the pleading boy. "It's been so long since I've walked within the realm of humankind. Those shapes are a prayer. A petition that the Creator protect the one who called forth power from The Song."

"That was *me!*" he said. "Another friend of ours had been almost cut in half by an *eku* who calls himself Marugan. Or Gozhira. Falthwën—Sharuyan, that is, of the Swath, had started to heal him. I—I didn't know what would happen, but I harmonized with him as he sang. There was heat and light: Shosafin—our friend— cried out, so I stopped singing; when he wiped away the paste Falthwën had smeared on him, his wound was gone! If what you say about those shapes on the wall is true, then your prayer was for *my* protection!"

"Is this true, I wonder?" Nanësra sheathed her sword and stepped toward Kalas. Roughly a head taller, she peered down at his upturned face and examined his features.

No, she's seeing inside *of me...*

"Maybe..." she whispered as she cupped the nape of his neck in one hand and, with the other, placed a single finger at the center of his forehead.

A radiating pressure wave, succeeded by pure white electric threads, pushed outward from between the *elu* and the boy. Kalas felt Nanësra *unlock* something within his mind as the wave's understated presence rumbled *through* everyone, rocked them on their feet without knocking them to the ground.

She could unmake *us all with a word,* Kalas believed.

"Maybe," she repeated to herself after a silent moment, having withdrawn her index finger. After wrestling with her thoughts, she released his neck and huffed, "You say this *traitor* has changed his ways? Yet he cannot use The Song! His *otherform* remains the wolf, yes? Yes, I thought so. You claim he's earned your trust, that he stood up to Marugan, but you don't—no, you haven't discovered *that* detail yet, have you?

"All right, fine! Let the consequence of your persistence be upon your own heads! I pray my runes weren't writ in vain, *Nalëndas!* Kadhëmba! We *will* meet again!"

With another pulse of light, Nanësra erupted in a spiraling column of white fire. Pristine silver wings spread outward from its writhing flames and carried the *fàrokelu* across the cusp of twilight and into the evening's first stars.

4.

"I thought I was gonna die!" Rül wheezed when Nanësra's radiance winked out. "Someone say something! I'm not so sure I didn't!"

"I felt it, too," Pava confirmed as she wrapped her fingers around his shaking hand. The others expressed similar sentiments and rubbed away the sting in their eyes as their fear and trembling subsided.

"She called you *Kadhëmba*," Nashmur said.

"Lad! What were you *doing?!*" Nïmrïk panted. Still kneeling, still weeping, he ignored the commander's observation. "Nanësra would have been well within her rights to slay me here and now! She's right: I am a traitor, as I told you once before. Not only that, but I was party to her attempted murder! Maybe you believe me— maybe Heshradan meant what he said, but…?

"What if Nanësra, in her zeal to cut me down, had cut you down, too, for standing in her way? She's an *elu*, lad! Her kind has never readily suffered the inconstancy of lesser beings! This world has been racing toward darkness from the beginning, and like the *erume* explained to you beneath the Vault, *you* are the only one who might bring about its restoration!"

Kalas just shrugged as he offered a hand to Nïmrïk. The *egu* accepted, and, still shaking, stood, with the young man's support.

"C'mon, everyone. The suns will set before long. Let's make camp and start again tomorrow."

"It's hard to believe it's been almost three months now since we left this place!" Rül marveled as he steered his team toward a break in the woods. The younger trees became the edge of a great and ancient pine forest whose tallest and oldest members blotted out the suns. After all that biting wind and frosted scrub, the warmer, gentler meadows and scattered copses had been welcome sights; now, as dark evergreens towered overhead, Kalas remembered the strange sense of *heaviness* that seemed to press down upon them from within its shadowed confines.

"Couple of days and we'll be home!" he continued. "I wonder how the farm's doing."

"I wonder what it looks like now. I know it hasn't been that long, but when we left, everyone seemed pretty busy clearing debris and fixing things," Zhalera mused. "I wonder what they did with Father's smithy..."

I wonder if my house still has a hole in the roof, Kalas considered. He shivered from the unpleasant memory.

"Cold?" Zhalera asked.

"In a way," he dismissed. "It's getting warmer though. Been getting warmer for the last week or so. Maybe Lohwàlar doesn't get as cold as I remembered..."

• • •

A day later, they reached the fork leading to Lohwàlar or Serular. When Kalas mentioned Shosafin's comment about the place, Nashmur chuckled, shook his head and offered his best wishes for any *dzhastur* imprudent enough to venture within its boundaries.

"Last I heard, some new religion—a cult, maybe—consolidated power there. No one we talked to—the queen-regent's sources, I mean—seems to know more than that. *Or…*they're more scared of their leader than they are Ësfàyami!"

"That's…this leader: he'd have to be pretty scary," Kalas admitted as he remembered Shosafin's blade against his neck while held in the queen-regent's deceptively delicate-looking fist.

"Rumors say he appears like a pillar of flame: crackling with fire, but not consumed. They say even the elements are subject to his authority. He's in command of some magical discipline, if you believe the reports."

Magic is magic…it's the wielder's intent *that determines its character,* Falthwën had said.

"Do you? Believe the reports?" said a voice from out of the shaded forest. Kalas had been so rapt within his thoughts that he hadn't acknowledged the subtle tickle above his shoulders.

"Shosafin?!" he said as he craned his neck toward the cab's open windows. "Rül! Stop!"

Rül had already drawn up the reins when Shosafin and Breaker somehow materialized in front of them. Kalas jumped from the coach and ran a few steps until he was ahead of Runner and Dancer.

"Shosafin! Where have you been?! You have no—"

The old soldier's face now bore a deep red wound across his cheek. His features retained their characteristic indifference, but something in his eyes had changed. Breaker, too, seemed more haggard than Kalas had ever seen him. Almost out of breath, as though he—and his rider—had been pushed too hard for too long.

"I—no, of course not, cousin!" Nashmur insisted. "I mean…

well, I haven't seen for myself, but—"

"Serular, lad," he said, ignoring the former commander. "Now's neither the time nor the place to have this discussion. Your fortunes have changed, it seems: where's your cleric?"

"He's…gone. We made it to Ïsriba, and—"

"No, lad: not here, not now. They'll be here before long—I thought you were them, at first!"

"'Them'? I don't—"

"I thought you would have returned long before now: I was on my way to Lohwàlar to look for you…Doesn't matter. Another day and we'll be there, and—"

"What have you done to Breaker?!" Rül demanded. "He's spent! You've run him—"

"He's got one more day in him, lad! Believe me! How about your horses? Will they last through the night?"

"Cousin, what's all this about?" Nashmur wondered as he squeezed Gilfën's ribs and trotted to Breaker's side.

"I'll admit, Nashmur: you've surprised me. I can't say I expected I'd ever see you out from under Ësfàyami's taloned shadow."

"That's fair, but a lot has happened. A lot has changed. You wouldn't believe it. You never did."

Shosafin cast a sidelong glance at his cousin, offered him a series of shallow nods.

"No, I never did," he admitted.

He might have said more, but confused and angry shouts, coming up from the south, from the direction of Serular, interrupted him.

"You can ride, yes, lad?" said Nïmrïk as he rolled from Dalafar's saddle.

"I'll manage, but why? What are you—?"

"Kalas! What's going on?" said Zhalera as she leaned out of the coach.

"All of you, continue toward Lohwàlar. I'll keep…whatever's behind us *behind* us!" the *egu* instructed.

Kalas grabbed hold of Dalafar's reins and tossed himself into the saddle. Dalafar sensed his unease, but Nïmrïk placed a hand on the black-and-silver horse's cheek, whispered something in his ear, and the blue roan relaxed. Shosafin watched in silence as the peculiar figure started for the road toward Serular. When he turned toward Kalas and insisted they hurry, his eyes shone with the faintest yellow aura.

"What's this?!" Shosafin muttered with a display of rare surprise.

"Not now! Let's go!" said Kalas as he gave Dalafar's reins a subtle flick and held them tight, his knuckles blanching as the horse snorted and followed the others through the woods.

5.

"Your friend back there. Where'd he come from?" Shosafin asked with casual indifference, though Kalas divined his real question.

"Nïmrïk's an *egu*, yes, but he's not like Dzharëth! He's not like the monsters that killed our townsfolk! You told me to abandon my naïveté, and I've tried—just ask your cousin!—but Nïmrïk saved our lives. More than once, and it's likely that's what he's doing right now, too. Who's this 'they' that's after you? What did you do this time?!"

For a moment, Shosafin said nothing, simply stared straight at the road ahead. Kalas decided he wouldn't bother pressing him: as much as he'd missed his presence, his company, he wasn't interested in wresting details from his reticence. The old warrior surprised him and began, "When I left you on the bank of the Hidden River, I backtracked for some of the smaller communities bordering Serular. Took a few shortcuts along the way, shaved maybe a week, maybe two, from what it would have taken had I stayed on the Highway. Anyway, long ago, Serular wasn't a bad place, but over the last few Sevens, that's changed. It's *dark* now, and I figured if anyone would know anything about…*ekume*, I'd find him in Serular."

"'*Ekume*,' cousin?" huffed Nashmur, just behind him. "I thought you didn't believe in such things?"

"You've been with this lot since Âivambar? You've been with them long enough to know how they excel at finding trouble?" Shosafin grumbled.

Nashmur laughed: "Too true, Ilbardhën! Too true!"

"I was right about *ekume*," Shosafin continued, ignoring his cousin's interruption. "Just not about Marugan. From what I uncovered, some ancient, almost-forgotten cult's been consolidating influence among Serular's elite. Something called the *Ragus pïni Tshaggul Kavar*—the Cult of the Deathless Flame. Townsfolk gushed about some figure 'circumfused in fire and shadow' making the rounds, performing impossible acts. They claimed he was the embodiment of the Deathless Flame, that he'd 'stepped out of history' for some 'special purpose.' Never learned what that was. They said when some of the old cult's more fervent adherents challenged him, he rained shards of light down on his accusers until every last one had been consumed. Most *Serularrinme* quickly fell in line.

"You're not wrong, cousin: had I heard all this *before* having met our young friend here, I would have dismissed their stories as just that. When I asked you if you believed the reports, it's because they appear to be true. I don't know who this Deathless Flame is, what his 'special purpose' might be, but having seen firsthand what his worshipers have done in his name—the horrors they've wrought within Serular and the surrounding homesteads, I'm convinced it's nothing good.

"I did discover a small network of people still practicing the older faith. In secret. Took quite some time to convince them I wasn't a spy for the *Tshaggul Kavar*. A young girl—just a child, really—said she'd overheard one of the *new* elders say something about a shrine far away to the North, in the Ice City of Galámur, across the sea.

"The Deathless Flame, whoever he is, sounds like he has the powers of the *ekume*. The *erume*. Whatever. I don't know if I'll find Marugan at Galámur, but I'm confident that I'll find *something*. Whatever's there might lead me to that *ilshandar*—that deceiver."

"He's working for Queen Ësfàyami," Rül said. "He was, at least…"

Shosafin cocked his head, canted it toward the farm boy.

"He says you killed King Rufàran and all his men. That you tried to kill him, too, because you'd made some deal with the *Potsobarut* emperor. *Kematu*, I think she said his name was," Kalas explained. "In the throne room, he…Commander Nashmur was taking us back to our cells, but he freed us instead. We got lost until we ran right into Marugan and more of his *shosayedhume*. Nïmrïk— the *egu* guarding our backs, who we met in Thosha—took one of his arrows: an arrow meant for one of us! Marugan got away—he just…you know when it's hot? You look out at the sand off in the distance, and the air kind of…shimmers? It was like that, except it wasn't *heat*, it was *darkness*, and POOF! he was gone.

"He might still be at Ïsriba. He might be at…Galámur, you said? He might be somewhere not of this world. Loradan *transported* us beneath a place the *erume* called the Vault of Stars: that's where the *erume* summoned Abarandal. That's where the *ekume* killed Falthwën…"

"I'm sorry for your loss, lad. You've endured a lot, it would seem. Loradan? Abarandal?"

"New friends," Kalas elaborated. "Actually, Loradan is Falthwën's *ilmazhas*. An *eru*, a member of the Great Swath. Also, Falthwën was the *eru* Sharuyan, overseer of earth and growth and gifts of life. He's the one who got rid of all the other *rudzhegume* in Lohwàlar that night. With his lightning. Forgot to mention that."

"There's some nasty stuff coming from those cultists," said Nïmrïk as he rejoined the group just before Tàfayan transcended the horizon. At some point, he'd assumed his lupine *otherform*, in which he still appeared. "I don't get the sense they're *ekume*, nor *Nalëndasme*, nor anything else with a history of privilege. Seems like they're just *edhume*, but without The Song, I can't really say for sure. I don't know how, but they're slinging some dark magic—that much I *can* say.

"Anyway, I think they're gone. For now. Not sure if they'll follow us. Mister Shosafin, not sure what you did to get their attention, but it might be a while before they forget about you…"

Pink clouds reflected predawn suns-light enough for Kalas to notice something peculiar glistening just behind Nïmrïk's shoulders. He tried to focus through the early morning haze at shapes that seemed to flutter with every step the *zhàrudzh* took.

"Nïmrïk, do you have—? Are those *wings?!*"

"Aye, lad. Oh, that's right: you've never seen them before. With dark magic involved, I thought it best to give those *Serularrinme* a good show—a good reason to turn and run away! I *think* it was enough, but for how long, I can't say.

"You look surprised! Nanësra had wings, remember? *Egu* have wings, too. *Elu* can use theirs to fly—actually, they don't *need* them for that…*Egu* can't. You once asked me if it *hurt* when I changed. The wings make it even worse. And they don't *do* anything, so I—most *egume*, really—usually don't bother. They mostly just get in the way. They're not as *elegant* as *elu* wings. More like Lady's wings, or—No! More like bat wings: leathery, almost translucent in the right light…"

"'Lady'? Is that the *gròma* you mentioned earlier? Extinct, aren't they?" said Shosafin, eyebrow raised.

"I thought so, too," panted Nïmrïk.

"The eaters under Deridzhas thought she was some kind of goddess, had her trapped down there! We freed her. Not sure where she went," Kalas supplied.

Shosafin shook his head and laughed.

"Noble," he said, sensing Kalas' curious gaze. "Rash, perhaps, but noble. *Âu* Nïmrïk, is it? Surely the boy has told you what happened in Lohwàlar? Surely he told you about the beasts that slaughtered his town? his parents? And surely he told you what became of the *nëshras rudzh* that murdered his father?"

"That he did, soldier. That he did. I understand your meaning, too. If you prefer, I'll keep as far from you as possible…"

"Nothing so drastic as that, wolf. I've learned that sometimes the boy sees things even I fail to recognize. Keep as close as you like: just know the lad is under my protection."

"Then it appears we have more in common than you know," said Nïmrïk.

6.

Before midday, an hour or two before the suns would meet at the top of the sky, they reached the outskirts of Lohwàlar. Nïmrïk abandoned his *nimegu* skin to disintegrate into smoke in the late morning light and resumed his human form. Kalas offered to return Dalafar to him, but he insisted he'd rather walk, and Kalas didn't press the matter. Ever since encountering the *elu*, the old man's resigned outlook turned darker, his rare smiles rarer still.

Nanësra saw something in him, I know it—that's gotta be why she let him live, he convinced himself. *Maybe she knows something about him he doesn't know about himself?*

From the Highway, everything looked almost the same as Kalas remembered: as they drew nearer, however, he noticed several new, low-roofed structures dug into the ground, and a pair of towers on either side of the road. A man holding an uncomfortable-looking sword appeared and, with a stern voice, called out: *"Àya, sàme! What's your business here?"*

I've heard that voice before…but where? When?

"Mister Hebul? Is that you?"

"Yes! How do you—Master Kalas? Tàran's boy? You've returned! Alive! I'll confess I didn't recognize you right away, but this one: he was part of the *Poyïsriba* garrison, *hish?* And this coach! This is not the old farm wagon you left town with!"

"No, sir, it is not! We've had…some adventures, that's for sure!"

"Indeed! Well, welcome home, young man! And welcome, friends of Kalas! Oh! Before you go: seems Azhëk was right! Tàran's name *is* at the top of the monument!"

"The…monument?"

"The memorial we were discussing when we last met?"

"Right! Of course! That's—thank you, Mister Hebul…"

"It wasn't up to me—not entirely!—but on behalf of Lohwàlar, you're welcome. Your father was a good man. We're diminished by his absence."

"These towers are new," Kalas led, willing tears not to accompany fresh thoughts of everything—every*one*—he'd lost, his father foremost in his mind.

"Yes! Tsharak—you know Tsharak, yes? Crazy—that is, the odd, uh, gentleman who lives out beyond…Never mind! Tsharak suggested we take perimeter security more seriously: said we'd grown too accustomed to the world's disinterest in Lohwàlar. He made some other suggestions, too. In fact, he's become something of a fixture within the Council Hall's corridors, meeting with elders and magistrates on an almost daily basis.

"Between the two of us, I'll admit that I'm surprised at how readily Sàrush accepted the old man's recommendations! I've never known the Magistrate to be so…well, I've never seen him so *solicitous*. I guess the tragedy of the wolves really changed him—for the better! Again: welcome home!"

They left Hebul to his duties and traveled along the spiral streets toward Lohwàlar's Crescent, the heart of its civic landscape. Rül reined in his team, and Kalas hopped down from Dalafar. Zhalera and Abarandal exited the coach, the former whispering something in the latter's ear. At one end of the curved mall stood the town's modest Council Hall, dozens—maybe hundreds—of Sevens more recent than the Sanctuary, but still an ancient structure. At the other end, between two recently planted cedars, stood the memorial Hebul described.

To some, the single slab of richly veined pink granite, cut and polished to a mirror-like shine, might have been nothing more than a casual chunk of prettified stone; to Kalas, having lived his whole life among these people, he understood its significance and the reverence with which it had been placed. He ran his fingers through the deep characters that spelled out his father's and mother's names. Gandhan's, too.

"It's almost surreal," Zhalera said from his side. Kalas nodded. Said nothing.

Abarandal placed one hand on his shoulder and another on Zhalera's. When they turned to look, she closed her eyes and began a soft melody. A requiem.

"Thank you," they said in unison.

The weather in the desert, while warmer than the lands they'd traveled, still contained traces of cold that caressed Kalas' face and made him sneeze.

"*Dàbirëthu,*" said Rül from his seat.

Kalas nodded his thanks. A moment later, he sighed, yawned, and suggested they visit the Council Hall.

"It'll be there tomorrow," Rül countered. "The horses—all of them, not just Breaker—are exhausted, and I still have a ways to go before I reach the farm."

"You're right," Kalas allowed with another yawn. "Let's meet up here tomorrow morning. A night's sleep—in actual beds!—should do all of us some good. Everyone can stay with me—uh, no, maybe not…"

"Why doesn't everyone stay with me?" offered Zhalera as she squeezed Kalas' hand. "I'm sure it's dusty after all this time, but hopefully it won't be so bad? Oh! Food though…"

"Keep the things we packed when we left the Gateway," insisted Pava. "Rül, your family will feed us, won't they?"

"You're coming with me?" he said, surprised, and a smile spread across his face. "No, I mean, of course! Mother would love to meet my—you! She'd love to meet you! Father, well, I've told you a little about him: he's…he might take some getting used to…"

"I'll go with you two," said Shosafin. He'd dismounted Breaker during their conversation with Hebul; now, he ran a soothing hand across the tired beast's withers. "I need to speak with Thara. I need to return her steed and offer my apologies for his condition. Don't worry—apart from that, you won't even know I'm there!"

"I'm sure they won't," Kalas agreed; then, remembering, he added: "I forgot! Shosafin, your sword!"

He unslung the soldier's borrowed weapon and handed it to him. Shosafin almost laughed as he reached for it and nodded his thanks.

"It drew the attention you intended," Zhalera accused as she aimed her head toward Nashmur.

"Ah, yes, that," Shosafin confessed with his typical indifference. "I wasn't sure this sword's presence would persuade my cousin to tear his mouth away from the queen-regent's hindquarters, but it seemed the only acceptable course."

Nashmur's cheeks burned, but he said nothing. Zhalera scolded: "Your—Kalas, what'd you call it? 'Pragmatism'? Your *pragmatism* nearly got us killed! What if—"

"But it didn't," he interrupted. "You're a resourceful lot. I knew you'd manage."

Exasperated, Zhalera fumed, and Kalas tried to hide his grin as she stormed toward the coach's boot to retrieve her things. With her bundles in hand and Valarandal strapped across her back, she headed for her home. Kalas grabbed his pack and motioned for the others to follow as he raced to her side and took one of her bags.

Contrary to Zhalera's prediction, her house seemed almost free of dust, as if someone had stopped by to clean while they were away. The door had been locked—she'd double- and triple-checked before they'd left—yet nothing seemed amiss. With Kalas' and the others' help, she restocked the larder, prepared an evening meal, and pointed out the rooms.

In the morning, after the best sleep Kalas had enjoyed since Thosha, everyone headed for the Crescent and waited for Rül and the others to meet them. Much of the damage wrought by the *rudzhegume* had been repaired: new construction mingled with old, the scents of mortar, dressed stone, and, rarer, sawdust peppered the air. Kalas' eyes wandered in the direction of his own home, and he wondered if anyone had thought to patch the gaping hole in its roof. The first sun had barely risen when they set out; the second appeared low on the horizon when Rül and Pava trotted into view astride an unknown horse. The *úrukilmukrit* girl sat in front of Rül and seemed to take up almost no room as he tightened the reins and brought his mount to a standstill. Shosafin was nowhere in sight, but that didn't necessarily mean anything.

"Father's dead!" Rül said as he alighted from his mount. He reached up for Pava and helped her down as well.

"Rül! I'm so sorry!" Kalas and Zhalera said as one. "Is Thara all right? What—what happened?" Kalas added.

"A week after we left, Mother found him face down in the barn. He was still holding his pitchfork. Mother rushed him to the Sanctuary, but she knew he was already dead. The clerics could only confirm it.

"His heart just…quit, they said. Combination of stress and working too hard. And paranoia, really. I tried to get him to talk to someone about it, but he refused! You saw it, right? You saw how he could be?! It was always tough trying to talk to him, but I thought someday…I mean, I never even said goodbye. I just stole his horses out from under him," Rül mumbled.

"Rül, you can't blame yourself," soothed Zhalera as she wrapped her arms around him.

"Of course I can!" he insisted even as he returned the gesture. "If I hadn't let him get away with his stubbornness…If I *made* him see a cleric—if I just brought one to the farm…Maybe he'd still be alive…"

"I know how you feel, and…I'm sorry," Kalas repeated as he reached up and placed a hand on his big friend's shoulder.

"How could you—? Oh, right," Rül remembered. He let Zhalera hold him for a moment longer, then stepped back and wiped at his eyes.

"How is…how is Thara taking it?" Zhalera wondered.

"I almost don't want to admit it, but she seems *at peace* with things. Not that she's happy about it! No! I just mean…he was a hard man to live with. A hard worker, a good provider, but difficult. The farm belonged to Mother's family for generations: she was her father's only child, so, of course, when Grandfather passed away, it became hers. Father had made some…well, he'd made some bad decisions. And his mistrustful nature didn't help things. He put the farm in trouble. Money trouble. We might have had to sell it if

Mother hadn't stepped in and fixed things without him knowing about it. I know she hated having to go behind his back, but he left her no choice.

"In her own way, I can tell she misses him, but in other ways, he's been gone a lot longer than a couple of months. Shosafin's still up at the farm, helping out. He knows his way around things."

"Son of a *rasak* weaver," Nashmur reminded him. "Your mother—Thara, right?—she must have been happy to see you!"

"Oh, she was! Until she saw her horses' condition! Shosafin tried to take the blame, but I don't think Mother believed him. Not entirely! She did thank him for getting me home safely—I think that's why she let him off easy. The horses will be fine—after some well-earned rest! I don't think Ascender here minds the change of scenery. She's a hard worker: loves to run, but doesn't get out as often as she'd like."

He worked his fingers across the chestnut mare's withers and ended with a loving pat behind her cheek.

"Shosafin will find us. He always does. It's a long way to Tsharak's place: if Hebul's right and he's been spending a lot of time at the Council hall, maybe we'll run into him there? And, Zhalera, maybe he's right about your grandfather..." Kalas whispered. She stiffened and turned away, and he opted not to press the matter.

"First, though, I want to visit the Sanctuary. Just for a minute. I think Vàyana should know what happened to Falthwën. None of you has to come with me. I'll catch up with you after I've had a chance to talk with her."

Zhalera cleared her throat and stood beside him. Abarandal sang a brief tune and joined them.

"Of course," he said. "I'm sure she'd love to meet you!"

He nodded when no one else said anything and turned toward the old temple.

• • •

"An *eru*," Vàyana whispered as she sat between her former charges. "Not just an *eru*—*Sharuyan* himself! I should have known!"

She smiled as she dabbed at her eyes before drawing both of them in for a shared hug. "My children…" she wept.

"I—we thought you'd want to know," Kalas said when she released them.

"Thank you." She considered him for a moment and added, "Prophecy and cruelty: one and the same where you're concerned, it seems. You have my sympathy, young man."

"This is Abarandal. Another *eru*. The Swath summoned her just before…all the bad things happened. She's part of the prophecy, too…"

"Abarandal? What a pleasure to meet you!"

The diffident *eru* bowed slightly and voiced a few notes in kind.

"She doesn't speak with words. Just song," Zhalera explained. "Only Kalas—and that *elu*, Nanësra, I think—can understand her."

"Marvelous!" Vàyana beamed. "And perhaps not so cruel after all? Tell me, children: what will you do now?"

"We'll speak with Tsharak. He hears The Song. Knows the prophecy—parts of it, at least, and he knows history. More than just Lohwàlar's, I'll bet. That…artifact—*vàsu*—buried in the Empty Sea: Tsharak has something of a similar make. It shares some of the same symbols, at least. He's not sure where it's from. He showed it to me before we left for Ïsriba, but I promised not to say anything. Falthwën said that thing Father and I discovered is not the only one of its kind. We told you about the things we saw beneath Deridzhas: someday, I'll go back there, collapse that mine shaft, and burn what's left of that village to the ground. Unless the *erume* get to it first. I understand now why they try to *unmake* such things. Things from before the world was cracked.

"If anyone can guide us now, it'll be Tsharak. It *has* to be. We need more than just The Song: we need someone who can interpret it. With Falthwën gone, I don't know where else to go."

"I wish you well, child. I wish I possessed such gifts—such *privilege* as you and Mister Tsharak. I wish I had something more concrete to offer you than prayers, but prayers are privilege in their own way, and you—and the tasks that await you—will remain in mine. To that end: *zhi Ilun—fìe id dàbirëzhu á enëzhu; hàsayihad—tsheth ëzhu im fìe id onò osaro:* may the Creator bless you and keep you and cause his face to shine upon you."

The suns met and parted ways before Kalas, Zhalera, and Abarandal returned to the Crescent. With the day well underway, numerous *Lohwàlarrinme* stared and pointed as the pair (and their curious companion) traversed the town. Most stopped to express both their grief over their losses and their certainty that from the ashes, a stronger Lohwàlar would emerge; some, however, simply scowled, muttering suggestions that Kalas and his father were responsible for the massacre the *zhàrudzhme* had inflicted. He tried not to let it bother him, but Zhalera must have sensed his discomfort: she grabbed his hand and gave it a brief squeeze.

"No one out here. Must still be inside the Council Hall," Kalas suggested when they finished exploring their immediate surroundings. "C'mon, Zhalera, let's see if Tsharak's in there, too."

"Fine," she muttered, abandoning the amiable air she'd adopted during their visit with Vàyana. Neither Kalas nor Abarandal said anything: they just looked at one another with eyebrows raised.

The Hall's warm, still air had a stale quality about it that seemed to coat Kalas' lungs as he breathed it in. This was only his second visit: his first was when Gandhan suggested Sàrush send some people to Ïsriba. The air hadn't seemed so *old* then.

Three months seems like such a long time ago!

He coughed, and a plump figure poked her head around a corner. Her features remained unchanged as she assayed Kalas and the *eru:* when she considered Zhalera, her eyes lit up and her pursed lips broke open in a wide smile.

"Zhalera, dear! You've returned! Your grandfather will be most pleased with your visit! You've no idea how much he's—"

"I'm not here for *him!*" Zhalera growled through clenched teeth and flat lips. The woman recoiled at the tart tone in the young lady's voice.

"Oh? No? Uh, I'm sorry! I thought—"

"Madam, we're here for, uh, Tsharak," Kalas intervened. "We heard he's been spending a lot of time here recently. Do you know if he's here today? Oh! And some friends of ours: they might have come in just a little while ago. Do you know if they're around?"

"Oh! Yes, of course! They're…well, they're with your friend Mister Tsharak! I—just down this corridor, past the main chamber: there's a room with green double doors. That's where—"

"I know my way to Grandfather's offices, Rïzina," Zhalera huffed. "C'mon, Kalas. Let's get this over with."

Kalas offered Rïzina an apologetic shrug as Zhalera thundered past. She hadn't gone too far when a mix of familiar voices interrupted and overshadowed her heavy footsteps.

"Zhalera!" said Tsharak, nearly dropping the sheaf of papers he carried. "Master Kalas!"

He slapped his papers at Nashmur, standing beside him, and rushed at the pair with his unusual grace and ease. Collecting them both in a wiry hug, he held them for just a moment.

"It's good to see you, too!" Kalas agreed. "But there's—"

"Falthwën, I know. When my…*tattoo* no longer shined with his light in time with The Song, I knew something must have happened. Those markings are less a tattoo and more an *imprint* of the Swath's energies. Your friends confirmed my suspicions. They've also explained—as best they can—some of your adventures! Oh! My manners! *Dàbiras nir, Shâu* Abarandal!"

The ancient man held out a hand, which, after a reluctant moment, the *eru* accepted. He placed a solemn kiss atop her knuckles and released her. She giggled at his manner, smiled, and sang her thanks to him.

"Ah, right! Only song, they told me. No matter. You have the most beautiful voice, my dear!

"Now then, why don't you join me while I finish up with the Chief Magistrate? Won't take more than half an hour, I think. After that, we can discuss *other* things. Come, this way!"

He gestured everyone toward Sàrush's offices while he lagged behind. Before Kalas passed him, he snared the young man with his gnarled hand and held him back a moment. When the others were beyond earshot, he whispered, "I've made some discoveries while you were away! I've learned some things about your artifact, I believe, and I've been waiting—impatiently, I confess—for an opportunity to share them with you!"

Chapter V

In the Belly of the Pump

Subtle electricity surged through the old man's callused fingers as he removed them from Kalas' arm. The tingle persisted for a moment before dissolving in a promise of adventure. Kalas thought about questioning Tsharak right then, but everyone was waiting for them in Sàrush's well-appointed offices.

Mortared stone wedged between crumbling vestiges of the building' original infrastructure spanned from wall to wall. The remaining wooden columns had been plastered and painted so many times it was difficult to tell where the ancient supports ended and the stonework began. Every polished surface sparkled in the combination of torch- and suns-light illuminating the area. Collections of shallow drawers and cubbies for scrolls lined almost every foot of floor space. Neat to a fault, except for the items Tsharak had retrieved from Nashmur and dropped on Sàrush's lacquered wooden desk, Kalas tried to picture Wodram's study arranged in similar fashion. Laughed when he couldn't. Zhalera grunted, but before he could explain, her grandfather emerged from some back office.

Shorter than Kalas remembered, but not as paunchy, the balding, tired-looking man offered everyone a smile—a genuine smile, it seemed—and sat down at his desk. He chided Tsharak with a good-natured air as he brushed away his latest drawings. As he made his introductions, Kalas saw Falthwën had been right in his assessment of the Chief Magistrate: his former haughtiness was gone; in its place was unfamiliar humility and, perhaps, contrition for his former attitude. As he spoke with the others, his eyes continually darted toward Zhalera, who took great pains to avoid his gaze.

"I had no idea," he marveled, his voice tinged with regret, when Nashmur and the others explained their encounter with Ësfàyami. "I was convinced she'd take our troubles seriously. I thought it'd be a simple matter. I—No: I thought I could achieve some small fame for myself by bringing the Falcon's attention to an otherworldly malfeasance within its borders. As if such a thing would merit such grandeur!"

He laughed at himself and shook his head, and so he missed Zhalera's cautious glance in his direction.

"Misters Rül and Kalas, and…Zhalera, my granddaughter: please forgive me for my failure as a leader. Kalas, your mother was right: had I listened to your father—had I possessed the courage to hear him when I had the chance, several *Lohwàlarrinme* might still be with us today…"

"*Âu* Sàrush, I'm not trying to be rude, but, well, what *happened* to you?!" Kalas blurted.

"Not rude at all, my son," he began with a rough cough, "and it's simple, really: I'd become nothing but a pompous *nagag,* a bag of hot wind more interested in power and perception than the true well-being of this town. Don't you see? While it's true the *rudzhegume* sowed death and destruction upon our town, their malevolence only took root because I, in my pride, prepared the soil for their murderous deeds. I will live with the shame of my hubris until I breathe my last, and, well…

"I tried to step down as Chief Magistrate, but for some reason, Mister Tsharak here persuaded the rest of the elders not to accept my resignation. He won't tell me why, and I've ceased asking. With his help, we—no, the townsfolk, really—have accomplished much, but there's still a lot of work to be done…

"Zhalera, my child, after Mister Tsharak and I have gone over his latest drawings for improvements to the Lower Quarter, would you permit me to show you something? I'll understand if your answer is no."

Zhalera said nothing, but she regarded him with a cool look and offered him a subtle shrug.

Tsharak explained his drawings to the Chief Magistrate and suggested redistricting portions of the old riverbed. He also pointed out how additional towers facing the Empty Sea could provide better coverage of the far side of town as part of his ultimate argument for a complete ring of equidistant lookouts surrounding the town's heart.

"Each tower will have a bell with a unique pitch, as well as a brazier holding a pyre of wood. Day or night, should anything approach the town, guards will be able to sound an alarm. And if we build those larger towers at the center of town—I know you're not crazy about the idea!—we could alert every citizen in a matter of minutes. Or less!"

"You and your towers, old man!" Sàrush laughed, and Kalas saw Zhalera scrutinize him with more care as he continued to display this most unfamiliar demeanor. "I understand your concerns, but towers in the middle of the Crescent?! I'm not so sure our citizens will agree to such an eyesore! The towers around Lohwàlar's borders make perfect sense: I can't imagine the rest of the Council finding fault with those."

"If the towers around the town are tall enough, why not add mirrors to focus light from the signal fires toward the *Crescent*—is that right?" suggested Pava. "At night, people would know something was happening when they saw your Crescent all lit up. You could even cut the mirrors in such a way that it'd be easy to see which tower—or towers—the warning was coming from, too."

Sàrush chewed his lower lip as he contemplated the idea. Tsharak just laughed: "What a *brilliant*—if you'll pardon the pun!— solution, dear one!"

Zhalera's grandfather seemed to agree. "It's worth considering, my child! Pava, yes? From under the Áthradho? I like it. I do! I'm just not sure where we'd find enough glass for all the mirrors we'd need…"

"I'll bet Miss Pava here has an idea," Tsharak winked.

"She could even help you get everything set up," bragged Rül with a hand on her shoulder.

"Yes, I'll bet she could," Sàrush allowed. "Something we'll be sure to mention at the next Council meeting! Tsharak, I'll make the initial motion: you'll second it?"

"Of course, Chief Magistrate!"

"Just *Sàrush*, please! That title…doesn't rest as comfortably as it once did…"

"As you wish, *Sàrush*," the old man said with a florid bow. At first, Kalas wondered if he grasped the sarcasm in Tsharak's gesture: when Sàrush shook his head with a self-deprecating laugh, he had his answer.

This is not *the same man!*

Tsharak continued: "All right, Master Kalas! And the rest of you! The Chief—I mean, we're done here for now. Let's—"

"Oh, Mister Tsharak, a word in private, please?" Sàrush beckoned. He nodded and waved the others into the hall.

"He's…different," Kalas nodded at Zhalera, hoping to gauge her reaction. She kept her mouth shut, but her body language shifted: her grandfather's new mien intrigued her in a way she couldn't disguise. She maintained a sense of caution, remembering, perhaps, some unspoken history she refused to discuss. Kalas had asked her about it—more than once—but she never elaborated on *why* she disliked her grandfather so much.

When Tsharak exited the Chief Magistrate's offices, he informed them he'd just been assigned another task. Said it wouldn't take long, that everyone should follow him, and so they did.

"Patched the hole in your roof," he said along the way, addressing Kalas. "Took care of everything else, too. Should be in perfect condition. I hope you'll forgive the intrusion—I made sure no one set foot in Wodram's study."

"I wondered about that. The roof, I mean," Kalas admitted.

"Where are we going?" said Zhalera as they followed Tsharak through Lohwàlar's streets. "It's almost like you're leading us toward what's left of Father's smithy..."

"Oh? Well, we're almost there. You'll see!"

He brought them around the corner of a partially-renovated building. Kalas could neither remember what it was nor bring himself to care when he saw what Tsharak intended them to see: where Gandhan's smithy used to be, someone had built a *new* smithy, resurrected its old stones and fitted all the gaps with new specimens. Its old hinges, blackened in the attack, had been scoured, rubbed, and polished; now, fastened to thick new slabs of resin-scented wood, they gleamed in the afternoon suns. Above the double doors, someone had replaced Gandhan's old shingle with a new one that bore Zhalera's name. Awed, she said nothing as she rushed forward and tried opening the doors.

Locked.

"Tsharak! What—who—how did this happen?! I have so many questions! Thank you! Thank you! Thank you *so much!*"

"Your thanks are misdirected, dear one," he said as he reached within the folds of his tunic. He produced a key that sparkled like the door's revitalized hardware and held it out to her. "When he asked for my help, I made a few—*minor*—contributions, but this is all because of your *grandfather's* dogged determination."

She paused, her hand halfway to the key in Tsharak's.

"He wanted to show this place to you himself. Sàrush explained to me—confessed, really—his unworthy treatment of your father, how he'd once believed Gandhan's trade was for lesser folk than himself. When his daughter died, he'd caught a glimpse of the family he'd cheated himself from knowing, but in his pride, he couldn't bring himself to admit that to anyone. Not even to your grandmother.

"When Gandhan died, he said it was like someone pulled a lever in his soul. He wrestled with how to approach you about it: he feared—correctly, it seems—that you'd be unwilling to hear anything he'd have to say. By the time he mustered up the courage to come to you, you'd already left for İsriba.

"He couldn't bear the thought of losing you, too. Even if you wouldn't tolerate his presence, you were still a part of Lohwàlar, and he'd bide his time, let you recognize the change in him—but you disappeared, and right away, he insisted the smithy be rebuilt. At first, the other elders insisted it could wait: Gandhan was gone, you were gone—and might never return—and other families had greater need. He agreed, but for hours at a time, in the early morning and again at twilight, he'd be out here clearing away debris, sorting damaged stones from others he could reuse…He didn't advertise his project, nor did he hide it, but little by little, other townsfolk asked if they could help. With gratitude none of them expected, he gladly thanked them for their assistance. I think he spent days trying to get those doors' fixtures as bright as possible!

"Those that helped him spread the word about this strange 'new' Sàrush. As you can imagine, most wouldn't believe it—until they visited the smithy for themselves. When everything was finished, he informed the Council elders of his decision to step down: but he'd achieved such a connection with the people—*his* people—at last, that none would hear it! Like Falthwën suggested, I brought my designs to Sàrush shortly after everything had happened, and he'd come to trust in me. It took some doing, but I persuaded him to remain Chief Magistrate, and, reluctantly, he agreed.

"That shingle—*your* shingle, dear one!—Sàrush drew with his own hand. Now, before you get the idea that he just rebuilt this place to buy your approval: he wasn't sure if you—if any of you—would survive your journey. He kept thinking about the *kelâme* who'd lost their lives on the way to Ìsriba before the wolves attacked, and he was almost sure you'd suffer the same fate. This place is yours—free and clear: you'll find the deed inside just waiting for your signature. If you choose not to speak to him, he won't press the matter.

"However, if I might offer a bit of advice? *Choose reconciliation!* Not because he's earned it, but because there are better ways to spend one's days than rehearsing bitterness until it becomes routine. And that's coming from someone who's almost attained one hundred twenty-eight Sevens, mind you..."

He pressed the key into Zhalera's trembling hand, wrapped her fingers around it, and concluded: "He asked me not to tell you any of this. I told him I was going to anyway. He knew not to argue about it and just handed me the key. If he got *his* way, this smithy's origin would remain a mystery to you."

Stunned, Zhalera squeezed the key. The key to *her* smithy. Her face surrendered all expression to a sort of numb listlessness.

"I...I didn't know. I never would have thought it possible..." she droned.

"That makes *two of you*," Tsharak huffed. "Tomorrow, *talk* to him. Learn for yourself what he's become. That's all I'm asking."

"That...I can do," she allowed.

"Excellent! Now then, why don't you show us around your smithy, and then we can discuss…ah…"

"They know," Kalas said. "The Swath told us there are even more of those things out there, under the earth!"

"I suspected as much!" Tsharak exulted.

Zhalera inserted her key and turned the lock. Gandhan, her father, had built it not too long ago, and as its tumblers shifted into place, she remembered his hammer blows with every click as the door unlocked.

"Come on in," she said as she wiped her eyes on her sleeve.

2.

The new smithy's interior still held the faint scents of pitch and naphtha, as well as those of charcoal, seasoned wood, and a few others: absent were the fragrances of creosote or burned oil. Zhalera took a few moments to explore: she removed her sword and set it on a drafting table as she poked around an arsenal of tools. That's when she noticed Gandhan's hammer, situated atop a huge anvil. The last time she'd seen it, it had been matted with blood and fur; now, cleaned and freshly polished, it gleamed. She looked around for other signs of Gandhan's former presence—and wasn't surprised when she found none.

"This place is wonderful, it is," she began, "but it's…it's just…"

"It's not Gandhan's," Tsharak finished.

"No, it's not," she confessed.

"It's *yours*," he reminded her. "Gandhan is and always will be a part of you: so, in some small way, it *is* his, too…"

Zhalera nodded and stared at the ground for a moment until the old man clapped his hands and suggested everyone find a seat.

"Here's as good a place as any," he said as he struck sparks into sconces along the walls. "Better than most, actually. I don't think we'll be bothered for a while."

Gathered around the drafting table, Tsharak reached within a pocket for the strange shape he'd shown Kalas almost three months ago. He set it down and gave everyone a moment to stare at it, to consider its lines and curves and markings.

"Doesn't look like much, does it?" he chuckled. "Kalas, if you and Zhalera had never shown that *artifact* to me, I probably never would have remembered that I had this thing!"

Nïmrïk looked at the symbols carved along the object's milky surface. He stood, shifted his position, then shifted again to gain a better perspective.

"You can pick it up. It's quite safe. I think!"

"Uh, Nïmrïk? Maybe…I mean…"

"No, it's all right, lad. I've seen what I needed to. It definitely looks like something from under Deridzhas. Those characters look familiar, too. Mister Tsharak, you say there's something similar not too far from here?"

"There used to be! Sharuyan caused a mountain to fall on it. It would take years—Sevens maybe!—to clear away all the rock. With *conventional* means, that is."

"Indeed," Nïmrïk nodded as he returned to his corner.

"Loradan of the Swath said *erume* tried to *unmake* such things whenever they could. Said they came from a time before the world was cracked. Falthwën said he'd been *marked* somehow by the *ekume* and couldn't risk anything more than a rockslide: otherwise, I think he would have *unmade* the craft—that's what he called it—at the bottom of the Empty Sea," Kalas informed Tsharak.

"Is it their policy to *unmake all* such *vàsume?*" Tsharak prodded.

"Uh, I think so? She said *usually,* I think. I don't know. My head hasn't been right for a few weeks now."

"I ask because I suspect the Pump is part of such an artifact!"

The *Lohwàlarrinme* said nothing, dumbstruck by the old man's suspicion. The others exchanged perplexed glances until Nashmur spoke up: "The…*Pump?*"

"This place is a desert," Kalas reminded him. "Didn't used to be, but, well, you've seen enough to know! The River used to run through the Lower Quarter—dozens of Sevens ago. Like any town, Lohwàlar would have died without water. Someone discovered the Pump and—well, Tsharak was there: he could tell you better!"

"*Dozens* of Sevens ago?" Nashmur scoffed.

"No one knew where the Pump came from. How it got into the Empty Sea," Tsharak explained, ignoring the soldier's skepticism. "We thought it was a gift from the *elume* or *erume,* though honestly, once we figured out how to redirect its output, we didn't care! For generations, its ceaseless activity has held this place together."

"People had to maintain it from time to time," Kalas continued. "My father was really good at it. Last time he was there, part of it had broken. That sort of thing happened once in a while. Tsharak, what makes you think the Pump is an artifact?"

"*Part* of an artifact, my boy! When the lot of you left for Ïsriba, I searched the archives under the Council Hall for old records, just in case I came across something that might help with reconstruction. I had no idea I'd come across a report from the first examination of the Pump!

"It was buried under Sevens of forgotten books and papers. Would have been easy to overlook, but throughout my years, I've developed an eye for such things—you've seen my home, so you know! Curious, I took a closer look. I don't remember the engineers and artists who scribed that volume, but their work is beautiful! Sàrush should put some of it on display!

"Anyway, something about the drawings seemed familiar to me. Not like remembering something I'd already seen: more like connecting two ideas I'd once believed unrelated. Maybe 'familiar' isn't the right word. I took a few trips into the Sea on my own, poked around the Pump's innards, and that's when I found it! Some kind of door, almost buried under a maze of gears and pulleys, pipes and conduits. It was—"

"—rusted shut," Kalas interrupted. "Oh! I'm sorry! I—"

"You knew about it?" Tsharak raised an eyebrow. "Why didn't you—"

"No! I mean, yes! I mean, Father told me he and Azhëk found something like that when they were fixing something. I don't remember what. Father said Azhëk tried to open it, but it wouldn't move. He—Azhëk—said it was *hot,* too. I asked Father about it, but he insisted it wouldn't open."

"Most curious," Tsharak mused. "Assuming Azhëk's door is the same one I discovered, he must not have spent too much time with it. I gave it a few sturdy whacks with a stick, and a crust of some kind chipped away from its surface. You know me: I gave it a few *more* whacks until I could get the end of my stick wedged under this crust. A few tugs and it cracked away like a shell! It seemed to me like something—the rock itself, maybe—had *melted* over the door and cooled. It wasn't that thick: maybe a quarter-inch at the thickest."

"I was still at the Sanctuary. The wolf attack. I think Father was anxious to finish up as quickly as he could," Kalas said.

"Had Azhëk spent just a few more minutes on it, he probably would have discovered it first: symbols like those etched across your *vàsu*—or the ones on your translucency, or the ones on *this* curious thing—had been painted or printed across the door. The colors were still so bright after all these Sevens! Millennia, possibly! And even though it looked like regular, half-rusted steel, it wasn't! It's something else! Not *exactly* like the *skin* on your artifact, but unlike anything I've ever seen!"

"What?! Why would no one have noticed it before?"

"That 'crust' was extensive. Almost like someone intentionally tried to cover things beneath a layer of slag. Unless someone went looking for it, he'd have no reason to notice it: I'm surprised Azhëk noticed anything! I suppose it's possible people *could* have noticed it and just thought it wasn't important. The Pump was new technology to us: almost *everything* about it was a mystery, a marvel, and it was a different age."

"I want to see it," Kalas insisted.

"I don't!" interjected Rül. "If it's anything like that nightmare under the mining town, count me out!

"That door. It's still closed?" said Nïmrïk from the corner he'd claimed while Tsharak shared his discovery.

"It is. With the 'crust' knocked away, I discovered a ring—part of a bulkhead, maybe—sticking out from the wall about half a foot. That ring had a small rectangle carved out of it, and inside that was a smaller, oblong indentation: I ran my hand all along it, but nothing happened. Since that smaller hole and this object here have consistent markings, I held this thing against it: same result. That's one of the things I most wanted you to see!"

"Let's say you *do* get it open. What if the air behind it is like the air in Deridzhas? What if opening that door poisons Lohwàlar and turns your people into *eaters*. Or something worse?!" Pava postulated.

Kalas opened his mouth to rebut the *úrukilmukrit* girl's concern, but in his mind he saw his father, doubled over and coughing blood; he saw his friends, stumbling through the mines as they choked on its deleterious atmosphere.

"I…that's a good point," he conceded with a wry frown. He furrowed his brow as he considered things. "I wish Falthwën were here…"

"If there were some way for *me* to get behind that door, I could let you know, but, given our circumstances, I don't think that's possible without opening it first," Nïmrïk said as he eyed Kalas, then Tsharak.

"How could *you* let us know? Wouldn't its atmosphere affect you, too?" the old man wondered, his eyes narrowed.

"I...uh...hmm," he floundered. Kalas held up a hand and explained.

"Tsharak..." he began. "Nimrïk is...not *edhu*...He's...he used to be an *elu*..."

"'Used to be,' you say?" Tsharak's eyes flashed toward Zhalera's sheathed sword. "So he's a *nëshras egu*, then?"

As he spoke, his voice increased in pitch and volume, his rage apparent. He glared daggers at the humble-looking figure, unmoving and staring at the ground.

"That's why I didn't say anything at first," Kalas sighed. "Look, Tsharak: I know you harbor no love for *egunàm*. Not after they destroyed Kësharan. And you—more than anyone—should understand how much Zhalera and I hate *egume*, too. Nimrïk is not like the others. If you'd been with us under Ïsriba, you would have seen him risk his life for us more than once! Heshradan, of the Great Swath, believes him. I do, too."

Nimrïk said nothing, and despite his earlier pleas that Kalas not feel sorry for him, the young man felt sorry for him anyway.

"When he learned what was happening in Kësharan, he tried to get there in time to prevent its destruction. He was too late—he can't hear The Song anymore—but he saw Falthwën rescue you. He kept an eye on you as best he could, until *erume* chased him away.

"And then there's Nanësra, the *elu* who confronted us on our way across the steppes. She intended to kill Nimrïk. *Kadhëmba*, she called him. But she didn't. In the ancient past, Nimrïk fought against her, and even *she* is reserving judgment. She's wary, but she's patient. If an *elu* can bide her time, give him an opportunity to demonstrate his remorse, surely you can, too?"

Tsharak took a series of deep breaths, closed his eyes and traced a pattern in the air until he'd tamed the visible elements of his fury. In forced tones, and after delivering a warning, he agreed he'd remain civil: "Keep your distance, *rudzh!*"

"*Kadhëmba* is what the *elume* called me when I was still among their number. Nanësra uses that name as a reminder of everything I've squandered. An insult. A richly-deserved insult," Nïmrïk explained. With a heavy sigh, he continued: "Mister Tsharak, if—"

"You're not going anywhere," Kalas interrupted with a dismissive wave.

"Uh, all right then, so…" Rül stammered. "What's next? What about the things Shosafin discovered in Serular? We still have to figure out what Marugan's up to, right? And what about that cult? That can't be good news! Where *is* Shosafin, anyway? Must still be at the farm…"

"I thought we'd solve the wolf problem in Ïsriba," Kalas admitted. "I had no idea what we were getting ourselves into. I knew nothing would be the same—not for me, not for Zhalera—after the attack, but I guess I thought, somehow, things would go back to the way they were. Mostly.

"I want to investigate the Pump, just to get it out of my head if nothing else, but just in case Pava's right, it's probably wisest not to open that door—assuming that's even possible—until we have a way of knowing what's on the other side. Right now, we should make Marugan our priority. Marugan and others like him, people bending the world toward war. I think heading for Galámur makes the most sense. I don't know if the people Shosafin talked to near Serular are trustworthy, but it's all we've got."

"Serular!" Tsharak exclaimed. He abandoned his smoldering gaze at Nïmrïk and cocked his head toward Kalas. "What were you doing in Serular? It's been a while, but last I heard, that was no place for…well, you're not *childen*, but…you know what I mean, *hish?*"

"Apparently, it's not the place for *anyone*," Nashmur said. "My cousin heard rumors that led him there. For some time now, it's been overrun by the *Ragus pïn*—"

"—*pïn Tshaggul Kavar. Eku* worshipers!" Tsharak interrupted as fresh anger danced across his face.

"Maybe. Maybe *eru* worshipers," the soldier elaborated. "Ilbardhën—Shosafin, I mean! Shosafin said the cultists described the Deathless Flame as wrapped in *fire:* the *ekume* we faced beneath the Vault were pure darkness. Not a shred of any kind of light."

"*Eru* worshipers?! *Erume* are no more worthy of worship than *edhume*—or even *elume!* Created beings, every one of us! I've encountered *eku* cults in my travels, but I've never known an *eru* to countenance such nonsense. If this has been going on for Sevens… If an *eru* is permitting such flagrant blasphemy, then the prophesied darkness is approaching much faster than I thought!"

While the heavens were silent, while the stars were black, Kalas recalled with a shiver.

"But you won't make it to Galámur before the year is out. Not through Gambarad's winters! If you left *today,* it'd probably take a few weeks to reach Tarular. Under the Standing Mountains, you'd have to deal with the ice and snow that blows in from the *Shadaún Ilarod.* Then, it's a hard slog through the only pass on the windward side: *Töthrismedas Kig,* it's called. It's rough enough in the summer, when the days are longer: this time of year, it'd be madness.

"On the other side of Trolls' Gap, you'd have a few more days on the road before you'd come to Melash-Niruk, the nearest port. That's where you'd have to charter a ship to sail you across the ocean. I've never been there, but I understand Galámur is no less than two weeks' voyage from Melash—assuming smooth seas and prevailing tailwinds.

"The forests between here and Töthrismedas Kig are prime hunting grounds for all kinds of scoundrels: the roads are slow going, and the crags give them plenty of places to wait in ambush. As anxious as I'm sure you are, you'll do no one—nor the prophecy—any favors rushing toward an icy death!"

"If I just understood how this whole *kalswàrafi* thing worked!" Kalas sighed as his shoulders sagged. "Tsharak, that story you told about Falthwën: what he said when he found you under Kësharan. 'There's magic in your blood,' right? Does that mean…what I want to know is…can *you* move through the *kalthesh?* Like the *erume?*"

"Alas, my boy, I cannot. I've come to believe that the magic he spoke of is the source of my longevity. Traveling after the manner of light is beyond my grasp of The Song."

"Then I guess we'll have to wait," Kalas acknowledged with a helpless grimace. "Wait and hope the world doesn't turn to ash before the winter ends."

3.

For the next week, Kalas and the others remained in Lohwàlar, allowed Tsharak—and, on occasion, Sàrush—to point out some of the progress they'd made rebuilding over the last few months. Including the repairs made to his parents' home. He discovered he could spend hours a day in Wodram's study, poring over ancient volumes and perusing ragged scrolls. He tried spending a night in his old room, but his memories made awkward bedfellows. Zhalera had been more than happy to share her empty home with him. Rül had opened up his farm, where Shosafin seemed to be spending an inordinate amount of time, but Pava, Nashmur, and the gruff soldier were the only takers: Abarandal and Nïmrïk stayed close to Kalas and Zhalera.

Some days, Zhalera would sneak away for hours at a time; when she returned, her floral fragrance mixed with charcoal smoke, Kalas understood she'd been at the smithy. His first instinct had been to volunteer whatever help she wanted; his second, better instinct had been to let her keep her secrets.

Maybe this time alone is what she needs right now to build her confidence…

He studied his grandfather's ancient tome, staring at each character and every woodcut and willing them to reveal their secrets.

Recalcitrant, each refused.

Back at Zhalera's home, just before drifting off one night, the shapes seemed to *move* as his eyes fluttered against sleep. Sitting upright, he stared at the pages again.

Nothing had changed.

That's when Kalas heard both *eru* and *egu* sharing songs from another room. Songs and laughter. He remembered Nïmrïk's song from Ïsriba's dungeons, but as he harmonized with Abarandal, its lachrymose underpinnings gave way to more hopeful strains. He and Zhalera, approaching from different angles, had tried to listen with as much discretion as they could manage; sensing their presence, however, Abarandal beckoned for them to join her and Nïmrïk, pleaded for Zhalera to sing with them, like she'd done on the road. Tentative at first, she agreed, gaining confidence as she rediscovered her voice. Kalas closed his eyes as the medicine in their music soothed his battered head and the thoughts contained therein. With his eyes still closed, he sensed an arrhythmic brightness tapping at his eyelids. Annoyed at first, he opened them, scanned the room for its source, and stifled a gasp when he saw Valarandal's blade pulsing within its scabbard. It only took a moment for its oscillating glow to synchronize with the curious trio.

"Guys! Look!" he whispered as he pointed toward the sword. "I'm sorry, I hate to interrupt, but I thought you'd want to see this!"

The singers stopped and turned toward the weapon. Not long after their last notes faded out, its subtle luminance disappeared, too.

"What do you think it means?" Kalas asked, excited. He'd directed his question to Zhalera, but Abarandal answered.

"But how can that be? Peradan said she was gone, caught in one of the *ekumedas* 'singularities,' he called them."

"No, she's right!" Zhalera insisted.

"She's—wait: can you understand her now?!"

"No! I—not really, but I recognized Valaran's name. I don't know how! I—Abarandal's right, though: *Valaran's alive!*"

"How can you be so sure?"

"Tsharak's tattoo!" she remembered. "He said *Falthwën's* light went out in it: he didn't say anything about Valaran's! Don't you think he would have mentioned that?"

"That makes sense," Kalas admitted. "He called his tattoo an *imprint* of the Swath. I wonder how it got there, on his hand like that. Remind me to ask him next time we see him! I guess Peradan must have been mistaken about Valaran's fate. I wish we had some way to let Loradan and the others know she's still out there!

"Nïmrïk, what do you think? You know more about the stars than any of us!"

Nïmrïk hadn't said anything since the bloom surrounding Val-arandal winked out. He maintained his silence, apparently choosing his next words with care.

"Valaran wasn't there, underneath the Vault. Not wholly. But whatever she'd imparted to that blade was enough to complete the summoning. What if placing that weapon—more accurately, that object containing the spark of her essence—on her symbol forged a connection with her, wherever she really is? What if that object has become a bridge for her, a means of communication? I'm only speculating, of course."

"We need to tell someone! Abarandal, can you reach out to the Swath? To any other *erume*? Maybe someone—"

"Maybe we should keep our secret for the moment," Nïmrïk

interrupted. "Sifuran was right, I believe: *someone* betrayed the Swath. Don't you find it *convenient* that the *ekume* appeared not long after the *erume* ripped a hole in spacetime and brought forth Abarandal? They were waiting for *her.* Abarandal, the *ekume* were waiting for *you.*"

The shocked *eru* shrilled a prestissimo stream of staccato notes until Kalas placed a hand on her shoulder and promised, "You know we'll do everything we can—more than that, if necessary—to prevent anyone or anything from *misusing* you, if you'll forgive my choice of words. It makes sense, though: just imagine how dark forces might *abuse* the *kathin kelësh* should it—should *you,* Abarandal, fall into their hands!"

Warbling between pesante and furioso styles, she stared into Kalas' eyes as she wept her next phrases.

"I know! It's all right! I understand! I'm still figuring out this prophecy business, too! Look at me! I know so little about The Song, about how to use it, yet here I am. You say you don't know what the prophecy means when it says *great power?* Something we have in common! Not even the *erume* who summoned you know. Not fully!

"We'll figure this out. Somehow. All of us. It'll be a while before we can head for…what'd Tsharak say? Melash-Niruk? That gives us some time to try to work things out. Tsharak, salty as he is regarding Nïmrïk, is a wealth of information. And my grandfather left a bunch of books and scrolls and stuff in his study. We can search through all that, too.

"I'll make a deal with you, Abarandal, because I'm guilty of the same things I see you doing. You doubt yourself. You doubt this prophecy. Or maybe your place within it. Maybe all of those things. Going forward, why don't we agree that the prophecy means what it says, that it *does* speak of us? I don't mean let's pretend we've got it all figured out: I mean, let's make whatever choices we can to bring light back to a dimming world. What do you say, Abarandal-Ilkelëshún? Will you make that deal?"

Bright and shining tears—fear, relief, something else: Kalas had no idea—brimmed within her eyes and spilled across her pale almond skin. With the back of one hand, she wiped them away; she wrapped the other around his wrist, held his gaze, and gave his forearm a single, solid squeeze. She neither said—nor sang—a thing, simply nodded with fresh determination in her glittering eyes.

"Perfect!"

In the morning, Kalas woke without the constant headache he'd experienced since Deridzhas. He felt better than he had in almost a month. As he helped Zhalera prepare a simple breakfast, he told her he planned to see if Tsharak would agree to show him the markings he'd discovered.

"I don't know if Rül and Pava—or Soshafin, for that matter—would be interested in coming with us, but I'll ask them anyway. All of you are welcome, too, of course!"

"Kalas, is that a good idea?" Zhalera prodded.

"No, I'm not going to open it! I'm not even going to touch anything! I've got that piece of *not-paper* with me, Tsharak has his stone—he never did say what he thought it was!—and, well..."

Abarandal sang her intention to come with him. Nïmrïk shrugged and nodded.

"It's more than just wanting to see that door," Kalas admitted. "For Sevens, Father maintained that Pump. In his own words, he told me how much he just seemed to *understand* it. It seems like forever since I was there, and I just want to see if I can...I don't know, *feel* him—some sense of his presence in his handiwork, I guess. It's selfish. I won't pretend it's not. And I could use a break from all this sitting around, staring at books full of stuff I can't make sense of."

"Yeah, I know how you feel," Zhalera confided. "I've been firing up the forge, pounding out a few simple pieces, just trying to remember everything Father had taught me…Maybe a break's not such a bad idea after all…"

"I'm glad you think so! Father kept all kinds of gear at the house. Tents and things. And tools—but we won't need those. I hope Rül's all right with us spending a night at his farm: it's too far to walk there and back and into the Empty Sea in a single day. We'll stop by the Council Hall, see if Tsharak's there. Leave word with Rïzina or someone if he's not. You could spend some of that time with your grandfather, too…"

"It's still weird," she said, almost embarrassed for some reason. "It's hard, letting go of a lifetime of anger in just a couple of weeks. I'm trying! I am!"

Kalas offered her a slow nod. Tàran and Màla had been the only family he'd ever known: their parents—Kalas' grandparents—had predeceased them Sevens before Kalas entered into their shared lives. Now that the people he'd called Mother and Father all his life were gone, now that he knew he shared none of their blood, he wondered about his true origins. Màla and Tàran would always be his mother and father. Their disparate biologies would never diminish the love they'd lavished on him: if anything, somehow, such incongruities amplified it.

"All right then, everyone. Let's pack up what we'll need, swing through the Crescent, and head up to Rül's."

Tsharak wasn't at the Council Hall, but Rïzina said she expected him later in the day. Zhalera asked about Sàrush's whereabouts, but his secretary claimed—with a touch too much insistence—she didn't know. Kalas could tell Zhalera doubted the woman's story, but she opted not to press the matter.

"Please tell Mister Tsharak we'll be up at Thara's farm for the day, then into the Empty Sea in the morning. To show our guests the Pump. I just…I thought he might be interested to know," Kalas finished.

"I wonder where Grandfather is," Zhalera mused when they'd left the Hall. "Was Rïzina acting strangely?"

Abarandal nodded. So did the others.

"We'll try again after we've seen the Pump," Kalas promised.

"Oh, you're here!" said Rül when Kalas and the others, panting, found him in the stables, rubbing down his horses. Runner's coat glimmered in the afternoon suns, and he whinnied hello when he saw them. Dancer snorted, impatient for the farm boy to continue his long, slow brushstrokes. "I would have told you tomorrow, but since you're here…"

"Told us what?" Zhalera said, her eyes narrowed.

"I—Pava and I—uh, well, I—we need to…I need to return her to the Áthradho. Just for a few days. A week at the most. We've got time before Tsharak said we should make for Galámur, so I thought it'd be all right. The steppes are cold, sure, but all things considered, they're not *that* cold. And we'll be back before you need to head north! I promise!"

"All the way to the Gateway?! And only for a few days? What's going on, Rül? Everything all right?" Zhalera pressed him.

"This seems…sudden," Kalas agreed.

Rül said nothing for a moment as he continued running his brush across Dancer's flanks. Unwilling—or unable, perhaps—to look either of them in the eye, he admitted, "I promised Rive. Maybe I should have told you, but I…everything happened so fast! And I wasn't—I'm still not…I don't know. I'm sorry!"

"No, Rül, I understand," insisted Kalas. "I mean, I don't, but it doesn't matter. It's a long trip. Will you be all right? Should we come with you?"

"No! Uh, I mean, Nashmur's coming with us, and without the coach, we can make better time. Mother and Shosafin have been teaching Pava how to ride: she and Ascender have really started to understand one another! That's where those three are right now. Besides, we won't be gone for more than a month."

"Is this what you and Rive were discussing? You two disappeared for almost a whole day," Zhalera remembered.

"No more than a month," he repeated, his eyes fixed on Dancer's hide.

"Right," said Kalas with a shrewd look in his eyes. "Speaking of Shosafin: I think I've seen him once or twice since we've been back. Has he recovered from whatever happened to him in Serular?"

"Oh, that. Yeah, he's fine. Better than fine, really! He's been helping Mother with farm stuff. Including the books: did you know he's really got a way with figures? He moved some things around and made some suggestions that should really help pay down Father's debt!"

"You didn't say anything about Shosafin going with you. Is he staying…at the farm?" Zhalera wondered with a sly grin.

"He said he was gonna talk to you about staying in town, but Mother wouldn't hear it! He didn't protest. To be honest, I think she's gotten used to having him around…and I think he's gotten used to *being* around. More than once, they've kept me awake at night, laughing and sharing stories. You know what's sad? I can't remember her and Father *ever* having conversations like that…

"Anyway, after I finish brushing out the horses, we'll find Mother, get you situated for the night. I guess we'll say goodbye in the morning."

4·

Thara was more than happy to provide a place for Rül's friends. She was also more than happy to push a broom or a shovel into each person's hands and point him toward his task. She tried to apologize to both Kalas and Zhalera for the way her late husband had treated them; instead, both thanked her for helping Rül pack up the cart.

That evening, after a meal that rivaled anything from Mbirin's Place, Rül and Pava, exhausted, said goodnight and shambled off toward their respective rooms.

"I suppose I should do the same," yawned Nashmur, stretching his vast arms and twisting his wrists in the air. *"Lushà hàf,* Thara, cousin, and the rest of you!"

Standing behind Thara on his way out of the room, he winked at Shosafin, who pretended not to notice. Kalas caught the former commander's signal and, with a smile, asked the old soldier: "Seems like you've stayed busy these last few weeks. Does Thara have you mucking stalls and shoveling manure all day, too?"

"Only some days," he said with an expansive grin. Kalas found the expression unsettling: at first he couldn't quite understand why, until he realized he'd never seen Shosafin *smile* before. Not like this. Not with genuine…*happiness.*

"I'll admit it: I like this kind of work!" he added as he dabbed a napkin at the corners of his mouth. "After all my years of stabbing things, it's nice to learn a few new tricks."

As he spoke, Thara regarded him with a curious gaze. She blushed when she realized Kalas had caught her stare: she cleared her throat and started piling her dishes.

Perhaps two, maybe three Sevens younger than Màla, Thara's unevenly suns-bronzed skin still had a glow about it. Choco-late-brown eyes glittered in the dim torchlight as she smoothed a dirty-blonde shock of wavy hair behind her ear. Like Rül's, her face had an inviting roundness to it: wearied from her recent losses and ongoing labors, she still possessed a subtle beauty not lost on Shosafin, if Kalas read things correctly.

"Let me get those," said the soldier, standing and scooping up his and Thara's dishes with his signature fluidity."

So he is *still in there*, Kalas noted.

"After all this time, you're saying people *can* change?" the young man suggested with a quick glance at Nïmrïk, who'd said almost nothing throughout the evening. Shosafin understood his implication, shook his head and laughed, and shrugged as he maneuvered his armload of dirty cups and plates toward the basin.

Before the suns had risen, Kalas helped Rül load his bales and tie them down across the horses' backs. He knew Rül didn't need the help, but the farm boy had come through a lot with him, and he hoped Rül would appreciate the gesture. Thara stood just inside the doorway, a steaming mug of something in her hand, and watched as her only son prepared for yet another journey.

Despite questions from multiple fronts, no amount of coaxing extracted new details from Rül regarding the nature of his trip. Adopting a resolve he'd rarely shown, he tightened Runner's straps and adjusted his tack in polite silence. Nashmur tended to Gilfën while Pava stroked Ascender's cheek.

"I thought you were taking Dancer?" Zhalera inclined her head toward the chestnut mare. "That's…who's that?"

"Ascender," Pava supplied. "Dancer's a great horse, but I don't think he knows what to make of me. Or maybe I don't know how to read him! That's probably it! Ascender, though: I understand her! More than Dancer, anyway!"

"Dancer could use the rest," added Thara. She passed her mug to Shosafin, who materialized from around a corner, and, still barefoot, stepped outside to help the cave-dweller girl into her saddle. "Runner, too, but he's more stubborn than his cousin. And a touch sturdier, if I'm honest. Ascender's a good fit for you—I could tell from the way you practiced riding with her. And she'll appreciate this opportunity to see more of the world beyond this farm! I… wish I were coming with you, but…the farm…Please understand!"

"Looks like we're ready?" suggested Nashmur, astride Gilfën. The ruddy creature snorted and tapped the ground with his hoof. Pava nodded, having offered Thara a grateful smile.

Before he climbed into his own saddle, Rül double-checked the straps holding Rive's *tëvët* in place. He'd rigged it to be accessible with just a simple stretch and a quick flick. Satisfied, he clucked his tongue and turned his mount toward the gate at the bottom of the hill. He hesitated, and Kalas thought he must have sensed Thara's mind somehow: she glided toward him, reached up for his hand, and held it for a moment. Neither said a word. Then she nodded, released her son, and stepped back.

"Shude, mën ar fisgiwares—ar paresëthu àrïv!" Rül promised. With a subtle squeeze against Runner's ribcage and a snap of his reins, he directed his horse toward the Áthradho. The others followed, Pava riding between Rül and Nashmur.

Kalas suggested they stick around the farm for a while, tackle as many of Rül's morning chores as possible. Zhalera and Abarandal agreed. Thara discovered their plot, however: while thankful that her son had such hard-working friends, she insisted they leave such tasks to her hired farm hands.

"You have someplace to be, yes?" she reminded them. "I managed well enough before, when Rül was away, after Barish…Thank you for your kindness, but please, make your investigations! The farm's been here for generations: I can't imagine it's going anywhere anytime soon!"

She tried to make a joke of things, but her sadness, her worry remained embedded in the subtle creases at the corners of her eyes. Kalas hesitated until Zhalera pulled him aside and suggested—loud enough for Thara to overhear: "We'll only be at the Pump for a day or two. Three at the most, right? It'll be at least a month before Rül returns. Plenty of time for us to help out until then…"

"Hey, that's right!" Kalas grinned.

Tàfayan had just cleared the horizon when the three of them finished packing up and departed the farm for the Empty Sea. Kalas tried to explain to Abarandal the object he and his father had discovered not too long ago. He described the Pump, recalling fragments of Tsharak's abbreviated history as he pieced together a rough timeline for her.

"Falthwën referred to the *vàsu* under the Empty Sea as a *craft*. It's unlike anything anyone—except the *erume*, I guess—has ever seen or heard about. No one knows where the Pump came from. Not really. It looks like it's made from ordinary…*stuff*, just like everything else. I just want to see this *door*. Zhalera, wouldn't it be the strangest thing if Lohwàlar's been sitting right on top of one of these artifacts for all this time?!"

"I think the strangest thing would be *Lohwàlarrinme* becoming soulless cannibals—or worse!—because of whatever's inside…"

Kalas paused, considered her statement, then remembered the curious, egg-like containers dangling from the destroyed craft beneath Deridzhas.

"That *would* be stranger," he admitted, "but I told you about that guy in that big room with the dragon? When his…pod, I guess, opened, I caught a whiff of the most *disgusting* odor! Sevens of times nastier than what we smelled from all that green goop inside the Empty Sea artifact! I have no way to know, of course, but I think Deridzhas' artifact was different from ours. The Pump could be yet another variation!"

"A *worse* variation," Nïmrïk suggested. "Just something to think about before 'I just want to *see* this door' becomes 'I just want to *open* this door.'"

"Ha!" Zhalera blurted with a crisp nod toward the *egu*.

"I know less about this place than you, of course, but I've made some…rash decisions in my past: one cannot always fully comprehend just how far-reaching our choices' consequences can be…"

"Noted," Kalas said.

"'Rash decisions'? That's perhaps the greatest understatement I've ever heard! In all my Sevens!" Tsharak cackled as he stood up from the rock on which he'd been sitting. They'd reached the Pump Road about a couple hours after leaving Rül's farm. Rïzina must have gotten word to him, because judging from the way he arched his back, the way his joints cracked and popped in the gentle, late-morning breezes, he'd been waiting there awhile.

"Tsharak!"

"So you intend to examine that door after all? I thought you might! With this cooler weather, we should make good time, reach the Sea just after the first sun outpaces the second in the afternoon!"

With those words, the old man stretched his limbs and started down the road again.

5.

Down in the Empty Sea, Kalas, Zhalera, and even Tsharak shivered when prompted by a chill wind. Nïmrïk and Abarandal seemed unaffected by the drop in temperature. Before making their descent, Kalas looked out across the treetops and noticed their bright green blanket of foliage had changed to orange, a mix of reds and yellows as the trees beneath him struggled against the waning suns-light.

"The suns, as weak as they are this time of year, don't have the opportunity to pump much heat into this canyon!" Tsharak explained. "These trees will *slow down,* one might say: that's why their tops take on those colors. Down by the riverbank, things will look pretty much the same as you remember. It'll be darker. And colder! Not so cold as, say, Ïsriba right now, but colder than back in town! Everyone ready? Let's go!"

After a while, they reached the remains of a stone archway. Vast and ancient, shrouded for unknown Sevens beneath thick underbrush and creeping vines until the last rainfire storm had feasted upon its natural camouflage, Kalas remembered it meant something to Tsharak. He hadn't dared to ask him about it then; now, other matters seemed more important.

The Pump—the *Machine,* the old man said it used to be called—hummed with rhythmic, mechanistic music as its various gears, pulleys, and inner workings performed their tasks, vital to Lohwàlar's continued existence. Kalas heard his father's work in every rising whine and falling whoosh as pipes and chambers filled and flushed: with a subtle tapping sound, the cycle reset and repeated its melody. Tsharak handed torches to everyone and guided them toward its deepest recesses, through shrinking passages and maze-like arrangements of machinery, and stopped only when he reached the "door" he'd described a few days ago. The door Kalas' father, Tàran, had told him about months ago. With nothing more than a wide smile, Tsharak swept his arm toward the presumed aperture. Protruding outward from the wall and studded with bolts or rivets, it bore little resemblance to the door within the craft.

Kalas examined the old man's find: he studied the symbols on and around its surface. Neither etched nor carved, the drawings appeared to have been painted on the curious material with precision only a master might have achieved. He didn't recognize these symbols, but their design bore unmistakable similarities to those from the artifact. Kalas reached out to brush away dust: he withdrew his hand before his fingers contacted its hot, pitted surface.

"Something wrong?" wondered Nïmrïk.

"No. I mean, I don't think so. I…it doesn't look like it, but if this *is* like the other artifact—or maybe that thing under Deridzhas…Weird things happened when I touched them. Remember that gross gas-stuff from that 'egg' in Lady's cavern? What if this 'door' opens and spills that stuff into the Pump? What if it gets into the water? Tsharak made that point not too long ago—about the other artifact, but if all of these things *are* related, I can't risk it! Not when Lohwàlar might pay the price for my curiosity!

"I'll admit it: I don't see the similarities, Tsharak. I don't think any of these look like the markings on the artifact—the craft, but I could be wrong. And now there's no way to check…"

"Too true, my boy, but there *are* identical symbols on *this!*" He held out the faceted *egg* and turned it over in his hands. It sparkled in the irregular torchlight. "Look right here: see this? And, if I turn it over, this? I remember this symbol from the artifact—craft, sorry! And *this* symbol is on the door here! Somehow, they *are* related! They have to be! Here, look how it fits into this little cup!"

As he spoke, Tsharak pushed the object into the shape beside the door, and, as he'd admitted before, nothing happened.

"Some of those symbols look like the ones on the *not-paper!*" Zhalera said, excitement catching in her voice. "Kalas, let's take another look at it!"

The young man bobbed his head, dropped his pack, and rummaged through its contents for the light-blue translucency gleaned from his grandfather's study. He inspected the icons and illustrations displayed on its see-through surface, ran his eyes across its edges—including the milky splotch where some unknown entity had bent a permanent crease into one of its corners.

"Hey, you're right!" Kalas exclaimed, his agreeable bobs becoming vigorous nods. "Tsharak! What do you see? Take a look at this!"

He handed the *not-paper* to the old man, who traded him for his *egg*.

"Hold this for me," he said, and as Kalas wrapped his fingers around its peculiar surfaces, its symbols, ignited from within, glowed a vibrant blue against the relative darkness all around them.

Abarandal whispered a few intense, rapid bars.

"Kalas…" cautioned Nïmrïk. "If that door should open…"

Door? Open?

Their warnings came too late. Before the young man could drop the egg-shaped object, it pulsed with heat and light, threads of lightning arced between it and the bulkhead, and a sympathetic glow of similar hue bloomed in the small depression. A hairline fissure groaned into existence from the door's center, followed by razor-fine threads of rich, shimmering blue that spread up, down, and out along its edges. Angular ribbons of multicolored brightness raced outward from the ovoid scoop. After a series of clicks and clunks, an odorless blast of air jetted from the widening crack as the painted surface split apart, and each half retracted into the wall with a faint, high-pitched whine. Then the cobalt-colored illumination blinked out.

"Is that—?" Kalas started: he was interrupted by a series of white lights as they buzzed into existence, their unexpected brilliance momentarily blinding him and the others.

As the impression of swirling clouds receded from view, he saw a passage, lit with bright circles lining its ceiling and cluttered with meaty black ropes and multicolored strands of what appeared to be twine or string. Gray, rectilinear surfaces jutted from the steel-plated walls. At the far end of the small corridor, barely visible, Kalas spied another door, more like the one from the craft.

No one spoke as everyone tried to comprehend the spectacle confronting them.

Nïmrïk edged his way toward the threshold, sniffed the air a couple times, and stepped inside. As if sensing his presence, some of the some gray rectangles hummed to life and started blinking out a periodic series of ever-changing shapes and symbols.

"Nïmrïk! What are you doing?! You don't—!"

"If there's death in here, let me discover it in your stead!" he insisted.

He took a few more steps, sniffed again, and waited. He looked from side to side, up, down, and back at the others. After less than a minute, he shrugged.

"This place doesn't have the stench of *wrongness* the mines had," he grunted, satisfied. "*That* kind of death, at least, is not present here. As for other kinds, I can't say…"

"I don't understand!" Kalas tried to explain. "I didn't touch it! I didn't touch anything! I—oh!"

Tsharak's stooped to retrieve his *egg,* dark again, and waggled it at the young man.

"But how?! Just touching this thing: how could that cause the door to open? And what's all that stuff inside? How are those— are they crystals? How are they glowing like that? Maybe they're mirrors, like Pava showed us?"

"*How,* I can't say," said Tsharak as he handed Kalas his *not-paper.* "Unless, perhaps, it's the magic in *your* blood?"

Abarandal interjected a stream of spirited notes. Kalas nodded.

"She's right: that wasn't *seranà.* Not from The Song, at least! I don't think it was, anyway! You would have heard it, right? If it had been The Song?"

"No, you're right," the befuddled figure agreed. "However it opened, it *opened.* If your *egu…friend* here is correct, maybe it's not the end of the world…"

"I just hope it's not the end of Lohwàlar," Zhalera muttered.

"These strange…crystals, you said? I've seen the *parafi-isadme* the cave-dwellers use: these might look similar, but I don't think they're the same thing. Other than that, I can't tell you what they might be. *Egu:* you've been around longer than I have! Tell us what to make of these animated panes of glass!"

Nïmrïk walked toward one of the luminescent items blinking with an angry, red light; he brushed a few copper strings from its surface—and yelped when a bright, hot filament leapt at his hand. Tsharak barked a laugh.

"Are you all right?!" Kalas took a step toward him.

"Fine! I'm fine! I just…watch out for any of these copper… things! There's energy in them, somehow…feels a little like weak *eruyâsru*…"

He tapped a finger on the object's surface—briefly, in case it might shock him, too. It gave slightly as a ring of light and a series of indecipherable symbols rippled outward from his touch.

"I'm not convinced they *are* glass," he replied. "Lad, when did your people discover the Pump?"

"Hundreds of years ago. Dozens and dozens of Sevens ago, I think. Right, Tsharak?"

Tsharak nodded. He turned toward the *egu* and regarded him with eyes slitted and brow furrowed. Despite his prejudice, he elaborated for the boy: "Roughly eighty, maybe eighty-five Sevens ago. Lohwàlar was green, once, before the rainfire storms and hot winds burned most of it away—but the Pump had been here long before that. No one knows exactly *how* long, but now, having seen… all this, it's obvious it predates the cracking of the world!"

"But the Pump isn't made from this metal!" Kalas contradicted him. "The Pump is wood. It's steel. How could it have survived such a cataclysm?"

"It's not *all* wood and steel," Nïmrïk said. "Here, come look at this!"

Kalas followed Nïmrïk's waving hand. Inside the strange hall, the *egu* pointed at the ceiling, toward a thick, uneven row of what appeared to be rotating discs and semi-elliptical plates. At regular intervals, rod-like devices descended from this primary shaft and through the floor into some invisible, unknown *below*. As the horizontal collection of not-quite-random parts turned, its motion alternately pushed and pulled the rod-things, their motion in perfect time with the workings of the Pump.

No, the music *of the Pump!* Kalas realized.

Tsharak had followed him into the cramped room; he, too, had looked up at the inexplicable components, his eyes awash in wonder.

"This place must be from some other, forgotten era," he suggested. His expression indicated a mind hard at work as he pursed his lips and cocked his head. "This shaft: notice how neither end is visible? One must connect to parts of the Pump we *Lohwàlarrinme* have always known: the other must connect to something on the other side of that *second* door—yes, I think that's what it is, too!

"Look at how smoothly it moves! When people first discovered the Machine, they tried to understand how it worked—why it never *stopped* working! I told you about injuries before: folks on *that* particular quest experienced a hefty number of them! After a while, people stopped trying to understand its every detail: we were just happy it worked at all!

"And those rod…things that disappear into the floor? There must be something *under* this place! I told you, my boy: things the world over aren't what they seem! Seems I would have done well to remember my own admonition! What do you say? Should we take a look at that second door?"

"I…no! Not right now! This is already more—much more— than I wanted to do today! We should be thankful we didn't uncover any of those can-egg-things like the *Deridzhasrinme!* We should be thankful that we didn't find toxic, broken…meat-bags like those in the craft downriver! No one's been here for…maybe since just after the world was cracked? Look at all this stuff: have you ever seen anything like it? No one has! Rather than fill the Sanctuary with fresh bodies, we should take our time to understand what we've discovered here!"

Tsharak wanted to protest: Kalas could read his thoughts in his sudden pout; instead, however, the old man laughed and shook his head.

"Such wisdom from one so young! Your mentors would be proud! You're right, of course." He winked, then chuckled and added, "Perhaps I could learn a lot from one like you?"

"I wouldn't go that f—The *erume!*" he interrupted himself, his eyes wide. "Everyone: remember, under the Vault! Loradan said they *usually* tried to *unmake* any *vàsume* they discovered. We know Falthwën had been to Lohwàlar before. He said something to me, about how the Pump sounded. I wondered, 'how would *he* know?', but he did! He knew about the Pump. The Machine. This place, too, probably, but none of the *erume* destroyed it!"

"Hey, you're right!" Zhalera exclaimed. Nïmrïk nodded as well.

"I wish Falthwën were still here," Kalas said, his tone sober. "I'll bet he—or Loradan! I'll bet Loradan could tell us more about this place, about why it's here, what it is—*was*—*before* it was the Pump…

"But he's not here. Neither is Loradan, nor any other *eru*. The suns will probably set soon, and we haven't set up camp. This place has been here for hundreds—maybe *thousands* of Sevens. It'll probably be all right for one more night."

6.

As curious as he was about the second door within the secret room behind the Pump, Kalas couldn't shake his memory from the other artifact: some unknown stimuli had birthed a punch of light that revealed a corridor strewn with desiccated corpses wrapped in well-preserved (and unfamiliar-looking) clothes. Everyone—even Abarandal—explored as much of the area as they dared, following Kalas' lead and attempting to touch as little as possible.

"After what happened at the craft, and again with the door here, I think I'll keep my hands to myself!" he clarified the next morning as he stood beneath the rotating shaft overhead, his hands in his pockets. "Better if I don't touch anything!"

The blinking, flashing "crystals," as he thought of them, continued to cycle through various images, casting a gray glow onto every washed-out face that examined their alien contents. What he'd believed to be ropes or strings proved to be bent and twisted copper strands encased in sheaths of brightly-colored, flexible material. Upon closer inspection, most crystals had numerous cables protruding from gold or silver ferrules attached to various points opposite their smoother surfaces. Nearly all of the inanimate crystals had similar cords dangling from them, too, but many of these specimens looked like they'd been cut or chewed through.

"Maybe there's nothing like the *wrongness* from the mines—or even the other craft—down here, but I can't shake the feeling that *something* bad happened here...or will! It's weird, this feeling. Irrational. Still, I think it's about time we return home."

None of the others seemed too disappointed in his decision (Tsharak excepted, perhaps), and it would be late afternoon before they reached Lohwàlar's outskirts.

When everyone had cleared the door, Kalas placed a trembling hand within the egg-shaped depression near its side.

Nothing happened.

He tried again. More pressure, this time.

Still nothing.

"Tsharak?"

"Hmm," the old man said as he scratched behind a white wisp

of beard. "Ah! Try holding on to this again?"

He handed the *egg* to Kalas, who cocked his head and arched an eyebrow as he accepted it.

"What am I supposed to do with this?"

"Honestly? I have no idea! I thought since the door opened when you held it last, maybe it'd close this time?"

"I wish it worked that way! I *wish* the door would cl—!"

Before he finished voicing his thought, each half of the door spun outward, and, with a subtle whine and faint whirring sounds, each assumed its former position. A thin streak of blue-white light flared along their edges as mechanisms within clicked into place.

"It was in my *mind!*" Kalas gasped as he threw the *egg* back at Tsharak.

"Wish granted?" the ancient man suggested with a smirk.

"*This* place *seems* all right," Kalas admitted as they exited the Pump onto the packed road, "but we still don't know what's behind that other door, and if we consider both of the other things like this, we're facing *terrible* odds. I think the *erume* have the right idea! Maybe we can't *unmake* things the way they do—and we can't just bury the Pump under a mountain!—but if we can keep it hidden behind this door, maybe that's enough for now. I want an *eru* to see it. One of the Swath. Loradan maybe, or—"

"Valaran," Tsharak said. "Such marvels as this place are her domain."

"Valaran?!" Zhalera started: "Peradan said she was dead, but—"

"*Dead?!* But how?! When?! No, that can't be right! I would have known…"

"Peradan said she died trying to rescue him from a…a…some kind of trap," Kalas explained. "He called it a *singularity*. Falthwën said he got caught in something similar—that's what happened to him before he showed up under the Temple that night. He said the *ekume* had marked him: that's why he couldn't make full use of The Song along the Highway."

"The other night: my *sword!*" Zhalera interjected. "Peradan must have been mistaken!"

"The *erume* aren't omniscient," Kalas admitted. "Falthwën often reminded me of that! Maybe she was just captured…It took Falthwën some time to recover, remember? And he had Loradan's help—wait a minute! What if Valaran knows who betrayed the Swath?! What if…what if *she* betrayed them?!"

"She did *not,*" Zhalera fumed, her nostrils flaring in the crisp canyon air. "No, I won't believe it!"

Nïmrïk spoke. "I think you're right, *Shâuín* Zhalera. We assume—correctly, I believe—that the world's dark forces want Abarandal's power to accomplish Ilnëshras' black desires. If the Seven Stars' betrayer *is* one of their number, it makes little sense that he or she wouldn't have been there when the *ilkelëshún* appeared. I'll admit I can't perceive the particulars of Abarandal's song, but the other night, the substance of her harmonies, in tandem with that soft, warm light—*Valaran's* light—transmuted my sorrow into something sublime. No traitor could have been a part of that! I can't explain why, not rationally, but I'd counter and suggest that Valaran—wherever she is, whatever her condition, is perhaps the only member of the Swath we can fully trust."

"You're an alliterative devil," Tsharak acknowledged, "and as much as it pains me to admit, I think you may be right."

"We have to find her," Zhalera decided. "Peradan made a mistake: she's out there, somewhere. I just *know* it. Somehow, I just do."

Miryan had disappeared by the time they reached Lohwàlar, her roseate remnants staining the few wisps of cloud pressed against the edge of twilight. Up from the Empty Sea, the air regained its relative warmth as everyone crossed the desert. When they neared the town, Kalas saw wide pits dug not too far from either side of the Pump Road. Vast heaps of earth and sand sat beside blocks of cut stone.

"This wasn't here yesterday," Kalas said.

"Mister Hebul's laborers, no doubt!" guessed Tsharak. "Looks like the Council approved Sàrush's request for more towers! Looks like they're preparing the foundations now. Must have started work this morning, while we were away. Won't be long before Lohwàlar has a solid network all along its entire circumference!

"Anyway, home is still a long walk from here, and I'd like to discuss a few things with your grandfather, Zhalera, before the Premier Sun disappears, too!"

"You're walking all the way home *after* you speak with Grandfather?" Zhalera repeated. "That's too far! No, why don't you stay with us? At least for tonight? While you're with Grandfather, we'll make supper. It'll be waiting for you by the time you get there!"

"You're very generous, dear one, but I—"

"No, she's right!" Kalas insisted, "I'm sure you're capable of walking all that way in the dark, probably better than any of us could do beneath both suns! Still, when there's no need…"

Tsharak hesitated, risked a glance at Nïmrïk, and mumbled, "I…can't accept. I'm sorry, I—"

Kalas followed the old man's flitting stare and watched Nïmrïk's face sag when the *egu* gleaned Tsharak's subtext. The young man hesitated, too: almost long enough for the crestfallen figure to repeat his offer to be elsewhere.

Almost.

With a quick finger jabbed at Nïmrïk—*Stay there!*—Kalas addressed Tsharak in low tones: "Maybe it's because you've had more than a hundred Sevens to hold on to your hatred. Maybe it's because of something else. I don't know. Right now, I don't care. For the longest time, I saw *Dzharëth* whenever I looked at Nïmrïk. Took some time before I saw him not for who he *was*—who he might have been—but for who he's *becoming*. Nïmrïk didn't kill your city, nor anyone in it. One hundred twenty-something Sevens is a long time to hate. How much longer must you keep it up?

"I know you weren't there when he took an arrow for us, or when he risked his life against the *ekume,* or when the *ilrâigme-edhume* almost unskinned him because he was trying to save Pava's family. I won't pretend to know his heart. As Falthwën was fond of reminding me, none of us possesses the mind of the Creator! I also won't pretend that his actions—his choices—haven't made their mark: if we knew he was an *egu* before Ïsriba's dungeons, before the Vault, maybe none of us would have given him a chance, either, but that's not how it happened. Again, Falthwën might have described it as an act of providence.

"We're all responsible for our own choices. Even—assuming such things exist—the little ones."

When Kalas began his lecture, Tsharak's cheeks took on a fiery color, like his blood was boiling; by the time the young man finished, his fury had bled out. Abashed and looking at the ground, he said nothing.

"Look," Kalas started, "I'm sorry for my tone, but not—"

"No, you misunderstand," Tsharak cut him off. He looked up, held Kalas' gaze for a long while, then shook his head and added, "It's not just because of Kësharan. It's more than that…but still, you're not wrong. Were green fire to leap suddenly from your fingertips, I don't think I'd be surprised: you sound more like Falthwën than I think you realize.

"I will come to Zhalera's when my business with Sàrush is completed. I will try to see this *egu* through your eyes, young man. Perhaps mine have become too dim to perceive things as clearly as they once did—yet not so dim I can't admit the possibility."

With a slight nod, the ancient man disappeared into town.

"Not a word," Kalas growled before anyone—especially Nïm-rïk—could say anything.

"Lad, help me to understand: first the Swath, then the *elu* Nanësra, and now Tsharak? I've helped out a few times, sure, but the way you've defended me to them? I don't get it."

He means, 'I don't deserve it,' Kalas intuited.

"Nïmrïk, if you're looking for a rational, well-reasoned argu-ment, you won't find one here. When summer started, my world was no larger than Lohwàlar: now, it's so much bigger and growing all the time. And I'm not just talking about geography.

"Maybe it's because I've only attained two Sevens, not Tsharak's one hundred twenty…eight? nine? Maybe that's why I can separate *you* from the *egume* that killed our parents, our friends and neigh-bors. Or maybe it's because I *felt* something in your song inside Ïsriba's dungeons. Maybe it's something else entirely. And maybe it doesn't matter. You've cast your lot with ours, and that means something.

"From your stories, I know you've tried to make up for things for millennia. Other *elume* have spurned you. Most *erume*, too. I imagine it would have been simpler for you to blame someone other than yourself for becoming what you are today, but instead, you've owned your sin—and its consequences. Like Heshradan, I don't know if you'll ever be an *elu* again—I don't know how any of that works—but I know I'm grateful our paths have…no, not *crossed*, but intertwined."

Nïmrïk nodded, held back tears, and sighed, "Master Kalas, after all these hundreds and hundreds of Sevens—thousands of years, I'm out of ideas. I don't know what else I can do *to* demon-strate my remorse, to attract the Creator's eye, that he might look upon me and approve my efforts. You're right, though: it *would* be simpler to blame someone else, just to retreat into the 'comfort' of that easy sin. Simpler…and *wrong*. I think I can admit this to you: I've considered it before. Not for thousands of Sevens, but still…

"I've conducted a few thought experiments—a series of 'what if?' scenarios: every imagined outcome felt like worms gnawing on the flesh beneath my skin."

As the four of them continued preparing supper from items purchased on the way home, someone started pounding on the door, fumbled with the latch, then let himself in.

"Zhalera?!" Tsharak called, his breathless voice underscored with worry. "Kalas?! Zhalera?!"

"In here!" she called, setting down her chopping knife and wiping her hands on her apron. "Tsharak, what's wrong? Did something—"

"Your grandfather! Sàrush! I found him unconscious on the floor of his office! A big gash across his forehead! He's with the clerics now. I ran here as fast as I could!"

"Grandfather? What happened? He seemed—"

"He's ill! Has been for a while—with what, I don't know. Rïzina knew about his ailing health, but Sàrush swore her—and Tshama— to secrecy. Even now, Rïzina was reluctant to tell me! She went to get your grandmother: I'm here for you. I tried to rouse him: his eyes fluttered, he mumbled your name, then he blacked out again. Come, dear ones! We must get to the Sanctuary!"

Chapter VI

Toward the Land of Living Winter

Sàrush's once rotund face looked gaunt, almost haggard in the Sanctuary's undulating torchlight. His chest continued to rise and fall with hypnotic regularity, but his eyes remained closed. A cleric had dressed his wound and applied a strong-smelling ointment. Dark red splotches ringed his neck where his inner tunic had absorbed much of his spilled blood. Tshama, Zhalera's grandmother, held one of his hands and waited for him to stir.

"Grandmother?" Zhalera said, her voice uncertain. Tshama turned toward the girl, revealing her glassy eyes and tear-stained cheeks as she tried to smile. Zhalera glided to her side, reached down, and squeezed her hand. Sàrush's hand, too.

"I wanted to tell you! Your grandfather wouldn't let me! I'm sorry, child!"

"No, Grandmother! Not now! I…How are you?"

Tshama didn't answer: instead, she shook her head, and with a knowing air insisted, "It's the same thing that took your mother from us! I just know it!"

"Mother? What? Grandmother, how could you know such a thing?!"

"He's been coughing blood! Not much at first, but still, Ferïn's sickness is the first thing I thought of when I caught him hiding it from me! Lately, he's been coughing more and more. I have no idea how long this has been going on, but I've known about it for over a year now! I should have said something! I'm sorry!"

A cleric entered the small room, set apart from the larger, less private corridors. Kalas looked up and smiled when he recognized Vàyana.

"Zhalera! I'm so sorry!" she said as she collected the young girl within the folds of her robe. "Your grandmother's right, I'm afraid. I remember Ferïn's last days…That Sàrush has managed to keep his illness a secret from so many for so long is something of an unfortunate wonder."

"Mother's last days? Does that mean Grandfather…?"

"A week or two, it would seem. I wish there was something we could do…"

The Song? Kalas wondered. He started to say something, but before any words came, he saw himself under the Gateway, struggling against a music that wouldn't quite bend toward his will.

Zhalera must have sensed his hidden thought: she turned toward him with a pleading gaze that threatened to break his heart.

"Zhalera, it's not that I don't want to…"

"Please, Kalas! After all these wasted years! You can do something! I've seen you! You can fix him!"

"I don't know what's wrong with him! And what about Rive? What if I can't control it again? What if I do something that takes away whatever time remains?"

Abarandal stood at the opposite side of Sàrush's bed. She leaned above the aged figure and whispered something over him, her notes resonating within the room's peculiar acoustics. She looked up at Kalas and sang an idea.

"You think so?"

"What'd she say?" Tsharak wondered.

Kalas didn't answer: instead, he followed Abarandal as she made room for him. He squeezed Sàrush's other hand until he felt the Chief Magistrate's pulse. Regarding Zhalera and Tshama without knowing how to disguise his misgivings, he closed his eyes and tried to *see* the disease within Sàrush.

"Zhalera, I don't…it's hidden from me. I'm sorry," he began as he opened his eyes.

That's when Abarandal took his hand and began a soft, lullaby-like tune, her voice faint and clear.

As the melody acquired…not in *volume* but in *presence,* something stirred within his mind, and for some reason he remembered Nanësra's touch and pictured her shimmering emerald eyes mere inches from his. He'd intended to blink away the image, but when his eyes closed, *shapes* coalesced within Abarandal's music.

Like on my birthday!

Nervous, he tuned the Song's harmonies toward his intent. The shapes—glittering motes of dust at first—swirled within his vision until each speck merged with a growing whole.

This is Sàrush? he wondered. *No, not exactly…*

He sensed, somehow, that this concretion was a representation of the man. He allowed himself time to remember Nïmrïk's assurance: he would *see* again. That's when he noticed not every glint of "dust" melded with the agglomerating effigy: these particles disappeared in lightless, root-like voids that wrapped around Sàrush's bones, clogged his heart and lungs, and even traveled through his veins and arteries.

Is this *his sickness?! It's everywhere!* Kalas lamented as the black masses seemed to writhe and sway with Sàrush's every breath.

I've never seen *things like this before! Not Shosafin, not Kadhëmba, not Rive…Abarandal! This is all because of her! Has to be! It—no, I'll think about that later: right now, I need to focus on Zhalera's grandfather! Except I have* no idea *what needs to happen next!*

Kalas furrowed his brow, integrated the fact that his physical eyes were still closed with the rest of his thoughts, and tried to picture part of the virulence dissolving in a flare of heat and light. In his mind, a concussive charge exploded against his will, surrounding everything with scintillating white. When it subsided, only unraveling threads of dusky malevolence remained inside Sàrush's lungs.

Is it working? It's working!

His eyes still closed, Kalas heard a tortured gasp as something crushed his hand. Startled, he opened them: Sàrush had woken; panicked, his involuntary muscles had contracted around Kalas' fingers. His wide, fearful eyes scanned the room, focused first on Tshama, then Zhalera.

"What's happening?!" he wheezed. "I can't feel my—"

"Kalas! That's too much!" Zhalera shouted.

Abarandal released his other hand. Sàrush's hard-fought breathing slowed as he realized where he was.

"It's not all gone!" Kalas protested. He closed his eyes again, but Abarandal gripped his shoulder and gave him an ungentle shake.

"'Too much'? I don't understand!"

You almost healed him to death...

"My legs! I can't feel my legs!"

What have I done?!

"Mister Sàrush! I'm sorry! I only wanted to...erase your sickness!"

"My sickness? So someone told you about that, I see! I—"

He took a deep breath, held it, and released it without urgency.

"Oh, this is much better! *Much* better!" he laughed as he swallowed additional gulps of air.

"But...your legs?" Kalas repeated, horrified.

"The Song. Too much, given his condition," Nïmrïk suggested. "Not your fault, lad."

"Husband!" Tshama exclaimed as she caressed his forehead.

Sàrush tried to sit up. He had to scoot himself back with his arms, but he managed. He stared at his unmoving limbs beneath his bed sheet. Vàyana looked at Kalas with a blend of fear and wonder, then examined her patient. When she looked up, she smiled.

"*Âu* Sàrush, it seems you'll be around a while yet! I have no idea what our young friend just did—nor how, but your heart and lungs sound…healthy!"

"Legs are nice…lungs are essential. Young Kalas, you've given me more time with my loved ones. It's a trade I'd make again and again, if such a thing were possible! I'm almost afraid to ask how you did…whatever it was you just did. No: I *am* afraid to ask! Nonetheless, please: accept my thanks!"

"I'm sorry," Kalas repeated, unable to meet the Magistrate's grateful gaze.

"Thank you, Kalas!" Zhalera whispered as she embraced him and would not let him go. Ashamed, the young man had escaped Sàrush's room with as little fanfare as he could manage while Vàyana performed a more thorough examination. Zhalera had followed him into the dim hallway.

"For paralyzing your grandfather? Yeah, you're welcome," he muttered.

"You heard him! You heard Vàyana! Because of you, he'll live! Longer than a week or two, I'll bet!"

"I don't know what happened," he tried to explain. "I guess after what I did to Rive, I wasn't sure how to handle things. With Abarandal there, The Song was…different. Stronger. *Easier.* I don't know. No, I'm not blaming her! I just…I think I tried to do too much, too quickly…"

"Grandfather is old. That's just a fact. Maybe there's a point where nothing can be done, no matter how someone uses The Song? Shosafin can't be much older than Rive—or the other way around—and Nïmrïk is, well, he's Nïmrïk. Overall, each of them is healthier than Sàrush. And I'm the one who pushed you to do it, so if you're going to blame anyone, start with me!"

"Zhalera, I—"

"Enough!" she whispered as she drew his mouth toward hers and placed a slow kiss against his lips.

2.

Kalas spent much of the winter tending to the Pump. Taking as many shifts as he could, he quickly realized most other *Lohwàlar-rinme* lacked his father's enthusiasm for its maintenance. Most preferred keeping close to home—especially since the Council had approved an aggressive schedule of construction projects: people seemed most eager to help with guard towers, walls, and gates. In between trips into the Empty Sea, Kalas stopped in to check on Sàrush, to see how he was doing *and* to look at Lohwàlar's future, drafted in two dimensions within Tsharak's annotated drawings. True to his word, Tsharak had struggled against his irrational hatred of Nïmrïk, even going so far as to share his indelible memories from the Night of Falling Skies. The *egu* couldn't hide the shame and horror that washed over him as the old man recounted the destruction of his birthplace, and Kalas suspected Tsharak understood the rough truth in Nïmrïk's visceral response.

He visited Zhalera at her smithy, offered to play the role of striker as she manipulated soft hunks of glowing metal, or to chop and pile wood for her furnaces. Abarandal helped, too. Despite her borderline ethereal constitution, she possessed amazing strength: Kalas had felt it in her fingers from time to time, but tasks that required *him* to pause to catch his breath, *she* performed without effort.

He said nothing about Zhalera's projects. If she'd been embarrassed by his admittedly effusive praise, he would suppress his impulse and appreciate her skill in silence. Some days, Zhalera seemed more flustered than others: at first, Kalas thought even his presence exacerbated her insecurity; when he mentioned it, she laughed and reassured him he was wrong about that. He'd tried to extract more detail from her, but she played coy, and he opted not to press the matter.

On some occasions, Zhalera accompanied him into the Empty Sea when he tended the Pump. She and Abarandal had developed a crude language comprised of simple musical phrases and hand gestures that allowed them to communicate increasingly complex concepts, though their discussions hadn't reached the sophistication afforded through direct speech. They managed simple stories and jokes, and more than once, Kalas caught himself on the outside of some experience shared between the two.

He passed several hours nestled within the peculiar comfort of Wodram's old study, poring over his collection in search of something either he or his father might have missed. Not just about the vàsu: about the Pump, too. Sàrush was only too happy to grant him access to Lowhalar's ancient archives, and Tsharak was kind enough to recreate the most relevant diaries and drawings for him to examine in greater detail. The ancient man's eyes seemed as keen as ever: his careful, gnarled and knotted hands translated every stroke with uncanny precision.

As he studied Tsharak's reproductions, he experienced an impression of reverent awe with every page he turned: these weren't originals, but woven within their sparse details were glimpses of uncertainty and adventure, of struggles and successes as Lohwàlar's people revivified their sere land through their imperfect mastery of the Machine. The Pump. Kalas absorbed every detail as best he could: he closed his eyes and pictured ancient men and women exploring and experimenting with its mechanisms, extracting water from the remnant of the Rumilswàr that no longer flowed along its primeval bed.

"I'm going back there," he said one night with such nonchalance that no one knew what he meant until he explained: "The Pump. That *room*—and the door behind it."

"Oh?" said Zhalera as she tried not to choke on her supper.

"I've been reading about what our ancestors had to go through in the Sevens before the Pump. It's just like Tsharak told us, only *more*. These people: they risked their lives for a better Lohwàlar. Some lost everything. It's *deeper* than we were ever taught in school…There's, I don't know, there's a *grittiness*, a *reality* that none of our lessons ever captured.

"What if the people who first opened the Pump—the Machine, they called it, remember? What if they'd been too scared to check things out? This town would have dried up and disappeared dozens of Sevens ago! The *erume* knew about it: remember when Falthwën handed Hàfilrifar to Loradan? How he said his search for it had brought him to Lohwàlar *'of all places'?* His words! And when I first met him, he indicated that he'd been here before. A long time ago."

"But Kalas! None of those people knew about other *vàsume!* They didn't know anything about that *craft* in the Empty Sea! They *certainly* didn't know about the horrors under Deridzhas! If they'd known what might have been waiting for them—"

"You're right, Zhalera: they didn't know, and, if they had, maybe things would've been different. I guess I'm just thinking that if the *erume* knew about the Pump and chose to leave it intact, they must have known about what lies beneath it."

"Maybe the lass is right," Nïmrïk suggested. Abarandal performed a deft series of maneuvers with her hands and fingers, eliciting a nod from Zhalera.

"The *erume* aren't all-knowing, Kalas!" she went on. "Falthwën himself made that point more than once! They left the Pump up and running. Good for Lohwàlar! What if one or more of them *did* know about Deridzhas? What if they *didn't know* it was what it turned out to be?"

"I thought about that—all right, not exactly, but listen: Abarandal, when we're *connected,* The Song is *visible:* I could *see* Sàrush's disease. I didn't understand everything at the time—I still don't!— but my head's been healed for weeks now, and I want to take another, closer look at that door and what might hide behind it.

"We'll need Tsharak's *egg,* and I imagine he'll insist on coming with us. We'll look for him at the Council Hall in the morning—if I remember correctly, I think he was working on updated drawings for some kind of training facility. A place where *Lohwàlarrinme* can learn how to become the soldiers Ïsriba failed to provide us. I think he'll be there.

"So what do you say? Will you come with me? Abarandal, if I'm right, it'd be a waste of time without you. Zhalera, Nïmrïk? Lohwàlar could—no, not just Lohwàlar: *I* would really appreciate your help…"

"I'll do it," Nïmrïk sighed through a subtle smile.

Abarandal looked to Zhalera, whispered a brief melody and danced her fingers through the air. The young blacksmith returned a slow nod and acquiesced: "We'll do it, too. I just hope you know what you're getting us into, Kalas!"

So do I…

"What changed your mind, my boy?" Tsharak wondered as he handed the "egg" to Kalas. Back at the Pump, behind its myriad elements, the old man grinned, intrigued. Kalas took the strange, smooth object and thought: *Door! Open!*

Lights. Beeps. Lightning. A subtle hiss as its mechanisms retracted then opened the door. Kalas didn't enter the small chamber right away; instead, he looked up and tried to picture where the massive crank within might interface with the more pedestrian, more familiar aspects of the Pump's workings.

It must connect somewhere. Maybe lots *of somewheres!* he conceded.

"Lohwàlar's ancestors were risk-takers. Makes sense: when everything they knew was dying, what did they have to lose? In some ways, we're in a similar place, only it's our *world* that's dying. Maybe I wasn't born to Lohwàlar, but I was raised here, and if I might borrow from her people's historic bravery, I will."

Past the threshold, he inspected each flashing crystal as its images flickered from one collection of bizarre shapes to another. He wondered, perhaps, if there was meaning in the rotating hues and shape-shifting blobs of color.

"This must mean *something*," Tsharak nodded as he stepped up behind the young man and peered over his shoulder. "No idea what, of course, but the way this and other, similar objects are arranged, I get the idea that someone—some*ones?*—kept an eye on each of them."

"There's no sign of anyone," Kalas countered. "That craft beneath the Empty Sea had bodies in it..."

"Maybe *that's* what's behind that second door?" Zhalera suggested. "Bodies. Or not. I have no idea! And I don't know what's worse: what's *really* on the other side of that door or just standing here worrying about it! If you're going to open it, *open* it! Otherwise, let's get out of here, shutter this place, and *never* come back!"

Kalas squeezed the egg-shaped item and approached the unopened door. He motioned for Abarandal to come with him. Curious, the others followed. Like the door from the now-buried artifact, the far wall of this blinking and beeping anteroom had a pearlescent surface that suggested similar filaments just beneath its skin. The whole thing might have remained invisible, but flameless overhead lights created just enough shadow to trace a feathery gray outline around its elliptical contours.

"This looks just like the door from the thing under the Empty Sea," Zhalera confirmed. In Kalas' peripheral vision, Tsharak nodded. "I'll bet you don't need that *egg* thing: I'll bet all you need to do is touch the symbols. Like before."

Zhalera was right: next to an unremarkable scoop, a faint series of familiar shapes marked the surface of the wall. Kalas handed the *egg* back to the old man and pulled his *not-paper* from his pack, unrolled it, and smoothed it out atop one of the inactive gray crystals. He studied the now-familiar shapes displayed within his translucent leaf, nodded, then rolled it up and put it away.

"Abarandal?" he whispered as he held out a hand. She obliged, and together, their voices low, they hummed one of the Song's abridged movements.

I don't see anything. No wrongness. *Not like all the other places. Maybe it's safe?*

Standing in front of the door, sweat beading on his brow, he let go of Abarandal's hand. He flexed his fingers and touched one of the symbols, then another, and another, until he'd completed what he hoped was the correct sequence.

"I wonder why it's so hot in here," he mused as he wiped away a trickle of perspiration.

"*That's* what you're wondering?!" Zhalera rasped in disbelief.

"Well, I just—"

Deep groans rocked the small room: punchy bass notes just above the threshold of human hearing reverberated from someplace far beneath the floor. Tight threads of bright green raced along angular pathways just beneath the skin of the wall. The lozenge-shaped door screamed as invisible mechanisms struggled against some obstructive force. Most of the lights exploded with sharp pops and puffs of sparks: bits of glass and metal rained down around them and collided with some of the planar crystalline surfaces, which hissed and snapped and spat fire until they fizzled out forever. With one last shudder, the door split apart: one half tumbled into the hall as thick black ropes of some muscle-like substance ripped away from their moorings and sprayed the floor with acrid green slime; the other imploded as elements beneath its skin tore loose and attempted to crush the entire shape into its intended position.

"Did it get hotter in here? I think it's—" Kalas began: one final tantrum, an outburst orchestrated in spark-tipped whips and gouts of goo, burned through the last of the construct's directionless energy before the room again turned silent.

Kalas and the others waited a full minute without a word.

"Maybe a *little* hotter?" Tsharak suggested.

With most of the overhead lights extinguished, most of the small chamber's illumination originated from the sole surviving display: the same one Nïmrïk had poked the last time they were here. It had glowed red then; now, though it looked black, it still emitted a faint gray light.

"The Pump!" Kalas exclaimed, ignoring the old man. "Did I break it? What if I just cut off Lohwàlar's water supply?! I thought I had the sequence right! I—"

"Pump seems fine," Nïmrïk assured him. "It *is* warmer in here, but I can still hear that shaft spinning overheard: sounds the same as before. Doesn't seem like whatever just happened fazed it in the slightest.

"And I don't think all that excitement was wholly your fault! I wasn't there when you opened that other object, but I suspect *this* place has been on the verge of collapse for hundreds—maybe thousands of Sevens. It has a haphazard quality to it, like it's built from parts—and eras—that don't really go together. The door that just blew up, for instance: looks nothing like the rest of this stuff out here!"

"Where do you think it all comes from?" Kalas wondered, accepting Nïmrïk's assessment for the moment. "How do those mirrors or minerals or whatever they are hold the light in those strange shapes? What's this colorful stuff with what looks like copper running through the middle? And those lights! Those weren't torches! Not suns-light, either—unless someone figured out how to capture it inside those glass globes or whatever they were?"

"Questions I can't answer, dear one," Tsharak admitted as he surveyed the room's recent destruction. He dragged his stick through a puddle of scintillating green slime and wafted its vapors toward his nose. With a sniff—and a cough, he recoiled, shivered, and said, "Not unlike the stuff under the Sea, but not quite as nasty. This place seems to lack whatever *wrongness* existed in the artifact there.

"There's a fragrance here, almost buried beneath the stink of what I assume belongs to that green stuff," Nïmrïk offered. "It's light...*moist,* somehow, and...floral? Plants, at least. My guess is it's coming from whatever's on the other side of that new hole in the wall..."

The dust had settled, revealing a black mouth where the door once stood. Stepping over the wreckage, Zhalera poked her head through its lightless aperture and took a tentative breath.

"Nïmrïk's right! Through here, I can smell...it reminds me of the forest after the steppes on the way home. Or maybe even the woods we passed on the way here, only in the summer..."

Kalas stepped into the darkness. His presence, or perhaps just his movement, inspired a sequence of crooked panels protruding from the walls to hum with a weak, green tint: after the first cast its light throughout the corridor, a staggered procession of subsequent panels hummed with similar luminescence. Someone from an unremembered age had cleared a path through the intrusive rocks and lacerated, muscle-like fiber bundles littering the floor; now, under feeble, aquamarine light, it beckoned them deeper into the eclectic blend of strange technologies.

3.

At the end of a short, curved corridor, lit by occasional banks of inconsistent sources, they reached a third portal at the top of a rusty, rickety-looking staircase. They'd passed numerous character sequences carved and painted on the walls—at least, that's what Kalas assumed they were: most were unlike anything he'd ever seen, but scattered among the shapes were symbols from the artifacts and Tsharak's *egg*.

"I wonder what this says," he muttered.

A smattering of light green blades of a grass-like plant formed a patchy carpet along the cavern floor, dotted here and there with pinpricks of pink, purple, and yellow. Tsharak knelt, ran his fingers through it, and pulled a coarse tuft from the earth. He rolled his prize between his fingers and took a deep breath. Nodding, he put it back where he found it.

The doors looked like someone had hacked them away a long time ago. Shriveled blobs of those rubbery black "muscles" hung in limp bunches, crusted with spiderwebbed flakes of hardened ooze. The edges of the hole where a door once stood bore signs of distress: thick, radiating lines of carbon scored various points along its perimeter; other places had an almost translucent, glassy appearance.

"This is weird," he said, mostly to himself. "Zhalera, Tsharak: nothing made a mark on that other artifact. Not rainfire, not Gandhan's hammer...Nothing. This one looks like it's made from the same stuff, so how did it end up like *this*?"

Neither had an answer.

On the first step, Kalas paused for a moment—just long enough to test his weight. Deeming it safe, he traveled the rest of the stairs with everyone on his heels.

Whatever's in here, we've already unleashed it. Might as well see this through...

Halfway down, a landing redirected them ninety degrees; at the bottom, they arrived at a stone-lined slash of track interrupted by yet another wall. Nïmrïk brushed away the dust to reveal a matte steel door nearly free from rust. Unlike the other doors, not quite halfway up, this specimen had a metal plate riveted to it. The *egu* pushed and felt the whole thing wobble just a little before it resisted. He shrugged and gestured for Kalas to give it a try.

The young man reached for its subtly textured surface: without any signs or symbols, he wasn't sure what—or where—to touch, so he ran his hands across its entirety. When nothing happened, he ran his hands along its frame, too.

Still nothing.

"Uh...anyone else?"

No one could persuade the door to open.

"I don't see any hinges: it has to open inward," Tsharak panted, resting for a moment after whacking it with his stick.

"I agree," Nïmrïk nodded. "Here, let me try again..."

Bringing all his otherworldly strength to bear, the *egu* half-crouched, maximized his potential energy, and launched himself at the steely slab that blocked their way. It didn't open, but Nïmrïk insisted he felt it give, insisted he try again.

On his fourth assault, his impact sheared the door from a set of bolts within the top and bottom of its frame. His momentum carried him into a shadowy space pocked with multi-colored strips of light: with a thud, he hit the floor. This new darkness vanished as other lights, somehow aware of his presence, buzzed and blinked into existence.

"Told you," Zhalera whispered with a subtle punch at Kalas'

shoulder. She pointed, and his eyes followed her finger toward a desiccated skeleton wrapped in rags and hunched over his or her last endeavor.

Long, illuminated bars dangled from the cave's ceiling, throwing light at occasional splotches of that flowery grass and disparate blocks of metallic crates or closets of varying design. Some constructs looked like they'd been built into the walls. Most were freestanding. Other apparatuses occupied a corner here or there—a bench, a low cabinet, something completely indescribable—each strewn with a dizzying assortment of lesser, equally unidentifiable accouterments. Dense clusters of color-coated copper strands, most protruding from the collection of metal constructs, crisscrossed the floor, climbed the walls, and even wrapped around the bars suspended overhead: almost all of them disappeared within a glittering bank of tiny lights, winking from a panel set within a wall of that exotic, pearlescent material, reminiscent of the artifact Falthwën had buried. Woven among the cables were various diameters of pipes or tubes: some transparent, others translucent, the rest opaque. Occasionally, a gout of cloudy gas or glowing liquid would surge within the conduits, never betraying its origin or destination.

Kalas pretended to wince from Zhalera's playful blow. As he explored the area, avoiding stepping on the subtle points of flora poking up from the ground, something beneath the arm bones of the clean-picked corpse caught his attention. He approached the remains, blew away a layer of dust, and gasped aloud at his discovery.

"Everything all right?!" Zhalera asked as she drew up beside him.

"Look at this!" he said, pointing to a pile of objects on the skeleton's work surface.

"Hey, these look like that…what do you call it? *Not-paper,* right? There's a whole stack of these things!"

With as delicate a touch as he could manage, Kalas tried to

extract the topmost leaf. His efforts upset the body, which disintegrated as it toppled from its seat, its skull rolling to a slow stop against what looked like another closet.

"Aswanthalu, sàyahal," he breathed. After a reverent moment, he shook the dust from the translucency and examined its contents.

Like the item his grandfather had discovered, numerous symbols and curious diagrams occupied most of its surface.

"I wonder…" he muttered.

"Wonder what?" Tsharak asked as he approached.

"Just watch," the young man said as he twisted the *not-paper,* turned it over and gave it a gentle shake.

The designs it displayed rearranged themselves as a small part of a larger drawing swelled to take up most of the page. New symbols—words, Kalas guessed—blinked into place and extended fine lines toward various points within the illustration.

"Ha!" he exulted. "That happened with the other *not-paper,* too! Slower, and not as obvious, before we left for Ïsriba! You all saw it this time, right?!"

"That we did, my boy," Tsharak agreed.

"How did it *do* that?!" Zhalera said, amazed.

"There must be dozens of these things!" Kalas noted as he grabbed a few and added them to his pack. "Just makes me wonder where Wodram got his sheet of this stuff. There's no way he could have discovered this place, is there? I mean, wouldn't he have taken more than one?"

"Maybe he didn't need to," Nïmrïk suggested as he held up two specimens he'd retrieved from the ground. Confused at first, Kalas took a closer look and noticed both pages looked identical. He pulled two random pages from his pack, poked and prodded either side with various gestures, and discovered each seemed to possess the same information: it didn't take him long to learn how to move between "pages," although he still had no idea what any of it meant.

"Still, I don't think Wodram—or any *Lohwàlarrin*—has ever known about these rooms beneath the Pump," Tsharak added. "It seems the source of his *not-paper* must remain a mystery!"

"Hmm. Guess I don't need all of these," Kalas admitted as he returned all but one to the table where he'd found them. "Grandfather's was broken, I think: it had a bent edge that might have messed things up. This one doesn't."

Abarandal sang a brief melody, and Kalas replied, "I don't know what we do now. Do we tell anyone about this place? I mean, that seems like the right thing to do: what if the people who discovered the Pump never told anyone?"

"That's a valid point," Tsharak began. "Nothing says we have to answer that question right now."

Zhalera, who'd been examining the flora underfoot, said, "Tsharak, what are these tiny flowers? Upstairs, you looked like you knew what they were, like maybe you'd seen them before? I don't think I've ever seen anything like them in town! We saw some wildflowers just outside of Thosha, but nothing like these—unless we did, and we missed them because of how small they are…"

The old man laughed and clapped a hand on her shoulder. "No, dear one, it's doubtful that you missed them: these flowers—a strain of grass, really—used to thrive all around Lohwàlar! Beside its streets, between its crops—almost everywhere! When the desert encroached, it was one of the last plants to go. *Srathafi gahwa,* we called it. 'Flowering grass.' As pleasant as it smells, it is just grass: people were more interested in plants one could eat! And there were better choices for livestock, too…It's been dozens of Sevens since the last of it disappeared from Lohwàlar! I never expected I'd breathe its fragrance ever again…"

"How did it survive down here?" Zhalera asked as she stooped to inhale its scent and run her fingers through it, like Tsharak had done not too long ago. "This place seems as dry as the desert, and it was dark until we came in and those lights—how *did* those lights get there? How could it be black in here one moment, then as bright as day the next?"

"Maybe it's these cables full of lightning, or these pipes sticking out of everything? What about these metal boxes everything's connected to?" Nïmrïk suggested.

"All good questions! None of which I can answer!"

"I'll bet *he* could have told us," said Kalas, pointing at the disassembled collection of bones. Seeing its skull near the other side of the room, he hurried over to it. "I just want to put this back. Show some respect…"

As he bent to retrieve the skull, he noticed a repeating swirl of muted light coming from behind a crack in the nearby closet door.

"Hey, what's this?" he wondered aloud. "Guys! There are more lights behind this thing!"

Nïmrïk reached the boy first. He knelt and pressed an eye against the almost imperceptible crevice, his movements chipping away flakes of rust. The *egu* gave the area a few light taps and succeeded in breaking off a respectable chunk of corroded metal. He stood and tried the door, but it wouldn't give. With stronger blows, he knocked away enough material to reach inside, rip out the lock, and pull the door open—and off its hinges.

"Guess I should have tried that first," he shrugged.

After a vestibule about three feet wide and nine feet deep, someone had hollowed out a rough, cylindrical alcove—probably the former owner of the skull he held in his hand, Kalas suspected. Perhaps eight or nine feet in diameter and not quite twice as tall, a five-foot diameter disc of metal? glass? some unknown substance occupied its center: its pedestal rose almost a foot above the ground, anchored with thick, black clusters of cabling; its hanging counterpart dropped about four feet from the ceiling. Pipes and tubes and finer cords entered and emerged from this larger construct as faint white lights followed one another around its circumference. Kalas stared up at it, watched the lights change direction, alter speed, and stutter through a spectrum of colors before the pattern repeated.

"What was that?!" Kalas asked. The others followed his gaze, noticed nothing, and shook their collective heads. "Again! That! What was *that?!* Between those discs: the air—space, maybe—it *flutters!* Like there's a beam—beams?—of light that are there and… aren't. Yes, I know how that sounds! Here, let me—"

"*DE!*" Nïmrïk shouted, and Kalas froze. "No, lad! Don't reach for it!"

"What? Why not? It's—wait! Do you know something? Do you remember?"

"I don't know. I don't think so. Maybe. Suddenly, I sensed… *gaaah!* All I can tell you is there's something…no, not *wrong* here, but…hmm…"

"Oh?" said Tsharak with a shrewd nod. "Kalas, may I see that skull?"

The boy handed him the macabre item: the old man hefted it a time or two and said, "Sorry, old friend," before lobbing it toward the emptiness in the midst of the contraption.

"What are you *doing?!*" Kalas exclaimed.

He didn't answer. He didn't need to: when the entire skull had crossed some invisible plane, a blinding column of aqua-tinted light flashed between the discs. It lasted just a fraction of a second: when it passed, the skull had vanished.

4.

Kalas stared at the empty, again-unremarkable space between the two strange discs. He stared at his hand and turned it over a few times just to ensure it was still connected to his arm. Horrified, he looked to Tsharak, to Nïmrïk, and back to the nondescript nothingness that had done…what, exactly?

"What just happened?" he whispered.

No one had an answer for him.

"If I'd put my hand in there…" He took a step back. Shuddered. "Nïmrïk, how did you know?"

"I didn't, lad. Not exactly. I saw you reaching for it, and—it's the strangest thing: I just felt like I had to warn you. No, not because I remembered something—I didn't…I don't *think* I did, at least! I just…It's almost like some external pressure insisted there was *danger* at the edges of that invisible column. I can't explain it any better than that…"

"Well, thank you!" he said as he absentmindedly rubbed his intact forearm.

"Perhaps we've seen enough for today?" Tsharak suggested. The others quickly agreed.

"Maybe it's a good idea if we *don't* tell anyone about this place. Not right now. Not until…I don't know, just…not right now…" Kalas stammered. "I understand the Pump was new technology all those Sevens ago, but this?"

"You're probably right, my boy," Tsharak nodded. "Gears and pulleys are one thing: 'spirit-light' that consumes things whole is another! This place has been here at least as long as the Pump. Longer, probably. Another Seven or so won't make much difference…"

As they retraced their steps, Tsharak paused to scoop up a patch of that flowering grass. He removed a cloth from his pack, moistened it with a splash from his waterskin, and carefully wrapped everything in a loose bundle. The others waited for him; his task completed, he smiled and gestured for everyone to continue.

Outside the door Azhëk and Tàran had discovered, Kalas reached toward the old man, who understood and placed his *egg* in the boy's waiting hand. After a moment of subtle whines and whirs, it closed and locked, and Kalas returned the ovoid object. The old man seemed to read his thoughts and said, "This door has been ignored for over one hundred Sevens. I'll speak to Azhëk: I imagine it'll be ignored for hundreds more…"

They moved quickly through the forest toward the Pump Road without much discussion. Zhalera tapped Kalas' shoulder, pointed out a doc and two fawns on the opposite side of the river. All three seemed to watch with mild concern as the party passed them by, and Kalas tried not to imagine the crazed—now dead—stag they'd encountered last summer.

I wonder if these are the deer we saw before. I wonder if their father's the beast who tossed Gandhan around…

When Abarandal saw the slender creatures grazing among a low thicket of berry-bearing shrubs, she warbled a song of joy and clapped her hands. Kalas thought the sound would frighten the skittish beasts, but after flicking their ears toward the *eru,* they relaxed and resumed their meal, indifferent to the strange figures observing them.

"Seems like they wanted to hear you sing some more!" Kalas whispered. Abarandal blushed. "I forget there's so much you haven't seen—and so much of what you *have* seen hasn't been pleasant. Maybe a day will come when that's not the case."

When they reached the base of the cliff, they paused: Nïmrïk held up a hand and scanned the horizon high above. He pointed, shivered, and mumbled, "There…"

A shape that hadn't been there before, immense and somehow familiar, seemed to watch their every move. For a moment, it remained in place, as still as the rocks on which it stood; then, with almost imperceptible motion, it launched itself from the rim of the Sea and hurtled through the air on vast, silvery wings. Mere feet in front of and above them, she stopped, hovered, and said, "Well met, Kadhëmba?"

"Nanësra," he bowed.

"Nanësra! What are you doing here?" Kalas blurted. The *elu* smiled.

"Bold as ever, young *Nëshriyilkursh!* I see you still have both hands…"

"Of course I do! Why wouldn't—oh!"

"Your doing, then?" Nïmrïk said as he stood.

"I might have made a suggestion," Nanësra confessed. "An intimation. Nothing more."

"You've been following us," Zhalera declared. The *elu* didn't deny it.

"You've piqued my curiosity. After uncounted thousands of Sevens, little else has."

"What was that thing? Those discs? That…*between?*" Kalas wanted to know. "What would have happened if I'd reached in there? What happened to that skull? You know, don't you? Why else would you have warned Nïmrïk? Are you—are you *helping* us?"

"You'll understand…when you need to," she said, alighting on the hard path. "Am I helping you? In the sense that all *elume* seek the fulfillment of prophecy, yes. More than that? I haven't decided."

Kalas grit his teeth, allowed himself a moment to collect his thoughts and wait for the fury welling up within to subside.

Why won't you speak plainly?! It's like you think this is all some kind of game!

He clenched and unclenched his fists, took a deep breath, and settled for: "Thank you, *elu,* for warning us about that thing under the Pump."

She smiled. Neither cruel nor kind, her striking lips curled around her perfect teeth as she said, "You've a fair tongue, young man! Despite your…frustration, perhaps? you possess yourself, and that's an admirable quality. Perhaps the world retains a measure of hope after all. Farewell, child! Farewell, Kadhëmba—and the rest of you!"

Kalas felt a subtle wave of warm pressure, a dazzling flare of white light as his eyes snapped shut against its brilliance. When he opened them, Nanësra was gone, the only reminder of her presence a fading thread of silvery particles dancing heavenward through the air.

"So that's an *elu*," Tsharak noted, still trembling, his eyes attempting to follow the disappearing glimmers that marked her departure. "In all my Sevens…"

Nïmrïk said nothing, though he, too, watched the last of the glittering dust fall to the ground. "An *elu*," he nodded at last. "The same one the boy told you about before. The same one I stood against in my pride and error. She *unmade* me—all of us who were there that day. I don't think I mentioned that. When I emerged from the *shosathesh*, dozens of…Sevens? seconds? Time is different there. When I acquired my *own* flesh again—No! I will never again steal someone else's skin!—I couldn't rationalize my transgression any longer. Thus began my unending quest for redemption. As you know, I can only *hope* such a thing is possible…"

"Nïmrïk, maybe it's just me, but I didn't hear the scorn in her voice this time. Not like last time, outside the well on the steppes. And it seems like she can *speak* to you, to your *mind*, across distances—do *elume* even worry about things like distance? You know what? I think she might be warming up to you! She didn't try to *unmake* you again just now—that's progress, right?!"

The *egu* kept his silence for a moment longer before responding with a bleak chuckle. "Lad, you find hope in the most curious places…"

5.

Another few weeks passed without apparent incident. Kalas spent more time with his grandfather's ancient books, including the indecipherable volume he and his father had been reading. Whenever he'd lose interest in a different work, he'd return to its intricate woodcuts and inscrutable symbols. He made notes about the frequencies of glyphs, about what patterns he could discern, but other than a few pages of syntactical curiosities and mathematical scribblings, he'd discovered nothing noteworthy. More than once, he fell asleep while studying, and on occasion, he dreamed, he supposed, the shapes trading places with one another, contorting into almost familiar forms as lines and strokes rearranged themselves into legible phrases. Each time, straddling the threshold of epiphany, he'd snap back to wakefulness, and the "vision" would disappear.

What is this book?! he'd wondered. Not for the first time. *I'll bet Nanësra could read this! That is, if she felt like it…*

Kalas had also visited Thara's farm and offered his assistance, but he quickly realized he was more of a hindrance than a help there. When he tried to apologize to Thara, she wouldn't hear it; instead, she thanked him for his willingness to lend a hand in Rül's absence.

Leaving one day, he felt a familiar prickle along the nape of his neck that had nothing to do with the cool, mid-morning air. He paused, looked around, and, with a sly smile, called out to Shosafin, who'd been observing him from beneath a wide straw hat.

"It's been awhile," he said as he approached the one-time soldier, now holding a pickaxe. Shosafin shrugged, planted his implement on the ground and leaned over it as he wiped away a thin film of sweat from his brow. Kalas assumed he'd been breaking up the ground for quite some time already.

"It has indeed," he admitted.

"So…you think this is where you'll be…for a while?" the young man prodded.

"For a while," Shosafin agreed. "At least until you and the others make your way north. If Marugan—Gozhira, whatever he calls himself—is hiding out in Galámur, I have to know. Even if he's not there, the Ice City is my only clue. If I don't find him there, maybe I'll find another lead."

"Oh…I…that sounds like you, that's for sure. I guess I'd gotten used to you…as a farmer, as strange as that sounds out loud! It just seems like you really took to this place. What will Thara say?"

"You're not wrong, lad. I *did* take to this place, and I have every intention of returning once I've…settled things with Marugan. I promised Thara I'd remain here until her son returned. I…may have promised her I'd look after him again."

"Oh?" smirked Kalas. Shosafin didn't have to look up to glean the subtext in the young man's remark: he paused just a moment too long before reaching for his pickaxe again.

"See you soon, lad," the old soldier dismissed him as he resumed his work.

Rül and Pava returned to town not long afterward, perhaps a month and a half since they'd departed for the Áthradho. About mid-afternoon on the day they entered Lohwàlar, Rül, Rive's *tëvët* in hand, stopped by Zhalera's place and invited them to the farm.

"There's lots to tell you!" he smiled as he panted—from exhaustion or excitement, Kalas couldn't tell. "But it can wait! Nashmur's already back at the farm. Let me and Pava get the horses home, get 'em rubbed down and taken care of—and get ourselves cleaned up! We'll tell you everything over supper!"

With that, he planted the heel of the *tëvët* in the ground, vaulted into Runner's saddle, and he and Pava cantered toward the farm, their mounts kicking up a low cloud of dust.

"Lots to tell us? Zhalera repeated when they were back inside. "I hope that includes why it was so important that they travel all the way back there so soon!"

"He said they'd tell us everything," Kalas shrugged. "Guess we'll see."

"He seems…different," Nïmrïk observed. "I'm not sure *how,* just…The lot of you have known him longer than I have. Maybe it's nothing."

That evening, having invited Tsharak to join them, Thara seated everyone around her table. Rül, who usually had a voracious appetite, only picked at his food while the others ate. Kalas thought he seemed tense, like he couldn't wait to say something. And he hadn't stopped smiling! Pava, for her part, enjoyed the meal Shosafin had prepared. His delicious dishes surprised everyone, it seemed. Except Thara.

"Besides, young Rül, your mother works her fingers to the bone. Sometimes, when she's distracted, I've managed to put a few dishes together."

Across the table, Thara tried to chastise him with her brow furrowed; however, her nascent grin destroyed any attempt at sincerity, and she laughed despite her best efforts. "You've figured out how things work around here! Don't sell yourself short, soldier!"

"However," he continued, "one thing Thara *insisted* on—"

"Hush, you!"

Shosafin nodded and stuffed a forkful of roast bird into his mouth.

When everyone finished eating, Shosafin cleared away the plates and disappeared into the kitchen. He returned with an enormous dessert atop a silver platter that struggled to contain the confection. With a wink at Thara, he placed it in front of Rül and Pava. Kalas' eyes widened when he realized what was happening.

"Is that—?! Did you two—?!"

"*Dzhibalafiyëhazh—fanaru tholumbitimu, dhemmeyahal! Okit-ëhazh—dàbiras fie nirimu!*" Thara beamed. And wept.

Zhalera squealed and nearly overturned her chair as she sped toward Pava's seat and squeezed her tight. "Why didn't you tell us?!" she demanded with a broad smile.

Abarandal whispered a song to Kalas, who nodded and affirmed, "That's right! *Married! Rül!* Is that what you and Rive were talking about?! Is that why he gave you his *tëvët?*"

"It is. I wanted to say something before, but I promised Rive I'd tell no one except Mother."

"I had no idea what was going on until we got there. I swear!" Nashmur insisted at a look from Kalas.

"*Úrukilmukritme* have a tradition—all right, we have *lots* of traditions, including those surrounding the right of succession," Pava explained. "As the only child of the *ëmîu,* when my father dies or relinquishes his claim—*fie zhi Ilun mbeshinidu!*—headship of our council of elders passes to me. You saw how Mother views *ilròumbume.* That's how most cave-dwellers feel about outsiders. My affection for Rül...complicated things..."

"Your father asked me how you and Rül were getting along," Kalas said. "Now I understand why!"

"When Rive took me aside, it was to get me to change my mind about his daughter. I think," Rül admitted. "He had lots of questions! You know me, though: I'm not a complicated guy. I answered as best I could, and somewhere in the middle of all that talk, I guess he changed his mind..."

"*You* changed his mind!" Pava insisted. "Father has always been wary of *ilròumbume,* but nowhere near as suspicious as Mother. Or most cave-dwellers, really. You didn't hide anything from him— blind or not, he's always had a way of reading people. You were honest and forthright, and he saw that in you. He wouldn't have given his *tëvët* to you otherwise! That's another tradition: cave-dweller fathers hand their weapons down to their sons-in-law. Not always immediately, but, as you've noticed, Father—his whole family, really—isn't so enamored with tradition that he won't part with it when he deems it…silly, I guess.

"That's one of the few things he and Mother disagreed on. She's always been…devout when it comes to our people's traditions. Father told her what he was thinking, and rather than risk…getting *angry* in front of everyone, she took to the Wastes to let the mist burn itself out.

"Were Father to come to an untimely end—were I or Mother to come to the same, before…uh, well…Legally, Rül would become the next *ëmîu*. Father's taken a liking to him, and he's not the only one who's wary of tradition for tradition's sake, but I know of no other *úrukilmukrit* who'd abide a *nimilròumbu* prince. Of course, there are procedures in place to transfer headship, should the need arise—that's how Father's house displaced Hwanzho's."

"So, Rül: do we call you *ëmîuín* now?" Kalas grinned. Zhalera, in mid-sip, fought not to spit liquid across the untouched dessert.

The farm boy's face drained of color: "Please don't!" he begged.

Tsharak stood, offered a brief speech that was part toast, part prayer.

"Congratulations, dear ones!" he concluded. "Now, *Shâu* Thara, if I might be so bold: this dessert appears unwilling to serve itself…"

"By all means!" she laughed. So did all the others, and Kalas tried to hold the moment in his memory in such a way he wouldn't soon forget it.

As the ancient man doled out slices of the dessert—a cake-like delight *Lohwàlarrinme* called *tsirosh*—Zhalera demanded Pava provide a detailed account of the ceremony. With a broad grin, she obliged.

"Rül says it's pretty different from *Polohwàlar* weddings," Pava concluded after regaling everyone with florid descriptions of the various rites and customs of the cave-dwellers.

"There's a *show*, I guess, where they work their mirrors in such a way that you'd swear the light is *alive!*" Rül raved. "For one scene, the way they swished it around looked just like the wings of an *elu!*"

"Mother was there," Pava said, her features softening to a grateful smile. "I was almost afraid to hope she would be. At first, I thought she was only there as Father's guide, but Sina later insisted that wasn't the case. We talked, and she admitted she had trouble dispensing with some of the old ways. Father had reminded her: according to the 'old ways,' they never would have met each other, much less gotten married, and I think, given time to consider things from that perspective, she relented. That's not to say she's suddenly become fond of outsiders, but she's taking steps…"

"She was kind to me," Rül defended his mother-in-law. "I mean, after a while…"

"You regarded her as more than *shëmiu* of the *úrukilmukritme.* More than just my mother. You regarded her with honesty and humility: the same qualities that won my father over. Should events require it, I think you'd make a great prince of our people, *eshudha!*"

Somehow, Rül blushed and blanched at the same time. "'Prince' is too great an honor for someone like me, *Milëlín:* hearing you call me *husband* is honor enough!"

When the *tsirosh* disappeared and everyone helped clear the table again, Rül transitioned to another topic: "When Rive and I were talking, under the Gateway, he said one of the reasons he'd prefer to see his daughter experience as much life as possible is because he's convinced the Death-bringer's gonna blot out the suns above the Áthradho, now that he knows the source of the murk. Its tremors have gotten stronger, more frequent—we felt a couple while we were there. As loose with tradition as his people might see him, he wanted his daughter to enjoy all the 'ancient and established trappings of a *nimúrukilmukrit* wedding.'

"Pava and I had become fond of one another, as I'm sure you could tell. By the end of our discussion, he drew out some deep things. Things I hadn't even realized. It's strange, but as hurried as everything seemed at first, I realized some *deeper* things: one, that even if this whole world is sliding toward darkness, that's no reason to bury what light remains! And two, some of that light comes from me and Pava. Together. From *all of us* who choose to live our lives in defiance of that darkness."

"Well said, my boy!" Tsharak thumped his mug on the table. The others concurred, Shosafin extending a subtle nod toward the strapping young man.

"We also discovered what Hwanzho had been doing," Pava revealed, "how he'd been conspiring with Gozhira—Marugan—to overthrow my father and assume the supremacy he believes is due his house. That's bad, but it's not the worst! It seems even Marugan has a master—someone with dark designs for the Gateway!"

6.

"After the wedding, a couple of Hwanzho's relatives approached us. I thought they just wanted to give me grief about my new husband, but it was our wedding day, and I wasn't going to let anything ruin it," Pava explained. "I was wrong about their intentions! Gidi, just a few years older than my five and two Sevens, complimented my dress, said I looked lovely. She said she was sorry to hear about Dese. I waited, sure she had more to say, but she didn't. Tafa, her younger cousin, sighed and said something like, 'See? I told you she wouldn't forgive us!' I'll admit, I was confused. I asked her what she meant, and Gidi blurted out a terrifying story about Hwanzho and some of his closer relatives.

"'We know better,' Gidi and Tafa insisted, 'but some from House Kado haven't forgotten the old hatreds. When your friend made the Great Collector shine, we knew Gozhira deceived us. I think most of our house did, but some—like Hwanzho—were too invested to admit that they'd been tricked.'

"Tafa said her mother, Falan, had intended to reveal Hwanzho's plot to my father, but his family threatened to kill Tafa while her mother watched. Then they'd kill her, too. Falan is not a weak woman, but without knowing the depth of Hwanzho's conspiracy, she didn't know who to trust. She loves her daughter…"

"Gidi put together a timeline for us," Rül continued. "Seems after Hwanzho murdered Dese and stole Falthwën's staff, he rushed off to meet with Marugan somewhere east of the Áthradho. Gidi knew how they'd threatened Falan, so she pretended to go along with Hwanzho—her uncle. She overheard him talking about Gozhira's master: someone he described as more fearsome than any mere *eru*. A wingèd wolf, he said. Petite. It wasn't her size that frightened Marugan: it was her iron *will*, her absolute lack of restraint regarding anything pitiable enough to come between her and her desires.

"Hwanzho didn't know we'd run into Marugan in Ïsriba: when he volunteered to come with us to rescue Rive and the others, it was to get closer to the *ëmîu*. Prove his loyalty. He never explained why he stole Falthwën's staff. Gidi heard him say Dese wasn't supposed to go with him: when Pava's uncle caught him going through our stuff, he panicked and struck him with it. Maybe that's why he took it with him? I don't know."

"According to Tafa and Gidi, this 'wingèd wolf' intends to conquer the Gateway with her army 'before the war begins,' whatever that means!" Pava finished. "That innkeeper in Âivambar told us Ësfàyami was—no, she told us *herself* that she was marshaling for war! And Nïmrïk, you said other nations had creatures in places of power turning the world toward war, but no one under the Áthradho seemed to know anything about that.

"Father rounded up the cancerous faction within Hwanzho's house. I don't know what will become of them, but if Gidi and Tafa have their way, it will be nothing pleasant. It's almost ironic: Hwanzho's attempt to reclaim House Kado's former glory drove most of it toward genuine reconciliation with House Murase! Falan made a convincing argument: if a *zhàrudzh* and her army are scheming for control of the Áthradho, a civil war would be a waste of time, resources, and lives.

"Whatever's coming, it's already on its way. We saw its foothold in Ïsriba. Rül and I discovered its presence even beneath the Gateway. Hwanzho wasn't among his tribesmen when the rest were captured: some time after his meeting with Marugan, he snuck back in—he knows as many secret passages as any dweller, I'm sure—and packed his things. Lots of heavy furs, Gidi said. She asked him where he was going—he still thought she was loyal to their house—and he said something about a place far to the west, across water as boundless as the Wastes. Gidi's a brave girl, but she's smart, too, so she let him go."

"'Water as boundless as the Wastes'? Sounds like an ocean," Nïmrïk mused. "Heavy furs?"

"Even if the lot of you weren't heading toward Galámur, I would be after hearing a tale like that," Shosafin said after a moment's consideration. "He believed this Gidi was still party to his and his family's conspiracy, yes? *Shëmîuín* Pava, how likely does it seem to you that Hwanzho—and his family—would use this opportunity to distract us from some greater evil? Stated plainly: how much do you trust this Gidi? Or Tafa?"

"I see what you're getting at, and it's a valid concern: historically, House Kado has been known for its cunning. That said, however,

I believe Gidi. And Tafa. Before we returned to Lohwàlar, I spoke with Falan. I spoke with Father, too. I said before he's always been good at reading people: as strange as it sounds, it's like losing his eyes has only improved his ability! *He* believes her, and he's had many opportunities to learn if she was up to something."

"Sounds like I could have learned a thing or two from your father," Shosafin admitted. "Galámur it is, then."

"Spring will be here soon. Were you to leave for Galámur in a week, two at the most, I believe you'd reach Tarular just after the first thaw of the season. Ascending through Töthrismedas Kig should be a lot easier—and safer—without having to worry about drifts as high as a horse's withers!" Tsharak suggested.

"Why do they call it 'Trolls' Gap'?" Kalas wondered.

"Because of the trolls, of course!"

"Trolls?!"

"You didn't think *töthrisme* were a myth, did you? Ah, my boy! Trolls are…a sect, I guess, of *erume* who surrendered to their darker impulses and sided with Ilnëshras. Unlike mere *ekume, töthrisme* became so attuned to darkness that *darkness itself* somehow manifested upon the skin of their physical forms. Most trolls are quite large and covered in dusky plates of rock-like crust. They're unable to merge with the *shosathesh* or exercise the privilege they once possessed. I understand most are slow-witted, too: perhaps a side-effect of their union—their *infection* with the dark?

"And that reminds me: another side-effect is their inability to endure the light of their estranged kindred—the *suns!* That's why it's best to brave the Gap during the late spring and early summer months, when the window of night is briefest."

"Trolls…" the young man repeated. Most of the others shared his horrified expression.

• • •

Kalas and the others passed the next two weeks finalizing their preparations and saying their goodbyes. He asked Tsharak if he'd be joining them this time, now that Lohwàlar's reconstruction was well underway. The old man smiled and thanked the boy for his invitation: "I appreciate the gesture, my boy. I do! I think Falthwën was right to bid me to remain in Lohwàlar late last summer; now, I'll stay because there's still much work to be done. *Âu* Hebul and his teams are hard workers, it's true, and possessed of keen wits and sharp minds, but that doesn't mean I have nothing to offer! No, I think my traveling days are through: like you, I wasn't born to Lohwàlar; like you, I was adopted by it. It's past time I show this place the kindness it's shown me over the Sevens, through its people. In fact, I think I've spent most of the last few months in town rather than at home! Vàyana has been kind enough to offer me her spare room, and I think I'll accept. That'll keep me closer to everything…and the Pump. Just in case."

"Well, be safe," he replied, and Tsharak laughed: "I might have recommended the same to you!"

Back at Zhalera's home, evaluating the contents of their packs, she confessed to Kalas: "All those times I snuck away to the smithy? I was trying to make a sword for you. I told you I would, but I couldn't get the metal to behave! I'm sorry! I kept it too soft or too brittle, no matter what alloys I used. You were curious about what I was doing there, I know, and I'd hoped to surprise you, but I got so frustrated I just burned it all to slag. I'm forgetting something… missing something, maybe. When we come back, I'll try again."

"Zhalera," he began. She cut him off.

"I've struggled with confidence ever since Father died. Before that, really: without his help, that knife you're so fond of would have probably ended up in the scrap heap, too. I've seen you struggle with confidence, trying to find your place within all this prophecy business. Unlike me, you've done all you can to rise to the challenge. You have faith in me: judging from your *persistence*. If the prophesied 'child out of time' believes in me, maybe it's all right if I believe in myself? Father used to say, 'The Creator bestows his gifts on whom he pleases, according to the kind intention of his will.' Watching me grind down the edge of your knife, he repeated that proverb with his big, goofy smile. I'll...I'll try again. Someday..."

Kalas brushed that errant lock of lemon-silver hair behind her ear, kissed away her tears, and held her tight.

"I'll wait," he whispered, "and it'll be perfect, I just know it. I don't say that to pressure you! I just...I will *always* believe in you—you know that, I hope!—but you need to understand this: your abilities do not depend on the belief of others! I agree with Gandhan—*o shelu fie id nir*—the Creator has no need of anyone's approval when he gives gifts. Neither do we when we use them for his glory!"

Everyone agreed to meet at the farm on the morning they departed Lohwàlar. Tsharak was there, too: although he'd spent many lifetimes' worth of Sevens isolated from regular contact with others, he admitted these last few months had rekindled within him a sense of purpose, of community he hadn't known for a long, long time. As the ancient man helped the others pack their things, Shosafin took Thara aside, and with heads bowed, he whispered something. She seemed grateful for his words.

A prayer, perhaps? Kalas wondered. *No, not a prayer—that's not his way...*

Rül hitched Runner and a new horse, a buckskin named *Diral-dïl-Lohwà*—Courser, Rül said, to the coach; Pava, from the box seat, waited for him until he completed his checks. Nashmur and Nimrïk waited astride their respective mounts. The first sun had crept above the horizon by the time Abarandal and Zhalera entered the cabin.

Shosafin finished cinching his bags, massaged Breaker's withers, and whispered something else to Thara. He'd placed a hand on her shoulder, and she'd wrapped her arm around it, clutching his callused fingers with her own similarly hard-worked hand.

"I'll bring him home—I'll bring them both home. I promise," Kalas heard him say. Stolid, Thara stood on her tiptoes and pulled the old soldier's face toward her own, whispered something in his ear, and let her fingers caress his jawline as he righted himself.

"Bring yourself home too, soldier" she demanded. He smiled— another genuine smile, unsettling in its rarity, and, in one fluid movement, swung himself into Breaker's saddle.

"Mën al paresëthu, shâuyahal," he said with a prim nod and a proper salute. *"Á al gabiresodhu!"*

Despite her storied toughness, Kalas thought he glimpsed the faintest trace of worry, tempered with hints of pride in both her son and his bride and the soldier on whom she'd come to rely, stretch across her brow and crease the corners of her mouth. He looked away and climbed into the coach.

"Take the Ruins Road toward Kësharan," Tsharak suggested. "Just past the Plains Gate—Oh! None of you knows where that is, do you?"

"I do!" Kalas corrected him.

"You do? Very good! Just past the Plains Gate, before you're inside what's left of the city proper, veer right, and follow the road for about half a mile. 'Road' might be a generous term these days. You'll come to another gate—I think! I haven't been back there in Sevens. Used to be called the Mountain Gate. Follow what's left of *that* road for a few miles north along the Sea of Jewel's coastline— that is, the rim of the Empty Sea. When you come to an old fork in the road, turn right again. There used to be signs, but it's likely those have long since disappeared. The rest of the way is up to you to discover!"

"Thank you, Tsharak!" said Rül, and Kalas could hear the excitement in his voice. "I'll see you soon, Mother!" With a flick of his reins, the coach lurched northward.

CHAPTER VII.

After Passing through Tarular

"ONCE AGAIN," KALAS SAID WITH A WRY GRIN AS the coach carried them through the desert, across the fragmented flagstones that comprised the Ruins Road, and past the remnants of Kësharan's Plains Gate. Rül turned right, per Tsharak's instructions, and followed a much worse stretch along the dead city's perimeter. Kalas peered through the windows at the compromised pavement, punctured here and there with indomitable trees bursting forth from beneath the earth. On a few occasions, he and the others had to stop and analyze the best way to navigate maze-like sections of their route: portions of towers and even the walls themselves had tumbled into the corridor between the city's various gates, forming labyrinthine puzzles. A few such "puzzles" required considerable effort to bypass, but just as the first sun descended out of sight, they reached what was left of the Mountain Gate.

"We should've made better progress," Rül grumbled.

"Nothing to be done about it," Nashmur offered. "Looks like it's been…well, it looks like no one's been here since Tsharak's youth. It's hard to believe he's almost nine hundred years old! Never would have thought it possible until I met all of you!"

Nimrïk began unloading overnight gear from his bags, but Kalas suggested, "Why don't we camp out in the city? It's destroyed, sure, but there are bound to be a few places where we could spend a single night, wouldn't you think? Father and I only saw a small part of it when we were here before, and that was on the other side of things, but some of the buildings we passed looked all right..."

"Falthwën said crystal from the Áthradho might have been used here," Pava remembered. "I'd love to see what's left of it: what a story for the people back home!"

"Is that a good idea? I mean, after everything that's happened here?" Zhalera countered. "Kalas, you remember what the *egu* did to my father's body..."

"I do, but everything that happened here was more than a hundred Sevens ago. Any *shosayedhume* would have probably moved on by now, right? It'd save us some time in the long run, too."

"Yeah...I guess," she allowed.

The moon, yellow-pink and somehow bigger than usual, had risen by the time everyone agreed on a suitable lodging place. On the Night of Falling Skies, Kalas assumed, something struck the middle of an immense tower built from precision-cut rectangular blocks: its top half lay in shambles, but its base seemed sturdy enough, even after all these years. He and the others examined its perimeter and visited its second and third floors: on the way to the fourth, a rotted wooden step crumbled to dust beneath his weight.

"I think there's enough room for the horses on the ground level, and we should be fine right above them," Kalas said as he picked himself up. Abarandal, who'd followed him, pressed against the walls: satisfied they'd hold, she smiled, and she and Kalas went downstairs. Rül was tending to the horses, trying to pacify the newest member of his team.

"This place seems all right," the farm boy nodded, "but Courser here seems a little, well, I've never known him to be skittish, but he seems a little out of sorts. Maybe it's just being away from home."

Kalas had discovered a small hearth, intact, on the second floor, and by the time the others returned from the shadows, he had a cheery fire blazing within. Zhalera, followed by Nashmur, Nïmrïk, and Pava, joined him and Abarandal and knelt before the fire. She rubbed her hands in its expanding warmth and muttered something about the unseasonable cold. Nïmrïk carried a pouch of foodstuffs with him: it took some doing, but at last he persuaded everyone to make room for him while he prepared supper. Shosafin had remained invisible until the fresh scents of stewed beef and warm *golfras* bread wafted through the city. As they ate, they discovered Nïmrïk was also a better-than-average chef.

"I must have picked up a thing or two from all those Sevens loitering around Mbirin's Place," he shrugged and joined them on the floor.

Once finished with the meal, with everything cleaned and put away and their sleeping arrangements made, Kalas and the others said goodnight before drifting off to sleep. Nïmrïk and Abarandal remained awake, tending the fire's remaining coals when the young man at last closed his eyes.

"Kalas!" the *egu* whispered in his ear. "Kalas! Wake up!"

"What? I'm—"

"Quiet!" Nïmrïk hissed as he placed a finger to his lips.

Kalas sat up and tried to see through total darkness: the fire had burned out, and his eyes perceived nothing.

"Nïmrïk?" he dared to breathe.

The *egu* grabbed his hand and led him toward the ground floor, where Shosafin and Abarandal peered through a broken window. Here, star- and moonlight illustrated their ribbon-like profiles with its glow and somehow intensified the concern in their shared stare. Kalas drew up beside them and tried to follow their gaze. Courser whinnied, his unease apparent.

In the distance, moving between the carcass-like bones of destroyed buildings, a pair of pale blue lights bobbed up and down, traveling the streets toward the tower in which they'd taken refuge.

Zhalera was right, Kalas acknowledged with an unnoticed frown.

The lights stopped and hovered for a moment near the remnants of an old fountain; soon, others rose up from a low mist now blanketing the ground. As the growing mob of despondent-looking shapes approached the tower, Shosafin reached for his sword.

"*De,*" Nïmrïk whispered as he placed a hand on the old soldier's arm. Shosafin ignored him and drew his weapon anyway.

The entities? things? creatures never reached their hiding place: seconds later, a morose breath of wind swept through the streets, wrapped the lights in suffocating fog, and blew away their every trace with a haunting sigh. Shosafin held onto his sword for a minute or two before returning it to his sheath.

"What was that, wolf?" he demanded of Nïmrïk, his voice still soft.

"*Shosayàódru,*" he said. "The manifest aftermath of what happened here nearly one thousand years ago."

"'Spirit-mist'?" he scoffed.

"The *Pokësharan kelâme* have been gone for more than a hundred Sevens now, but vestiges of their shared anguish remain trapped in this world. I didn't know what it was when I woke you, lad. I'm sorry. The mist can't hurt us. Not *physically,* anyway."

Kalas shuddered. Although the amorphous lights looked nothing like people, he imagined Tsharak's birth parents among the throng. *Lights,* he decided, was too strong a word: rather, the indistinct shapes seemed more like a *parody* of light, a subtle *half-darkness* pretending to be something it wasn't.

This is what we're trying to undo, Kalas affirmed. *Horrors like* shosayàódru *were never meant to exist. Nor the tragedies that made them possible in the first place…*

"It's all right, Nïmrïk. In a way, I'm glad I got to see them. It reminds me why I—why all of us are out here. I've doubted my place in the prophecy before. I still do, if I'm completely honest, but if there's a way to bring about a day when sorrows like these might cease…"

The *egu* nodded, but Kalas sensed something lachrymose in the gesture.

"Should you accomplish your part in this prophecy's fulfillment, they will cease…for a time. Come, there are still several hours before the first sun rises. You—you too, Shosafin—should get some sleep."

2.

Before morning came, Kalas, still flush with thoughts from his near-encounter with the disembodied half-shadows, grabbed a few buckets and a pole and made his way across the city toward the trail that would lead him into the Empty Sea. Abarandal, having never slept, it seemed, followed him and offered to carry a couple of buckets. Remembering her curious strength from their days at Zhalera's new smithy, he nodded and handed her a pair.

When they returned to the city, their buckets filled, Miryan had just ascended the horizon: Kalas had to pause for a moment as the Song washed away the world around him. Abarandal had sensed his sightlessness and leaned into him before he could stumble. When the blur of white subsided, he thanked her with a smile and a sidelong glance. Soon, Kalas heard voices nearby.

"Falthwën said something about this, I think," Pava said with a twinge of sadness. "I guess he was right: after all these Sevens, there's not much left of it."

"When I searched the wreckage for Sharuyan after the *Hàfpïn*

Vâlafi Zhàme, I remember coming across this place: then, about a quarter of it had been destroyed. It was still quite a spectacle."

As Kalas and his *eru* companion rounded a corner, they saw Pava, Rül, and Nïmrïk studying thin metal strips and shards of colored glass—no, crystal—still nestled within the crumbling remnants of a collapsed tower. Pava held onto one of the larger fragments, its blue tint blunted by the second sun's amber light.

"Hey guys, what's this?" Kalas asked as he set down his buckets and wiped his brow: despite the lingering winter chill, hours of climbing had warmed his blood.

"Kalas! There you are! Zhalera's been looking for you!" Rül exclaimed.

"She has? I mean, yeah, I probably should have said something…"

"I told her you were probably fetching water," Nïmrïk added. "Nothing to worry about."

"These crystals," Pava explained: "I think they came from the Áthradho, maybe hundreds of Sevens ago! I just wish I could have seen them whole."

"Hundreds of Sevens ago? And your people still talk about it?" Kalas marveled.

"Well…the *Kësharanrinme* weren't exactly honest in their dealings with the *úrukilmukritme,*" she confided. "In fact, that's one of the reasons most of us don't care to deal with *ilròumbume.* Not just because of how the people of Kësharan treated us: other kingdoms, too, had been abusing our kindness for Sevens. Kësharan's bad faith was the tipping point. That's why we still talk about it from time to time.

"Anyway, it looks like there isn't anything here to see. Not really. And the others are waiting for us. Nïmrïk, thank you for showing me all the same!"

"I'm just sorry there wasn't more to see, lass," he sighed.

"Pava's right," Kalas said as he looped his buckets across his pole.

"Time to get going. We've got a couple hours before noon—and a couple weeks, maybe less, before we reach Tarular."

Rül nodded, and he and Pava started for the tower where they'd spent the night. Nïmrïk let them get some distance ahead before he whispered, "You haven't said anything about the *shosayàódru*, I take it?"

"I haven't. I don't want to worry anyone."

"I don't suppose it matters either way."

"I mean, well, what are the odds that such mists would form in Lohwàlar?" Kalas continued. "The *rudzhegume* fell upon us, too..."

"That they did, lad, and I can't say the mists *won't* form in Lohwàlar, but I suspect you'd perceive it as an occasional, inexplicable *sadness* when walking through the places that endured the worst of the *rudzhúnthal*—the wolfstorm.

"The Crescent, then," Kalas nodded. *And my own home...*

Zhalera regarded Kalas with a curious look as he and the others returned. She said nothing at first as everyone packed up and piled into the coach or climbed into his saddle: when they started moving, she asked him how he'd slept. He confessed he'd had better nights.

"You might have been right. You'd think I'd have that figured out by now!" he said with a sheepish grin. "We probably would have slept better in tents..." Zhalera responded with a grin of her own and admitted she'd grown accustomed to sleeping in her own bed the last few months.

Not too far from the Mountain Gate, the desert sands turned hard, the scrub gave way to sparse hardwoods, and dunes became sandstone slabs and immense boulders as the team ascended the narrow road; half a day north and the forest deepened as towering pines and shaggy firs displaced the oaks and aspens. As they traveled across the subalpine plateau, Kalas wondered what stories Falthwën might have shared had he been with them. The *eru* cleric's knowing smile glinted in the boy's memory as he erupted in a shower of sparks and fire.

Kalas sat upright and realized he'd fallen asleep.

I had no idea just how exhausted I was—and am…

"Nice nap?" Zhalera said as she tried to stifle a yawn.

"I'm awake now," he insisted. "Why don't you get some rest? Looks like we've got a few hours before suns-down, and I think both of us need more sleep than we'd like to admit."

Zhalera curled onto his lap and wriggled herself comfortable, wrapping an arm around his waist. Mere minutes later, Kalas felt her breathing slow and adopt a measured rhythm as he ran his hand in slow circles across the rise and fall of her back. From the opposite seat, Abarandal stared out the window as the coach traveled past the warm browns and nascent greens of the coming spring. He couldn't divine her thoughts: a blend of sadness and uncertainty, it seemed, occupied her otherwise delicate features, though Kalas admitted he might have misread her expression. She turned toward him when he took a breath: he held it for a moment, tried to formulate his questions, then just sighed and shook his head. She smiled, nodded like she somehow understood his unspoken intent, and turned back toward her window.

I wonder what the other erume *think about this world, what it's become. I wonder what it was like before it cracked. I wonder if they're as scared as I am about what may—or may not—come to pass…*

Sifting through such thoughts, he fell asleep again.

Days and nights seemed to smear together like smudges between dusks and dawns as they approached Tarular. Seven, maybe eight days after Kësharan, it rained in the morning; by mid-afternoon, the rain had turned to snow, and, despite the cold, Zhalera begged Rül to stop the coach so she could experience it from the footman's narrow rumble. Kalas laughed at the happiness in her features as she reached out to catch the thick, wet flakes tumbling from an iron sky.

"*Snow*, Kalas!" she said, as though he had no idea what was happening. She marveled as the whitish crystals landed in her hand and melted into the ridges within her fingertips. When Rül stopped for lunch, he unhitched Runner and Courser, who seemed unsure about this strange accumulation beneath their feet; Gilfën and Dalafar, however, pranced about, pressed their powerful bodies against low, snow-covered branches, and enjoyed the cold against their skin: taking their cues from them, Rül's team—Breaker, too—soon followed suit.

Back on the road, its lazy curves became aggressive angles as the terrain inclined toward the first peaks of the *Taruúnme Ilkâshkit*. Traversing the switchbacks sapped most of their speed: Rül suggested they might not reach Tarular for a few more days. The snow stopped after a few hours, and Zhalera sighed when Nashmur explained that it would most likely disappear within a day or two.

"These mountains…they're the same mountains responsible for those biting winds on the steppes, right?" Kalas wondered. "I think that's what Falthwën said…"

"Yes, the Standing Mountains form the continent's northernmost boundary," the former commander confirmed: "they reach from the mouth of your Empty Sea to the far side of the Ilvurkanzhime. Their range spans hundreds of miles: actually, some people claim part of it slid into the Bejeweled Sea when the world was cracked, but, as you know, that was a long, *long* time ago…"

When both suns had set, everyone made camp, enjoyed a light supper, and retired early. Shosafin excepted: on foot, he disappeared without a sound. Their fire—and the forest—kept most of the chill wind from seeping into their bones. Soon, after scattered fragments of conversation, the other humans fell asleep, lulled by the soft strains of an impromptu lullaby whispered between Abarandal and

Nïmrïk.

After a restless night fraught with unremembered dreams, someone's heated discussion roused Kalas. Rül had brought them a short distance from the road: as the young man followed his ears toward the owners of the angry voices, he discovered Shosafin blocking two men wearing travel-stained blue robes.

"*Âu* soldier, please! Let us pass!" one figure insisted. His hooded clothes obscured his face, but the color in his voice described him as an older man.

"We're on our way to—ah, Melash-Niruk! Yes!" said the latter when the former elbowed him in the ribcage. "Melash!"

"What's going on?" Kalas said as he approached the soldier.

He waited a moment before Shosafin explained: "*Serularrinme.* Members of the Deathless Flame cult."

"Sir! You are mistaken!" the younger-sounding traveler protested. The older man held up a hand and cleared his throat.

"Not the cult! The *Randa pïni Sifumilël!*"

"Melash is a long way from Serular," Shosafin growled.

"We're traveling the *Sifuyerudas Kayu*—the Path of Sifuran. It's...call it a pilgrimage."

The old soldier held the travelers' gaze for a long, silent moment, his eyes naught but slits as he considered their claims.

"C'mon! We can't block the road like this!" Kalas pleaded.

After a brief pause, he shrugged, stepped aside, and said, "We *can,* but we won't..."

The older pilgrim presented him with a low bow; the younger figure managed a slight nod, but before the pair was out of earshot, he turned and muttered something both menacing and indiscernible. Without looking back, his older, wiser companion placed a hand on his shoulder and whispered something in his ear: as he listened, the malcontent's eyes widened, his head whipped forward, and his pace quickened.

Once they disappeared around a bend in the road, Shosafin sheathed his sword.

"What was—?" Kalas began. The soldier interrupted him: "They're lying," he spat.

3.

"What makes you say that?! I mean, how do you know?" Kalas wondered as he followed the swordsman back to camp.

"I told you some of my story before, about the skills I acquired after King Rufàran disappeared. I've been shoveling manure for the last few months, but I'd need a much bigger shovel for all the horse—"

"They said they were on a pilgrimage!"

"Empty words. With their mouths, they told lies; with their bodies, they told the truth: they're from Serular—their accents— and they *are* members of the *Ragus pïni Tshaggul Kavar*. I don't know what their plans are for Melash-Niruk. I don't believe Melash is their true destination. Sure, it makes sense: it's on the coast, surrounded by water, but there's a subtext, a tell in the way they spoke…"

"All right, if that's true—if you're convinced they're *really* cultists, why'd you let them pass?"

"They recognized me from Serular. I know it—that's what the older man said to his companion, judging from his response. They're cunning enough to avoid any unpleasantness for now. If they want to play a long game, let them: two cultists' deaths, out here on the road, gets me no closer to Marugan. Not today. I suspect they're not the only cult members on their way…north."

Kalas gasped when he deciphered the subtlety in Shosafin's cryptic reply.

"Galámur! Wait—that's where Hwanzho's heading, too! Do

you think Hwanzho joined up with the *ragus?* Why else would he be headed there? Galámur's far from Lohwàlar: it's even farther from the Áthradho! Unless…You don't think Marugan is the *Tshaggul Kavar,* do you? I wonder what he's up to…I wonder what the cult is up to…"

"That's something I intend to learn—and the main reason I didn't strike down those 'pilgrims' where they stood. Melash is nothing more than a way point for them: I'm sure of that. And no, Marugan is *not* the Deathless Flame: I'm sure of that, too. However, it seems improbable that both Marugan and this so-called *Tshaggul Kavar* would have unrelated business at the same time and in the same place. Especially somewhere as distant as Galámur. Understand, lad: if Marugan's involved, whatever the cult is up to—whatever this Hwanzho character is up to, I'm sure it's nothing good.

"Come, let's get back to camp and get on our way. We should reach Tarular before the cultists—before they can warn their fellow true-believers about me, but to do that, we'll need to move quickly!"

In short order, Kalas and the others packed up camp and started out again. A subtle drizzle, a mist, really, made everything damp and miserable, but at Shosafin's insistence, Rül and the others followed him and Breaker across the grueling and slippery terrain.

"I *assumed* things about Marugan in the past. Nearly died because of that, as most of you know. I won't make that mistake again," he said when the others shared looks with one another.

"He's probably right," Kalas allowed. "Thinking about the way they carried themselves, something was…*off,* I guess. We need to get to Galámur anyway, and the sooner we reach Tarular, the sooner we reach Melash. I just hope there's a boat waiting for us when we get there!"

Within a few hours, even though no one else noticed anything, the old soldier announced the "pilgrims" were somewhere behind them, but they'd do well to maintain their pace: as he'd explained to Kalas, he repeated his concerns that additional cultists would soon descend upon the mountain town.

"We won't get a full night's sleep tonight. Not in Tarular. We'll resupply and rest for a few hours, then make haste for Melash-Niruk. A few more hours at a moderate pace should give us adequate lead time," he outlined for the rest of the party. With a snap from Breaker's reins, the pair disappeared behind a spume of mist and mud.

The high walls of Tarular poked the muted gray-purple of the evening sky with sharpened wooden posts, every point formed from repeated scraping and blackening with fire, then polished to a satin-like finish that gleamed in the dull light of the setting suns. The walls' steel-banded doors rested open on their hinges; their towering watchtowers seemed devoid of human presence. Past the threshold, he noticed a few people walking the streets: a couple here, a family there, a solitary man or woman enjoying an evening stroll.

"Seems a little cold for a night out, doesn't it?" Zhalera wondered. Nashmur laughed.

"Cold to you, maybe, but these are the first hints of spring for these people! Some *Poyïsriba* winters have been so cold it seems the very air is trying to burn away your face: I imagine in a place like this, that's what every winter feels like. I'll bet most *Tarularrinme* would consider this evening downright balmy!"

"Hmm. Well, I still say it's cold!" she shivered.

Kalas agreed with a nod. He was about to say something when out of the corner of his eye he noticed a blue-robed trio slinking into an alley just a couple of blocks away."

"Uh, Shosafin," he hissed, and the soldier dropped back and approached the coach's windowed door. He said nothing about the out-of-place figures; instead, he nodded and offered Kalas his peculiar salute.

He saw them, too...

At Nïmrïk's suggestion, Rül steered his team toward the remotest inn available: "If Shosafin is correct—and there's no reason to doubt him—I think it'd be prudent to minimize our presence for the night. And yes, I know the exterior of this place leaves much to be desired, but that should work to our advantage: most of its patrons are probably hoping to maintain some semblance of anonymity, too."

"Nashmur, why don't you make arrangements for the night while the rest of us wait outside? And give me your sword. Just in case," Shosafin proposed. "No need to advertise we're from...out of town."

The former commander nodded, handed his cousin his weapon, and stepped into the low, dirty light seeping from the tavern's greasy windows.

"I'll make a supply run; then, I'll spend the night with the coach and our horses," Nïmrïk added as he eyed a few seedy-looking characters loitering near the shadows. "Anonymity has its disadvantages, too."

When Nashmur returned from the belly of the tavern—*The Dancing Bear*, according to the flaking letters carved into the cockeyed, weather-beaten sign dangling above its door—he nodded again, accepted his sword from Shosafin, and said, "It's as bad as it looks—maybe worse—but it'll suffice for one night. No blue-cloaks inside—none that I noticed, anyway. If we keep our heads down, we should be all right: pretty much no one but the proprietor paid me any mind. A good sign, all things considered.

"That said, we'll definitely need to keep our weapons covered: sitting toward the back and only slightly drunk, I saw a soldier from Gambarad. Someone with a sword bearing the crest of the Iron Bear, at least. It's possible he's got friends nearby. I bought us a few rooms: they're small, probably disgusting if they're anything like the common area, but nicer than, say, Ïsriba's dungeons!"

He smiled at Pava, who laughed as she recalled their old conversation. Most of their belongings had traveled into the darkness with Nïmrïk: each person carried what remained in small bags as Nashmur held the door for them. Across its threshold, the reek of stale beer and unwashed bodies mingled with the tantalizing aroma of roasting meat. Kalas breathed deep and pictured himself tearing into a plate full of sizzling beef strips. Rül sniffed the tantalizing air, too, and smacked his lips.

"That smells *so* good!" he mumbled. The others nodded.

Nashmur led them toward the back of the common area and a fragile-looking staircase that led to a small second story. At a nearby table, his eyes subtly glassy, sat a heavily bearded man wearing his *Pogambarad* sword. Kalas' eyes lingered on its crest—a snarling bear depicted with angular shapes and bold lines—for a moment too long. The soldier caught his gaze and, with one hand, raised his tankard; the other he placed atop his weapon's hilt. Kalas looked away, but not before the stranger smiled.

"Well met, friend! No—*friends!*" he slurred as he took in the rest of Kalas' companions.

"Uh, well met, mister soldier!" Kalas stammered as he tried to push toward the stairs.

"Hey, where you going? C'mon, sit down! Have a drink with me!"

"Uh, thank you, sir, but I—"

"Oh? Think you're too good to be seen with the likes of me? Why, I'll have you know I—"

"Easy, friend! The boy meant no disrespect: he merely assumed your invitation was a pleasantry intended to be declined," Shosafin soothed. "We've got some time. Time enough for one round, I'd say…"

When the old warrior spoke, he did so with an accent most would have mistaken for a native *Tarularrin*. Kalas didn't think Shosafin had ever been through these parts of the world before: the ease with which he affected the local linguistic color was nothing short of incredible. He grabbed a chair and gestured for Kalas to do likewise. At the same time, he glanced at his cousin, who nodded and continued up the stairs with the others.

"You'll have to forgive him," Shosafin explained. "He doesn't get out much…"

"Oh, no worries, friend! None whatsoever!" Their host set his cup down and snapped his fingers for the solitary barmaid: she glanced at him, smiled weakly as he twirled a few circles in the air above their table, and disappeared within the amber haze mellowing beneath the room's rough-hewn beams.

"Gidra will be back in just a minute. She's good—even if Bandag overworks the poor girl! Been telling him for years he needs more help, but does he listen? Bah! Of course not!" The man shook his head and released his grip on his sword.

"Nice-looking hilt," Shosafin noted with a casual air. "You been a soldier long, mister…?"

"All my life," the windburned man replied with a faraway look in his ice-blue eyes. "Until recently, anyway. Oh, the name's Obën. And you are…?"

"Shadrïs. The boy's name is Garat. 'Until recently'? Sounds like there's a story there…"

Gidra returned and slapped three frothy mugs on their table. Kalas jumped. Obën laughed and grabbed a new vessel. He raised it, puffed at the foamy head floating above his drink, and downed almost all its contents in a single swig. He thumped his not-quite-empty mug and wiped at his coarse, gray-blond mustache. Shosafin did the same. Kalas took a tentative sip, grimaced, and forced himself to swallow some of the bitter yellow liquid that snapped at his face. When he pushed his cup away, Obën shrugged and claimed it for himself, imbibing its remains with another singular draft.

"You're right, friend. There *is* a story there. It's…it's boring, really, and it's impolite to bore people. Especially new friends."

"Can't argue with you there," Shosafin agreed.

After a few minutes of insignificant niceties, the old soldier stood, placed a hand on Kalas' shoulder, and said to their host, "Thanks for the drink. Here's hoping your steel stays bright, friend. Come, Garat: time to go."

The young man stood, nodded, and followed Shosafin toward the stairs. He thought about looking back at the curious figure when Shosafin whispered: "Eyes forward, lad."

How—?

Subtle needles pricked at his awareness: a slight stinging sensation he'd experienced too many times to ignore that told him someone was watching him.

Be wary!

He fought not to breathe too sharply as he stumbled up the stairs.

Why is he watching us? What's his interest in us? Are we in danger?

4.

"He was evaluating us," Shosafin explained once he and Kalas reached their rooms. "Trying to gauge how much he could trust us—with what, I'm not sure, but if your friend Nïmrïk is correct, if people like Marugan have been starting fires in the hearts and minds of the world's sovereigns…I suspect our friend Obën sees more, understands more than he let on.

"We need to be careful here. *Everywhere,* really, but that should come as no surprise. Obën's tone, his body language, suggests he wishes he were still a soldier, though it's possible he was just testing us while pretending to be addled. I suspect he's figured out I used to be a soldier, too. A *Pogambarad* soldier, if we're lucky. Too bad there's no such thing as luck."

Shosafin's eyes sparkled with a light Kalas hadn't seen since their meeting beneath the bridge above the Óronas Lohwà, and the young man understood he'd never ceased his calculating assessment of the world around him, not even during his months as one of Thara's farm hands.

"He probably pegged Nashmur right away: it'll take more than a few months out from Ïsriba to grind away all those years of martial mannerisms," he continued. "It's probably a good thing your friend is with the horses. We should keep watch tonight, too. I'll wake you when it's your turn."

"No, you won't," Kalas said. "I'll keep watch. You have work to do in the morning: me, I'll probably be sleeping in the coach anyway. Might as well do *something* useful while we're out here..."

The old soldier smiled and shrugged. "If you insist, lad," he said as he eased himself onto one of the beds and closed his eyes: almost immediately, his breathing slowed; in less than a minute, he was asleep.

"What trouble did you two get into now?" Zhalera half-teased: Kalas didn't miss her cautionary tone.

"No trouble. Not really." He sighed and sat down on another bed. "I guess we'll find out."

"I don't have anything to do while we're on the road either: I'll stay up with you. If you'd like some company, that is."

"You know what? I would," he said, his thoughts elsewhere.

It was still dark when Shosafin shook Kalas awake: he and Zhalera had fallen asleep on one another's shoulders. They roused the others and made their way downstairs, taking pains to keep quiet. Before they reached the door, the soldier stopped, cocked his head, and looked around: after a moment, he cracked a wry smile and gestured for everyone to keep going.

"There's no coach house—none associated with The Bear here, anyway," Nashmur explained, "so Nïmrïk is probably near the stables. It's just a street away, according to the innkeeper. This way."

When they reached the stables—a low structure with a high, steeply-pitched roof—Nïmrïk was just strapping Dalafar's saddle atop his back. Gilfën was already saddled, and Runner and Courser had already been hitched to the coach pole.

"Breaker didn't seem interested in my help," he observed as Shosafin finished brushing down the coal-colored stallion before draping a blanket over his spine. "Otherwise, he'd be ready to go, too." The soldier said nothing, only shrugged as he finished securing his gear. Breaker pawed the ground and snorted, his hot breath steaming and his silver blaze shimmering in the weak, early morning light.

With everything ready, Rül gave his reins a gentle snap and eased his team onto the road. Nashmur and Nïmrïk followed and flanked the coach while Shosafin brought up the rear. The first sun had yet to breach the horizon, Kalas judged, looking at the low and irregular stripes of red-orange clouds. Surrounded by mountains, it would be some hours before the sun's direct rays fell upon Tarular. He shivered, grabbed a couple of furs, and handed one to Zhalera and wrapped himself in the other. She leaned into him as their vehicle bounced along the mountain town's cobbled streets. Abarandal, who'd been staring out one of the coach's windows, trilled a sequence of surprised-sounding notes as her sterling eyes widened.

"Something wrong?" Zhalera asked. "What'd you see?"

The *eru* whispered a few more bars and pointed toward a yawning alley, still dark. Kalas and Zhalera both tried to see whatever had spooked Abarandal: after contorting themselves into position, they looked and saw…nothing.

At first.

"I don't—" Zhalera began.

"There!" Kalas hissed and squeezed her arm. "Did you see that swish of bright blue?"

Abarandal sang softly and nodded.

"No, I—yes! Right there!" Zhalera said as a hooded figure popped into view from around the corner: a moment later, he disappeared.

"I wonder if they're with the two we, uh, met on the way here," Kalas mused. "I wonder if Shosafin saw them: no, *of course* he saw them! I guess there's nothing to be done about it now. Let's hope their plans keep them in town for another day or two."

Nashmur's prediction proved accurate: most of the snow had melted; now, only a few shrinking drifts tucked beneath broad-branched evergreens remained. When they stopped for a brief lunch, Kalas shared his concern with Shosafin, who had indeed observed the blue-robes' ineffective attempt to conceal themselves. In between bites of boiled, salt-cured venison, the soldier nodded and echoed the young man's conclusion.

"It's unlikely that our friends from yesterday reached Tarular before we did; somehow, these guys have noticed our presence. Maybe they're from Serular, too, and set out before the others? Yes, that has to be it: if they're from elsewhere, if they didn't recognize me from last fall, they'd have no reason to give me—any of us—a second look."

"There's another possibility," Kalas said, collecting words in his head and trying to decide how to voice them. "Somehow, *erume* can move as fast as light: their *thoughts* can move from one to another at the same speed. Maybe faster. I don't know. There were times when I could *hear* Falthwën's thoughts. Pieces of them, at least. If the Deathless Flame is *nimeru*, then I suppose it's possible he'd be able to do the same. Maybe he's got...what did Falthwën call me? *'Ilhadzhalas'?* Maybe there are privileged ones in league with him?"

Nïmrïk started, considered the boy's suggestion, then nodded. "It does make sense," he allowed. Shosafin seemed reluctant to consider such outlandish ideas; at last, he shrugged and allowed an *improbable* scenario such as Kalas had described wasn't necessarily *impossible.*

"*How* doesn't really matter right now," the soldier decided. "We'll need to be doubly aware of our situation from here to Melash. And beyond. All right, everyone: let's get back on the road. We'll reach Töthrismedas Kig in a day or two, judging from the maps I studied. We'll pitch camp about a half-day's journey from the Gap. I want a full day's worth of suns-light to navigate its mysteries: lots of twists and turns through swamps and mountain marshes."

"Is that so?" said Kalas, his eyebrow raised. "I mean, sure: sounds like a solid plan to me. I guess there's no reason to risk crossing the Gap at night...The terrain, like you said..."

Shosafin offered him a quick glance and a grim smile: his eyes never quite met Kalas'. Within minutes, everyone filed onto the narrow road and resumed the journey north.

The first sun, hanging low in the sky, splashed yellows, pinks, and oranges across a canopy woven from stringy rags of clouds; the second sun had disappeared hours ago, its exit from the heavens pealing softly within Kalas' thoughts. Some quality in the Song's subtle music suggested discretion.

"It'll be dark soon," he began. "Wouldn't it be a good idea to get off the road—and cover our tracks—while there's still a little daylight? We should still have enough time to cross the Gap before the suns set tomorrow if we get an early start."

"How are we gonna get this coach off the road and into this forest?" Rül protested. "The ground around here looks pretty soft: if we get stuck, we'll have more trouble than just a couple of *mafame* in blue costumes!"

"We'll manage," insisted the soldier. "Kalas, get out and collect some fallen branches. Lots of branches. At least as thick as your arm: thicker is better. I'll scout around, find some place for us to keep concealed. I'll be right back."

Less than half an hour later, Shosafin returned, dismounted Breaker, and showed Kalas what to do with the branches he'd piled up: "We'll lay them out like this as Rül drives his coach over them. I'd suggest a makeshift corduroy road, but given this wet environment, I don't want to risk injuring the horses should a log slip. We'll keep moving branches as the coach passes: the ground gets firmer in about a quarter mile."

Kalas started placing logs. Nashmur and Nïmrïk joined him and Shosafin, and within another half hour, they arrived at a small crevice formed by a slab of rock that had sheared away from its much larger parent. Panting, Kalas headed for the road to remove all traces of their presence while the others prepared the site. Zhalera followed, and the two of them leveled out the deepest depressions with rocks and pine cones: they walked backwards toward camp, erasing their tracks with makeshift pine-bough brooms and scattering twigs and needles.

By the time they reached the others, Nashmur had a low fire smoldering on the ground: they wrapped themselves in its flirtatious heat and snacked on bits of stale bread and hunks of dried meat. After almost an hour of methodical, uninspired biting and chewing, Shosafin's cousin kicked out the fire as most everyone wrapped himself in furs and hunkered down for the night. Nïmrïk disappeared for a moment; soon, a black, somber wolf padded into view, climbed over rocks and roots, and leapt onto the barrier slab.

"A few *Serularrinme* saw me like this last fall, but I figure all *rudzhme* look the same to most people: should one or more of the *sifu-ilmikasme*—blue-robes—catch a glimpse of me in this state, well, there's nothing out-of-place about a wolf in the forest in the mountains! I'll keep my eyes—and my nose—tuned to our immediate surroundings. The rest of you: get some sleep. If we stick to Shosafin's plan, we'll have a long day ahead of us tomorrow!"

"No argument from me," mumbled Rül as he stifled a yawn. Pava yawned, too, and followed him under a tarpaulin tent stretched taut and low. The others burrowed into similar structures: despite his fatigue, Kalas chuckled when he heard the *egu* suggest Shosafin get some sleep, too: "You're the show-runner, *âu* soldier! Perhaps you more than anyone need to be fresh for tomorrow!"

"I'm rested enough," he countered. Nïmrïk cut him off.

"You don't trust me. Nor, for that matter, does your horse." He bounded onto the ground and sat, gave himself a moment to scratch the skin behind his ear with a hind foot.

"I get it. I do," he continued. "After uncounted Sevens of similar reactions from all manner of beings, your reluctance is…typical. No, that's neither judgment nor condemnation—just an observation. Stay awake if you must: I'm in no place to dictate your choices."

Abarandal glided over to him and ran a delicate hand beneath his other ear. Nïmrïk almost lost his balance as he leaned into her welcome touch. The *eru* sang something soft, subtle, and sympathetic.

"Lass, I have no idea what you just said, but…thank you!"

"Maybe you're right," allowed Shosafin. "All right, wolf: keep watch, then. Wake us if anything catches your eye. Or your nose."

The old soldier disappeared within his shelter. Nïmrïk watched him go, then turned to Kalas, offered him a wolfish wink, and ascended the slab again. He paced its length a time or two before choosing a place to sit. Abarandal stood nearby and whispered soothing phrases from the Song. Nïmrïk's head swayed in time with her melodies, and as Kalas' eyes closed, he wondered if he heard her soulful strains with his ears or with his mind.

5.

Something hot and wet nudged the back of Kalas' neck, half-waking him from a deep sleep. He moaned and rolled away, dimly aware of soft and hurried paws on the ground around him. Before he drifted off again, one such paw slapped his chest as Nïmrïk huffed, "Lad! Get up! Someone's coming!"

"Someone—what? What's going—?"

"Hush! Wake the others: I'm going to get a better look. Keep your knife ready…just in case!"

Fully awake now, Kalas pressed the heels of his hands against his eyes, shook his head, and stood. He stumbled through the camp toward Shosafin's resting place, but the old soldier's bed was empty. It looked like it hadn't been slept in.

"Kalas? What time is it? Why are you—?" Zhalera mumbled as she lifted the corner of her tent.

"Shh! Someone's coming! Nïmrïk's scouting ahead. I'll wake the others. Got your sword? Good! Be ready!"

Zhalera nodded and crawled back inside her shelter while Kalas roused Rül and Pava. Nashmur had already unsheathed his sword: Abarandal, not unlike Shosafin, was nowhere in sight. With everyone awake and alert, they waited beneath the cool, pearlescent light of the waning moon.

Minutes—maybe mere moments later, Nïmrïk padded into view, his yellow eyes glinting from between the trees as he approached. He seemed cautious but unhurried, his bushy tail carried

230

low and an ear turned toward his rear.

"It's a soldier. From Gambarad, from all appearances. He's trying to keep a low profile, but he's in a hurry, and he's making some careless mistakes. Shosafin's tracking him now, but I—"

"Shosafin?" Kalas whispered. "I thought—"

"He makes his own choices," the slinking *rudzh* seemed to shrug. Kalas nodded with a shrug of his own.

"Obën!" the young man hissed. "The soldier Shosafin and I met inside The Bear. Shosafin suspected he knew we weren't who we claimed…he also suspected Obën had a sense about the *hidden things* taking place within the kingdoms of the world. He said he'd been a soldier all his life. Until recently—he wasn't ready to tell us just *how* recently. Or why. Do you think *he's* looking for us? He kept an eye on us the whole time we were at The Bear…"

"Can't say, but I'm sure we'll find out soon enough!" With a swish of his tail, Nimrïk bounded onto the rim of the natural ledge, sniffed the air and flicked his ears, and waited.

Nothing made a sound as they remained tense, wrapped within the unsubtle chill winding through the night. Rül looked at the sky and ran his gaze from side to side as he hefted the *tëvët* that used to belong to Pava's father.

Trying to figure how long until the suns rise, Kalas supposed. He figured they had another five, maybe four hours before the first sun would reveal its presence in stark reflections against a blue-gray mountain dawn. He looked toward the sky, too, and realized Nimrïk had abandoned his perch. Kalas opened his mouth to call out for the *egu,* but at that moment, some inexplicable urge commanded all his focus:

"*Âu* Shadrïs? Master Garat?" wheezed a gruff voice coming from the road. The young man guessed its owner had strayed from the relative predictability provided by the highway and into the deepening woods. After a minute, maybe two, it came again: closer, this time, and Kalas knew it was Obën. He risked a glance at Nashmur, who raised an eyebrow:

That him?

The young man nodded in reply.

A moment later, at the edge of Kalas' perception, the trees writhed with sudden violence as dark gray whirl tumbled toward their camp. When the snarl untangled itself, Nïmrïk stood over a crouching Obën, who held his empty hands in the air. He hadn't noticed the others, it seemed, his focus on the wolf's bared teeth.

"Easy, friend wolf! Easy now!"

Nashmur cleared his throat, but Obën seemed unable to tear his eyes away from the hulking beast assessing his every move.

"Mister Shadrïs?" he guessed.

"Not exactly."

"That's too bad! Maybe you'd be willing to, ah, give me a hand here?"

"Who's this 'Shadrïs' you're looking for?"

"A—uh, someone I crossed paths with not too long ago. If you're not him, then it's none of your concern. Does that mean I'm on my own here?"

"Not necessarily," Kalas said as he stepped into view, his knife in hand. Obën sighed, relieved, as the young man flanked the wolf; his relief descended into horror when Kalas returned his blade to his belt and stroked the gigantic wolf behind an ear.

"Murdas gunme! What are you—Master Garat? Master Garat, where's Shadrïs? And…*why* are you…*petting* that monster!" Obën paused, cocked his head, and continued, "And why isn't it tearing you apart? That's not a *typical wolf,* young man! Maybe you're not familiar with—"

"Egu," Kalas supplied as he moved his hand toward the back of Nïmrïk's skull and gave the fur between his ears a gentle tousle. "You're right: he's *not* a typical wolf, *Âu* Obën. You weren't keen on

telling Nashmur why you're looking for…Shadrïs. I respect that. Maybe you'd tell me?"

Nïmrïk ceased his snarling and sat on his haunches. Obën risked a glance in Nashmur's direction, his eyes widening when he recognized him.

"You were at The Bear, too!" he exclaimed. "All of you! Forgive me: it seems I've lost my touch in recent months…Anyway, yes, Master Garat, since you and Shadrïs were kind enough to share a drink with me: I watched you go upstairs, kept an eye out for you—*for* you, not *on* you! I missed you on your way out, so I rushed over to the stables.

"That's when I noticed a pair of figures spying on you. Blue-robes. Lots of 'em have passed through Tarular recently. Do you know about the *Ragus pïni Tshaggul Kavar?*"

Kalas' eyes darkened as he returned a curt nod.

"I'm not surprised. I suspect your friend—and you, no doubt—know there are things shifting just beneath the surface of the world we see. When I was still a soldier, I brought my concerns to King Mödus, but once he expressed his doubt—his *considerable* doubt—I lost what little support I had. Pretty soon, I didn't even have a place within his court."

"Sounds familiar," said Shosafin, Obën's sword in hand and his face expressionless as he separated from the forest.

"Shadrïs! Where did you—? Your skills are sharp, friend! Sharper than mine, at least!"

"Call me Shosafin."

Obën offered the old soldier a wry grin, as though he'd suspected *Shadrïs* had been an alias.

"Oh, uh, call me Kalas," added the young man, his cheeks reddening in the dark.

"I take it you heard everything, *Âu* Shosafin? Yes, well, those *sifu-ilmikasme,* they're part of these things, whatever their scope.

I realized too late they'd gained favor with King Mödus' court: whispered promises of secret power, immeasurable fortunes, and the like. When I saw they'd taken an interest in you, I wasn't sure what to make of your relationship with the cultists, but I stayed close on the off-chance I might find new allies…"

"…or eliminate new enemies," the old soldier remarked without inflection.

"Well…yes," Obën shrugged. "Wouldn't you do the same? I'd like to think I've encountered the former—although I'm curious how you find yourselves in the company of an *egu!*"

"That's a long story," Nïmrïk said, eliciting a startled gasp from the *Pogambarad* man, who'd only just regained his feet.

"Of that, I have no doubt! And as much as I'd like to hear it, there's no time for such things! The blue-robes are no more than a few hours behind me: when they made camp for the night, I snuck past them. Whatever your destination, we should keep moving lest they come upon us unawares."

"You're not wrong, but 'we'?" said Shosafin, a solitary eyebrow slightly raised.

"I assume you're on your way to Gambarad. The capital, that is, and I know that place well! I grew up within its walls, explored its every—But you don't care about that, do you? Because you're *not* headed for Gambarad, are you?" Obën interrupted himself as the subtleties in Shosafin's expression shifted.

"Not Gambarad…Hmm…The nearest town is Melash-Niruk… By sea! Of course! Friend, listen: I passed through Melash on my way south, and from what I've uncovered, Melash is where the *ragus* first established its foothold this side of the Standing Mountains!"

"Is that so?" Shosafin prodded. Obën understood something in his demeanor, however, and continued with a twisted grimace.

"You know where they're from, don't you? Somewhere far to the south, unless I miss my guess. I've never been south of Tarular.

Sir, as a friend—as a soldier, if nothing else—please: tell me what you know! Like I told your friends: this world is on the cusp of change. I've heard reports of the middle kingdoms marshaling for war against the Far East, and I've…I've learned appearances aren't always what they seem…"

Seem…

"Things the world over, under, and above," Kalas repeated, mostly to himself. Obën's eyes widened as he wheeled on the young man.

"What did you just say?!"

"What? I—Nothing! Just something someone told me a long time ago!"

"Indeed," said the soldier through slitted eyelids. "A 'someone' of my own told me the same. Soon after, she was murdered…Mizh had become something of a mother to me in the years after my own had died. That's also a long story, but in short, somehow, she saw past all the gilt and gleam others hid their wills behind. She saw the ugliness at the end of their endeavors and helped me learn to make critical distinctions on my own. *O shelu fie ith nir…*"

"Should we…should we fight them?" Rül wondered as he worked his fingers across the surface of his weapon. "I mean, how many are there?" He inclined his head toward Tarular and tested his balance, shifting his weight from foot to foot. Gauging the farm boy's resolve from the corner of his eye, Nashmur offered him a half-nod.

Shosafin considered their would-be companion a moment longer before he turned toward their camp: "Doesn't matter if there are five or five hundred: even if we struck them all down, even captured one or two, we'd diminish—or lose—our opportunity to understand their endgame.

"All right, everyone: let's strike camp and get on the road while we still have some hours between us. If we maintain a good pace, by this time tomorrow night, we should find ourselves at Trolls' Gap."

"Trolls' Gap!" Zhalera exclaimed. "What about the stories Tsharak told us? Do you really think—"

"Doesn't matter what I think, lass. Doesn't matter what *Tsharak* thinks. *Töthrisme* or not, we're out of options."

Chapter VIII

Between the Teeth of Trolls

The grizzled old soldier wove his inscrutable circles in front of and behind Rül and his team, between Nashmur and Nïmrïk, as he tried to impress upon the others his desire to reach the Gap before suns-down. When asked, he insisted he wasn't concerned with Tsharak's mythical beasts; rather, his concern centered on his unfamiliarity with the lands through which they traveled.

Kalas wasn't convinced.

"Maps are one thing. Experience another. That's why you're here, Obën, and not standing on the side of the road where we found you," Shosafin said when they stopped for a hasty breakfast. The *Pogambarad* veteran rode with Kalas and the others in the coach: Shosafin had instructed the boy to keep a hand on his knife and an eye on the man. For the last few hours, the exhausted figure had done nothing but sleep; however, Kalas remembered Shosafin's uncanny ability to maintain his situational awareness while he rested, and he wondered if Obën might have similar skills.

"I understand," Obën nodded at Shosafin. "I'd be wary, too, were our roles reversed."

"What can you tell us about the road between here and Töthrismedas Kig?" the boy asked.

"There's a stream just ahead. Should be nice and high from the recent snowmelt; the mountains rise a couple leagues after that. We'll traverse an exposed ridge where the weather's fickle: sunshine one moment, driving wind and pounding rain—or blinding snow—the next. Late in the day, we'll drop down into the forest again. We'll have to ford a different stream—a shallow river, really: the bridge that used to span its banks is gone.

"I wish I could suggest making camp for the night once we cross the river. The *Dombayilkibas,* it's called, wraps around all kinds of rocks poking out of the ground. Some people call those rocks the *Gunínme*—Little Teeth, not to be confused with the *Gunme,* the *Töthrismedas Gunme*—jutting from the earth at the heart of the Gap. I'm getting distracted: too frequently, the woods along the Rockwinder's shores provide concealment for the boldest—if not the brightest—brigands…

"I gather from what the girl—young woman, sorry!—said earlier that you're aware of the legends surrounding the Gap? They're true. No, I haven't seen a troll for myself, but I've heard stories from trustworthy sources, men whose word is unimpeachable, and if there were any way to avoid the Gap at night, I'd strongly recommend it. But there isn't. Not if we want to reach Melash before the blue-robes.

"Friend Shosafin, if you'll excuse my boldness: it seems you've made an impression on the cultists. One they're not likely to forget any time soon. What happened? Where are they from? You talked about their endgame: if you had to guess, what would you say they're up to?"

"Serular," he grumbled at last. "Near the southern coast. That's where I ran into them last year. I was…looking for someone. An old…friend. That's where I learned about the cult. And where I first attracted the attention of the *sifu-ilmikasme.*

"If my former 'friend' is involved with these blue-robes, they're up to nothing good. You're right, though: there's no time to waste.

Let's keep moving. There's no reason to let them continue to close on us."

"Won't they have to rest, too? They're on foot, right? Surely we'll cover enough ground to avoid the Gap at night, won't we?" Pava wondered as she helped pack up.

"Not a chance worth taking, lass," Nïmrïk, again in human form, responded. (Aghast, Obën hadn't known what to make of him when he emerged from the tattered remnants of his lupine shape.) "Shosafin's right: if this Deathless Flame were merely human—I intend no offense!—perhaps we could rely on his followers' frailties to delay them as yours delay you, but Kalas made a wise observation the other day: perhaps they do have privileged ones among their ranks who might whisk them across the *kalthesh*. And before you ask: 'Why haven't they traveled the light-realm already?' Maybe they're interested in our 'long game,' as Shosafin might call it. Maybe they *have*, for distances short enough to escape our notice. Maybe they're similarly unwilling to reveal the extent of their power until they deem the time aright.

"And maybe they're just hapless adepts hoping to exact some reward or boon from the object of their devotion. The truth is, the only way to know for sure is to reveal to them our own secrets: we'd learn much from such an encounter, but not enough. In this, I agree with Shosafin. It seems the most attractive choice among a clutch of unattractive options is to face whatever mysteries Trolls' Gap harbors in the dark."

The old soldier spared a glance at the *egu*, and Kalas thought he glimpsed surprise in his shrouded gaze as everyone finished securing the rest of their gear.

With a snap, Rül guided Runner and Courser onto the road again. He stopped only briefly when he reached the first stream Obën had described—just long enough to replenish their water stores; then, the party began the long, gradual ascent out of the trees and onto the bare rock that stretched for unnumbered miles toward the north. The second sun joined the first atop a cool, clear sky, bringing with her the soft peal of chimes that echoed within the recesses of Kalas' mind. He closed his eyes, gathered his will, and tried to access the privilege Falthwën had described to him.

"Kalas?" said someone next to him.

Zhalera? Zhalera. Who else?

He felt fingers—soft, delicate, and improbably strong—brush his forearm; he felt his follicles pucker and the fine hairs therein stiffen as Abarandal reached across the space between them and whispered something within his thoughts.

A warning? I don't understand…

He opened his eyes: the dark-haired *eru* held him with her silver gaze. When she withdrew her hand, his skin felt like it had been doused in ice and fire and lightning all at once. Kalas sucked in a sharp breath and risked a look at what he feared would be a fresh wreck of flesh, but his arm was just fine.

"What was that?" he uttered as the sensation subsided.

Abarandal sang a few phrases, mixing in a few gestures of the kinetic shorthand she and Zhalera had created.

"They might hear you!" the young blacksmith acknowledged. "'They'? Hear you…what? I didn't—Oh! The Song! Of course! That night, on your second Seven: didn't Falthwën say he—and others like him…or like Nïmrïk…*heard* The Song *through you?*"

He did…

"Song?" prodded Obën, his eyes still closed.

Kalas smirked: *I knew it!*

"Zhi *Helim,*" he corrected him. "The 'cord of Ilun's intent,' as a friend once described it. It's *The* Song the Creator began when he established the world and everything in it and beyond."

"Ah. *Ilunasdas Yahir.* 'Creation's Prayer,' Mizh called it."

"Have you…what does it sound like?" Zhalera quizzed the man.

Obën laughed.

"Friend, you're asking the wrong soldier! Can't say I've ever *heard* it. Anything I know about it—which isn't much—I learned from Mizh. Most everyone considered it nothing but a story. Not her. She described it as, well, a mix of things, if I remember correctly. She didn't talk about it much: I think a lifetime of strange looks and hushed whispers in the streets took its toll. She did say it had different...*moods,* if you will: language that changed from time to time but meaning that never wavered. No matter the context, no matter how fleeting its surface idioms, Mizh always believed the Prayer revolved around a singular theme:"

"Hope," Kalas breathed.

"Indeed..." said Obën as he opened his eyes and observed the boy with a shrewd glance.

2.

Before midday, the few deciduous trees along the road disappeared, displaced by towering evergreens; not long after, even those surrendered to the elements as the party ascended above the timberline. Exposed atop the ridge, not even the confines of the coach could obviate the irrational sensation of watching eyes all around. Peering through its windows, Kalas marveled at the steep slopes descending either side of the trail and hoped no other travelers would approach from the opposite direction: the narrow path—nothing more than a haphazard-looking arrangement of poorly fitted stone slabs—seemed barely wide enough for their vehicle, let alone another of similar proportions. On one side, far to the west, he saw the suns-light sparkling atop the distant waves of the *Shadaún Ilarod*—the Roiling Ocean; on the other, rising opposite a narrow, densely-wooded valley, he saw numerous rougher-looking peaks, shrouded in gray mists.

The Wastes-that-Devour must be somewhere on the southeastern side of those mountains, he reasoned.

"This is the best route?" Zhalera wondered with a sidelong glance at Obën. The *Pogambarad* soldier mimed a yawn as he sat up and followed her gaze out the window. "I mean, why does the road come up across this ridge? Why not build it somewhere, well, safer?"

"I think there was a lower road, once, but that would have been before my time. Probably not worth maintaining or something. This route isn't exactly well-traveled, as you might have noticed."

"I wondered why we hadn't seen anyone," Kalas admitted as he returned to his seat.

"Most trade and travel between the North and South takes place over water. Not too many people are—and I beg your pardon—foolish enough to make *this* trip—and not just because of the terrain. Say what you will about *töthrisme*, but the highwaymen that roam these parts are plenty real!"

"If this road is hardly ever used, what's the point in lying in wait all the way out—*up*—here? Melash isn't more than a few days from here, right?" Zhalera said.

"Fair question, friend. I don't have a good answer. I've run into them a few times myself: wild-eyed and reeking of filth. More animal than human in some respects. Most times, I've been fortunate enough to stay beyond their reach: other times, I've had to put a few of them down…I don't think I'll ever get used to that haunting, lightless stare in their eyes…

"I'm sure you're all capable of handling yourselves, too? You all have a way about you. A way that says you're familiar with violence."

"When necessary," Kalas defended.

"Of course," Obën shrugged. "Anyway, let's hope this is all just academic. Conjecture. We should reach the Rockwinder just after the first sun sets."

• • •

Aside from enduring some powerful blasts of wind rushing up its sides—and enjoying some extreme views of the lands between the mountain ridge and the far away Roiling Ocean, traversing the *Shâk ohi Zhàdas Dath*—the 'Knife at the Sky's Edge,' according to Obën, proved otherwise uneventful. Kalas shrugged off the impression of someone or something observing their passage and tried to enjoy the scenery. On occasion, a bird would streak past the coach windows, shrilling a high-pitched screech as it sliced through the mild afternoon air.

Kàsh hil nira. Ilrâidh-fin, Kalas noted, his thoughts turning toward Ïsriba, its national identity replete with falconine symbolism, when another raptor buzzed the coach. It circled the forest at the far side of the Knife, then adjusted its wings and coasted over the distant trees toward the ocean. He watched it a while longer until it disappeared behind a series of clouds gathered just beneath the ridge. As he turned his attention toward his traveling companions, Kalas blinked and whipped his head around—there, not too far from the forest they would enter within the hour, he spied an angry swirl of purple high above: before he could mention his suspicions aloud, a stab of orange-white fire forked through the sky. Additional bolts followed.

"Rül! Stop!" he insisted as he crammed his head through the small window behind the coach box.

"Uh, Kalas?" the farm boy said as he drew up his reins.

"Rainfire in the woods just on the other side of the ridge! *Ilâeg-sal!* It'll burn us alive if we get caught in it—and there's no protection out here!"

"You're right, lad, but we're still some distance from it," Shosafin insisted as he brought Breaker alongside. "Let's give it a few minutes, see if it passes…"

Zhalera clutched Kalas' arm as they climbed down from the coach and beheld the ravenous spectacle ripping through the clouds and plummeting toward the earth.

"Where's it coming from?" she wondered. "What's that—? Look! I see something—is there something *in there?!* Looks like *pieces of something* falling with the rain?"

"I don't know," he said after squinting for a moment. "Maybe it's just smoke? Or the lightning creating shadows on the clouds? Or maybe you're right. I just remember being scared when Father and I were almost caught in it. Obën: do you get a lot of *ilâegsal* storms in Gambarad?"

"Not often, friend. I've heard others speak of them—I've seen the results—but this is the closest I've ever been to such a storm. Sounds like you've been through one before?"

"Last summer. I had a shovel—an almost-new metal shovel, and the rainfire ate right through it. I had a friend, and his father…the rainfire ate right through his face, too."

"Looks like it's over," Nashmur said when the clouds surrendered their violet shade and the breeze blew away the orange color in the air. "Kalas, any words of caution?"

"No: afterward, Father and I just saw blackened earth and a few smoldering trees. I think the worst of the storm just burns itself out in the sky. The ground was safe enough to walk on, if that's what you mean."

"We need to keep moving," Shosafin interjected, his face marred with the slightest trace of a scowl. Kalas sensed he did *not* appreciate the delay, no matter how necessary. "That storm cost us half an hour. Cost the cultists nothing. Let's go."

Kalas watched the sky like a hawk—like a falcon, perhaps— for any sign of the rainfire's return as the party dipped below the timberline again. After a few miles, and after the second sun had disappeared, he caught the taint of sulfur on the wind: an acrid sting that lodged in his nostrils and would not depart.

"Hungry rain must have hit somewhere near here," he coughed, and soon, toward the valley side of the mountains, he saw the amber glow of fire glinting from downed trees. Heavy smoke blanketed the forest floor and pooled between rocks and roots, where the lengthening shadows swallowed its remains. Kalas shuddered as Ëlbodh's ragged face and terrified, single-eyed stare flashed across his thoughts.

When they reached the Dombayilkibas, the last rays of the first sun reflected from a canopy of high, puffy clouds and filtered through the trees with soft, diffuse light that lent their surroundings an otherworldly glow. Loath to stop, Shosafin raised an arm and suggested they replenish their water supply while they had the chance as he and the other riders dismounted.

Obën's description of this portion of the road had been perfect: numerous black slabs protruded from the ground, and Kalas marveled at the peculiar shapes and angles held in their various edges. He paused for a moment, set his buckets down, and ran his fingers across their almost polished surfaces.

"Obën, these *Little Teeth*…did someone put them here?"

"I don't think anyone knows for certain! They don't look like any of the other rocks around here, do they? And from a certain point of view, they almost look like they're aligned in rows. There have been more than a few suggestions that someone should arrange a scientific expedition, perform surveys and experiments and the like, but no one seems keen on spending that much time so near the Gap!"

Kalas shrugged and retrieved the water he'd been carrying when a sound like voices seemed to flutter overhead. His eyes wide, he looked to Shosafin, who placed a finger to his lips and gestured for everyone to hurry. Kalas wondered if the blue-robes had reached them already when he recognized a familiar cackle.

"Highwaymen!" Obën hissed as he helped Abarandal and Zhalera into the coach.

Kalas shook his head as he closed the door behind him: *"Eaters!"* he insisted.

3.

"What do you mean, *'ilrâigme'?*" Obën wondered as the coach stuttered over the rough, uneven road on the far side of the Rockwinder.

"Not that long ago, we uncovered…there's a town—Deridzhas—probably just south of the Standing Mountains: some of Pava's people were captured by eaters-of-men. Yes, cannibals! We… far underground—Deridzhas was a mining town—we discovered something too unbelievable to describe right now, but the place was swarming with *ilrâigme-edhume*. I don't know if your 'highwaymen' are the same thing as the eaters, but that laugh…

"Tell me, Obën: have you ever heard of anything…strange about this place? Stranger than teeth or trolls, I mean? Maybe some other weirdness no one's been able to explain?"

"I don't know what you mean, friend," Obën apologized, his features bent toward recollection. "I guess trolls are enough to worry about for anyone unfortunate enough to pass this way!"

"I wonder if the eaters will cross paths with the cultists," Zhalera wondered with a subtle smirk.

"They most likely will; however, that only means we'll reach the Gap when it's darkest—and tonight's a new moon."

"Nïmrïk can see in the dark. Better than us, at least, when he's, well, when he's a wolf."

"You call him 'wolf,' not *'egu,'* I've noticed," Obën prodded.

246

"Not at first," Kalas explained, and provided him with an abbreviated account of how they met, taking pains not to mention some of the more sensitive details.

"I never would have thought it possible after what happened back home," he finished, "but I've learned a few things since then. And I've learned there's a lot *more* to learn, too…"

Obën listened to the boy's tale without interruption, nodding now and then as his story unfolded. He winced when Kalas showed him the scars still visible across his chest, wept when he told him about Màla's death, and grinned when he outlined Lohwàlar's ongoing renaissance.

"Someday, I'll have to make a trip to the southern end of the continent," he began: before he could continue, something rocked the coach hard enough to toss Kalas and the others through the air. Abarandal pealed a question, her song incalzando.

"I don't know!" he replied as he helped her to her seat. "Obën, any idea what—"

Before the *Pogambarad* warrior could speak, something else hit the coach: a moment later, a pale arm streaked with oozing sores reached through one of the windows and groped the air. Its owner had almost grabbed a fistful of Zhalera's hair when Kalas heard a subtle ring, followed by a maniacal shout. The highwayman's severed hand collided with the coach's floor as angry gibberish faded into the night. He turned to see Obën's sword, slick with blood and glittering with hints of starlight. Outside, additional voices rose up from the darkness as Rül stopped his team and shouted something to Pava.

"We must be near the Teeth!" Obën observed as he wiped his sword across his leg.

"C'mon!" Kalas instructed as he bounded from the cabin, his knife in hand. Zhalera unsheathed Valarandal with a yellow flash as she and the *eru* followed him into the night with Obën bringing up the rear.

"It's *hot!*" said Zhalera.

"What's hot?" Kalas wondered.

"My sword! It feels like it's fresh from the forge! It's—no, it's cool now. That was strange! It's never done that before!" she explained as she studied her weapon for a moment. "Pava! What are we dealing with?" she added when she caught sight of the cave-dweller woman.

"Looks like *ilrâigme!*" she confirmed as she scanned the woods for movement. "Nïmrïk turned *rudzh*—he chased a few into the forest. Shosafin and Nashmur: I don't know where they are, but they must be close. Rül's protecting the horses as best he can: without them, we'll never cross the Gap—never mind reach Melash!"

An eater—a highwayman, an adversary—flung itself from beneath the coach and snagged Abarandal by the ankle. She screamed—

Even her fear is music!

—and wrenched her foot away from her assailant with enough violence to dislocate its shoulder. Kalas dropped to one knee and plunged his blade into the side of the figure's ash-colored neck.

"No idea if these…highwaymen operate the same way as the eaters south of the Ilvurkanzhime, but if they do, we've got our work cut out for us!" Pava warned as she hurled her *tëvët* toward another attacker's chest: in a blur of motion, she danced across the side of the coach, pivoted, and, in a single move, retrieved her weapon and lanced the creature's abdomen. Kalas tried not to choke on the ensuing stench.

"Abarandal! Get back in the coach!" Kalas said. She raised her voice and insisted she be allowed to stay and fight.

"I know you can handle yourself! That's not it! It's—if something *happens* to you…It's the *world* I'm worried about!"

Before she could protest again, Zhalera agreed: "He's right, my sister! We—most of us—aren't that important in the grand scheme of things! If—"

Abarandal glared at her and breathed a flurry of notes…then disappeared within the confines of the cabin.

"What was that?!" Zhalera asked as she sized up a fast-approaching enemy.

"She said *every one of us* is important," Kalas answered. He spared a quick look at Zhalera's and Obën's swords, stifled his jealousy, and remembered the axe Rül packed away.

"I'll be right back!" he shouted. "Rül! Where's your axe?!"

The farm boy shouted his response, and Kalas dug into the compartment his friend had indicated. After rifling through its contents, his fingers wrapped around the axe's well-worn handle: he gripped it tight and turned—

He *tried* to turn: a highwayman slapped his shoulder with a studded club fashioned from the fire-hardened remnants of a tree stump.

"What—?" he began when the man jabbed at his stomach. Kalas' question decayed into a series of pained gurgles as he doubled over. He braced his back against one of the coach's wheels as he collapsed and found himself staring up into a pair of bloodshot eyes framing yellow-white irises and pinhole-sized pupils: in the dark, that was all he could discern.

Obën's highwaymen are *eaters, then. Maybe there's a* vàsu *buried beneath this ridge somewhere? Maybe—why does it matter now?* he laughed aloud.

His would-be murderer paused, surprised, perhaps, with the young man's outburst. When Kalas sighed, the disheveled figure raised his club and—

Staccato thunder echoed through the night as the forest split apart, sundered by a vast wall of slouching darkness that swept trees aside like twigs. The *ilrâig* dropped his weapon and looked up: he screamed as something hauled him skyward; he disappeared within a dull, almost purple mist high above.

Another highwayman shouted something—a warning to his companions, Kalas guessed, as they scattered. He stood and picked up the axe he'd dropped. Other voices screamed as additional colossal, colorless shapes seemed to materialize out of nothing.

"Did he just say—?" Zhalera whispered from the other side of the coach.

"*Töthrisme!*" Obën confirmed. "Trolls!"

"They're *huge!*" Kalas gasped as rock-like fingers groped the dirt in search of prey. "Tsharak said they were big, but *this?!*"

"The suns have just set: if the old man was right, we're in for a long night," said Shosafin as he separated from the shadows. "Looks like the trolls chased away most of the eaters: if we're going to survive the Gap, we need to push through!"

The *Poyïsriba* soldier led everyone along the serpentine route as it cut between towering granite pillars. He'd always had a way with Breaker; now, he demonstrated his rapport with the other horses as he coaxed them through the nightmare unfolding all around. With one hand, he stroked Courser's withers; with the other—and without breaking focus—he ran his sword through a highwayman who lunged at him from behind a tree.

"Obën, how much longer before we clear Töthrismedas Kig?"

"At least a league, friend. The Zhàshâk might have leveled out, but either side of this forest is bounded by impassable cliffs. The road is the fastest—the only way, really, through these mountains. If we can make it another mile, maybe—"

A *töthris* crushed their *Pogambarad* companion within its stony grip before he finished speaking. Too horrified even to gasp, Kalas watched as the life drained from Obën's eyes; he watched as they stared forever forward, glassy, as the troll shoveled his corpse into its purplish maw. Its face had neither eyes nor nose—none visible, at least: just an insatiable mouth. The troll reached down to grab Kalas, too, but Zhalera dropped her sword, launched herself at him, and shoved him out of the way.

"Kalas! C'mon!" she shouted. She waved a hand across his face; slapped him when he showed no response. "Kalas!"

Still reeling from the shock of Obën's death, he ignored the sudden flash of light bursting from within the coach: he tuned out the whoosh of wings beating within his mind. Abarandal, ignoring Kalas' and Zhalera's prior warnings, glided from the coach and bounced lightly onto the rough flagstones over which they half-ran, half-stumbled.

"He's—it just *ate* him!" he protested as though Zhalera hadn't been there, too.

"I know! And it almost ate *you*, too! Now c'mon! Stay sharp!" She helped Kalas to his feet, picked up her sword—suddenly coruscating with threads of citrine light, and noticed the *erushátem* as she turned around.

"Abarandal! What are you doing out here?! Get back—!"

Sensing, perhaps, the distant similarities in their compositions, the troll shifted its focus toward the otherworldly woman with shimmering skin. Flexing its thick fingers a time or two, it reached for her: as one, Kalas and Zhalera screamed a warning that came too late. Time seemed to stretch—through no magic of the Song this time—as the troll's plated hand wrapped around Abarandal's tiny frame. When she disappeared within its grasp, Kalas realized she'd been glowing: now, not even the stars' frail light seemed capable of blunting the dark.

4.

Gone! She's…Undone! The prophecy's undone! What hope remains?! Kalas agonized as the ever-present subtleties of the Song ceased within his mind.

Not even seconds later, a pulse of heat and cold and threads of fire cracked the agglomerated black crust clinging to the troll's fingers just moments before the pieces flew apart. The forest blazed with innumerable colors as sizzling rays of visible light, flung from Abarandal's hovering, translucent form, split the night. The rest of the troll crumbled into dust as its essence—its *rilâ*—shriveled into gossamer ribbons before the lightstorm blew them away, too. A discordant bass note shook the earth before its sour waves succumbed, overpowered by the triumphant chords welling up from soundless sorrow, and Kalas realized what he'd mistaken for the Song's cessation was naught but an extended fermata, a transition between its movements.

Drawn, the other *töthrisme* approached the shining star, considered her exalted presence, and attempted to crush her as they had numerous highwaymen.

And poor Obën.

Every effort ended the same: countless Sevens' worth of reified darkness disintegrated into biting bits of dust borne away on sudden blasts of wind. Each *unmaking* exploded in Kalas' head with furious orchestral abandon: a solitary chord composed of soulful strings, bright and lively horns, and ethereal woodwinds—underscored by deep drums' resounding thunder. He squeezed his eyes shut as blood trickled from his nose, and he remembered the way the Song felt when the *Kel Erume* first summoned Abarandal:

A sense of something wrong *looming within the music the* erume *sang…There's* wrong *here, too, but it's not from Abarandal's song: it's from the* töthrisme, *from their unmaking. It's…I don't know, a* necessary *wrong, maybe: like a wound so deep, so profound, that healing it brings back the hurt from when it was inflicted.*

*If all this…work she's doing makes me—*privileged *or not!—feel like this, then what does* she *feel?! It must be agonizing! And yet she's* *glowing—no, blazing! Like a miniature sun!*

When the trolls were gone, Abarandal descended toward the earth and turned opaque as her undulating aura surrendered its vibrance to the remains of the night. Her feet hit the ground, and Kalas, sensing her imminent collapse, rushed forward to catch her, to ease her as she fell.

"Is she...?" Zhalera wanted to ask as she placed a trembling hand on Kalas' shoulder.

"No, she's all right. Weak, I'd guess, but she'll recover. I don't know if any of you heard it—*felt* it the way I did, but this was more than just rescuing us from these *töthrisme*. So much more! I don't know how else to explain it..."

Abarandal's eyes fluttered, her chest heaved, and she smiled as she looked into Kalas' face. She looked toward Zhalera and the others, too; then, with Kalas' help, she stood and took a few steps. She opened her mouth to say—to *sing* something, when some preternatural sensation arrested her attention. She turned and walked with purpose toward the edge of the forest.

"Abarandal?" Kalas wondered, following at a close distance.

She ignored him and raised a hand toward the night, toward something within the woods, and sang what sounded like a requiem.

"Abarandal?" he repeated, his voice barely a whisper.

The trees parted as yet another troll trudged toward the beckoning *eru*. Its steps were measured, however. Almost reluctant. Nashmur rallied the others and prepared to attack, but Kalas held up a hand of his own.

"Wait!" he insisted as he turned toward the others, his expression a mix of uncertainty and trust. "Just...wait..."

"Kalas, are you sure?" Zhalera wondered, her features illuminated by Valarandal's blade as she worked her fingers along its hilt.

"Of course not, but this...this is different. This *töthris* is different..."

When it reached Abarandal, rather than try to squeeze her—to make any contact whatsoever—the troll knelt and bowed its head before her. Abarandal touched its cheek as her tune shifted keys, and suddenly its mournful minor notes turned subtly optimistic; she altered tempo and added hope and joy. As she sang, the troll's face cracked apart, and purple, oily streams poured from where its eyes should have been.

Her song complete, the *eru* sang a brief coda that Kalas understood as an invitation for the troll to stretch out its hand to her. If it understood, it made no indication, and Kalas wondered if *töthrisme* could speak at all. She repeated her invitation: timorous, the troll obeyed.

Abarandal sang a new song when she placed her outstretched hand atop the heavy black crust that covered the troll's. As before, the congealed darkness split apart, chipped and peeled; this time, however, there was a curious kind of *peace* about it—not the violence described by the others. With every measure, another chunk cracked and sloughed away, dissolving into nothing more than dust; with every note, the darkness lessened as a nascent, feeble light within gained strength.

"The troll's getting smaller!" Rül observed.

"It sure is!" Nashmur agreed.

"What…what's happening?" Nïmrïk wondered, awed. "Is that… *light* inside?"

"No idea! I've never seen anything like this!" Pava said.

When she finished her melody, Abarandal held the wispy fingers of an emaciated figure composed of weak, sputtering luminance. She beheld its insubstantial form for a moment and breathed a wordless prayer as the light condensed and collected within her cupped hands; after cradling its glow for a moment, with tears and a smile, she thrust her arms toward the sky. Kalas heard a tinny, muddy-sounding chime as the light—stronger now, it seemed—

raced up, up, up toward the heavens, gaining strength and purity during its ascent. It hovered high above them for a moment, glittering brightly as the chime turned clear and resonant before the radiant spectacle twinkled out of sight.

"What…what was that?" Nïmrïk repeated.

While the others stared at the sky, Kalas steadied Abarandal as she stumbled, exhausted. When wingbeats rustled in the sudden stillness he risked a look around, but the darkness kept its secrets.

"You…you *healed* it, didn't you?" he accused. She smiled again and ran a hand across his face as her eyes closed. She sang to him— just a few phrases—before she passed out against his shoulder.

"Is she…*asleep?*" Zhalera wondered as she helped Kalas carry their friend toward the coach. "I've never seen her sleep before. I didn't think she had to!"

"Not asleep. Not exactly. Recuperating, I guess."

"What did she say? What happened to the troll?"

"The troll: she reminded him that the Creator has always known his heart: unlike the others, he'd come to understand and repent of the wrong he'd done. Now, he's '*ihi alasdrame fisgiwara*'—'returned to the heavens,' she said. No longer *töthris*, no longer *eku*—a light again shining for the Creator's glory.

"All the trolls that were here have been *unmade*, but others remain. The Gap might be safe for a while, but not forever. Let's get Abarandal back inside the coach and get out of here!"

"Healed him…" Nïmrïk muttered under his breath, his wide, wolfish eyes glinting in the dark. "I never would have believed it! How…how is such a thing even possible?"

"You'd know more about these things than any of us," Kalas reminded him. "You'll have to ask her when she wakes. Whenever that might be…"

5.

No one had much to say as they hastened through the remainder of Trolls' Gap and waited for the suns to rise. Kalas reflected on Obën's untimely end and wondered what other stories he might have told, what other knowledge he might have shared had that troll not devoured him. Expressionless, he stared at the empty seat beside Abarandal's still-unconscious form.

Àd kelâihad fie zhi Ilun zhîam shir, he prayed. *May the Creator have mercy on his soul.*

After a few miles, the twists and turns between the Teeth straightened out, and the party descended the northwest side of the Taruúnme Ilkâshkit in relative peace. Shosafin insisted they try to make up what distance they'd lost to the brief confrontation: yes, he said, he knew the horses were tired; yes, he acknowledged, a recent acquaintance—a likely ally—had just died a most horrific death; all facts that would not slow the cultists at their heels. At first, Kalas marveled at the old swordsman's dispassion; after a moment's contemplation, however, he understood more practical matters occupied Shosafin's attention. The luxury of mourning would have to wait.

"Obën—*o shelu fie id nir*—said the blue-robes first set foot on the northern shores of the continent at Melash-Niruk," Kalas reminded him. "How can you be sure we're not rushing from one doom toward another?"

"I can't," Shosafin admitted, his response monotone. "It's too much to hope more *töthrisme* might appear and waylay the cultists. It's quite possible—probable, even—we'll have to exercise the utmost care when we reach Melash. Whether they have…what's the word—*ilhadzhalasme?*—privileged ones with them is irrelevant: Melash is the fastest route to Galámur. The port city is a big place, judging from the maps I studied in Lohwàlar. Much larger than

Tarular. And it's unwalled: we should be able to sneak in without raising any eyebrows. Once we get there, we'll evaluate our options."

Abarandal woke the next day: Zhalera held her close when she sat up, then at arms' length as she chided her for scaring them. She laughed when *eru* apologized.

"No! No, my sister! I'm just happy to see you're all right!" she explained. "But why *did* you leave the coach? What if…something bad had happened to you?"

Abarandal responded with an allegretto melody, her fingers dancing a frenzied sequence. Zhalera tried to follow along: "That's too fast!" she interrupted when she could no longer keep up.

"Wings," Kalas translated. "Wings and light. I heard them, too. I thought it was just my imagination."

The *eru* smiled and nodded at Kalas.

"'Wings and light'?" Zhalera's eyes narrowed.

"She says something—some*one?*—compelled her to confront the *töthrisme,* to *unmake* the darkness…"

Abarandal nodded again and sang another string of notes.

"She…afterward, before we kept moving, she heard—no, *sensed,* I think—that last troll…the one hiding in the woods. I don't think she knew what would happen. Not exactly."

"Wings and light…" Zhalera repeated as she stared through the window toward the sky.

When they began their descent toward the fringes of Melash a couple of days later, a light, almost sulfurous scent flavored the air: Pava took a few curious breaths and tasted its salty tang.

"I can't tell if it's disgusting…or if it's amazing," she admitted as she wrinkled her nose one moment and breathed deeply the next. "Maybe it's just…*different:* it's nothing like the smells under the Áthradho!"

"It has that effect," Nashmur laughed. "When I was younger, I spent some time near Ralothova's shores—far south-southeast of Ïsriba. That was the first time I saw the ocean, and it took a few days to appreciate it; when I returned home, however, I discovered I actually missed its fragrance. There's something soothing about the sea…

"Talking about these things reminds me…I'll try to spare you the political details, but I was part of a small envoy to Ralothova's *shelïgar,* Dàgandzhu. We were only there for about a month, but in that time, I learned *Ralothovarinme,* like their queen, are a peace-loving people. That's why we were there: Dàgandzhu had proposed a treaty in which Ïsriba would provide for Ralothova's defenses in exchange for…I forget what, but it doesn't matter. Bluntly stated, they're ill-equipped for war: despite the fens and swamps between them, if Ësfàyami makes good on her threats against her neighbors, it won't be long before she crushes Ralothova beneath her talons."

"That's why I…we *need* to find Marugan," concluded Shosafin. "That's why we need to learn everything we can about the *Ragus pïni Tshaggul Kavar,* too, and how they're connected."

By midday, the narrow road widened, its neglected surface improved, and the party passed an eclectic collection of low, steep-roofed houses. None shared the same color as its neighbor, but Melash's overall palette trended toward dark reds and browns; bright teals, blues, and greens; and, most prominent, fiery yellows. The distant ocean they'd glimpsed atop the ridge had disappeared when they'd reentered the forest; now, the subtle, metered music of its surf pounded against an unseen shore. Abarandal's ears perked as she studied the white noise carried in the crash of every wave. She must have sensed Kalas' eyes on her: she turned toward him and tried to explain the nuances she heard—*felt*—in every frequency.

He nodded, his expression an admission that he didn't share her experience. She tried to describe her thoughts in greater detail, but Kalas stopped her with a wave and smiled, "It's all right: no need to explain! It's enough just to see you so...*alive!* Especially after Trolls' Gap!"

Soon, they found themselves sharing the road with others: a mix of *Pomelash* natives and visitors, Shosafin said as he appraised each passerby. The highway coming down from the Standing Mountains approached the port from the east, placing the city between them and the sea. As traffic picked up, the old soldier guided everyone toward the side of the road, dismounted Breaker, and started undoing the lashings securing some of their gear. He suggested they stagger their entry into the city:

"I'll go first, approaching from the south. Give me an hour. If I don't return, Nashmur: approach from the north; after half an hour, Nïmrïk: approach from the south, too. Rül: we'll reach Melash proper soon. Sell your coach and—"

"*Sell it?!*" Rül exclaimed. "I can't! It's not—how will we carry all our gear? How will we—"

"Sell it. Abandon it. I don't care. We can't take it with us. And if there's any gear we can do without, sell that, too. Breaker can carry some of it, but we'll need to minimize our footprint before we charter passage to Galámur. Runner and Courser have hauled the coach—and the five of you—without complaint for all these miles. Let Pava ride Courser—I've seen how her skills have improved, and even though he's no Ascender, I'm confident they're both up to the task. They'll appreciate your sacrifice, I'm sure."

Kalas thought the old soldier winked at the farm boy before he turned to address him and the others.

"Zhalera: Runner's capable of carrying both you and Abarandal: if you'll forgive my indiscretion, even together, the two of you impose a lighter burden than that coach!

"All of us must take great pains to keep as close to the shadows as possible. As you've already pointed out, Kalas, the blue-robes were in Melash before they were anywhere else north of the mountains. You spoke of *privileged ones,* and whether or not you're correct, we need to keep our faces, our identities as secret as possible—not just you and me, but *all of us.*

"Somewhere between two or more lighthouses out in the harbor, Lohwàlar's maps showed a tall, circular structure jutting out over the water, high above all the piers. Tsharak says it's the customs house: strangers shouldn't attract too much attention in such a place. Wait inside, and I'll find you. Should you glimpse any *sifu-ilmikasme*…ignore them. *Ilhadzhalasme* will most likely already know who you are: others will probably be drawn to any sudden action. The *busyness* of such places becomes a kind of camouflage. Part of blending in is tuning out those around you, adopting a self-important air."

Shosafin checked his knots, and Kalas caught the faintest suggestion of reproach when Breaker whinnied. The gruff old soldier chuckled and stroked the animal's withers, collected his reins, and, with a flourish, walked toward the busier parts of Melash-Niruk. His companions watched him until he disappeared.

6.

After Dalafar, bearing Nïmrïk, cantered toward town, Kalas suggested they find a secluded place in the nearby woods and hide the coach, rather than sell it. Rül quickly agreed, and the five of them spent roughly an hour caching the vehicle within a thick stand of firs.

"Good idea, Kalas," Rül huffed as Pava leapt onto Courser's back. "We won't get any money for it this way, but I think we'll manage!"

"I don't know if we're coming back this way or not," the young man admitted. "Maybe I'm overthinking it—maybe enough trade happens here that it wouldn't attract much attention—but if cultists got a look at our coach back in Tarular, it'd be pretty easy to spot in a place like Melash. We don't need to give away our presence—even incidentally."

"I just hate the thought of selling it when it was a gift, really. What would Yëlisha say?"

"She'd understand, I believe," Pava concluded. "Her inn might have made her wealthy, but I got the sense that *people* were more important to her than property."

Zhalera nodded as she helped Abarandal onto Runner's back. With Kalas' help, she vaulted into place in front of the *eru*. She fidgeted for a moment, then admitted, "Wouldn't be a bad idea to sell or trade some of our stuff for saddles! It's been a long time since I've ridden without one! I forgot what it was like!"

"No argument from me," Pava said as she squirmed a little.

"Looks like it's no more than a few miles from here," Zhalera added. "We'll manage, but if we're going to be riding much once we reach Galámur, saddles are a must!"

"I don't remember the maps as well as Shosafin. I guess we'll see once we reach the island. *Avëlöth*, I think it's called," Kalas noted. "I think he described it like the top of a mountain sticking out of the water."

Both Pava and Zhalera confessed their backsides were tender by the time they reached a trading post and procured a pair of saddles and the necessary tack. Kalas did his best dickering with the shopkeeper, but afterward, he figured he'd been outplayed. Both Pava and Zhalera confessed their backsides were tender by the time they reached a trading post and procured a pair of saddles and the necessary tack. Kalas did his best dickering with the shopkeeper, but afterward, he figured he'd been outplayed. Rül shrugged and suggested he not worry about it: he told him they could still afford some saddlebags.

Outside, the farm boy saddled their horses. With everything in place, including bits and bridles, Rül and Kalas packed up their remaining gear and buried it within the bags they'd acquired.

"These are *deep!*" Kalas remarked. Rül beamed and suggested they'd seem a touch shallower once they divided Breaker's burden, too.

"I guess me and Pava will head out first?" Rül wondered. "The shore will be on the other side of the city, right?"

"That's right," Kalas assured him. "We came down opposite the water. Just head west and I'll bet you'll come to that building—customs house, right?—Shosafin was talking about. If it's as big as he says, I'll bet you can't miss it! In between a couple of lighthouses, he said. We'll be right behind you. Well, half an hour behind you, anyway!"

"We'll be fine," insisted Pava as she collected Courser's reins. "C'mon, *eshudhayahal!* Let's go!"

Rül blushed and grabbed hold of the buckskin's lead and merged with the constant bustle whirling all around them.

"Looks like we're next, *shâume!*" Kalas said when the others were out of sight. "We've got some time: any interest in exploring a few side streets before we work our way to the customs house?"

"We should probably—" Zhalera began. She paused and cocked her head when a sound arrested her attention.

"That sounds like hammers! On an anvil!" she said. "Coming from…north of here? If we're careful, maybe we could see what *Pomelash* smithery looks like?"

Abarandal looked from one to the other with uncertainty in her expression. She opened her mouth to sing something, then clapped a hand over it and held Kalas with a look.

She doesn't want anyone to hear her voice. Smart thinking!

"I understand," he nodded at her still-covered mouth. "We'll be careful though. Discreet. We'll keep our distance: we'll—"

"Hold on!" Zhalera warned as she loosened her feet and twirled down from the saddle. "I'll walk, too: I want to get close enough to see what's going on! It's been…it's been too long since I've watched another blacksmith at work…"

"I understand that, too," Kalas nodded. Abarandal seemed to wilt beneath the mournful quality in her friend's voice. She made no objection as Kalas led Runner toward the rhythm of ringing blows against steel.

Traversing Melash's streets, Kalas marveled at the engineering skills on display as vibrant structures jutted out from terraced slopes in defiance of gravity. He wondered how some of their balconies and upper stories stayed aloft. Larger, better maintained boulevards switched back and forth on their way to the sea; the avenues they took to the north followed straighter paths. The blur of voices—a mix of angry shouts and raucous laughter atop a steady stream of even-toned conversation—made it difficult to focus on the noises emanating from the smithy, but Zhalera—unsurprisingly—had an ear for them: "Take the next left…now right…now—no, straight! It's right up ahead!"

As they turned a corner toward the source of subtle music comprised of hammers, tongs, and bellows, Kalas drew in a sharp breath and did his best not to jerk Runner's lead as he quickened his pace.

"Kalas! It's right—"

"We don't have time, uh, *Tshedra…*" he whispered as he walked toward a side street that would lead them toward their rendezvous.

"Uh, K—what's going on?" Zhalera hissed. She turned to look around when Kalas grabbed her elbow and muttered, *"Sifu-il-mikasme!* Eyes forward!"

She obeyed.

"I'm sorry," he continued, his voice nearly inaudible, "but we're not the only ones interested in the blacksmith's work. I saw two cultists across the street—at least, I *think* they were cultists. I don't think they saw us, but I didn't want to give them the opportunity. It's probably best we just…wander toward the shore."

"I understand," she said. He didn't miss the regret in her tone.

"Maybe I was wrong," he allowed, "and I'm sorry I—"

"No, it's the right choice. It's…it's not like I've never seen a furnace before," she laughed. Kalas cringed at the forced, mirthless noise.

"I'm sorry," he repeated.

"Who's *Tshedra?*" she whispered when they'd crossed a few streets, when the sounds from the smithy melded with the overall timbre of the city.

"Today, she's you!" he explained. "It was my grandmother's name. My mother's mother's name. I never knew her, but Mother always spoke highly of her. Anyway, when we were south of here, Sh—Oh! Call me *Garat* while we're in town."

"And her?" Zhalera said with a glance at Abarandal.

"Hmm. How about…"

"*Ásira,*" Zhalera declared. "Ásira."

Kalas looked back at Abarandal, who chuckled at her suggested alias.

"You don't like it?" Zhalera asked. The *eru* shook her head and indicated she was quite pleased with it. Through their gesture-language, she asked Zhalera what it meant.

"Ásira was my father's mother. I told you about Gandhan. He was a big man with a bigger heart. So was his mother. My memories of her are few, but they're strong—vibrant, like the woman herself. It seemed like a fitting name. I'm glad you like it!"

"Shosafin used the name *Shadrïs,*" Kalas supplied. "No idea what it means—assuming it means anything! He came up with that and 'Garat' pretty quickly. Guess he must be used to it."

The second sun hovered just above the distant gray line that was the horizon as Kalas gaped at the unending ocean beneath the promontory on which they stood. He closed his eyes for a moment and tried to recall the chasm beneath Kësharan or the canyon between the walls of the Empty Sea. Even in his mind's eye, he'd never seen so much water.

Somewhere between the sky and the shore, the ocean turned from an unbroken line into a series of short, uneven curls. The steady lap of waves against numerous piers and the syncopated knock of docked ships bumping against their pilings suggested he relax his guard: tempted to succumb, someone barked an order at someone else, breaking the maritime enchantment, and he glanced around for any blue-robes who might have noticed them. It seemed no one paid them any mind.

"This is…it's almost *unbelievable!*" Zhalera breathed. Abarandal had joined them on foot; she, too, marveled at these new, peculiar environs. Aloud, she said nothing; with signs and gestures, she shared in their amazement. Kalas followed her gaze across the jittering path of light rippling on the waves toward its source: Miryan. When the *eru* stared straight into its golden beams, he touched her elbow and suggested with a whisper, "Uh, better not look directly at it! Don't want to burn your eyes out!"

She laughed—covered her mouth again when she heard the music in it—and shook her head. Her hands and fingers danced a quick series of steps, but he'd never understood many of the signs she and Zhalera had created.

"It's…she's all right," Zhalera translated. "Doesn't have the same effect."

"Oh…right!" he nodded. Too vigorously, perhaps. Both women

laughed. Abarandal twirled her fingers again—more slowly, this time—and Zhalera explained each sign.

"Ilmazhasahwu is…I don't understand that one…an authority figure? No? Something like that, I think…Anyway, let's get inside and meet up with the others. Surely they're here by now? Probably waiting for us!"

The dominating domed structure Shosafin called the customs house contained all of Melash's governmental offices, spread throughout its floors, according to a directory posted near the entrance. After tying Runner to a post, the three entered its ancient stone halls and wandered toward the rotunda: overhead, the first sun shed silver beams through amber-tinted glass. Until he stood within its light, Kalas hadn't realized how cold he'd been. He shivered.

"I don't see anyone: do you?" he whispered.

"No one," Zhalera affirmed.

"He said he'd find us. Should we wait here? Probably not out in the middle of the room like this?"

"There are benches against the walls. Let's take one and wait there. I just hope we—"

"Hope you what, miss?" Shosafin said as he turned away from the crowd.

"Sh—uh, Shadrïs, *hish?* How do you—" she gasped.

"*Âu* Shadrïs! You remember *Tshedra?* And *Ásira*, yes?"

"Of course! *Tsheth ëzh dàbirafime nir, shâume!*" he nodded without missing a beat. "Now, come! There's an inn next door. I've secured us a couple of rooms. The others—*most* of them—are waiting."

"What aren't you telling us?" Kalas accused, sensing some unspoken news beneath the old warrior's placid expression.

"You're learning well, Master Garat!" He allowed the faintest trace of a smile. "It seems your *friend*—"

He means Nïmrïk…

"—discovered something on his way here. Some*one.*"

"Oh?"

"Yes, an…old acquaintance. They're…catching up down by the docks, I believe. It's most fortunate: he's still holding onto that *staff* he…borrowed."

'Staff'? 'Borrowed'? Does he mean Falthwën's *staff?! But that was stolen*—Hwanzho! *Hwanzho is here?!*

Chapter IX

On the Waters of the Roiling Ocean

"Does Pava know? Has she seen him?" From Shosafin's expression, he knew he'd guessed correctly about Hwanzho. "I don't envy the pain he's invited upon himself..."

"Not yet, on both counts. The rest of them are in those rooms I mentioned: when I couldn't find your friend, I went looking for him. It's probably Hwanzho's screams that gave away their position. I was on my way up to give Pava the good news. Good for *her*, that is...not so good for Hwanzho!"

Both Rül and Nashmur had trouble restraining the feisty *úruk-ilmukrit* woman when she learned of her estranged countryman's presence: for a fleeting instant, Kalas saw Tsana in her twisted features, her livid scowl. When she regained some small measure of composure, she managed to spit: "Take me to him. *Now.*"

"Uh, Pava—*Milëlín*—is that the best idea?" Rül countered. "Dese was your uncle, I know, and I would never pretend to understand exactly what you're feeling, but...but...Kalas! I mean, when the skydogs attacked his family, he didn't..."

"I wanted to," Kalas finished as Rül ceased his gainless attempt to reason with his bride. "Tsharak stopped me. Dzharëth would've ripped me to pieces if he hadn't. I think that's what Rül's trying to say, Pava: not that Hwanzho's capable of ripping you to pieces, but maybe a little perspective will—"

"You're not helping!" Zhalera shook her head. "Telling her to calm down? That's not what she needs to hear right now!"

"No, I—" Kalas defended until he recognized the rising fire in Zhalera's eyes. Wisely, he shut his mouth and held his tongue.

"I just want to *see* him," Pava insisted, her tone too measured, too controlled. "I want to know—Shosafin! You—where'd you go? Shosafin wants to know, too, right? He wants to know what business Hwanzho had with Gozhira! Marugan! Whatever his name is! And what if Nïmrïk—what'd you say, Kalas? 'Rips him to pieces'? What if there's nothing left of Hwanzho when the *egu* finishes with him?!"

"That's out of context! And Nïmrïk would *never*—"

"Tell that to the *ekume* he destroyed! To the *ilrâigme* he eviscerated under Deridzhas!"

"That's different, and you know it!" Kalas roared.

"Hey now, watch your tone!" Rül demanded: "That's my *sheshudha* you're talking to!"

"*Shâume! Âume!* Please!" Nashmur begged as he raised his hands, releasing his grip on Pava's arm in the process.

Like an arrow loosed from its string, the agile woman bolted from the room: Kalas could only admire the shrewd grace she displayed as she ducked every swinging arm, avoided every flailing leg.

"Nice work!" Zhalera grumbled.

"Well? C'mon, Kalas! We need to find her!" said Rül as he clapped a meaty hand atop his friend's shoulder.

"'We'?" he retorted.

"I—well, yeah, I mean—" Rül began. He paused, stared at the ground for a moment, and continued, "Look, I'm—"

"No, you're right," Kalas sighed. "I'm...I shouldn't have yelled at her. *Aswanthalu...*"

"Of course, *sà*. It's been a long day. A long couple of months!

Just…a lot going on, right?"

"Can't argue with you there…"

"Lose something, gentlemen?" Shosafin said as he marched Pava back into the room. Defiant and still scowling, she glared at everyone in turn. Maybe it was a trick of the rippling candle light, a deception demonstrated by the last rays of the remaining sun, but Kalas caught flecks of red glinting from her incensed and haunting eyes.

"*Yash àódru?*" he whispered.

"'Red mist'?" Nashmur repeated.

"Like your mother?" wondered Kalas, his voice low.

"No! I…I just…" Pava began: with a sigh, she abandoned her fight against the soldier and collapsed atop one of the room's narrow beds. She held her head in both hands and took several deep breaths. After a brief silence, she started to cry.

"Mother warned me this might happen someday," she sniffed as she pressed away her tears. "The mist never hit me before…I thought I'd been spared! But you're right, Kalas. You're right. I can feel it in my blood, bubbling up and tainting—and *heightening*—my every perception. It's like Sevens upon Sevens of hot needles pricking all my senses!

"Nïmrïk called it a curse, and he's right. For generations, women from my mother's line would sometimes find themselves swallowed by bloodlust. Not all of them, not every daughter born from her ancestors' lineage, but enough for people to see a pattern.

"It's…according to Mother, when she's '*ibi àódru*'—'in the mist,' the colors of the world *shift*. I never knew what she meant, but just now, everything took on a red tint; each of you had a bright, yellow-orange aura about you, too. Lines seemed sharper, time seemed slower…

"When I first met all of you, I told you we weren't fighters. That's true, but it wasn't always that way with us. A long time ago, my people had another name, another purpose. *Sulumilmukritme.* Mother told me what she knew, but even that wasn't much. All I know—and *know* is a strong word—is that our ancestors used to be fearsome *shagabme*—warrior-assassins.

"Somewhere in our ancient past, the power we served grew suspicious of our strength and sought to rid the world of us, one woman at a time. Sooner than he anticipated, the *sulumilmukritme* figured out what was happening and turned against him. He'd been thorough, though: not enough remained to stand against the rest of his forces.

"The surviving families begged the Creator for deliverance, but nothing changed. Desperate, they turned their attention to darker forces. Someone—some*thing*—heard their cries and bestowed the *yash aòdru* upon them. With faster reflexes, sharper vision, and increased strength and endurance, our ancestors overcame their would-be destroyers.

"But the mist wasn't the blessing it first appeared to be. Those who stayed *ibi aòdru* too long discovered their lifespans many Sevens shorter than their forebears. Others had trouble stepping out of the mist: always angry, always ready for a fight—even to the death—over the silliest things. When the *sulumilmukritme* understood what was happening, they repented of their bargain and cried out to the Creator again.

"He sent an emissary, an *elu*…Mother never told me the particulars, but the Creator had *not* been ignoring them: what the *elu* showed them was something none of them ever would have imagined. Cut to the core of their being, they begged her to lift the curse of the red mist. She said she'd been granted such authority, and thus undid the ruin inflicted by their impatience.

"Such a boon from the Creator, she warned, wouldn't remove all consequence. She said from time to time, the mist would build above the heads of choice women. Most *sulumilmukritme* didn't care—the worst of their ill-made deal had been undone! They were free! Well, *most* of them…"

Rül sat next to his bride, wrapped an arm around her shoulders, and collected her hands in one of his. Like the others, he was too stunned to say anything.

Hesitant at first, Kalas carefully considered his words before he spoke: "Falthwën told me something once. The details aren't important now, but I think his point was this: the Creator's arm is neither too short to reach us wherever we are, nor too weak to build new and beautiful things from the wreckage we leave in the aftermath of our worst decisions. The red mist isn't your fault—it's not your mother's, either, but maybe—just maybe!—someday, he'll make something amazing from your grandmothers' folly because of *you*."

Zhalera looked up at him, her eyes glistening in the waxing candlelight. She nodded, her expression full of thanks. Abarandal took a step toward him and touched his arm: she said nothing, but he sensed she approved of his remarks.

"Does that mean you won't…live for very long?" Rül wondered. "Not that it changes anything! I just—"

"No, I don't think so. I don't know. This is the first time I've ever been *in the mist*, but I think I'll be all right…"

"You will be. *We* will be," Rül promised with fierce solemnity. Pava leaned into him.

"Do you really believe that?" she said. Not to Rül: her eyes hadn't left the floor, but Kalas knew she was talking to him.

"I do, Pava. I didn't understand what Falthwën was trying to tell me back then, but I think I do now. At least a little better than before. Sometimes the Creator keeps his handiwork a secret for a season…even *Sevens* of seasons! I've come to believe he reveals his secrets at the proper time."

2.

"It's quiet now," Shosafin observed as he led the others down stairway after stairway toward a row of ramshackle structures set back some distance from the waterfront. "I guess we'll learn soon enough if that's a good thing…"

A gust of salt-scented air whipped through Kalas' hair: he shivered despite his best efforts to ignore the cold. Behind them, the noise of waves and an indiscernible glut of voices folded over one another until neither had any meaning. The buildings where Shosafin said Nïmrïk was "catching up" with Hwanzho had known better days. Occasional strips of peeling paint suggested they'd been as brightly colored as most of Melash's other constructs some time ago; now, their yards littered with what looked like discarded maritime equipment—some rusting, some rotting, they resembled little more than coarse parodies of their former selves. Surrounded by the consequence of sheer neglect, Kalas wondered how Shosafin had discovered anything in such—"

"Blood," he muttered as a dark red stain, then another, and another, caught his attention. The trail, subtle as it was, pointed toward a gray-brown shack with pitted trim and a collapsing roof.

"That's right," Shosafin nodded. "Like I said: you're learning well. Let me—no, Kalas: why don't you go first? The *egu* seems to trust you more than…more than he trusts me. The rest of us will wait."

The young man looked to Pava, who shrugged, sighed, and nodded. Responding with his own nod, he pushed aside the unlatched door and stepped into the room's twilight-smeared semidarkness.

He realized he hadn't given much thought to the building's interior until his eyes adjusted and he realized how *long* it seemed, how far away from the opposite end he stood. Kalas said nothing at first: he studied the room for some sign of Nïmrïk or Hwanzho.

Something in the shadows fluttered, and he heard a faint panting sound coming from the far wall. He took a step across the cracked flagstone floor, rousing someone's attention in the process.

"Is someone there? Help! Please!" cried a weak voice. Kalas drew nearer to its source and discovered the *úrukilmukrit* kinslayer, his bloodied arms tied above his beaten head and suspended from a metal hook. When he recognized Kalas, his swollen eyes widened: in mid-sentence, his begging turned to sobbing.

"The soldier send you?" Nïmrïk growled from out of the shadows as he padded his way to Kalas' side. He'd assumed his wolfish *otherform,* and his yellow eyes glowed hot against the dark

"The others are right outside," he nodded. "We weren't sure what, uh, we might find when we got here, so…"

Nïmrïk chuckled. "Hwanzho is just fine. All right: no, he's not, but he'll live. For a little while, at least. I wanted to be sure Pava had a chance to…*talk* to him. I wanted to be sure he would *listen.* He's been going on and on. Mostly nonsense, I suppose, but still, I'm sure Pava has words for him."

"Let me get her," Kalas offered, and retraced his steps. On his way out, he saw Falthwën's staff leaning against a support column. *Hwanzho must've held onto it after…Dese,* he noted as the captive's renewed sobs echoed from wall to wall behind him.

"*Ràk-iltshidh,*" Pava seethed when she stood before her uncle's murderer. She held herself together, but everyone appreciated the great effort such a feat required—including Hwanzho, who flinched at the sound of each deliberate syllable. "Why? *Why,* Hwanzho?!"

"*Shëmîu,* I'm sorry! I—"

"You're sorry you got *caught!*" she spat. "Don't pretend otherwise! I'm not interested in your excuses: you can tell me the truth, or you can hang there in Nïmrïk's capable hands. Paws. Whatever."

"I didn't mean to kill your uncle! He just…I panicked! I only wanted…Gozhira told us—"

"You wanted my father's title!" Pava interrupted. "You—your house!—never accepted your place among our people! You were so blinded by ambition and the praise of men that you sold yourselves to darkness! Did House Kado learn *nothing* from the burden of the *yash àódru?!*"

"*Shëmîu,* please! I never wanted any of this! I—"

"I'm embarrassed, really," Pava continued, ignoring Hwanzho's guttering entreaties. "I really thought you—more than all your kinsmen—had acknowledged Father as the *úrukilmukritmedas* rightful *ëmîu.* House Murase as the rightful seat of power. What a fool I was! I should have—"

"Tafa! Tafa—or maybe Gidi? Gidi told you where I was headed, yes?"

"—what?" said Pava, her former train of thought interrupted. "How did you—?"

"That's what I've been trying to tell you! Please, listen for just a moment! If you don't like what I have to say, I'll accept whatever doom you decide for me."

It only took a moment for Pava to regain her fiery demeanor. Somehow, Kalas could *feel* the mist rising in her blood. He assumed the others could, too.

"I'm listening," she permitted as her piercing eyes narrowed to wary slits.

Hwanzho sighed, tried to lick his cracked and bleeding lips, and took a labored breath before he began: "I never wanted any of this to happen! I—no, all right, I mean—that's true, but I know a few words won't convince you. I…okay, you're right: House Kado still believes that headship of our people belongs to them. Maybe I should have said something before…it doesn't matter: it's too late now…

"I hoped I might set an example for Dzhavo and the rest of

my father's household by entering into Rive's service. I hoped they might see he wasn't the enemy they believed him to be. Maybe I should have known better, but it didn't work. They regarded *me* as an enemy. If Gozhira had never come to the Áthradho, maybe...

"But he *did* come, and that's when House Kado sought me out again. I was naïve and believed they'd seen the error of their ways, that maybe they thought I could help broker peace between our houses. Instead, they told me the *Ilosar* had returned to the Gateway, that he understood the 'unjust indignity' they'd suffered. He told them he'd come, in part, to restore their former fortunes. And, of course, they believed him.

"Part of his scheme required a spy within House Murase's ranks. Dzhavo—Father's always been an opportunist: you know that!—insisted I become that spy and pass information back to the family. Just minor things, I thought, and *Shëmîu*, I'm sorry, but it had been so long since my father—since *any* of my family, my house—had said a word to me! I can't imagine you know what that's like..."

"I can," Nïmrïk muttered.

"Over time, his requests became more pointed, and I found myself too willing to obey. Soon, the *'Ilosar'* himself wanted to meet with me, to discuss his intentions for the *úrukilmukritme* and how he needed *my* help to create a better world for us cave-dwellers. He said he had plans for us. Can you believe I was haughty enough to believe his lies?! What am I saying! Of course you can! I'm embarrassed at how little effort it took for him to poison my thoughts. It counts for little—for nothing, I know—but I truly believed I was helping our people! The *iltithme-kal* had been dim for so long, and he did make them brighter...

"Then *you* showed up," he said as he inclined his head toward Kalas, "and I knew right away I'd believed a lie. When you vanished, Pava, I told Father I wanted no further part of Gozhira's plan. He wouldn't hear of it, of course. Gozhira had disappeared sometime before all this, but not long after *you* disappeared, he returned and claimed *he* had done away with the 'illegitimate *shëmiu.*' I wasn't there beneath the *Kathin Iltith* when Kalas made it shine, but I learned—too late—that Gozhira was lying. Again.

"When Rive went looking for you, I…I hoped he *wouldn't* find you. I'm sorry! I hoped—even though I knew better by then—that *maybe* there was *some* truth to Gozhira's words. Then you came back…"

"He's *not* the *Ilosar*—I know that now—but he *is* a being of power! He put words in my *mind* from…I have no idea *where* he was—I just know I heard him in my thoughts! I tried to resist his will, but I wasn't strong enough: I couldn't even resist my father—a being of mere flesh and blood. What chance did I have against an *ilalasdra?!*

"When all of us returned to the Gateway, Gozhira instructed me to search your possessions for something he called the *great power.* I had no idea what he meant. I don't think he did, either. Not exactly. I thought my failure might be a chance to prove my *uselessness* to him. Looking back, he probably would have killed me for it, but at the time, I was so tired of everything…I hoped if I failed he'd just…leave me alone.

"Dese…If he'd just done something—anything!—other than follow after me! I tried to be discreet, but he figured out I was up to something. He reached for his *tëvët:* that long white was staff right there, and I…I never meant for *any of this* to happen! I ran toward the Wastes, where I met with Gozhira and told him what I'd done: after such an incident, House Murase would see me for the spy I was, and, I thought, he'd have no purpose for me—at last! Again, I was wrong.

"He said I'd proved my loyalty. He told me his mistress—and I'll never forget the way he looked when he described her—had plans for me. I didn't think *ilalasdrame* knew terror, but it was written across his face in bold strokes. I guess whatever happened under Deridzhas answered some question for her. He said we would travel to Galámur, but not why. Not exactly.

"Falan—Tafa's mother, Gidi's mother's sister—is one of the few people in all of House Kado who sees this infighting for the nonsense it is. I wanted to speak my concerns to her, but there never seemed to be a good time. I snuck beneath the Gateway to collect some things for the trip, and I made sure I ran into Gidi. She and her cousin have always been close friends, so I dropped as many subtle hints as I could, hoping she'd somehow piece things together and…I don't know, I just…It was the best I could do! I don't know if Gozhira can *read* thoughts as well as he speaks his own within another's—"

"He can't," Nïmrïk volunteered.

"—but she *did* piece things together! I mean, here you are! Pava—*Shëmîu*—I'm telling you the truth! I'm sorry I lacked the courage to say something before all of this, before I…Dese…I'm sorry. *Su pirathëthu—su pirathëzhu: aswanthalu!*"

For a moment, Hwanzho tried to hold Pava's gaze; when she said nothing, he let his head droop: from shame or sudden weakness, Kalas couldn't tell.

"You're just a victim?" Pava coaxed. "Just a pawn in Marugan's—Gozhira's schemes?"

"Yes! Yes! Exactly! I had no choice!" Hwanzho rallied. He raised his head in a half-nod when he glimpsed her scornful scowl.

"You could have made any number of better choices, Hwanzho! You know better than any of your family how little *Ude* regarded some of the old traditions. The old prejudices. Father would have welcomed you into House Murase! Such things have happened before!"

"Maybe *you* could have made any number of choices, *Shëmîu*. *I* made the only choice available to me. As misguided as Father is, he's still my father, still head of our house. Maybe *Ëmîu* Rive would have understood. Not Dzhavo. *Never* Dzhavo. That's what's wrong with my family, Pava. That's what's always been wrong with them—and always will be."

The young *shëmîu* shook her head and sighed.

"This…*all of this* was so unnecessary!"

"*Shëmîu—*"

"So you're more than half-way to Galámur," Pava cut him off: "what's waiting for you there? Did Gozhira clue you in? Or does he keep his thralls uninformed?"

With his eyes again staring at the filthy ground above which Nïmrïk had suspended him, Hwanzho shed fresh tears that caught the last shreds of twilight.

"All I know," he wept, "is Gozhira's mistress summoned him to a place on *Mbizhad Dal Taru*—Glass Sword Mountain—wherever that is! She has plans for him and the other *ilalasdrame* she's bent toward her will. He said something about an *eru* who would—"

"An *eku?*" Kalas offered.

"Gozhira is *eku;* no, he said *eru,* someone with knowledge who—"

He hiccuped, winced, and resumed speaking: "an *eru* who'd actually seen—"

He belched this time, and Kalas thought he saw tendrils of smoke waft from his wrinkled grimace.

"I'm sorry, I—something's not—*AAAGH!*"

His last syllables were wrapped in smoke that jetted from between his lips. Hwanzho's insides seemed aglow as he screamed and twisted against his bonds.

"It burns! *Im màr! Im màr!*" he gurgled as hot blue flames clawed their way out of his throat and seared the roof of his mouth. As his clothes started smoldering, Pava, who was closest to him, tried to pull his shirt away, but most of it had already melted into his flesh.

Dark, electric patterns scribed themselves across his bubbling chest as his eyes sizzled and burst in a gout of sparks. Fresh fire leapt from his empty sockets and licked away the skin stretched taut across his face.

"What's happening?!" Nashmur shouted as one of Hwanzho's arms split apart and separated from his shoulder. Somewhere underneath his thoughts, Kalas sensed a grating cacophony, a perversion of the Song woven within the flames' every sinuous motion. As the burning man's weight shifted, he worked his jaw in one final, fruitless attempt to speak. His smoking skull lolled forward with enough momentum to rip the bones of his remaining arm from their scorched tendons and charred skin, and as his blackened corpse fell toward the floor, Kalas watched the fire that had devoured Hwanzho retreat within its victim. When his remains hit the ground with an oily thud, the suns had wholly set. In perfumed darkness, scented with a heavy, greasy sweetness, no one said a word.

3.

"Kalas! What happened?" Zhalera demanded when the silence became too much to bear. "Did you—?"

"Me?! No! Of course not! I—wait! I *did* hear something, though! The Song. *Almost.* A mockery of it, maybe. I don't know. But it wasn't me!"

Abarandal placed a hand atop his shoulder and nodded: she'd heard it, too.

"*Egu. Eku,* maybe. If Hwanzho was telling the truth, even *eru.*" Nimrïk agreed. "I heard it too, lad: that terrible *noise.*"

Shosafin drew his sword, produced a flint, and struck sparks onto a pair of torches. He handed one to Nashmur and knelt to study Hwanzho's still-smoking body, prodding it a few times with the tip of his blade.

"Cousin, what are you doing?!"

The old soldier ignored him and continued his examination. Kalas watched him trace the lines wrought by the fire, and as his torch bobbed and swayed, it cast its gleam across Falthwën's staff, still propped against the column. The young man collected it and held it at arm's length for a moment. He squinted, just in case…

Nothing happened.

He ran his fingers along its polished length and tried to remember the shapes his old friend had carved in the darkness. He twirled a few haphazard arcs through the air and remained unsurprised when, again, nothing happened. With a sigh, he joined the others.

"It looks like the fire burned him from the inside," Shosafin suggested as he handed his torch to Pava.

"From the *inside?!*" she gasped. "How—?! I mean, is such a thing even possible?!"

"These burn marks: there's something strange about them. A non-random regularity…Nashmur, help me flip him over. Carefully!"

Nashmur handed his torch to Rül. When he tugged on the dead man's shoulder, what remained of his deltoid muscles sloughed away from his frame. Disgusted, the former *Poyïsriba* commander grumbled something impolite as he wiped fragments of broiled flesh from his hands.

"I said *carefully!*" Shosafin scolded.

"Right…" Nashmur muttered.

They tried again, and, succeeding, the grizzled soldier offered the others a grim nod.

"I'm not surprised," he said as he stood. "Pava, a little light?"

The *úrukilmukrit* woman took a few steps toward the macabre scene and played her torch over Hwanzho's corpse.

His blackened, eyeless skull still bore strips of melted skin, and even without cheeks or lips, Kalas read pain and horror in his features. Rül and Pava moved their torches up and down, instinctively following the blistered tracery that had arrested Shosafin's attention.

Improbably clean lines formed a strange, discrete shape—a symbol, maybe—across Hwanzho's chest and stomach. Kalas cocked his head and considered the marks from numerous perspectives. Overall, the design suggested a crude representation of a fanged flame:

"It's the mark the *ilragusme* use. The cultists. I saw several examples scattered throughout Serular. Sometimes for communicating with one another, sometimes for terrorizing anyone who disagreed with them. The *Tshâdunas Kavar,* people called it. It seems the rumors of the Deathless Flame's power are true."

"*Sharuyandas Âsru,*" Kalas said. "Zhalera: you saw it, back in Lohwàlar, right? You told me lightning tore through the roof and consumed the *zhàrudzh* who killed your father. And my mother. I only saw glimpses of it in the sky that night. This wasn't the same thing—not exactly, but it can't be a coincidence that at the moment Hwanzho started to tell us about a meeting between dark forces, about an *eru*—an eru!—involved in Marugan's mistress' plot, that fire from within would devour him!"

He looked around from one concurring nod to the next. After a moment's consideration, he continued, "It looks like your *Poserular* source was right, Shosafin. And Pava, despite his sins, I think Hwanzho was telling the truth, too."

"That doesn't—!"

"I'm not saying it does! I'm just saying maybe things were more complicated than we realized..."

His assessment complete, Shosafin stood and retrieved his torch. "Nïmrïk," he said, "you never did tell me how you crossed paths with Hwanzho..."

"Coming into town, I caught his scent on the wind. It was subtle—at first I thought Pava had reached the city ahead of me, but I followed it until I reached what I'm guessing was an older part of Melash. I tied Dalafar to a post—Dalafar! I left him there! I—"

"I'll get him," Rül offered, grateful, it seemed, for an opportunity to remove himself from the lingering reek of human smoke. "Just point me in the right direction."

"I'll come with you," said Pava, and in the torchlight, Kalas thought she looked tired. Exhausted. No suggestion of the *yash aódru* remained within her eyes as she reached for Rül's arm. Nïmrïk told them where to find his horse as Nashmur handed his torch to the farm boy. The *Poyïsriba* soldier watched them for a moment, then followed after them at a short distance.

As the trio dissolved into the shadows, Nïmrïk continued: "I'm sorry. I knew it was him right away—he was still holding Falthwën's staff! I followed him down a few streets, watched as he tried to secure a berth on one ship or another, but by then the suns were setting, and even though I can see—and smell—pretty well in the dark, I didn't want to risk losing him. I grabbed him, and I knew from his eyes he recognized me.

"I searched for a place without the taint of recent human presence: that's how we ended up here. I knocked him around a little—all right, *more* than a little—and tied him to this hook. I made him watch as I ripped myself free from my human skin. He *really* didn't like that! Not long after, you showed up."

Shosafin nodded. "'Glass Sword Mountain.' None of Lohwàlar's maps described a place with that name. If Hwanzho was booking passage on a ship, Galámur is still his most likely destination… assuming he was telling us the truth."

"He was," insisted Kalas with a shudder.

"Yes, lad, I suppose you're right," he sighed.

The soldier paused for a moment, his thoughts turned inward, then nodded to himself and said, "It's possible we'll be here for a few days before a ship bound for Galámur weighs anchor. I'll learn what I can about this Mbizhad Dal Taru. Kalas, you have a thing for books: in a city like this, there's bound to be a library, a school—something with maps. Records. Whatever you do, be discreet: I don't want to raise anyone's suspicions."

"We saw a couple of *sifu-ilmikasme* on our way to the customs house," Kalas informed him. "No, they didn't see us—I'm *pretty* sure they didn't see us!—but even if they did, isn't it moot? The *Tshaggul Kavar,* after what he did to Hwanzho…surely he knows we're here by now?"

"The Deathless Flame, maybe, but not everyone in Melash is an adherent! Yes, take pains to guard your identities and intentions, pay attention to your surroundings: I'm confident the three of you can handle yourselves. Come, let's get away from here, get back to our rooms. We'll discuss our next steps after we've all had something to eat."

"I'm…I'm not hungry," Kalas mumbled.

4.

Shosafin—predictably, Kalas observed—had already disappeared by the time the young man woke the next morning. Nïmrïk had abandoned his *rudzhsheth*—his wolfskin—before departing the docks the previous evening; now, he sat in a small chair and guarded the door. Except for the slow rise and fall of his shoulders, his stillness suggested sculpture, and Kalas assumed he'd been sitting there all night without sleep.

"Lushà ahwumeyan, lad," the *egu* grunted without shifting position. "Shosafin left about an hour ago. Didn't say much. Didn't say *anything.* Your *eru* friend's awake in the other room, but no one else is up. Unless you can think of a better use for me, I think it's best I keep a low, low profile today. I wasn't exactly…discreet yesterday afternoon.

"To be honest, I'm not sure how well I handled things with Hwanzho. Not just because of what happened to him, no: it's more…I guess it reminds me too much of the path I used to walk. I felt the same way after I killed—murdered?—Liro, Mbirin's father, all those Sevens ago.

"I've told you I've done all I can to make things right, to atone for my past sins. I do well for a while—for Sevens upon Sevens, sometimes—but then something like Hwanzho or Liro happens, and I realize *why* I remain everything I am…and everything I'm *not.*"

Kalas wasn't sure how to respond. He frowned, took a breath, and—

What was that?!

—he swiveled on his heels: he thought he'd glimpsed *Nanësra* standing across from the *egu* at the opposite end of the room. When he allowed himself a closer look, he discovered naught but empty space.

Was she—? No, of course not…

"I wish I knew the magic words to set your soul at ease, Nïmrïk, but I'm not convinced such words exist. Just now, I thought I saw Nanësra, standing right over there. I didn't, but it reminded me of our conversation on the steppes—and the one outside the Pump. I really do think she's starting to see you for the *elu* you used to be. Less the *egu* you've been in the past, at least."

"That's perhaps the kindest thing anyone's ever said to me, lad, but Nanësra is not the Creator, and thus I retain my curse."

"You know, Nïmrïk, maybe you're trying *too* hard? Maybe… maybe you're trying to achieve something no created being could ever hope to achieve?"

His shoulders sagged as he murmured, "If you're right—and I'm afraid you are—then my plight is hopeless."

Kalas sighed. "No, Nïmrïk, that's not what I'm saying."

He paused, unsure if he should continue the discussion, when his thoughts traveled toward the night Abarandal freed the *töthris* from its accreted darkness. He wondered why that scene had thrust itself toward the forefront of his consciousness and looked around for Nanësra again. All he saw was Nashmur and an oddly-shaped lump he presumed to be Rül, both still asleep.

"What about that troll Abarandal…helped?" he said at last, his voice low. "I didn't see it *do* anything special. I don't know if it even *said* anything: I just know Abarandal said the Creator knew his heart. If—"

"That's the problem! The Creator knows *my* heart, too!"

"Nïmrïk—no, *Kadhëmba,* do you really believe your capacity for rebellion is greater than the Creator's ability to restore?"

"You mock me…"

"Just the opposite, *sàyahal.* You've called yourself *Nïmrïk* for so long, you've forgotten who *Kadhëmba* is. Know this: when I call you *Kadhëmba,* I'm referring to the *elu* you were at the dawn of time—

the *elu* I believe you'll be again someday." Nïmrïk said nothing as large tears plumped within the corners of his eyes.

"Anyway, I'm on my way to get Zhalera and Abarandal, see if we can find some mention of Glass Sword Mountain. Shosafin's probably right: there must be schools or libraries or both in a city as big as Melash. We're bound to discover something! In fact, now that I think about it, I'll bring along that book of mine that no one seems to understand: maybe someone here can help?

"And please, think about what I said. Maybe you *haven't* done everything you can to demonstrate your remorse: maybe the one thing left to do is *accept* the Creator's forgiveness?"

The former *elu* shrank into his seat, his head cupped within his shaking hands. As he rocked back and forth, his whole body wracked with quiet sobs, Kalas closed the door behind him and padded from the room.

Turning toward the hall, he gasped when he caught Nanësra's profile again in his periphery. He blinked, assuming the apparition would be gone when he opened his eyes: instead, Kalas found himself confronted with the inescapable solidity of her imposing presence. He dropped his book: she knelt, plucked it from the floor, and, after puffing away the dust from its pages, handed it to him. Kalas gasped when a buzz of electricity leapt from her fingers to his. She'd traded her armor for a simple, shimmering tunic, cinched at the waist and ending just above her knees; her greaves for silver-strapped sandals twining around her calves.

Not my imagination, then...

"Nanësra! Uh, thank you!" he managed as he accepted the book from her hand. He wasn't sure what else to say.

"Well-met, Master Kalas," she replied with a subtle nod.

Neither said anything nor moved for what felt like forever. From Kalas' perspective, at least.

"You're wise beyond your years, my child."

"I am? Uh…I mean, thank you," he repeated, and she *smiled*.

"A child of two Sevens, and you've understood what Kadhëmba has not."

'A child of two Sevens'? Where have I heard that before?

"I…what?"

"I told you before: you've piqued my curiosity, and I'm interested to see what stems from your future discourse with the *vâlas elu*. You've thanked me twice just now: allow me to thank you in return."

"Thank…me?!"

"For standing between my sword and his skin."

Seized with sudden boldness, Kalas rifled through the pages of his book until he reached the woodcut featuring Nanësra beset by a pack of *zhàrudzhme*. He held it up for her to see and asked, "Both of you are in this picture, right? What does it say? I've been studying this book for months now, and I can't understand a word of it!"

"No?" she said, bemused and with an eyebrow arched.

"No!"

"Not a word?"

"That's right!"

"Is it?"

"What are you getting at? You, Falthwën, Heshradan: none of you speaks plainly!"

"That's fair," she allowed, and the rising suns-light flashed within her deep green eyes. She laughed—genuine, happy laughter that somehow retained the full weight of her voice. Before she shimmered beyond his power to perceive her presence, she promised: "We will meet again. You've a great many ordeals ahead of you. I wish I were permitted to deliver you from them—from one that will seem particularly cruel."

"What?! What are you talking about?! Tell me—!"

"You know it doesn't work that way, my child! I'll leave you with a plea. Remember this: the Creator sees things from perspectives none of us—neither *elunàm* nor *edhunàm*—can fathom: we never know when the shape of tragedy we glimpse from one perspective might assume the shape of blessing from another."

"I don't understand! Why must every *ilalasdra* keep so many secrets?!"

Nanësra provided no answer. With knives of light stinging in his eyes and chords of power ringing in his ears, she vanished in a blur of beating wings.

"Kalas?" wondered someone behind him. He turned to see a sleepy-looking Zhalera standing in the doorway of her room. "I thought I heard you talking to someone."

"I was. She—Nanësra!—she's gone now…"

"Nanësra! What was she doing here?"

"I…I don't really know. She was…*nice* this time! She actually *thanked me* for stopping her from slaying Kadhëmba!"

"Who?"

"Nïmrïk. I'm going to call him by his true name from now on."

"And she *thanked* you? That doesn't sound like her!"

"Doesn't it? We don't know *what* she 'sounds like.' Not really. When we first met her, we were with someone who tried to *unmake* her who knows how many Sevens ago! Just now, she told me we have a rough road ahead of us, that she wished she were allowed to protect us from some of the things we'll face—and she meant it."

"Did she say anything about your book?" Zhalera added when she noticed it in Kalas' hands.

"I don't know…"

"You don't know?!"

"She speaks in riddles!"

"Ah, right…"

"She seemed surprised I couldn't read it. Or maybe not *surprised,* but…I don't know how to explain it. It's like she wanted to tell me something but just…didn't. Maybe she *couldn't*. I was on my way to grab you and Abarandal to see if we could learn something about Mbizhad Dal Taru. I thought I'd bring my book along, too, just in case *someone* in this city might understand it. Worth an attempt, at least."

"I see," she nodded. "Abarandal's up. I think she's fully recovered from whatever happened at Töthrismedas Kig, and—"

"That reminds me: Zhalera, remember at the Gap, I mentioned hearing wingbeats and seeing a light inside the coach right after the trolls attacked us?"

"Wingbeats? Light? Right, you did say something, but I still don't remember: there were so many things happening all at once!"

"I wasn't sure what to make of it then, but now…I wonder if Nanësra was there. I wonder if *she* persuaded Abarandal to defend us from the trolls. I'll have to ask her the next time I see her."

"Oh? You two have plans?" Zhalera smirked.

"No! She said we'd meet again. She didn't say *when*."

"I'm only teasing! Let me get dressed—and grab my sword! We'll get some breakfast—after that, we'll explore Melash some more, find out what we can! And…*maybe* visit that forge…"

She winked as she withdrew into her room. Alone in the hallway, Kalas revisited Nanësra's warning: *You've a great many ordeals ahead of you…one…particularly cruel.*

5.

With the first sun well above the horizon, the second a half-circle bisected by the sea, the atmosphere surrounding the port city had an otherworldly quality: Kalas thought it had a pink tint as he and the others traversed Melash's streets. Zhalera agreed and said the puffs of low-hanging clouds looked orange to her. Kalas considered them, remembered Tàran's assessment from what felt like ages ago, and decided they weren't the right clouds for rainfire. The suns were bright, too: had there been no ilragusme to worry about, it would have been a perfect day—despite the cold.

They had no idea where to begin, and each looked—and felt—out of place among the meandering crowds of *Melashrinme*. Abarandal, with her fair skin, bore the closest resemblance, but her dark and multi-colored hair made a definite impression. And, her most serious impediment, of course: she couldn't speak with words. Zhalera's exotic golden tones had already begun to draw attention, too, so Kalas did most of the talking (in his best approximation of a *Potarular* accent) while the others kept their hooded cloaks drawn tight. To his surprise, most people seemed eager to help: he framed his quest as a search for *Pomelash* histories, and thus received directions toward the northeastern quarter of the city.

"There's the Maritime Academy, down by the customs house, but if it's history you're interested in, Niruk Tàlar University—oldest one in Melash—is that way, just past the river. The *Dzhinilmor*—the Icespitter, that is! Less than a mile from here," one kind old woman informed them.

"*Ágazhëthu, shâu,*" he said with a polite bow. She chuckled at the foreign gesture. Kalas blushed as they said goodbye and headed toward the Dzhinilmor.

"My 'accent' isn't cutting it," Kalas observed, dismayed.

"It's…not *that* bad!" Zhalera insisted. With a giggle. "I mean, it's probably our mannerisms more than anything: we don't *move* like the people here! We don't know their customs or turns of phrase…"

Kalas returned a wry grin. After looking at his book, he turned toward the northeast, where the kindly woman had directed them, then toward the coast and sighed.

"I *really* want to go to the University, but the Maritime Academy sounds like it'd have maps and charts and things."

"Maybe," Zhalera acknowledged, "but if the Mountain is part of Galámur, maybe the University would have better resources after all?"

"Hwanzho *was* looking for a charter, so there has to be ocean travel involved, but maybe you're right? What I mean is as much as I want to ask someone about this book, I don't want to waste our time. And I don't want to be out in the open any longer than necessary!"

"I understand that, but I vote we start with the University: we've already made our way inland, and Sho—*Shadrïs* said he thinks it'll be a day or two before we ship out. The Academy will be there tomorrow!"

Grinning now, Kalas accepted Zhalera's reasoning and led them up and down several streets, across an elaborate bridge that spanned the floe-covered Icespitter, and onto the grounds of Niruk Tàlar University. Nestled at the base of sheer basalt cliffs, it seemed almost like a part of the mountains despite its striking exterior. They followed signs toward the administrative offices, made a few inquiries, and received directions to a Professor Tomush's quarters.

The unnamed woman had indicated that the University was the oldest one in Melash: from the ancient trees and weathered structures purposefully arrayed upon its grounds, Kalas wouldn't have been surprised to learn it was the oldest university almost anywhere. They traveled a well-worn cobblestone walkway beneath a series of elaborate arches onto a vast quadrangle. Slabs of dark, almost black granite and cream-colored limestone carved with ornate reliefs decorated every façade. Woody, deep green ivies clung to cracks within and cornices atop each robust wall: Kalas first thought their vines grew randomly; a closer look, however suggested landscapers tended them as meticulously as the manicured emerald lawn blanketing the quad. Twin reflecting pools with notched corners, constructed of the same dark granite as the rest of the campus, occupied either end of the oblong plot. A breed of bird Kalas had never seen before stood along the coping stones capping one of the pools: it held his stare with its bright, yellow-orange eyes for just a moment before it flexed its powerful barred wings and vaulted toward the sky. He tracked its ascent, admiring the suns-light glinting from many-paned windows and the multihued slates staggered across the steeply-pitched roofs as he watched the creature disappear behind the clouds.

These windows. The roofs. Reminds me of Kësharan.

The atmosphere within the quad felt warmer to him. Zhalera concurred when he mentioned it: Abarandal thought about it for a moment before she shrugged and smiled.

"This grass: I wish we had this back home!" Zhalera said as she paused and ran her fingers through its feathery blades. "I guess it wouldn't do too well with all the heat. Nothing does…"

"Tsharak found that…what'd he call it? *Srathafi gahwa?* He said it used to be everywhere. Maybe it will be again someday?"

"Lohwàlar was different back then. The whole *world* was different back then!"

"*Some*day. Not tomorrow, not the day after, but who knows?"

Despite the University's predictable layout, navigating its long, repetitive corridors and stairwells proved disorienting. The history department, someone told them, was on the north hall, third floor, toward the northwest corner tower. Intricate stained-glass windows interrupted the walls' otherwise unremarkable solidity, allowing multicolored suns-light to cascade onto a loose assortment of well-used desks and chairs situated on the ground floor. As they ascended each riser, their footsteps echoed through the broad and mostly empty space, and Kalas wondered where everyone was.

"It's a school, right? Seems like we're the only ones here! I hope that woman was right: I hope Professor Tomush is around!" he said as they stepped onto the balcony and peered across the grounds below.

"It does seem—" Zhalera began.

"Professor Tomush?" A tall, severe-looking figure clad in heavy, flowing robes interrupted her as he materialized within the doorway of a nearby classroom. His shrewd, light brown eyes flitted from face to face beneath his canted brows. "What business do you have with the professor? The year is over, and you're not students here…"

"No, we're not, uh, we're just…we had a question—a few questions we wanted to ask him! He's—we were told he might be able to help us!" Kalas stammered, unnerved by the chilling austerity the man exuded.

"Hmmph!" he grimaced. He was about to dismiss them when he noticed the book in the young man's hands. "Professor Tomush is…What is that you have there? Give it to me!"

Something more than the rudeness in his demeanor gave Kalas pause. He looked at his book, at the old man's twitching fingers, and at Zhalera and Abarandal. His friends had expressions that mirrored his own suspicions.

"Uh, no, mister…I'll hold on to it. Thank you. Uh, Professor Tomush?"

"Hmmph!" he spat again, his eyes darting toward Zhalera's sword, "I've other matters to attend to anyway!"

With an arrogant flourish, his vestments swished from side to side as he brushed past Kalas. As he moved, the young man thought he glimpsed a flash of color beneath his black outer garment. After his clipped, quick footsteps ceased echoing through the almost empty walkway, Kalas took a deep breath, only then realizing he'd been holding in his last.

"Maybe the University was the wrong choice after all," he conceded. "That guy—whoever he was—there's something—"

Abarandal completed his sentence with a burst of low, discordant notes.

"—exactly!"

"I don't know what you just sang, but I agree with both of you!" Zhalera admitted. "I'm sorry, Kalas: I thought this place might be our best option."

"I did, too, remember! It's all right: there's still the Maritime Academy, and we have to pass that way any—"

"Psst! *Demme!* This way!" a warbling voice commanded. Kalas looked around for its source. Toward the end of the hall—their intended destination—a round old man with frazzled white hair jutting from the sides of his otherwise naked head motioned for them with repeated sweeps and flexures of his index finger.

"What do you think?" Kalas whispered to his companions.

"We're here…" Zhalera suggested. Abarandal nodded.

"Uh, hi?" Kalas managed as they reached the peculiar little man. His outer robes resembled those worn by the other stranger, but as his wrist rocked back and forth, Kalas glimpsed brighter colors within.

"I'm sorry about Professor Rahwi. He's, ah, well, he's somewhat renowned for his less-than-sunny disposition! And I'm sorry again for eavesdropping, but you're looking for Professor Tomush?"

"Well, yes…" Kalas hedged. The wizened figure interrupted him:

"What I mean to say is: you've found him! *I* am Professor Tomush! How may I be of service?"

He thrust a hand forward, revealing an elegant, gold-colored ring set with irregular yellow stones on his little finger. Something more than its beauty arrested Kalas' attention as suns-light blazed within its facets. The young man held onto his book with one hand and accepted the professor's greeting with the other.

"Excellent! Now, it seems you've brought me a book? A history, perhaps, if someone directed you to me?"

"We're really trying to find a way to Glass Sword Mountain," Kalas said. "None of the maps—"

"This way, *dhemme!*" Tomush interrupted as fear soured his once jovial expression. He traced a curious series of shapes and circles in the air as he ushered the trio into his room. Once inside, he shut the door, secured it with a series of heavy bolts, and turned to address his company in the silence—the secrecy—of his chambers.

"Mbizhad Dal Taru," he said, after a lengthy pause. "Seems there's been a lot of interest in that place in recent months. No, *years!* Sevens! Though not all at once. Forces of—interested parties are growing bolder. Tell me, child: what's *your* interest in the Mountain?"

"We, well…we're looking for someone. That's where we think we'll find him."

"I see."

After an appraising look, Tomush slapped a meaty hand against his liver-spotted forehead and apologized for his poor manners. He cleared stacks of books and scrolls from a few wooden chairs and offered them each a seat, which they gladly accepted. Zhalera unslung her sword, placed the tip of its scabbard between her feet, and leaned forward as the professor chose his words.

"Glass Sword Mountain is…a place of power."

"An…*amplifier?*" Kalas suggested. Tomush stared at the young man for a moment, his surprise plain to see.

"Yes, actually, although that's a curious way to put it!"

"Oh? I—a friend once described such places that way."

"A friend, you say? Indeed…Is this friend whom you hope to find at Glass Sword Mountain?"

"We won't be finding him *anywhere.* He's dead."

"My condolences," offered the professor as he traced his circles in the air again.

"What's that shape?" Zhalera asked Tomush. "The one you keep drawing with your finger? It's familiar, somehow. Kalas: doesn't it look familiar?"

"You…recognize a pattern there, do you?" said the professor as he curled his other hand around his dancing fingers and hid them behind his back.

"Of course!" she remembered: "The Vault! It's the mark where Valaran would have stood—"

"Valaran?! Vault?!" Tomush gasped. "How do you know such names?!"

The professor took a step back and nearly tripped over a pile of thick volumes scattered across his floor. Kalas studied the man and tried to discern his thoughts and intentions.

He couldn't, of course.

"Kalas! Tell him!"

Taking into account the plump figure's jeweled ring, the symbol he'd been carving into the air, and the shimmering gold fabric beneath his professorial frock, Kalas revealed to him a portion of the truth: "Abarandal, would you say hello to the professor?"

The *eru* girl smiled and sang her salutation. Tomush cocked his head, squinted, and regarded her more closely.

"Forgive me, child," he said as he collected himself and took a step toward her. "I mistook you for a *Melashrin,* but you're not from around here, are you? None of you hails from Melash. Nor Gambarad. I'm from…somewhere else, too. Your song is lovely— perhaps the most beautiful music I've ever heard—but I don't grasp your meaning."

"The *Kel Erume* summoned her from within the Vault of Stars," Kalas explained. "Valaran—one of the Seven with whom you're acquainted, judging from your ring and the shapes you've been making—wasn't there. Not entirely…"

"She was there in part, though," Zhalera continued as she unsheathed her sword. *"Valarandal.* Passed down through my family across uncounted Sevens. Her essence, a portion of her *rilâ,* maybe, inhabits this blade. Tell me, professor: what do you know about Valaran?"

"May I—may I see your sword?" he asked, his fingers timid yet twitching with anticipation.

Zhalera considered his request for a moment, then handed him the hilt. As his hand closed around it, honeyed efflorescence swirled within its blade. Tomush gasped and almost dropped it.

"Gili erume! It's heavier than it looks!" he marveled as he re-turned Valarandal to Zhalera. "I'd heard of such objects—many, many Sevens ago—but I never dared imagine I might hold one! Some of my ancestors, I'm told, enjoyed the *valaderudas* favor, but that would have been a long, long time ago: before dark forces made them flee their homes."

"What about that ring of yours?"

"Only topaz stones in gold settings, I'm afraid. Designed to mimic her corona, to acknowledge her gifts as an educator, but otherwise unremarkable. As for her symbol, I discovered it Sevens ago while conducting my research. At some point, I started writing it in the air when I got nervous. Or excited. Or both!

"Mbizhad Dal Taru. History describes it as a place of power. A *kelëshdiru.* Glass Sword Mountain waits atop Avëloth's highest peaks, toward the tip of its northernmost cape. Because of how it rises from the ocean, the island's interior is inaccessible from all directions except the underground port carved into its southeastern cliffs at Galámur. Finding a ship to take you there might prove difficult: for some reason, like I told you, for months now, the Ice City's been a point of interest for unsavory characters from all across the earth."

"We have a friend who's trying to find us a ship right now," Kalas admitted. "We *need* to get there! To find out what Marugan, his mistress, and their ilk have planned! If their schemes come to pass, there's no telling what might happen to the world!"

"Marugan? I've heard that name before! Not too long ago, in fact: he visited the University. Something about the man seemed… tainted, maybe. Wrong. And not just his scarred face. I thought he was here to see me, but no: Professor Rahwi met with him. Rahwi is also a professor of history: he's had his eye on my chair for Sevens now. I stick around just to spite him: honestly, I would have surrendered it years ago—I've attained a healthy number of Sevens—but Rahwi wants it *too much*. I've never trusted anyone with such unbridled lust for authority. Not that chairing the history department at the University carries much prestige, but in principle…

"Anyway, Rahwi told him much of what I've told you. If Mbizhad Dal Taru was Marugan's destination, he's probably on Avëlöth as we speak."

"He wouldn't need a boat," Kalas mumbled.

"No?"

"He's…*eku*. A star, once, like Valaran, but corrupted."

"Ah, yes, I'm aware of the stories. A history professor, you know!" he laughed. Turning serious, he added, "It's possible he *kalswàra*, then. Can you imagine: traveling along paths of light? Moving vast distances in the twinkling of an eye? Wouldn't that be nice?!"

"Yeah, that'd be something," Kalas sighed. He hung his head and remembered his book. "Hey, Professor, since we're here…have you ever seen anything like this before?"

He opened his volume to the scene with Nanësra standing against the wolf-demons and held it out to the old man. Tomush gasped again and took the item from the young man's hands. Taking pains to treat each leaf with utmost care, he examined a few pages, sniffed its ink and bindings, and hovered a shaking finger above each wandering line.

"Where…" he breathed.

"My grandfather. I don't think anyone knows where he found it. Not even Tsharak—his oldest friend, I mean. I've been trying to understand it for months now! Sometimes, it seems like the writing *almost* makes sense, but then it's just random shapes again."

"It's *old!* Older than anything in my library! In our entire collection! Young man, I hesitate to ask, but would you consider loaning—perhaps even donating this volume to the University? To *me?* I can't read it—I'm not sure anyone here can—but it's possible the mathematics department might discover something through frequency analysis or decryption algorithms. Assuming this text is written in a *known* language, of course…"

Nanësra's mercurial smile flashed across his thoughts, and Kalas couldn't elude the impression that he wasn't quite finished with Wodram's book.

"It was my grandfather's," he said as he reached for it.

"Of course! Of course! I respect that! As someone untethered to his own history, I understand your desire to hold onto it better than most, I believe! If I might be so bold, then, allow me to make a request: you said the writing almost makes sense to you sometimes? When it *does* make sense to you, will you remember me? Will you communicate your findings? The woodcut: above the *elu,* I see the Seven Stars confronting *zhàrudzhme.* There's no way to know for sure, but I wouldn't be surprised if this work was created mere Sevens after the Creator cracked the world."

"You know about that?!" Now it was Kalas' turn to gasp.

"I'm an historian," Tomush shrugged. Almost as an afterthought, he added, "Tell you what: if your designs conflict with those of this Marugan character—and Professor Rahwi, I want to help. In your travels, have you heard mention of a sect called the—"

"*Ragus pïni Tshaggul Kavar,*" Kalas spat.

"I'm not surprised. It's mostly *ilragusme* who are trying to reach

Glass Sword Mountain. Because we're between years, I imagine Rahwi will join them soon enough."

"The Professor is a cultist?!"

"He wouldn't describe himself as such: he claims he follows the *Sifuyerudas Kayu,* but his ambitions align more closely with those of the Deathless Flame."

"Beneath the Vault, *ekume unmade* one of our friends—the *eru* Sharuyan. Others suggested the Swath had been betrayed. I've been trying to figure out who would have done such a thing," Kalas told Tomush. "We met a few cultists on the way here. They, too, claimed they were on the Path of Sifuran. I wouldn't have thought Sifuran was the traitor: he seemed most eager to summon Abarandal against the world's end...

"Valaran wasn't there, under the Vault: Peradan said she'd been caught in a...a *singularity,* he said. Was he mistaken? Was he lying? Maybe an *eru* not of the Swath betrayed them."

"Those are questions I cannot answer. As for Galámur, give me a day or two: I have a friend—a captain—who owes me a handful of favors. I'll see to it that he provides berths for you aboard his ship on his next voyage. How many of you are there?"

"Really?! Professor Tomush, thank you so much!" Zhalera gushed. "Uh, let's see...there are...eight of us. Plus four horses. And our gear."

"*Eight* of you?! And horses? Hmm..." The professor raised an eyebrow.

"We're grateful for any help you can give us. Maybe our friend will find other transportation for the rest of us."

"It may come to that, but I'll do what I can!"

Shosafin returned to their rooms later that evening, long after the suns had disappeared. He tried to hide his frustration when he revealed he'd been unable to find a ship willing to ferry them across the sea, so Kalas and the others ignored the color in his voice. Zhalera told everyone what the three of them had discovered at the University, and about Professor Tomush's seafaring friend.

"If he can't provide passage for all of us at once, we'll have to make separate trips. Inconvenient, perhaps, but actually not a bad idea," Shosafin said. "I've been pursuing Marugan for almost a year now: you'll understand if I *insist* that I am on the first boat headed for the island?"

"Who goes with you?" Kalas wondered.

"Depends on how many berths your professor friend can get. Nothing we do tonight will change that. Might as well get some rest."

6.

"We'll see you in a couple of weeks. Three at the most," Nashmur said as he clapped a hand atop his cousin's shoulder. Rül and Pava stood with him and nodded.

"I'm sorry there isn't room for all of us," Kalas apologized, "and I'm sorry we have to leave the horses behind!"

"Not your fault, lad," the former commander said. "I'm just grateful your professor friend was able to make our travel arrangements, staggered as they might be!"

"It'll give us time to find a place to board the horses. Guess we won't be needing those saddles after all," Rül added.

"In a city like this, there must be a reputable place for them. Probably more than one. There'd better be: Thara will have my hide should anything happen to Breaker! I'm confident you'll find what we need," Shosafin suggested to Rül. "Anyway, we'll only have room for essentials. Not a bad thing, really. It'll shrink our footprint, help us blend in better."

The five boarded a three-masted tall ship named *Zhiamdas Salo-*

rosh, helmed by one Captain Dzholëf. Kalas felt all the blood in his face pool somewhere in his lower extremities as the black-stained vessel rocked upon the waves. Nausea bubbled its way toward his throat, but he closed his eyes, placed a hand against his mouth, and breathed in the salty air until the sensation passed. Zhalera tried not to laugh. She failed. Even Abarandal giggled as the young man tried to steady himself.

"Stone and water," Shosafin muttered as he followed the others up the gangplank. "Let your body sense the rhythm of the water, adopt its shape. Let its movements inform yours…"

"Whatever you say," he groaned from between his fingers.

Two days after meeting with the professor, Tomush sent a pageboy to the inn with news that his captain friend would be sailing for Galámur in two days aboard the *Salorosh*. When Kalas questioned his bona fides, the messenger drew Valaran's sigil in the air. He explained the professor had secured four "berths"—little more than closets, really, although he suggested it might be possible to fit two people in the largest. Zhalera volunteered to double up with Kalas. She'd tried to couch her choice as a matter of necessity, of *pragmatism*, but Pava understood her subtext, snickered, and gave the young, blushing man a sidelong glance.

"It'll have to do," Shosafin acknowledged, and the party finalized their plans.

The next morning, he and his cousin scoured the city for a ship willing and able to transport three people to Galámur. Curious, Kalas followed at their heels.

Inside a dark, seedy tavern—little more than a narrow hallway lined with taps, benches, and drunkards—they met a weasel-faced man who called himself Bayal.

"Three people to Galámur, *hish?*" he said, his nasal voice drawing out the last syllable. "Make it worth my while, and I'll get it done," he insisted. "I'm first mate aboard the *Kandha pïni Bethrume*. The captain's probably on her backside around here somewhere. Don't worry: *I'm* the one who does most of the sailing! So…what are we doing here?"

"Thank you for your time," Nashmur said with a heavy, disgusted sigh as he stood to leave.

"A moment, friend," Shosafin smiled. Kalas remained seated and tried not to cough as pungent odors swirled up from around his ankles. While the cousins exchanged heated, indecipherable whispers, the young man examined the small room disguised as an alehouse. Finding it unremarkable, he turned his attention toward the slight figure seated across the table from him. His clothes, while wrinkled and slightly soiled, still looked like they'd been cared for, like their owner took some measure of pride in his bearing. Bayal pretended not to listen to the soldiers' discussion, but he couldn't hide the intense interest behind his small, bright blue eyes as he tried too hard not to pay attention. Sensing Kalas' analytical gaze, he turned toward the boy and smiled, revealing a mouth full of polished, crooked teeth. He removed his cap and smoothed back a shock of greasy blond hair.

He's hiding something. I bet everyone here is hiding something; that, or hiding from something. Bayal looks like a travel-stained mariner, but there's something underneath all that. He's not what he seems…

"Shadrïs," Kalas interrupted. Nashmur looked around for a moment: Shosafin turned toward him without missing a beat. Adopting a bored, disinterested air, the young man continued, "Maybe the *Bethrume* isn't the *best* option we've got, but I *like* Mister Bayal here. I'm sure we can come to some arrangement?"

Shosafin flashed a brief smile. Nashmur cocked his head and sighed again in disbelief. "I suppose you're right, lad," said the old soldier. "All right, *Âu* Bayal, what are you thinking?"

• • •

"I think I see the *Kandha pïni Bethrume* across the bay," Kalas said once he and the others had boarded the *Salorosh* with what few belongings they could carry. "Bayal said it had bright blue sails: before the wind changed, I thought I saw sails like that on that ship over there."

"Get a good look, lad: once Dzholëf's crew weighs anchor, you'll be spending most of the next few weeks below decks," Shosafin reminded him.

"I know, I know," he groaned again, just a moment before vomiting his breakfast over the *Saloroshdas* railing.

"Tomush's proxy said we'd have to earn our keep," Zhalera reminded the soldier once they'd been directed toward their quarters. "Any idea what we'll be doing?"

"Someone'll need to swab the decks: Kalas, that's you," he grinned.

"It's…it's only fair, I guess," he nodded as his empty stomach gurgled.

"Abarandal will help: given her…quiet nature, it seems best to minimize her interaction with the crew. At least we're on a commercial vessel: no other passengers to worry about.

"Zhalera, you and Nïmrïk will work the galley. I'll work the rigging."

"You know how to do that?" Kalas raised an eyebrow.

"In part," Shosafin admitted. "I've sailed before."

"You have? When? Where?"

"Nashmur's not the only one who's been to Ralothova!"

Kalas struggled less and less with the ever-shifting surfaces beneath his feet as days turned into weeks. The air retained a sizable amount of winter's chill, but one day, under the suns' concentrated light, he had to remove his shirt while swabbing the main deck. When a series of fast, towering waves rocked the *Salorosh* without displacing him, Captain Dzholëf, a wiry, middle-aged man with red, leathery skin almost buried beneath a mass of tattoos, noted his improvement. He, too, worked bare-chested in the afternoon heat.

"Got your sea legs at last, swabby!" he laughed.

"*Hish*, sir!" Kalas replied. He'd never heard the phrase *sea legs* before, but he understood the captain's meaning.

"Professor Tomush must hold you in high esteem: I left two of my crew back at Melash to make room for you," he laughed again.

"I'm sorry, sir! I had no idea!"

"Well, to be fair: you're better with a mop than the man I left back in town! Still, I wonder why you're so intent on reaching Galámur. Other ships would have been available within a week or two, a month at most…"

Kalas wasn't sure how to respond. He didn't want to be rude, but he didn't want to reveal too much. He maintained a polite silence while Dzholëf stared him down. When the uncomfortable moment passed, the captain nodded, smiled mechanically, and turned to go. That's when Kalas saw a familiar shape within the intricate network of lines and fills inked in tints, tones, and shades of blue across his naked back.

"Uh, Captain. Sir," he said, unsure how to address the man. "That shape on your back: I've seen it before…"

"Which one? You'll have to be more specific!" he laughed, although Kalas perceived he remained guarded.

"The blue one. A triangle with a circle on every side, wrapped in a bigger circle. It looks old—older than the rest, I mean, but it's so well done! If you'll forgive my saying so, it's a beautiful piece!"

"You like that one, do you? Strange you'd notice it…or maybe not? You're right: it's the first tattoo I ever received. There's a story behind it—there's a story behind all of them! Tell me, have you ever heard of the…no, no: of course not. Seems no one remembers the old wisdom…"

"The what?" Kalas prodded, forgetting himself for a moment.

"Sifuran," Dzholëf said and watched Kalas for his reaction.

The young man paused his mopping a moment too long.

"You've heard this name before? You know it?" he plied when Kalas tried too hard to pretend he didn't know what the captain was talking about.

"I…yeah," Kalas admitted.

"Nowadays, not many do. Tomush does: you know that, I'd wager. I'll say no more about it." Dzholëf paused in his work and surveyed the flat line of the horizon: dark blue below, light blue above. Kalas matched his movements and saw nothing but water; roiling moments ago, now it resembled an endless pane of glass as *Zhiamdas Salorosh*—*Mercy's Triumph*—sliced across its surface.

"Five more days," the captain declared as he returned his mop to its bucket. "Five more days and we'll reach Avëlöth. And Galámur. Don't forget your shirt: when the suns set, that cold will come up fast and sure, and we don't need you catching ill!"

Kalas offered Dzholëf a weak smile and continued his work until the man and his strange marks disappeared below decks.

Chapter X

Across a Phantom Threshold

VËLÖTH ROSE FROM THE SHADAÚN ILAROD LIKE A vast black monolith set against Tàfayan's faltering rays. Rays that draped the clouded sky in sheets of gold veined with hints of pink. One by one, sparks of light flickered into being as the *Salorosh* sailed closer to the island's sheer sides. A thin line of luminous orange seemed to stretch and widen as the ship rounded a promontory to expose a gaping, half-moon-shaped cavern cut into its bluffs and lit with numerous signs of activity. Soon, even in the twilight, Kalas caught the flutter of ships dousing sails or maneuvering into position to cast lines or drop anchor.

Galámur!

True to his word, Dzholëf's interactions with Kalas for the last four days consisted of little more than details surrounding his duties or snippets of polite conversation. Something about his mien, however, had changed, and the young man suspected the sea captain regarded him with a strange, almost expectant curiosity. On more than one occasion, he commented on the water's uncanny stillness contrasted with the wind's favorable bearing, as though Kalas understood such considerations. Dzholëf laughed and explained they'd reach Avëlöth ahead of schedule: "Wind and water don't always work so well together. Not this time of year! If conditions persist, we'll shave a day, maybe more, from our travel time. It's almost as if the arbitrators of all things elemental are shepherding us along our path! It's a good omen, regardless!"

As the maw-like port swallowed *Zhiamdas Salorosh*, a sudden wall of cold closed in around the ship. Standing on the main deck, Kalas shivered as gelid air rolled across his frame. Zhalera wrapped her arms around the fur cloak she'd been wise enough to grab before ascending from below decks. Abarandal remained as she ever was.

Shosafin and Nïmrïk assisted with furling the sails and heaving lines to longshoremen waiting on the pier. Despite the frenzy of snaking hawsers and shouted commands volleyed from ship to shore, the speed with which Dzholëf's crew and the *Galámurrinme* moored the *Salorosh* surprised the young man. Once secured, other longshoremen bridged the gap between land and sea with a gangplank, and Dzholëf granted permission for his passengers and some of his crew to disembark. The old *Poyïsriba* soldier led the way: Kalas knew he was assaying his surroundings, searching for signs of trouble. The young man gestured for Zhalera and Abarandal to precede him. Before he could follow, Dzholëf placed a rough, callused hand on his shoulder and demanded a moment of his time.

"Master Kalas, maybe I'm no historian like Professor Tomush, but I've sailed enough of this world to understand we're living in interesting times. I've heard tales about 'wolves' and trolls…even 'lions' and lights in the sky. Used to hear 'em once in a while as a boy; now, it seems like *everyone* has a story. I'll bet you have stories of your own. You're reluctant to speak about such things, and, as much as it pains me to admit, that's probably to your credit—I do love hearing such tales!

"You probably know as well as I do—better, perhaps!—that not everything is what it seems. Not everyone is *who* he seems."

"You're not the first person to say so," Kalas admitted.

"Whatever your business is in Galámur, never forget that," the captain smiled as he withdrew his hand from Kalas' shoulder.

"*Ilun-alavri,* swabby!"

Dzholëf doffed his hat, spun on his heels, and descended toward the lower decks. The young man remained still until Zhalera's insistent calls registered at last.

"Yeah, on my way!" he mumbled as he joined the others on the ground.

Underneath almost impossible arches carved and sculpted into Avëlöth's foundation—immense cliffs barely blunted through untold Sevens of tides and storms, Galámur buzzed with a peculiar normalcy as dockhands worked the piers, loading and unloading cargoes and passengers—a few clad in bright blue robes. Groin vaults as wide as Lohwàlar's Crescent, supported by stout columns fraught with decorative reliefs, divided the artificial harbor into seven neat sections, each teeming with a dazzling array of huge ships, modest dinghies, and everything in between. Motifs woven within the architecture evoked hazy memories of some other place, but Kalas couldn't decide from where. Along the water's edge, peddlers at their stands or in front of their carts hawked an eclectic blend of wares. Most seemed peaceable enough, but a few had more aggressive ideas on how to conduct business. One such man—a weedy old fellow with sallow skin and bulging eyes—displayed surprising speed as he leapt in front of Shosafin and waved a gaudy glass bottle beneath his nose.

"Good sir! You look like a man in desperate need of *halâ pïn dzhin srathi!* Just a few drops of this most potent elixir is guaranteed—*guaranteed!*—to summon untapped reservoirs of virility and puissance from wearied bones like yours!"

Shosafin ignored the man, but even as he stepped to the side, the persistent peddler mirrored his movements.

"Ah, a man of discerning taste, I see! Tell you what, friend! Today—and just for you—it's *two* bottles for the price of one!"

Shosafin attempted to step around the figure a second time without success.

"You've got a good eye, my friend! A good eye, indeed! And I have good news: you've passed the test!" Adopting a conspiratorial tone, he added, "Someone as well-trained as you would never settle for novelties like ice-flower essence nor stone's blood nor even powdered iron-bear baculum, would he? No, you're looking for something stronger—*much* stronger, am I right? Of course I am! As fate would have it, you're in luck! I have such a potion right here! It's—"

"Pashad! You've been warned!" a booming voice exclaimed. Kalas had been so rapt with the strange little man's hard-sell that he'd failed to notice a band of three or four children scattering like wind-driven dust devils. When he looked again, the peddler had disappeared as well.

"Check your pockets, *sàme*. Pashad and his troupe of miscreants run a well-organized operation, much to the harbor master's chagrin."

The voice's owner, a towering figure dressed in oiled leather breeches waggled his sinuous sword toward the shadows. Gleaming greaves and gauntlets crafted from hammered metal protected his shins and forearms. His heavy, ursine cloak retained most of its original facial features; now, however, polished black gems glittered from the dead bear's eye sockets. Kalas looked around and noticed other, similarly attired figures distributed throughout the port. None so large as this man, however.

Shosafin offered a subtle nod as the soldier returned to his patrol.

"Who—who was *that?!*" Kalas wondered aloud.

"Port authority."

"He's huge! Glad he's on our side!"

Shosafin turned toward Kalas, his expression severe: "Make

no mistake, lad: he might have scared away 'Pashad,' but we've no assurances he's on 'our side.' It's best if we maintain a…*polite distrust* while we're on this island. There's no telling who might be servants of Marugan. Or the Deathless Flame."

The young man gulped and nodded.

As they resumed their trek, Kalas remembered the patrolman's admonition and ran a hand through his pockets and his pack.

"Pashad had *five* accomplices. I secured everything before we left the *Salorosh*. None of those urchins made off with anything of ours," said the old soldier without looking over his shoulder. "That said, there's no harm in double-checking."

"I wonder when Rül and the others will arrive," Kalas mused.

"We'll wait in town for a few days—up to a week, maybe—for the *Kandha pïni Bethrume* to get here. You're welcome to wait longer, if you choose: that's as long as *I'm* willing to wait," said Shosafin.

"A week? But if Marugan knows we're here, what's to stop him from…Kalas, what's that word? What if he…*kalswàr* away from here? If he's in league with the Deathless Flame—and it seems he is—surely he already knows something of our plans?" Zhalera countered.

"Good point," the soldier conceded. "Three days."

Navigating the shifting corridors of people, animals, and vehicles teeming along the harbor's streets, Shosafin led them away from the water toward a broad stairway draped in light streaming from overhead. Airborne particulates hung suspended or danced in lazy spirals within the column of brightness that seemed to ripple in the rising wind.

"Reminds me of the *parafi-isadme* under the Áthradho," Kalas noted, "but I don't see any reflectors or light-collectors…"

"There aren't any, from what I've been told: high above us, there's an artificially-faceted glacier that directs suns-light this way. Galámur is a divided city. Neither east-west nor north-south: *top-bottom*. The 'topsiders'—what Dzholëf's crew call the people at the top of these 'Great Stairs'—consider themselves *above* those who spend their lives hidden away from the suns. And not just literally. That said, the *tsumayumbume*—topsiders—are wise enough to acknowledge that their way of life depends wholly on the *nirukumbumedas* good graces."

"That sounds terrible!" Zhalera fumed. "Why would the portsiders tolerate such bigotry? They control the waterfront, right? Why not refuse to cooperate with the topsiders?"

"They tried that. Once. According to a *Pogalámur* crewman who grew up portside, King Mödus' army—one of his grandsires, that is—made short work of the *nirukumbume* resistance. The portsiders tried to block off the Great Stairs, but there are other, secret avenues throughout the island. The topsiders had the suns: they had light and enough resources to survive. The portsiders had the sea—until the topsiders started attacking incoming ships with trebuchets, ballistas, and similar engines...

"The whole island was a mess for years until everything was resolved. In part, anyway; now, there's at least cooperation between the upper and lower classes. The *nirukumbume* figure if the *tsumayumbume* want to waste their energy looking down on them, that's their choice.

"Bïrug—the crewman who told me all these things—was quick to add that King Mödus doesn't hold the same perspective as his ancestors. Says he even took his queen from among the portsiders. 'The old prejudices will take time to die,' he said, 'but Mödus has struck a powerful blow against them!' It'll be...interesting to see what becomes of this place over the next few Sevens.

"When we get topside, we'll find a place to wait for the others. Bïrug gave me the names of a few establishments where we might avoid curious eyes and ears."

2.

Galámur's "topside" reminded Kalas of a colder, less organized version of Âivambar. Mortared stone and wood-paneled buildings looked like they'd been piled on top of one another at first glance, but a closer look revealed their foundations had been erected atop the island's irregular surface, most designed to maximize its natural rills and ridges. Contrasted against the damp, pervasive chill beneath, suns-light seemed to pour warmth into the valley above the Great Stairs. Flagstone-paved streets spread out from a ringed wall encircling the aperture, connecting the city's disparate sectors like a spider web's radius threads. Again, the reliefs carved into the limestone blocks suggested something almost familiar to Kalas: despite his best efforts to sift the designs and architecture from his memories, he couldn't.

"Come," Shosafin instructed as he paraded them past rows of shops and storefronts. "The place we're looking for is…this way." He selected one of the thoroughfares emanating from the "wheel," as Kalas considered it, and set off.

"What are we looking for?" Zhalera wondered.

"A man named Daór on the Northwest Spoke. Supposed to run a nice place. Nicer than The Dancing Bear, at least. Bïrug knows him well, told me to give this Daór fellow his name. We'll see what happens."

The "Spoke" curved around an uplifted glut of what looked like residential spaces: with his view unobstructed, Kalas caught his first glimpse of forested mountains far to the north. Thick black thunderheads surrounded the highest peaks, and faint blotches of lightning strobed from within their banks.

"Mbizhad Dal Taru must be up there somewhere," Nïmrïk suggested as he observed Kalas' stare. The *egu* had remained rather quiet, almost distant, since their last conversation. He made a sound like he had more to say; instead, he exhaled, shook his head, and kept his eyes trained on the electricity writhing through the clouds.

Shosafin spent most of his waking hours over the next three days pacing the stout, polished wooden floors of the third-story rooms Daór had provided them. Heavy, plastered walls blunted most of the noise from the metered rhythm of his booted footsteps. On occasion, he'd stop, peer through the narrow windows, and frown when the others failed to appear. Kalas couldn't remember him ever betraying his emotions with such frivolity, although the soldier had come close on the banks of the Hidden River west of Thosha.

"They'll be here," Kalas insisted with as reassuring a smile as he could muster. Shosafin spared him a glance, ignored his optimistic façade, and remarked, "Oh? You're a prophet now, as well as a pawn of 'prophecy'?"

Kalas' expression conveyed his hurt with more clarity than words ever could have managed.

"Kalas, I'm sorry," Shosafin apologized. "I'm usually much better at this sort of thing. Waiting. Exercising patience. Knowing—believing, I suppose—how close I am to Marugan has me unbalanced. I'm not used to that, and I'm more disappointed in myself than anything—or anyone—else. I keep reminding myself it's been Sevens since King Rufàran disappeared…I know—I was *sure* that Marugan died with the rest of the king's company that day! Ever since I learned he's still alive…

"I'll scout the port again, use the time to…reevaluate my intent. My approach. Why don't the rest of you continue to learn what the locals know about Glass Sword Mountain?"

"Kadhëmba, you want to come with us?" Kalas prodded as he grabbed Falthwën's staff. The *egu* winced at the sound of his own name. He sighed, donned his coat, and followed as everyone except

Shosafin headed for the street.

Most *Galámurrinme* with whom they spoke breathed a hurried prayer or imprecation when Kalas asked about the Mountain: "No one goes up the Mountain, *átem!* No one interested in living out the remainder of his natural life! Besides, no one *really* knows which one of the Blades—the range that makes up most of Avëlöth's north end—is the *genuine* Glass Sword Mountain!"

"We're...we have business there," Zhalera explained. "What's so bad about the...*Blades,* you said?"

"'Business'?" repeated the old man with whom they'd been speaking. "You're not a buncha flame-chasers, are you?"

"'Flame-chasers'? I don't—Oh! No! Absolutely not!"

"No, I didn't think so," he admitted as he gave the four of them an appraising glance. "You don't have The Look about you...All right, listen: Galámur doesn't get many visitors. Not as many as we've seen in recent months, what with all them *ilpuzhritme-kavar* traipsing around, that's for sure! In recent years—probably about the same time those figures started showing up—there's been a shadow over the *Tsikme*—the Blades. An endless shadow whose substance blots out the suns. Some days, when the sky is low and leaden—like today—you can just make out its shape as it treads above the clouds."

"You've...you've seen this shadow?" Zhalera wondered.

"Oh, no, not me personally, but a friend of a friend of mine who lives at the foot of the mountains says some of her flock's gone missing. Told my friend she and her husband waited up one night, thinking it was bandits. It wasn't, she says.

"Anyway, this was a few summers ago, when the weather here's about as warm as it gets, and they'd built themselves a nest of sorts from furs and blankets to ward against the cold. My friend's friend says they must have drifted off: she woke from a dead sleep to horrified bleating—coming from *above* her! She looked up just in time to see one of her ewes sailing overhead!

"She tried to rouse her husband, but by the time she managed, the shape—and her sheep—was gone.

"That's just one of the stories. There are others. Some less fantastic, I suppose, but the *forests* on the Blades' slopes are dangerous in their own right, too: bears (we *are* a part of Gambarad, remember!), wolves, catamounts…and don't forget the terrain! There might be a handful of game paths here and there, but almost everyone who's crossed the Ravine has disappeared."

"The Ravine?" said Nïmrïk, his eyebrow raised.

"Oh yes! A couple of leagues into the woods, just before the Blades turn sharp, the ground just…disappears! On clear days—lots of fog down there most of the time—you can see the other side, maybe sixty, seventy feet across. There might be a few makeshift bridges still around, but like I said…the Ravine stretches from shore to shore. It's hard to tell, but from the ocean, if you look closely, it looks like someone tried to cut Avëlöth in half—and failed, but just barely!"

"*Almost* everyone?" Kalas questioned.

"I only know of one woman who people say ventured over the Ravine and came back. Legend says—and it *is* considered something of a legend nowadays—maybe five, five and a half Sevens ago, this woman believed her child had wandered away from the farm. Convinced he'd ignored her warnings and gone into the forest, she ran after him. When her husband returned from the fields, he asked his farm hands where she was: none knew exactly what had happened, but after comparing stories, it wasn't hard to guess.

"He rounded up his men and made a search of the woods where he thought his wife might have gone. She couldn't have been gone for more than a few hours: he searched as far as the Ravine, he and his farm hands and neighbors, long into the night, but it seemed like she'd just been plucked from the earth! They scoured every last inch of those woods: they found her shawl near the Ravine, but nothing else.

"The ironic thing? Their boy had been at home the whole time, playing a game with some friends. His hiding place had been so good, he'd fallen asleep waiting to be found. Never heard his mother calling for him…

"First thing in the morning, his father took up the search again. All day, stopping only for a few sips of water, he looked high and low for his bride. Nothing! Did the same thing for the next few days.

"When he'd almost lost all hope he'd ever see her again, he made one last journey into the woods, all the way out to the Ravine again. And he *found* her! *Alive!* In body, if not in spirit: her mind was…just *gone*. Her clothes were tattered, her face and hands scraped and scratched, her fingers bleeding from clawing at something…She was raving, spouting nonsense. Her husband carried her home, hoped the sight of their son would cut through the cobwebs wrapped around her thoughts, but nothing seemed to help.

"The farm's still there: the couple's son runs it now. His father died a few years back. The mother's still alive, still…addled. Her son tends to her as best he can."

"That's…wow," Kalas said when no other words would come. "Thank you for your time, good sir! I'm almost afraid to ask, but would you tell us where to find this farm?"

His distaste for their endeavor writ plainly across his face, the old man shrugged and explained how to reach the place. He warned them the woman's son was wary of strangers—foreigners especially, and suggested that even if he didn't chase them from his land outright, he probably wouldn't let them speak with his mother.

"I understand," Kalas acknowledged, "but I think it's worth a visit. C'mon, everyone: let's head north. Maybe…maybe there's something we can do for her?"

The *eru* responded with a sad, uncertain smile as the four of them parted company with the old man. He was still shaking his head as he turned away and disappeared into the city.

3.

"Is this the best idea?" Zhalera wondered as the four of them walked toward the farm the old, unnamed man had indicated. "I mean, if someone came to me asking questions like that…"

"It's probably not the *best* idea, but it's the only one we have right now. Everyone else we talked to—*tried* to talk to!—couldn't get away from us fast enough when they found out we were looking for the Mountain!"

"We'll be respectful, of course," Nïmrïk elaborated, "but I agree with Master Kalas. And if he and the *erushátem* might help this woman, we may learn more from her than from the rest of Galámur combined."

Abarandal sang a few muted bars and placed a hand on Kalas' arm. She looked up at him with a blend of hope and apprehension he wasn't sure how to dispel.

"We'll figure it out," he said. *I hope so, anyway…*

Pogalámur farms had a different mood than Rül's farm back in Lohwàlar—or even the fields surrounding Thosha's western border. Here, workers tended terraced plots of land, turning over shovelfuls of soil along some and evaluating early growth poking up from others. They passed a gate on their way up a long, steep hill. Zhalera noticed a smear of black swipes defacing on one of its posts and pointed out how much it resembled the scorched lines burned across Hwanzho's corpse. Someone had tried to scrub away the stains, but the impressions remained.

• • •

"Hi!" Kalas grinned as they approached the nearest farm hand. "We're looking for…uh, well…we're looking for the owner. Never did get his name. Actually, all we know is that his mother, well…"

"You're looking for *Diza* Hëk." The man jerked his head toward a well-worn path without looking away from his work. He seemed so focused on his task he never bothered asking about theirs.

"Hëk, is it? Thanks!"

At the top of a long, well-compacted road, standing sentry over seven or eight terraces, a middle-aged man sat beneath the eaves of a small, well-maintained home. Even with his head hanging between his shoulders, Kalas thought he looked about as big as Gandhan. Maybe leaner. Seated in a well-weathered chair, he'd been resting against the work-worn handle of a giant pickaxe. When he heard their approach, he raised his weary head and bored into them with his piercing hazel eyes. Kalas caught his stare and held it as he and the others drew nearer. Summoning his best smile, he slowed his pace when he came within a few feet of the structure's shallow porch. The tired-looking farmer stood—

He's taller *than Gandhan,* Kalas corrected himself.

—and…said nothing. He watched, impassive aside from the subtle fire smoldering in his eyes.

At least a full minute passed with no one breaking the strange silence.

"Kalas?" Zhalera whispered as she raised an elbow against his ribs.

"Kalas, is it?" said the farmer at last. He blinked, breaking his stare for the first time since the young man became aware of it. "What can I do for you, Master…Kalas?"

"Good day, sir! Look, we're sorry to bother you, but we're looking for Hëk. *Diza* Hëk. Is…is that you?"

"What's your business with Hëk, young man?"

The farmer hadn't admitted anything, but Kalas suspected this towering figure was indeed the farm's owner and proprietor.

"I…we're…we're searching for some…thing. Someone. Someone told us they might be headed for Mbizhad Dal Taru, and—"

"Get out of here," the man said. Growled. "You flame-chasers aren't welcome here!"

"No! We're not—"

"I've been patient. Polite. I've endured your nonsense for too long now! If you won't leave of your own accord…"

Hëk hefted his pickaxe, tested its weight against his callused palm.

"Mister—*Diza* Hëk, I promise you we're not involved with the cult! We heard about your mother, about the time she got lost in the woods near the…the Ravine, someone said, about how she—"

Hëk swung his tool at Kalas' head, but the young man had anticipated the gesture. Nïmrïk crouched and Zhalera's hand flew to Valarandal's hilt, but before either could make another move, Kalas waved them off. Hëk's momentum cost him his balance: with his borrowed staff, Kalas applied the slightest touch against his shoulder. The farmer couldn't compensate in time: he started to fall, but Kalas pivoted around him and again redirected his trajectory; relieved him of his pickaxe as Hëk thudded into his chair.

"We're not *'ilpuzhritme-kavar,'*" Kalas said when the farmer looked up from his empty hands in disbelief. "but the person we're looking for is. We think. He's involved with the *ragus* somehow. It's our goal to put a stop to…well, whatever it is the Deathless Flame has planned.

"We've only just learned that the Blades are impassable, separated from the rest of Avëlöth by a ravine. *The* Ravine. We heard about what happened to your mother when you were a child, too…"

"Did you now?" said Hëk as his eyes narrowed.

"I—you have no reason to trust us, which you've already made clear, but my…friend and I would appreciate a chance to speak with your mother."

Both Hëk and Abarandal protested at the same time.

"Out of the question!" he spat.

Abarandal fired off a barrage of prestissimo notes requiring no interpretation.

"Mother's suffered the unkindness of Galámur's imbeciles for almost my entire life. You might be fast, boy—faster than me, but I'll run my pickaxe through your skull before I let you have your fun at her expense!"

"You misunderstand," Kalas sighed. He flipped Hëk's pickaxe and presented its handle to the farmer. "You don't need me to tell you this, but I will anyway: be thankful for your mother. Mine—my father, too—passed away not too long ago. Whatever's become of your mother—whatever happened to her at the foot of the Blades, at least you have her with you. C'mon, friends: looks like we'll be searching the forest by ourselves."

"Wait…"

Hëk led Kalas and the others through the dim interior of his home. An ancient home that seemed part of the earth, like it had sprouted from the Blades' foothills Sevens of Sevens ago. Though the place was unmistakably old, Hëk had done well keeping everything in order. He ushered them into a small room toward the back of the building, about as far from scrutiny as possible, Kalas guessed, and drew back a few inches of drapery. Faint streams of suns-light filtered through the rough, uneven glass and cast a fanciful combination of caustic networks and curved shadows across the profile of a seated, stationary figure.

"Mother?" Hëk cooed as he approached her and tucked a strand of gray-white hair behind her ear. Her unfocused eyes seemed to peer into the distance far beyond the walls, windows, and woods outside. She didn't flinch or react in any other way as he placed a large and gentle hand atop her tiny shoulder.

"Mother, some…visitors have come to see you! No! Not like… not like any of the others! I promised you, and I meant it! They— the boy, he lost his parents not too long ago. The girl, too. Young man and woman, really…

"I'll be honest: I don't know what they hope to learn from you. Sevens ago, all you wanted to talk about was fire and shadow and monsters in the dark. Now, seems you don't want to talk at all. I told them as much, but, well, here they are anyway."

"*Shâu…?*"

"Mohral," Hëk volunteered, his eyebrow raised.

"*Shâu* Mohral," Kalas continued, "thank you for your time. I—we—we just wonder what you can tell us about Glass Sword Mountain. We've been told it's somewhere high beyond the *Tsikme.* Beyond…the Ravine…"

Mohral turned toward Kalas when he said "Ravine." A light—a fire of sorts—danced across her eyes as they focused on his expect-ant gaze. She opened her mouth, worked her jaw as though she intended to speak, but the only sound she made was a hollow sigh. Tears welled up within the corners of her pale brown eyes. She raised a weak hand to wipe them away and tried again to speak: this time, she managed a pained sob. Her arm collapsed upon her lap as she slumped forward.

"Mother?!" Hëk bellowed as he pushed Kalas away from Mohral.

"Mister Hëk, I'm sorry!" Kalas apologized.

The farmer ignored him for a minute while he examined his mother. Finding nothing amiss, he stepped back. Kalas sensed the man was moments from expelling the lot of them from his home. As Hëk took a breath and prepared his tirade, the young man in-terjected: "I know it's asking a lot, I do, but please: before you ask us to leave, I have a request. A small thing, really! I promise none of us will say another word to your mother. Not unless she says a word to us first!"

Flustered, Hëk, sputtered for a moment before he laughed and spilled bitter tears of his own.

"Mother hasn't said a word for Sevens! That croak you stole from her throat is the most vocal she's been in years! You want another minute with her? Why would I allow that?! You saw the pain in her face just now! What kind of son would I be if—"

"Not another word. I promise. And my promise is as good as yours."

"Is it now? All right then, I'll give you another minute: when I tell you it's time to go, it's time to go, and don't think for an *instant* I won't remind you with steel!"

He underscored his meaning with a wave of his pickaxe. Kalas nodded and approached Abarandal.

"I know, I know," he agreed when she whispered a few frail notes. "I don't have any idea what we'll find *inside,* either, but you saw that light in her eyes, right? She's in there, somewhere. I think we can find her. I think we *have* to find her! Will you help…like with Sàrush? Only not her *body:* her *mind?*"

Abarandal drew a deep breath. She regarded Kalas with a look of childlike fear—and trust—before she allowed him to guide her to Mohral's side. Kalas knelt and caressed the hand she'd tried to raise with his own. He closed his eyes.

It's dark *in here,* he acknowledged as he explored the immaterial substance of the elderly woman's scattered thoughts. *No wonder she can't communicate! This place is filled with snatches of her past—trees, rocks, lightning, and darkness! Wait! What was that?! A hot light running between all these…these* pieces, *preventing her from putting her thoughts together.*

I can see the edges of each wrecked memory…Some of them look like they might fit together! Like a living puzzle!

In the dark gulfs between fractured remembrance, Abarandal's song suffused the gaps with soft, healing light. Inside Mohral's broken thoughts, the illumination wrought by the *eru* suggested green tones, and Kalas wondered if such…*wavelengths,* if that was the right word, were Sharuyan's—Falthwën's—portion of the summoning song made manifest. The staff in his other hand hummed with hints of energy.

With Abarandal's help, Kalas willed the disparate fragments into place until he found two pieces that seemed to share an edge. He held them together, but when he sought other pieces, the former fell apart.

Abarandal! Help! he begged.

She sent a pulse of yellow fire that coruscated along the fragile seam, leaving thin marks in its wake as it welded the pieces together.

Ágazhëthu! That worked!

Kalas collected as many pieces as he could *see* and arranged them as best he could: Abarandal joined them together until Mohral's mind resumed some semblance of its prior wholeness. All the while, threads of angry electricity lashed at their efforts, and he suspected some other will had intruded upon her consciousness long ago. Together, he and the *eru* extinguished the disruptions as they assembled the shards of the old woman's mind.

As the honey-colored energy sizzling between each suture cooled, Mohral's thoughts, memories, and intimations of self turned opaque, obscuring her innermost being from Kalas' view. Abarandal suggested they'd done all they could: Kalas released his grip on the Song and let the swirl of colors, notes, and energy flit away, until his surroundings resolved into the comfortable interior of Hëk's home.

He blinked a few times and braced himself with Falthwën's staff until the curious shapes and shadows disappeared, then stepped back. The *eru* guided him toward Zhalera, who took his arm and wrapped it in her own. Mohral inhaled sharply and scanned the room, her once-distant gaze now focused.

"What did you…what just happened?" Hëk breathed.

"This isn't…The Blades! The door within the rocks! The fire—Oh! The *fire!*" Mohral exclaimed as she straightened in her seat.

"Mother?" the farmer whispered. "Mother…?"

"Hëk, *adathahal?* Is that you? No, no: my son is just a child! And you're not Ukan, though you do favor him. Tell me, sir: where is my son? my husband?"

"Mother, I—it's me! It *is* me! Hëk, your son! It's been…it's been years since you…went away, in your mind…"

"Hëk? My son? Then…it's true, isn't it? Everything I saw, everything that happened…"

The farmer nodded, and despite his imposing stature, he suddenly seemed so small, so fragile.

"Hëk!" Mohral exclaimed as she stood. She almost lost her balance, but her son was there: he caught her in his powerful arms.

"Mother!" he cried and held her against his heaving chest, taking pains not to crush her in his joy at her return. Turning toward Kalas—and Abarandal—he asked: "How did you…I don't understand! I—and I don't care! You've brought my mother back to me! Not even the Creator could do that!"

"You give us too much credit, Mister Hëk! Any…powers or abilities we possess are gifts *from* the Creator! You think you know his—"

"Hmmph. I still don't care!"

Kalas sighed and opened his mouth to protest when Nimrïk placed a hand on his shoulder and interrupted him: "Perhaps *Shâu* Mohral would be willing to share with us what she remembers about…what happened all those Sevens ago?"

"No! She's been *away* for too long!"

"Nonsense!" Mohral interjected. "I've been trapped inside my head for how many Sevens? I've tried to get out—to *come back*, maybe, but it wasn't until these young people showed up…

"I tried to share my story for Sevens! No one seemed interested in what I had to say—not even your father! Speaking of Ukan, where is he? No, it's been too long, hasn't it? You must be six or seven Sevens now, yes? Surely my husband has gone the way of all living things: returned to the soil…

"Anyway: after years of no one *listening*, I…stopped trying. It was easier that way. For a while, I forgot how to speak, I think. Maybe I just couldn't. As kind as these young people have been— and as grateful as I am for their…service, there are still *holes* in my recollection. No matter: if they have questions, I will provide what answers I can! Ask away, young man!"

4.

"It was darker in the forest than I thought it would be," Mohral began. "I was so focused on finding little Hëk—he *was* little, once!—that I didn't pay too much attention to where I was going. I got lost. Before you reach the Ravine, there's a slight dip in the foothills that lead to the Blades. I thought I was returning to the farm when I slipped on something and tumbled downhill, toward the edge. I remember taking hit after hit as I bounced over the ground. I remember my surprise when the next hit didn't come: I must have closed my eyes, because when I opened them again, I was falling into darkness, falling toward the bottom of the Ravine.

"I closed my eyes again, waiting for the inevitable, but instead of coming to a swift end, I landed on something…hard, but with some give. Here's where my memory gets sketchy: there was a jolt, and suddenly I was moving *sideways*, carried along by some fast-moving object. Something *huge!* Reminded me of some of the stories my great-great-grandmother used to tell about ancient creatures long forgotten…Whatever it was, I didn't have long to think about it: moments later, I tumbled from its scaly back and rolled into a door of sorts.

"A *door!* At the bottom of the Ravine! At first I thought it was just a natural opening. The mouth of a cave, maybe. But there were designs, and something…I can't quite describe it: *soft*, maybe? No, but that'll have to do: the *space* around this 'door' was…*soft*, somehow. Not the rocks: the *emptiness* between the rocks! I know how it sounds: numerous *Galámurrinme* made sure of that! How could *space* be *soft?* I have no idea! I just know that's the best way I can describe it! I'll admit I was dazed from my fall, but I know what I saw, what I felt. Thinking perhaps Hëk had gotten down here somehow, thinking maybe he was lost in this cave, I walked into the 'softness'…and immediately, everything went black. I thought it had been dark at the bottom of the Ravine: on the other side of this door, I learned the true definition of darkness.

"I couldn't see a thing. For a while, I wasn't convinced I could *feel* anything, either! The floor—not the ground: the floor!—was smooth. *Too* smooth. Every step echoed across what must have been a vast space. There was wind—just a little—and even though Avëlöth is at the northern edge of the land of living winter, for the first time in my life, I felt *cold*. In spirit as well as in flesh.

"I called out for Hëk: If *I* was scared, I couldn't imagine what he must be feeling! He never answered, of course, but right after I said his name, fire…*crackled* into being! At first, I was grateful for the heat and light, but my gratitude turned to horror when a towering shape chased away the shadows with its glow. A figure without substance, taller than a man and composed of living, hot-blue flame, stretched out a hand and said something—I don't remember what, I'm sorry—as he touched my mind. His face was a mouth full of fangs, twisted horns sprouted from his forehead, and every last inch of him was *fire…*

"I think there might have been others in that place with us. I don't know. The next thing I remember is finding myself outside again. I must have climbed up from the Ravine—I don't know how, but I see glimpses of my bleeding hands and broken fingernails…I remember Ukan found me, but I blacked out as he carried me home. The next few days…or weeks or months, really, are a blur. Too many faces. Too many voices. I tried to tell everyone what I remembered, but no one believed me! It was so hard to hold my thoughts together. I think the kindest suggestion was that I must have hit my head on my way to the bottom of the Ravine. Most people just laughed and said I was too much like my great-great-grandmother. In a word, crazy…

"Not long after, I just…shut down, I guess. The Sevens came and went and I didn't even notice! All the while, there was lightning in my thoughts, a searing sensation that compelled my silence. I fought it at first, but after a time, it became too great a struggle: it was easier to sit and watch and keep quiet. Whatever you two did must have broken whatever power bound me. Thank you! I hope that answers your questions—at least in part!"

"Thank you, Mohral," Kalas bowed. "I could see a little—just a little!—of your thoughts while we were putting them back together, but not for long: I can't read minds—no one can, as far as I'm aware! I know it's been a long, long time, but do you think you'd remember where you were before you ended up in the Ravine? Do you think you'd be able to show us?"

"Out of the question!" Hëk roared as he pushed Kalas away from his mother again. "The farm has been the entirety of her life since Father discovered her in the forest all those Sevens ago, and—"

"—and it's time I saw the world beyond its borders again!" Mohral insisted. "Hëk, my son: it's precisely *because* I've been confined to this place for so long that I need to—"

"The farm? Sure. But the woods? the Ravine?! Mother, I can't allow it!"

"Are you going to restrain me, child?"

"I—what?! No! Of course not! I just mean—"

"I know you mean well, my son, but for the first time in ages, I'm in my right mind again. I've answered a few questions for these people, yes, but their gift deserves more than mere words!

"Now, the day is old, and it's a long walk back to town. Hëk, please prepare rooms for our guests. Tomorrow, when the second sun ascends above the Blades, we'll take them to the place they seek. Perhaps the earth will reveal more than I've been able to."

"I'll bet Shosafin would like to be here for that!" Kalas acknowledged. "Kadhëmba: you're...faster than the rest of us. Would you be willing to hunt down Shosafin and let him know what we've learned?"

The *egu,* still not used to the sound of his old name, paused for a moment before he nodded and disappeared within the lengthening shadows.

"Mother," Hëk said, his tone subdued, "I...I'm sorry for everything that's happened to you! I'm sorry I—"

"Enough, child! Let's not waste what years remain to us on might-have-beens!"

"Of course, Mother. Of course. Kalas, yes? Right this way..."

Mohral seemed like a different woman as she moved about her kitchen in the morning. Kalas' stare elicited a chuckle from Hëk as he bit into a crusty slice of bread.

"Twice a day, I'd guide her through the fields, explain to her what was taking place throughout the year. I never knew if she understood what was going on, but she's always been fond of the outdoors. Seemed wrong to leave her trapped inside all the time. In fact, yesterday, when you showed up, we'd just finished our afternoon walk.

"I'm…I could have treated you—your gift to Mother—with greater kindness. I'm sorry."

"If it were my mother…" Kalas nodded. He never finished his thought; instead, he shook his head and ate another forkful of eggs. "You thought we were *ilpuzhritme-kavar* when we first showed up. Have cultists been coming around here lately?"

"A few," Hëk said. "Even a few's too many. Most of 'em are on their way to the Mountain, same as you—that's why I thought you were with the cult. The first bunch seemed interested in Mother's story—and they were, but for all the wrong reasons. Don't get me wrong: if they want to waste their days worshiping a walking fire, let 'em! When Mother couldn't answer their questions—you saw her condition—they got huffy. Belligerent. Started calling down curses on her! I tossed 'em out…beat a couple of 'em pretty bad: seemed like they wouldn't listen otherwise!"

"Calling down curses?" Zhalera repeated. "Before coming to Avëlöth, we discovered an old…acquaintance in Melash. We…had a conversation with him, but before he could tell us much about the Deathless Flame, he started burning—from the *inside!*—and when he was gone, marks like those on your gate were burned into his chest!"

"Is that so?" Hëk remarked, neither surprised nor concerned. "Seems to me those chasers' curses were just words."

"I wonder why your mother didn't, well, why she was just trapped inside her own mind instead of…something worse." Kalas mused. "Maybe she doesn't know anything concrete, like Hwan-zho—our 'acquaintance'—did? Or maybe she was left in that state as a warning to anyone curious about the Ravine?"

"Then there must be *something* at the bottom of the Ravine," Zhalera agreed.

"A door," Mohral insisted as she cleared the table, "where space is *soft.* Looks like everyone's finished here, *hish?* I'll show you what I remember—maybe a starting place will suffice?"

"It's more than we had before we met! We're grateful for your help. And for your bravery!"

"And *I'm* grateful for a chance to prove—after all these Sevens—that I'm *not* crazy! Come! Follow me!"

5.

"Do you think Nïmrïk and Shosafin will be able to find us?" Zhalera wondered as Mohral and Hëk led them through the woods behind the farmhouse, over several subtle inclines, and toward a gradual downhill slope. The trees here, a thick mix of various species, formed a narrow, natural trail across the terrain's inconstant contours.

"If Kadhëmba can find Shosafin, I'm sure, together, they'll be able to find us! I would have preferred waiting for him—I know how much he's been waiting for this, but were our positions reversed…He'll understand. I hope…"

A few hours later, Mohral advised everyone to watch his step and pointed at a rotted wooden bridgehead. Its supports had succumbed to the ravages of time: only a handful of planks remained, jutting a few feet over the yawning expanse; the rest had collapsed into the Ravine's murky depths.

"I think this is it," she said, uncertainty coloring her voice. "I wish I could be sure, but I'll admit I'm not. I *think* I remember that bridge—looked about the same, even Sevens ago—but I don't know. There was *a* bridge nearby, at least: I thought Hëk might have tested his courage against such a thing: he was always a brave—if sometimes foolish—young man!"

Hëk's already suns- and windburned cheeks darkened. Zhalera stifled a giggle and thanked Mohral for her help: "This is more than we could have accomplished on our own! Now we just need to find a way down. These walls are *steep!*"

"They're no steeper than the cliffs under Kësharan," Kalas added as he leaned over the chasm's rim. He stepped back before a sudden wash of vertigo upset his balance. "Oh, right: you've never been that way, have you? Of course, there was a trail—not *much* of a trail, but a trail nonetheless!—cut into the rocks behind Kësharan.

"I wonder, though…Mohral: you saw a door down there, at the bottom of the Ravine, right? You're sure it wasn't just some rectangular rocks that might have fallen just so? No, I'm not doubting you! I just…well, if someone built a door down there, then they must have built a way to reach it, right?"

"There was nothing natural about it, child! *Super*natural, maybe, but neither nature nor human hands created that…that *portal!*"

"All right. Let's look around: maybe we'll find something by the time Kadhëmba and Shosafin get here?"

"I don't know if it's really a path, but I think we might be able to climb down over here," Zhalera said after searching the area for almost an hour and a half. She'd lowered herself onto a slight ledge—no more than an inch or two of cloven rock—and called out to Kalas and the others. "There's a bunch of 'steps' like this, it looks like. I don't know: I can't see all the way down—too foggy, but this is the closest we've seen since we've been out here!"

I was sure Kadhëmba would've returned with Shosafin by now, Kalas frowned. *No matter, I guess. They'll get here when they get here…*

He nodded at Zhalera and followed her onto the almost imperceptible ledges. Abarandal followed him without hesitation: the way she moved, Kalas wouldn't have been surprised had she turned ninety degrees and simply *walked* down the sides of the Ravine.

Mohral clung to Hëk's massive hand as she watched them go. She expressed one desire to follow them, to see for herself the door and the "soft" space beyond; she expressed another to return to the familiar confines of her farm, where great beasts and fire-clad figures were naught but stories conjured by her great-great-grandmother. The latter desire won the day.

"I thought I could do it. I thought I could come back here and, well, I don't know. I'm older than I was, unable—unwilling, at least!—to brave the Ravine a second time! Please: take care of yourselves! Be safe—as safe as you can, given your circumstances! I hope you find what you're looking for!"

"Kalas, Abarandal: thank you again for returning my mother to me! I never thought I'd know her this way again," Hëk said, gazing at them through misty eyes.

"Don't thank me: thank the Creator!" Kalas nodded before his head dipped below the chasm's edge. "And please, If it's not too much trouble: if Kadhëmba—the surly old man from before—comes looking for us, will you point him in our direction?"

"We can do that," Mohral promised while Hëk rolled his eyes at Kalas' mention of the Creator. The old woman squeezed her son's fist: when she had his attention, she nodded toward the three figures perched at the rim of the Ravine.

"Uh, yeah, all right, sure," the farmer agreed.

After navigating carefully selected hand- and footholds for about an hour, Kalas looked up at the thin white smear of sky snaking overhead. He panted, craned his neck to wipe his dripping forehead against his shoulder, and called out to Zhalera, about twenty feet below: "Any sign of the bottom? We must be a mile down by now!"

"It's almost pitch black in this Ravine!" she protested. "I can barely see my own fingers! If we don't reach the bottom soon, what should we do?"

"Keep going!"

"I knew you'd say that, but seriously: my fingers are getting tired. Cramped. It won't be long before I can't trust my grip. And…I don't know if you can hear it up there, but my stomach's been rumbling for a while now! Seems like all this climbing's already burned through breakfast! Without a break, getting topside's going to be difficult!"

"Let's try to make it a little farther. If we don't reach—"

"We're here!" Zhalera interrupted. "There are designs carved into *smooth* walls that widen out: about ten or twelve feet beneath that, there's a *floor*. There are a few rocks here and there, some tree branches, it looks like—and part of that bridge!—but there's no way this *floor* could have happened on its own! Look: even though the mouth of the Ravine curves away a few hundred feet above us, you can still see suns-light reflecting from the floor's surface!"

"Mohral must have been right about this place," Kalas allowed as Abarandal helped him descend the decorated walls: some of the reliefs provided just enough purchase for his hands and feet. He unslung Falthwën's staff from his shoulder and tapped the ground with its heel. A curious ringing echoed through the corridor. "Let's see if she was right about this *door* she described…"

After a few minutes of walking, silent except for the subtle sound of their footsteps on polished bedrock, Zhalera cried out: "Ugh! What is that *smell?!*"

"It's…there's something familiar about it," Kalas said as the odor lodged in his nostrils.

"It's not like that stuff leaking from the *vàsume*," Zhalera clarified: "it's, well, it's gross, but it's a different *kind* of gross!"

"*Lady!*" Kalas blurted.

"Lady?"

"The dragon under Deridzhas! This reek reminds me of the cavern where Nïmrïk and I found her. Not quite as nasty down here, but similar. Mohral said her great-great-grandmother told stories about a 'great beast,' didn't she? Nïmrïk thought they'd all disappeared from the earth until we found Lady; and that old man who pointed us toward Hëk's farm, he said something about a shadow that blotted out the suns. What if they're describing a *gròma?* What if one of them has been living beneath the Ravine—like how Lady was living under Deridzhas—for thousands of Sevens?!"

"Are we in trouble?" Zhalera gasped at the thought. Even in the semidarkness, Kalas watched as she whipped her head from side to side in search of such a creature.

"I…I don't know. The eaters had tortured Lady, so she was a little…ornery. If there *is* a dragon down here, I think we'd do well to be careful. That's a big *if,* though…I'm not sure how one could've gotten down here anyway: these walls are pretty close together, and the Ravine's too narrow."

"Maybe, but what if whatever's down here has been down here since it was *little.* Smaller, at least? Or what if it smashed its way underground for some reason—Lady ripped her way out of the mines, remember? Or maybe these walls aren't as close together as they seem?"

"I hadn't…yeah, that could be…Well, we'll just have to be careful," he repeated as his flushed cheeks surrendered their color to Zhalera's horrific idea. A slow shadow passed overhead, punctuating their fractured understanding of their circumstances.

"Uh, c'mon! Let's find that door!"

Kalas hadn't been paying attention when he bumped into Abarandal, who'd stopped moving through the twisting route.

"Oh! Sorry!" he apologized as he brushed her shoulder. "It's hard to see down here. Something wrong? Why'd you stop?"

For roughly half an hour after reaching the ground, the three had explored the Ravine. Some of the elaborately designed walls had sheared away from the cliffs, collecting on the floor in ragged heaps and exposing rough, undressed rock underneath. The inconstant shadow lurking in the space above them seemed closer, the malodorous air a touch thicker. The *eruín* whispered a few tremulous notes, raised a shaking hand, and pointed toward a subtle bluish glow coming from a bend in their path. Kalas stepped in front of her and traced the aura to its source.

A door between two unadorned columns, capped with a heavy, squared lintel, yawned into a separate void within the Ravine. Half-light flickered at the aperture's periphery; darkness consumed its center. Kalas reached toward the space: he stopped himself when he remembered the machine? device? construct? deep within the Pump. Instead, he picked up a rock and tossed it into the opening. It seemed to hover, suspended for a moment, before rings of white-blue light rippled from its impact.

The rock was gone.

"Soft?" Kalas wondered.

"This must be the place. How did Mohral ever find it?" Zhalera wondered.

"Maybe she didn't," Kalas postulated. "Maybe someone—something—found her..."

"Kalas, I don't like this," Zhalera shivered. Abarandal agreed.

"Me neither," he admitted. "We have a little time, I suppose. We can wait: maybe Kadhëmba will bring Shosafin soon? Maybe they'll have a better idea what's in store for us?"

While he spoke, the lingering tang that had haunted their travels all along the Ravine intensified. Pebbles cascaded from above. The shadows deepened and a growl, a hiss interrupted the heavy stillness.

"Kalas?"

A massive, claw-tipped forelimb pawed the air as the dragon struck at them. It missed by mere inches, the wind of its swipe upsetting Abarandal's sparkling hair. Larger rocks gave way as it repositioned itself for another blow.

"Lady was big: this thing looks bigger still!" Kalas warned. "It won't be long before it reaches us! Kadhëmba said they're usually peaceful unless threatened: I don't know how *we* could've threatened *that*, but I don't think now's a good time to ask it! I don't think we have a choice: it's the soft space on the other side of that door or the claws of this great beast!"

Abarandal screamed a song at him, her fear almost tangible in her notes.

"I know! I know! I don't trust this place either, but we're trapped: if we stay where we are, we're doomed; at least there's the possibility of safety on the other side of that door!"

"He's right, my sister," Zhalera pleaded. "None of us likes our options, but he's right. Come on: hold my hand! I'll try to be brave for both of us!"

The great beast snorted fire and filled the chasm with greasy smoke. The tawny-eyed blacksmith grabbed one of the frightened stargirl's trembling hands. Kalas grabbed the other. With a gruff nod, he led Zhalera and Abarandal across a film of stinging steel-blue light and into abject darkness.

PART II.

Chapter XI.

Opposite Another Vault

"I can't see!" Zhalera gasped, her voice echoing throughout the curious, somehow familiar space. Every vestige of suns-light filtered through the fog at the bottom of the Ravine was gone. Not even the buzzing rime of blue light hovering atop the film through which they'd passed offered any illumination: it too was gone. "And it's *cold* in here!"

Kalas nodded—and laughed when he realized she'd never see the gesture in the lightless room. "Yeah, I can't—The door! It's gone!" he shouted at the darkness. Abarandal breathed a few low phrases, the tremolo in her minor chords a clear summation of their shared apprehension.

"I don't know," he replied, "but Mohral got out: there's got to be an exit somewhere."

"Kalas, it's pitch black down here! If we start wandering around blind, who knows what dangers we might run into?!"

"True, but we can't—"

"We can't just stand around, either. You're right. If we take slow, small steps, maybe we'll find a wall—or a light, or a door…"

Abarandal sang a new song, a subtly brighter melody, and even though no one could see him, Kalas' cheeks reddened at her question.

"Falthwën—I wish you could have known him! He conjured

light and fire from this staff, yes, but I can't! I've…I've tried. A couple of times. Kadhëmba said it didn't work that way."

The *eru* fumbled in the dark for Kalas. Finding his arm, she groped her way toward his hands and the twisted staff gripped therein. After a brief squeeze, she whispered a few more notes, traversed his arm and shoulder with her fingers, and caressed his cheek.

"I wondered!" he admitted.

"Wondered what?" Zhalera demanded.

"Inside Mohral's mind…it's hard to put into words, but when we were putting her thoughts back together, part of The Song Abarandal sang reminded me of Falthwën. I saw it as threads of green energy; when she fused the broken pieces together, I thought about the light that runs across your sword sometimes, and even though none of us has ever met her, I thought about Valaran, too.

"I've been trying to remember the shapes Falthwën used. Even back in Lohwàlar, at the Sanctuary, he traced it in the goop he made for Ëlbodh. When he brought the mountain down over that artifact in the Empty Sea, he traced it in the air. And again in Deridzhas, he made the same shapes. Remember?"

"Yes, actually, now that you mention it!"

"I don't think the shapes themselves have any special power—he always described his abilities as *privilege*, but maybe there's *something* about them. Professor Tomush wouldn't stop drawing Valaran's symbol, either, and Captain Dzholëf, he had a symbol—Sifuran's symbol, I think—tattooed across his back. Not like Tsharak's markings: the captain's was just an ordinary tattoo, I think. Ever since the Vault, I've been noticing those symbols more and more."

"Why don't you try again?" Zhalera suggested. "Nïmrïk said Falthwën's staff didn't work if he hadn't granted its user permission. *Privilege*, if you prefer. It could have never been anything except a piece of wood in Hwanzho's hands, but in yours…?"

"That's a nice thought, but I've *been* trying to…do something with it ever since we recovered it! Seems like it's nothing but a piece of wood in my hands, either!"

Abarandal sang a few bars of encouragement: she agreed with Zhalera.

"Why not?" Kalas muttered as he closed his eyes. He laughed at himself: *Why did I do that? It's already dark!* He focused on the cleric's thin silver instrument in his alcove, on the air above the rock he infused with explosive magic outside the artifact, and on Falthwën's—*Sharuyan's* last exertion against the *ekume,* until he recalled the lines and curves of his departed friend's sigil:

Fan kal nir! he thought against the darkness.

A punch of white-green radiance erupted from the tip of Falthwën's staff, hung suspended in space above them, and exploded in a wash of non-localized illumination.

"Too much!" Zhalera exclaimed as she shielded her eyes.

"Sorry!"

Kalas willed the light to recede—just a little—until his and Zhalera's vision adjusted to the sudden influx of radiance. Abarandal's eyesight, it seemed, required no adjustment.

"Why didn't it work before?" he wondered aloud.

"Maybe time and place matter?" Zhalera suggested. "On the way to İsriba, where Falthwën said something about such things.

And even Professor Tomush said Glass Sword Mountain was a place of power."

"You're right," Kalas remembered. "Then maybe the door we passed through brought us all the way under the Mountain? But from outside, it looked like we had miles to go before we reached the Blades' peaks…"

"Nashmur wondered why no one had ever found the Vault under Ïsriba: Falthwën said it wasn't *exactly* beneath it. Maybe something similar happened here? Maybe that's why the door just disappeared? Of course, it doesn't explain how the door got there in the first place, but I'm just throwing things out…"

"That…makes sense," he admitted, his brow furrowed. "Doesn't explain how we got *here,* of all places, but one thing at a time! Next question: *what* is this place?!"

Kalas stepped across the gleaming floor, shivering as whispered winds wheeled throughout the room. The others followed, and soon, they reached a faceted wall cut from a curious substance, veined and sparkling like a slab of polished granite. Following its contours, they came to another, similar wall.

"Is there something familiar about this place to either of you?" he asked as he stepped back. He willed the light to rise, to reach high above them and reveal the wider room's secrets, but his eyes proved unequal to the task. Before his friends could answer him, he stumbled over something interrupting the floor's otherwise unbroken smoothness.

"It's like the Vault!" Zhalera marveled. "It's—Kalas, are you all right?"

He picked himself off the ground and examined its discontinuity: despite lacking red gems, the shape suggested Yayan's symbol. Kalas followed a line extending from its boundary and discovered Heshradan's symbol, likewise devoid of precious stones.

"It…I think it *is* some kind of Vault!" Kalas said. Abarandal harmonized her agreement. "Falthwën said there were others, that the one beneath Ïsriba wasn't the only Vault. This one looks… abandoned, I guess. There's no dust here, but I don't think this place exists in the same way the rest of the world exists! I'll bet these symbols used to be filled with jewels…but how could someone—"

"Quiet!" Zhalera hissed as she drew her sword. Bright, white-yellow ribbons writhed along its surface. She herded them toward the opening and explained: "I thought I heard something! Voices, maybe! This way! C'mon!"

2.

"Voices?" Kalas wondered. "Down here? If this is a Vault—and I'm pretty sure it is!—then the voices must belong to *erume*, right?"

Abarandal suggested otherwise.

"You're right," he acknowledged: "Mohral found her way down here. So did we, for that matter! I guess those voices could be from anyone. Or anything…"

"Quiet!" Zhalera repeated as she led them across the Vault. A short distance from the symbols, they reached a door cut within one of the faceted walls. "I don't remember anything like this under Ïsriba," she added.

"Yeah, there weren't *any* doors in that place, but you saw all the stuff we had to climb over to get here: maybe this Vault is, I don't know, 'broken,' somehow?" he whispered.

"You're asking *me?!*"

Down a long, dark corridor, Kalas and Abarandal followed Zhalera, Falthwën's staff throwing shadows at the walls as they searched for the voices' source. The passageway's acoustics played tricks on their ears: one moment, Kalas was sure they were right on top of it; the next, the indiscernible conversation seemed impossibly distant.

We could end up walking right into whoever—whatever!—is down here...

He voiced his concern aloud and willed his staff to dim. Zhalera confessed she had no idea how or why her weapon sometimes glowed, sometimes blazed: sheathing it seemed the only way to blunt its gleam.

"I just hope I'll be able to draw it fast enough. *If* such a thing becomes necessary," she sighed as she returned it to its scabbard. Even then, subtle yellow light seeped from its hilt.

"Feels like we've been walking for quite a while," Kalas said. He figured it had been about an hour, maybe less, since they'd discovered the Vault. "If we weren't under Glass Sword Mountain before, I'll bet we're close now!"

Abarandal stopped short, mumbled a few breathless phrases, and clutched Kalas' arm.

"Darkness?" he repeated. "You're not talking about a simple absence of light, are you?"

"You must be right," Zhalera agreed: "we must be close now. To what, I don't know, but I feel it, too: an *unpleasantness* all around me. And I think the voices are getting louder! I think—"

She stumbled over something, stifled a cry as she braced herself against the wall, and instructed Kalas to play his staff across the ground. He did, and its soft green glow revealed a pristine sword with peculiar contours and glittering edges.

There's something familiar about this! Have I seen it before? No, that's impossible! Isn't it?

He knelt, brushed away a light rime of dust, and picked up the weapon.

"Ouch!" Zhalera jumped. Despite Kalas' concern, she unsheathed Valarandal and held it away from her body. "It's hot again! Hot and...excited? Anxious? I don't know!"

The sword in Kalas' hand responded, jagged orange slashes erupting along its length.

"I've—we've seen this before," he muttered. "It's hot, too, and… *angry?!*"

Abarandal had no idea what he meant: Zhalera, after another glance at Valarandal, suggested, "The Vault under İsriba! Peradan!"

"No, he had a spear," Kalas insisted. "I remember he—No, you're right! When he *first* arrived, he *did* have a sword! *This* sword! He said he lost it battling *ekume*. The *erume* never told us where they went nor what they were doing in the moments before they summoned Abarandal, but Yayan and Peradan ran into dark stars. I figured they were just trying to make sure nothing interrupted them. Is it possible *this* is the place where the *ekume* almost got Peradan?"

"Then wouldn't there be a *singularity* around here somewhere?"

"I…maybe? I don't even know what a *singularity* is, much less what one might look like!"

"Well, we should be careful. Doubly so," Zhalera decided. "C'mon!"

Before they took their next steps, Abarandal cried out. Kalas turned toward her, Peradan's sword still in hand.

"Abarandal? What's wrong?"

She said—sang—nothing, but her eyes remained fixed on the angry orange blade wavering in the air. Kalas followed her gaze.

"This sword?"

She risked a few pianissimo notes.

"It's been…touched by darkness? Oh! Of course! Peradan lost it in a fight with *ekume.* Hey, I remember now: under İsriba, you said the same thing about *him.* Is that it? Is that the darkness you're talking about?"

"Kalas," Zhalera interrupted, "under İsriba, when the *ekume* appeared: Sifuran suggested the Swath had been betrayed. Before that, when he and the others disappeared, neither he nor Heshra-dan encountered anything. Like you just said, though, Peradan was almost captured. What if…what if Peradan *wasn't* fighting an *eku* when he lost the sword you're now holding?"

"Zhalera, what are you saying?"

"The fire that killed Hwanzho had a bright blue tint to it. The magic between the Ravine and this Vault glowed blue, too. And then there's the cultists' robes. Haven't you noticed? Falthwën—Sharuyan, whenever he'd use that staff, we'd see green. Same thing with the lightning he rained down on Lohwàlar. Loradan, when she *kalswàra* us out of the dungeon and into the Vault, everything was violet. And from the first time Falthwën did that thing with my sword—infused with Valaran's essence—it glowed yellow. Every *eru* of the Swath has a color. I don't think it's a coincidence that everything associated with the *Ragus pïn Tshaggul Kavar* is blue."

Kalas said nothing while he stared at the waves of heat rolling from the sword they'd discovered. He grit his teeth and tried to piece things together in his thoughts: "I've said it before: Sifuran *did* seem a little too eager when the Swath summoned Abarandal, but I figured it was because of what they *didn't* do when they had the chance before the world was cracked…

"But that doesn't explain why he would have attacked Peradan *before* beginning the summoning: without the entire Swath, they wouldn't have been able to call her out of the heavens: they barely managed without Valaran, and even that would have failed if you hadn't—

"Oh no! Peradan said Valaran sacrificed herself to save him from a singularity. He was wrong—we think—but maybe Sifuran only *pretended* to be excited about Abarandal? What if he thought getting rid of Valaran would have been enough to corrupt the calling? But Professor Tomush, someone devoted to Valaran, introduced us to Captain Dzholëf, someone with Sifuran's symbol tattooed across his back! Why would the professor—no friend of the cult—set us up with someone devoted to Sifuran? Remember how he felt about Professor Rahwi?"

"What if the captain tricked the professor?" Zhalera suggested. "Or what if he's not part of the cult, just a devotee who doesn't know Sifuran's darker identity? His *is* the *guilt* of water, among other things, right?"

A cloud of concentration hovered above the *erudas* face while Kalas and Zhalera propounded their theories. Before Abarandal could say anything, Kalas remembered: "Rül! Pava! Nashmur! The *Lord of Winds'* sails had Sifuran's symbol painted on them! Maybe it's like you said: maybe it's just because, y'know, it's a boat, but what if it's not? Nashmur didn't like the looks of Bayal, the *Winds'* first mate, but I thought there was something…I don't know how to describe it: there was something *off* about him, but in a *good way!* Nashmur wanted to walk away, but I convinced him not to! What if I was wrong? What if something happened to them? What if that's why they haven't reached Galámur?!"

Abarandal shook her head and opened her mouth, but Zhalera spoke first: "Kalas, it's not your fault! There's no way you could have known!"

"We have to get out of here! We have to find Shosafin! Kadhëmba! Maybe even Nanësra, somehow! We—"

The *eruín* latched onto Kalas' arm—the one in which he cradled Falthwën's staff—and spat a flurry of frenzied notes at him. She shook her head, but her music was too fast to parse.

"Abarandal, slow down! What are you saying?! *Who's* not—?"

Rough hands reached out of the darkness and grabbed Kalas and the others. Despite the muddy mix of orange, yellow, and green illumination, he recognized the all-too-familiar shade of blue in the hem of their assailants' robes before someone tied a coarse sack around his head.

3.

"Where are you taking us?!" Zhalera demanded, her voice muffled. Kalas assumed she couldn't see their surroundings either. He tried to count his steps, to keep some approximation of the distance they'd covered, but every push, every shove made it almost impossible. It felt like the path's slope descended toward the heart of the Mountain, where the air abandoned its chill as an unnatural warmth encroached.

"*Dâethëthe!*" one of the cultists roared. Zhalera yelped when someone slapped her, and Kalas' blood surged with heat that had nothing to do with the corridor's rising temperature. He stopped: when one of their captors collided with him, he drove his elbow back as hard as he could. He stifled a laugh when he connected with what felt like someone's abdomen: he grunted when, presumably, that same someone struck him on the nape with a blunt instrument and kicked him toward an unknown destination.

"Do that again! C'mon!" someone with a reedy, singsong voice wheezed.

"Enough!" another insisted. "The *Iltshâdunas* has designs on them! Let's stop wasting time before *we* end up burning from the inside out!"

Another half an hour later (or maybe an hour: it was hard to tell), a cultist ordered Kalas to stop. They'd descended a series of stairs, arranged in what felt like a wide spiral, and exited onto a smooth, flat plane. Not long after the last step, a din of murmured voices and muted whispers corrupted the cavern's stillness. He couldn't discern specific words or phrases: neither could he escape the taint of malign triumph rising up around them.

Every snatch of conversation ceased when a blue-white flare exploded across the space. He squinted and tried to look away: not even the sack still covering Kalas' eyes provided adequate protection. A repeated rustling spread out around him: after a moment, he suspected the cultists were prostrating themselves in the presence of the Deathless Flame.

"Well done, my children!" he boomed, his voice a grating mix of ill-matched frequencies. Kalas struggled to remain standing against the physical pressure waves the entity's presence projected. He bristled, braced himself, and hoped Zhalera and Abarandal held their ground, too. More than mere speech, the Deathless Flame suffused his words with dread and power, and despite his strength of will, Kalas' legs threatened to give way.

Pretending his courage was not, in fact, fast departing, Kalas insisted: "You can't win, *Sifuran!* The rest of the Swath will stop you! And I'll never—"

Someone jabbed at the back of his knees with the flat of a blade, and Kalas fell. That same whiny, almost musical voice from before raged, "You will not speak thus to the *Tshaggul Kavar!*"

Kalas stood. Discovering his hands weren't bound, he undid the cord around his neck and whipped away the sack. The ladies—still standing—weren't too far away, but Kalas' attention gravitated toward the gaunt figure aiming Peradan's sword at his chest. The young man raised his arms and hoped he'd be able to protect himself with what little hand-to-hand training Shosafin had taught him. The cultist raised his sword, but before he struck, familiar white-blue fire erupted from his eyes, his mouth, his chest, and he dropped the weapon. As fire consumed him from within, his last expression hardened in uncomprehending surprise.

"None shall touch them!" the Deathless Flame commanded his worshipers. "Not unless I give the *explicit* word! Presume to know my will and perish!"

No one moved. No one except Kalas, who turned to face the source of the harsh light and harsher voice.

The Deathless Flame, perhaps fifty, maybe sixty feet away,

towered above a waterless sea of prostrate blue. Standing almost thirty feet tall, his horned head nearly reached the chamber's ceiling. Searing fire and sinuous lightning snaked across his frame, twining up from around his feet, slithering across his consummate physique, and undulating in mirrored electric spirals across his head and shoulders. One hand remained outstretched: a warning, perhaps; the other held what Kalas presumed was a weapon, though its features remained wreathed in flame.

Is that a sword? a spear? an axe?

The living conflagration raised his arm, then brought it down in a sharp slice, and the ocean of adherents parted: between their groveling shapes, he approached Kalas and—

No, he's headed for Abarandal!

The young man *thought* a warning at the *eruín* and hoped she'd understand. She did, and quickly removed her sack. He risked tapping Zhalera on the shoulder, and she, too, pulled the item from her head. She glanced around the room, hoping—without success—for a glimpse of Valarandal.

"Yělò ar shus, Kathin Kelësh!" said the Deathless Flame as he stooped and cupped Abarandal's chin in his smoldering grip. She tried to be brave, Kalas could tell, but shreds of fear belied her pretended courage.

'Again'? Then he must *be one of the Swath…*

If his flames burned her, she gave no indication; instead, she held his gaze—and her silence. The sparks and fire leaping across his fingers—his entire arm—sputtered, acquired an orange tint, and disappeared for a moment before new flames took their place. The *Tshaggul Kavar* snatched his hand away and stared at it, taken aback, it seemed, by the consequence of contact with Abarandal.

He wasn't expecting that! Kalas observed. *Still, I need to watch myself: just because he wants* her *alive doesn't mean he won't boil my intestines where I stand!*

The object in his other hand seemed to flicker, and Kalas suspected he'd seen it before. He decided it wasn't a sword; rather, it was longer: a pole weapon, perhaps. He tried to remember the battle under Ïsriba, to picture the weapon the sapphire *eru* wielded against his allies as a part of his great deception.

Sifuran had a sword—no, he had two *swords. Short swords. Not a…a spear? a pike? And one of the* ekume *would have* unmade *Sifuran if Nïmrïk hadn't stopped it…*

"No: *not* Sifuran," he said aloud, and the Deathless Flame whirled on him. Abarandal nodded and sang a different name.

"*Peradan?!*" Kalas repeated with a shout. "*That's* why Abarandal drew back when you touched her! Not because you were *fighting* darkness: because you're *serving* darkness!"

Orange lightning chased away the blue fires shrouding the massive figure with a violent surge. He smiled, revealing a mouth full of needle-sharp fangs. The nearest cultists risked a glance in Kalas' direction: Peradan consumed them in his twisted wrath. As their bodies burned and filled the chamber with the fetor of charring flesh, time *stopped*.

Confused, Kalas looked around at the fires frozen in midair, at the unchanging expressions of pain and surprise on the faces of the Deathless Flame's victims. Behind him, Zhalera and Abarandal remained standing and unmoving. A peculiar light—a *half-light*—bloomed within the room, and Kalas allowed himself a moment to appreciate the architecture's intricate design, its detailed friezes and reliefs.

A sanctuary? A shrine? A…temple?

"Welcome to the *kalthesh*, young Cursebreaker!" Peradan said as the fires surrounding him burned away and he assumed human-like proportions. His spear—the same one from under the Vault at Ïsriba—cut the half-light with a wicked gleam as he aimed its tip at Kalas.

"We're in between moments: the world around us is *paused*, you might say, but you've been here before, haven't you? Oh, not *here*, not in this nasty *cave!* You've traveled the light-realm before! Yes, now I recognize your vibration—your *frequency.* I'm surprised I—"

"Loradan! Where is she? Where are the others? What did you do to Valaran?! If you—"

Peradan tweaked his spear. That's all it looked like to Kalas, but sudden fire gnawed at the flesh beneath his ribs. Wincing, he risked a glance at his abdomen and saw a fresh, cauterized gash.

"How noble! Or perhaps merely unimaginative?" he mocked the young man with another flick of his weapon. "Whatever Loradan did to you affected the rest of us, too: truthfully, I have no idea where they are—no thanks to the *ekume* I charged with breaching the Vault! Those fools have never been the brightest stars in the sky—if you'll forgive the pun!—but it's not like I could reveal my designs to the *erume!* Nor the *egume!* Why, they're no better than the *elume!* Arrogant dotards, every last one of them, prowling the cosmos like they're *better* than us. Better than *me!* For thousands of Sevens, we've been looked down upon as the heavens' servant caste. No more! Now that I possess the starchild, I will rise above my pretentious 'betters' and demonstrate the superiority of *my* will! *my* power!"

"Why on earth would you do this?" Kalas asked, impotent against the raving *eru.* "When Ilnëshras rebelled, the world almost fell apart! Would you risk another cataclysm?!"

"'*Why on earth?!*' Listen to yourself! You think I care about this worthless planet?! Child, I am a *star!* Thousands of times as grave as this pathetic ball of filth you call home! You and your kind possess less significance than motes of dust obliterated by my solar wind! It's bad enough I've been tasked with overseeing your well-being. Once, your kind esteemed us as minor deities; today, too few *edhume* recognize their insignificance when measured against our ageless, inestimable might! Too few among the *ilalasdrame* recognize the magnitude of their dire need for us! Soon, *edhunàm* will understand its place—its low, low place—in the hierarchy of creation! Soon, even *elunàm* will understand the error of its presumption!"

"Valaran sacrificed herself so you could escape an *eku* singularity, and you—"

Peradan laughed. "Haven't you figured it out?! Valaran sacrificed nothing! We've carried out our shared duties across more aeons than you could possibly comprehend: when I explained our designs to her, she intended to reveal my 'faithless blasphemy' to the others. As much as I loved her—and I did love her, you know—I couldn't allow her to interfere. A singularity seemed the most...*humane* means of disposing of her. After that, I knew I had to take pains to disguise myself among you humans. Under Ïsriba, you saw how Sifuran seemed most anxious to begin the ritual? He's always been headstrong. Cocksure. That's why I chose his color for the *Tshaggul Kavardas* flames. It seemed like the perfect ruse..."

"How could you do such a thing?! How could you betray the— wait: you said *our designs:* how long have you been working with Marugan?" Kalas asked as he tried to fathom the extent of Peradan's maniacal treachery.

"Marugan!" Peradan spat. "We were friends. Once. That all changed when his faction sided with Ilnëshras and everything fell apart. He thinks he can rise above his station: he thinks he *needs* to transcend his created state, to surpass what he perceives as his *nimeru* limitations. He's wrong, of course: *erunàm* is no less—"

"Is such a thing even possible?" Kalas wondered despite his circumstance. "It is, isn't it?! Might be, at least! Falthwën said something about—" His interruption invited another quick twist of Peradan's searing spear. Across his cheek this time.

"Why should it matter if it's *possible?!* It's *unnecessary!* He's attached his service to Tsathrâuda, Ilnëshras' chief lieutenant. Yes, *that* Tsathrâuda! The one who slew the *elu* prophet! He believes she possesses the power to 'elevate' his very nature! Again, he's wrong!

"Despite the differences and distrust between *erunàm* and *ekunàm*, both still exist within The Song. When Marugan learned of my designs on the 'great power,' he sought me out, invited me to cast my lot with them. I played along, curious to learn exactly *how* they intended to perform the impossible. Abarandal is *more* than just another *eru*, Kalas! We stars might have called her from out of time and space, but she surpasses all of us—even if she doesn't yet realize it herself! Tsathrâuda has convinced Marugan *she's* the key to unlocking his potential. She's convinced him that *eru*—even *edhu*—possess within them a divine spark, that apotheosis only requires the proper catalyst: Abarandal."

"Do you...do *you* believe that?" Kalas dared to ask.

"Utter nonsense! Tsathrâuda is simply appealing to his avaricious vanity: Marugan should know better! Then again, he *did* align himself with the Accursèd One...

"No, I'm quite content to remain *eru*. Haven't you been paying attention? There's no *need* to become other than what I already am, what I've always been! My goals are simpler. Attainable, even! All I want is the *respect* I'm entitled to! The respect and adulation *all erume* deserve from the children of men! The...attention of the Creator!

"You're confused. I'm not surprised. When Ilnëshras, a created being like the rest of us, declared himself a peer of the *Ilrunonòa*— the Uncaused—did the Creator crack the heavens? Did he wreck the firmament? *No!* Not even Nalun's death goaded him into action! Yet when your kind aspired to the very divinity Marugan is pursuing, he destroyed the world! For Sevens upon Sevens upon Sevens, I've tried to understand what makes *edhunàm* more worthy of his interest than *ilalasdranàm!*"

"You're right: I don't understand!" Kalas confessed. "I know the Creator 'cracked the world' in ages past. No one I've talked to knows—or cares to explain—exactly what that means, but you *must* know—better than I do—it was *not* a good thing! You're an *eru!* You were *there!* You said something about your duties: surely you've seen the horrors unleashed by the artifacts left over from before the world was cracked?! It sounds like you're frustrated that Ilun didn't...what, crack the *heavens?!*"

"Understand, child: despite your youth, you've traveled vaster portions of the earth than most. You've endured numerous hardships: physical, emotional, even spiritual. Yet nothing you've seen compares to the depth of suffering your world has known—and *will* know again. As horrific as these things have been—and will be, none of it compares to the depravity, the corruption percolating through the immaterial!

"*Yes,* I want the Creator to 'crack the heavens,' as you say! Humanity has his attention. *I want it.* If I have to sacrifice my *rilâ* for the benefit of all *ilalasdranàm:* I will! If I have to align myself with the raving schemes of a delusional dark star: I will! If I have to corrupt entire populations of your race to get it; if I have to burn away your entire world to attract his eye, believe me, child: *I will!*

"I can see those slow wheels turning in your mind. You're wondering why I'd reveal this to you, yes? I'll tell you: we're going to be partners, the two of us—make that the *three* of us! There's rapport between you and the starchild. The entire Swath noticed it! Of all created beings, it seems you alone possess the ability to ken the meaning in her song. You will be the interface between us. You will ensure she understands precisely the nuance required of my designs. You will see to it that she executes my will without hesitation, without question...because if you refuse, you'll look on, helpless, while Zhalera's innards boil into vapor. Slowly. Painfully."

"No! You can't! Why—?!"

"First, though, we'll *kalswàr* across the surface of the earth while I visit shock and fire and fury upon everyone you've ever known, anyone who's ever done you the slightest kindness. Perhaps, when at last you've understood the irrevocable gravity of your error, I'll permit you to die. Then again, perhaps not. The choice remains within your blessed hands, child. I suggest you make it *quickly.*"

4.

Kalas' breath caught in his lungs. A red wash bloomed along the corners of his peripheral vision as he considered Peradan's ultimatum.

I can't! I can't agree to this! If I do, how many people—how many heavenlies—will die? And if I don't…Zhalera! Falthwën said I'd face a choice: is this what he was talking about?

Peradan must have understood the conflict unfolding across Kalas' fluctuating features. He smiled, his perfect teeth sparkling in the strange light. Kalas risked a glance at Abarandal. At Zhalera.

I condemn one of them no matter what—no matter who I choose!

He studied Zhalera's motionless form and the terror reflected in her eyes. Kalas wondered for a moment—for *just* a moment—if Peradan would kill her quickly if he went along with his designs: *She'd see Gandhan again. Fërin, too. Even Tàran and Màla…And what would she tell them about me? About what I'd done? No, I can't do it! I* won't *do it!*

He considered Abarandal as her haunting silver stare bored into his soul and touched the very center of his being. Kalas tried to imagine what atrocities Peradan might compel her to perform: *Even if Peradan permits us to live, there's no way Zhalera would ever forgive me for betraying her friend. Her sister. And, if I'm honest: no, there's no way I'd forgive myself. No, I can't do it. I* won't *do it!*

"I said *quickly,* child!" Peradan seethed. His impatience with Kalas' indecision manifested as tongues of flame curling around the stony contours of his hard-featured face. "Make no mistake:

360

you're a convenience, not a necessity! Abarandal *will* understand my desires whether or not I understand her!"

Kalas said nothing. Exasperated, Peradan closed his eyes, took a deep breath, and sighed. Time slipped its restraints and resumed its familiar pace. The fires the *perayeru* had ignited within select adherents' bowels lapped away their lives; their convulsing bodies staggered to the floor, their screams unraveled in the room's unsteady atmosphere. Zhalera scanned the area for some sign of her sword. Abarandal continued regarding Kalas with her steely gaze: at first, he thought she was angry with him—maybe she'd glimpsed his thoughts as Peradan made his demand? When he considered the entirety of her rigid face, her set jaw, he recognized steadfastness and strength of will. Not anger. Together, the three of them would find a way to—

Kalas felt time stretch again: something pulled at his extremities—his limbs, his core, and sucked everything toward a reified intimation of lightlessness. It felt like hours passed as he attempted to raise his head and shout a warning to the others. When he finally managed, Zhalera, too, was caught in whatever force was *absorbing* him. He couldn't see Abarandal anymore: he tried to turn his head, but what few photons the room possessed stretched out like luminous spider silk before somehow splintering against the swelling black sphere: he couldn't see a thing. Before the last vestiges of conscious thought surrendered to the dark tumescence, Peradan laughed inside Kalas' mind: "A singularity, child! Opposite its event horizon, time will stand still! You'll only have a moment—less, really—to reflect on this, but while you're in there, I intend to visit such destruction upon your world that *erunàm* and *elunàm* alike—to say nothing of *edhunàm*—will pine for the day the Creator merely cracked it! When you see your world again—what remains of it—you'll understand the fullness of your folly! You'll understand you—"

No! Kalas tried to scream, but his mouth, his throat and lungs no longer felt the same. He wondered if he still *had* a mouth as the singularity stretched every synapse within his brain beyond his neurons' ability to function. The last thing he remembered thinking: *Even if there's a way back from this, I've failed! Abarandal: I'm sorry! I thought I could protect you. Protect the prophecy. I've—*

Kalas' atoms and molecules, his cells, tissues, and organs—every facet of his body slammed together, and he couldn't understand how or why his *kelâ* remained coupled to his physical self. The room's gelid air wriggled across his form: as each draft passed, it left the memory of fire in its wake. Fire and electricity, like the subtle evidence of some elemental chimera's clandestine presence. He sweat and shivered as his brain tried to parse the conflicting data. When his eyes could see again, he realized he was still within Peradan's chamber. He turned, stumbled, and fell. That's when he noticed Falthwën's staff, still clutched within the waxy remnants of someone's fingers.

Professor Rahwi?!

He wrenched it free and used it to regain his feet until he remembered how to hold his balance. Assessing his circumstances proved challenging until the rest of his mind and body renegotiated communication.

Peradan was gone. So were the cultists who'd survived his petulant ire. Those whom the *perayeru* consumed remained where they'd fallen, their carcasses sending up bits of ash as wind pirouetted across the room. Someone coughed, and he noticed Zhalera enduring similar straits.

"Zhalera! Are you all right?!" he shouted as he raced to her side.

"I...I think so! What happened? Kalas, what was that?!"

"A singularity! Peradan said some terrible things about his—"

"Peradan?!"

"Right! The Deathless Flame isn't Sifuran! It's Peradan! You were saying: every *eru* has a color—an aura, right? Well, I don't know how, but Peradan must have altered his. Probably to convince people he wasn't the *Tshaggul Kavar*. And it worked…"

"Kalas, where's Abarandal?! She was here just a second ago!"

"That's the thing about a singularity: Peradan might have been lying about a lot of things, but I don't think he was lying about that! We could have been in there for minutes or hours or Sevens and not know it! Peradan wanted me to work with him, to convince Abarandal to serve his ends—he's insane! I don't see either of them: that cannot be a good thing!

"I don't think we've been 'gone' for too long, though," he continued as he knelt over a corpse and held his hand above its smoking fragments. "There's still heat in this guy. Maybe a couple of hours, at most? You're right: we have to find Abarandal! Before he pulled us into his singularity, he touched her face—you saw that, right?— and as scared as she was, I don't think Peradan expected…whatever it was that happened. I don't think she'll be as easily controlled as he's anticipating. I *hope* not!"

"She's tough," Zhalera affirmed. "Tougher than she looks."

"No argument from me! Somehow, though, she's delicate, too. Maybe not in a physical way—she's impossibly strong, you know that, but…I don't know how to describe it."

"I know what you mean," she admitted, "but it doesn't matter: we still have to find her! C'mon!"

Zhalera grabbed onto Kalas' hand, squeezed it just a little too tightly, and hauled him to his feet. They'd traveled no more than a few steps when something glinted in the odd, lingering light. She tugged Kalas toward the source of the gleam and kicked away someone's blackened arm.

"Peradan's sword!" she exclaimed. "I wonder if my sword is somewhere nearby?! Kalas, please: help me find it!"

He nodded, and each explored a different portion of the chamber. After searching through numerous heaps of blackened body parts, Kalas found Valarandal. Its scabbard bore fresh scorch marks; when he drew out a few inches, its blade seemed unscathed. And warm.

"I've got it!" he cried, and Zhalera scooped it from his hands. "I know it looks a little rough, but I don't think the sword itself is damaged. Makes sense: you said nothing your ancestors tried had any effect on it, right?"

"Right, but none of them were stars!"

"Oh…yeah. Right…"

Zhalera unsheathed her weapon, and, exposed to the atmosphere, it flared to life as sheets of white-gold fire played along its sides and spiraled from its edges. Kalas had never seen it so luminous. Even from a few feet away, he could feel uncharacteristic heat rolling from Zhalera's sword. Valarandal glowed so bright and hot, he had to shield his eyes.

"How are you still holding it?" he marveled.

"What do you mean?"

"You don't feel that heat? Even from here, it feels like I could burst into flame!"

"Really? I mean, it's hot, but it can't be *that* hot!"

"How about that light? It's blinding!"

"Well, it's bright, sure…"

"It doesn't have the same effect on you," Kalas observed. "Anyway, I'm glad you have it back! I know how important it is to you!"

"Hey, why don't you take Peradan's sword? Maybe it'll do until…y'know…later?"

She handed it to him, and he tested its balance and examined its edges. He hacked the air a time or two, carved a few swirls in space, and danced it across the back of his hand before catching it in his grip with a deft flourish. Zhalera marveled at the skill Kalas displayed with his manipulations; shocked, she grunted when he tossed it to the ground.

"What are you doing? Is something wrong?"

"I shouldn't be surprised: that sword is almost perfect. Maybe it *is* perfect. Light and fast, and it looks like it could cut through just about anything!"

"Then why'd you throw it away?!"

"Because it was Peradan's! I can't—I don't want to carry something that used to belong to him!"

"What?! That's…What does it matter who it *used to* belong to? It's a sword!"

"But what if it's got a piece of his essence? Like how Valarandal has a piece of Valaran inside? The thought of holding on to a fragment of his treachery is too much!"

"Let me see," Zhalera insisted. She retrieved the discarded sword and explored its contours under the light emitted from her blade. After a few minutes, she nodded and handed its hilt to Kalas.

"I don't think so. In fact, after comparing this sword with mine, I think Valaran created both of them. Father would've known for sure, I'll bet, but despite their differences, there are enough cues to convince me that this thing is more Valaran than Peradan.

"But even if it's not: just because he used it for ill doesn't mean you can't use it for good! A sword's no different than a…a *shovel*: it's a tool! Like *seranà*. It depends on how you *use* it—isn't that what Falthwën said? And I'll bet unlike anything I know how to make—probably anything I'll *ever* know how to make, *this* sword will prove effective against *ekume*. And *erume*…

"Hold onto it. Give it a name—you're big on names, I know! Let it be a memorial to Falthwën, the way he died to preserve you, to protect the prophecy: in your hands, let it remind you of everything we've learned and everything we've yet to accomplish. Let it remind you that we face more than mere flesh and blood: we face powers we still don't understand—*and*…we're friends with a power greater than any the world has ever known!"

"All right, all right! You've made your point!" he huffed with a wry grin. *"Sharuyandas Tshandu.* That's what I'll call it."

"'Falthwën's Justice.' It's fitting," said Zhalera. "And speaking of our friend: either Abarandal is around here somewhere, or she and Peradan *kalswàra* somewhere else! Even if we wanted to search the 'light-realm' or whatever, we'd be wasting time without knowing where they're headed! If we're gonna find her, our best bet is to examine this place first. C'mon! Let's get to work!"

5.

"It looks like there's only one way in or out of here," Zhalera said after she and Kalas spent some time examining the room. "Unless they did that light-thing, I don't know where else they might have gone."

"There's a place over here where the wind feels *different.* I know that probably doesn't mean much, but it's…here, let me just show you!"

Kalas guided her toward a series of deep striations cut into part of a wall. He held out an arm and waved it across its surface. He frowned when he couldn't find the disruption he'd described.

"It was right here!" he pointed. "Or…was it over here? Maybe here? It should be—"

About a foot from his fingertip, the grooves etched within the rock rippled: they seemed to lose solidity as they broke apart with a subtle, iridescent shimmer. He drew back his arm as someone pried apart the wall from the inside.

"What?!" he exclaimed as he stepped back and raised Peradan's—no, *his* sword.

A delicate-looking hand, streaked with grime, pushed through the flexing stone and groped against the sudden absence of obstruction.

"Abarandal!" Zhalera shouted as she lowered her own sword and grabbed the young woman's arm. She braced herself and pulled: Kalas dropped his weapon and did what he could to help. The unnatural qualities of the rock faces proved difficult to understand, and after a few seconds, another force applied itself against their efforts: Abarandal's arm retreated within the stone.

"No! No!" Zhalera cried and redoubled her efforts.

Maybe I still don't understand my part in the prophecy, but it can't be just a coincidence that Abarandal escaped from Peradan! And I can't let her—our hope for a better future—just end *like this, trapped inside a mountain!*

"Zhalera! Stand back!" he ordered. She refused.

"I can't let go! Something's pulling her! She'll—"

"Trust me!"

She whirled on him, her resistance blooming; it wilted when she perceived something in his bearing—maybe the way he held Falthwën's staff, because she hollered an apologetic warning as she released Abarandal's hand and leapt out of the way.

Kurshëthu, he commanded, and white-green fire vaulted from the tip of his outstretched staff. It collided with the wall, penetrated the vacuum between its atoms, and seemed to ripple underneath its stony surface before the point of impact exploded in a cascade of fragmented rock. When the dust settled, Zhalera tabled her amazement at what Kalas had done and rifled through the debris in search of her friend: "How did you—? Never mind! Help me find her!"

The young man had already dropped his staff and started heaving away the pieces. After just a few minutes, they heard Abarandal's song through the rubble: despite some coughing, its music sounded clear, vibrant, and…excited?

"*Zhi Ilun tsavár!*" Zhalera exulted with a broad smile. "What's she saying?"

"She's all right! She's—she'll tell us later, but she…*found* someone?! She found a man, she said! A man balanced along the cusp of a…an *event horizon?* I don't know what that means! Peradan used that phrase—Falthwën did, too, once. Doesn't matter right now! Let's get them out!"

They kept digging.

In about half an hour, Kalas and Zhalera had cleared an opening large enough for Abarandal—and her new companion. Still shaken, the young woman stumbled into the room, where the pair held her upright until she regained her balance.

This isn't mere physical weakness…

"First trolls, now this?!" Zhalera chided with a relieved twinkle in her eye. "You've gotta stop scaring us like that!" Abarandal shrugged and smiled.

"I hope I didn't hurt you!" Kalas apologized. The wearied star assured him he hadn't.

"How did you defeat Peradan's trap?! Not even Falthwën could do that! How did you escape?"

She cocked her head as her thoughts retreated inward, searching, perhaps, for an explanation Kalas might comprehend. At a loss, she shrugged, and her smile took on an apologetic twist.

"You said you found someone?" he reminded her, doing his best to ignore his unanswered questions. "Trapped, too, from the sound of things?"

The *eru* nodded and looked over her shoulder, toward the spherical chamber where she and the figure she'd discovered had emerged from their curious prison. As he considered its polished, glass-like walls, Kalas wondered if she'd somehow *unmade* just enough of the material world to accommodate their presence within the mountain's roots, or if he had somehow—subconsciously, perhaps—hollowed out just enough room for their survival.

It doesn't matter: she's safe! That's *what's important!*

"What—*how* did you—?!"

She began a snatch of song as the man staggered from the opening. Mature, perhaps seven or eight Sevens, with salt-and-pepper hair and a well-trimmed beard to match, he scanned the larger room with haunted eyes that marred his otherwise regal bearing. He focused on Abarandal, his gaze flagging Kalas as they sought the young girl. Before Abarandal could communicate more than a few bars, the figure's stare locked onto the sword in the young man's hand.

"You!" he bellowed as he lunged for Kalas, who only then discovered the new arrival had a sword of his own. Caught off guard, he failed to avoid his crazed attacker's shove.

"What have you done to my men?! What have you—where are we?! Where are *they?* What sorcery is this?!"

"Sir?" Kalas managed as he blocked the man's wild blows as best he could. Quick as lightning, Abarandal hauled Peradan's former prisoner away from Kalas. She whispered a brief lullaby in his ear: distracted, he loosened his grip on his weapon long enough for the young woman to pry it from his fingers and restrain him while Kalas stood and brushed away the dust. He raised his sword—Zhalera raised hers, too—and noticed the man's eyes flicker between its flashing edges and the young man's perplexed expression.

"It's this sword, isn't it?!" Kalas understood. "It's familiar to you?"

The man cackled: "You jest! Why, mere moments ago, you pressed that fiery blade against my throat! We were in the woods! I don't know where we are now, nor how you brought us here, but I—"

"The woods? Above the Ravine, you mean?"

"The woods! You—The what? Ravine? This is a trick…"

"No, *âu!* Not a trick!"

"You reek of broiled flesh! You have the gall to insist that your designs are not deceitful with a sword—*that* sword—pointed in my direction?!" He struggled against Abarandal's grip. Failed to escape her grasp.

"Look, mister: you were caught in a singularity—a trap, I guess, that the *ekume* construct. We just escaped from one ourselves: in there, time stands still; when we got free—Zhalera, how *did* we get free?"

"I thought you did something! Something with The Song! You're telling me you didn't?"

"No! Not that I remember! Abarandal! Did you—? No? I thought—? No, we'll figure it out some other time…"

He made a show of lowering his sword, relaxed his stance, and gestured for the *eru* to release her grip. He glanced at Zhalera, who'd already gleaned his intent and lowered Valarandal. Kalas continued, "Like I was saying: when we were freed, maybe a couple of hours had passed. How long—no, you couldn't answer that, could you? What's the last thing you remember?"

The fierce light in the stranger's eyes slackened as he observed as much of the room as possible without looking away from Kalas.

"All right, fine," he muttered, risking a glance in Abarandal's direction as she let him go. He straightened his impressive frame, smoothed away the wrinkles in his dark gray overshirt, and adjusted his rich green leather scabbard before he spoke: "Hunting. One of my *kindume* told me he'd heard rumors of great wolves prowling the countryside. The dogs—usually noble creatures, unafraid of anything—mewled like whelps and fled! I suspected whatever frightened them *had* to be worthy prey, so I gave chase.

"In a small clearing—no more than a break between the trees, really: that's when I first saw them. Eyes as large as dinner plates and bright as gold. That's when I *smelled* them, too: a most malodorous stink that lingered in my nose and mouth! I drew my sword as the forest…came *alive!* Shadows turned into wolves—monsters!—and surrounded me. I'd already drawn my sword, but somehow, by the time I raised it, the wolves were gone! Before I could turn around, I felt something cold, hard, and sharp against my neck. Something glittered in my eyes: at first, I thought it was setting suns-light reflected from some brigand's sword. I risked a glance and saw fire racing along its edge—the same fire clinging to it even now!

"But you know all this! It *just* happened! Do you deny it?!"

Kalas didn't address the man right away; instead, he asked Abarandal to hand him the huntsman's sword. He ran his eyes along its unsettlingly familiar blade, admired the skilled craftsmanship displayed within its hilt, and gasped when he examined its green-gold pommel.

Its green-gold *falcon-crested* pommel.

He dropped his weapon, knelt and bowed his head, and returned the now-confused stranger's sword, hilt first.

"Aswanthalu, elïgarahal! You've been…you've been away for so much more than a 'mere moment'!"

"Kalas! What are you doing?!" Zhalera hissed. "Get up! Why—who *is* this man?!"

"Look at his sword!" he instructed. "Look at the symbol on the pommel! At the emeralds in its eyes!"

She shrugged and did as Kalas asked.

"That's strange! It looks like Shosafin's sword! What would—"

"Shosafin! You know my servant Shosafin? What have you done with him? Where is he? Where are the rest of my men?!"

"King Rufàran!" Kalas begged. "Please, receive your sword—and with it, my humblest apologies!"

"King Rufàran?!" Zhalera knelt, too.

Chapter XII

Against an Absent Enemy

"Young man! Explain yourself!" the king demanded. When Kalas didn't move, he grabbed his sword with a vulgar huff and rapped the young man's head with the flat. Kalas stood.

"If you've done something—*anything*—to my men, know this: your life is forfeit!"

"King or not, he could show a little gratitude!" Zhalera muttered.

"He doesn't understand!" Kalas interceded. "He's—O King, believe me, please! Sevens have passed since you were captured! Shosafin is—the wolves you were chasing: of all your men, he's the only one of your men who survived their attack. No, that's not accurate, is it? All right, uh…Your daughter, Ësfàyami, rules Ïsriba now, and she's—Marugan, one of your lords, right? Marugan's been steering her toward war with Tsobarut! Ralothova! All the—"

"*Lies!*" Rufàran insisted. "My daughter is far too young to assume the throne! Far too naïve to understand the subtleties of statecraft!"

"You don't understand," Kalas repeated, his head sagging. "I don't know how to convince you, not down here, separated from the world like this, so here's what I suggest: come with us. Hopefully Shosafin is waiting for us back in Galámur. Maybe he can persuade you of the truth? What do you say, King Rufàran?"

The king reared back, raised his sword high, and sliced at Kalas' neck.

Kalas leaned away from the intended blow, rolled along the ground, and retrieved his sword: when Rufàran recovered and aimed another blow at his ribs, Kalas parried it with ease; rather than counterattack, he remained guarded and waited for the next strike. The king whirled and redirected his momentum; having adjusted his feet, he feinted twice, then lunged. Kalas anticipated every advance and countered with deft maneuvers.

"How are you avoiding my sword?!" the king wondered aloud. "You're just a boy! No more than, what? two Sevens? Yet you move like one of my *tanagme!*"

"One of your soldiers instructed me," Kalas tried to explain. "Shosafin, in fact!"

Rufàran scoffed and came at the young man again; this time, Kalas knocked the sword from his hand, pivoted, and swept his legs out from under him: when Rufàran landed on his back, he placed the tip of his weapon at the king's throat. The surprised man glared at Kalas—then burst into laughter.

"All right, all right: I yield! Maybe Shosafin *did* have a hand in your training..."

Kalas withdrew his sword and offered his arm to the beaten king. Rufàran eyed him with suspicion for a moment, looked around at Zhalera and Abarandal, and finally accepted.

"Shosafin—Ilbardhën, in the days after your disappearance—hasn't been idle during the all Sevens you've been...gone," said the young man. "He blames himself for what happened to you, you know..."

Abarandal had retrieved Rufàran's sword: she handed it to Kalas, who in turn handed it back to the king. This time, he accepted it with grace.

"Sevens have passed, you say? Understand: I don't believe you, but you've been…accommodating, I suppose, and since we're obviously *not* in the woods outside Ïsriba, it seems I've little choice but to accompany you. I could wander around this…this cave alone, I suppose, but no. I'm curious to understand your endgame…"

"Fair enough, I guess," Kalas shrugged. "All right then: there's only one way in or out of here—that has to be the same route the cultists used when—"

"Cultists?!" Rufàran interrupted.

"A lot has changed, your highness," Kalas reminded him. "There weren't any forks in the passage we followed, but who knows what we missed when our heads were covered! And some of Peradan's followers—the ones he didn't destroy!—might be running around here, too! We'll need to be careful. Come on, everyone!"

The young man tapped the heel of Falthwën's staff on the ground and willed soft light to bloom from its tip. Amazed, Rufàran stepped back and gasped: *"Seranà!* Sorcery indeed!"

"Not sorcery, Your Majesty! *Privilege.* That's what Falthwën—a friend—called it. The tunnels are dark, but we should have enough light. Stay close! Once we find an exit, once we're outside, in the Ravine, we—The dragon! What if he's still out there?!"

"Dragon?!" Rufàran spluttered. "This is a trick! There are no dragons in the world today!" He took another step back and raised his sword again.

"A lot has changed," Kalas repeated. "I really want you to come with us, but I can't force you to do anything. If you'd rather wait here or search for some other way out, that's your choice. I won't lie to you, but I won't pretend the last few Sevens haven't happened, either. The world is…at a crossroads, I guess."

At a crossroads…and somehow it's up to me *to decide which way to go?!*

Abarandal trilled a brief passage, and Kalas shrugged. "I don't know—Kadhëmba said they were normally peaceful. He must feel threatened."

"Your voice!" Rufàran gushed. Abarandal's porcelain cheeks reddened even in the dim light.

"She—we'll talk about it on the way. Assuming you choose to come with us," Kalas began. "Shosafin and Kadhëmba have no idea there's a *gròma* patrolling the Ravine. Let's hurry!"

The rediscovered king said little on their way through the tunnels toward the "door" in the wall of the Ravine. He kept his peace, did his best to restrain his incredulity, and tried to listen while Kalas and Zhalera outlined as best they could the events of the past few Sevens. However, when they told him about how his daughter had treated them, he gushed his strident disbelief. Kalas shrugged. He assumed Zhalera did, too, because neither said much afterward.

What cultists had survived Peradan's tantrum—assuming he'd left any alive—must have taken alternate, unknown passages, because neither Kalas nor the others discerned any sign of them.

Of course, it is *dark in here. Wouldn't be hard to miss someone if he were hiding...*

"We must be getting close to the door," he said aloud. "We've been walking for quite some time now. I just hope it's really there this time!"

"What do you mean?" Rufàran wondered.

"It was like a sheet of something, like a semisolid...*emptiness,* I guess, in the Ravine. Yes, I know that makes no sense! Once we passed through it, it was gone: there was no door on the *inside* of the cliffs. If it's still not there, we'll have to find some...other means of escape."

"Do you have something in mind?"

"I...uh, maybe," he mumbled.

"Oh?" said Zhalera.

"First, let's see what's there..."

• • •

"I don't see anything," Zhalera observed when they reached the end of the narrow trail. "Looks like the path here just ends. Same as before."

"Really?" Kalas queried as he ran his hands across the rocks. "You don't see that shaky light seeping through the cracks?"

"I don't even see the cracks you're talking about!"

"What? They're right there! About the size and shape of the door, I'd say!"

"But you didn't say anything about it before! I didn't think any of us saw anything then!"

"No, you're right, but it goes from here…to here," he said, tracing its outline with the tip of Peradan's sword. "Oh! Maybe that's it?!"

"Maybe what's what?" demanded Rufàran.

"Zhalera, hold this," Kalas said, ignoring the king for the moment as he handed her his weapon. He turned to look again, but the luminous, spidery threads had vanished.

"Oh! I see!" Zhalera exclaimed. Nodding, she passed the sword to Abarandal, who reached for it, shuddered, and refused to take it. Instead, she passed it to the king.

"Oho! What is this?!" he marveled as he raised his fingers to the portal's shimmering plane.

"Wait! No!" Kalas shouted. Rufàran recoiled, then regarded the young man with a cool, expectant glare.

"Apologies, Your Majesty, but we don't know what might happen if you touch it!" he explained as he reclaimed his sword. "Try throwing a rock, or—actually, throw *this* rock! Zhalera, Abarandal: it's the rock I threw from the Ravine! King Rufàran: see what happens when you throw this rock through the wall!"

Kalas picked up the stone and handed it to the bemused king.

He took it, hefted it, and, with a shrug, heaved it toward the strange phenomenon.

It just bounced and rolled away along the floor.

"Now what?!" Zhalera sighed. "Hey, Kalas, you said you had an idea! Well? Let's hear it!"

"Falthwën's staff," he began as he retrieved the unremarkable missile and traced lazy circles across its contours with his thumb. "Kadhëmba says it's just a stick in anyone else's hands. When I found it back in Melash, I tried to make it *do* something. Nothing happened. Then I remembered what you said about The Song: I needed a goal. Something specific. That's the key, I think. I still don't know. Not really…

"Anyway, remember the rockslide in the Empty Sea? That was Falthwën's doing. When everyone else had left, he drew something in the air above a rock, then he picked it up and threw it at the craft. I saw it *change*, mid-flight: a few minutes later, BOOM! You saw what happened when we went back for a closer look!"

Despite the insufficient light hugging the tunnel's walls, Kalas watched the color drain from Zhalera's face: "That's how you freed Abarandal and King Rufàran, isn't it?"

Although neither Abarandal nor Rufàran were present when the mountain crumbled over the ancient *vàsu*, it seemed they understood the implication. The three of them exchanged uneasy glances with one another until Kalas dropped the rock, raised his hand, and shook his head.

"We're not there just yet!"

He flexed his fingers around his sword's pearlescent grip and studied the shimmering space: he handed Falthwën's staff to Abarandal, scooped up the infamous rock, and hurled it through the outline framed in scintillating blues. The wall rippled where it hit: a moment later, the stone vanished with a flash of light.

"How—?!" the king spluttered. "Young man! Explain!"

"This sword doesn't just allow us to see the door: it allows us—and, it seems, the objects of our will—to pass through the barrier here. I guess we won't need to blow up the Ravine from the inside after all!"

"That's a relief!" Zhalera acknowledged, "but you said it yourself: this is the only way in or out of these tunnels! Peradan didn't kill *all* the cultists—at least, if he did, there wasn't any sign of them, and we checked every crevice of that big room! They must be down here still!"

"North of Serular, Kadhëmba said some of them were using magic. I wonder: were they *ilhadzhalasme?* Or can Peradan—can any *eru*—extend his *privilege* to others? I guess that's moot right now: this is the only exit *we* know about," Kalas elaborated. "We'll have to worry about the cultists later. Zhalera: stand right…step to your left, to your—right there! Abarandal: behind her, please? And King Rufàran, behind her? Good! Now, when I say your names, touch the wall. And…*brace yourselves!*"

2.

After the others blinked away, Kalas, with his sword outstretched, touched the inconstant portal. His body—his physical, material substance—acquired inexplicable new properties, and despite his perceived absence of lungs, he gasped.

It's another singularity! he chided himself. *How could I be so careless?! How—? Wait! No, this* isn't *a singularity…*

Naught but a stream of energized consciousness—the distillation of his *kelâ,* he thought—he explored the bizarre world assaulting him through a host of impossible senses: traveling across a strange admixture of time and space, colors caromed across his vision—no, his *thoughts;* here, some otherworldly sense supplanted sight, though his ability to perceive remained intact. Light frequencies hummed and droned within his ears—their analogs, anyway—and wrested from him any hint of *whereness.*

I've…I have been here before, he remembered. *It's like Peradan's singularity, but…different. The light-realm! The* kalthesh! *But it wasn't like this above the Gateway! Or even under Ïsriba! Here, I don't know where I'm going. I could be outside, at the bottom of the Ravine, or just about anywhere else, I guess! How will I know?!*

The colors surrendered their saturation and descended toward homogeneous gray.

Anticolor.

The discernible frequencies dissolved into an all-encompassing, atonal din. Kalas felt his extracorporeal sense of self coming apart, fraying like a tattered cloak; soon, he thought he might become nothing but a smear of ineffective will within a universe of nothingness.

The mental effort required to construct a single thought—much less a logical progression of ideas—became almost too much to bear. Before he abandoned himself to the merciless void, a fiery streak of energy forked across the gray and permeated his immaterial substance. It swooped and banked, revealing iridescent green along its glancing angles, and rushed upon him again: a moment before the inescapable wash of brightness collided with him, he shut his eyes—

—and opened them when he hit the polished ground at the bottom of the Ravine. Zhalera and the others were waiting for him. She started to say something, but he threw up before she finished speaking. With his index finger raised, he beckoned her to wait while he collected himself.

"Kalas! Are you all right?! What happened?!"

"I…I don't know! I thought I was coming apart! Not just my body: my soul, too! I think I almost…this is a weird way to put it, but it felt like I was melting! More than just my flesh and blood!"

He shuddered. "None of you felt that? All of you are all fine? No cultists? No dragon?"

Abarandal nodded. So did the king.

"Yeah, I was gonna say: it *stung* when we went in; it was nothing like that when we came out! No cultists, no dragons: the three of us are fine! Kalas: you're *sure* you're all right?"

"I am now, Zhalera. I might not have been if this string of light hadn't *pushed* me out of the *kalthesh*. It reminded me of part of a dream. It's different, I think, from what happened above the Áthradho. Or what Loradan did under the Vault. I don't know how else to explain it."

"I'm just glad you made it out," Zhalera whispered. She helped him stand, wiped away flecks of sick still clinging to his chin, and held him close.

"What's this for?" he asked as he returned the gesture. Even drenching sweat and the film of cloying smoke failed to eliminate the quintessential *Zhalera-ness* in her fragrance. When he considered what odors might be emanating from his person, he preemptively apologized: "Uh, I'm sorry if I stink!"

"Just because," she smiled before letting go. "Ever since we were children, we've been a constant part of each other's life. I guess I just assumed we always would be. I thought we'd…I mean, well, with everything that's happened to us…I want you to know I don't take you for granted."

"I…I know what you mean," Kalas stammered. He held her tawny gaze for a moment before the fire rising in his cheeks bade him look away. Rufàran whispered something to Abarandal, whose cascade of bright notes suggested laughter. The king nodded.

"Uh, the suns," said the young man, ignoring the *erudas* exchange with Rufàran. "There isn't much light left in the sky, and given how difficult it was to get down here, I suggest we wait until morning before we try anything foolish."

"Yes, well, I also prefer to try foolish things in the light of day," the king said. "No, you're right: you three have the benefit of experience—limited, perhaps—with this…Ravine, but it's *freezing* down here, and I'm suddenly hungry! I don't suppose you've got anything to eat, do you?"

"I'm sorry, Your Majesty, we don't. We…well, today's been… we weren't expecting anything like this! If we follow the Ravine, we should be able to collect enough wood for a fire. At least then, we'll be *warm* and hungry. When the suns rise, we can work our way out of this place."

The four of them scoured the ground for fragments of firewood, and after about half an hour, the skin at the back of Kalas' neck rippled as some preternatural sensation gave him pause. He stood, listening for signs of whatever presence had aroused his suspicion. Not wanting to alarm the others, he worked his way toward Zhalera.

"There's something in the dark," he hissed. She nodded, dropped a few of the sticks she'd discovered, and kept a hand on her sword. He cleared his throat to gain Rufàran's attention: when the king looked up, Kalas jerked his head toward Zhalera's sword, placed a hand on his own weapon, and looked over his shoulder toward the source of his disquiet. Rufàran followed suit. He was about to warn Abarandal when someone interrupted him:

"*There* you are," grumbled Shosafin as he and Nïmrïk left the secrecy of the shadows.

"I'm glad you're safe, lad!" Nïmrïk said, relieved.

"Kadhëmba! Shosafin!" Kalas exclaimed. "You'll never guess what—*who*—we found! He's been—"

"Shosafin?!" the king repeated as he joined the young man.

When the gruff old soldier glimpsed his long-lost king, his almost-impervious façade collapsed and washed away in a rush of sudden tears. He sank to his knees and bowed his head as he tried to collect himself.

"My liege," he managed.

"No, not Shosafin!" he said, turning to Kalas. "My chief body-guard is just a couple of Sevens older than you, I'd wager. This man is clearly too old to be him!"

"Much has changed, Your Majesty," Shosafin said, his eyes still focused on the ground.

"Seems that's what everyone keeps saying," Rufàran complained. "Oh, get up! Get up!"

He obeyed. "It's true: it's been Sevens since you disappeared from the woods beyond Ïsriba, since my failure bereaved the Golden Falcon of her king…and so much more. If you'll forgive my impudence: where have you been all these Sevens?"

"You, too? As I've told your young friend here, I was hunting only moments ago! The dogs ran one way: I ran the other, toward—"

"Toward the wolves, right. The wolves *Kindu* Marugan told us about…"

"How could you know about the wolves? None but my most trusted soldiers knew what we were hunting or where we were going!"

"It's been many Sevens, my liege. To the best of my recollection, you haven't changed since the day you disappeared. I don't—"

"A *singularity,* I think," Kalas interrupted. "The traps Falthwën told us about, the kind the *ekume* use. Turns out *Peradan* is the Deathless Flame! He's the one who captured King Rufàran! In a singularity—hovering along its 'event horizon,' he said, time stands still. From the king's perspective, it really *has* been just a moment since he was in the woods outside Ïsriba!"

Shosafin considered Kalas' revelation for a moment before he continued, "Marugan's impossible speed: when he ran me through, was I caught within such a snare? And Peradan: one of the Swath,

I thought you said?"

"I think *erume*—and *ekume*—can exist in a state that, to us, makes it feel like time is standing still when it really isn't. I don't think you were trapped so much as Marugan moved across the *kalthesh* to reach you so quickly.

"And yes, Peradan is—was?—a member of the Swath. Somehow, he altered his corona to make people suspect he was Sifuran. I'm ashamed I believed his deception. He trapped me and Zhalera in one of his singularities, but only for a few hours, I think. I still have no idea how we escaped! Abarandal must have been in one, too: or the light-realm, maybe, and somehow, wherever she was, she discovered the *Poyïsriba* king!"

Shosafin nodded, shrugged, and laughed before he addressed Rufàran again: "You heard the lad. A *singularity*. A trap. I'm still not convinced he's correct, but, better than any scenario I can conceive, it explains—at least in part—what we're experiencing here and now.

"*Kindu* Marugan, it turns out, is an *eku*. I've since learned it was his design that all of us should be set upon by *egume* and devoured. If you've been trapped for all these years, then it's my unhappy duty to inform you—"

"—the wolves murdered them all. Yes, the boy told me. I didn't believe it. Even speaking it aloud, the words feel all wrong! Kalas told me Marugan has been influencing my daughter, too..."

"He has, my liege, and not for the better, from what Kalas and his companions—including my cousin, Commander Nashmur—have told me. She's queen-regent now—oh, so you've heard? Of course...

"Kalas, one question: If Marugan intended for all of us to die between the teeth of demon wolves, why did they attack *him?*"

"It's a long story, but it seems an *egu* called Tsathrâuda promised Marugan something if he worked toward her ends. Marugan and

Peradan have known each other for millennia. Hated each other for almost as long. When he discovered Peradan had plans of his own…

"Peradan thinks Marugan's a fool. From what King Rufàran said, I think it was Peradan's duty to send the wolves, and I wouldn't be surprised if, for some reason, he 'forgot' to point Marugan out to them before they attacked."

The old soldier nodded again. Turning toward his king, he said, "Were there some means to convince you of the truth…but there isn't. Not here, not now. Maybe when we return you to Ïsriba…"

Kalas thought Shosafin might have said more, but instead he turned his focus to their immediate needs: "You've been gathering firewood. Good. Even in the best light, it would be difficult for most of us to scale this Ravine. We should camp down here for the night. You probably reached the same conclusion yourselves."

"We passed a few crevices—not caves, really, but better than nothing—on the way here," Nïmrïk said. "Might be a better place to build your fire than out here in the…well, 'open' is too generous a word!"

Between the walls of a narrow crack, seated around a soaring fire, Kalas shivered despite its warmth. He yawned, too. He had no name for his experience traversing the *kalthesh*—Peradan's perversion of it—but it had drained him more than he'd been willing to admit. Zhalera, watching him, yawned, too, and smiled when he caught her gaze. Despite his insistence he wasn't tired, Rufàran had already fallen asleep.

"Given what happened to Rufàran's men, maybe it's best if I remain in human form for now," Nïmrïk suggested. No one contradicted him. "In fact, maybe I'll patrol the area. You said you weren't sure where the cultists might have gone. Wouldn't be a bad idea to make sure they're *not* still around…"

The *egu* offered a half-nod and let the shadows swallow him while Shosafin stared at—no, *through*, Kalas decided—the shifting flames struggling against the deepening cold. As the young man studied the gruff soldier's features, without altering his posture or expression, Shosafin, aware of Kalas' scrutiny, observed, "You've acquired a sword."

"Oh, that? Yeah, it was Peradan's. He had it in the Vault, before the Swath summoned Abarandal, but he told us he lost it. I guess he left it under Glass Sword Mountain. You weren't there, under Ïsriba, when…everything happened, but Zhalera's sword—Valarandal—could cut through the *ekume* that attacked us. Your sword couldn't. I think this sword would've been effective against them, too. I wonder: if you'd had Zhalera's sword, or maybe even this sword—maybe when you slit Marugan's throat, he would have stayed dead…

"I named it *Sharuyandas Tshandu*. If Peradan had a name for it, I don't know what it was. Don't care. I'll hold onto it until Zhalera forges me a sword of my own."

"May I see it?"

Kalas handed him his weapon. Shosafin examined its contours, the jagged vein of orange-tinged crystals along its spine, and tested its weight and balance with a few deft maneuvers. He nodded his approval and handed it back.

After a few quiet minutes, the soldier sighed and, without looking away from the fire, admitted, "This changes things, lad."

"I—what? The sword?"

"No, not the sword," he clarified, his voice monotone. "Our reasons for traveling north have always been our own. For a while, they complemented one another; now, however, mine have changed. Understand: I'd hoped—against all probability—that the king was still alive, but tonight, seeing him in the flesh—the very same flesh from so many Sevens ago…I'm…reassessing my goals.

"King Rufàran needs to return to Ïsriba. Right away. I've studied you long enough to believe what you—and my cousin—told us about the queen-regent. Had I been a better soldier in the days before Marugan corrupted Ësfàyami, the last several Sevens might have unfolded very differently. The king might have never been abducted, secreted away in one of Peradan's traps..."

Kalas listened, rapt, while Shosafin spoke. When he resumed his pensive silence, the young man remembered something Falthwën had told him.

"If you had been a 'better soldier,' as you say, then lots of things would've been different, it's true. For one, I'd be dead."

"Oh? Explain."

"If Rufàran hadn't disappeared; if you hadn't become *Ilbardhën;* if you hadn't come to Lohwàlar with Valderïk, then Dzharëth would have ripped me apart in the streets."

The soldier nodded. He still hadn't looked away from the flames and their frantic dance. When he said nothing, Kalas continued: "I mean, I'm sorry for everything that happened to you, to the king—even to the queen-regent, but at the same time, I'm grateful. If you go back to Ïsriba with Rufàran, what will become of Marugan? He's still out there, somewhere, working to turn the world toward war. What will become of—

the prophecy

—us? We barely escaped Ïsriba without you!"

"But you *did* escape. You withhold too much credit from yourselves. And too much has changed. *Decayed.* Ësfàyami projects poise and strength, but the kingdom is a wreck. A wreck I believe only her king can restore. If you're right about the world being at a crossroads, you'll need a sure foundation from which to formulate and execute your strategy. There's none better than Ïsriba, the *Nimkosra Kàsh,* when she's in peak form. Yes, I'm biased, but in this, I'm also right. One day, I *will* recompense Marugan for his treason against the Golden Falcon, but not today. Nor tomorrow."

The fire swelled as something within its embers popped and sizzled. The haphazard stone ring shifted, spilling red-orange coals onto the polished ground. As hot waves fluttered along their edges, Kalas rubbed his eyes when the fire expanded in a rush of heat and sparks. He blinked, disbelieving the figure suddenly standing at the center of the broken stones.

"'Not today'? 'Nor tomorrow'? How about *now?!*" said Marugan as he aimed his bow at Shosafin and fired.

3.

The old soldier exhaled an abbreviated grunt as the *ekudas* arrow pierced his forearm. Kalas figured Marugan had been aiming for Shosafin's head, but even caught unawares, his reflexes provided the extra moment necessary to avoid the worst of his adversary's attack. The shadows' edges frayed and split apart as *shagabme* oozed into the small circle of firelight. Terrified, Kalas realized the shadows contained other horrors as inky black snakes of *nimeku* malevolence slithered across the ground and through the air toward their prey.

Too stunned to speak, he willed his hands and feet to *move*, to rouse Zhalera and Rufàran before the living darkness consumed them. One tendril, thicker and more solid than the others, discovered the *Poyïsriba* king and coiled itself like a serpent about to strike. Before it could unleash its accumulated potential energy, a wolf snarled its way through the night and vaulted into the air. Nïmrïk caught the malign appendage in his gleaming teeth, wrenched his head from side to side, and wrestled with the *ilnàfel* until it withered into smoke between his jaws. Without a glance at Kalas or the others, he lunged into the dark: flurries of wet tearing sounds and a noise like a thousand screams echoed from wall to wall as the *rudzhegu* gnawed and slashed at the lightless stars.

"Zhalera! Rufàran!" Kalas managed at last. He sliced through another tendril as it tried to wrap around the *eruín*.

"Abarandal! Look out!" he cried. For some inexplicable reason, though her eyes were open, she had the look of someone *elsewhere*. Kalas spared a moment to squeeze her shoulder, to try to reach her, but a *shagab* intervened: he swung his sword across its chest and willed his assailant into dust.

"Kalas?! What's going on?!" Zhalera said, gripping Valarandal as its blade rippled with golden threads of frenzied energy. She hacked at a tendril and, her question answered, added: "Where'd they come from?!"

"Marugan!" he shouted as he dodged a blow from an "undead" assassin. Nïmrïk reappeared and bit the man in half.

"I didn't sense their presence until…I'm sorry, lad!"

"Never mind! Marugan hit Shosafin! His arm—his *sword* arm! I don't—"

"Oho! What's this?!" raged King Rufàran, awake at last. When Kalas turned toward his voice, he saw an attacker slump and slide from the king's black-stained blade.

Shagabme! Kalas explained. "Let me and Zhalera handle the *ekume*—your sword's ineffective against them!"

The king ignored Kalas' warning as a sinuous strand of darkness twined itself around his ankles. He fell, slicing at the appendage with increasingly panicked strokes. Zhalera, closest to him, rushed to his aid: Valarandal sang—Kalas heard its exultant song within his thoughts—as her blow severed the *eku* from its intended victim. Amazed, Rufàran mumbled his brief thanks and turned his sword upon the vivified warriors.

The young man risked a glance in Shosafin's direction. The gruff soldier had gained his feet, and, despite his wounded strong side, he continued to defend himself against Marugan's repeated attacks. Kalas understood that the scar-faced man considered Shosafin naught but an amusing plaything: he permitted the injured warrior just enough time to anticipate the *ekudas* next move before he renewed his attacks.

"I'll admit, *shël sà*, it's refreshing to abandon the caul of commonness I've had to wear through all these Sevens!" Marugan cackled, his dead gray eyes glinting in the fire's flickering light. He reached into his quiver, and Kalas realized it was empty: before he could tell Shosafin, a faint line of black wavered between Marugan's fingers, and in almost no time, he'd nocked another arrow. He let it fly just proud of Shosafin's left side: the flagging old man blocked it with his sword, but he staggered from the effort.

How much longer can he go on? The nimnàfel seranà *must be poisoning his blood: if such an injury almost* unmade *Kadhëmba, what will it do to a mortal man?*

Kalas took a few deep breaths, raised his sword, and *almost* took a step toward Marugan. Shosafin, anticipating, perhaps, the young man's intention, made a subtle gesture without shifting focus: *Stand fast!* he instructed.

Kalas obeyed.

Bored, it seemed, Marugan tossed his bow and drew a *Poyïsriba* sword from his hip. He made a show of examining its balance. He ran his finger along its edge until purple-black ichor dripped and sizzled from the cut it left behind.

"Your favored weapon, yes? I'll admit: I don't see the appeal…"

"That's no surprise," Shosafin panted. "That a craven like you would prefer to snipe his betters from the shadows makes perfect sense."

"Cute," Marugan huffed. "Enjoy your last few breaths, old friend! Oh, don't worry: your friends—How odd! That a man like you would acquire *friends!*—Your friends won't have long to grieve. As soon as I've cut you down, I'll finish what I started under Ïsriba!"

"You talk too much!" Shosafin panted as he made a clumsy

thrust at the smirking figure. Marugan swatted his blade aside with a snide chuckle.

Loath to abandon Abarandal, Kalas knew the old soldier wouldn't survive against the brunt of Marugan's full might. He called out to Nïmrïk: "Kadhëmba! Protect the *kathin kelësh!*" and hacked and slashed his way to Shosafin.

"You!" Marugan recoiled when Kalas reached him. "No, it doesn't matter! Not even one of the *Nalëndas* can stand against Tsathrâuda, against Hatred's Right Hand! Hwanzho, yes? I'm not surprised that faithless poltroon would reveal my designs to you— he betrayed his own people, after all! Still, I—"

"Shosafin's right. You talk too much!" Kalas agreed as he vaulted toward Marugan. As he sailed through space, one of the *eku* evaded Nïmrïk's maw and twisted its black ropes around the young man's waist. His momentum arrested, he lost his grip on his weapon: "No!" he cried as inertia wrenched it from his fingers. He wilted as it clattered across the chasm floor.

"Not even one of the *Nalëndas!*" Marugan laughed, his voice a grating concretion of ice and gravel.

The living dark dragged Kalas away from the gloating gray-eyed man, away from Shosafin's panting form, and toward some ignoble end. He struggled, hammering at the tentacle constricting him, but his blows were useless.

So...this is how it ends...

Not today, lad, Nïmrïk growled within his thoughts. The wolf, shimmering and somehow airborne, descended upon Kalas' captor and raked its poisoned claws across the *ekudas* peculiar surface. Kalas felt it shudder. Sensing an opportunity, he pushed with renewed vigor against his otherworldly bonds until he freed himself. He hit the ground, rolled like Shosafin had taught him, and lunged for Falthwën's staff, still propped against the wall where he'd left it. From the corner of his eye, he witnessed a puff of brightness as

Nïmrïk ripped apart the *eku*.

"Not again!" Marugan raved at the meddling *egu*, shifting his attention away from Shosafin. Space around him seemed to slide apart, like it had outside the Vault under Ïsriba not too long ago.

I can't let him escape! Kalas understood. He turned his will toward Marugan as his physical form surrendered its solidity to the immaterial. To his surprise, the *eku* ceased diminishing; rather, the world around them seemed to lose substance. Opposite a milky haze, Nïmrïk, wings unfurled, hovered above another dark star; Shosafin, favoring his wounded arm, waited, frozen, on the other side of their fire's immobile flames. Sheets of black blood hung like slick curtains suspended from nothing as Zhalera's sword made and maintained contact across a *shagabdas* neck; Rufàran, almost prone and inches above the ground, held his sword with statuesque stillness—as did the inhabited assassin standing over him.

Abarandal's song echoed through the *kalthesh* as Kalas intercepted Marugan before he brought his sword down on Nïmrïk's outstretched neck. He barreled toward the raging figure and collided with his ribcage. The *eku* missed his target, and as suddenly as reality had paused, it snapped into its familiar rhythms as Kalas and Marugan tumbled from the light-realm.

Too afraid—yes, *afraid*, Kalas realized—to speak, Marugan stared, horrified, at the still-shining young man. He scrambled to his feet and aimed his wavering sword at Kalas, but Shosafin batted it away, despite his injury.

"Tsathrâuda promised me I—! No! This can't be! She said the prophecy was nonsense! Just something—"

"Enough!" Shosafin roared with uncharacteristic fire in his eyes. "Enough of your lies! Your twisted words! You've *failed*, Marugan! With Ïsriba's rightful ruler restored to power, everything you've built over all these Sevens will come undone! Without Ïsriba to underwrite your wars, your designs will be unmade! *Revehwa ihi*

Kàsh—"

Sword in hand, he raised his weakened, blackening arm. Marugan's labored breathing slowed, his eyes regained their former soulless reserve, and with a superhuman flick of his wrist, he sliced at Shosafin. Despite his injury and his human limitations, the seasoned warrior almost sidestepped the blow.

Almost.

"*Now* who talks too much?" the *eku* grinned as Shosafin's severed arm hit the ground with a dull thud, his white-knuckled fingers still wrapped around his sword.

The maimed man staggered back and stared at the space where his limb used to hang. Blood jetted from his shoulder, where Marugan's blade had wrought its clean-edged malice. With color seeping from his face, Shosafin stumbled and leaned away from the *ekudas* rising weapon.

"*No more!*" Kalas shouted. His hand burst into flame: operating on sudden instinct, he grabbed onto Shosafin's spurting stump and willed an eruption of heat and light into the wound. Everything within his field of view swelled with luminance; every line seemed sharper, more discrete, as his friend cried out. Eyes ablaze, he let go and whirled on their adversary. Marugan lunged at Kalas, but the young man, capable of the same violence of motion, dived out of the way. The energy, the *seranà* he'd expended had left him weakened. Before Kalas could right himself, the savage *eku* glowered over him. For a moment, he neither spoke nor moved; when the moment passed, he raised his sword again.

"I...I wasn't finished," Shosafin muttered from behind.

Surprised, Marugan hesitated and turned toward the sound of the wheezing old soldier.

"*Revehwa ihi Kàsh! Á salorosh i* ëligar*ihath!*" he thundered as he revealed his weak side and drove *Sharuyandas Tshandu* through Marugan's still-grinning face. "Glory to the Falcon! And victory to her *king!*"

The *eku* tottered for the briefest instant before he collapsed onto his back. Shosafin's borrowed sword extended about a foot through his skull: inch by inch, Marugan's head slid down the blade—slow, like a caress—until it reached the ground. Light-like particles buzzed about the fringes of his mortal wound as his corporeal substance disintegrated into wayward sparks. Directionless gusts whipped them through the air, where they died against the froth of night.

4.

With effort—and after coughing fit, Kalas managed to regain his feet. He wobbled and wondered, "Shosafin! Are you—?"

"Fine, lad. Fine. For now. Hope you don't mind that I borrowed your sword…"

"Your—my sword? No, of course not! Your arm, though!"

"I'll survive, thanks to you. Again."

Without headship, the remaining *shagabme* shambled along the Ravine. Rufàran maintained his onslaught, but the soulless revenants poured into the chasm without ceasing. Zhalera held back the worst of the *ekume,* but Kalas knew they'd never last the night. Even Nïmrïk's repeated assaults required lengthening pauses in between.

He pried Shosafin's weapon from his rigored fist and traded it for Peradan's. The wounded warrior nodded and completed the young man's unspoken thought: "We're not through here, lad. C'mon, let's get back to work!"

"You're not serious?!" Kalas scoffed. "You're—look: *sit down!* Rest! You've spilled enough blood—mostly your own—for us! Let us—"

"No, *you* look, Kalas! I can read it in your expression: you know your friends are getting tired! You can barely stand! You *need* my sword if any of you hope to see another suns-rise! Let me—"

"What's that?!" Kalas interrupted. Shosafin squinted and cocked his head. "You don't hear it? Don't *feel* it? Like—"

A river of light swept through the Ravine, its shining currents wrapping around the *ekume* and toppling the *shagabme*. As the surge enveloped and extinguished the remains of Marugan's dark army, *music* reverberated from wall to wall, an arpeggiated wash of melody ringing with the dissolution of every grim combatant. Like Marugan's remains, hot wind sloughed theirs away, consuming every clot of viscous filth with celestial fire. When it passed, Shosafin accused Kalas with an arched eyebrow.

"No! Not—I mean, I have no idea what just happened! Unless Abarandal did something? Maybe? She was…she looked lost in thought, I guess, when everything started…"

The *eru* had crept up behind Kalas: with a tap on his shoulder and a soft, whispered phrase, she dismissed his suggestion. She managed a few more notes before the whoosh of beating wings drowned out her song. Sharp pinpricks of *presence* raised the hairs on the back of Kalas' neck, and he turned toward the descending *elu* as her sandaled feet caressed the dust-choked canyon floor.

"Nanësra. Of course," Kalas nodded. "*You* must have rescued us from the singularities! How long have you been here? Did you— how did you know to come *here?* How did you know we—"

"What he means," apologized Zhalera, having drawn up beside them, "is *thank you* for your help!"

"Right! Thank you! I thought I…No, no, I didn't, did I? We're grateful for your help!"

Abarandal completed her interrupted song with a brief passage and a deferential nod toward the gleaming, wingèd woman. Nïm-rïk, still wearing his *nimegu* shape, padded over, still panting with belabored breaths.

"Kalas! What happened? Did you—Oh!"

When he recognized Nanësra, the wolf folded his leathery wings, tucked his tail between his legs, and turned his large, yellow eyes toward the dirt.

"So that's what you were doing, Abarandal? Summoning her?"

"Not exactly," the *elu* ceded.

"I…I thought I heard a cry for help," Nïmrïk admitted without looking up. "Faint. Indistinct, but nonetheless a voice in dire need."

"Why didn't I hear anything?" Kalas wondered as he turned toward him. "Maybe with everything going—Kadhëmba! Your fur!"

"My…fur?" He raised his flattened ears.

"It's silver!" Zhalera explained. Abandoning any semblance of decorum, she knelt and ran her fingers through his thick, glittering coat. "It's so *soft!*"

"Does this mean you'll openly help us now?" Kalas wondered. Nanësra shook her head.

"The dark stars have transgressed their proper bounds. Enforcing such restrictions has always been within my purview."

"That's not 'no,'" Kalas noted.

Nanësra ignored his observation and turned her attention to Nïmrïk. She knelt opposite Zhalera and worked her fingers within the scruff of his neck, massaged his overworked muscles, and moved her hands toward his face. She paused for a moment, and Kalas guessed she'd discovered the scar from the wound Marugan had inflicted.

"There's never been a *swënrudzh*—a silverwolf—from among the fallen *elume* before, Kadhëmba," she said as she released him and stood to her full height. "And lest your deeds here tonight tempt you to believe that *they* are the reason for your altered appearance, don't believe them! You remain a *wolf*, after all…"

"No? What, then?" he managed as he tried to glimpse his own

backside with a few slow, sharp circles.

Nanësra hesitated, opened her mouth, and, with a sigh and a flash of sorrow, added, "You'll learn. That's my hope for you, at least." She gave him a sad smile and turned away.

Sensing her imminent departure, Kalas blurted, "Wait! Before you go! If you're not going to help us, will you at least tell us why you freed us from Peradan's traps?"

She stopped. With a slow turn and a shrewd expression, she admitted, "I'm not the one who abetted your escape. Until Abarandal revealed your plight, your *kelâme* were shrouded from me: I couldn't…*see* you. And when I did arrive, it took time to cut through all these *shagabme* and *ekume* to reach you…"

"It wasn't you?" Kalas murmured. "Then who…?"

Nanësra tried to hide a subtle smile as gleaming wings unfurled behind her back. She rose into the night, her aura radiating rays of brilliance that caught and danced within invisible crystals scattered through the rocks on either side of the Ravine. Before she disappeared, she raised her sword and let its edges glitter in her light: *"Lasas yëlò ar shus!"* she boomed as a burst of white stung their eyes. When it passed, darkness pressed in all around them, frustrated only by the fading embers of their fire.

5.

Kalas woke from a fitful sleep when a shadow and a rush of wind passed over him. Staring into the ribbon of sky overhead, he caught the swish of something vast and distant in his periphery, but it disappeared before he could get a better look. Around him, most of the others had already risen: Shosafin sat next to the fire, poking it now and then with his sword. Kalas winced at the difficulty his gruff friend endured while adjusting to his weaker left hand.

"Good morning," Zhalera said when she realized he was awake.

397

"Good morning," he returned. "I thought I saw the dragon—maybe its tail, at least—somewhere above us, but I don't know."

"We've seen it, too," she confirmed. "No, I don't think it has any interest in us. Not anymore! I was thinking how you said the eaters under Deridzhas had captured their dragon…made me wonder if maybe Peradan or Marugan did something to the creature guarding this place. With both of them free…?"

"Wouldn't that be something," Kalas mused.

"Wouldn't *what* be something?"

"Oh! I was just thinking: what if this *gròma* and Lady crossed paths someday?"

"I…hmm, I'm not sure I like the idea!" Zhalera confessed.

"Well, what's the likelihood they'd ever meet, anyway? We're half a continent away from Deridzhas!"

Shosafin dropped his sword. Kalas looked over to see him shaking his hand and flexing his fingers. The soldier said nothing, nor made eye contact with anyone, but he couldn't disguise his frustration as he leaned over and retrieved his weapon.

"How's he doing?" Kalas whispered. "I mean, how's his shoulder?"

"You saw all the blood he lost. He's tired. It'll be some time before he's at his peak. I think he's afraid of what his 'peak' might have been reduced to," said Zhalera. Shosafin, aware of their presence, stopped working with his sword and tried to return it to its sheath. Kalas looked away as the disfigured man struggled with his task. Abarandal, who'd been watching, breathed a stream of melody and canted Shosafin's scabbard just enough for him to reach.

"You'll get there, she says," Kalas explained.

"Morning's almost over. Time to go," he said, ignoring Abarandal and Kalas. "Once we're back at Galámur, we'll charter passage to the mainland and—"

"You mean *after* Rül, Pava, and your cousin arrive, right?" Kalas insisted.

"I must get King Rufàran to Ïsriba! Nashmur knows how to handle himself. He'll keep your friends safe. He'd understand…"

"Oh yeah? Would Thara understand?" Zhalera piped up. "Seems to me you made a promise to protect her son! You can do that all the way from Ïsriba? Even when he's somewhere on the ocean?"

"Thara…" he began, but his petulant retort died after her name escaped his lips. "We'll find the others first, then return to Lohwàlar. My liege, it will delay us, but—"

"If you made a promise, you must keep it," Rufàran interrupted. "I'll go on ahead of you. It's—"

"No! I mean, forgive me, my liege, but Ësfàyami believes I had a deal with Emperor Kematu of Tsobarut. A deal that involved your head…not necessarily the rest of you. If you were to return without me…"

Rufàran gasped. "My daughter truly believes such nonsense?!"

"I'm sorry, my king: I understood too late that her counselors didn't have the kingdom's best interest at heart. Under their perverse tutelage, she's been…she's been misled."

"Then I'll wait. If it's really been Sevens, as all of you claim, then I can wait until you've fulfilled your promise. Lohwàlar, you said? *Rivertown.* Sounds like a lovely place!"

While the others prepared for the long, hard climb, Abarandal wandered toward a deeper crevice cut within the walls. Kalas watched as she ran her hands across its rough surface, as she furrowed her brow and hummed a few tentative bars. She reached a nondescript place, whistled a couple of notes, and, with a nod, placed both hands against the rock and…remained motionless.

"Abarandal? Everything all right?" Kalas wondered. She hadn't realized he'd been watching, and jumped when he called her name. Frustrated, she motioned for him to join her, to place his hands against the same stones. Curious, he obliged.

"What are you—?"

She placed a finger to his lips and arched an eyebrow.

"Sorry!"

With Abarandal watching him, he shrugged, closed his eyes, and tried to *see* or sense whatever captured the insistent girl's attention. He let the noise of their companions drift away from his conscious consideration; he let the dull hardness of the rocks transcend the sensitivity in his fingertips. When nothing happened, he opened his mouth, but a sudden *pull*—or was it a push?—pressed his entire body against the wall. Eyes wide, he pushed himself away, and, catching his breath, exclaimed, "What was that?!"

Abarandal didn't answer. Not even with a snatch of song. Instead, deeming his reaction confirmation of some undisclosed hypothesis, she cracked her knuckles—Kalas had never seen her do that before—and stood square to the rocks. She paused, issued a brief warning, and raised her voice.

"'Hold on'? Hold on to what?! What's going—!"

Her music was *command.* An inviolable instruction issued to the earth itself. Kalas stumbled as an unknown force impelled him toward the *eruín.* He worked his fingers raw as he tried to grab onto something, anything: at last, his hands found purchase, and he cried out when his feet left the ground, drawn toward Abarandal. The stargirl and her song became a nexus, a focus—an irresistible force not unlike one of Peradan's singularities.

"Abarandal!" Kalas shouted. She never heard him: the imploding sphere of spacetime ripped his voice apart before it ever reached her ears. Rocks from the cliff snapped like twigs and sheared away, enveloped by the burgeoning ball of energy and light. He tried again: "Abarandal! What are you—?!"

He fell.

After righting himself and dusting himself off, he watched as the last few threads of Abarandal's effort unraveled in a trick of light. She turned toward him when he called her name a third time: she stumbled when she tried to walk to him.

"Easy! Easy!" he cooed as he caught her and helped her stand. "What was that? A singularity? Look at the cliff! It's like someone carved a bowl into it! And *polished* it!"

She panted—other than the night at Troll's Gap, he'd never seen her so exhausted. In between gulps of air, she did her best to explain.

"You...altered your density? increased your gravity? I don't— how?! What—*why?!* What's in there? You saw something, didn't you? Felt something, maybe?"

Abarandal's breathing slowed and deepened as she recovered from her exertion. She shook her head and tried to answer Kalas' questions. Almost nothing she said made sense.

"Another *eru?* Is that what you're saying? Is that what I felt? And he's still inside the Mountain? You thought you could...what? Draw him...out?"

She picked up a piece of rock, held it at arm's length, and let it fall: before Kalas could interrupt, she held up a finger. Taking a deep breath, she closed her eyes, made and released a fist a few times, and held her outstretched hand above the stone. Kalas felt the pull again. Subtler. The shapes and colors around her fingers—light itself—*bent,* and the object rose up until she wrapped her fingers around it again.

"That's...*wow!*" Kalas stammered. Abarandal smiled and slumped against his side.

"Hey, I said easy!" he teased as he draped her arm around his shoulder. "C'mon, let's get out of this Ravine, get you back to the city, where you can take a nap!"

She managed a few phrases insisting Kalas let her try again, but he refused: "You can barely stand! Another try and you'll rip *yourself* apart, never mind these rocks! Maybe we can try again when you're rested?"

Too tired to argue, she complied. They'd only gone a few steps when a sharp crack reverberated through the chasm. Kalas jumped; then, abashed, looked over his shoulder for the source of the excitement. A jagged crevice, reaching beneath the ground and disappearing above the subtle curves of the Ravine, had split the "bowl" Abarandal's prior energies had made.

"What was—Abarandal! Is she all right?!" Zhalera rushed to her side and draped her other arm around her shoulders.

"She's fine. I think. She will be. Just needs some rest."

"Rest?"

"Yeah, I know, I know! She believes there's another *eru* inside the Mountain. She wants to try again, but look at her!"

"He's right, my sister: you *do* need rest! Here, it's nothing like our lodgings back in town, but sleep. Even if only for a little while. We'll be here when you wake."

6.

Kalas opened his eyes a few hours later: he, too, had needed the rest, though he wouldn't have admitted it. He stood and approached Abarandal and Zhalera: the latter worked her fingers in a blur while the former considered her movements. Shosafin and Rufàran examined the Ravine, the warrior shifting his weight from side to side, attempting to gauge his best approach. Nïmrïk padded into view from one end of the corridor and said, "It's not 'flat,' but half a league or so back that way, this polished floor turns into dirt and rocks, and the ground slopes upward. I only climbed a short distance, but it looks like there's a pretty severe forest above the rim. There's still ice and snow, but I think it's our best option..."

The wolf flicked his eyes at Shosafin's shoulder, at his *missing* arm. He looked away and added, "I could smell the ocean, too. It's still far away: the lot of you probably won't even notice."

"Then let's move," the rough soldier insisted as he stepped next to Nïmrïk.

"What were you two discussing?" Kalas asked Zhalera once underway. "I still don't know either of you make sense of all that finger-waving!"

"She woke up before you did. You—both of you, you've been through so much, and I didn't want to wake you. Anyway, she dragged me to that big crack in the wall. I don't think she found what she was looking for: she looked confused, like maybe she'd made a mistake about something. She asked me to get out my sword, so I did. It was weird: for a second, Valarandal glowed, and I felt like something was pulling me toward the mountain! Then it stopped. Faded, maybe. I'm not sure.

"I asked her what she thought would happen, but I think she was embarrassed. I don't know. Sometimes, I think I can read her pretty well; other times, I have no idea. She didn't want to talk about it. I was probably a little *too* persistent. I think I upset her..."

"Oh yeah? Well, I'm sure you two will work it out."

When everyone exited the Ravine, the suns had surpassed their zenith and began their subtle descent toward the horizon. Despite his injury, Shosafin offered no complaints nor demanded the others wait for him.

He knows Kadhëmba chose this route specifically for him, Kalas noted. *He's working harder than he should just to prove he won't be a burden, that he won't slow us down.*

"Hey, we're out of the Ravine! Let's...let's take a little break, all right? I...I could sure use one!"

"If you insist," Shosafin sighed, well aware of Kalas' intent.

"You lost a lot of blood," Rufàran reminded him. "You—"

"I know!" he roared, panting from his prior exertions. "I know! And I've...I know. Forgive me, my liege. Kalas: forgive me, lad. I'm...unaccustomed to accepting help from others. It's...it's humiliating."

"Humiliating? Or humbling?" the king sought to discern. "There's no reason to judge yourself humiliated. No reason except pride.

"And all of us—*all* of us—need to be humbled from time to time. Why do you think I made *you* my chief bodyguard? Oh, don't look at me like that! You *earned* your status: *other* captains believed themselves worthy of greater honor just because their *fathers* were men of renown. Such men need to be reminded from time to time: *service* merits honor! Not birth!

"Now: *rest.* Consider it a command. It'll give me a chance to learn more from your friends about the changed state of things. I'll admit I'm curious to learn more about this *rudzhún* with whom you've allied yourselves!"

"No, I—I mean: of course, my liege," he acquiesced. Finding a nice, thick tree, he leaned against its trunk and closed his eyes.

Nïmrïk guided them west along the rim of the Ravine until they reached the destroyed bridge; from there, he tracked his way toward Hëk's farm. Kalas considered a short visit, an opportunity to reassure Mohral, but given the party's condition, he said nothing.

When they reached Galámur and Daór's establishment, Kalas and Zhalera—and Rufàran—made quick work of an early lunch, doing their best to ignore the unsubtle murmurs from the tavern's other patrons. Shosafin's glistening wound still reeked of blood, sweat, and seared flesh, and the others bore their share of cuts and scrapes as well. From the overarching thread woven between each whispered conversations, Kalas gathered that only portsiders presented themselves with such ignominy.

Having finished eating, Rufàran insisted Shosafin get some sleep. The gruff soldier assured his king he'd be fine, that he'd undergone similar "treatment" not too long ago without adverse effects, but the *Poyïsriba* king remained adamant. Shosafin obeyed.

Before he and the others could stand from their table, a wiry fellow pulled up a chair and plopped down next to him. It took Kalas a moment to parse the curious familiarity in their guest's demeanor: when he flashed a twisted smile filled with polished, crooked teeth, he gasped.

"Morning, *shâume á âume!* Morning, King Rufàran! Welcome back!"

"Bayal?! You—!" Kalas managed.

"Indeed!"

"The *Kandha pïn Bethrume?* That means—!"

"Aye, and I'm sure you have questions. Come with me: we'll see how many I can answer."

"Wait! You know King Rufàran! But he—I mean, *how*—?"

"Not here, child! Not…not here. Besides, my, ah, *crewmates* are anxious to hear what you've been up to, too!"

CHAPTER XIII.

While Dreaming on the Water

PAVA VAULTED FROM THE EDGE OF HER SMALL BED AND wrapped Zhalera and Abarandal with her wiry, trembling arms. Rül offered more subdued greetings when Bayal ushered Kalas and the others into the cramped quarters he'd secured. Nashmur eyed his cousin through narrow slits, his stare an unspoken accusation: *I tried to warn you!* When he noticed Shosafin's missing arm, he abandoned his glower. The old soldier answered Nashmur's inquisitive gaze with a half-shrug.

"Looks like you've been through some stuff," the former commander began. He wagged a finger at his cousin's injury. "What... well...what happened?"

"Marugan."

"Marugan! You found him? He was here?!"

Shosafin allowed a wry grin. *"Was* here, yes."

"Oh? I see. Your side: it looks…it's *healed!* How is that possible?"

The old soldier said nothing. Sensing his reluctance, Kalas interjected, "The Deathless Flame! He's not just some random *eru:* he's Peradan! Of the Swath!"

Bayal, who'd been rearranging the room, dropped a small stool when he heard Peradan's name. Kalas looked up to see a harsh streak of blue surge within the first mate's eyes. He apologized and said, "I'm sorry: you said *Peradan* is the *Tshaggul Kavar?"*

"Yes! We asked around and learned about a farm, a woman…it's a long story, but she told us about a place at the bottom of the Ravine—someone said it almost looks like a slash through the north end of Avëlöth: *Galámurrinme* call it the Ravine. She—Sevens ago, she…anyway, we found a 'door' in the wall. The floors: they're *smooth*, polished, I'd say. That's not important, is it? All right: this 'door' was more like, uh, more like—"

"Mohral—the woman at the farm—called it a *soft* space. That turned out to be a pretty good description," Zhalera supplied. "We walked into it, and suddenly we were *inside* the Mountain! In a space like the Vault under Ïsriba, only—Oh! You couldn't know about that, could you?! It's—"

"It's all right," Bayal insisted, the faintest trace of impatience puckering the corners of his mouth. "Please: go on!"

"Yeah? All right, well, we got caught—cultists—and the Deathless Flame, towering over everything and dripping with hot blue fire, trapped us in a *singularity!*"

"Before he did," Kalas added, "he held me in some kind of…not *bubble*, not really, but maybe 'bubble' works? He told me about his plans for Abarandal. He threatened Zhalera—everyone, really—if I refused to help him. It seemed like an instant, but when we got out, hours had passed."

"You 'got out,' did you?" Bayal queried, his eyebrow raised.

"None of us knows how! I thought maybe Abarandal did something—*I* sure didn't! She said it wasn't her, though: she was stuck inside another wall, in some kind of shrine-like room! I can't explain it, but after a while, we…got her out of there—her *and* King Rufàran!"

"And you're sure the *eru* posing as the Deathless Flame was Peradan? Not, say, Sifuran? Heshradan? Some other, unnamed entity?"

"I thought it probably *was* Sifuran, now that you mention it,"

Kalas admitted. He's one of the Swath, one of—wait: do you know about the Great Swath? The—"

"I've heard the stories," Bayal dismissed.

"All right, so Sifuran: his aura is blue, right? Since the Deathless Flame is described as rippling with blue flames—not orange or yellow or some 'normal' color—I just assumed it was Sifuran. Under Ïsriba, Sifuran seemed most anxious to summon Abarandal from…actually, I don't know *where* she's from. Not exactly. I guess it's not important right now…

"Anyway, the cultists' preferred color is blue, and the few we crossed paths with all said they were following the Path of Sifuran, part of some pilgrimage or whatever. In the Vault, the *Kel Erume* had a long talk with each other—none of the rest of us knows what it was about—but after that, before they brought forth Abarandal, they disappeared for a while. We have no idea where they went. When the *ekume* attacked, we figured someone had betrayed the Swath. Like I said, if the traitor *was* part of the Swath, I figured it had to be Sifuran…

"Inside Glass Sword Mountain, though, we found this: *Peradan's sword!* He had it with him when he first materialized under the *Poyïsriba* Vault; later, he said he lost it in a fight. *Ekume.* But yesterday—two days ago? Whatever! When he shed his flames, he had a spear with him—the same spear he had *after* he lost his sword."

Kalas drew *Sharuyandas Tshandu* and held it aloft.

Stunned, Bayal's eyes remained fixed on the glittering blade, his expression an unlikely blend of horror, surprise, and dawning realization. Myriad emotions flickered through his features before coalescing in a gout of apoplectic laughter.

"He's good!" the sailor managed at last. "Oh, he's good! Never suspected a thing! I should have, I suppose, but, no…Or maybe… maybe I just didn't want to…"

"What are you…what do you mean?" Kalas wondered with his head canted.

"What? Oh, nothing. Nothing! Young Kalas, may I see that weapon you've recovered?"

"The sword? Right! Of course! Here you go."

Bayal took the blade and twisted it in the suns-light filling the room. Bright sparks arced within each crystalline facet shifting along its spine. He cut a series of deft swipes across the air, smiled and nodded, and presented its hilt to the young man. Something in his movements seemed familiar, and Kalas tried to remember why.

"Definitely one of hers," Bayal muttered as Kalas tucked the sword into his belt.

I'll have to get a sheath for this!

"One of…hers?" Zhalera prodded.

"Oh, this sword was most definitely Peradan's. I wondered if it might have been a forgery, but—"

"Shosafin here killed Marugan with it!" Kalas insisted.

"—but no, it's definitely the sword Peradan carries. *Used* to carry. You already know it's capable of cutting down *ekume*—something no mere copy could do! Only—it seems only *Valaran-unas* weapons possess that trait. Whatever his purposes, it seems the Creator bestowed such authority on no one else…

"Looks like you could use something to keep it in, yes? I might have something suitable lying around, if you'd be interested."

"Yeah! I am!"

Zhalera cut him off before he could continue his story: "There's more to tell, of course—Marugan, Nanësra, and—"

"Nanësra?" Bayal said with a start.

"You know that name?" Kalas asked.

"We can talk about all that later," Zhalera continued. "*Zhiamdas Salorosh* and *Lord of Winds* left Melash on the same day, almost at the same time, but we got here days before you did! What took you so long? What happened?"

2.

"Like most people who make their living from the sea, Captain Lâris devoted herself to Sifuran via the *Randa pïni Sifumilël*. Not too long ago, she sailed the *Winds* into Serular. The cult's influence had been increasing for Sevens, and from what I've been able to piece together, she more or less subscribed to their manifesto: it's probable she believed Sifuran to be the Deathless Flame—not unlike you, Kalas—and sought to gain power or privilege by pledging her allegiance."

The young man noticed a shudder of disgust ripple across the old salt's face as he described Lâris' motivation, like her choices offended him on a personal level.

"Her *former* first mate wanted nothing to do with the cult. According to the crew, he confronted the captain: he'd lived his early Sevens in Serular, before the cult acquired its present status, and he begged her to cut ties before 'Sifuran himself tears the *Winds* apart.' She cut him down where he stood, wiped her blade on his shirt, and made sure everyone on deck understood what happened. And *why*. Every member of her crew cast their lot with the cult after that, though I suspect most 'conversions' were more pragmatic than profound. I'd heard rumors about the Deathless Flame, about his presumed identity, and I made it my goal to discover who would dare profane…Sifuran's good name. I played along with Captain Lâris' ambition, learning what I could as the *Winds* sailed the oceans.

"I didn't learn much, not at first, but after a while, we heard about a gathering, a summons, I guess, of people devoted to the self-described *Tshaggul Kavar*. One of his contemporaries—Marugan—had recently fled his prior environs. Secret whispers suggested anyone devoted to the cult should travel north, and so we did. We docked at Melash to rest, resupply, and…wait. We had no idea where we were headed next. The captain visited with a professor from the university: Ravi? Rahi? No, Rahwi! Professor Rahwi, himself a member of the cult, if my guess is correct. Afterward, she told us we'd sail for Avëlöth in a couple of days. Said she had some business to attend to first. I followed her into that alehouse where Nashmur found me and discovered her 'business' consisted of little more than 'getting drunk.' I don't know—it's nothing I could rationally explain, but I think she sensed a coming change. Probably *not* the change that came—for her, anyway—but then again…?

"I watched the *Salorosh* leave the harbor: it's good for you that you escaped—yes, escaped!—Melash when you did! A couple of hours later, before the *Winds* hoisted her sails, a mob of cultists swarmed the docks and demanded passage on any ship bound for Avëlöth. All the way north, Captain Lâris didn't know exactly when or where she and her ilk would meet their false god.

"Peradan! I still can't…Never mind! Somehow, the cult as a whole decided they had to make for Galámur *that day*. Maybe Peradan appeared to them in a dream. Maybe that professor character goaded them into action. I don't know.

"The captain made as much room as she could, but even she realized the *Winds* was dangerously overladen. Before Serular, she'd taken on bale after bale of heavy equipment. Weapons components. Things I haven't seen since…uh, well, anyway: even the captain realized she couldn't accommodate any one else. We pushed back dozens of would-be travelers before we just cut lines and put out into deeper water."

"It was crazy!" Rül interjected. "The three of us tried to keep out of the way, but it seemed like every last inch of every single deck was crawling with blue-robes! A few of 'em took an interest in Pava…a very *unhealthy* interest! I knocked a few heads together, and I'm not ashamed to admit it!"

"Lest the boy give you the wrong idea, we did keep a low profile. Overall," Nashmur clarified. "For the first few days, we carved out a hiding place in the hold. Seawater kept that place cold—almost as cold as Ïsriba in the depth of winter! Even down there, I knew something was wrong with the ship: I'm not a sailor, but I have sailed before, and I could feel the *Winds* listing to port. Or was it starboard? The point is: something was wrong with the ship! I told Rül and Pava to stay hidden while I went to investigate. I probably should have stayed hidden, too. I heard shouting. Screaming, really. I sought its source and discovered cultists and crew members alike bleeding out all over the place. We were in the middle of a mutiny!"

"Turns out Lâris understood the *Winds* would never reach Avëlöth with everyone and everything on board, so she started… tossing excess weight overboard," Bayal continued. "I've encountered many dead-hearted creatures across my Sevens, but Captain Lâris was a rare breed. She cut down blue-robes left and right: I'm surprised her arm never tired! And the way she *grinned* the whole while! She *enjoyed* it. Even after she and her crew had trimmed the ship, she seemed bent on culling every surviving passenger. We did our best to quell her bloodlust, and I thought we'd succeeded, but I suspect I'm not the only one who kept a close eye on things afterward.

"I hadn't known the captain for very long, but something in her manner suggested instability: after the passengers' ill-fated uprising, she considered every imagined slight a prelude to mutiny. Maybe a day or two later, I woke to the sounds of screaming: by the time I got there, a couple of crew had pinned her arms, but not before she'd cut down a hapless deckhand. She *almost* wrenched herself free, insisting the dead swabby had purposefully splashed water on her boots earlier that day. Other crew showed up and bound her hands and feet—but not without a struggle! We tossed her in a closet—the *Winds* has no proper brig—and barred the door as best we could, but Lâris knew her ship. Most of her crew realized she'd abandoned her sanity; one unfortunate soul, however, discovered it the hard way: she convinced him to let her go, and she thanked him by stealing his sword and driving it so deeply into his chest that she couldn't pull it from his bones…"

"She found us!" Rül elaborated. "She was sneaking around below decks, headed where, I don't know, but I think we surprised her: she sure surprised us! I was half asleep and she grabbed my *tëvët!* It's a good thing Pava can see pretty well in the dark: she heard me struggling with the captain, woke up, and knocked the *tëvët* out of her hands!"

"She slipped away after that," Pava continued. "Bayal put Nashmur on guard duty, said he remembered his initial distrust from their first meeting—I didn't know what he was talking about. I guess it doesn't matter now. Anyway, we searched the upper decks and told Nashmur the captain was free!"

"We told him what had happened, and the three of us went looking for Bayal. The commander's idea," continued Rül. "We didn't see him on the main deck, but before we could find him, we felt the whole ship just *rumble,* like something exploded! I almost fell overboard—Pava and Nashmur grabbed me before I did. We couldn't tell *where* the explosion—whatever it was—had come from, so we hurried below decks to check the hull. That's when we found Bayal, standing over Captain Lâris. She…she was dead!"

"There was water *everywhere!*" Pava added. "Water and a black, iridescent sludge. I thought maybe the *Winds* had a hole in it, but Bayal—Bayal, you seemed unconcerned! Anyway, she'd gotten her hands on another sword: Bayal kicked it away, knelt down, and… You whispered something, didn't you? I couldn't make it out. The look on your face: I thought it was a prayer."

"It…yes, it was a prayer. After a fashion," Bayal allowed. He paused, his focus somewhere else for a moment, before he sighed and shook his head.

"I didn't say anything then—didn't want to worry anyone, but there *was* a breach. I told the crew to patch it as best they could, but the *Winds* needed to be drydocked for proper repairs. I…hoped if we cut speed, we'd eventually make it to Galámur…"

"You never told us how she died," Nashmur said, and Kalas sensed the soldier had been waiting for an opportunity to pose his questions: "What happened to her? Were you, uh, *there* when she…I mean…how *did* she die?"

3.

"'How did she die?'" Bayal repeated, his eyes focused on something—some*when*—far away. "Her peculiar 'allegiance' to the Deathless—to Peradan—became a door too enticing for her to ignore. Somewhere between Serular and Melash, she tethered her *kelâ* to an *egu*. She—"

Kalas gasped as images of Dzharëth, sallow and sitting in a wreck of tattered flesh, vaulted up from the depths of his subconscious. Bayal appraised him with a pause and a raised eyebrow. With a knowing nod, he continued: "When I found her, she wore the blackened form of a hairless wolf, gnashing her yellowed teeth and beating her bloodied wings against the hull. We fought. Briefly. In all my Sevens, it's always been the *egu* whose strength of will maintains their malign symbiosis—no, parasitism, really. Yet *Lâris* seemed the dominant figure in this tethering! Her will remained resolute, I'm sure, but with the fast-approaching dissolution of her *kelâ* from her flesh, the *egu* sensed an opportunity to flee: the energy of their opposing wills manifested as explosive power. The three of you appeared soon after."

415

Awestruck from the unimagined details Bayal provided, everyone seemed at a loss for words—considering, perhaps, what other dangers remained just beneath the surface of their daily lives.

We roam the detritus of a broken world, Loradan said beneath Ïsriba.

Judging from the other's introspective expressions, Kalas assumed they were most concerned with Captain Lâris' secrets; however, he sifted through the particulars of Bayal's story from a different perspective.

"Your clothes," he said. Almost mumbled.

"Come again?"

"There's not a drop of that black stuff on you. Nor the stink of burning flesh. It seems you know an awful lot about *egume* for a first mate. I've only known a few others who understood the union between *edhu* and *egu,* who described it like you did: a *tether.* You said you *fought* her. How? With what? No mortal blade can stay the arm of the immaterial. Not for long. You said as much yourself! And anyway: you don't have a weapon on your person! You're hiding something from us. You have been ever since that rat hole on the docks at—"

"Master Kalas, I assure you—"

"—at Melash. No, I know—somehow, I can't explain—you're… not *safe,* but…I've only attained two Sevens. Until last summer, I'd never left my home. Tell me: why does it seem like we've met before?"

"Uh, I…"

"Not in Lohwàlar, no. I know everyone there—by face if not by name. You've never been to Lohwàlar. Not in the last two Sevens, anyway. Not in Thosha. Nor Âivambar. In Ïsriba, we were surrounded by Ësfàyami's minions—as Commander Nashmur knows full well…"

With a sigh and a sly smile, Bayal, replied, "That's not entirely true, is it?"

"Yes, it's—wait: what?"

"*Under* Ïsriba, after Marugan's *shagabme* threatened to overpower you. After that…?"

"There's no way you could know about that! About *any* of that!" Kalas insisted, hastening to his feet. "Not unless—"

"Unless I was there. I was."

"Impossible! You'd have to be one of—"

"The *Kathin Sâash*. The *Kel Erume,* if you prefer. Here: allow me a moment…"

In what seemed like an ephemeral twist of light, Bayal's face contorted—no, relaxed, as though it had been contorted the whole time. His eyes, already as blue as the open sea, shone with a deeper, purer blue, and his grinning, once-crooked teeth formed a perfect curve within his steadfast jaw. Even his clothes *shimmered* in the late morning suns-light before the twist refracted the image away.

Again, Kalas gasped.

"Did you *see* that?!" he demanded of the others. "It's—how? *Why?*"

"See what?" Nashmur wondered with subtle glances across the room.

"Kalas?" Zhalera prodded.

Most of the others offered puzzled looks all around. Nïmrïk chuckled. Abarandal sang.

"Hey, I've heard that before!" Zhalera said, catching the last few notes. "Somewhere. I can't remember where…"

"It's his name," Kalas understood. Abarandal nodded.

"Whose name? Bayal's?" Rül suggested, attempting to piece things together.

"In a manner of speaking, I suppose it is," Kalas allowed. He remembered the moment beneath Lohwàlar's Sanctuary when Tsharak divined Falthwën's true name. The eccentric old man had kept the mysterious cleric's secret then; Kalas would keep Bayal's now.

"Unless he says it's something else," he shrugged.

"You harbor discretion beyond your years, young man! Perhaps I should have understood a *Nalëndas* would discern things others would not. It's been so long since I've crossed paths with someone so *gunagas*—blessed *and* cursed at the same time..."

"Bayal, who *are* you?" Pava wanted to know.

"No, I suppose there's nothing to be gained from excessive discretion," he sighed as he held her gaze, winked, and filled the room with a blast of blue-white light.

Gasps abounded as Bayal's seafaring garments fluttered in a breath of sudden wind and resolved as scintillating robes; his salty features assumed other, familiar contours.

"*Sifuran?!*" Pava exclaimed—and clapped a hand over her mouth. "What are you—what are you doing *here?!* Have you—?! You've been with us this whole time! And you never said a word! It can't be mere coincidence you just *happened* to join up with Lâris' crew! What happened to the other *erume?* I mean Loradan, Yayan, Heshradan. There were so many *ekume!* Did they...?"

"I don't know, but I believe—I *choose to* believe they're well," Sifuran assured her with a wave of his hand. "Loradan's...call it a *spell*, although that's not quite right: it seems her *spell* chased everyone and everything from the Vault. Hers is the realm of the immaterial, after all...

"We knew we'd been betrayed—but not by *whom*. Not one of *you*—not even you, Nïmrïk: I knew that much even then, despite Peradan's contrarian insistence. I'll confess: even now, it's hard to believe he's a traitor to the Swath. Oh, how foolish! How self-important we *Erume pïni Sâash* have become!"

Sifuran choked on a spate of unhappy laughter, wiped at his teeming eyes, and continued: "No, my child: not coincidence! Everything I've told you—then and now—is the truth. Our discussion under the Vault, before we summoned Abarandal: we discussed the Deathless Flame. Among other things. Maybe it's because he chose *me* to parody—or maybe it's because of my delegated gifts—but I intended to discover this pretender and put an end to his chicanery. Now, mine is the *guilt* of *water,* among others…

"After the world was cracked, the *Randame* were intended to serve as tangible symbols of the Creator's presence, conveyed through us, his intermediaries. His servants. And we are *all* his servants: as members of the Swath, *our* service was to tune the hearts of a world without music to the strains of The Song. To reunite their *kelâme* with that ancient and eternal melody. When the world remembered *Zhi Helim* again, we assumed the *Randame* would cease to be. We were wrong. The cataclysm served its purpose, but the sickness in men's hearts lingered: succumbing to that sickness, it wasn't long before they corrupted their way upon the earth yet again!

"We professed our failure before the Creator. Shamed, we offered to *unmake* the *Randame* and suffer the 'death of light'—the cessation of our exalted station—should such sacrifice atone for our inability to carry out his will. Our maudlin gestures weren't of interest, however: instead, as though he *foreknew* how things would happen, he nodded and dismissed us with a kind word."

"You—you've seen the Creator? Face to face?!" Kalas marveled.

"Of course not!" Bayal exclaimed as every vestige of color drained from his expression. "Not exactly. It's hard to explain to someone whose entire existence has been encumbered by flesh, whose soul has yet to experience the eternal, unbounded by time. He made his will known to us. That's about as plainly as I know how to state it. And so the *Randame* persisted. For a time. Some—most—became shadows of their former glory. Others were abandoned altogether. And some—like the *Randa pïni Sifumilël*—devolved into heretical cults. Many, *many* Sevens ago, I struck down the most ardent sects. It seems time and inattention provided fertile ground for those old sentiments to smolder—if you'll forgive the pun!—until Peradan—*nëshras fie hòyihad nir!*—assumed the avatar of the *Tshaggul Kavar*..."

He sighed and added: "Looks like I'm on my way to Serular. Again."

"You're welcome to come with us!" Rül offered. "I mean, we're not going to Serular, but we are heading south. I think. Kalas, we're heading south, right? Y'know...home?"

Rül's friend looked from face to face across the cramped room. Most eyes turned toward him, expectant. Shosafin's remained focused on the floor.

"South," Kalas nodded. *"Home.* Marugan is gone, but Peradan is still out there. And remember what Obën said: other wills are guiding other kingdoms toward war, too. I don't know what we can do about that, but I intend to learn...

"Zhalera: Professor Tomush. At the university. I think he'd be interested in hearing about what we've discovered. I'm...I'm pretty sure I saw what was left of Professor Rahwi under the Mountain, too...

"Sifuran—Bayal? We'll need to check in with the harbormaster, but I don't know when the *Salorosh*—the ship that brought us here—is expected back. It might be a while. If it's any consolation, I think her captain observed the old ways. The 'old wisdom,' he said...Is the *Bethrume* seaworthy?"

"Oh yeah: I guess we'd need to go with *you,*" Rül acknowledged.

"The *Winds* needs some repairs, it's true, but I think she'll hold together. Truth be told, it doesn't really matter! Why don't you spend the rest of the day recuperating: I'll go portside and get things ready. If all goes well, we should be sailing by this time tomorrow."

4.

Despite the unmistakable remnants of her recent misfortune, the *Kandha pïn Bethrume* glided over the Roiling Ocean. Contradicting their namesake, the glass-like waters mirrored the bright blue sky as the ship sliced across their surface. Kalas watched, transfixed, as their keel bled out a thin, symmetrical line of white as accommodating winds shepherded them toward Melash. Sifuran's *theme* hummed along the precipice of perception, assuming prominence within the Song.

Not magic. Privilege, Kalas reminded himself.

"What's on your mind?" Zhalera asked, suddenly at his side. He'd been so engrossed with his thoughts about recent events he hadn't heard her approach. She giggled and placed a hand on his shoulder when he started.

"I mean, of *all* the things that must be on your mind, which stands out the most?"

"This water," he said, inclining his head. "It's impossibly calm. Or maybe it isn't. We're desert-dwellers: what do we know about water?! Still…Falthwën's *gifts*—his *guilt*—had to do with healing. Among other things. Sifuran's have to do with water. Among other things. These conditions must be his doing."

"Water? You're thinking about water?" Zhalera repeated.

"No, not really," he sighed, "but it's easier than thinking about what comes next. Marugan's gone, but it seems like he might have been the least of our worries. Peradan's out there. And Tsathrâuda, too! I was thinking: remember, back in Lohwàlar, when Pava said Hwanzho's…friends? relatives? I don't remember, but they said something about a wingèd wolf: that I *do* remember, and I think maybe they—Hwanzho—was talking about Tsathrâuda.

"I don't know what to do, Zhalera. It's been months, and I still have no idea what I'm supposed to do regarding the prophecy the *erume* told us about. I'll bet Tsathrâuda knows, and, given what the Swath told us about *her*, I'll bet she'll stop at nothing to make sure I never learn. I'm not ashamed to admit I'm scared. I'm a *little* ashamed to admit I'm grateful for these delays—Melash. Serular. Lohwàlar. It'll give me time to keep studying that book. The book Tomush seems so interested in. Yes, the book I can't read. I guess I'm hoping something will, I don't know, *click* one day. There are times when it seems like I'm *this close* to understanding parts of it."

Zhalera opened her mouth, held her breath for a moment, and opted not to say anything. She worked her fingers across his shoulder and smiled before she, too, turned her gaze toward the sea.

After a while, Abarandal joined them. Kalas thought she was about to sing something when she paused, arrested by the melody woven within the waves. She smiled, allowed herself a moment, then cleared her throat and whispered a subtle phrase at the young man.

"Oh? Uh, yeah, sure. I'll, uh, I'll be…I'll see you later!"

"Kalas?"

"Abarandal has something she wants to ask you. Privately. I'm gonna see what Rül and Pava are doing—no, I'm gonna see how Shosafin's holding up. Or—No! I'll study my book. Now's as good a time as any."

Below decks, Kalas rifled through his gear until he found the indecipherable text. He thumbed through its pages and stared at the characters like he had so many times before.

With similar results.

He sighed, clapped it shut, and headed for the main deck.

Maybe suns-light and fresh air will help me think more clearly?

Kalas risked a glance toward the bow, where Abarandal and Zhalera remained engaged in an animated conversation. Even from afar, it seemed to him like the substance of their discussion trended toward the unpleasant. He turned toward the stern. Finding a comfortable spot atop a pile of sailcloth, he situated himself beneath the suns and opened his book again. Instead of flipping from page to page, he studied the faded gilt worked into its covers and traced a finger over its contours. Soon, lulled by the salt-scented air and the rhythm of the waves, he fell asleep.

A wisp of chilled wind twisted across his face, and Kalas opened his eyes with a start. He blinked a couple of times at the curious pink color permeating the atmosphere and, acknowledging something peculiar in his peripheral vision, turned his attention toward the star-strewn sky. While swollen strings of puffy clouds stretched low across the horizon, the bright blue of midday dissolved to black. Bright and shining, sparks of light danced across the firmament, and Kalas suspected he'd found himself suspended between realities, neither awake nor dreaming. A harsh red streak traced an angry line through the middle of the overhead expanse: leading the trail of dissipating residue, he thought he discerned a discrete shape—something he shouldn't have recognized, yet some indescribable aspect about it insisted he'd seen it before. His world was impossibly *quiet*.

Its brilliance died out, and Kalas realized he was still holding his book. Heavy before, now it seemed its weight had increased sevenfold. Its covers gleamed in the warm light suffusing his strange environs. Traces of…fire? energy? raced within its gold and silver embellishments as he turned to the first page. Intrigued by its familiar, illegible markings, he wondered if he'd ever unlock the secrets they withheld. He wondered if Nanësra had any idea what she—

One of the strokes glittered like a star, twinkling against the night. He held his breath when another flared up, then another. It seemed, from his perspective, these lights existed *behind* the strange words drawn across the page. Kalas angled the book and marveled at the shifting planes revealed within its inked lines. Unable—unwilling, perhaps, to look away, his mind's eye followed the stars within the text until a string of glyphs tore themselves free from the page and wrapped him in their strokes. Their touch felt like ice and fire on his skin. He struggled against his improbable bonds, but the shapes leapt upon him with increasing speed: they lodged within his ears; choked the air from his lungs; and, at the apex of the horror rising in his thoughts, pierced his eyes like slender thorns. As the last character sped toward his face, reflected against the back of his mind, he saw the world—the *planet*—wreathed in blue and white and suspended from nothing.

Still bound, he felt the words writhing across his flesh and searing his skin. Intimations of meaning pounded at his thoughts—*creation* and *communion*, woven within the shapes for *harmony*—the root chord of the Song. *Corruption* and *curse* intertwined with *dissonance*. He watched a singular sun rise above the darkness and illuminate a world already green and thriving: an instant later, heavy clouds emerged out of nowhere and blotted out the light. He watched the seeds of arrogance—cast from a bitter hand—bloom within the hearts of men and bear the black fruit of pride.

Thunder resounded beneath the canopy of sky, followed by the rush of water and the ringing out of gut-dropping cracks as the earth split. Mountains erupted, spraying sheets of molten rock across the never-ending night. Lightning chafed against the overwhelming veil of shadow, each forked blast at last succumbing to a superior foe. Revealed within their feeble lights, Kalas watched, helpless, as the world rent itself apart and died between a war of fire and water.

Despite the unending turmoil revealed by the second skin of glyphs still clinging to his frame, the unanswered *quiet* unnerved Kalas the most. As each scene pressed itself upon his thoughts, a unique collection of characters—*words*, he supposed—assaulted his senses. As wave after wave of catastrophic power rose up and ripped the light from the stars, a wave of another sort crashed against his mind: an inescapable dread that all was lost.

He sighed. Sobbed. Stared blindly into the eternal night thrust upon him. He didn't notice the coded swirls and slashes peeling away from his skin until he could no longer bear the incessant pricking sensation marching toward the forefront of his thoughts: when the last glyph extracted its barbs from his eyes, he knew he was free, but freedom seemed unimportant in a universe unmade.

A silent blast of fierce white light soared out of the darkness, away from the ruined surface of the earth, gaining magnitude and strength as it arced toward the heavens. The darkness shriveled at its passing, reeling from the glow trailing in its icy wake. Kalas was not prepared when an ear-splitting *BOOM!* collided with his chest and sent him careening through spacetime.

Another light—warm and golden—twisted into view, and the former light *embraced* the latter. Commingled, their brilliance suffused the shrinking black. Kalas felt his substance…*slip away*, but before the waxing radiance overshadowed what thready vestiges of sense he possessed within this realm, the word-shapes that once held him burst into flame. Unconsumed, their constituents rearranged themselves into ordered rows and columns, and, for a fleeting moment, the young man understood their meaning.

5.

Kalas said nothing about his waking dream while the Winds sailed ever nearer Melash-Niruk. He tried to camouflage his excitement, his altered perception as he continued to peek between the covers of his book whenever possible: he worried his renewed focus would raise eyebrows, and, for some inexplicable reason, some compulsion urged him to keep his secrets for a time. Would Zhalera notice? Would Abarandal?

Over the next few days, he discovered his friends had secrets of their own. Something in their dynamic had shifted, but when he asked, neither wanted to talk about it. Indeed, their close friendship seemed strained as they kept a polite—albeit peculiar—distance from one another.

"I don't get it," Kalas admitted one morning. "Just a few days ago, you two boxed me out of a long conversation! What could have happened to—"

"I said I don't want to talk about it," Zhalera reminded him with an edge in her voice.

"I'm sorry," Kalas apologized. "I was trying to…I just…you two have become like sisters. It makes me sad to see something come between you."

"How could someone like me think of someone—some*thing* like her as a sister?! Kalas, she's so *different* from us. From *me,* anyway. Higher. *Better.* She asked me…never mind. I'm sorry it's taken me so long to create a sword for you."

"What? No, don't worry about that! What are you talking about? I mean, why mention it now?"

"Never mind," she repeated with a sigh and shook her head.

Kalas said nothing for a while; instead, he reached across the railing for her hand as she stared at the crisp horizon. He remembered a time when she massaged the webbing between his thumb and forefinger and did the same for her. She relaxed—just a little—with another sigh.

"When Peradan had me in that singularity, he said some things. Mostly garbage, but on one point, I agree with him. Marugan thought Tsathrâuda was going to, I don't know, change him into an *elu* or something. And I don't know if you remember, but Falthwën once told us about a woman—an *edhu* woman—who became a star. Anyway, Peradan said it didn't matter: from his perspective, *elume* were no more important than *erume*. Now, I know he reached a different conclusion from that observation, but I think I understand what he was getting at: the Creator made each of us *elu, eru,* and *edhu* for a reason. Did Abarandal give you the idea she believed herself 'above' you? Me? Anyone?"

Zhalera maintained her silence, but Kalas felt the slightest twitch ripple down her arm and into her fingers.

"I didn't think so," the young man nodded. "I won't say anything else about it, but I hope—no, I *know* you two will find a way through this."

"Kalas, you have no idea what she's asking! She wants me to— but how could I?! I can't! I won't! It's impossible! It's…There's no way I could ever measure up, meet the standard she demands!"

"I hoped you would overcome your self-doubt," Kalas lamented. "Maybe you haven't yet, but you *will*—I know it! Even if you don't. Abarandal is like a child in some ways, but in others, she's fathomless. If she asked something of you, she must believe you're capable of it."

He pulled her away from the railing and turned her toward himself. He took her other hand and waited until she met his gaze.

"I believe you can do it, too."

"You don't even know what she asked!"

"I don't need to."

He let go of one hand and traced the hard knot of tight jaw muscle just below her temple. He smiled and willed his confidence in her to manifest within her own breast as he kissed her forehead.

Melash-Niruk looked the same as it had when they left: ships coming and going or waiting for longshoremen to load and unload their cargoes; passengers thronging along the various piers, some boarding, others debarking. Despite the activity, things operated with a practiced and efficient normalcy. Kalas said as much, and Rül and Pava laughed: compared to the frantic scene they'd endured, the waterfront looked downright placid.

"My friends, why don't we retrieve the coach you told me about? From what I've gathered, it's still where you left it," Sifuran suggested. "Master Kalas: I've brought the Winds as far as she'll go. You said you knew a captain who might sail us toward Serular?"

"Dzholëf," he nodded. The *eru* grinned—he knew that name, it seemed. "I'll find him. If he's around! Maybe Professor Tomush would know? I...I'd like to have a word with him anyway..."

While the others followed Rül and Pava, Kalas insisted Zhalera accompany him and Abarandal. It took some doing to persuade them both to abide one another's presence—not because of animosity; rather, it seemed, because of abject deference: neither wanted to upset the other. With an impatient sigh, Kalas cut through their strained interaction: "I don't know what's going on. I'd ask, but it's really none of my business. Things are awkward, I get that, but it doesn't change your friendship, does it? No, I didn't think so! So c'mon: we have things to do, and not a lot of time!"

Neither woman met the other's eyes, but both followed as Kalas led them across the bridge that spanned the Dzhinilmor and into the hills where the University stood. They skipped the main office, dodged the returned student body as it undulated through the ivied columns and thronging halls, and headed straight for Professor Tomush's quarters. Kalas did his best to ignore his own pangs of insufficiency: he wondered how someone from his unremarkable beginnings might compare with the serious-faced souls whizzing by.

The professor didn't answer when they knocked on his door.

"He's probably in class," Zhalera muttered.

"You're probably right," Kalas admitted. "He is a professor, and school's in session. I'm sorry I rushed us all the way out here! Do you want to go back, or do you think we should wait here?"

"We're already here, and we don't know what his schedule is: walking all the way to town seems unnecessary. Let's wait," Zhalera suggested. "You know, I'll bet his classroom's around here somewhere. Why don't we see if we can find it?"

"Yeah, good idea," Kalas said. "Why don't you lead the way? I'll be honest: I'm surprised I remembered where Tomush's quarters were. I'm afraid I'll get us lost!"

Zhalera's dour expression cracked into a subtle grin as she grabbed his hand. "C'mon then, you two!" she said as she guided them through the corridors. "Let's check down here…"

"How'd you know he'd be here?" Kalas marveled when she stopped them just outside his door. The professor's warbling voice lilted through the windows, describing some ancient war and the geopolitical situation that precipitated such hostilities. He mentioned the "southern continent" and something about a strange blue metal: these topics held Kalas' interest, but when Tomush added border disputes and collapsed trade negotiations, he started counting all the stones in the nearest wall just to keep himself awake.

"I didn't, but it seemed a logical choice. This wing, this floor is where they keep the history department—I remember that from last time. What do you think he meant when he was talking about *zhi iltshagdâgme*—the houseless ones? Almost sounds like Pava's people."

"Oh? I guess I stopped listening. Guess maybe I'm not cut out for university…"

"What? That's a strange thing to say! I only meant—Oh! Looks like his class is out! C'mon!"

Although he wasn't expecting them, Tomush welcomed Kalas, Zhalera, and Abarandal into his classroom when the last of his students shuffled toward some other destination. Rapt, he listened while they outlined their adventures since their last meeting. He seemed unsurprised when Kalas told him about the late Professor Rahwi.

"It's ironic: that the 'god' he believed would grant him…whatever boon or beneficence he anticipated would be his downfall! And Sifuran himself was here in Melash! The company you keep!"

The young man asked the professor if he knew when Captain Dzholëf might return. He didn't, but suggested it wouldn't be more than a few days.

"If that's not soon enough, there's likely other ships bound for Serular?"

"I'd rather wait," Kalas confessed. "A few days won't make too much difference…"

They talked a while longer, until Tomush said he needed to prepare for his next class. As they stood to leave, Kalas wondered if he should mention his dream or vision or whatever it was regarding his grandfather's old book. He hadn't said anything about it to anyone, although he'd wished—more than once—that Falthwën had been around to walk him through such things.

But he isn't. Nor will he be…

"Uh, Professor, real quick: do you remember this book?" he prodded as he removed it from the small pack he wore.

"Of course! It's probably too much to hope you've changed your mind about leaving it with me?" Tomush smiled.

"Yeah, sorry," Kalas apologized. "I just wanted to tell you: I had a…well, not a *dream,* not exactly, but…I thought I fell asleep, and I saw…I saw some strange things. Anyway, the words from this book came to life and…well, before I woke up, I *knew*—somehow, I *knew* what they said!"

6.

"I saw the world beneath a singular sun. I heard The Song—Creation's Prayer—without any taint of brokenness. And then I watched while everything fell apart. Before I could breathe again, thousands of years had come and gone, and I saw shadows rise up and eat the light. I remember feeling helpless. *Hopeless.* Darkness was everywhere.

"Then, with everything silent, light exploded from the ground, and the sun—Nalënahwu—tore apart the black as the second light—the second sun?—hurried toward him. The Song came back, and when it knocked me…awake, I don't know, as the words sped by, I understood them!"

"You understand them?!" Tomush almost whispered, his fingers drawing lines in the air.

"I…I did. For a moment. I've been studying the shapes every chance I get, but the glow, that white fire is gone, and looking at the words feels like looking at a memory I'm not sure was ever mine. Still, I remember the story—the history I learned from that moment. At first, I thought I was only seeing things. Making stuff up in my head, maybe. Now, though…I can't explain it, but—"

He whirled around when he thought he heard beating wings just outside the classroom. Peering through hazy-paned windows, he saw nothing notable, but he smiled as he turned toward his friends.

"I see," he muttered.

"Kalas!" Zhalera almost shouted. "You never told us this!"

"I wasn't sure I had anything to tell," he deflected. "Even until now, I think I'd convinced myself I'd imagined the whole thing!"

"'Until now'?"

"When we got to Melash, after that unpleasantness with Hwanzho and before someone told us about the University, do you remember finding me in the hallway? Holding this book?"

"I…Maybe? I must've been half asleep when—No, I do! You said you'd just seen Nanësra! You two had been talking about—!"

"Yes! And just now, I thought I heard her right outside!"

Tomush, who'd leaned against his lectern, straightened and rushed toward the door. He flung it open to reveal a growing crowd of confused students.

"Professor? We still have class now, don't we?" a young woman wondered. "Your door was closed…"

"Yes, yes, of course! One moment!" he grinned before closing the door in her bewildered face.

"She's gone. If she was ever there in the first place," Kalas observed. "Anyway, I'm glad I held onto it! It seems almost cruel to tell you this mere days before we sail for Serular, but I thought you'd like to know."

"Young man, I'll admit I'm more interested in your book than ever, but given the things you've all been through, the, ah, *otherworldly* company you keep, I consider it a kindness that I've been allowed some small part in this unfolding story! I agree with you: I'm glad you kept your book! Well…*mostly!*" Tomush admitted with a quick wink.

When they returned to the customs house and the rooms they'd secured, Rül and the others weren't back yet. Rufàran, disguised in a close-fitting hood, stared out the small window at the busy streets below. Shosafin slept—or pretended to: Kalas still couldn't tell, and Nïmrïk waited off to one side of the door. The young man set his book on a small table and suggested they visit the smithy while they waited for news of Dzholëf's arrival. Zhalera bristled and risked a quick glance at Abarandal, who pretended not to notice. Her expression flickered for a moment, then she headed for the door.

"Anyone want to come with us?" Kalas offered. Rufàran shifted position, intending to rise, it seemed, until Shosafin's gruff voice insisted he stay behind.

"It's not my place to tell you what to do, my liege, but even though we're in a foreign land, even though most of the cult is gone, I believe it's wisest if we keep to ourselves as much as possible. While Peradan held you captive, who can say how many of his followers knew about your presence? Remember: he had eyes in Ïsriba long before you disappeared. Were we to pass someone—or some*ones*—who recognized you along the streets of Melash, I can't...I can't predict how events might unfold."

Not asleep, Kalas noted. *And still convinced he can't protect the king...*

"No? Well, why don't you—"

"We could tell you if we see anything interesting," Zhalera interrupted as she jabbed an elbow into Kalas' ribs. "But it's just a smithy, right? No matter how many Sevens it's been, it's still just heat and metal!"

"It's up to you, Ilbardhën."

Zhalera took Kalas' arm and steered him toward the door. "Why'd you call him that?" she whispered. When Abarandal followed them, she tensed. The *eru* sang a brief phrase with an inquisitive quality.

"No, of course not! There's no reason you should stay behind," Kalas assured her.

The peal of hammers hitting heated steel softened Zhalera's rigid demeanor well before they reached the canopied workspace. Vast bellows breathed on bedded coals, coaxing as much heat as possible while a blacksmith—a giant who bore more than a superficial resemblance to Gandhan—worked a glowing length of material atop his anvil. Every blow created a cloud of sparks. Kalas couldn't prevent his eyes from blinking with every impact, but

Zhalera seemed entranced and unable to look away. She took a step toward a low wall to better examine things. The man noticed her interest and paused for a moment. Kalas thought he was going to yell at them, but his blackened face broke into a wide grin when he assayed the young woman's motives.

"Not your first time by the fire, lass, unless I miss my guess!"

"No, sir," Zhalera admitted, her eyes never leaving the dull orange object he gripped with his tongs. "Uh, better not let us keep you: that piece you're working on—looks like it's gonna be a sword: soon, it'll be too cold to work, and you're not even close to finished!"

"'No, sir' indeed!" he roared, his smile broadening. "Yes, now that my eyes have adjusted, I see it: you've spent some time over an anvil! Tell you what, lass: why don't you fetch an apron and give me a hand with this sword?"

"Oh, I'm sorry! I didn't mean to—"

"Sorry for what? You're right, after all! It's been a long day, and this heat gets to me after a while! Come, show me how you'd do it."

"We've got time," Kalas said, responding to the question in her look. When she turned toward Abarandal, the *eru* smiled and looked away. "Go ahead! The others aren't going anywhere without us!"

Zhalera's cheeks blossomed in a bright shade of self-effacing red as she handed Kalas her sword, entered the stall, and accepted an apron from the blacksmith's immense and callused hand. He offered her a hammer: she accepted it, tested its weight, and shook her head. She set it down and chose another, then another, until she found one with the heft and balance she wanted. Satisfied at last, she gave the piece a few light taps. And grimaced.

"Too hard," she grunted and returned it to the fire. When she deemed it proper, she moved it to the anvil and gave it a few more taps. Happy with the tones her blows produced, she started shaping the blade in earnest while the blacksmith observed.

"Where did you apprentice, lass?!" he wondered with approval.

"In Lohwàlar, with my father. He's…he's gone now. Maybe it's the light—maybe it's the environment, but you remind me of him…"

A strange electricity seemed to hang in the air as the trio headed toward the inn. They walked without speaking for a block or two, but Kalas detected something different in Zhalera's step. Something lighter. He cleared his throat and suggested, "So that blacksmith was pretty impressed with you!"

She tried to hide her widening grin; when she couldn't, she admitted, "It was nice to work on something again. I've been away from such work for too long. Impressed, though? No, I think he was just more tired than he let on!"

Abarandal, her eyes focused on the road, whispered a brief melody, and Kalas laughed.

"Or, like Abarandal says, he recognized ability when he saw it! I agree with her! You did your best to keep your work hidden, back home, and I understand it's because you were working on a gift for me, but after watching you just now…Peradan might have trapped us in a singularity, but even then, time didn't stand still like it did while I watched you work! I've said it before, and you know I'll say it again, but you have a gift with metal, Zhalera!"

Abarandal placed a hand on her friend's shoulder. When she turned toward her, the *eru* girl danced her fingers in a blur and sang a low, almost subvocal strain. Zhalera's color drained and she insisted, "I'm sorry, my sister, but I—"

Abarandal pressed a finger against the young woman's lips and repeated her song. Harder this time. Higher. Yet not in anger nor frustration; rather, in almost desperate hope.

"I…I'll think about it. I will. I promise," Zhalera managed at last. Abarandal held her gaze for a moment, then smiled and wrapped her in her arms.

"'Lest the stars forever dim'?" Kalas repeated, confused. "That's what she said, I think, but I don't understand."

"Me neither," Zhalera confessed, working her silver-colored shock of hair between her fingers while she pondered his translation. "Me neither, but I'm working on it."

Chapter XIV

Above the Plains of Serular

C APTAIN DZHOLËF DIDN'T SEEM TOO SURPRISED WHEN Kalas and the others discovered him in port a few days later. When the young man explained their situation, the grizzled tar nodded and told them to wait for just a little while. Two days later, having shifted his responsibilities to other ships, he said *Zhiamdas Salorosh* was at their disposal. He grinned and risked a glance at Bayal, who pretended to be too focused on loading up the coach—and their horses—to notice.

"Just like that?" Kalas scoffed. Wary, he, too, looked to Sifuran for reassurance.

What if Peradan wasn't the only one who betrayed the Swath? The prophecy?!

"Not exactly," Dzholëf countered. You asked me about one of my tattoos the last time we sailed. Remember? Well, Mister Dzhuran—sorry, Bayal, right? Whatever he goes by these days: he's the one who inked it!"

"Oh?" Kalas gasped, surprised. The captain laughed.

"He's got other names, too. You're familiar with them, I'm sure. Anyway, it's a long story—a *good* story, but a long one! The crux of the matter is this: long ago, I told…our friend if he ever had need, he only had to ask. That said, this is the first time in, what? five Sevens? five and three or four? that our paths have crossed again."

"The old wisdom?" Kalas wondered, recalling the phrase Dzholëf had used before.

"The old wisdom," he concurred. "Now then: when everyone's aboard, we'll weigh anchor and put out."

"How long will it take to reach Serular?"

"It'll be faster than traveling over land! I'll admit I'm surprised you made it, considering everything you had to pass! Highwaymen? Trolls? No thank you! Now, let's see…given the season, with prevailing winds, it should take us less time to reach the southern capes than it did to reach Avëlöth! A couple of weeks, should everything go smoothly. Less, should things go smoother still!" Dzholëf said with another wink in Sifuran's direction. "If you're worried you'll get bored, I'm sure your mop is around here somewhere!"

Away from the ruddy glow thrust up by the twin lighthouses and myriad signal fires burning throughout Melash, the stars glowed like blazing embers against the dark cloak overhead. The Crown, a well-known constellation made up of seven stars, glittered with uncharacteristic brilliance as the *Salorosh* carved its way through the Shadaún Ilarod toward the southern continent.

"Which one is you?" Kalas asked when Sifuran walked up and stood beside him. The *eru* chuckled and shook his head.

"Afraid I'm below the horizon, lad! I won't be visible from this part of the world for months yet."

"Is it strange?"

"Is…*what* strange?"

"Being…well, being *here,* while also being *there?* Or does it not work that way? I mean, you have a body, right? A human body. Don't you also have a…I don't know, a *star body,* too? I have no idea how any of that works! It just seems like it'd be strange!"

"You're not wrong, but it's more than that. More than merely two…*bodies,* to borrow your phrase. I'm not sure you'd understand it even if I could put the concepts into words your kind can parse."

At first, Kalas thought the mercurial figure meant he *wouldn't* explain more than he *couldn't* explain, but after chewing on his lip for a moment, he clapped a hand on the young man's shoulder and turned him a few degrees.

"See there? Just above the water?"

"I can't tell where the water ends and the sky begins!" Kalas admitted.

"Oh? All right: the waters are calm tonight, but not perfectly still. See how they shift from side to side with the waves? And see where they don't? Got it? Good! Now, follow me: see where I'm pointing, just above the horizon? Yes! That's it! See the bright, white-green star? That's *Zhi Lihwa.* The Shepherd. You probably know him better as Sharuyan. Even though—"

A wave of something straddling the cusp of pain and sadness rippled through Kalas. Sifuran held his tongue when the young man sucked in a deep breath. The *erudas* hand still atop his shoulder felt like weight and fire as he stared at the skyborne entity. He blinked away hot tears, and the sudden film between his eyelids made it seem like Sharuyan's celestial self—still wreathed in emerald—walked upon the distant waves. Kalas shivered, willed his composure to return, and prompted, "Even though...?"

"I'm sorry, lad. I forget sometimes that...no, never mind. Even though Sharuyan is...*gone,* he's...*not* gone: we can see him, but it's *not* him. Not wholly, I mean. It's...Forgive me, lad: it seems I can't find the words according to the tongue of *edhunàm.*

"It's not *strange* from the perspective of the *erume,* but I can see how you might think it would be. We're unique in that regard, I suppose. *Elume* have their peculiarities, as do *edhume,* but only *erume* are thus divided. And no, *divided* isn't the right word, either! One day, though, there will no longer be the need for such division."

"The prophecy?" Kalas guessed.

"In a manner of speaking, I suppose," Sifuran conceded, "though not the one that's taken you so far from your home! No, not even the prophecy spoken before the *elume* so many Sevens ago."

"There's a *third* prophecy?!"

"'Prophecy' conveys too limited a concept. All the words I know fail to contain it, as a matter of fact, but perhaps 'prophecy' will have to do for now. One thing I can tell you is that this greater *prophecy* contains all other prophecies within itself."

"It…what?"

"Exactly!"

Kalas laughed. His face still wet—and cold without the suns to blunt the northwinds' chill, he rubbed away his tears and looked toward *Zhi Lihwa* one more time.

"I miss him, Sifuran," he said without pretense.

"So do I, lad. So do I."

2.

"The coach was right where we left it," Rül was explaining when Kalas joined the others below decks. "It was covered in ice and snow, but I guess it froze before water could get inside the wood and fabric and ruin everything. We dug it out, hitched it to Courser and Runner, and, well, here we are!"

"Tell me something, lad," Shosafin said to Kalas, "if your new friend is…like Falthwën, why are we *sailing* toward Serular? Why aren't we *kalswàr?* That's what you called it, right? Light-traveling?"

"Under the Sanctuary, when Falthwën returned from his captivity: you remember what he told us, don't you? How he'd been marked by the *ekume?* When Peradan held us in his singularity, he said he recognized my frequency—whatever that means. I don't know how it all works—you know that: remember what happened when we came up through the Gateway?! Anyway, with his alter ego unmasked, I have no idea what Peradan might try next. If he can sense us through the *kalthesh,* it just seems like a better idea to use ships and horses instead. It takes longer, sure, but it makes it harder for others to find us, too. You of all people should appreciate that!"

"Fair enough, lad."

"It's ironic," Kalas added after a moment's consideration. "You're the only one of us who wasn't there: neither under the Vault nor under the Mountain. Peradan wouldn't recognize your frequency—your vibration, I guess. If it were possible for you to travel the light-realm, you wouldn't be 'seen' like the rest of us. And as much as we're all looking forward to getting *home,* your desire outstrips the rest of ours combined!"

"You're not wrong. Seems you've become quite adept at discerning the tells we all exhibit."

"I had a good teacher," he shrugged. "Oh! That reminds me: it'll be a few weeks before we reach Serular. I'm ready for more sword lessons if…if you are…"

Shosafin had started for the door; now, he paused. Despite the poor light, Kalas knew the old soldier tensed, and the young man couldn't ignore the aura of embarrassment he exuded. Without a word, Shosafin took another step.

"I mean it," Kalas said. The rigid figure stopped again. "You've been…struggling ever since everything that happened in the Ravine. I won't pretend I understand what you're going through. I—with what little I was able to learn from you before, I was able to hold my own against some pretty rough characters. I'll bet your weak side is better than most others' strong side! There's so much I can learn from you! If…if you'll stop feeling sorry for yourself. If you'll focus on what you *can* do instead of what you *can't.*"

With a quick twist of light, Shosafin's sword was at Kalas' throat: "You have *no idea* what you're asking!" he growled through gritted teeth.

The young man held his ground without flinching. And smiled.

"See? What some might call your weak side is really just…your *other* side: you think your injury has made you weaker. That's why you didn't want Rufàran to come with us into town: you thought— you *believed* you wouldn't be able to protect him. Well? Look at us now! How quickly did you draw your sword and cross the room? And where's *my* sword? Still slung across my back! That's what I'm talking about! You have so much to teach, and I have so much to learn. If…if you don't *want* to teach me, that's one thing, but believing you *can't* is another.

"Physically, you're diminished. I'm not pretending otherwise. However, unless everything you told me about your history was a lie, you'll adapt. That's who you are. That's what you do. No matter the scenario, you rise above it and build a better, stronger version of yourself. These circumstances are another *opportunity*. This time, though, no one's snubbing you—no one but yourself. If you need *permission* to borrow strength from others—what little we have to offer—you have it."

Shosafin held Kalas' gaze for what seemed like minutes: the young man knew it couldn't have been more than a few seconds. He felt the soldier's energy shift with his weight as he returned his sword to its sheath.

"Main deck. Before the first sun ascends above the rails," he said as he disappeared within the shadows.

For the next several mornings, Shosafin was right where he said he'd be, working his sword against the air. The scene reminded Kalas of his first "lesson," conducted in silence upon the thinning grasslands east of Lohwàlar. For the first few days, the soldier's movements lacked their prior grace and balance, and Kalas contented himself through observation. Soon, however, as Shosafin rediscovered his feet, he demonstrated his familiar fluidity. Indeed, he displayed a new, asymmetrical appreciation of his shifted gravity as he moved across the ship's creaking boards. One morning, satisfied it was more than mere suns-light flashing in the gruff figure's eyes, Kalas joined him. He said nothing as he did his best to mimic Shosafin's steps, working up quite a sweat before the second sun revealed itself. When the rest of the ship's crew dragged itself to work, the soldier sheathed his sword and headed for the stairs. Kalas watched him stop before he descended.

"Thank you," he muttered, just loud enough for the young man to hear. And then he was gone.

By the time *Zhiamdas Salorosh* sailed within sight of Serular's rocky coast, Kalas found himself enjoying the endless horizon and the sometimes unpredictable undulation of the waves beneath the ship. He laughed at himself when he remembered his first day aboard Dzholëf's vessel.

"I've gotta admit I'm surprised at how much I think I'll miss the ocean!" he confided in Zhalera. Even from hundreds of feet away, Serular's cliffside waterfalls sparkled like diamonds raining down through suns-light. "I mean, yeah, I'm glad we got to see so much water: I used to imagine the Empty Sea when it was still the…Bejeweled Sea, Tsharak called it? I wasn't even close! Still, in those first few days without solid ground underfoot, I'd had enough! Now? Living on the sea, surrounded by water, doesn't seem so bad…"

"I won't miss it at all!" insisted Rül as he heaved his lines and helped reef the mainsail. He wiped the back of his meaty hand across his sweat-beaded brow. "You had it right, Kalas: solid ground all the way!"

Nïmrïk, across the deck, had been staring at the ocean: without apparent cause, he winced and jerked his head. Abarandal, standing next to him, whispered a few soothing yet otherwise indiscernible phrases. That's when Kalas heard it, too: sforzando trumpets stabbing in his ears—no, his mind—as pieces of the Song rose up and pierced his thoughts.

"I heard it, too," he assured the old wolf, now massaging his ears. "That was…*sharp!*"

"Not a normal part of The Song," he agreed.

"It feels—no, it *sounded* like someone in an orchestra played their part too loudly," Kalas explained to the others. Nïmrïk nodded.

"Friends," Sifuran began, emerging from the aftcastle, "I'd intended to travel with you for a while, to attempt to succeed Sharuyan in some small way, but my intentions are irrelevant. Peradan's roots run deep here, and it will take vast amounts of time and effort to undo the malfeasance he's wrought upon the *Serularrinme.*

"It seems none of us knows what's become of the other *Erume pïni Sâash.* Peradan told you the truth in that regard. I have no idea what Loradan did under the Vault. Nor how. Whatever it was, its effects are more severe than anything I've ever known…

"It's my guess, however, that I'm not the only one wary of traveling the light-realm. When we reach the shore, I'll wear a different face for a while: after Lâris' last display here, I'm sure even the shortest memories have grown, and my work requires anonymity. For now.

"Lohwàlar is less than two days' travel: if I learn anything, I'll send word. Young man—all of you: you have your own, unenviable tasks to attend to. I might have doubted your resolve not so long ago, when we first met; now, I harbor no such reservations! Wield the heavens' great power with care and wisdom, young man. When we debark, we must seem as strangers to one another, so I'll say this now: *tharan bethrume á thòënthar shadame,* my friends. Fair winds and following seas…"

3.

Kalas had never seen so many stairs—nor so many waterfalls—in one place. Woven together in an almost magical rope of marble steps and powdery cataracts, elaborate stonework wrapped around and in between several natural arches, creating an intricate framework of lace-like tracery designed to complement the endless whitewater torrents cascading from above. From his ship-side vantage, the cantilevered casings gleamed like gemstones in the midday suns. The *Salorosh* waited on the open sea until Serular's harbor master assigned her a berth; when they reached the shore, however, Kalas noticed Sevens' worth of dirt and grime had rimed the stairs with a matte patina in some places; drab mosses and silvery lichens covered others. A few piers—many fronted with peculiar, tower-like edifices—looked like they'd recently caught fire.

He decided Serular's infrastructure wasn't haphazardly *stacked* like Âivambar's, as he'd first suspected; rather, it seemed the city's architects had squeezed every suggestion of utility from the difficult geography. Indeed, its buildings almost flowed like waterfalls themselves from one plane to the next. Kalas discerned something familiar in the city's lines—despite their unfamiliar orientation—but he had no idea why.

Sifuran—or Bayal, or Dzhuran, or whatever name he'd chosen—remained aboard the *Salorosh* while the others gathered their belongings. As he'd intimated, he wasn't there when Kalas and the others stepped onto solid ground, and the young man wondered if he'd recognize the *eru* should their paths ever cross again.

Probably not.

Huge box-like constructs ascended and descended throughout the city: elevators operated via thick chains and wheeled pulleys enabled *Serularrinme* to transport goods (and themselves) from one level to another. Kalas followed the mechanical components to an enclosure populated with several donkeys, each yoked to a stout spoke protruding from a vast wheel around which the chains wound and unwound as necessary. A bank of bell-shaped apertures studded the space's periphery: when disembodied voices shouted piped commands from parts unknown, the animals' overseers would goad them into action.

All these chains and pulleys: that's a lot of moving parts! he acknowledged. *Almost as complex as the Pump. Bigger, at least!*

"Kalas! There you are!" scolded Zhalera when she discovered him standing awestruck beneath a convoluted mesh of gears. "What if…you-know-who came back to Serular to…I don't know! What if he came back here and he sees us?! You can't just wander around… alone! None of us can!"

"No, I…no, you're right," he agreed. "Sorry! I just wanted to see how all these moving platforms worked! But I don't think Peradan is here. Even if he was, I get the sense that he's moved on from here. I think that's what the *eru* who showed up on the ship told Sifuran, too.

"The what? How could you know that?"

"Oh, right! I guess only Kadhëmba, Abarandal, and I heard it. I wasn't trying to eavesdrop, but his alterations to The Song were so *loud!* Not all *erume* have been, I don't know, *marked*, I guess, but Peradan knows the frequencies of every member of the Swath. It makes sense for Sifuran—the others, too, probably—to communicate through go-betweens."

"We should find a place to stay," Shosafin said as he steered Breaker toward Zhalera. "Rül's got the coach hooked up. He and the others should be right behind me. Things seem…quieter than the last time I was here. I have an idea."

A few minutes later, Runner and Courser trotted into view, hauling the coach bearing Rül and Pava. Nashmur and Gilfën, Nimrïk and Dalafar brought up the rear. Kalas and Zhalera hopped into the cabin and took their familiar seats next to Abarandal.

"This way," Shosafin instructed when everyone was ready.

The old soldier guided Kalas and the others through crowded thoroughfares and lesser-traveled streets and into the higher, rural parts of the city. Along the way, stationed between a curious collection of fire-blackened buildings, they passed an unusual number of *Poyïsriba* soldiers. Nashmur tensed when he noticed them and did his best to stare at the ground, the collar of his cloak turned up to hide his face.

"They're not here for us," Shosafin dismissed, sensing the shared discomfort spreading throughout the party. "See their eyes? They're watching the city itself. They'll ignore us unless we give them a reason not to."

"How can you be sure? Why else would they be here?" Nashmur countered.

"Don't know. Exactly. Maybe Náli can tell us."

"Who's Náli?" Pava wondered.

"Náli's the young woman who told me about Galámur last winter. Her family lives up this way: they have a few acres of... well, not *flat* ground, but it's less inclined than the rest of Serular. We'll stay with them for a day or two, if they're all right with it, and get a read on what's going on in this part of the world again. *Something's* happened here since I left..."

A few minutes later, the ground surrendered its steepness and emptied them onto a terraced, bald-like area bordered by thick stands of old and new trees. Toward the back of the plot, a small house hid beneath and between a few of the largest pines; a small barn sat behind the house. A trio of bored-looking goats munched on tufts of grass poking up from the earth in random places. One acknowledged their presence with a momentary glance and a disdainful bleat before returning to its meal.

"There's no one here," Rül whispered.

"Isn't there?" Shosafin said, his eyebrow raised. He motioned for the farm boy to drive his team toward a space not too far from the main building.

Kalas exited the coach and approached Breaker. He ran his hand across the creature's withers and looked around. In low tones, he mentioned the several pairs of eyes peering out at them from above. Shosafin returned a subtle nod.

"We'll wait. Give them some time to assess our intentions. It's likely none of these people know what's become of the Deathless Flame. Or maybe they *do* know, somehow, and have other fears to consider. We can afford a little patience."

A few minutes later, a small girl stepped out of the trees and walked up to the old soldier's massive horse. She held Shosafin's gaze for a moment until her curiosity about his missing arm proved too much to suppress. Her eyes widened and she stepped back.

"*Zhi Tshaggul Kavar?*" she wondered, her raised and shaking finger pointed at his stump. "*Gâëhath—il zhi Tshaggul Kavar kima?!*"

"No, Náli: not the Deathless Flame. One of his…an acquaintance of his, yes, but he's dead now. Hmm: Garat, *is* he dead?"

"Uh…*unmade,* at least. I think that's how the *erume* would have put it, yes."

"*Erume?!*" Náli gasped. "*Unmade?!* You possess the strength to *unmake* such beings?! Then why—*why*—didn't you protect us from the *ilragusme* the last time you were here?!"

As the young woman spoke, her voice cracked, and Kalas figured she had two or three fewer years than he did. She pawed at sudden tears and did her best to look angry, but her posturing only revealed her fearful sadness."

"Náli, is it?" Kalas soothed and took a step toward her. Quick as lightning, she pressed a rust-spotted knife against his chest. He stopped and raised his empty hands.

"Náli, we're not here to harm you or your family—nor whomever you're hiding in these trees," he continued with as much calm as he could muster. "Shosafin—Shadrïs, maybe: I'm sure he did all he could to protect you from—"

"No, she's right," Shosafin admitted as he dismounted. "I was so focused on learning whatever I could about Marugan, about his whereabouts, that I was careless. Náli, I'm sorry for whatever damage my indiscretions caused you."

"I don't know if you've heard," Kalas transitioned, "but the so-called Deathless Flame is the *eru* Peradan. His followers are—"

"Peradan?!" someone interrupted. Kalas looked over Náli's shoulder and saw a wiry man. Judging from the bits of bark clinging to his clothes, Kalas assumed he'd been watching them from the trees, too. "You're telling me a member of the 'Great Swath' resurrected the old cult? Why?"

Other figures appeared, each curious to understand Kalas' strange revelation. The young man told them what he could, condensing the relevant points into a concise narrative and concluding with Peradan's disappearance and Marugan's death at Shosafin's hand. He took pains to accentuate Náli's newsworthy contribution: "Without your help, Sevens might have come and gone before we knew where to look, and who can say what power the cult might have acquired in that time?

"Anyway, mere steel can't hurt *ilalasdrame* in any meaningful way: we had no way to fight back until we recovered Peradan's sword—a sword forged by Valaran herself. Shosafin wouldn't have known that when he was here last: I don't know if he told you, but he almost severed Marugan's head the last time they met: it knit itself whole in minutes!

"But the cult is coming undone. Word is on its way: you could say it's already arrived, if you'll believe our report. Either way, I suspect you'll hear other accounts soon enough. Whatever fear you've endured at their hands, it's nearly over."

Náli kept her blade against Kalas' throat while he spoke. When he finished, she hesitated and glanced at the man behind her: quick as a flash himself, the young man pivoted away from the blade and captured her arm in a hold. She dropped her weapon, and he caught it before it hit the ground. He held it for a brief moment, then handed her the hilt.

"None of us is here to hurt you," he promised. Náli scowled and grabbed her knife before stomping toward the house.

"My sister's discovered a strange new fire in her belly," explained the man who'd been standing behind her. "Cultists lit it for her when they killed our father, Niv. Two days after you left us, *Âu Shadrïs*. Or *Shosafin,* your friend said? Shosafin, then."

"Niri…"

"I figured Serular had seen the last of you, but no, of course not. I'm not that lucky! You probably want something, don't you? Ha! Your silence says I'm right! Well, c'mon: it's getting late in the day. Might as well get inside. Oh? You're wondering if I'm on the level? Maybe Náli's forgotten the particulars from the last time you were here, but I haven't. I'm pretty good, pretty quick: you might have lost an arm, but I remember how you moved. I'm not stupid! You've got nothing to worry about from me. Can't say the same about Náli…"

4.

Niri, the oldest surviving sibling, told Shosafin and the others what had happened in recent months. Niv had been one of Serular's few remaining members of the *Randa pïni Sifumilël*. He did his best to keep clear of the cult: Niri said he recognized the old error they espoused. A longshoreman by trade, he'd abandoned his livelihood long ago, before Náli was born, and retreated upland to put some distance between his family and the *ragusdas* rising influence. He feared—correctly, Niri insisted—his entreaties for discernment would seem like disagreement, if not blatant opposition, and so he chose to disappear.

"It wasn't enough," Niri continued. "Not everyone belonging to the *Randa* saw things the same as Niv…"

For a couple of Sevens, he explained, Niv managed the balance between the old and new "wisdom," as both *ilsifumilëlme* and *il-ragusme* referred to their collective traditions. Despite his practical disengagement from Serular's festering sectarian differences, he kept informed. Niri said he'd been diligent to communicate the old wisdom to his children, to explain the flawed thinking that spawned the cult in ages past, before its current renaissance.

"It all came to a head one night. I'm not sure we'll ever know *why* they did it—I'm not sure they know anymore than we do… Náli blames herself, but I think it's just bad timing. There's no way anyone could have known what she told you, soldier: not unless one of *you* said something! Náli's smarter than that…

"Anyway, I suspect the rest of us will be with him soon enough. You must have seen it on your way up the streets? Soldiers everywhere—same sword as you? Burned buildings? Not long after most cultists set out for…Gambarad? Galámur, right? Not long after that, *ships* appeared off our coast. They captured some of the vessels leaving our ports; others, they just destroyed. They waited on the water for days, maybe weeks. I wouldn't call it a siege—the rest of the continent is just above us, after all, but soon, they attacked us. Not with arrows or ballistas: with something new and terrifying! May Father forgive me for saying so, but until then, I never believed in magic like he did. I don't know what else to call it! Beams of unwavering red light were just *there,* punching holes in our city, widening with every subtle ripple of the ocean. Anyone hit by the beams just turned to ash—that's what everyone says, and really, I have no reason not to believe them!

"We called for aid when the first ships were taken, but we had to go over land, and it takes our fastest riders weeks to reach Ïsriba—especially in winter. We sent riders for Ralothova, too—they never returned: Ralothova's farther away, yes, but their ships are faster. In the end, it didn't matter: I don't know why—no one does, it seems—but after a while, the ships just sailed away. No one knows where they came from nor why they attacked. Now, Serular sees a lot of ships: most even I can recognize, but not even the saltiest *Serularrin* seemed to know anything about them. Not long after they left, a regiment arrived from Ïsriba—faster than we thought possible, but not fast enough. Their troops are still here, months later. Doing what, no one really knows."

"Watching the city," Nashmur mumbled, mostly to himself.

"Now that you mention it, yes, it does seem that way. It's like they're sizing things up, getting ready for something, maybe," Niri said, his features twisting into a frown. "Maybe they're expecting those ships to return?"

"They're getting ready to steal our city out from under us!" Náli spat, having abandoned her aunt in the kitchen. "You didn't believe me when I said the cult-men were moving north, but I was right about that! Wasn't I…Shosafin? I was right! I'm right about this, too. I know it! *You* know it, too, don't you…Nashmur, right? I can see it in your face!"

"Náli, Serular is *part* of Ïsriba! What is there for them to steal?!" Niri started to remind her, but his pale, blue-green eyes widened when Nashmur shrank away from her words.

"So it *is* happening," the former commander muttered.

"What's this?" Niri demanded, his eyes shifting between Nashmur and his sister.

"Marugan, the man my cousin was hunting: he's been part of

the *Poyïsriba* court for a long time. Those who knew him thought he was a loyal subject—a friend, even, but it turns out his true loyalties lie with a fallen *elu*. Tsathrâuda, she's called.

"Part of Marugan's plan for Ïsriba involved starting a war—no, *wars* with neighboring kingdoms. If detachments have gained a foothold here, if they're establishing a new presence in Serular, building strength…You say the first soldiers arrived sometime *after* those ships disappeared?"

"Convenient, wouldn't you say?" Shosafin grumbled.

"'Convenient'? I don't get what you're driving at," Niri admitted.

"You're the ones who requested a presence from the capital, are you not?" Nïmrïk added. "A presence that got here a little *too* quickly, by your own assessment?"

"It sounds like you're saying Ïsriba was behind those mysterious ships! That they possess…weaponized magic capable of vaporizing entire buildings in a single pulse! That they attacked us just to trick us into inviting them here! Like I said: Serular already belongs to Ïsriba! Why would they do such a thing? *How?!* How could Ïsriba launch even a single ship—she doesn't border any ocean! Even with the cult running roughshod across Serular, we heard rumors that things weren't all right in the capital, but I never would have suspected Queen Ësfàyami capable of such…such—"

"Malice," Rufàran growled and caught his sinking head between his hands.

"Maybe Ralothova has already fallen? Maybe those ships used to belong to the Great Whale of the South?"

"No, like I already told you: they weren't any *Poralothova* configuration anyone here's ever seen!" Niri insisted. Addressing Rufàran, he said, "Malice. Well…yeah. That. But where would the queen get her hands on such weaponry? I mean, let's be real: we all know magic doesn't exist! Not *really*, right? And what could she hope to gain by sacking a tiny little city like Serular? A city already under her rule?! We haven't been a notable power for Sevens upon Sevens!"

"You're the coast. Cliffs behind you, water before you. A prime location for a forward operating base for a future offensive," Rufàran began. "If things are as bad as I've been told…I have a question for you, Mister Niri: have the *Poyïsriba* soldiers started constructing scout towers above the cliffs?"

"You know, now that you mention it, I think it's possible! Let me see…yes, probable, even! With all the reconstruction taking place, I guess I just didn't think twice about skips full of building materials ascending above the plateau. No one did—no one I've talked to, anyway. You haven't been up there, have you? No, you still have the scent of the sea about you. How could you have known?"

"It's what I would have done," Rufàran shrugged with sadness in his voice. "To answer your question: I have no idea where my—where the *queen-regent* might have found such devices you describe. Nor where these ships could have come from—assuming they *are* hers. There's the river that runs beneath the capital, but it's no place for ships that size!"

"I might have an idea about those weapons," Kalas offered, drawing all eyes toward himself. "Pava, you told us that it had been many Sevens since you'd had any encounters with the *ilràigme-edhume*, right? We learned from Hwanzho that Tsathrâuda held an interest in Deridzhas, that all the things that happened there answered some question for her. From what you've just told us, Niri, I suspect that 'question' revolved around, uh, well, an *artifact*. A remnant from an older world. Part—or parts of one, at least. We've learned that the heavenlies usually *unmake* such things when they encounter them, but there are still things even the stars have yet to discover."

Nashmur seemed to shrink in his seat as the others discussed Serular's recent excitement. He looked from Rufàran to Kalas, from Niri to his cousin, and, after a while, stood and paced the floor.

"I can't stay here," he said aloud.

"None of us is staying here," Shosafin insisted. "In a day or two, we'll head north and west, toward—"

"No, I can't stay *here,* away from Ïsriba. Not while the world around us is coming undone! Kalas, I was right to trust you: you've demonstrated remarkable integrity from our very first encounter. I hope you've learned to trust me, too. I hope you—I hope all of you will understand why I can't return to Lohwàlar with you."

"Cousin, Ësfàyami will have your head separated from your shoulders before you reach Thosha. You know that. So no, I don't understand! I don't—"

"I should have seen it coming," he raised his hand and continued. "I'd heard whispers about the queen-regent's building projects, each more ambitious than the last. I just assumed—I *wanted to believe*—that they were all for the Falcon's glory. There were times when conscience tempted me to listen more closely, but I guess I'm more my mother's son than I'd care to admit sometimes: a slave to duty without regard for the rightness—or the wrongness—of *someone else's* cause. I'd whine about what I wish I would have done, but that won't change anything: I can only hope to change what hasn't yet come to pass. If I'm close to the source of infection, maybe I can find a way to...*fix* things, in some small measure.

"It's funny you mention Thosha. Yëlisha keeps an eye on things. Several eyes, I imagine, with all the information that passes through Mbirin's Place! I'm not as adept at disguise as you, Shosafin, but I've learned a lot in the last few months. I'll just have to trust it'll do. And let's be candid: I'm not all that useful to you. Not really. As much as I wish it weren't true, you don't *need* me. You—"

"Nashmur," Kalas tried to interrupt.

"Please, young sir! What I mean to say is this: there's *no reason* I should come to Lohwàlar with you. In Thosha, maybe Âivambar— or even Ïsriba itself, I can gather intelligence. Do some advance scouting and better prepare you for your arrival. Don't try to talk me out of it: Kalas, your nobility, if you will, proved the catalyst that pushed me into action. I choose to believe there must be other *Poyïsriba tanagme* whose hearts are torn as well, who need a similar push to turn away from the error the kingdom has embraced. Because if we're alone, in the grand scheme of things, no matter how just our cause—how *noble* our intentions, it won't matter."

5.

Two days later, Kalas and the others woke to find Nashmur gone. Náli claimed she helped him pack and guided him to the main road, toward the route that joined up with the King's Highway.

"The last time I helped one of you," she glowered at Shosafin, "cult-men cut down our father!"

"Náli," Niri cautioned with a weary sigh. She spat.

"I just want you gone! Maybe Niri's right, maybe the cult-men would've come for Father anyway…but maybe he's wrong."

"Náli, I know the cult has more or less controlled Serular since before we were born, but that's all changing now! Our guests were right: I've listened in on conversations near the docks, and something happened up north not too long ago: their story checks out. The—"

"If it's not the cult, then it'll be the soldiers! Weren't you listening? They're hiding from the crown! I thought about leading the big one right to them, but I'm not gonna do their jobs for them! Sounds like he'll get caught soon enough anyway. At least it won't be my problem when he does!"

Before Niri could chide his sister, Shosafin raised his remaining hand and said, "Can't say I blame her for her choices. Can't say I'd have done much different were our roles reversed. Náli, you're not wrong, not exactly, about the soldiers. I've been exploring the city at night, and your brother's right: the cult's influence is a shadow of what it used to be, even a few months ago."

"I suspect, uh, a friend of ours had a hand in that," Kalas offered. "Seems there's been renewed interest in the *Randa pïni Sifu-milël* since we got here. The *true* Order of the Sapphire—not that 'Deathless Flame' nonsense. You won't take our word for it, nor should you, I suppose, but we're telling you the truth."

"*Âu* Niri, *Shâuín* Náli: thank you for your hospitality," Rufàran said, standing. "We'll be on our way before suns-down this evening. Shosafin, I know you have a promise to keep, but I understand your urgency. I've seen precious little of this changed world, but what I have seen alarms me. I'm unashamed to say it. I'd address these soldiers myself, but it's been so long. Too long. The sooner we—*I*—confront my daughter, the sooner we might disabuse her of her delusion."

"Your *daughter?*" Náli piped up. "Who are you talking about?"

"Miss Náli, you're much too young to remember, I'm sure, but Sevens ago, before Ësfàyami was queen-regent, her father, King Rufàran ruled Ïsriba and its surroundings," Nïmrïk explained.

"*Rufàran?* Isn't that *your* name?" she said, addressing the man. He nodded.

"Father told us stories," Niri confirmed as he looked the king up and down. "You're welcome—for our hospitality. I don't know if you expect me to bow or grovel or lick your boots, but I'll decline the honor. All my life, Ïsriba has never paid Serular any mind. You'll forgive me if I respond in kind?"

Shosafin opened his mouth, but before he could speak, Rufàran nodded and said, "I will. Forgive you, that is." He sighed and looked over Niri's shoulder, into the future, or perhaps the past, Kalas thought, and continued, "The spoils of my forefathers' ambitions have outpaced the Golden Falcon's ability to maintain them. I've wondered for some time now if there might be wisdom in dividing the kingdom into smaller, confederated states. *Temme temme nirest,* after all, in dire need of accountability and consequence. That's the way it was before Ïsriba's first king, you know: an alliance of lesser kingdoms, though not without its own problems. I've come to understand that wise rule requires a degree of *intimacy* with one's subjects, an intimacy unobtainable with too long, too impotent an arm."

"You would *give up* your kingdom?" Náli rephrased, not convinced.

"*My* kingdom?!" Rufàran laughed. "Child, Ïsriba hasn't been *my* kingdom for some time now! Even before I...disappeared, I understood the creeping weakness in the kingdom's grasp. I was foolish enough to say something about it, too. Truth be told, that's probably why my advisors poisoned my daughter's mind, why Marugan's claws gripped her so readily, so deeply.

"That's not what you asked, though, is it? Yes, I would give up my kingdom if that was the best way to serve my people."

"*Serve?* I don't think you understand how this whole *king* thing works!" Náli scoffed.

"You know what, young lady? You're probably right," Rufàran winked. "I know some lords who'd agree with you!"

Late the next day, having exited Serular just after the suns parted the prior afternoon, Rül reined in his team when they reached the divided highway and the immense and ancient tree. The same traces of signage poked from beneath its coarse bark, and bright green buds already peppered its branches. Shosafin drew up just behind Runner and Courser and waited.

"Straight ahead will take us toward the steppes," Rül reminded him.

"And left will take us toward Lohwàlar," he added.

"It'll take us toward the steppes...and the Gateway," Rül

amended with a sidelong glance at Pava. Kalas, listening through the coach's open window, caught the plaintive note in the farm boy's voice.

"We'll only be in Lohwàlar for a little while," he insisted. "Just long enough to…well, I don't know, all right? But Nashmur will be fine! The *úrukilmukritme* will be fine! For a time, at least! It's not like we won't be coming back this way soon! We still—"

"I still have to return to Ïsriba," Shosafin interrupted. "Maimed as I am, I guarantee there's blood to be shed along the way, from here to the kingdom's throne, and I…You'll most likely be in my way…"

"I see," said Kalas, biting his lower lip.

"You do?" whispered Zhalera, beside him.

"Well, I guess we'd better keep moving then. There aren't many places for shelter between here and Lohwàlar, and we're not going to reach her before suns-down," he said for Shosafin's benefit. For Zhalera's, once the coach started moving again, he explained: "I don't think he's cared about *anyone*—or had to—for a long, long time. He doesn't know how to let on that he's concerned about us. Nothing we say will change his mind, so I'm not gonna waste my time. Doesn't mean we're not going with him when the time comes!"

Soon after the first sun dipped beneath the undulating horizon, rippling in the rising heat of spring, Shosafin directed the company toward a small embankment and suggested they make camp. After a light supper peppered with inconsequential conversation, people parted ways for the evening. Kalas said good night and disappeared beneath his tent; before he'd fallen asleep, however, Abarandal, with Zhalera's help, stumbled over to him and collapsed. Her fair skin, sticky with a light film of perspiration, had acquired a sallow tint. She righted herself, wiped her forehead, and turned toward the young man with fear in her watery eyes.

Or maybe it's not fear? Maybe it's…confusion? Maybe it's something else…

"Abarandal! What's wrong! Zhalera! What happened? What's going on?"

"I have no idea! I heard her cry out, I tried communicating with her, but she just kept singing the same phrase over and over! I still don't understand her, but it sounded like *this:*"

Zhalera sang the short piece of music. Despite her beautiful tones, Kalas couldn't discern anything specific within its notes.

"I'm sorry!" she apologized when she witnessed Kalas' nonplussed expression. "That's the best I can do! I don't know—"

"No, it's not your singing! We're not stars: we don't—we *can't*—use music the same way they do!"

"*Some* of us can't," Zhalera accused with a wry half-smile. Kalas blushed.

"Abarandal," the young man soothed as he daubed at her cheeks and forehead with a cloth. "Abarandal, what's happening? What can we do to help?"

The young woman convinced the pair to help her toward a place just beyond a nearby rise in the earth. When she beckoned them to stop, they obeyed. She sucked down vast quantities of fresh, chilly air, and seemed to regain some strength. She insisted she could stand on her own, and Kalas and Zhalera, after exchanging concerned and helpless glances, released her.

"You're sure you're all right?" Kalas wondered after a tense yet uneventful minute. Abarandal smiled. Indeed, she'd ceased sweating, and her skin displayed its familiar warmth.

"If you say so," Zhalera shrugged.

Before they turned toward their camp, the stargirl cried out, and something flung Kalas to the ground. Zhalera, too, and the young man remembered the strange scenario at the bottom of the Ravine, where Abarandal believed another *eru* had been imprisoned. He tried to stand, but an invisible force prevented him. Dark red fingers curled around the fringes of his vision, and his limbs felt like rocks. *Heavy* rocks. He willed his head to turn toward Zhalera: she, too, lay sprawled on the ground.

What's happening?! he tried to shout as his lungs collapsed.

He was flying. Hovering, at least, a few feet above the dirt. The force had surrendered its iron grip, and a welcome shudder of euphoria radiated across his body. Between him and Zhalera, Abarandal floated, too, centered within a golden nimbus reflected from the sandy ground. In the distant north, beyond the plain and above the stringy clouds, a violent bloom of energy as bright as day ripped the night apart and draped the world in a caul of flaxen light.

In sudden darkness, Kalas hit the dirt with an abrupt thud. Spiraling suggestions of color writhed within his sightless eyes until the aftermath of the flash subsided. When he could see again, Zhalera was rubbing her eyes, too. Abarandal, still aloft, descended toward the earth, her eyes aglow with the last traces of the golden light.

"Abarandal! My sister! Are you—you're all right?" Zhalera wondered as she staggered to her side. The *eru* nodded with a broad smile.

"What just happened?!" said Kalas, massaging the back of his head. "What was that *light?!*"

Abarandal didn't answer: her attention remained fixed on Zhalera, whom she glided toward and whose hands she captured with her own. Kalas caught a few notes from a whispered song, but he couldn't divine the message. The *eru* kissed the young blacksmith's forehead, then dragged her to Kalas and placed one of her callused hands in his. Without a backward glance nor any explanation, she retraced their steps toward camp, leaving the bewildered couple in her wake.

"She sang something to you," Kalas observed as the two of them followed Abarandal. "I couldn't make it out…"

"I…it's nothing. Nothing I want to talk about right now."

"Wait—did you *understand* her? Could you make sense of her singing?!"

"No! I—well, I don't know! I just…it's more like I know what she means, and *that* is what I don't want to talk about! Not…not right now. Maybe someday.

"I don't understand what this was all about though! That light! That push—that *pull!* I couldn't breathe! For a moment, I thought we were gonna die!"

"It's like what happened in the Ravine," Kalas explained, and he repeated his story. "Anyway, we should get some sleep. Tomorrow, we'll be back in Lohwàlar. After that? We've still got a lot of work ahead of us…"

Chapter XV

Beyond the Bonds
of Fellowship

NOT LONG AFTER THE FIRST SUN JOINED THE SECOND above the horizon, Rül nodded at the man standing guard at the foot of a new tower just outside Lohwàlar. Broad at the base and tapering toward its peak, flecks of mica glinted from its dun-colored sandstone construction. Kalas exited the coach and stretched his legs, still sore from the effects of the prior evening's gravitational flux. He looked up at a broad, clear plate of faceted crystal suspended just beneath the tower's roof.

"Hey, Pava! Rül!" he gestured. "Look! They set up those *iltithme* you brought back from the Gateway!"

"Oh, those!" the sentry nodded. "Took a little doing to get them situated, but we managed, with Rofe's help! I think—"

"Wait—*Rofe?* Why do I know that name?" Kalas interrupted. Pava reminded him: "We rescued him from under Deridzhas, re-member?! Oh, I wish I'd been here to greet him! I'd love to know how he's doing—and learn what's been taking place beneath the Áthradho!"

"Oh, he's still in town!" the guard explained. "I'll be honest: we're a stubborn lot, and we figured we'd know how to get all these...*collectors,* right? We thought we had it all under control! Well, we didn't! It's a good thing Tsharak invited your friend Rofe to stay with him and Vàyana! Even better that he agreed!"

"Tsharak's still at Vàyana's place?" Zhalera noted. "That's a surprise!"

"Oh? Ha! Well, it seems they've become rather, ah, *fond* of one another since you left! Right, so these collectors: it doesn't take too long to get 'em installed," the man continued, "but you have to adjust 'em over the course of a couple of days. When the seasons change, we'll have to do it all again!"

"Rül! Take us to Vàyana's place!" Pava demanded.

"Of course, *Milëlínahal!*"

"Uh, thanks, Mister…Othar, right?" Kalas said as he climbed back into the coach a moment before it lurched toward town.

A peculiar *newness* lingered over Lohwàlar's ongoing reconstruction, and Kalas marveled at the industry his neighbors had exerted over the last few seasons. The townsfolk they passed waved enthusiastic greetings, pointing and whispering to one another as Rül headed for Vàyana's small home not far from the Sanctuary.

"So this is…*Rivertown*," Rufàran said, confused. "Am I missing something?"

Kalas and Zhalera laughed. "Sevens and Sevens ago, the Rumilswàr ran right through the middle of Lohwàlar. Things have changed since then: the river changed course and the land became a desert."

"The Curvewanderer? Interesting. Well, your people seem… nice?"

"They are, Your Majesty," Kalas agreed.

"Tsharak and Vàyana?" Zhalera mused, her thoughts on Othar's unexpected revelation.

"Friends of yours, I assume?" Rufàran queried. Kalas nodded.

"It's weird, right? Well, I mean, maybe it's not: Vàyana lost her husband some Sevens ago, and Tsharak…well, I don't know his story, but I don't think he's always been alone. I don't know why, just a feeling, I guess…"

"No, it's great!" Zhalera insisted. "I mean, I know Tsharak is, what, nine hundred years old or something like that? I just wonder how long, well…It doesn't matter! I just hope they're good to each other!"

For whatever time remains to them. To her, Kalas inferred from Zhalera's abrupt shift.

"I'm sure they will be," he agreed.

"Nine hundred years?!" Rufàran spluttered. *"*That seems unlikely!"

"More or less unlikely than anything you've seen since we stepped out from the inside of the Ravine?" Kalas smirked. Rufàran chuckled and inclined his head.

"Interesting," he repeated.

Abarandal, her thoughts returning to their earlier conversation, laughed aloud, her light, sparkling melody filling the cabin as they rode.

"Well, sure, but what's the likelihood of *that?!*" he wondered.

"Ahem?" Zhalera cleared her throat.

"Oh! Abarandal's just wondering: what if Vàyana had a life span akin to Tsharak's? What if she has, say, eight or nine, even ten Sevens, and has yet to acquire dozens more? I guess it's a fair point: I wonder when Tsharak realized he wasn't like most other people?"

"But she told us she didn't hear The Song, right? If she *was* like Tsharak, wouldn't she know it? Wouldn't she be able to hear it, too?"

"You're right," Kalas admitted. "Well, Abarandal, seems like there's your answer!"

The stargirl responded with another brief phrase and shrugged, smiling all the while.

"I guess we will," he conceded. Changing the subject, he added, "Hey, what happened last night? You looked sick—not like with the trolls…maybe a little like you did in the Ravine, but after that light and the weird floaty stuff, you seemed better than ever! I'll be honest: my head still hurts, and everything's still sore from getting tossed around!"

"Yeah, I wondered that, too," Zhalera confided.

Abarandal neither said nor sang an answer, but the way her smile *shifted,* the way her ice-colored eyes darted toward Zhalera, Kalas knew she knew more than she seemed willing to reveal.

Before he could press the matter, Rül brought the coach to a halt. "We're here," he shouted, rocking its suspension as he jumped down from his seat. When they stepped outside, Tsharak, Vàyana, and Rofe were there to meet them. The latter embraced his kins-woman—and quickly apologized for his familiarity. Pava laughed and told him not to bother with such things. Rofe even offered Rül a polite bow: when the farm boy looked to his bride for instruction, she laughed again and returned the gesture.

"*Shëmîuín,* it's so good to see you!" he gushed.

"You as well, Rofe! You look well! I'll admit: I'm surprised to see you here! I mean, I'd be surprised to see *any* cave-dweller so far from home! What convinced you to come all this way?"

"Our people have regarded outsiders with distrust for too long, and I don't exclude myself from that observation. We've had our reasons: I was there when those soldiers came down through the Áthradho. But it was *ilròumbume* who risked their lives to rescue us under those mines; it was an outsider who powered up the *Kathin Iltith,* and if our princess can overcome our ethnic prejudices—I mean, you took an *ilròumbu* for a husband!—maybe the rest of us can, too.

"So I thought traveling a little might be a good way to start. We haven't had much contact with anyone for Sevens—not since I've been alive! I wondered where to go, but when I heard about the mirrors you'd ordered for Lohwàlar, I volunteered to deliver them. Mister Rül, your people have been most gracious! Well, once they accepted my help! Our people can be pretty stubborn, too, as you already know!"

"Mister Rofe has been a *great* help," Tsharak piped up. "We're still finishing some of the observation towers—we had to raise them several feet to provide a clear path for light to reach the Crescent, but the mirrors we *have* managed to install are working perfectly! In fact, with some expert grinding and polishing, Mister Rofe shaped them to paint lighted arrows on the ground pointing toward the source of trouble—just like you suggested, Miss Pava!"

"*Dhemme*, it's so good to see you again!" Vàyana said, wrapping each in a tight hug. "You've been gone for quite some time! And to the distant North, I understand?"

"I promise we'll tell you all about it," Kalas assured her, "but first, we need to get Rül back to his farm: Shosafin has a promise of his own to keep."

"Ilbardhën, your arm!" Tsharak gasped. "What—"

Rufàran joined the others, and when Tsharak saw him, his eyes widened: "King Rufàran?! Can it be?!"

The rediscovered king paused, mid-stretch, and cocked his head.

"You…know my name?" he said, surprised.

"Of course! It's been Sevens since we met—well, we never really *met*, but I was there, at your coronation: you look exactly the same! Here in Lohwàlar, we don't often hear about what's taking place all the way to the East, but we did get news of Queen Helëstal's passing. My belated condolences."

Rufàran inclined his head, placed a hand on Tsharak's shoulder, and said, "Thank you, kind sir. Tsharak, is it? Nine hundred years old, the lad says?"

"Close enough, I suppose," the old man shrugged.

"Remarkable!" the astounded king shook his head.

"We'll tell you everything," said Kalas, addressing Tsharak, "but we really should get Rül back to his farm. The sooner we're done

here, the sooner we can return with King Rufàran to Ïsriba and…
do what needs to be done. I'm sorry, your Highness. I wish there
were some other way…"

Shosafin, his jaw tight, insisted, "The king and I will sort it out
when *we* get to Ïsriba."

2.

Thara would not stop weeping with joy when Rül pulled up to
their squat, sprawling farmhouse. She buried her face within the
folds of his travel-stained tunic and held him close. She reached
for Pava after a moment and absorbed her daughter-in-law into her
inescapable embrace. Rül whispered something only the three of
them could understand, and the cave-dweller laughed. Thara wiped
her eyes and laughed, too, until she registered Shosafin's injury.

"Your arm!" she exclaimed.

"Marugan," he replied. "He's dead now, I think, but he didn't
go quietly."

"Does it…does it hurt?"

"Even though it's not there, sometimes, it *does* hurt. Most of
the time, it's…fine, I guess. It's a wonder I didn't bleed out at the
bottom of that ravine. Good thing the lad was there."

"The lad?"

"Kalas. He—oh! Hmm…" Shosafin looked at Kalas, who felt
unseasonable heat prickle in his cheeks and across the back of his
neck. "He managed to stop the bleeding before that happened."

"I, uh, yeah…I'm just glad he's all right," Kalas stammered.
"Hey, I'll tell you what: it's good to be home again!"

"It sure is!" Zhalera agreed.

"Uh, let's get what we need unloaded from the coach," Rül
muttered. "Then give me a few minutes to tend to the horses, and
we'll—"

"I'll get someone else on it!" Thara insisted: "You've been away for too long! Take what you need, then get inside and get cleaned up—all of you! Including *you,* whoever you are! Shosafin, it seems you've exchanged your cousin for someone new. Where *is* Nashmur? He's not...? I mean, he isn't...?"

"No, no, dear lady! He...ventured east ahead of us. He had some things he needed to sort out for himself. We'll meet up with him soon enough."

"Oh?" said Thara, her eyebrow arched.

"I'll explain, I promise."

"You've kept the last few you've made," she smiled, although her eyes weren't in it.

Shosafin overlooked her wariness and said, *"Shâu* Thara, permit me the honor of introducing you to King Rufàran, rightful ruler of the kingdom of Ïsriba!"

"King Rufàran?! I thought he was—"

"Most people seem to think so," the king nodded as he wrapped his sturdy fingers around her workworn hand. He knelt and pressed his forehead against the skin above her knuckles. "Including, I've heard, my own daughter."

"But the queen-regent is, well, she's a mature woman now! At *least* your age, if appearances can be trusted! There's no way—"

"Appearances can *not* be trusted. Not in this instance, if your friends are correct," Rufàran said with a broad smile. "I'll be honest with you, good woman: I'm still trying to make sense of it myself! Now, you said something about us getting cleaned up? It's been a long journey!"

"Of course! Of course! Right this way!"

Kalas woke from an impromptu nap to hear Nïmrïk outlining a portion of their recent travels. Thara, rapt, seemed unable or unwilling to move, lest she break his spell. He looked to Zhalera and Shosafin as his tale progressed. The young man noted he didn't share every detail: whether for brevity or some other purpose he could only guess.

"The *shagabme* just kept coming," he said. "The lad distracted Marugan long enough for Shosafin to wake us all from the nightmare, at the cost of his arm. Yet we had other help, too: light that poured through the Ravine like the waters of an insurmountable flood! An *elu*, an old…ah…an acquaintance of mine…"

Shosafin offered reluctant nods and disinterested grunts from time to time, and Kalas wondered if Nïmrïk's retelling provided an alternate perspective of events he hadn't considered. The gruff warrior mumbled indiscernible things whenever the shaggy raconteur praised his endeavors in any slight fashion.

When everyone finished relating his or her portion of the story, Thara, seated between her son on her right and Shosafin on her left, his injury between them, had no words. She made a show of squeezing Rül's hand, grateful he'd returned to her safely: she reached for Shosafin's missing limb; when she didn't find it, she laughed at herself and wrapped her arm around the remains of his and leaned into his shoulder. He tried to pull away, embarrassed, it seemed, but Thara would not let go: "Stop it," she commanded with a tone that settled the matter.

"*Zhi ëligar pïni Nimkosra Kàsh,*" she marveled, addressing Rufàran. "Gone for all these Sevens; now, in *my* house of all places!

"Shosafin, I understand your desire to return the king to Ïsriba—I haven't forgotten the things you told me last winter. When you've restored Ïsriba's rightful king, when you've regained your good name: make me one more promise. As you said, you've kept the others—even when we were strangers, when I had no right to demand such things from you. Maybe I still have no right to make this next request, but I'll make it all the same—such things have never stopped me before! When you've completed all your labors…

return to me. Come…*home. And stay.*"

Maybe everyone in the packed room gasped at the same time. Maybe just Kalas, but judging from the astounded expressions scribed on every face, he guessed the others held their breaths as well.

"My dear lady," Shosafin began. He sucked in a breath and held it. He looked away from Thara's entreating eyes and toward the stump she gripped with iron determination.

"My dear, dear lady," he continued, softening, it seemed, "I promise."

"Good," she nodded, self-assured. She regarded Rül, still awe-stricken, and patted his leg; with her now-empty hand, she massaged the cheek beneath Shosafin's scraggly beard. Her eyes brimming, her expression raw, she pulled the soldier toward herself and kissed him. Abandoning his gruff demeanor—for a moment— Shosafin responded in kind and wrapped his remaining arm around the small of her back.

"Uh…Mother?" Rül croaked when no one else seemed willing to speak. Pava tugged on his arm and breathed something in his ear.

"C'mon, everyone," she said, her eyes sparkling. "Let's figure out what to eat: I can't be the only one who's had enough of stale bread and salted fish!"

"Kitchen's this way, right?" Nïmrïk gestured and exited the room. "Let's see what we can cook up!"

"I should have expected as much," Kalas confided to Zhalera as he helped her wash the dishes after the veritable feast Nïmrïk had prepared. "The way Thara looked at him before we left. The way Shosafin looked at *her*, when he thought no one was looking! I wasn't spying! Not *really!* I just…some things you just notice, y'know? Sometimes you don't know what you've seen until something else ties everything together."

"Something like Thara grabbing Shosafin and—?"

"Something *just* like that," Kalas agreed. "He thinks he's less of a man, you know, without an arm. You could hear it, couldn't you? How he thought about *not* opening up to her? Maybe after Sevens of putting up with someone like Barish—*o shelu fie id nir!*—Thara figured out how to make herself understood. I don't think any other woman would have been as capable. I'm happy for them both, and if I can help Shosafin keep his promise to her, I'm going to do it. We *will* go with them to Ïsriba, of course! I'm not naïve enough to think getting Rufàran back on the throne is the end of things: other kingdoms have their own 'Marugans,' as you know. I can't imagine what it'll do to Rufàran to see what his daughter's become, what his kingdom has become beneath her reign. Getting her to step down should put this part of the world on a path toward peace."

"Let's hope you're right," Zhalera nodded as she chewed on her lip.

"It's funny you should say that: I know you don't hear it, but you asked me about The Song a while back, under all the stars above the Empty Sea. Do you remember how I described it to you? Do you remember the thread that runs between every movement, every chord, every note?"

Zhalera thought about it, her eyes distant as she accessed the memory. At last she smiled: *"Hope."*

3.

Over the next few days, Kalas and the others made their rounds throughout Lohwàlar: they exchanged pleasantries with Sàrush and Tshama one night; the next, they detailed their recent adventures to Tsharak and Vàyana over a meal. It seemed obvious that the ancient man had explained much of the world's unsettledness to

Vàyana, yet both of them expressed shock and dismay when Kalas told them about Peradan's betrayal.

"In all my Sevens," Tsharak shook his head and rubbed at the tattoo-like symbols that dotted his leathery hand.

"You're doing it again," Vàyana whispered with a nod. "Does it still itch?"

"What's that?" Kalas wondered.

"Oh, nothing," Tsharak insisted. "A few days ago, this mark on my hand felt like it was burning. I must have cried out in my sleep and woken Vàyana despite the distance between our rooms: she applied a salve that muted the worst of it…"

"A few days ago?" Zhalera repeated, her eyes narrowed.

"Yes, that's right. The night before you got back, I believe."

"I see," she said with a subtle glance at Abarandal. The *eru* stared at the ground; the others—Kalas included—looked at one another.

"The night the sky turned to gold?" Nïmrïk arched an eyebrow.

"It's…no, never mind," dismissed Zhalera with a wave of her hand.

"I made a few more trips into the Empty Sea," Tsharak admitted after a conversational lull. "To the Pump, too. I don't know what put the idea in my head, but something nagged at me about the way the *craft* and the Pump are situated. Since I've been helping redesign the town, I, ah, 'borrowed' some surveying equipment and took a few measurements. I can't be certain, not without getting under all that rubble Falthwën brought down upon the artifact, but based on my best estimates, the Pump and the artifact lie along similar axes. I did some exploring, some digging, too, and I discovered gouges in the landscape that might easily be mistaken for natural features: on closer inspection, however, it looks like something *scratched* at the earth with terrible claws. Had the Empty Sea remained the Sea of Jewels, I doubt anyone ever would have noticed."

"You think they're related," intuited Kalas, having constructed a mental picture. "You think the artifact and the Pump are…what? connected? the same thing?!"

"Your words, not mine, my boy!" the old man laughed. "The truth is, I don't know, but I'm confident both were there before either Sea existed."

"That's what Father thought, too," Zhalera said, remembering Gandhan's observation with a wistful look.

"If you're right, then that room behind the Pump makes a lot more sense," Kalas admitted. "That thing behind *that* room, though? What do you make of that?!"

"Without your…unique abilities, I've been unable to get a closer look: which is probably just as well! I am an old man, after all."

Kalas shivered: "Sometimes, in dreams, I see that skull sailing through the air and *staring* at me, even though it has no eyes, just before it disappears…"

"Abarandal and I have something we need to talk about," Zhalera said a day later, as she and the *eru* prepared for a trip to her smithy. "And I'm sorry, Kalas, but it's something just between the two of us. When I can, I'll tell you all about it—about everything she's asked of me, but right now, I can't. I hope you understand…"

Kalas nodded. "I do, Firebird. I do. I mean, I have no idea what you two have been talking about, but I'll be ready when you are."

"Will you, though?"

Puzzled, the young man said nothing, and Zhalera, perhaps mistaking his stunned silence for reflection, squeezed him for a moment before she and Abarandal exited her late parents' home.

Nïmrïk, watching from the shadows, stood behind the young man as he tried to make sense of things.

"Enigmatic," he said, and Kalas nodded. "Any idea what they're scheming?"

"None whatsoever. It looked like she was packing items for the forge, but I have no idea why Abarandal had to go with her for that. She's been working on a sword for me. Or, she *had* been! I was probably a little obnoxious about it—no, I was a *lot* obnoxious about it, but I thought I'd made things right. Maybe not?"

"Looks like you've got the morning—maybe the day to yourself?" said the *egu*, abandoning the mystery surrounding the women.

"I guess I do," Kalas realized. "Rül's got something on his mind—something *other* than Shosafin and Thara! Something I think he'll need to sort through on his own, whatever it might be. And speaking of Shosafin, I suspect he and Thara need to have a talk, too. We've checked in on Sàrush, spoken with Tsharak…I am tempted to go back to the Pump, but it's too late for that, and I don't even know what I'd be looking for…"

In his mind, he saw the dessicated figure slumped over a stack of translucencies. He pictured himself holding one up to the light and studying its effects as its symbols changed. As the pictures in his imagination shifted form and position, he noticed something: "Kadhëmba, I figured out what I'm doing today! Nanësra did something to my mind—or maybe just my book, the one with the woodcuts in it. I had a dream, a vision—something, I don't know what. I didn't say anything about it at first, but just now, I was thinking about that *not-paper* my grandfather had, about the similar items under the Pump, and just now—I don't know how or why, but I think the *not-paper* and the unreadable book are somehow related! No, not in the way they look *now*, but in the way the book—its characters—looked in the dream-thing. I didn't see it at the time, or maybe I just didn't realize it.

"I'm taking both items back to Wodram's study. I don't know if there's anything else to discover in there—Father and I made a pretty thorough search, and Falthwën and Zhalera and I searched again after that, but he had a lot of *stuff* lying around. It's possible we missed something: before we left, I spent a lot of time in there, but I was so focused on the book and that other thing. Maybe it's worth one more visit?"

"If you'd like some company, I'll come with you. Otherwise, I'll wait here until you or the ladies return. I don't think it's a good idea to move around town without a guide: unlikely as it is, if someone were to figure out what I am…"

"Yeah, of course, c'mon," Kalas said as he grabbed Falthwën's staff and collected his things.

Despite its recent repairs, the air surrounding Kalas' house suggested something tomb-like as he and Nïmrïk approached its dusty exterior. The second sun had already separated from the first and hung about halfway between its zenith and the horizon. With a deep sigh, he pushed open the heavy door and entered into the gloom. After giving his eyes a moment to adjust, he headed for Wodram's study, stepping reflexively over the place where the *rudzhegu* had felled Gandhan. He paused when he reached its threshold.

"Something the matter?" Nïmrïk wondered and glanced around the rooms.

"No, I don't think so. It's just…I'll be right back. Or you can follow me: it's up to you."

Kalas dropped his pack beside the door to the study and entered deeper into his old home. Nïmrïk followed.

"My old room," he acknowledged, his eyes lingering on the sconce Màla often reminded him to extinguish. He continued the tour: "The kitchen. Mother was a great cook. Father, too, on those rare occasions when he found himself in here. That's where I found her—where Zhalera found her, right before she died…"

After checking the remaining rooms—for what, he had no idea, Kalas returned through the great room: "That new-looking patch in the ceiling? *Sharuyandas Âsru* tore a hole through the roof, but

Gandhan was already dead. Mother already dying…Kadhëmba, maybe this wasn't such a good idea, coming back here! Last time, I could put all this out of my mind, but today? I don't know why, but it's harder to bear for some reason."

"Lad, you're going to find some days are easier than others. You're going to find others are harder, and the worst part: you're going to find you won't know the difference until later. Sometimes *much* later. You know what I am, what I've done, so believe me when I say I understand—in principle, if not in particulars. If you think being here, today, will make your task more difficult than being somewhere else, I'm content to follow you elsewhere: if you want to stay, I'm content to do that as well. Sometimes a change of scenery helps lift one's mood. Sometimes…it does not…"

"I appreciate that," Kalas said after another heavy sigh. "We're here, and so are Wodram's old books, so we might as well stick around. Who knows? Maybe you'll uncover something none of the rest of us has!"

Nïmrïk shrugged and began a slow walk around the disheveled space. Scrolls and codices still littered the shelves. And the floor. Portions of the ancient stone table Falthwën had shattered still occupied the center of the room. As he lit a cobwebbed candle jutting from the wall, he asked, "Hey, Kadhëmba: you see all these pieces of rock? They used to be a table. I was just thinking…I'm not sure if you were awake yet: you'd just been shot by Marugan, under the Vault, but Falthwën said he found Loradan's weapon Hàfilrifar inside part of something he called *The Arch*. Was he talking about this table? What is The Arch, anyway?"

Nïmrïk shivered and dropped a book he'd retrieved from the floor. He squared himself with the broken stone and raised his hands in a protective gesture as his eyes flashed hot and yellow. He growled, and Kalas, for the first time since the *egu* had become a member of his peculiar family, felt afraid. He raised Falthwën's staff and adjusted his stance.

"Kadhëmba?" he ventured, his eyes locked on the bristling figure.

Nïmrïk must have noticed the young man's movements in his peripheral vision: he sniffed the air and turned to include him in his field of view. When he noticed Kalas' posture, when he smelled Kalas' fear, he seemed shocked, like he'd been somewhere else—some*one* else—for a moment. He relaxed, and the shine in his eyes subsided as his mien softened.

"Forgive me, lad: it's been a long, long time since I've heard mention of The Arch! Millennia ago, when the heavenlies defeated Ilnëshras, *elume* and *erume* constructed a prison from the wreckage of their wars. *The Arch.* Many of us endured Sevens upon Sevens confined within its walls. You've been held within a singularity: there, you're blissfully unaware of time's passage. You're simply removed from its flow, practically speaking. Within The Arch, the opposite is true. Seconds pass like centuries, and one remains keenly aware of everything from which he's been abstracted.

"I don't know what happened to The Arch. I suppose no one does. One day, my cell was my world; the next, I was adrift in space, high above the earth. Perhaps a different world altogether? It doesn't matter. When I discovered I was free, my first thought was gratitude toward the Creator: my second thought was *where did the first come from?!* Peradan wasn't wrong when he wondered why no other *egu* has tried to regain his first estate. To this day, I'm the only one that has—that I'm aware of, and, if pressed, I still couldn't tell you *why*...

"That a piece of my former prison should have found its way to your world—and into your home—beggars belief! Those fragments look like nothing more than bits of stone to me, but my...*senses* aren't what they once were.

"It did look different before it broke," Kalas informed him.

"And Sharuyan discovered a weapon—a *nimeru* weapon—inside the table?"

"Yes, the thing he used to call out to Loradan. The weapon she used when the *ekume* attacked us. You were injured: you might not remember. I couldn't lift it, couldn't even budge it! Falthwën said it had been elsewhere—and else*when*. I didn't know what he meant."

"This is strange stuff, lad! Strange indeed!"

Hours passed in inconsistent silence as Kalas pored over his grandfather's collection. Again. Nïmrïk interrupted him on occasion as he examined one discarded work after another. When the single candle burned itself out, the young man realized the suns had set a while ago.

"How long have we been here? I mean, quite a while, obviously, but it doesn't seem like it! There's all kinds of history in here: I got sidetracked more than once! Never did find anything that might tie the *not-paper*—and the craft buried in the rocks—to the book. I guess I didn't really expect we would, but it's still disappointing. I should see if there's another candle around here somewhere… Maybe—"

Kalas stopped speaking when a dim flicker oozed past the door to the study. He held his breath as a chill wrapped around him and sapped the warmth from his bones. The flicker gained strength as it seemed to veer toward the great room, just down the hall. Intrigued, and despite his rising fear, he followed it.

Hovering over the place where Gandhan died, a gauzy half-darkness cast a strange *feeling* across the space.

"It's like the…what'd you call it? Those things in Kësharan? *Shosayàódru?* Is that what this is?" Kalas whispered.

The unnatural manifestation of sorrow lingered a moment longer, then drifted toward the place where Màla died.

"He was *inhabited,* Falthwën said. After the *rudzhegu* got him.

Would that make a difference?"

"Maybe. Maybe not. I don't think it really matters."

The spirit-mist, attracted, perhaps, by their exchange, altered course again, and floated toward the pair.

"You said these things couldn't hurt us, right?"

"Not *physically...*"

The half-darkness thinned out and curled itself along Kalas' body, and he understood: he experienced an emotional pressure that threatened to gouge a valley through his psyche. He stiffened, and the sensation intensified. Mustering all his will, he breathed out deep and slow and closed his eyes.

"Lad! Are you all right!" Nïmrïk hissed.

"It's all right," Kalas mumbled, addressing the mist. "You're not Gandhan. You're not Mother, either. I don't know *what* you are, exactly, but you don't belong here!"

"Kalas, I don't think it understands! It's neither a person nor a 'ghost.' I'm not sure words mean anything to the mist."

The young man cocked his head, then nodded. He took a deep breath and collected phrases from his deepest sorrows, his greatest losses, and arrayed them in his mind as the foundation for a requiem. Next, he willed the Song to assume the shapes of his brightest memories of Màla and Tàran, of Gandhan and all of Lohwàlar; he layered his melodies in soft, sweeping movements; he juxtaposed the somber and the serene, and, caught within the counterpoint of wreck and rapture, the *shosayàódru* burned away like fog in the rising heat of day.

Dark silence abounded. A gust of wind crept into the room and traced an icy path across his cheek: that's when he realized he'd been crying. At his side, Nïmrïk's muffled sobs percolated through the quiet. Kalas could feel the old wolf's eyes on him, but the grizzled figure said nothing as he shambled out the door and into the night.

4.

He caught up to Nïmrïk just before they reached Zhalera's smithy. No lights shone through its windows; no smoke ascended from its stout chimney: Zhalera and Abarandal must have returned home. Exasperated—overcome, it seemed, with syntheses he'd been unable to express, the egu plopped himself on the steps in a heap. He buried his head in his hands and shook while Kalas waited.

"I didn't know such things were possible," he mumbled. "Has it always been thus? Have I just been ignorant of The Song's potential? From the dawn of time, I've never heard such…I don't even know how to describe it!"

He raised his head, wiped away fresh tears, and continued: "I'm not talking about the roughness in some of your choices…or maybe I am? I guess the whole of your arrangement—imperfections and all—touched some part of me that's been dead for millennia. Some part of me I'd forgotten about, honestly. I know you were… *communing,* maybe, with the spirit-mist, but I also heard—no, I was immersed within that expression of The Song.

"Lad, I don't think you realize: neither *elunàmdas* rigid lawfulness nor *egunàmdas* chaotic anarchy has ever tapped into the utter substance of The Song the way you, a mere *edhu*—forgive my condescension—just did! This wasn't like before, when you healed me under Deridzhas: this was…well, I have no idea what this was! When I told the Swath how I'd come to be in Thosha, dangling from the gibbet, do you remember I said I recognized Sharuyan? Do you remember I said I recognized *you,* too? I'm starting to wonder: maybe it wasn't you, the man, I recognized. Maybe it was something else, something yet unrealized? But that's irrational, isn't it? Illogical? I don't know—maybe I never will—but more than ever, I understand why Sharuyan believes you to be necessary for the prophecy's fulfillment…

"Maybe it's not my place to say, but woven within your melodies, I discerned threads of uncertainty. That's not a condemnation! No, I only mean I sensed…I don't know, a secret fear, maybe, that you haven't shared with anyone: the anticipation of some dread event. I perceived it as an understated counterpoint, a line of shadow intended to accentuate your otherwise luminous harmonies. As someone who's entertained fear for uncounted Sevens, I'll just offer a word of caution: take pains not to let it swallow your hope! We *elume*—forgive me: we *egume* know the prophecy, too:

*To bring the light
Or to banish it;
To bring the day
Or embrace the dark*

And:

*Surrender us to darkness
Or hasten us toward day?
Bind the world in shadow
Or cover us with glory?*

"I trust you have your reasons for keeping your secrets. I've kept my own for thousands of years, and as someone who's dabbled—who's *embraced the dark* before…If you decide you'd prefer to share your fears with someone, as flawed as I am, I'd consider it an honor. Understand: I'm not asking you to divulge anything you're unwilling to. I just want you to know you don't have to bear these things by yourself. Whether it's me or someone else, promise me you'll ask for help before your uncertainties overwhelm you! Had I done the same—when I had the opportunity…"

You've a great many ordeals ahead of you…one…particularly cruel,

Nanësra had said to him. Her lament had lodged in the back of his thoughts from the moment she uttered those words, but until now, he hadn't realized her sad secret had metastasized into something darker within his mind.

"You…you got all that from whatever happened at my house?" he managed after a stunned moment. Nïmrïk nodded once.

"All right, well…thanks. Uh, Zhalera's not here. Probably headed back to her place. We should do the same, don't you think?"

"As you wish."

"Doesn't look like they're here, either," Kalas frowned when they reached Zhalera's home. "I hope they're not worried about us—we were gone for quite a while! You don't suppose they went all the way up to Rül's farm, do you?"

"You'd know better than I would," Nïmrïk replied. He sniffed the air and tried to taste which direction they might have taken. "I don't think so, however: what's this way? Vàyana's place? The Sanctuary? I still haven't figured my way around this town!"

"Both, actually," Kalas nodded. "You go past the Sanctuary on your way to Vàyana's. I hope nothing's happened! C'mon, we should go!"

Nïmrïk nodded and followed the young man as he jogged through Lohwàlar's darkened streets. They passed a few people along the way, and Kalas stopped and asked each one if they'd seen or heard anything about Zhalera. None had, although as they approached the Sanctuary, someone coming from the opposite direction said he'd heard a commotion of some sort: "I probably wouldn't have thought twice about it if you hadn't asked," he admitted.

"*Ágazhëthu!*" Kalas panted as he raced toward the old temple.

"Uh, right: thank you," Nïmrïk repeated.

He didn't slow down when he reached the threshold: instead, Kalas barreled through the doors and startled the receptionist.

"Zhalera!" he demanded. "Zhalera! Abarandal! Are they—"

Abarandal sang his name and interrupted him, and he turned toward the *eruín* as she half-dragged, half-coaxed Zhalera into the front room. Grasping the concern in his features, she added her assurance that everyone was all right.

"What about your chest?!" he countered, pointing at the charred bits of blood-soaked cloth above her heart. The young woman glanced down, blushed, and tried to rearrange the folds in her blackened clothes.

"This is a place of *healing!*" the disgruntled receptionist insisted with quiet urgency.

"Right! I'm sorry!" Kalas apologized.

Abarandal addressed Zhalera with a rapid string of notes, then released her and beckoned the others to join her outside, where she offered her cryptic rationale.

"But you're *not* fine! You wouldn't have come here if you were! Was there an accident at the smithy?! No? Then what? I don't understand!"

Abarandal insisted she'd said enough. Too much, perhaps, and deferred to Zhalera, who at last emerged from within the Sanctuary.

"Zhalera? What—you're crying! What happened! Please—"

"Nothing!" she spat, and Kalas discerned a curious blend of embarrassment and fear in her retort. A few people enjoying the evening's brisk air stopped and turned toward the sound of their discussion. She looked around and realized she'd attracted an audience. "I don't want to talk about it!"

Kalas had no idea how to respond, so he just nodded. Zhalera, perhaps anticipating some rebuttal or insistence that she dialog with him, opened her mouth to shout him down: when she realized he hadn't said anything, nor was he about to, she huffed an angry sigh and stomped toward her home. Abarandal cupped a hand around Kalas' ear, whispered a brief spate of notes admonishing patience, then followed after her friend. The young man and the *egu* exchanged confused glances before they, too, retraced their steps.

"What do you think—?"

"I don't!" Nïmrïk interrupted. "And neither should you! Give her time. Give her space. You'll gain nothing if you demand an explanation: indeed, you might lose something."

"That's pretty much what Abarandal said," Kalas admitted. "I'll do my best, but…Did she look *hurt* to you? Not Abarandal—yes, *she* looked hurt! I mean Zhalera! No, not physically…I don't know… something else…"

"Leave it alone, lad," Nïmrïk growled.

When the first sun rose the next day, Kalas, heeding Nïmrïk's advice, said he planned to visit Rül's farm. He sat at Zhalera's table, carving a scrap of wood with his knife. She hadn't emerged from her room, and, after a timid (and unanswered) knock at her door, he hoped she'd be all right. Abarandal communicated she'd remain in the house, too. Kalas discerned a strange timbre in her music: he said something about it, but she insisted he had nothing to worry about.

"What about your—?" he began, but she took a deep breath, let her lungs expand without impediment, and smiled. He laughed and admitted, "That's right: you're a star, aren't you? Not given to the same frailties as us! Well, *me,* at least! Would you believe, despite everything, I forget that sometimes?"

The young girl deflected with a smile.

"I don't suppose you'd wanna tell me what happened, would you?" he plied, pointing at her chest, where he'd seen unexplained scorch marks the day before.

Her smile faltered, as though she contemplated saying something, but after a pause, she opted not to say anything.

"Didn't think so. All right, then, I'll be back before suns-down.

Kadhëmba, wanna come?"

"Master Kalas, if you'll indulge an old man, I think I'd like to remain here, too…"

"Oh? Hmm. Should I stay, too?" he wondered aloud. Both Abarandal and Nïmrïk seemed ill-at-ease, and he couldn't understand why. Hoofbeats outside interrupted the awkward silence before either dared respond.

"Rül? Shosafin?" Kalas said as he stepped outside. Behind them rode Pava, Rofe, and Rufàran. "What's going on? Is everything all right? I was just on my way to see you. Things here are—"

"It's time, lad," Shosafin interrupted. "I've kept my promise to Thara; now, I keep my promise to myself. To Ïsriba. Given the season and the strength of our mounts, we should reach the capital in three weeks at the latest."

"You're leaving? Right now?! But I thought—well, Rül! Pava! What are you doing? You're not going to Ïsriba too, are you?"

"No, Kalas, we're not," Rül mumbled. He'd been staring at the ground since the quintet arrived at Zhalera's place; now, he raised his head, stiffened his back, and, having established eye contact with his friend, explained: "We're returning to the Gateway."

"Oh? How long will you be gone?"

"Kalas, *sàyahal*…we're not coming back."

Stunned, the young man had no idea what to say. Rül, perhaps interpreting his silence as a request for details, elaborated: "It's one of the things Rive and I discussed on our way down from there last year. I've discussed it with Mother: when I learned what had happened to Father…I wasn't going to say anything to her, but she figured I was holding something back, and I'm not good at that, as you know. When she learned Pava and I were getting married, she demanded I keep my word. She's been a farmer longer than I've been alive—a point she was quick to drive home—and insisted she'd manage.

"I didn't know about her feelings toward Shosafin. Or his feelings toward her. I know about them now, though, and it just seems like things are falling into place. We'll ride with Shosafin as far as the Áthradho. Pava's become quite comfortable with Ascender, and I think Courser will enjoy not having to haul the coach anymore!

"This is the right time, the right choice, Kalas. We've been through a lot, there's no denying that, but with Marugan gone, with Hwanzho's treachery revealed—and with him gone, too, the cities under the Gateway need our help. *Pava's* help. It's still *the* major crossroad between East and West, and more than ever, people are gonna want to control it. Pava knows the Houses, all the crazy stuff that's happened there—and she's traveled vast distances from it! No other *úrukilmukrit* can say as much! No other cave-dweller can say she's traveled with the *Ilosar,* either!"

Kalas tried not to cry as the farm boy presented his rationale. Until this moment, he hadn't entertained the likely ramifications of Rül and Pava's union. Nothing overt had changed. Still, the more the farm boy said, the more Kalas understood where he was coming from, and as much as it pained him to admit, he recognized the wisdom in his intent. He considered begging them to stay, to build their lives in Lohwàlar. He wanted them to understand how much he needed their strength and friendship, and he wondered if perhaps they hadn't understood the depth of his gratitude. Instead, all he said was: *"Kasraf nir, sáme.* Be safe."

"As soon as King Rufàran has addressed…the corruption in his court, when the kingdom's been restored, I'll be back: it seems I've acquired a penchant for making promises to a certain woman in this town," he said with a subtle glance at Rül, who smiled this time. "You'll see *me* in Lohwàlar soon enough, lad. Consider that a promise, if you like!"

"Is Abarandal here?" Rufàran wondered. Perhaps divining his request, the young girl stepped out of the house.

"Ah! There you are!" he nodded as he hopped down from Runner, his borrowed horse. He knelt, took her hand, and said. "Thank you, lass, for freeing me from that prison! I must apologize for my reluctance to believe you—all of you—at the time, but it's clear to me that things are not what they used to be. Perhaps they never were. Perhaps they merely *seemed* a certain way..."

Seemed.

Kalas cleared his throat. Rufàran didn't seem to hear.

"My liege," Shosafin prompted. The king kissed Abarandal's hand, stood, and climbed into his saddle.

"What's all this?" said Zhalera, at last emerging from her home.

Pava dismounted Ascender and explained everything. Numb, Zhalera responded with a weak nod and a vacant stare. Like Kalas, she tried to prevent tears; like Kalas, she failed. With a heavy sigh, she mumbled something indiscernible and disappeared inside. Abarandal sang her goodbyes and followed after her.

"Chin up, lad!" Shosafin insisted as he maneuvered Breaker closer to the young man. "You've proven yourself quite the enigma. Usually, I don't like enigmas: I like understanding what I'm up against—especially when my adversary doesn't know what *I* know about what *he* knows! With you, though? I stand by what I said a long time ago now: there's something *noble* about you, and despite the...inexplicable stuff that follows you wherever you go, I still believe that.

"You've been a quick study—surprisingly so, I'll admit—and not just with a sword! I'm confident you're capable of handling yourself between now and whenever we meet again. Until that day, young sir, stand strong. Keep an eye on things while I'm away. Look in on Thara from time to time, *hish?*"

"I can do that," Kalas acceded.

Shosafin nodded, his features grim. Before he raised his veil and wheeled Breaker toward the Highway, he flashed a brief smile; then, with a squeeze against the stout beast's ribs, he led the others toward the rising hills east of Lohwàlar. Kalas followed them around the corner of Zhalera's house and watched until they disappeared behind a dusty cloud. Wind, warmed by the suns, whipped it away, along with any trace his friends—his *family*—had ever passed him by.

5.

"I guess it's just us now," Kalas noted as he let himself back inside. He held the door for Abarandal, who offered him a weak nod and a weaker smile. Disgusted with herself, she shook her head and spat a stream of frantic notes.

"I know, I know! It's *not* all right, but I don't know what to do about it! It…it should be all of us! It *has* to be all of us! But Shosafin's not wrong, either: King Rufàran has to reclaim his throne. If I'm honest, those two probably spent *too* much time here. Rül and Pava, too: she's the *úrukilmukritmedas* princess—even if she hates that title—and now Rül's their prince. He's right, too: pretty soon, armies will fight for control of the Gateway, and the houses need to know what's coming; they'll need to know what happened across the world above them. How can they if no one tells them?

"I wish I knew what the other *erume* were up to! We still have no idea what's become of Loradan, after she did her thing. Nor Heshradan. Nor Yayan. Maybe…maybe in a few days, we can go back to Serular? Bring Tsharak with us? Maybe Sifuran will…I have no idea! I just…I don't know what we're supposed to do next!"

Abarandal sighed and nodded. It seemed she had nothing else to say, no words or notes of encouragement. Instead, she placed a hand on his shoulder and pressed her forehead against his, like she did when communicating strong emotions with Zhalera.

"Zhalera!" he breathed aloud and took a step back. "I'm not

489

taking this news well, I know, but you saw how she *changed* before she turned around and went back inside? That's not like her! C'mon, let's make sure she's all right. Well, none of us is 'all right,' but you know what I mean! C'mon!"

When Kalas and Abarandal went inside, they called out for Zhalera, but she didn't answer. Kalas headed straight for her room, where he discovered her seated in a patch of suns-light on the floor. She didn't acknowledge his presence—nor Abarandal's, when the *eru* appeared behind him. The pair looked at one another, neither sure how to proceed. At last, Kalas offered Abarandal a curt nod and seated himself next to Zhalera. Without speaking, he pried her clenched fist from her lap and wrapped his fingers around hers. Abarandal joined them, and the three sat motionless until their silhouettes stretched into spindly caricatures of their former selves.

Kalas' stomach gurgled loud enough to wrest a gasp from his lungs. He pretended the abrupt noise hadn't echoed through the dimming room—until Zhalera tried (and failed) to choke back a laugh.

"I'm...I'm really hungry," he confessed. She laughed, her eyes spilling over with tears, and she relaxed her fist and squeezed his hand.

"It's been...a long day," she admitted. Rising to her feet and helping Kalas do the same, she added, "C'mon, let's eat. Maybe after that, we'll figure out what happens next."

A day later, Kalas busied himself with his books—and his *not-paper,* attempting to remember what he'd glimpsed before, to cement his grasp on what he believed to be visions from the world's distant past with the hope that such knowledge would provide some advantage for the present. And the future.

Like so many times before, his library—he'd ceased thinking of it as *Wodram's* library, or even *Tàran's* library—refused to cooperate. Tsharak stopped by to help Kalas catalog and organize his collection: he offered his vast wealth of knowledge, his colorful tales from Lohwàlar's earlier days, but even his accumulated anecdotes failed to provide new insights into the mystery concealed within those curious letters.

"Nanësra knows what it says," grumbled the young man, "but she won't tell me! When we first met her, I thought she was gonna destroy us all; then, something changed—I don't know what, not exactly, but it seemed like she wanted to help us. *Wanted* to, but maybe *couldn't*. Not directly, anyway. I don't get it! I'm convinced there are important things in here! Things we need to know! I don't understand why she won't—or can't—just tell us!"

"Neither do I, dear one," Tsharak commiserated. "Like our departed friend, however, I presume she has her reasons. Her restrictions, perhaps. Maybe there's some yet unknown benefit you'll only realize through this kind of mental exertion? I don't know, it's just a guess. More of a hope, I suppose."

"Maybe…" Kalas admitted with a heavy sigh as he returned to his work. "And maybe I'm going about this all wrong? I've been staring at these symbols off and on for months now: I recognize patterns here and there, repeated sequences that—I'm guessing—represent similar words or concepts, but I don't know languages! I don't know codes! Coming back to the mainland from Melash, I just sort of…*fell* into the shapes on the page. Later, at the University, when I was telling Professor Tomush about it, I heard wingbeats… Maybe you're right: maybe she's doing as much as she can, given whatever *restrictions* she's dealing with. Did I tell you she seemed surprised when I told her I couldn't read this book?

"I just…I wonder if I'm trying *too hard* to force these words to mean something? Does that make sense? Maybe I should wait for…I don't know, call it *divine illumination* or something: since no one knows this language except the *elume,* that sounds about as rational as staring at these shapes and believing I'll magically understand them!"

"If you're simply thinking out loud, have at it, young man! If you're expecting a reasoned response, I'm afraid I've none to give."

"Hmm?" Kalas said, distracted. Tsharak laughed and scratched at the marks on his hand.

"Indeed. Well then, I'll leave you to it. I have a few things to run by Sàrush before the suns set. Perhaps I'll see you tomorrow."

"Right, right," mumbled Kalas, his eyes closed, his attention elsewhere.

Maybe Nanësra expects too much, Kalas frowned as he opened his eyes in the dim study. Tsharak had been gone for…hours? He'd lost track of time, but the suns had set, their only trace a faint half-light filtered through a narrow window. He stood and stretched his legs, then lit a few candles and returned to his chair. He sat, his movement sending perturbations through the flames, and as their yellow-orange tongues lapped the swirling air, Kalas glimpsed something in the dust where his grandfather's table—a fragment from a celestial prison—used to stand.

Just a speck of something, he realized when he took a closer look. *Still, I wonder: how did Loradan's sword end up in there? How did the whole thing end up here?*

Contemplating such mysteries, his eyelids heavy, he suggested to himself it was time to leave lest Zhalera and the others worry about him. The candles flickered again, and he looked up at Abarandal, standing in the doorway.

"Oh! Have I been gone too long?" he said as he stood.

The young woman said nothing as she glided across the small room, her diaphanous robes shimmering with unnumbered colors. When she reached him, she took his hands and placed them on her cheeks. Her silvered gaze seemed to bore into him as the immaterial substance of their *connection*—first manifested beneath Ïsriba, when he alone seemed able to understand her song—gained strength and threatened to consume him. Her. Both of them.

Abarandal! What's happening?! What are you doing?! he thought as he tried to ignore his welling panic.

Violent wind rocked the study: Kalas was too confused to care where it came from. His candles winked out, and in the dark, Abarandal's hands felt as cold as steel. Thunder cracked the wind-whipped silence as forks of lightning raked across his vision. The *eru* turned toward the sky, her movements quick and sharp, like a flashing sword. She spoke—not in song, nor in words, but in ringing, metallic echoes. When she turned again, her skin coruscating beneath her robes, her eyes aflame, Kalas had to look away from her burgeoning brilliance. Ice and fire and crackling energy writhed across his hands and along his arms. Abarandal opened her mouth to speak and—

Kalas awoke with a start. His candles had shed several inches, and the suns had wholly set.

Another dream? Vision? Had to be, he insisted: *What else?!*

Standing, he stretched to work away the nascent aches lodged within his neck and lower back.

"This chair's not the most comfortable place to sleep," he acknowledged aloud. He studied his hands and remembered a time when Abarandal's touch had conjured similar sensations. He rubbed his arms and shivered.

Guess I'd better get back to Zhalera. And Abarandal. Abaran…dal. Hmm…

Chapter XVI

Inside Zhalera's Smithy

"Where have you been? The study?" Zhalera wondered when Kalas at last entered her home. Her face still bore streaks of dust and ash, and her cheeks still glowed like burnished bronze from the heat of her forge. She had undone one bun coiled atop her head and started working on the second.

He nodded, his thoughts still focused on his most recent *episode:* he wasn't sure what else to call it. "Going through the books and scrolls, still trying to make sense of *this* book." He held it up with a sheepish smile. "Tsharak was there—for a little while, anyway, helping me catalog everything—well, *some* things: there's a lot of *stuff* in there! I thought he might recognize something, but I don't think he did. Nothing about this book or the artifact, at least. He had to go before suns-down. I mean, he seemed to be in a hurry to get back to Vàyana's place before she did. Makes you wonder, doesn't it?

"Anyway, you've been spending lots of time at the forge, yeah? You must have quite the project on your hands! How are things?"

Before Zhalera could respond, Abarandal looked away: Nimrïk, listening from the kitchen, paused his chopping and sucked in a breath. Kalas understood at once he'd asked the wrong questions.

"No, I'm sorry, I don't—" he tried to say.

"Kalas, it's hopeless! *Hopeless!*" she wailed as she burst into tears. "The metal won't…it won't *obey* me! Things aren't like they were when Father was around! The metal *respected* him! He could shape it into anything! He made it look easy! Maybe *too* easy! I thought I could do it—do something, I don't know, but now I'm starting to think that knife of yours—you know, the one you won't stop talking about—is the best I'll ever manage!"

"Zhalera, that's not—"

"I thought things would change, that they—that I'd get better at this! You're always telling me how great you think that knife is, and after a while, I started to believe you knew something I didn't! And the blacksmith at Melash: he acted like he was impressed with me, and again, I thought maybe I could rise above my doubts—but no matter how much I believe in myself—no matter how much *anyone* believes in me, it doesn't change the fact that I'm just not up to the task!" She glanced—no, *glared* at Abarandal and added: "Even if a stone believes with all its might that it can swim, if you throw it in the river, it *sinks!* Every time. *Every* time!"

"Task?"

"Will you just *stop?!* Just once?!"

"Zhalera, I'm sorry!" Kalas insisted, and Zhalera softened at once: perhaps she glimpsed the pained concern in his wounded expression.

"I…I know! I *know!* And somehow, that makes it *worse!* Your knife was the first piece I made all by myself, the first piece I was truly proud of—and even then, despite your praises, all I could think about were my mistakes! Before, when I was trying to make a sword for you, all my efforts produced were mockeries of my intent! I melted everything down: I hoped to burn away my shame, but it didn't work. I've tried to act like I believe in myself, and for a while, maybe I did, but then Abarandal asked—but I don't. *I don't.* Not now. Not anymore!"

Kalas had no idea how to respond. He knew words, no matter their substance, would only make things worse. Unwilling even to nod or shake his head, he stared at Zhalera and the red fire in her dirtied cheeks. His mind still replaying recent events from his study, he tried to change subjects and said, "Hey, you know that dream or vision or whatever I told you about on the way to Serular? Well, I had another one—I think—some time after Tsharak left!"

"Tonight?" Zhalera prodded, her curious tone a vast improvement over her previous tirade. Nïmrïk resumed his work in the kitchen, and Abarandal stepped into the light to listen.

"Yeah! At first, I didn't realize it was a…I'll just call it a dream. I was tired, I knew that, but I thought I saw Abarandal standing in the doorway! She didn't say anything, but she *floated* over to me and pressed my hands against her cheeks. Her hands were cold, like iron in the morning, before the suns have risen. I asked her what was happening, but instead of singing, she made these strange noises, like…well, like ringing metal. Wind—I don't know how it got in there, but it was a dream…Anyway, wind blew out the candles, and in the dark, there was lightning: like Falthwën sent, only *different*, somehow—that's not helpful, is it?"

Addressing the intrigued woman, he continued: "When it flashed, before it faded out, Abarandal: you turned, and all I could think about was someone twisting a sword! Your skin, your eyes: they started glowing—or maybe that's just when I noticed, but you opened your mouth to say something. Something dreadful, it seemed, but that's when I opened my eyes and…woke up, I guess.

"I don't know why I never realized it before—I'll bet everyone else did!—but your name: Abaran…*dal*. Part of your name means *sword!* Strange that something like that would come to me in a dream, but I—"

"You said you wouldn't say anything!" Zhalera roared as she turned on the young *eru*. Abarandal's already porcelain features surren-

dered what little color they possessed as she blurted out a staccato rebuttal: even if Zhalera had been capable of understanding her frightened song, Kalas suspected she wouldn't have listened. "I told you not to tell him, and you said you wouldn't! And then he tells us about this *'dream'* of his?! *Why,* Abaran*dal?* Why would you betray my trust?! You were like my sister!"

"She didn't!" Kalas interjected. "She didn't say anything to me! She didn't tell me anything! Zhalera, I don't know what you're talking about! Please, listen! I don't know why you're so—it doesn't matter! Please, just tell—"

"Just *what?!*" she demanded, wheeling toward him now. "It's not enough she guilts me into wounding her?! Now she's whispering her dark sayings in your ears, too? Abarandal, I don't know how to make it any clearer: I *can't* do what you ask of me! I tried! *Zhi Ilun—fie id aswanthalu,* I tried! I...I'm sorry! I just...I..."

The young blacksmith's outrage disintegrated into apologetic sobs as she unleashed her frustrations on her friends. She wiped away her sudden tears, smearing gold-toned streaks across her face, and pushed her way through the door and into the night. Kalas looked at Abarandal and wondered, "What was she talking about? Do you think she'll be all right?"

Abarandal sang a brief reply, and Kalas shook his head: "No, of course not! I'm not asking you to betray her confidence! I know you would never do that! I don't know why *she* thinks you would! I...I'm embarrassed, really: I should have known my attempts to build up her confidence only made her feel less capable."

The young woman trilled a retort.

"Maybe you're right, but just because she internalized everything doesn't mean I shouldn't have been more observant. I don't know. I just wish one of you could have said *something* to me about... whatever secret exists between you two. Maybe I wouldn't have made things worse..."

Nïmrïk abandoned his chopping knife and stepped into the great room. He wiped his hands on his apron, then removed it and suggested, "Lad, Abarandal: perhaps we should follow her? There's an undercurrent of something manic in her display. It's not your fault, but she bears watching. Come on, let's see what she's up to."

"Her smithy," Kalas ascertained. "It sounds weird, given what she just went on about, but even if she has no faith in herself or her abilities, and even if she says she can't do whatever she thinks she needs to do, she'll work herself into the ground just to prove to us—no, to *herself*—that her doubts are justified. That's where we'll find her, so yeah, let's go!"

2.

Through muted tones and broken phrases, Abarandal insisted, contrary to Nïmrïk's assertion, that Zhalera's present state of mind was all her fault. Kalas had no idea what she meant—right now, he didn't care: an indescribable, inexplicable thread of panic twined around his thoughts and knit itself into a cloak of all his worst imaginings. Urgency impelled him toward the smithy at a pace even Nïmrïk had trouble maintaining.

The streets shouldn't be this empty, Kalas noted, the observation an embellishment along the hem of the panic-cloak knit within his thoughts. In his haste and concentration, he neither saw Tsharak nor understood his companions' warnings until he ran into the old man and both hit the ground.

"Tsharak?" he said, offering a hand. The ancient figure accepted, and even in the thready moonlight, he saw sputtering lights swoop and swirl along the contours of his curious tattoo.

"You sense it too, my boy?" Tsharak wondered as he regained his feet and brushed away the dirt.

"Sense…? What? Yes, I—No: Zhalera! We're headed for her

smithy!"

"Then lead on!" he exclaimed as he massaged his glowing hand.

The air turned thick and smoky as they approached the stout structure with its many chimneys, each expelling heavy clouds as Zhalera—who else?—stoked her fires. Kalas knew how hot the furnaces could get, but he'd never seen their heat warp the *outside* air with undulating waves like this; indeed, beads of sweat had already accumulated on his brow.

"Zhalera!" he called out, coughing from the ash listing toward the earth.

How did she get the fire so hot so fast?!

"As hot as things are, I'd be surprised if she could hear you above the roar of her forges!" Tsharak suggested. Kalas nodded. He tried the door when he reached it, but Zhalera had barred it from the inside.

What if she's passed out from the heat?! What if she can't hear me?!

"Zhalera!" he tried again, banging on the door with both hands. Perspiration poured down his face, and as he wiped it away, he wondered how anyone inside could endure such heat without succumbing. "Zhalera! There's no way it's safe in there! Your fires are too hot!"

Underscoring his concern, one of the stones framing the doors snapped: Kalas winced as a whizzing shard of shrapnel sliced his cheek. Knocked back, he scrambled to his feet and rushed the door again, but it still wouldn't budge. Tsharak cried out: Kalas spared the old man a glance and saw Nïmrïk and Abarandal had already reached his side. Focusing on the smithy—on Zhalera again, he schemed in vain for some way to breach the doors.

I left my sword at Zhalera's place! There's no time to go back and get it: I have to think of something else!

"The light-realm!" he shouted, not caring whether Peradan had marked him. "It's the only way!"

He closed his eyes and tried to picture the space opposite the shop's heavy doors. He tried to remember his state of mind within the Áthradho, when he first entered the *kalthesh,* but his memory wouldn't cooperate. He tried to remember the phrases from the Song he'd employed, but the melodies remained inaccessible.

I can't—I won't *let it end like this!*

Summoning the Song within his fist, he drove his hand against one of the wooden doors, which splintered from the impact. The fires inside, emboldened by the sudden supply of oxygen, surged with strength. Kalas tried to peer through the hole he'd created, but intense flames prevented him.

"Zhalera!" he screamed and delivered another blow. Frantic, he reached through the ragged opening and fumbled with the latch, but the hot metal rebuffed his touch.

"It's too hot!" he shouted as helpless tears now mingled with his sweat. He closed his eyes again and willed himself next to Zhalera.

"Kalas?" he thought he heard her whisper, despite the roaring flames surrounding him. He wasn't sure where he was: fire abounded, yes, but something convinced him he—*they*—were somewhere other than the smithy.

"Zhalera!" he exulted, no longer concerned about their precise whereabouts. "Zhalera! I—"

His existence exploded, and he felt his consciousness dissociate from his corporeal form. He experienced a vague suggestion of motion, but without his physical senses, he couldn't reconcile the contradiction.

Where am I? he wondered. *Am I in the light-realm? Did I—but where's Zhalera?! Did I really hear her say my name? Why isn't she with me? Or is she with me, and I just don't know it? How is this—*

The colorlessness that had consumed him vomited him into a whirl of oranges and blacks: he crashed into Nimrïk and knocked him to the ground, too.

"Easy, lad!" the gruff figure said as he helped the young man stand. "You vanished for a minute! At first I thought you'd found a way inside, but…well, here you are…"

"Kadhëmba? What do you mean? Why do you sound so—?!"

Kalas aligned his gaze with Nïmrïk's stare: moments ago the smithy had been a bright and shining testament to Lohwàlar's vigorous renaissance; now, it was nothing more than a smoldering heap.

"Zhalera?!" he called.

No one said a word.

"*Zhalera?!*" he roared and vaulted toward the charred doors and broken stones.

Nïmrïk, anticipating his reaction, caught him: the *egu* grunted from the strain of staying the young man's fevered energy.

"Did she get out?! Did you find her?!" Kalas demanded as he struggled. When no one answered, he roared again.

"The place just exploded," Tsharak said without regard for his own tears. "I had to step back because of the heat: it's a wonder you weren't consumed yourself! The fires were too strong: there were flames coming from the chimneys, too! I saw you shining—no wonder Pava's people call you the *Ilosar*—and right when you disappeared, a too-bright blast of…magic? I don't know, but something more than mere fire tore through the smithy: something bright and golden, like a sun! Even Nïmrïk and Abarandal had to step back from that! And then there you were, hurtling through the air…"

"Where's Zhalera?" he repeated, though he suspected he already knew.

"It's still too hot—for you," Nïmrïk said as he relaxed his grip. "Here, let me…"

Kalas stood by and denounced his human frailties as the *egu* approached the debris. He picked his way through fragments of broken stone and blackened wood.

"Oho! What's this?!" he exclaimed and whisked his hand away from some of the wreckage. "It's…it's too *hot*, even for me! No, not *hot*, but…I don't know, exactly. Mister Tsharak, perhaps you were right: there is something strange here. And…I'm sorry, lad: apart from *this*, I can't find any sign of Zhalera…"

"That's her hammer! Her four-pound hammer!" Kalas said. "She *was* here! What if she's trapped—you said it's too hot for you to check everything, right? What if she's caught under a stone? Or… or…I don't know, an anvil or something?! What if—"

"Lad, if it's too hot for *me*…"

"No! No, she has to be in there! We have to help her! We have to get her out of there! We—!"

Kalas bolted for the smithy's smoking remains, but Nïmrïk spoke the truth: he couldn't get half as close as the old wolf before residual heat stung his eyes and seared his skin. Still, he might have continued to throw himself toward certain destruction had the *egu* not placed a hand atop his shoulder and ushered him away from the pyre. Neither Nïmrïk nor Tsharak nor Abarandal said anything as curious townsfolk appeared along the fringes of the dying firelight. Someone called for sand and water; someone else mentioned Sàrush. The rising din became a tinny thrum in Kalas' ears as he studied Zhalera's abandoned hammer. He held it close to his chest despite its uncomfortable warmth. With his free hand, he wiped away his most recent spate of tears and wandered into the dark.

"Lad?" Nïmrïk whispered as he jogged toward the young man's side. Abarandal and Tsharak caught up to them.

Without emotion, he muttered, "Zhalera's place. I don't have anywhere else to go."

3.

Kalas didn't remember falling asleep, but he woke when the first sun's rays pressed against his eyelids. He blinked and wondered where he was before he remembered everything from the night before. He sighed, sobbed, and slammed himself into his borrowed bed. He shivered despite the gentle heat wrapped within the midmorning air.

People outside the room in which he found himself must have heard him: soon, Tsharak knocked at the door and whispered, "Kalas?"

The young man said nothing.

Perhaps sensing his quiet attention, the ancient man added: "We'll be right outside, my boy. Right outside…"

Kalas listened without moving until Tsharak's footsteps faded away a few minutes later. Staring up at heavy wooden beams, he sighed again and tried to rein in his sobs.

"Particularly cruel," lamented Nanësra. Kalas started and stared toward the dim corner of the room where the *elu* stood. She smoothed her shimmering robe and sat at the foot of his bed. Recovered, Kalas sat up and glared daggers at the woman.

"You knew," he muttered. "You…*knew!*"

Nanësra met his gaze and maintained her silence.

"You…surely you could have *done something?!*"

She looked away, her expression clouded. Kalas waited. After a tense moment, she admitted, "I…I don't know, child. You must understand: I'm not used to *not knowing*. It's true: I knew this event would come to pass, but I didn't know the particulars. I didn't know…I don't know everything. Maybe I know very little, all things considered?

"I'll tell you this, though you'll despise my words: were I here, were I able to 'do something,' still, I might have chosen not to. Too many of your kind prefer action—any action, even a *wrong* action—to careful contemplation. Too many of your kind consider naught but the moment: you ignore—or refuse to entertain—anything beyond the immediate slice of time in which you find yourselves. Perhaps it's because you're finite? Still…"

"What?! You mean—are you saying you would have let Zhalera *burn to death?!*"

Nanësra laughed.

"You—?! That's *funny* to you?! How can you—"

"You misunderstand!" the *elu* insisted with an impatient flare. "You phrase your accusation as though I *delight* in her immolation!"

She stood, the scintillations in her robe revealing gleaming armor underneath—no, not *underneath: intertwined* somehow, as though both occupied the same space and time. She reached behind her shoulder—

For her sword, Kalas flinched.

—and, with a sigh, returned her empty hand to her side.

"Kalas, do you trust the Creator?" she demanded.

"I do," he hesitated. "I did. I *thought* I did. I…I don't know."

"Because he's repurposed that which he's allowed you to enjoy? Because he's permitted this tragedy? Because things stopped going your way?"

"Nanësra, things stopped going my way when a devil-wolf buried a knife between my father's eyes! When another ripped the life from my mother! When others wrecked my town!"

"We roam the detritus of a broken world, Kalas: instrument of prophecy or not, why should you receive exemption from its thorns and thistles?"

'The detritus of a broken world.' That's what Loradan said…

"But why?! What purpose could Zhalera's death serve?! My parents' deaths, for that matter?!"

"It was never intended to be this way," Nanësra said, her eyes far away.

"No? Then tell me why it *is* this way! He's the Creator! Can't *he* do something about it?!"

"There you go again," she noted with a wry smile. "Perhaps you're asking the wrong question: the same question numerous *edhume* have asked from the dawn of time. You assume he *isn't* doing something: maybe it's wiser to acknowledge that we're not omniscient, that his mind is not ours to know. Is it possible the Creator chooses not to burden us with infinite detail regarding the things he *is* doing?"

"Well…I mean, couldn't he at least give us *some* details?! Some idea of…I don't know! I just…it'd be nice if he'd let us in on the secret from time to time!"

With coy kindness, she smiled again and said: "Would you dictate terms to the Creator? Would I?! Not every man, woman, or child who inhabits this injured earth receives the same largesse as you! Few mortals have ever glimpsed my kind—nor Valaran's kind, yet here you are conversing with an *elu*—and not for the first time—as though I were flesh and blood!

"I can't tell you the Creator's purpose regarding Zhalera. And I won't pretend her passing won't continue to affect you deeply. Deeper than you know, I suspect. I offended you when I laughed: I apologize. I'll allow that I chose a poor moment for my…indiscretion. That said…I'm no prophet, but I predict, in the fullness of time, your sorrow will end. *This* sorrow, anyway…

"May I make a request? I'll admit, I'm not used to asking anything from anyone—much less someone so…temporal! It's a flaw, a prideful indulgence—common, it seems, among *elunàm*, our reluctance to admit we need *community* as much as anyone…

"Anyway, my request: *Trust your Creator!* I know you're struggling right now. Even *elume* have had their faith tested. Some have passed such tests, some have failed, and some…well, some still haven't discovered their own resilience! But you're neither *elu* nor *eru,* and I'll confess: your brevity is something I find difficult to understand. Perhaps I'm asking a lot from you, but I believe you're capable of greater things than even you realize."

Kalas waited for the austere figure to finish. He tried to meet her gaze, to promise her he'd forsake his doubts, but such a vow wouldn't come. Instead, he substituted fresh tears for words.

"It's too much. Too soon," Nanësra said to herself. "No matter. Kalas, understand: I'm not making this request for *my* benefit! Know this as you process these things that have most cruelly come to pass."

She placed her hand on his shoulder, sending a hot thrum of energy through his entire body. He remembered her touch from their first meeting on the steppes by the well, how she'd somehow sifted his mind. He remembered their encounter outside his room in Melash, when she'd returned his dropped book to him. This time, her touch was different. Amplified. He sensed some unspoken purpose in the way she slid her hand along the side of his neck, trailing luminous particles as she reached his cheek and turned his downcast eyes toward hers.

"I've said and done all I can, Kalas. I suspect it seems I've said and done precious little from your perspective, but I have to believe it's enough for the things yet to come. You're perceptive: you've kenned my presence at times and in places others have not, and that's no small thing. Remain perceptive. Investigate your suspicions, your unanswered questions, and continue to learn everything you can about the world in which you find yourself. Who knows what strange mysteries you might unravel?!"

She withdrew her hand, and the soft light and subtle heat rippling across his cheek subsided. The energy oscillating through his frame diminished, sapping his strength as it disappeared. Spent, though he'd done nothing more than stand, Kalas' knees buckled, and he caught himself on the edge of the bed. When his sudden rapid breathing slowed, he looked for Nanësra, but she was already gone.

4.

"I have to see for myself," Kalas insisted when at last he joined his friends. Tsharak sat next to Vàyana, across from Sàrush and Tshama, whom the ancient man must have summoned. Nïmrïk and Abarandal kept their quiet distance while the others sought to mute their shared misery through fond recollection.

"I should be grateful for our mended relationship, but I confess: I feel the bitterness more keenly for it!" Sàrush admitted from his peculiar chair: someone had bolted an axle beneath his seat, and he ran his tired fingers across its stout, iron-banded wheels.

Tshama nodded. "I know what you mean: I thought when Zhalera finished traipsing the breadth and depth of creation, she'd come back, fire up her shop—it was a beautiful shop, dearest!—and, well, I thought we'd have more time! Especially after Kalas healed your lungs! Still, I *am* grateful—and I know you are, too—that the two of you got things sorted: even a little time is better than none!"

"I looked through the plans until the early morning hours: I checked, double- and triple-checked my annotations. I haven't dared to voice my fears aloud until now, but what if the smithy collapsed because of some flaw I introduced? What if it's *my fault* my granddaughter—my only granddaughter!—is...no more?!"

Tsharak made a disgusted noise that Sàrush's sudden sobs almost overpowered: "Listen, Chief Magistrate! *I* approved those plans! I—and a host of others—examined your handiwork while you built that structure! I'm confident it's not your fault the smithy collapsed! Grief can make you think horrible things. *Believe* horrible things. I know. I've struggled with my own from the days when the

River roared between the banks of the Lower Quarter. The fact is, none of us was there. Inside, I mean. Fire is a mercurial creature, old friend: always hungry, never sated."

"Peradan must have done this! He *must* have! It wouldn't take much for an *eru*—even one so treacherous—to know how to find us: I suspect he marked us when he trapped Zhalera, Abarandal, and me within his singularities..."

Abarandal, grieving in her own way, glided over to him and caressed his arm as she sang a question.

"There's no way to know for sure, but remember: he told me what he'd do to anyone who'd done me the least kindness if I refused him. We still don't know how we got away from him, from his traps: what if he *let us go?* You didn't do it. *I* didn't do it..."

She plied him with another question, and he retorted, "All right, all right: maybe it wasn't him. So what?! He's still out there, still pitting kingdom against kingdom! We have to *do* something!"

Too many of your kind prefer action...to careful contemplation...

"Kalas, I'll go with you, if you want," Nïmrïk offered. "To the smithy, I mean. If you'd rather go alone, I understand."

"Yeah, that's fine...that's fine," Kalas nodded, his focus lingering on Nanësra's remembered words. He wandered into the kitchen, spied a slice of *golfras* bread, and stuffed it into his mouth. Between bites, he said, "You ready? Let's go."

Neither Nïmrïk nor Kalas spoke as they approached the still-smoldering wreckage that had been Zhalera's smithy. Despite the heat rolling from the ash heaps, and despite the suns' warmth, a chill rippled down the young man's spine. The stones framing the doorway remained standing, although the door itself had succumbed to the fire's appetites. Charred portions of some of the walls had spilled into the streets in haphazard piles. The whole scene suggested a violent explosion, and as he surveyed the damage, he wondered why he hadn't been consumed when the light blinded him and threw him from the door.

"I don't get it," he sighed at last, after walking the shop's blackened perimeter. "Zhalera's so careful about her work! She takes it very seriously! Something she learned from her father, no doubt. It doesn't make sense she'd...well, I don't know *what* could have happened!"

"I saw the look in her eyes when she left the house. It's been my experience that people can become...forgetful when they've got a lot going on. And, lad, she had a *lot* going on inside that head of hers. I'm sure you don't need me to tell you."

"Maybe...Still, it doesn't sound like her," Kalas hedged. He stood beneath the doorway and looked inside where her work surfaces had been. A twist of wind snaked past him, and as he turned, something glittered in the corner of his eye.

"Hey, what's that?" he asked himself as he entered the unsound structure. Suns-light, cast as dusty columns from holes burned through the roof, dappled its warped floor.

"Kalas! I don't think it's safe!"

The young man remembered a similar warning from Vàyana not too long ago. He remembered Zhalera's undaunted desire to search the ashes of her father's smithy and the gleam in her eyes when she recovered her four-pound hammer. Despite his sorrow, he smiled. When he rounded on the object, he gasped.

"Kalas? Lad?" Nïmrïk called as he jogged toward him. Kalas stooped, picked something—some*things*—up from the floor, and held them out to the *egu*.

"That looks a lot like Zhalera's sword, Valarandal!" Nïmrïk breathed. "But *broken?!* How is that possible?"

Kalas stared at the spidery cracks radiating from the edges of each piece and struggled to suggest an answer. When Zhalera held it, honey-colored ribbons of energy writhed across its surface; now, in his trembling hands, all he saw was gray. He tried to come up with some idea about what might have happened, but as he aligned the pieces and stared through an asymmetrical hole ringed with black scorch-marks, no ideas would come.

"It's not! It *shouldn't* be," he admitted at last. "Zhalera said her ancestors tried everything they could to work this metal: nothing they did left any kind of mark! No amount of heat could soften its lines; no amount of hammering could alter its shape! Kadhëmba, I don't think it was a normal fire that did this! Abarandal didn't seem to think Peradan had anything to do with this: I wonder what she'd say if she saw *this?!*"

"Maybe he did, maybe he didn't. I know I've offered you a lot of advice recently, and you've been kind enough to endure it with grace. I'll presume upon that grace and offer you another morsel: your primary mission—*our* primary mission, if you'll suffer a little boldness—is to present a better direction for the kingdoms Peradan and his ilk have endeavored to corrupt. Striking down Peradan would only postpone the war he wills for humankind: were he banished from this plane, surely another would rise up and take his place. Until your kind—and not just your kind: *all kinds*—desire a better way, the world will turn from war to war in an endless cycle."

Nïmrïk paused, smirked, and added, "It only took me…several hundred Sevens to figure that out! Hopefully, others are faster learners!"

Kalas nodded, although he was only half-listening as he carried the shattered halves of Valarandal across the smithy. He glanced at the ceiling with its broken beams, its cracked and canted chimneys; frowned; then walked to another place and repeated the gesture.

"One of the new towers!" he said, and Nïmrïk cocked his head. "Lad?"

"Sorry, I was listening—really, I was!—but there's something, I don't know, *off* about the way everything's strewn about in here, about the burn marks through the ceiling. I can't see them all at once—there's too much stuff in the way. I think I could get a better perspective from one of those new towers!"

"Oh? Uh, all right, if you say so," Nïmrïk shrugged.

"C'mon! Let's go!"

Giras, the middle-aged man posted at a nearby tower—and grateful, it seemed, for the respite, traded places with Kalas. He wiped his brow when he reached the bottom of the sandstone steps and admitted the guard platform made an excellent collector for the suns' reflected rays: "Gets hot up there! Look around as long as you like—take your time!"

Kalas climbed onto the platform—Giras was right about the heat—and craned his neck for an adequate perspective of Zhalera's smithy. From below, Nïmrïk cautioned him not to lean out too far. Kalas assured him he'd be all right.

Although Giras' tower was the nearest, tallest structure, Kalas realized it was still too far away. Even standing on the rails, he could only get an oblique view of the holes eaten through the roof, which had shifted from its compromised supports. Still, despite the imperfect presentation, he thought he saw a pattern in the charred remnants. He leaned out a little more—

That almost looks like—!

—and screamed as he lost his balance. And his train of thought. Nïmrïk, anticipating Kalas' stubbornness, had already positioned Giras and himself beneath the young man: the pair caught him before he hit the dirt.

"Well? What did you see?" Nïmrïk said when they'd righted him.

"I…I don't know," Kalas admitted. "For a moment, I thought I saw a pattern. Something unnatural, I guess, but maybe it's just the way the beams were fitted together? Reminded me of the symbols under the Vault, with all their circles and triangles, but I didn't get a good look.

"Probably doesn't matter: even if it *did* look like something, what's the difference? Zhalera's...gone, and I have to accept that. I don't have to like it—and I don't!—but I know no matter how much it hurts, no matter how much I know I'm going to miss her, I can't bring her back. *No one* can bring her back..."

"That's...Kalas, you have my sympathy," Nïmrïk whispered as he did his best to ignore Kalas' subtle tears. "Few people I've met—no matter how many Sevens they've acquired—have displayed such wisdom. It's a travesty you've come by it while still so young."

"If you'd known me when my parents died, you'd know it's wisdom hard-earned. Wisdom I wish I never knew. Wisdom I wish no one had to know. Kadhëmba, I don't know if it's wisdom or a kind of numbness or maybe...something else. I'm not sure it matters. I just...I miss them. All of them. *So much...*"

The young man wrapped his arms around the *egu* and wept, embarrassed at his inability to check his emotions in front of a stranger like Giras. Nïmrïk returned Kalas' embrace and held him without reservation.

"Uh, it's all right," Giras said. Muttered, really. "When the wolves attacked, my grandparents...didn't make it, either. They got my sister, too. I've heard the stories about Tàran, about how Dzharëth—whatever he was, uh, did what he did. It's not the same, I know, but I understand—a little, I think, what you're feeling. I... you're braver than I am, Kalas. That's one of the reasons I volunteered for guard tower duty: up and away from anything else that might happen to Lohwàlar..."

"That doesn't mean I'm braver," Kalas said as Nïmrïk let him go and he wiped his face.

"Sometimes," Giras continued, through tears of his own, "when the suns go down and the sky turns red, I think, 'What if the wolves come back?' I don't—I can't face that again! And then I think, it'd be easy—*really* easy—to just *fall* out of this tower, like you just did…"

"But you haven't, have you? You're still here! That means you're still fighting: that means you're still winning! Giras, I'm sorry for what the *rudzhegume* did to your family…for what they did to *you*, and I know it's not easy. *I know.* I've learned everyone has battles of his own. Some people fight theirs from the outside; others, from the inside. *Keep fighting,* Giras! You are braver than you know!"

Kalas clapped a hand on Giras' slumped shoulder. The man stiffened, straightened, and dabbed at his eyes. He looked the young man in the face and nodded.

"I…I think I can do that," he considered, and Kalas suspected he was talking more to himself than the others. "I can try…"

"No one can ask more of you," Kalas affirmed with hints of lightning in his eyes. Giras stepped back when he noticed, then smiled, nodded again, and returned to his post.

When the watchman disappeared, Nïmrïk retrieved both halves of Valarandal, handed them to the young man, and wondered, "What's next, lad?"

"Home. *Zhalera's* home," he said, staring at the broken sword. "I suspect Giras isn't the only *Lohwàlarrin* warring against his despair, and maybe there's nothing we can do about that. Then again, maybe there is…"

5.

"I'll call a meeting," Sàrush decided when Kalas and Nïmrïk returned and described their encounter with Giras. "Lohwàlar's leadership needs to address the underlying dread still coursing through the lifeblood of our town: its people. We've been so busy rebuilding, so busy constructing this façade of normalcy that we've—that I

514

have neglected the fear and uncertainty so many of us must still be dealing with! I don't know what to say…not exactly. It's…it feels like it did when Fërin passed away. May she be at peace! *O shelu fie Zhalera nir! O shelu fie sashin-odh nir!*"

The Chief Magistrate, overcome with revivified memories, clapped his hands against his face and sobbed. Tshama, never far away, wrapped an arm around his convulsing shoulders and drew him toward her side.

"That's a respectable start," Tsharak agreed, his focus somewhere else, it seemed to Kalas as the ancient man returned from conferencing with his inner thoughts. "With the confusion of the wolves' attack well behind us, we've all had time to entertain our baser fears. The opportunity to voice such things aloud, to know we share a collective dismay—to know we're not alone, might hasten the healing process." He nodded toward Vàyana, who took his hand and squeezed it.

"Most of the physically wounded have recovered, but I—and other clerics, I'm sure—sense that the unspoken mental and spiritual injuries seem slow to mend. Maybe what you propose, Chief Magistrate, is the catalyst we clerics have been praying toward…"

Kalas listened for a while as the others made their plans, but despite his efforts to remain engaged, he tuned them out and turned his attention toward Zhalera's shattered sword. Whether saving their lives or even summoning Abarandal, he'd come to think of Valarandal as an extension of her *kelâ* the more Zhalera wielded it; now, staring at its impossible ruin felt like staring at *her*. He put the pieces down with a heavy sigh and tried to join the conversation again, but his thoughts lingered elsewhere.

A few days later, when Sàrush hosted his gathering and confessed the anguish with which he still wrestled, the *Lohwàlarrinme* responded with refreshing, communal candor. Kalas, from his seat at the back of the Council Hall, smiled when Giras stood and shared his dark imaginings. Others had been dealing with similar issues, it seemed, judging from the reactions he received.

After Sàrush adjourned with a prayer for perseverance, he stayed put as the rest of the townsfolk returned to their daily lives. Someone had built a ramp for the Chief Magistrate, who, spying Kalas, wheeled himself over to the young man. Tshama accompanied him, but after a discerning moment, he patted her hand and suggested she go home: he promised he'd be along soon. She glanced at Kalas, offered him a sympathetic smile and clutched his shoulder, then nodded and disappeared.

Neither figure said anything for a long while. Neither needed to. Kalas hadn't spent much time with Zhalera's grandfather, but now, he appreciated his company. At last, struggling against an intangible weight wrapped around his heart, he said, "After the wolves killed her father, she told me that as much as she missed him, she wouldn't wish him back, even if she could…She only told me a little about her mother, about Fërin, but she said they were together again, and she wouldn't take that away from either of them…

"I thought we had more time. I've been told there's some heavy stuff the world's about to face, but even with all of that, I never thought…I didn't think I'd be sitting here, without her. Not like this. And now I can't even tell her…I mean, I'm sure she knew—I'm sure I'm not as subtle as I think I am sometimes, but I never told her…

"When the wolves killed my parents, even after Falthwën spoke with me, I don't know what might have happened if she hadn't been there to lend me her strength. I know we've told you some of what happened to us while we were away from Lohwàlar, but those stories are incomplete: there's so much *more* underneath it all, and even now, I can't find the right words!

"Everyone else knew: Mother, Father…even Gandhan. They'd

tease me about it from time to time: that day we found Ëlbodh in the Empty Sea; before that, when the *ilâegsal* chewed through my shovel, Father—no, never mind…I don't know why it's so hard for me to say the words: *I love her,* Sàrush. I can't remember a time when I didn't. I can't fathom a time when I won't, no matter how many Sevens I have left. The years will be lesser with her gone, but greater than if I'd never known her. I keep thinking about all the times I should have said something: either here, before all this craziness happened; or even in between Ïsriba or Avëlöth! Maybe I should have followed Rül's lead: he and Pava didn't waste any time! At first, even though they've got a few years on me, I thought they were too young to get married, maybe rushing into things, but now…?"

"You're right about one thing," Sàrush nodded as Kalas trailed off: "Everyone else *did* know how you and Zhalera felt—no, *feel*— about one another! I watched my granddaughter mature from a distance—my pride, as you know—and even if it was only from the edges, you were always there, in her periphery. I'm ashamed to admit I had the same arrogant disdain for Pump workers as I did blacksmiths, but the breadth and depth of your love was inescapable. I…that's one of the reasons I refused to see your father when he came to me, before the wolves attacked. Things might have been different if I'd been less of a pompous twit. Maybe it's too much to ask, but I beg for your forgiveness all the same, young man."

"The circumstances might have been different, but the outcomes? They'd probably still be what they were. None of our defenses would have kept the wolves at bay," Kalas conceded. He stared at the floor for another minute before he cracked a smile: "I was that obvious?"

"You *both* were! Had things been one-sided, it wouldn't have mattered to me. It's clear that things were decidedly *not* one-sided! Ah, Kalas, my son: I am sorry for the man I've been! To your point: there are so many things I would have pursued with greater intensity had I known what evil lived within the future. None of us does, though, do we?"

"Agreed," Kalas said. "Except I'd say that evil doesn't just live within the future: it lives within the present, too. Maybe there's a way to *unmake* it today, to cripple its potential tomorrow? Maybe that's why the *erume unmake* so many of the things they find? *Âu Sàrush*, thank you for your time. It's given me some things to think about, some ideas about what comes next."

"Please, if it's not too presumptuous: call me *Grandfather*. It seems…*right*, you know?"

"I…I've never had a grandfather," Kalas stated. "Both Màla's and Tàran's fathers passed away before I was…before I ever had a chance to meet them. I…all right, uh, *Grandfather,* thank you for your time."

6.

"I've been seeing Nanësra in my dreams. At least, I *think* it's in my dreams," Nïmrïk confessed to Kalas a week later while the latter busied himself with his books. "I thought I was just…that is, I, uh, well, never mind. She reminds me of my ancient past, when I wore the lion-skin: even though it's impossible, I see it shining in the infinite, unbridgeable distance. I reach for it, and, without fail, I fall into a bottomless abyss. I know you believe otherwise, but I can't help thinking she's taunting me…"

"Dreams?" Kalas said, surprised. "I didn't think you slept! At least, I've never seen you sleep!"

Abarandal, despite her benumbed sorrow, giggled.

Nïmrïk smiled. "Maybe it's a little different from what you'd consider sleep, but while tethered to the material world, we're subject to at least a few of its limitations."

"I see," Kalas contemplated. "She's always been…cryptic. No denying that! Most of the time—no, pretty much *every* time I see her, whether in dreams or in person, I never understand her meaning. Not until later. I think she *has* to be…confusing. Falthwën used to say the *erumedas* memories weren't intact. Incomplete. I think Loradan said as much, too. Maybe the *elume* have, I don't know, restrictions of their own? That's what I think: no idea if I'm right! What if she's not taunting you? What if she's…stretching you? Goading you toward something you don't think you're capable of?"

"Well, there are innumerable things I'm incapable of," he conceded with a wry grin. Abarandal giggled again and shook her head. "Anyway, how's your 'research' going? I'm sorry I can't make sense of these things: I hope the historical vignettes I've supplied have been useful."

"They have. They've been interesting, anyway! Father knew a fair amount—I'm sure he picked up a lot from his father, and more from Tsharak, but neither's been around as long as you have. As for my 'research,' it's…I'm stuck. It feels like Nanësra unlocked something in my mind. It's like a door with a keyhole that used to be dark; now, there's light shining out of it, but when I look directly at it, I'm blinded. Staring at these pages hasn't resulted in any new clarity, that's for sure!"

The *eruín* put down her most recent book and sang a few phrases in response.

"Maybe, but from our prior conversations, I think she's done all she can. All she's permitted. As dumb as I feel sitting here with my eyes closed, I think she put everything necessary in my head. Somewhere. I just have to find it. And, if I'm honest, it's…*something else* to think about…"

He closed his eyes again and sighed, retreating within his thoughts as Abarandal vocalized an encouraging melody. With her every note, the shifting suggestions of color swirling within his darkness acquired form. He gasped and looked around, but the shapes had vanished. Abarandal stopped singing.

"Sing that again! Uh, I mean, *please!*"

She obliged, and as he closed his eyes again, the colors resumed their former configurations. Subtle, easy to miss against a background rife with spark-like visual noise, he wondered if perhaps these distillations had been inside his mind for some time, now revealed in the sympathetic vibrations generated through Abarandal's music. He opened his eyes and the symbols—more pictographs than words, he decided—shimmered in the air. He stood and circled them, and thus discovered they possessed a third dimension. As his perspective shifted, he discerned a singular image coalesce—a thought or concept, maybe. Something about its contours seemed familiar—so very familiar—but he couldn't quite place it.

I know these shapes! This image! At least, I think I do! I know I know what I'm looking at, but at the same time, I can't contextualize it! Maybe from another angle…

He continued his slow circle, and, too late, Nïmrïk called out: "Watch yourself, lad!"

Kalas tripped over a short stack of books. Sprawled across the polished stone floor, he cried out as the spectral display flickered into nothingness when Abarandal ended her song and rushed to help him up. On his feet again, he squinted at the center of the room and willed whatever he'd beheld to manifest itself again.

It refused.

"You saw something?" Nïmrïk prodded.

"Something," he confirmed. "What, I don't know. It started out as words—shapes and symbols, at least, but when I walked around them, they *changed*. No, they didn't *change:* I just saw facets—dimensions—I never knew existed. Words on surfaces are only two dimensions, but these…they had *depth*, too, and, strange as this sounds, maybe something else, some other dimension! *Dimensions!*

It's hard to explain."

Abarandal took up her refrain again, and Kalas studied the empty space at the middle of the study, but whatever he'd seen refused to return.

"It's gone," he said, shaking his head. "It seemed to move without changing shape or position—that makes no sense, I know! Like I said: hard to explain! Your singing, Abarandal, made it—them?— visible for a moment. I don't know if it was the melody, the tone in your voice, or both—or something else entirely!"

She sang a few more bars. Kalas laughed under the weight of her epiphany: "Why didn't I think of that?! You're probably right!"

"Uh…lad?" Nïmrïk wondered.

"What? Oh, right! Abarandal said maybe my direct approach was too much, that when I was only *half-thinking* about it, things once invisible revealed themselves by degrees. It makes sense, and it fits. Of course, now the trick will be 'half-thinking' about it. Subconsciously, I guess. Maybe there's—"

"Kalas?" someone shouted from the great room. "Kalas?!"

The young man picked up his sword and exited the study— and almost collided with Rofe. Covered with dust and sweat, the *úrukilmukrit* man caught himself and leaned against a wall. He held up a finger, then panted: "Your friend Nashmur…from the sound of things, there are reliable reports that Peradan's been sighted near Ïsriba! Nashmur almost drove his horse to death trying to reach the Áthradho! We hadn't been home for more than a few days—Pava and Rül are fine!—when he tumbled through the upper gate and told Rive what had happened. The *shëmïuín* told her father about Hwanzho and Peradan's treachery just the day before. Now, as you know, we cave-dwellers have long memories: if one of the guards hadn't recognized Nashmur from his prior visits, it's probable he would have been cut down on the spot. Fortunately for him—for all of us, I deem!—*I* was one of the guards that day!

"We—no, Rül, really—tended to his horse and his exhaustion, and before Nashmur slipped into a deep sleep, he insisted we get word to you, Kalas: Âivambar already looks like an extension of Ïsriba, its fortifications enhanced and its gates swarming with *tanagme* loyal to Ësfàyami. He thinks maybe one of them, passing through Thosha, recognized him despite his precautions.

"It seems Peradan has replaced Marugan as the silver tongue tickling the ears of the queen-regent. Maybe one of his cultists. He wasn't sure, and before he could say more, he lost consciousness. I got here as fast as I could: I'm not a great rider, but Master Rül's horse seemed to sense my urgency."

"Wait!" Kalas halted everyone on their way out the door and into the burning suns-light. "If Peradan's in Ïsriba, even nearby, what about Shosafin?! Rufàran?! What if they're—"

"Peradan never met Shosafin," Nïmrïk reminded the distraught lad.

"They traveled through the night," Rofe said: "They were well away before the dawn of the second day."

"Remember?" Nïmrïk continued, "He wasn't with you beneath the Vault, nor in the Ravine—in either sense—until *after* the spessartine *eku* (so I deem him!) had already departed. Yes, Peradan knows the king, but I trust Shosafin knows his way around the shadows. None of the heavenlies is omniscient, and it seems out of character for 'Ilbardhën' to overlook such a detail. Had any harm befallen them, I'm sure Nashmur would have known and would have said something."

"That makes sense. I hope you're right! Anyway, we're no help to them all the way to the West like this. We have to get to Ïsriba. It'll take too long over land. The season's right, though: maybe Sifuran's still in Serular? Maybe he'll sail us to Ralothova? I think it's our best move."

Abarandal questioned him with her song.

"No, that's a fair point: we don't know if he's still there…but I have an idea! Sometimes, Falthwën would touch my mind with his, through The Song. I don't know if I can tune its harmonies to such ends, but with your help, maybe we can communicate with Sifuran? Not in words—I don't know if that's possible, but I think we can let him know we need his help."

"You're probably right, lad," Nïmrïk nodded. "Certainly worth a try. While you two work on that, I'll—well, hmm. Maybe I'm not the best choice to tell Tsharak what we're up to? I know he's tried to see me through your eyes, but I'm not—"

"I'll go with you," Rofe offered. "We got to know one another pretty well while working on the mirror system. And…I think he might surprise you."

The *egu* arched an intrigued eyebrow but said nothing. With a gesture, he beckoned Rofe to follow him through Lohwàlar's dusty streets.

"All right, Abarandal. Let's give this a whirl. I'll be honest: I have no idea what I'm doing. You probably figured that out a long time ago."

The stargirl smiled, shook her head, and clasped his tanned hands with her fair fingers. With her eyes toward the sky, she closed them and began a soft, contemplative melody. Kalas closed his eyes, too, and willed his thoughts, borne upon her ethereal strains, toward Serular.

Chapter XVII

Under the Unending Stair

"Tell me again, my boy!" Tsharak prodded the next day. Nïmrïk, buoyed by Rofe's encouragement, explained their intentions to the ancient man. "Tell me how you reached out to Sifuran, how you think he's waiting for you in Serular…"

"Through The Song, through Abarandal's manipulation, I think—I *think!*—I touched Sifuran's mind. His thoughts, at least. I wasn't prepared for what I saw—no, not *saw*, but *sensed*, I guess. I've been thinking of the *erume* like people. *Regular* people: not stars! Falthwën must have done something to conceal aspects of himself when he reached out to me. The *erume* are so…so *big!* That's not the half of it, but the sheer *immensity* of Sifuran's presence almost crushed my spirit. I might have collapsed beneath its weight had he not recognized me—or maybe my frequency?—and quickly shrouded his celestial attributes.

"I tried to communicate our need for haste across the oceans, and I *think* he understood: his reply knocked me back—it's a good thing Abarandal was holding onto me! Maybe it's just wishful thinking, but I got the sense that he's been waiting for us. And that's really it. I admit I might be imagining things. I've never tried anything like this before! Still, I think we need to go. If we leave tomorrow morning, we should reach the plains before the suns set on the second day: you know how far away it is, and we don't have the luxury of horses this time."

"I see," Tsharak nodded as he massaged his tattoo. "That's not the *strangest* thing I've ever heard! Well, Vàyana and I would be happy to help however we can."

"Thank you. Both of you. I need to let Sàrush know what we're doing. I don't know how much he knows about the prophecy, or the role the *erume* think I have to play, but I wasn't going to speak to that. Regardless, I need to say goodbye to him and Tshama. I might—

never see him—nor any of you—ever again

—be gone for quite some time, and he's made all kinds of efforts to atone, maybe, for his past actions: with his family gone, I think he sees me as the next closest thing. Even asked me to think of him as my grandfather! After paralyzing his legs, it's the least I can do."

"He did say something about that," Tsharak nodded again, his mouth curving into the slightest smirk. "I suppose he'll insist the lot of you remain with him and Tshama this evening. I suggest you do it. Vàyana and I will be there before the suns breach the horizon. We'll prepare breakfast: you won't leave Lohwàlar on empty stomachs!"

"Mister Tsharak, neither I nor the lass *needs* to eat," Nïmrïk demurred. "Not after the manner of *edhunàm*. Make what you will for the lad and the cave-dweller, but there's no reason to—"

"We'll see you—all of you—in the morning," Tsharak insisted, his voice firm, although his eyes focused elsewhere.

"It's so good to see you!" Tshama gushed when Kalas and company arrived at his "grandfather's" home. He'd never been inside it, but he remembered his father's unflattering descriptions of its exterior: "Too showy. Too pretentious. Too big," Tàran had said, and now, examining its features in greater detail, the young man wondered if perhaps his father had been "too jealous" to some small degree. Not quite as old as the Sanctuary, its exposed wooden elements had been chipped away in some places and embedded with mineral sands in others. The structure stretched high above most others in Lohwàlar, having been built in greener years, before the suns' copious heat directed its architects to pursue other, cooler designs.

The interior's ground floor, the first of three, boasted numerous artifacts: ancient tools and earthenware, articles of historic costume, and similar curiosities from eras long forgotten, all neatly arranged. Sàrush must have divined Kalas' unspoken thought, because he laughed and acknowledged, "No one's really sure what this place used to be, but now, well, it looks like a museum, doesn't it? Actually, for a while now, we've been fine-tuning plans to convert this place into one. Tshama and I don't need all this space, and, given my, ah, condition, I don't need all these stairs! If I'm honest, I can't remember the last time either of us has visited the second or third floors! We discussed these things even before my illness, but we—I kept coming up with reasons not to do anything. Those reasons seem silly, now…Anyway, we're glad you're here!"

Kalas had trouble sleeping. The house, more plush and well-appointed than any he'd ever been in, seemed rife with curious energy that stirred his already unquiet mind. As he climbed out of bed and wandered the moonlit halls, he understood what Sàrush meant by "all this space."

When he reached the stairs, an intricate helix spiraling into the darkness above, he tried the first few steps: a sharp, deafening creak gave him pause. He waited, certain the entire household heard the noise. When no one investigated, he tried a few more, then another, until he gained the second floor.

At the far end of the narrow corridor in which he found himself, Kalas saw subtle hints of moonlight glinting from the spines of numerous books. On either side of him, he saw the shapes and shadows of several doorways. Focused on the books, he walked toward their shelves until he barked his shin on something abandoned on the floor. He did his best not to cry out, and as he sucked cold air through his teeth, he tried to guess what he'd walked into. Moonlight reached neither him nor the source of his injury: he discerned naught but darkness.

Should've brought a candle. Or Falthwën's staff, he acknowledged. *Sàrush said it's been a while since anyone's been up here. I'll have to ask him about it in the morning. Tsharak, too: maybe he knows more about this place? Lohwàlar has always been my home, but there's so much I don't know about it! There's so much I don't know about…so many things!*

Loath as he was to leave a mystery, the pain now throbbing in his shin reminded him just how tired the rest of his body was. With a broad yawn, he felt his way down the stairs and shambled back to his room. Atop his bed, he closed his eyes and did his best not to think about anything. Anything at all.

2.

"Good morning!" Sàrush beamed when Kalas stumbled into the home's large kitchen. The Chief Magistrate and his wife sat at one end of a heavy-looking table. Despite its size, it seemed small, somehow, surrounded by so much empty space. Tsharak busied himself above a bubbling stove while Nïmrïk and Vàyana engaged in polite conversation. Rofe, from a small nook, looked up from his pack and nodded. Abarandal brightened when she saw the young man and sang a welcome. Kalas sat down beside her and cupped his head in his hands. Not even the fragrance of Tsharak's sizzling breakfast seemed to blunt his fatigue.

"Uh, right. Good morning," he managed after a moment.

"Pardon me for saying so, but you look awful, Master Kalas!"

"Couldn't sleep."

"That's…perfectly understandable," Sàrush admitted.

"I ended up upstairs," he continued. "Couldn't see much, but I thought I saw books everywhere. I tried to get a closer look, but I hit my leg on something and decided I'd just go back to bed."

"Oh! Sorry about that!" Tshama apologized. "As Sàrush said, we rarely go up there anymore."

"I studied those books while you were away," Tsharak supplied as he tended his pots and pans. "I don't think there's anything… useful to you in them."

"No? Well, anyway, it got me thinking: I've lived in Lohwàlar almost my whole life, and I know so little about it. The Sanctuary? This place? Even New Lohwàlar, buried in the sand west of here. There's so much history I don't know, and as little as I *do* know about this place, I know even less about the world beyond!

"I said *almost* my whole life, because I realize I don't know *where* I'm really from. Heshradan said he brought me to my parents—to Màla and Tàran, I mean, but he didn't say from where. Maybe it doesn't matter, but I…I mean, Tsharak: you've lived in Lohwàlar for hundreds of years, right? You think of it as home? But when I hear you talk about Kësharan, there's a catch in your voice—a fondness that remains even after all these Sevens. You *know* where you come from. Now, with my parents gone, with…with Zhalera… *gone*, I just…it feels like I don't belong, like anything and everything that ever kept me, I don't know, *grounded*, has been torn away, and what does that mean for me? Saying it out loud, I know it sounds selfish—and maybe it is—but what I mean is I feel…*abandoned*. That probably sounds like a slap in the face to all of you, doesn't it? I don't mean it that way, I promise…"

"Maybe it doesn't matter where you come from," Nïmrïk said after a brief silence. "I have the opposite 'problem,' one might say: I know *too well* where I come from, what I've done. It's taken a long, long while to figure it out, but I think I understand; now, I have to worry less about where I've come from and focus more on where I'm going. Less on what's behind and more on what's ahead. That's my hope, anyway."

"Did…did your eyes just *glow?!*" Tshama wondered aloud, her hands tightening on Sàrush's shoulders.

"Probably just the suns-light," Tsharak dismissed from his place at the stove. Nïmrïk glanced at the old man, but he didn't react: busy, it seemed, scrambling eggs and browning sausages.

After breakfast, Sàrush and Tshama said their goodbyes and watched Kalas and the others go. Tsharak and Vàyana escorted everyone toward the southeastern outskirts of Lohwàlar: the cleric seemed less timid than Kalas remembered, though she often looked to the ancient man for reassurance as they followed the rocky remnants of a little-used road.

"Tsharak, will you keep these?" Kalas asked, handing him Falthwën's staff and both halves of Zhalera's shattered sword. "You have a knack for collecting things…"

"Of course! I know just the place for these!"

"I think Falthwën would want you to hold onto his staff. Who knows? Maybe it'll respond to that 'magic in your blood,' too? And Zhalera's sword: maybe it'll never get fixed—it can't even be melted down! And maybe that's all right: it's so much more than just a sword—even broken like this. I thought about leaving it with Sàrush, but I thought it might be too painful for him to bear…"

"Maybe, maybe not," said the ancient man. As Vàyana glanced at the town behind them, undulating in the late morning heat, he continued, "Seems this place is still capable of surprising even me! Anyway, this is as far as we go, dear ones."

"Tsharak, why did you…When Tshama caught the *gleam* in my

eyes…?" Nïmrïk wondered.

Their guide said nothing, his eyes on the ground. Vàyana, bemused, shook her head and explained, "Attitudes cultivated over many years—many Sevens—don't just disappear! Still, Tsharak knows you care about the boy—the young man, I mean; that you've risked much to protect him. Even more, he knows *Kalas* trusts you. Relies on you. And you—"

"Vàyana! I can speak for myself!" Tsharak insisted, the deep tan in his cheeks darkening.

She laughed and placed an arm around his shoulder. "You can, I'm sure, but you won't! All I mean to say is that it's hard for you—like it would be for anyone—to reconcile past prejudices with present experience. In other words, Nïmrïk, Tsharak's trying to say he's sorry for the way he's treated you."

Tsharak kept quiet. Nïmrïk, too. At last, Rofe interrupted the awkward silence: "Uh, I'll go with you until the Highway divides. No reason why we can't travel together!"

"No reason," Kalas repeated with a nod.

Rofe helped Abarandal into his horse's saddle: at first, she protested, but the *úrukilmukrit* man held firm until she agreed.

"Mister Nïmrïk, may I…may I ask you something?" Vàyana ventured once everyone had started eastward. He motioned for the others to continue while he lingered. When they'd gone a short distance, Kalas looked back: Nïmrïk had shed his human form; Vàyana, kneeling, massaged the wolf beneath one ear and scratched the base of the other. Tsharak, despite his fearlessness when facing Dzharëth, seemed almost afraid to touch the patient creature, his silver fur sparkling in the rising suns' shifting light. The young man gasped. Then smiled.

3.

"Vàyana," said Nïmrïk, still a wolf, when he caught up with the others. His belongings, once worn across his back, now hung in separate bales from his sides. "Tsharak told her what I was. She'd seen flashes of my kind on the Night of Angry Wolves—that's what they're calling the attack on Lohwàlar—but only flashes. Tsharak told her about me, and I guess whatever he said must have piqued her curiosity. She's been very kind, hasn't displayed any animosity toward me—which I don't understand, I'll admit. I saw no reason to deny her request. And she was kind enough to rearrange my pack: it's actually quite comfortable!"

"I know what you mean: she has that quality about her. Probably what makes her such a good healer," Kalas agreed. He considered Nïmrïk's altered appearance as he trotted along the road and asked, "What did Nanësra mean, back in the Ravine, when she said there had never been a *swënrudzh?* The way she said it, it sounded important."

"Skydogs have always been *nathrudzhme* with fur as black as night—not like natural wolves, who come in all kinds of colors..."

"How—*why* did your fur change from black to silver?"

"I have no idea—not because of anything *I've* done," Nïmrïk sighed after thinking about it. "Nanësra made that much clear."

"So what's it mean?"

"I don't know. I'll be honest: when I glimpse myself like this, everything seems surreal, like I'm in someone else's skin. *Fur,* I mean! It's...weird."

"Maybe that's it? Peradan, despite his treachery, said there's never been a *rudzhegu* like you. Maybe you *are* the only one who's sorry for following Ilnëshras?"

"If it were as simple as that, why *now?* Why not hundreds of Sevens ago, when I first recognized my error and sought some way to make atonement?"

"You've got me there," Kalas shrugged. For some reason, he thought of something Falthwën once said: something about a "hypothetical" situation considered from an external vantage point. He wondered what Kadhëmba's experience might look like from such an expanded perspective.

"Black? Silver? What's it matter?!" Rofe interjected. "When I look at you, I just see someone who helped save me from crazed cannibals! *And* a dragon!"

Late in the day, they reached the sign-swallowing tree and searched for a suitable place to camp. Their cave-dwelling companion considered riding through the night, but the others persuaded him to wait until morning: contemplating the unnatural stillness of the lightless forest ahead, he shuddered and agreed. A tangle of low-hanging branches provided a natural framework for a simple shelter, and after an uncomplicated meal of cold rations, Kalas fell asleep.

The next morning, after tending his horse and helping the others pack up, Rofe said his good-byes: "I'll get word to Nashmur, let him know your plans. And I'll tell Pava and Rül the unhappy news about your friend: again, Kalas, you have my sympathy."

"Be safe, Rofe," the young man replied.

Once the woods absorbed the *úrukilmukrit* traveler, Kalas yawned and suggested the three of them continue toward Serular. The first sun had only recently climbed above the horizon and penetrated the forest's fringes: it would probably be beneath the world again before they reached the plateau above the city.

"I wonder if we'll run into anyone," he said out loud. "Last time we headed east, we didn't see anyone on the roads until we reached Thosha. I know we're not going that way now, but even when we came up from Serular before, it seemed there was almost no one around. I wonder what Sifuran's been up to…"

"Guess we'll find out," Nïmrïk growled, still wearing his *other-form*. He ranged ahead of the others, sometimes disappearing into the thinning woods and reappearing on either side of Kalas and Abarandal—or even behind them.

"Why did…when I commented on your name, why did Zhalera react the way she did?" the young man dared to ask the stargirl after a leagues-long silence. "She thought you'd told me something, that much I get…I guess I'm just wondering if I hadn't said anything, maybe she wouldn't have run off, and maybe…*maybe*…?"

The young woman reached out for Kalas' hand and wrapped her fingers around his. She squeezed and pressed it against her face before releasing her hold on him. Pianissimo, she whispered a few cryptic phrases of reassurance and regret.

"No, I know—even now, I wouldn't ask you to betray her confidence! I just…I wonder if I hadn't said anything, maybe—"

Abarandal cut him off with a staccato retort. Despite his sadness, he smiled: "That sounds like something she would have said! After the…what did Kadhëmba call it? Oh! Right: after the Night of Angry Wolves, I wondered: if I'd done things differently, maybe things wouldn't have turned out like they did. Zhalera was just as disinterested in 'what-ifs' as you are. Still, it's hard *not* to think like that. I don't know why."

"Be grateful for friends willing to call you out when you do!" Nïmrïk barked. "I've spent an unhealthy majority of my existence wallowing in 'what-ifs.' It crushes one's soul. Paralyzes one's ability to choose, to learn, and to move forward."

"Fair enough," Kalas agreed.

On the road south, they crossed paths with naught but a few indifferent parties, and Kalas figured it was just as well. Nïmrïk let them know whenever he sensed others headed north, then made himself scarce. One time, a band of three seedy-looking characters hesitated long enough to give Abarandal an uncomfortable leer. They sized up Kalas, judging his abilities, it seemed. He let the suns glint from the jeweled pommel of *Sharuyandas Tshandu* and stared them down until one swatted another on the shoulder and whispered something to his companions. The three men stepped aside and let Kalas and Abarandal pass without incident. A few seconds later, they heard a howl of surprise; a few seconds after that, Nïmrïk, grinning, padded into view.

"Just in case they thought about getting clever," he insisted, eyes gleaming, when Abarandal gave him a reproving look.

No other travelers gave them any trouble, and not long after the first sun followed the second behind the horizon, they reached the edge of Serular.

"All right, we're here," Kalas observed. Unnecessarily. "Now we just have to figure out where to find Sifuran. He never told us what he was doing here, so I have no idea where to look. And there's probably still *Poyïsriba* soldiers around: best not to let them see us, I'm sure."

Nïmrïk pulled himself free from his wolf shape, pushing apart its jaws from the inside until his skin split apart. He wrapped the fragments around himself and stood there for a moment, dripping and steaming in the twilight while shreds of the otherworldly substance evaporated. He shivered, worked his hands through his greasy-looking hair, and cleared his throat.

"Oh! Right!" Kalas nodded and turned away while the old man rifled through his pack for a change of clothes. "Uh, if I remember right, we're not too far from Niri's place. Neither he nor his sister—all right, *none* of his family seemed pleased to make our acquaintance, but their father was one of Sifuran's true acolytes: I think it's reasonable to assume Sifuran might have sought them out?

Or maybe they'd catch wind of his presence? (No pun intended!) Even if I'm wrong, I don't know where else to go…"

"That's as good a plan as any," Nïmrïk growled as he finished getting dressed. "Lass, what do you say?"

Abarandal, lost it thought—or postponed grief, perhaps— didn't respond right away. Instead, she looked toward the horizon, shimmering in waves of heat surrendered from the earth. Kalas followed her gaze just in time to see a bright flash splash the sky with angry pink. Before he could ask the others if they'd seen the same thing, two more flashes—one lasting at least a full second, another half as long—followed the first. When he glanced at his friends, he knew he hadn't imagined things.

"Pink…*lightning?*" he mused.

"No, lad, I don't think so," Nïmrïk disagreed.

Abarandal whispered a syncopated refrain and quickened her pace.

"That's right," Kalas frowned as he and the *egu* matched her speed: "Niri said he'd heard stories about red beams of light turning things to ash."

"From the sea. From a fleet of unknown ships," supplied Nïmrïk. "I don't think that's mere lightning."

4.

They followed the main road until it split and took the spur that would lead them to Niri's land. In the dark, Kalas sensed a nearby presence. He paused abruptly enough for Abarandal to bump into him and apologized. Staring at the fringe of trees whose needles rippled in the subtle wind, he added, "Hi, Náli."

"Oh, it's you," she said as she rose up from the shadows, her knife in hand. "I didn't think I'd see you again. Or maybe I just hoped I'd be so lucky!"

"That's enough, *shehwiín*," Niri warned as he returned a short sword to its sheath. He conducted a brief assessment of his visitors and remarked, "You're missing people."

Kalas winced and conceded, "Things have…yes, we are. Commander Nashmur, you'll remember, lit out before we did. Shosafin and Rufàran returned to Ïsriba. Rül and Pava had business elsewhere."

"What about that other lady? The smart one with the pretty hair?" Náli demanded.

"She…there was a fire. An accident. She didn't…there was nothing left of her," Kalas confessed as his eyes pooled and overflowed. His young inquisitor stiffened but said nothing else.

"Looks like you told the truth last time you were here," Niri segued. "You probably saw it on your way down the plain, right? Bright red flashes over the sea? Since you first arrived in Serular, there have been a few similar incidents, but something's blunting their destructive power: I've seen it for myself! The ships keep their distance, but there's a hum that travels through the water before the beams strike. Rattles the teeth in your jaw. Now, though, something—some kind of…invisible wall blocks their malice from reaching our shores. Magic? Science? Something in between? Maybe it doesn't matter, so long as our people are safe.

"No one I've talked to knows if Sifuran has really come to Serular, but like you predicted, the cult-men have fled; the *Randa* our father knew has enjoyed a modest renaissance. Still, everyone's on edge: people who used to think us strange for living so far above the city have started looking for places like ours.

"Anyway, what brings you back this way? When your commander-friend disappeared, when Shadrïs—no, Shosafin, right?—when he talked about heading east with the 'king…' Well, like Náli said…"

"Mister Niri, I'm sorry for just showing up like this, but we're here for Sifuran. Believe—or don't—what you will, but you said something about the *Randa pïn Sharumilël:* I know it's an imposition, and we have no right, but I don't know what else to do. There's no one else to talk to. Your father, you said, was loyal to the *Randa?* To Sifuran? If the Order of the Sapphire is restored, maybe you know where we could speak with the *ilrandame?*"

"'Restored' is a stronger word than I'd use. I suppose I could show you where they used to gather. You think one of them will know where to find Sifuran? You really think he's around here somewhere?"

"Yes. To both questions."

"All right, well, no one's going anywhere tonight. C'mon, let's get inside, get you something to eat. We'll head into town in the morning."

"Thank you, Niri," Kalas started, but the wiry fellow dismissed him with a grunt.

Náli lingered, her once-rusty knife glinting in the lazy moonlight. Kalas waited with her and remarked, "You polished your knife. Almost looks brand new. Tell you what: you press *that* against someone's throat, they'll think twice about getting in your way!"

"You're making fun of me!"

"I'm not. I promise…Hey, you wanna see something?"

Wary, the young girl waited, and Kalas raised a hand, then reached for his birthday present. He twisted it to catch the light, then handed the hilt to Náli. Her eyes wide, she held it up, slashed the air a few times, and marveled at its lines. Kalas smiled.

"Wow, this thing is amazing!" she gushed. "Where can I get a knife like this?"

His smile shattered. Startled by his sudden dejection, Náli apologized.

"It's not your fault," he insisted. "Zhalera—'the smart lady with the pretty hair'—made it for me. For my birthday. She was a talented blacksmith—like her father. Would have done great things if she…Anyway, this knife is all that's left of her work…"

Náli pressed the weapon into Kalas' hands, then wrapped her arms around him and squeezed him with more strength than he thought she possessed. He felt the subtlest sobs wrack her tiny frame when he returned her awkward embrace. She pulled away and wiped her eyes.

"I'm sorry about your friend," she said as she regained her composure. She fidgeted before blurting out: "It's not your fault the cultmen killed our father. It's…it's not Shadrïs' fault, either. No, the *mafame* who took his life: it's *their* fault. I'm just a kid: I couldn't do anything to them, but still, I needed someone to blame. Someone to *hate*, y'know?"

"I do, actually. When devil-wolves—*rudzhegume*—killed my parents, I couldn't think of anything except how much I wanted them to suffer.

"Did they? Did the dogs suffer, I mean?"

"One of them got cut down by…magic lightning, I guess; the other, Shosafin—Shadrïs cut off his arm, then *unskinned* him, so yeah, I think he suffered…"

"Good!"

"You know, that's what I thought when I first heard about it, but even so, my father was still dead. My mother, too. Now, I'm not saying I'm *unhappy* they're gone: I just…I don't know. It's strange, talking with you like this: until now, I don't think I realized how…I was going to say, 'how *sad* it makes me,' but that's not it. Not exactly. I guess it all just seems so *unnecessary*."

"Yeah, I know, I know," Náli admitted. "But I don't want to be *sad!* I want to be *angry!* When I'm angry, I can push it all down and pretend there's something I can *do* about it. But there isn't, is there? There's *nothing* I can do! There's nothing *anyone* can do!"

Moved with pity—and glimpsing himself in Náli's outburst,

Kalas hugged her and said, "Someone told me once: 'We roam the detritus of a broken world.' I think that means things weren't supposed to be the way they are. Not everything, anyway. I mean, if you're gonna call something *broken,* you have to have an idea of what *whole* looks like, right? Maybe someday, things will work the right way again. That's what we're working toward. That's what I'm hoping!"

She nodded, considering his words: "Maybe someday," she agreed.

After the simple supper Niri's and Náli's aunt—Nasha, Kalas learned—prepared for everyone, Niri pointed the young man toward a pile of skins on the floor. Exhausted, he collapsed atop their well worn surfaces, too tired to complain. He realized he'd expected an earthy smell—why, he couldn't have said; instead, he breathed in a pleasant, woodsy fragrance. He closed his eyes against a twinge of envy that neither Nïmrïk nor Abarandal seemed to require sleep like he did. Before slumber severed him from his waking thoughts, Náli's pert voice demanded, "Hey! What are you doing sleeping out here?"

"What? It's where Niri said I could get some rest. I didn't—"

"No, no, no: this is no good!" she clucked. "No, come with me!"

Too tired to disobey, Kalas followed the young girl through the low structure and into a small room. Despite his fatigue, he sensed a floral-scented subtlety throughout the space and discerned it belonged to Náli.

"The skins are fine: you don't have to—"

"Get in," she instructed, pointing at a small bed wedged in a corner. Again, he obeyed.

"That's better, yeah?"

As well-brushed sheepskin furs caressed his face, he nodded.

"Of course it is," she agreed as she pulled the topmost layer over him. For the second time, he closed his eyes. Before Náli left her room, she issued one last decree: "Get some rest, Kalas. You'll need it for tomorrow.

5.

"Looks like you've made a friend?" Nïmrïk remarked when Kalas stumbled into the broad gathering hall at the center of the house. The young man massaged the back of his neck and worked his jaw a few times as series of mismatched windows filtered the early suns-light. Moments ago, Náli roused him from a deep and dreamless sleep and dragged him from her room. She'd since disappeared, and Kalas, only half awake, had no idea where she'd gone.

"Yeah, I guess," he allowed. He yawned and breathed in the lingering fragrance of flowers and…farm animals—the sheepskins, he surmised. "We discovered we have some things in common. She's a good kid. Fiery. Feels things deeply…"

Nïmrïk nodded. "Well, good. You—*we* could all benefit from gaining friends. It's a welcome change from losing—I'm sorry! I…I should have been more delicate! I didn't—"

"I know what you mean," Kalas stiffened, then slumped into a nearby chair with a heavy sigh. He stared at the curious caustics refracted from the windows' eclectic panes for a while, then continued: "You're right. Náli said we've got a lot to do today. It'll be good to have her along."

Nasha entered the room bearing a tray filled with eggs, meats, and other breakfast items and set it on a low table. She offered Kalas a reproving glance, then shook her head. Before she turned to leave, Náli reappeared. Perplexed by Kalas' expression, she looked to her aunt—gleaning *her* expression, she huffed, "Aunt Nasha, it's all right. These people aren't…they want…I think they can make Serular better, like it was when Grandfather was a boy—"

541

"What do you think a few sand-treaders can do for Serular?!" Nasha demanded. "Maybe the cult is weaker than it used to be, but you're a fool if you think that means it has no more influence! Your father would still be alive if he'd just…gone along with things instead of thinking they'd ignore his dogged adherence to the old wisdom!"

"You don't mean that!" Náli snarled through gritted teeth, her jaw clenched. "Father saw the cult for what it was: he saw what it did to Serular, to our friends and families! You're saying he should have been a part of that?!"

"…if it kept him alive," Nasha whispered with tears swelling in the corners of her eyes.

"How can you—what kind of life would that be?!"

"You sound so much like him, but you're young. You don't understand—"

"I understand well enough! If Father made any mistake, it was thinking the *ragus* would ignore him if he just kept quiet: he should have called them out! Publicly! Loudly! If they were going to kill him anyway, he should have made it cost them something!"

"You're young," Nasha repeated without conviction.

"I can't believe you think so little of your own brother," Náli smoldered, her cheeks flushed.

"I just wish he were still alive…"

Dabbing at her eyes, the young girl's aunt bumped into Niri as she hastened from the room.

"What's all this?" he wondered with an accusatory look at his little sister.

"Nothing," Náli assured him. "Nothing. Grandfather would've understood…"

"How can you know that? You never even met him!"

"Maybe not, but Father told me about him, about—"

"Father told us a lot of things. Is that…is *that* what made *Shade*

Nasha so upset? Náli…"

"Don't tell me you think everything was fine when the cult was in charge?!"

"Of course I don't, but I…Look, never mind. There's no reason to get into all of this again, especially with…guests around. When you're done with breakfast, come find me outside, and we'll venture into town. And…be kind to Nasha. Niv was her brother long before he was our father…"

Draped in borrowed woolen cloaks to shroud their faces, Kalas, Nimrïk, and Abarandal followed Niri and Náli into the stacked streets of Serular. Several *Poyïsriba* soldiers patrolled its alleys and avenues, and the young man tried not to attract their attention. As they moved through the city's terraced environs, *Serularrinme* continued rebuilding from the wreckage wrought by the mysterious ships and their incomprehensible weapons.

Hundreds—maybe thousands of stairs later, having passed through residential, commercial, and industrial districts, Kalas' knees threatened to collapse. His ragged breathing must have registered with Niri: after a backward glance, he whispered something to his sister and beckoned everyone else away from the streets and their bustling traffic. Náli nodded and disappeared.

"Doesn't matter where you're from: these streets take some getting used to," their guide assured the young man. "We'll wait here. Just a few minutes."

"I'm fine," Kalas gasped and leaned against a building. "Don't… don't stop on my account!"

"You think we stopped just for you?"

"What? You—? No! I mean, well…all right, maybe I—"

"Ha! I'm only teasing."

"Oh! I…I didn't know…"

"Why would you? We're not friends: you probably think I'm

always staid. Aloof. But you don't know me. And I don't know you."

Kalas said nothing as he nodded at Niri's apt summation.

"Náli needs to check on something for us. *Without* us. And no matter how loudly you deny it, you—your knees need a break. We've got *lots* more stairs ahead of us."

"Do you think we could be? Friends, I mean?" Kalas asked while they waited. When Niri didn't respond right away, the young man figured he had his answer.

"Náli seems to think so," he admitted after a long silence. "Me? I don't know. I don't…up from the city, away from everything, I don't get to know people. No, that's not true: I don't *want* to get to know people. Before they killed him, Father warned us about the cult. I understand he was trying to keep us safe, but a lifetime of mistrust doesn't disappear just because people—people I don't know—say things are different now."

"Growing up in Lohwàlar was so different," Kalas said. "Everyone knew everyone. I had to learn how *not* to trust people. Shosafin, I'm sure, would say I still haven't mastered that 'skill.' And he'd be right. Still…I hope we can be friends someday."

"*Why?*" Niri wondered.

"Why not?" Kalas countered. Nïmrïk, listening, chuckled and shook his head. "Devil-wolves. Magic boats. Fire cults. There's too much misery in the world to bear it alone."

Just then Náli appeared. She whispered something to her brother, then started down the street. Niri stood and motioned for the others to follow her as she led them deeper into the city. As they wound beneath its twisting structures and interconnected arcades, Kalas thought of Serular as a vast stone tree twining its rigid limbs in and around the surrounding cliffs. Extending the metaphor, Náli's route carried them past the city's more recent buildings as they descended into its roots.

"Nàvan said the patrols won't be in these parts of the city this morning," she explained as she looped them around another bend. "He's got a pretty good idea of how they move. We should be all right."

"Nàvan?" Nïmrïk wondered.

"One of Father's brothers," Niri grunted. "Works the lifts toward the upper reaches, but he grew up down here. Knows these alleys well."

"I bet he'd like you," Náli mused. "Yes, I think he would. He'd pretend not to, but he would! Anyway, we're almost at the *Randadas* meeting place. Just another—"

Ice and fire traced hurried fingers across Kalas' neck. He raised a hand for Náli to stop talking and placed the other on his sword. Nïmrïk sensed it too: catching the young man's eye, he nodded, motioned for the others to continue, and let himself fall behind.

"What are you doing? What's going on?" the girl whispered and drew her own knife.

Abarandal: stay close! he *sent* toward the *eru*. She nodded and placed a hand atop his arm.

"Nàvan made a mistake," he hissed.

6.

Náli quickened her pace and insisted, "Are you sure? I don't see anyone! And what happened to your friend?"

"He can handle himself. And he'll find us—he's got a great sense of, uh, direction. Right now, we need to get off these streets—and fast!"

"All right, uh, this way!" she said, guiding them down an alley almost too narrow to fit through. "There's a taproom not too far from here. Nàvan knows the owner. Who are we running from?"

"I don't know, exactly," Kalas admitted, his eyes darting from shadow to shadow. "Something…unwholesome. Maybe we won't—"

Náli gasped as an awkward blow sent her reeling to the ground. Kalas hacked at the air where she'd been standing. He connected with something—some*one*, but his foe never made a sound; instead, a gout of sour smoke wafted into the alley.

"*Shosayedhume! Rungula shagabme!*" he warned as he readied himself for another blow. Náli's attacker, missing an arm now, took another step toward her. Kalas sliced across its abdomen, and its entire substance crumbled.

"Náli, are you all right?" he asked as he reached out. Before he could help her up, Niri cried out—too late: another ghost-like figure rammed his shoulder. He dropped his sword and careened into a wall. Náli scrambled to her feet and plunged her short knife into Kalas' assailant again and again with little effect. The young man struggled as the thing wrapped its cold fingers around his neck and raised him off the ground.

Niri tried to pry Kalas free, but the creature's rigored grip proved too strong.

"What is this thing?!" he marveled.

"My sword!" Kalas rasped. "Get…get my sword!"

Niri ceased striving, nodded, and vanished from Kalas' collapsing field of view.

My knife! he remembered. He fumbled at his belt for his birthday present until he felt its familiar contours. *Even if I can't end him with this, maybe I can buy Niri a few seconds…*

On the verge of losing consciousness, Kalas slashed at the *shagabdas* wrist. He'd expected a twitch, maybe a momentary spasm as insensate flesh suffered mechanical injury: what he had *not* expected was twisting threads of yellow-white light twining just beneath its skin, knitting themselves around bone and sinew as they impeded its will. The inhabited *Poyïsriba* soldier released the young man and examined his wound when otherworldly fire erupted within its core and consumed every shred of its physical existence.

What's this?! How is this possible?! he marveled as he examined the blade Zhalera made for him. *That's never happened before…or has it?!*

The *shagabdas* ashes collapsed in a heap. Niri, wielding *Sharuyandas Tshandu*, stood behind its powdered remains.

"Who—*what* is after you?!" Niri demanded, his expression a conflicted blend of horror and amazement.

"There might be more! Be on your—"

"I think that's the last of them," said Nïmrïk, bloodied and rimed with dust, as he appeared from behind a corner. He sniffed the air and explained, "I put down a few others, and I'm not sensing any more."

"Everyone all right?" Kalas asked after accepting Nïmrïk's appraisal. "Náli, you took quite a tumble…?"

"Just a little shaken…and maybe a little scared!"

"There's no shame in that! Abarandal? You all right?" She nodded and sang a brief melody.

"He—it wore kingdom armor! Is every accursèd soldier one of…one of *those?*" Niri wondered as he poked at the heap on the ground.

"Not likely," dismissed Kalas. "The last few times we ran into them, someone else was controlling them. Guiding them, maybe. When he—Kadhëmba! Does that mean Peradan is near?! Or something worse?!"

"Doubtful, lad. The ties that bind these creatures to their masters aren't limited by distance—not the way you perceive it. No, with Sifuran still around, Peradan wouldn't risk it. He's a schemer, not a fool. And speaking of Sifuran, we'd do well to reach the Order without delay."

"We're almost there," Náli promised. "Just a few more blocks, a few more stairs—all right, all right: a *lot* more stairs, but really, we're almost there!"

Niri returned Kalas' sword to him. Now, abreast of Náli, the young man held it up to help light their way. The first sun had only surpassed the second by an hour, but the unfathomable number of structures stacked above them blotted out most of their rays. They passed beneath a split waterfall, each redirected cataract a veil on either side of an endless staircase. Kalas, flagging, revived a little when a cold mist, unwarmed by the shielded suns, fell upon his sweating skin.

"The Unending Stair," Niri offered. "This run surpasses all others throughout all of Serular.

"Does it now?" Kalas sighed.

Hours passed. At least, Kalas could've sworn hours had passed when Náli exclaimed "We're here!" At the end of a long and narrow chasm carved between towering foundations stood a tall iron door, black with scorch marks. Despite its decrepit condition, its reluctant hinges still moved, and the company traveled down a low-ceilinged corridor and into a small, seven-sided anteroom. Spent, Kalas rested against a wall. Náli gave him a sly smile: she and the others seemed unaffected from the numberless steps through Serular's present to the roots of its ancient past. The farthest wall featured an immense barrier constructed from heavy-looking wooden planks banded with iron.

Looks like the room below the Sanctuary, he noted. *No murals though.*

"This is where Father used to come. I don't know what you expect to find—it's been Sevens since the Order's been here. Their last gathering was before Náli was even born. I told you: they're gaining numbers, but slowly; they're still too afraid to revisit their old haunts—especially after the *ragus* burned some of them alive down here! I'm not sure we can even get this inner door open.

Looking at it, I'm not even sure it is a door!

"I don't think we'll have to," Kalas countered. "He'll know we're here. Abarandal, can you…reach out to him? I'll try, too, but I'm no—I mean, maybe between the two of us, we'll have better odds?"

Even in the orange light of Kalas' sword, the color in her cheeks deepened, but she nodded and mouthed a haunting requiem. The young man took her hand, tuned his thoughts toward the Song, and willed his request toward Sifuran.

"Your voice!" Niri gasped and, drawn, took a step toward the singing woman.

"Hush!" Nïmrïk growled. Niri stood still. Náli, similarly enchanted, closed her eyes and absorbed as much of Abarandal's song as possible.

As the stargirl sang and the young man cast his intention toward the absent *eru,* the gentle sound of lazy water—like the Curvewanderer in late summer—bubbled in his ears. Suddenly, the noise of roaring torrents devoured that of unhurried gurgles, and Kalas wondered how he hadn't drowned. He opened his eyes—without remembering when he'd closed them—and saw the door-like object shimmer.

Like the thing at the bottom of the Ravine!

Kalas glanced at Abarandal, at Nïmrïk, Niri, and Náli, and, judging from their expressions, assumed everyone heard the same sounds of water. He looked back at the unsubstantial plane, its edges glittering with a faint blue gleam.

Maybe we're supposed to touch it? Kalas hypothesized. He stepped toward it, hand raised, and a wave picked him up and washed him away from the light. He stood, sure his clothes and belongings would be soaked through, but other than his own perspiration, he remained dry. The wood-and-iron device had disappeared.

"Well met, *sàme!*" Sifuran boomed, his voice like an ocean gale. Despite his subtly altered features, Kalas still recognized him. His *presence.* Or maybe his *frequency?* "I've been waiting for you! You want to get to Ralothova, *hish?*"

"Yes! I just hope we reach it—and Ïsriba in time! Peradan's there, and—"

"I'm well aware, my boy! You told me when you reached out not too long ago!"

"I did? I don't remember—I don't know how any of this works. Not really."

"You also told me about Zhalera: child, you have my sympathy."

Kalas nodded and fought back tears. He looked down, and Sifuran considered his companions.

"Father! *Su pirathëthu, aswanthalu!*" Niri stammered when the *eru* met his fearful gaze. "I refused to see the world through his eyes—and now his world sees me through mine! *Âu* Sifuran, forgive my hardness of heart!"

"Forgiveness is neither mine to give nor to withhold, Master Niri."

"You know my name?!"

"*Âu* Niv made mention of you, yes..."

Niri cried out and sank to his knees.

"You're the lord of justice, right?" Náli accused. "Well then, why did you let the cult-men murder our father?!"

"'Lord'? No, my child. Not the way you mean it. However, among other things, I am delegated the *guilt* of justice. Like you—all of you, I know only the things permitted me to know by the Creator, and—"

"Okay, then why didn't *he* save my father?!"

"You presume the Creator makes the entirety of his incomprehensible will known to me? I won't pretend I—"

"Náli, the Creator has his reasons," Kalas obtruded. "That's a stupid answer, you're thinking—I know: I thought the same when another *eru* said much the same to me. Let me ask you this: do you think it's stupid—I'm putting words in your mouth: forgive me, but do you think it's stupid because it's unreasoned, or just because it's not what you want to hear?"

"It's stupid because my father's dead!" she demanded.

"I'm not saying you have to *like* the answer! I'm only saying— Oh! I interrupted! I'm sorry!" he said, realizing what he'd done.

Sifuran chuckled. "I miss Sharuyan, too, my boy, but it's obvious the two of you spent some time together: for a moment, just now, I could almost hear his infuriatingly rational, peaceful voice. He's right, Náli my child, even if it's maddening to admit it sometimes. Oh? I guess I'm still thinking about Sharuyan…"

Nïmrïk cleared his throat and asked, "The ships with their death rays: did you put a stop to all that?"

"Yes. No one is supposed to have that technology anymore. I—"

"'Technology'?" Kalas repeated. "From Niri's description, I thought it was magic!"

"Maybe the two aren't so different?" Sifuran suggested. "Then again, maybe they're irreconcilably different, and maybe what divides them is infinitely subtle?"

"Uh, all right, okay. I guess. I mean, if you say so," Kalas shrugged. "By the way: did you know there are *shagabme* prowling the streets? We ran into a few on our way here!"

Sifuran's brow furrowed and hot blue fire flashed across his eyes.

"I did not," he admitted. "No doubt Peradan—or perhaps his handler—has minions the world over. I don't think he knows with certainty where we are…unless some *privileged* cultist noticed your arrival. When Loradan flung us from the Vault, I thought the consequent silence a bane; now, I'm inclined to think it a boon! Still, we should get underway with all speed. Before the suns rise tomorrow, meet us at the Korut district's southernmost pier."

"'Us'?" Nïmrïk repeated.

"We'll have plenty of opportunity to discuss things once we're asea, old wolf! Until then, get these people home, make whatever preparations you must, and get some rest!" Sifuran turned toward Kalas as he mentioned *rest,* and as humbling as it was to admit, the young man knew he needed it. The *eru* raised a hand, closed his eyes, and, a moment later, added, "The streets are free of soldiers: go now! We'll see each other soon!"

Chapter XVIII

On the Way to Ralothova

Despite the midsummer season, Kalas shivered in the damp salt air blowing through the masts and sails rocking alongside the fortified pier and slab revetments where Sifuran had said he'd meet them. Neither Nïmrïk nor Abarandal seemed much affected. Náli, at least, wrapped her arms around herself and massaged her ribs. Niri, cold or not, peered out over the ocean.

"Korut," he'd said when they'd all arrived. "Serular's oldest surviving district. Jutting out from the cliffs like this, it's been attacked time and again, although, until recently, not for many Sevens. That's why the walls are so thick, why there are so many watchtowers. They used to call them castles—that's what they look like from overhead. Those are Father's words, not mine: his family used to live closer to the water."

Inside many of the "castles," Kalas glimpsed movement as the *Serularrinme* on duty kept watch for—

The ships, Kalas realized. *They're watching for those ships with the… what did Kadhëmba call them? 'Death rays'? And what did Sifuran mean about technology? Surely such a thing doesn't exist?!*

"Any idea when he'll be here?" Náli wondered. "The suns—the first sun'll be up soon."

"Why are you so concerned?" Niri demanded of his sister. "It's not like you're going with them! No, you and me: we need to stay in Serular."

"Really? Why?"

"We need to do our part to restore the Order of the Sapphire. You were right before: Father should have said something. He saw the cult gaining strength: he neglected his opportunity while the Order still had some of its own. We—I won't make that same mistake."

"Niri, where's all this coming from? You never believed in all the things Father taught us—I'll admit, I doubted more than half of them myself!"

"Under the Unending Stair. Witnessing the glory of an *eru* firsthand, it…opened my eyes. Maybe that sounds trite. Maybe it *is* trite, but it's the best I can do. Yesterday, I was content to grope around in the dark; today, I see things in the light, and I have a lot of work to do."

"Work is not enough," Nïmrïk muttered.

"I'm sorry?"

"What I mean is I've spent…a long time trying to make up for things I've done; no, things I was. As much as I might have accomplished, it's still not enough…Forgive me, I don't mean to blunt the sharpness of your newfound zeal! Who knows? Maybe it'll be different for you: you didn't, uh…your sins are less than mine, I'm sure."

"Stay in Serular if you like," Náli pouted. "I'm going with them!"

"No, *shehwiín,* you're not! Let's not do this again! Not now! I mean, you haven't even attained your second Seven! You said it yourself: neither of us respected Father's devotion. We owe him! We owe Serular—we owe Sifuran!"

"Maybe *you* do…" she pouted. With a heavy, angry sigh, she added, "Fine! We'll stay in Serular! In fact, I'll go home right now!"

She wrapped her arms around Kalas and squeezed; when she

released him, she whispered, "I'm…I'm sorry about Zhalera…"

"Náli! It's not a punishment!" Niri shouted after his sister. Whether she heard him or not, she disappeared between the castles and the tangy mist rising off the water.

The four waited in awkward silence until a shadow cut through the fog, an indistinct blur that gained substance as it neared the pier. Something about its contours seemed familiar, Kalas thought, and as deckhands tossed mooring ropes over the rails, at last he recognized *Zhîamdas Salorosh*.

"Ahoy!" Dzholëf thundered from above. The young man returned the captain's greeting as he and the others secured the ship. With the gangway in place, Dzholëf and a few others debarked.

"Lushà ahwumenul!" Sifuran seemed to materialize from out of the brume and, with a flourish, winked toward Dzholëf. "He's agreed to sail us all the way to Ralothova!"

"I have, have I? That's a funny way to put it," the captain shook his head—and returned Sifuran's wink. "Care to explain just what I'm doing here?"

Sifuran pulled him aside, and the two shared a whispered conversation. Dzholëf nodded, shook his head, nodded again…When they finished, he said, "All right then, I suppose I have. Agreed, that is! Come along: let's get your gear aboard. You'll find your rooms right where you left 'em! My crew will need to refresh our supplies in town, but that won't take long. Enjoy your final moments on dry ground: we'll weigh anchor within the hour."

Dzholëf boarded his vessel and disappeared amidships while several sailors ventured into town. Niri's gaze remained fixed on Sifuran, who seemed not to notice. When the *eru* said he had business in the city as well, the *Serularrin* cleared his throat and begged to accompany him.

"Young man, you're free to move as you like: this is your city, not mine!" Sifuran said with a touch of annoyance.

"Oh, uh, of course, of course!" Niri stammered. "Forgive me, *Kathin Sifuyeru*—my father tried to teach me the rites, but I was unwilling to listen. I have so much to learn…so much to atone for…"

Sifuran placed a hand on Niri's shoulder, pivoted the uncertain man to face him, and, in gentler tones, said, "Niri, son of Niv, listen—I deem you mean well, but understand one thing: that obsequious note in your voice? I hate it! It's the same tune the *ilragusme* sang when gushing about their idol. Unlike Peradan—*hòyihad*—*fie im nëshras nir!*—I will *not* permit my name to be the substance of such blasphemy! I sing The Song in the presence of the Creator, yes, but so do countless others—everyone of us a mere *creation!* Maybe Peradan let *his* head swim with dreams of misbegotten glory? Or maybe the seed of self-importance took root in him in aeons past? Maybe one day, we'll know with certainty, but I—"

"I don't understand!" Niri wilted. "Father spent his whole life worshiping you, yet when—"

"*Not* true!" Sifuran railed. "He…respected me, yes, but he *never* worshiped me! None of the Order *ever* worshiped me! Until Peradan's betrayal, no *ilranda* worshiped his patron *eru!* Not with said *erudas* approval! Such a thing would have been unthinkable! Understand *two* things, then: *no created thing is worthy of your worship!*"

"What am I supposed to do?! I don't know where to begin!"

"Seek out what few adherents remain within Serular. Like Niv, they sought to disappear while the cult held sway; like Niv, they know the old wisdom. Let them teach it to you…Here, hold up your hand."

Niri did as he was told, though his head hung limp between his shoulders. Sifuran whispered something Kalas couldn't understand, then gripped Niri's wrist with one hand and scribed something on his upturned palm with the other. The man cried out as puffs of blue flame jetted from the *erudas* fingertip. When he let him go, Niri stared as his handiwork. Curious, Kalas sidled up beside him: Sifuran had carved his symbol into Niri's flesh. Subtle strands of blue-white light still glittered along the edges.

"The fire should burn itself out in a matter of days. In the future, when you see this mark upon your hand, remember this encounter. You do well to desire the rebirth of the *Randa pïn Sifumilël*—so long as you hold fast to its true purpose: all of us—*elume, erume, á edhume*—exist for the glory of Ilun.

"Now go. I'll impress upon a remnant to gather at the place beneath the Unending Stair: they'll be waiting for you when you arrive."

"Thank you, *Âu* Sifuran! I'll go right now! Oh! But what about Náli? If only she could have been here as well!"

"Here is where your path—and your sister's—diverge, my eager friend…"

Niri, wearing a confused expression, nodded and turned to go. He managed a few steps before he stopped and turned back: "Maybe we could be, Kalas. Friends, I mean." He offered the young man a weak smile, then resumed his pace.

2.

Kalas' quarters aboard the *Salorosh* seemed much the same since their trip to Galámur: spare, yet clean. He stowed his modest provisions, then headed above board. Sifuran opted not to join them on their journey: "If Niri's any indication, I can't have well-intentioned yet ill-informed people offering worship to me—to *me!* Ha! No, lest this renaissance result in another cult, I'll remain in Serular. *Tharan bethrume á thòenthar shadame* until we meet again!"

Walking the deck, he glimpsed neither Nïmrïk nor Abarandal, so he sought out Captain Dzholëf and found him on the quarterdeck, issuing orders for his crew to weigh anchor and get under way. The weathered salt acknowledged the young man with a nod as his vessel left its berth and put out into deeper water.

"It's good to see you, Master Kalas, though I'll admit, I hadn't expected we'd ever meet again!"

"Yeah, I was surprised to see the *Salorosh!*" Kalas agreed. "How'd you get here so quickly? I mean, we only arrived a couple of days ago: unless you were already on your way, it doesn't seem possible."

"It's strange—or maybe it isn't—but we were making our usual rounds between Avëlöth and the mainland when I got this sense I needed to head south. I explained it to my crew—most of 'em have been with me for a long time now, so they're used to the occasional interruption in our typical routine—and we turned around, put in at Melash, and shuffled things around. It's not ideal: we'll lose considerable profits, but whatever damage my reputation suffers on the mainland, my crew's become accustomed to being taken care of. And as necessary as profits are, there are a few things that are more important.

"As we got closer to Serular, out under the suns, I felt the mark on my back—the one you noticed when we first met—start to burn. It never does that! I figured the *Sifuyeru* was reaching out to me, and it wasn't long before I saw the fortified piers of the Korut district whenever I closed my eyes. I was probably more surprised to see *him* standing on that pier than you were to see me!

"I understand a few of your crewmates have gone on ahead of you to Ïsriba, that things there are not good, and that your friends are quite probably in grave danger. More than that, I understand you have…work of your own that needs to be done. Sifuran also told me about your lady friend: Master Kalas, words cannot convey my sorrow…"

"I just…if Ïsriba's somehow acquired an armada—or maybe Niri was wrong: maybe Ralothova's already been overrun? Either way, we have to get to Ïsriba!" Kalas agreed. "They say Peradan's there: if he is, we have to stop him! I don't know exactly what his plans are, but he wants humanity to destroy itself. Our friends must be in Ïsriba by now—if they aren't, they will be soon! How fast can we get to Ralothova?"

"We run a fast ship—you should remember that! Especially when we're as light as we are. And I suspect Sifuran might bend his will toward the water on our behalf. If only Loradan would bend hers toward the wind! That said, we should reach the Great Whale in roughly two weeks. Faster, if the *erume* intervene."

Kalas chewed his lip and nodded, his thoughts already occupied by the future's uncertainties, and said, "I hope it's enough," before he descended toward midship.

When he reached the main deck, he paused, abaft of beam, and leaned over the railing as the Second Sun thrust its subtle warmth across the sky. As the Song rippled through his mind, he closed his eyes and tried to picture its melodies and harmonies as the shapes and colors he remembered from his second Seven.

Why me? Why am I the one stricken with this…this curse? *If I never heard The Song, if I never learned what it was, Zhalera would still be alive. Mother and Father and Gandhan, too.*

All true, a voice agreed, haunting him with how familiar it sounded. *Your loved ones* would *still be alive. For a season. Perhaps for the rest of their natural lives. And what of the rest of the world? Would you condemn it to death and darkness for the sake of your serenity?*

Who—? No! That's not what I meant! I just—

Isn't it, though? the voice insisted. *You know the prophecy: you heard it beneath the Vault of Stars under Ïsriba. You know the stakes! And you know our present circumstances, as painful as they can be sometimes, can serve as guideposts toward a brighter future. You've suffered much—none would deny that—and it's possible you've yet to suffer more; but consider the unexpected blessings, too! Unlikely friendships and alliances. A deeper understanding of the wound from which the world suffers—and a chance to* unmake *its injury! Ah, my child: perhaps it's 'unfair' to require so much from one still so young, yet here we are! Here* you *are! You have my sympathy…*

"Falthwën?!" Kalas started. He stood, opened his eyes, and looked around.

He was alone.

No, of course not. I'm probably just hearing his voice inside my head because if he were *here, he'd probably say something just like that.*

"And he'd be right," he admitted with a sour look. A passing deckhand offered him a quizzical look.

"Oh, no, I'm just…thinking out loud," he assured the man, who shrugged and continued on his way.

Kalas laughed at himself and turned toward the stairs leading below deck. The Second Sun, half above the horizon, glinted from something metallic not quite buried beneath a pile of sailcloth. Curious, he altered course to investigate.

The source of the glint shifted—and so did the shape of the heap.

"What's this?!" he wondered aloud. With one hand, he reached for his knife; with the other he reached for the edge of a sail. He hesitated for a moment, then yanked the material aside.

"Náli?!" he gasped. "What—? How—?"

"Hush!" the young girl begged and wrestled the sail from Kalas' grasp, the exposed edge of her blade flashing with her movements. She covered herself again and, her voice naught but a hoarse whisper, insisted: "Throw some ropes over me or something! Someone else might see me!"

"Náli, come out!" Kalas ordered.

Silence. And restless fidgeting.

"Náli?" he repeated with a hint of iron in his voice.

"All right, fine!" she groused as she slid from underneath her hiding place. "But I am not going back! Let Niri contend with the Order! Me, I wanna help! You're gonna kill…what's his name? Peradan? You're gonna kill him, right? I want in!"

"It's not that simple, Náli! Peradan's not a man—mere steel won't hurt him. Not for long! I don't *want* to kill him, but I'm afraid you're probably right: that's what it'll come to. I don't think we can reason with him, not after what I saw under the Ravine."

"The…what?"

"Some place north, a little like the place—It doesn't matter! You shouldn't be here! I'll talk to Captain Dzholëf: maybe we're not so far out we can't turn back…"

"Kalas, *please!*" Náli implored. "I…I'm young, I know—one and six—but even before the cult-men murdered Father, I was making plans to get away from Serular. I couldn't stand living in hiding like we had to. I couldn't stand being trapped at home, like some kind of prisoner! Remember when Shadrïs first brought you to our land? We were in trees! *Trees!* Why? Because that's what we always do when someone comes up from the city! That's the way Father taught us. I didn't know any different, but it still seemed ridiculous to me! Sometimes I'd sneak into the city and poke around—that's how I learned about Galámur. Among other things. And guess how many people I saw hiding? *None!* And even after Father died, *Shade* Nasha demanded we keep doing it! Niri—I love him, but as hard-nosed as he seems, he's a pushover, really. At least where Nasha's concerned!

"I can't go back. I won't! Even if you turn this ship around, I'll…I'll go north! No—east! Yeah! I'll go to Ïsriba on my own, maybe confront Peradan by myself! So…so *please:* don't make me go home!"

Náli's high-pitched voice increased in frequency as she made her case—and her threats. Kalas watched as her eyes, the same shape but a deeper green than her brother's, welled with tears that hesitated before spilling onto the deck.

"You'll never make it to Ïsriba before we do," Kalas sighed and sheathed his knife. He leaned against the rail again and looked out at the interplay of suns-light sparkling on the water and said, "There are no guarantees. I can't promise you safety. I can't promise you success—I can't even *define* success! It's possible one or more of us will die before we reach Ïsriba—it's possible we won't even reach Ralothova, much less Ïsriba! And even if we all survive all the way to the queen-regent's throne, it's possible Peradan will have noticed what we're doing and…I don't even know!

"You *should* be headed home, but we'd lose too much time turning around. And I know how you feel. Maybe better than anyone aboard this ship. You're still a child…but even though I've attained my second Seven, I am, too, in so many ways. I can't make your choices for you. I'd like to, but I think you're hard-headed enough to actually try to *walk* all the way to Ïsriba! You're not concerned what Niri will think when he finds you're not at home?"

"He'll figure it out. It's not the first time I've gone missing. And Sifuran'll be there. I heard him when he said my brother and I had different paths. What if this is what he meant?"

Kalas sighed again. With a wry smile, he turned toward the young girl and said, "All right, well, here we are. C'mon, let's at least tell the captain he's got a stowaway. You ever swabbed the deck before?"

3.

As they sailed through the next few days, Náli became something of a fixture on the main deck, sweeping her mop across its weathered boards. One of Dzholëf's younger hands—probably Kalas' age—discovered myriad ways to cross paths with the girl that defied probability: Náli didn't seem to mind, especially when he offered to swab half the deck for her. The captain tried to hide a smile when Kalas brought her to him, and the young man suspected he'd known about her presence all along.

On the fourth day out of port, the lookout bellowed out a warning: "Two—no, three ships! Corsairs! Thirty degrees to port, about a league distant! Making…four, maybe five knots!"

"Colors?" the captain wondered.

"None! Black sails. Unusual hull configuration, too. Not like anything I've ever seen!"

"Have they seen us?"

"Aye! They altered course about the same time I spotted them!"

"Pirates?" Kalas wondered, having overheard all the shouting.

"Guess we'll find out," Dzholëf muttered. "Trim the sails, lads! Let's see if we can put some distance between us!"

"I swear, Captain, they weren't there a moment ago!" the lookout insisted. "It's like they just *appeared* on the water!"

For a few tense minutes, *Zhîamdas Salorosh* hummed across the water. The crew adjusted lines and sails to coax another knot or two from their vessel, but the unidentified crafts continued to close the gap. Náli, who stopped her work to watch the spectacle, suggested, "What if they're the ships that attacked Serular? I never saw 'em, but, well, you heard Niri: no one knows where they were from, either!"

"I thought the same thing," the captain admitted. "Right now, we can only hope we're wrong. I've heard the rumors, too. It seems they don't want anyone to know where they're from: I think it's safest to assume they intend us harm. We'll have to hope we can outrun them!"

Dzholëf closed his eyes and moved his mouth, but no sound escaped his lips.

He's praying, Kalas thought. Directing his attention toward the black smudges shifting in and out of focus as they rocked atop the waves, he closed his eyes and willed a message toward Loradan, *guilt-bearer* of the winds. No one, mortal or otherwise, it seemed, knew anything of her whereabouts or activities after she flung them from the Vault under Ïsriba. From all accounts, Kalas wondered if whatever she'd done had somehow torn the fabric of the *kalthesh*. Altered it, at least, in some fashion that hindered the medium.

"They're gaining on us!" the lookout shouted without trying to hide his apprehension. Kalas opened his eyes to see three distinct shapes rolling toward them, their coarse black sails full of malign wind. Metallic-looking turrets mounted on their forecastles glinted in the suns. As the crafts navigated crests and troughs, sinister red light swelled from within gaping cylindrical maws directed at Dzholëf's ship. Kalas didn't know the complexities of water, but the captain confirmed his fears: "Of all the times for the wind to shift! They'll reach us in under a minute! All right, lads! Make ready! Prepare for boarders!"

"We won't be boarded," Nïmrïk lamented with an outstretched arm indicating the hot glow rising through the turrets. Like many others, he and Abarandal had been drawn above board by the shouts of crew and captain. "They intend to destroy us with their death rays. Seeing those things *almost* reminds me of something, and while I don't remember specifics, I do remember *fear.*"

A beam of hot, pink-white light lambent with electric arcs lanced the sky with a high-pitched whine. It missed the *Salorosh* by about a hundred feet.

"*Erume mbeshinaru!*" Dzholëf exclaimed and wiped cold sweat from his brow. Kalas felt the hairs on his arms stand up straight.

"They won't miss again," Nïmrïk predicted.

One of the other ships fired; it, too, missed—by about half the distance of the first.

"Of course, I'm happy to be proven wrong!" he laughed without humor.

The third ship sailed between the first two, its otherworldly weapon primed. Before it fired, somehow, Kalas *knew* it wouldn't miss. Gathering all his impotent courage, he stared down the bore and waited for his end.

Maybe there's some other 'child' who can fulfill the prophecy? he wondered as his world erupted in a wall of light.

4.

The deck beneath his feet shuddered; indeed, individual air molecules seemed to smack against one another, unleashing an acrid tang. Kalas opened his eyes and saw what he could only describe as puckered discs of pink light clinging to an invisible sphere encircling the entirety of the *Salorosh*. For a moment, the discs, still attached to their attackers' ship by snaking snarls of blue-purple light, spiraled around the impossibly solid sky; then, with a pulse that sucked the wind—the *life*, it seemed, from Kalas' lungs, the discs, trailing their serpentine umbilicals, receded toward their source with lightning speed. They disappeared within the turret—

How did—?!

—and the craft exploded in a cloud of shattered wood and shredded metal. Shrapnel ripped into the other two vessels and into their unknown apparatuses, triggering similar results. Before the shockwaves of their destruction reached the *Salorosh*, Kalas grabbed Abarandal, who'd joined him near the rail; drawing her toward his chest, he turned his back on the spectacle unfolding abeam.

When nothing happened, he released her, offered an apologetic smile, and turned toward the sea again. Naught but a few smoldering planks—and an iridescent black film—remained atop the ocean's surface. He gave Abarandal a quizzical glance, which she dismissed with a staccato flurry. He looked to Nïmrïk, whom he discovered was regarding *him* with similar suspicion.

"No! I don't—I wouldn't even—I have no idea what just happened! I thought—I don't understand how we're not dead!" Kalas insisted.

"*Erume mbeshinaru*," repeated the captain. "That was *close!* All right, lads! As you were! Best speed for Ralothova!"

As the crew, still shaken from the inexplicable events they'd just endured, returned to their stations, Kalas assessed his friends: "Uh, everyone all right? Náli? You okay?"

Náli, leaning so far over the rail Kalas thought she might topple into the sea, turned toward him with a grin that stretched from ear to ear: "*That was amazing!*" she shouted.

"So…yes, then?" Kalas chuckled.

"Amazing!" she repeated. "Those ships *have* to be the ones that attacked Serular! A few of them, anyway! And they just—*BOOM!* I don't care how—I'm just glad they're gone!"

"Indeed," Nïmrïk agreed, "but from Niri's description, there were more than three such vessels. We would do well to remain vigilant. I'll offer to take a shift keeping watch: my constitution provides me an advantage, after all."

"Your what? What do you mean?" Náli wondered. Nïmrïk ignored the question.

"Good idea," Kalas affirmed before the young girl could press the matter. "Maybe there's something the rest of us can do, too? I'll ask around, see how we can best help. C'mon, Náli, why don't you come with us?"

"Anything's gotta be better than swabbing the deck!" she nodded.

Late in the day, well after the second sun had set, Kalas walked up and down the port side of the ship. Again. He lost count of how many times he'd circled the deck, his eyes fixed on the cliffs, the horizon, and the cliffs again. The lookout seemed only too happy to trade places with Nïmrïk, warning him, "Just so you know, it's rough up there—every wave feels about a hundred times stronger!" Nïmrïk assured him he'd manage.

Dzholëf thanked Kalas—and Náli, who'd insisted on following him—for wanting to help: "I appreciate the offer, lad, lass, but we run a tight ship! My crew knows its duties. We'll reach the Whale fastest if you let them do their jobs. Tell you what, though: more eyes on the horizon—even on these cliffs—won't hurt. Give word if you see anything that seems out of place. Just keep clear of the crew and pray we're favored all the way south and east!"

Náli, accompanied by the deckhand who made no secret about his interest in her, shared a laugh as they approached from the bow. Neither seemed to notice Kalas until the young man almost bumped into him. He cleared his throat.

"Oh! Hi, Kalas! Kávi was telling me about some of the places he's been! He's—oh, don't make that face! I'm not keeping him from doing his job! We're doing what the captain said, we're looking for other ships."

"Have you seen anything? I haven't," Kalas asked.

"Can't say that we have, *Âu* Kalas," Kávi replied. "Just a few seals sunning themselves on the rocks."

Kalas laughed. He couldn't remember anyone addressing him as *Mister* before. Before he could ask about the seals, Náli tugged Kávi's sleeve and, gesturing toward the cliffs, said, "Hey! What's that?"

"What's what?" both men wondered.

"Not a ship or anything, but I thought I saw light coming from the cliffs! I don't see it n—Right there! See? See?!"

Kalas squinted and strained to see what Náli saw. About to dismiss her claim as nothing more than reflected suns-light, he saw it, too: a subtle, shimmering sheet of water illuminated from below. Had they passed this place when both suns were in the sky, they never would have noticed it, he reasoned.

"I see it!" he affirmed.

"What do you think it's from?" Kávi asked.

"I'm from the desert: I have no idea! Looks like a waterfall—maybe it's just a reflection?"

"The light doesn't look right," countered the deckhand. "Looks like it's coming *up from under* the waterfall. Behind it, maybe?"

"I don't know," Kalas admitted. "I'm not familiar with…wherever we are! Hey, maybe Captain Dzholëf would know? I mean, he's sailed more than any of us, right?"

"Then we should ask him!" Náli insisted and started for the captain's quarters with Kávi in tow. Kalas stared at the out-of-place luminance for a moment, then followed after them.

5.

"Light coming from under a waterfall? You're sure it wasn't just a reflection? Light sometimes misbehaves when there's water involved!" Captain Dzholëf suggested. He'd been discussing rigging with his first mate—a rotund gentlemen named Bolá—when Náli, dragging her new friend behind her, barged into his quarters.

"Begging your pardon, Captain, but it didn't behave like a reflection," Kávi countered: "something about it seemed off, but none of us is familiar with this part of the coast."

Dismissing Bolá, Dzholëf rifled through his collection of charts and said, "All right then, let's see where we are…"

It took him a few tries to locate the right chart: he admitted he rarely traveled this part of the world; when he did, he unrolled it onto a table and traced the coastline with his finger.

"Serular is…*here*. That means we're right…*here*," he said as he traced their route with his finger. "North of us is…Ïsran."

"Ïsran?"

"It's a small city—a large town, maybe?—a few leagues south of…Ïsriba, it seems."

"That can't be a coincidence!" Kalas blurted. Náli nodded her hearty agreement.

"Those ships *must* have come from Ïsriba!" she said.

"But how?" Kávi posed, studying the captain's chart. "Ïsriba is leagues and leagues from the sea! There's a river here—the *Ridësh-ilnush*. That must be the source of the waterfall. If this chart is accurate, it's too small for a ship the size of the ones that attacked us! Looks like it opens up before it drops, but there's no way any ship—any*thing*—could survive those cliffs!"

"Ïsriba's roots run deep," Kalas said, sorting his thoughts as he thought out loud. "When we were prisoners there, we were deep underground, and I think its passageways ran deeper still. I wonder if there's something down there that no one knows about. No one except the queen-regent. Nashmur said she had all kinds of construction projects going on.

"The…beam weapons mounted on those ships: what if she has other, similar devices? What if she's found a way to take her projects *underground?* Hey, Náli: King Rufàran said there's a river that runs *beneath* Ïsriba, remember? Kávi, you said it looked like the light was coming from under or behind the waterfall. What if Ïsriba did something? Changed the river's path somehow?"

"That's a lot of 'what-ifs' based on what might just be a trick of light! And it would take unimaginable effort to redirect such a river!" Dzholëf scoffed. He started to roll up his chart when he paused, gnawed his lip, and unrolled it again. He tapped at the squiggly line representing the river and added: "Then again…I don't know how accurate this chart is. It's old, and, like I said, I rarely travel these routes, but look at this indentation on either side of the river: a natural harbor, I'd say, capable of sheltering a ship or two. Maybe three."

"What if there's a cave or something behind the waterfall? Something large enough to hide a ship—or two? or three?" Kalas suggested.

"It would have to be a *very* large cave! Regardless, there's nothing we can do about it tonight, but I'll mark it on my chart. We'll ask Sifuran about it when next we meet. Still, even if you're right—even if Ïsriba is staging ships along the cliffs—*inside* the cliffs, it doesn't explain how they got there, not without someone noticing…"

"Maybe they started in Ralothova? Nashmur said something about an agreement between Ralothova and Ïsriba," Kalas informed them. "I know those ships don't look like Ralothova's—I mean, that's what everyone says: I wouldn't know one way or another!— but what if Ïsriba…I don't know, *modified* them somehow? Maybe in that harbor?"

"'What if'? 'Maybe'? Too much speculation, lad! Too much indeed! The saddest thing? Given the way the world is turning lately, it's almost plausible! Anyway, there's nothing for us to do between here and there: when we reach the Whale, we're sure to learn more."

A few days later, Nïmrïk spied two more corsairs, astern and gaining on them. With all the sails rigged for maximum speed under prevailing conditions, the *Salorosh* could do nothing except anticipate another confrontation.

"Behind us this time," Dzholëf remarked. Bolá nodded. "Aye, Captain! Where do you think they're from? Nearest western port is Serular—unless they weighed anchor a day or two after we did, there's no way they could've caught up to us! The *Salorosh* might be a cargo ship, but she's faster than most, and we're high in the water!"

Kalas, listening, caught the captain's glance: *Maybe there's merit in your suspicions*, it said. Abarandal stood against the rail and stared out over the water. Indeed, it seemed the specter of impending doom captivated nearly everyone. The young man discovered his prior dread never came; instead, he considered the ships with cool anticipation. When they closed on Dzholëf's vessel and charged their weapons, Kalas' skin prickled as the hairs along his arms stood straight; a buzz rattled between his ears, and he stepped toward Abarandal and placed his hands atop the rail.

"Here we go again," he smiled, unsure—and unafraid. She covered his hand with her own, held him with her silver eyes, and breathed a brief melody.

"I guess we'll see," he nodded.

White-hot impulses ringed with bright red light vaulted from the corsairs' turrets and seemed to plow through space until, as before, some invisible force manifested all around them, collected each writhing strand of energy, and redirected each assault toward its origin. Like their predecessors, these ships disintegrated in a blinding conflagration of wood and metal.

Sifuran must have a hand in this! Kalas decided. *He must have done something, 'exercised his privilege,' as Falthwën might have described it.*

"It seems it wasn't just good fortune, then," Dzholëf mused with a wink at the young man.

"Let 'em come again!" Náli shouted from the main deck. The young firebrand wrapped Kávi in a violent hug; then, realizing what she'd done, she pushed him away with an awkward shove and punched him in the shoulder.

"She may get her wish," Kalas frowned. "I just hope you're right. About our 'good fortune.'"

"Two more days and we'll reach Ralothova. Three if the winds refuse to cooperate. You know, it occurs to me that maybe Ralothova's own fleet has been attacked, too: something I hadn't considered until now. Well, we'll know for sure soon enough."

• • •

Rocky slopes studded with strands of leafy palms, followed by rolling hills and broad plains displaced the cliffs that separated most of the southern coast from the sea. White, black, and, on occasion, brown sheep grazed green, quilt-like meadows as the *Salorosh* sailed ever closer to Ralothova. Despite their distance from the shore, several raised their woolly heads as the ship rolled across the main. Kalas imagined being surrounded by so much grass and remembered how much Zhalera enjoyed her brief exposure to the lush quadrangle at the university in Melash.

She would have loved to see this...

Warm breezes rising off the ocean rippled through the palm trees, and, following the wind's path, he raised his gaze toward the horizon and frowned when he discerned dark gray clouds collecting above the interior. Something unnatural, unwholesome thronged beneath their leaden canopy. The first sun would disappear within the hour, and in its unsettling twilight, random spates of dirty orange and yellow light flashed against the iron-colored ceiling. Not lightning—not *eruyâsru* either, Kalas deemed. Something from the mind and hand of man. Something fearsome.

Nashmur described Ralothovarinme *as a peaceful people, but that sky...There's nothing peaceful about it!*

"Captain!" Nïmrïk shouted from above. "Several ships approaching—and fast! *Poralothova* configuration, if memory serves, but their hands are full of steel and fire. Be wary!"

"Ahoy!" someone shouted as one of the ships drew up alongside. "Drop your sails and prepare to be boarded!"

"Captain?" Bolá deferred.

"Aye, do it."

The first mate issued orders to the crew as Dzholëf addressed the man in the other ship: "What can I help you with, friend?"

The dour figure said nothing as several sailors emerged from below decks bearing hooks and grapples. Archers with arrows nocked waited above board. With the vessel secured, a six-man team with flickering oil lamps and drawn swords ascended a rope ladder, made a quick survey of the deck, and nodded at their captain. Four headed for the lower decks while the other two remained topside. A tall and imposing presence, the *Poralothova* ship's spry captain sheathed his sword and scaled the ladder with practiced ease. He remained silent until, some minutes later, his four men reappeared on the main deck. One shook his head, but all six men kept their weapons ready.

"You'll forgive us, *friend*, for exercising a little caution, *hish?*" he said at last. Lamplight glittered from flecks of salt crystals caught in his chest-length blond beard as his mouth curled into a thin smile. A smile that stopped short of his hard, iron-oxide brown eyes. "Carelessness costs, you know—especially these days, it seems! In recent months, these waters have been plagued with evil ships—ships armed with unimaginable weapons! Get caught in one of their barrages, and you're as good as dead!"

"We've…heard stories of the same," the captain admitted.

These sailors would never believe what happened on our way here, Kalas understood.

"Your vessel is a *Pogambarad* configuration, right? We don't see the likes of her around here often. You're a long way from the Iron Bear…"

"Aye, that's correct, Captain…?"

"Call me Thurën."

"Captain Thurën, then. Captain Dzholëf, at your service."

"Tell me, Captain Dzholëf: what brings you all the way to Ralothova's shores?"

"It's those very ships you mentioned. We were in Serular, where several vessels matching your description wrought havoc upon her people. We wondered if perhaps the *Ikin pïni Kiwan* might know more about them?"

"You mean you wonder if the People of the Whale are *responsible*. Serular is a *Poyïsriba* protectorate: why travel all this way? Why not ask your queen?"

"You've a sharp mind, friend," Dzholëf conceded: "we did consider whether the attacks on Serular came from Ralothova. Ïsriba, as you know, has no ports—and besides: why would the Golden Falcon attack her own people? Serular *does* belong to Ïsriba, as you've already mentioned."

Abarandal, standing next to Kalas, sang a few soft notes.

"Are you sure?" he whispered. She nodded. "All right, I'll say something. I hope you're right!"

The young man jogged up the stairs leading to the quarterdeck. He hesitated for a moment, glanced back at Abarandal, and, at a nod from the adamant *eru,* cleared his throat and said, "Uh, Captain Thurën? Sir?"

"Aye, lad? Speak!" the *Poralothova* captain demanded, his eyes never moving.

"Uh, sir, I—well, I think you should know: Queen Ësfàyami can't be trusted! *That's* why we're coming all the way around the continent to Ralothova instead of traveling over land. It's true, we weren't sure if the death-ships were yours or someone else's—we wondered if maybe they came from Ïsriba somehow, or if, well… We wondered if Ïsriba had broken her treaties with Ralothova and captured your ports…

"Some friends of ours—also at cross-purposes with the queen-regent—were headed there not too long ago. Since they left us, we learned—well, we think they might be walking into a trap! Look, I know you have no reason to care, but our quarrel isn't with Ralothova. It's with Ïsriba. With Ësfàyami and…her court. We're not here to cause—"

"There it is!" Captain Thurën beamed, examining Kalas at last. "I admire your forthrightness, boy! Saves us so much time! Don't you agree, Captain Dzholëf?"

At a nod from their captain, the soldiers who'd boarded the *Salorosh* sheathed their weapons and returned to their own vessel.

"He…Yes, yes, I suppose there's something to be said for the lad's candor."

Thurën beckoned for his first mate, who handed him a blue-gray square of cloth and nodded when his captain whispered a command; Thurën then handed the object to Dzholëf: "All right then: hoist this flag and no *Poralothova* craft will interfere with you. You're not carrying anything like the wreckage we recovered from prior incursions, and your ship—as lovely as she is, I'm sure—isn't built for the kind of speed and maneuverability necessary for those devices.

"Your cabin boy's not wrong about Ësfàyami. It's true, we do have agreements with Ïsriba, but we're not as helpless as the Falcon believes! No, we—"

Thurën stopped himself, his wide eyes flashing in the lamp light. He chuckled again and added, "Ah, enough about politics! Hoist that flag, friend, and no one will bother the *Salorosh* while she remains in *Poralothova* waters. I'll sail with you the rest of the way: my ship, the *Rahingun,* will follow us. Just to make sure there are no surprises between here and there. Permission to come aboard, Captain?"

"Granted," Dzholëf muttered with a sweeping and insincere gesture.

6.

"This does *not* look like Ralothova! Not how I pictured it after listening to Nashmur describe it!" Kalas confided to Abarandal and

Nïmrïk, who'd descended from his perch and joined the others on the quarterdeck. "He described them as peaceful, unable to protect themselves without Ïsriba's help—but look at all these warships!"

Captain Thurën directed them toward a well-protected bay boasting stout fortifications. He instructed Bolá to furl sails. Dzholëf's first mate hesitated until his captain grunted his assent. Guards observing from tall, iron-faced towers kept their bows trained on the *Salorosh* until they noticed Thurën's banner. Someone shrilled a blast from a trumpet, and Kalas felt something move beneath them: a rush of tremulous waves, illuminated with torch- and moonlight, rippled through the water.

"What was that?" he wondered. Thurën smiled but said nothing about it; instead, he gestured toward a pier. Dzholëf nodded and instructed his crew to dock there.

With the ship moored, Thurën asked, "Permission to leave the ship, Captain?" Kalas thought Dzholëf didn't want to smile, but he did: "Aye, granted!"

Before he left, he offered some advice to the captain, his crew, and his passengers: "The Whale prides itself on its peaceful history, but don't mistake our *preference* for peace as an unwillingness to protect our interests! Tell me, Captain: as a sailor, you're familiar with various kinds of whales, yes?"

"I'm familiar."

"Of course you are. The Great Whale is a *baleen* whale. Those who would threaten our sovereignty are krill. You understand?"

Dzholëf nodded. Thurën smiled, polite and cold. *"Tsheth zhi Kathin Kiwan shelu nir!"* he said. Threatened. Kalas looked from one captain to the other, not sure what the *Ralothovarin* meant. Addressing the young man, he said, "You're worried for your friends. I respect that. And it seems you see through the Falcon-queen's veneer: would that more of her people were so perceptive! Even so: be wary between here and there! The land is treacherous, yes, but more so the spirits who rule the fens and marshes between the lowlands and the mountains. Avoid them at all costs, and you just might reach your friends intact!

"I see no reason to impound your vessel, nor harass you while you remain our guest. Like I told you: keep that banner flying, and no one will bother the *Salorosh,* but know this: return it on the day you leave our waters, or we *will* take it by force. Now then: welcome to Ralothova!"

"I've done what Sifuran asked of me, but I must return to my routes," Dzholëf told Kalas and the others. "I'm sorry to leave you here, on your own, but I—"

"We're grateful," Kalas interrupted. Nïmrïk, Abarandal, and Náli nodded. "There's nothing to explain."

They waited on the main deck for Thurën to disappear into the busy throng living and working Ralothova's ports. Kalas wondered if they were in Ralothova proper, or just one of its properties. He decided it didn't matter.

"We'll find out if anything's happened to Shosafin. To Rufàran. I know they're intent on confronting the queen-regent, but if Peradan *has* appeared in Ïsriba, if he *has* replaced Marugan in the court, then they'll need our help: their weapons are useless against *ekume!* Tell Sifuran about the ships—and tell him we said *thank you!"* Kalas requested.

"Aye, lad, I understand. Oh, before you go: take this! Back pay for keeping my deck sparkling clean," Dzholëf said and handed him a heavy purse.

"Captain Dzholëf! I can't—"

"We'll resupply and shove off from Dzharasa—this city—in a day or two, weather permitting," the captain continued, ignoring Kalas. "Above those dark clouds, I saw red skies, and that's usually a good sign. I imagine it will be a long while before our paths cross again, but I'd like to believe they will! And under better circumstances!"

"Good-bye, Kávi," Náli said as she parted ways with her new friend. She hesitated, then, with a resigned sigh, *punched* his cheek with her mouth. "Like Captain said: we'll meet again!"

Dzholëf suppressed a laugh. "Farewell, friends!"

Kalas and the others debarked *Zhîamdas Salorosh* and ventured into town, weaving through Dzharasa's bustling waterfront districts while searching for an inn. Along the way, they discovered the source of the thick clouds collecting low over the city: despite the moon's choked light, several furnaces blazed in the early night's rising darkness. Hammer blows rang throughout the streets, and every strike reminded Kalas of Zhalera. Without intending to, he stopped and watched one blacksmith pound out a curved sheet of metal while another drifted holes through a glowing steel slab. The former wiped his brow and noticed Kalas' stare. He grinned and waved before returning to his work.

"Weapons?" the young man wondered aloud. "Just look at all these forges!"

"Thurën implied Ralothova was better equipped than İsriba suspected," Nïmrïk reminded him. "Obën—may he be at peace—suggested King Mödus of Gambarad had someone tainting his decisions like Marugan tainted Ësfàyami's. It makes sense that someone—some*thing*—would discolor Queen Dàgandzhu's perspective as well. Treaties, after all, are only words: their power is the threat of retaliation against faithlessness. When one party no longer fears retaliation, those words lose all their power."

Abarandal, listening, breathed a single phrase, an arpeggiated minor chord, and Kalas and Nïmrïk stumbled as a curious force pulled them toward the girl. The young man reached out to steady himself and caught her arm: when he touched her, a subtle charge traced an uncomfortable route along his nerves. He glanced at her and thought he saw the faintest trace of light fading from her narrowed eyes.

"Uh…Kalas?" Nïmrïk queried as he righted himself. Náli seemed confused, too.

He means, 'What was that?!'

"I'm fine. We're fine. We're fine, right, Abarandal?"

She seemed to return to herself, to the present, and smiled at the young man. She patted his hand, still attached to her arm: he flinched; when nothing strange happened, he blushed and let go of her.

"You're probably right," Kalas admitted, addressing Nïmrïk. "Abarandal seems to think so…I *think*. I get the sense she's *offended* by the way all these kingdoms are, well, *faithless*, like you said. No, it's not like she's surprised by it, just…saddened.

"Let's find a place for the night. In the morning, we'll figure out what's next. We'll need supplies. And horses: it's a long way to Ïsriba, and we'll never get there with enough time to make a difference if we're on foot. We need to understand what's between us: Thurën said something about fens and marshes…and spirits."

"We'll need to choose our words carefully," Nïmrïk pointed out. "When *Ralothovarinme* learn we're headed for Ïsriba, we're bound to raise a few eyebrows."

"Abarandal, you knew when you asked me to speak up about Ësfàyami that Thurën would react the way he did, didn't you?" She shrugged, raised an eyebrow of her own, and tried to hide a wry smile. "I'm not sure *how* you knew, but all right. That's probably how we need to position ourselves as we gather resources: we are unhappy subjects with grievances against the queen-regent. And it's true, too. Well, *mostly* true: unlike me and Náli, I'm not sure if either of you could rightly be considered *subjects* of any mortal authority!"

The young *Serularrin* yawned, and Kalas, succumbing, did the same.

"I'm tired, too, Náli. And hungry. I'll bet those words don't describe you two, but speaking of mortals, well…C'mon, it looks like there's an inn up ahead."

Chapter XIX

Through the Greedy Fens

"Seems like I *did* learn something from traveling with Rül," Kalas marveled as he finished tacking up his recently acquired horse, a bay stallion named Daram. He adjusted Daram's bit and massaged his withers before he swung himself into his saddle. Abarandal laughed, her notes bubbling over like an easy waterfall as she and Náli waited atop a light-colored mare named Belënshaf. Kalas blushed.

"You know, I've never heard you talk," Náli began, addressing the *erushátem*. "You don't say much, but when you do, you're always singing! I guess if I could sing like you, maybe I'd always be singing, too…"

"Náli, there are probably some things you should know," Kalas admitted as Abarandal cupped a hand over her mouth. "Tell me: have you ever heard anyone describe the world as *cracked?*"

"'Cracked'? No, I don't—Wait! Yes! Father said something about that. A long time ago. I was young: I don't remember exactly what it was. Probably because I wasn't really listening…"

"Did he ever tell you anything about a prophecy?"

"Hmm…I don't know. Again, I wasn't the best listener. Me and Niri, we thought his stories were only stories. I guess we should have listened better. Believed him more," she suggested, her eyes brimming. Kalas nudged Daram toward Belënshaf and patted her shoulder.

"I'm sure all of us could have appreciated our mothers and fathers a little more. Maybe a *lot* more, but that's not why I brought it up," he soothed. "Sifuran, the *eru* your father esteemed: he's a member of something called the Great Swath. The Seven Stars. Not too long ago, I traveled with another member of the Swath: Sharuyan—Falthwën, when I first met him. They told us there's some dread event on the horizon…They told us about a prophecy…

"Under Ïsriba, in a place they called the Vault of Stars—a place a little like the one under Serular where Sifuran met us, they summoned Abarandal. All the *Kel Erume* were supposed to be there, but Peradan—that treacherous *perayeru*—trapped Valaran within what the stars call a *singularity*. She wasn't there, under the Vault, when the stars lifted up The Song—"

"The…Song?" Náli repeated.

"Ah! Okay…Hmm…All right, The Song is, well, it's complicated! Anyway, we think because Valaran wasn't there, something went wrong with the summoning, and that's why Abarandal doesn't—can't use words. Only music. I say *'think'* because none of us knows for sure."

"So…*stars*…*summoned* Abarandal? Why? From where? Who is she?"

"Fair questions. I don't know from where, but the prophecy speaks of a *great power*, and the *erume* believe it's her. They believe I have a choice to make, and I think it'll have something to do with her: it'll have something to do with wielding this 'great power,' but I'll be honest with you: I still have no idea what that means!"

Náli didn't seem to know how to respond. She stared, awed, invisible wheels turning within her thoughts. At last, she shrugged, gripped the horn of the saddle she shared with Abarandal, and said, "All right then! Are we gonna ride toward Ïsriba, or are we gonna sit here all day?! Nïmrïk! You're sure you don't want a horse? How will you keep up? There's plenty of money left over from what Captain Dzholëf gave us!"

"I'll manage," he insisted with a sly grin. "I had a horse not too long ago. Dalafar. He's back in Lohwàlar. He…he understood me the way few others would, I think. I appreciate your concern, but I'll be fine. Navigating the fens might be easier this way, too."

"They called them the *Nimshirag Shaladme*—the Greedy Fens. What do you think they meant by that?" Kalas pondered.

"Thurën said something about *spirits,*" Náli recalled. "Maybe that has something to do with it?"

"Maybe. Kadhëmba, have you ever been through the fens?"

"Not…in recent years, lad. Nashmur mentioned *fens,* but he never said anything about *spirits.* Maybe it's just a *Poralothova* superstition?"

"Like those *töthrisme* north of Kësharan?" Kalas countered. Nimrïk offered him a dry chuckle.

"Why do you call him *Kadhëmba?*" Náli wondered. "I thought his name was Nimrïk?"

"Oh? Well, you're not wrong, I guess. Nimrïk is what he calls himself, but Kadhëmba is his given name. Someone who's, uh, known him a long time calls him that, and I guess it just stuck with me."

"You people are weird," the girl muttered with a shrug. Kalas inclined his head—*You're not wrong, Náli!*—and squeezed Daram's ribs. With a snort, he and Belënshaf carried their riders through the swirling smoke rising from Ralothova's furnaces, past the city's outskirts, and toward the northwest and its storied wetlands. Nimrïk followed at a distance for a while; then, he disappeared. When Náli noticed his absence, she said, "Stop! Stop! Nimrïk's gone!"

Kalas laughed. "He's closer than you think. He'll catch up. In fact, he might even be ahead of us. Hard to tell sometimes."

"Weird," she repeated when Kalas declined to elaborate.

. . .

A day's worth of travel took the party through flat, sandy plains studded with shallow pools, coarse grasses, and gnarled, wind-shaped scrub. By the time both suns had set, lesser vegetation gave way to older, sturdier copses surrounded by placid black water. Curious knobs resembling tree stumps polished to a matte, reddish-brown finish poked through its inky surface, providing places for strange waterfowl to alight. A stout specimen with feathery horns and intense red eyes studied them for a moment, then spread its vast wings and dissolved within the deepening sky. Eerie creaks and subtle splashes spooked the horses, and as Kalas and the others prepared a fire, Nïmrïk, who'd reappeared just before the first sun vanished, did his best to reassure them.

"I think Thurën was right," Náli shuddered. "Feels like we're being watched!"

Kalas nodded and looked around. He closed his eyes and tried to hear the subtler harmonies of the Song, to divine any presence waiting just beyond the circle of their firelight; nothing untoward tainted his perception, but he sensed Náli wasn't wholly wrong.

"Seems there aren't too many places off the main road suitable for making camp, but we'll be all right, I think," said Kalas. "We'll take turns keeping watch. I'll go first. Why don't you get some sleep? Someone'll wake you when it's your turn."

"If it's all the same, I'd rather sit with you. Just…just in case…"

"As you wish," he said, inclining his head.

With their fire nothing more than a smoldering bed of dull embers, Kalas did his best not to wake Náli as he stirred to place another log on the fire. She fell asleep with her head on his shoulder after no more than an hour or two, nearly four hours ago, he guessed. He wished he had Rül's innate sense of time. Overhead, a faint red light raced across what little sky he could see, then disappeared. It seemed familiar for some reason.

"See anything?" he whispered as wolf-Nïmrïk padded into view, his pale gold eyes catching the light.

"Nothing worth getting excited about. Náli's half-right: we *are* being watched, but not by spirits. *Edhume.* I smelled at least ten people, but there could be more: the scents in this place are strange. Confusing. I don't think we need to alter our plans, our route, but I thought you'd like to know."

"Yeah, of course. I wonder if they're just curious, or if they're waiting for us to venture deeper into these fens before they try something?"

"I'm sure we'll find out," concluded Nïmrïk. "Now then, why don't you get some sleep? I promise I'll wake you if the watchers demonstrate ill intent."

"Yeah, okay," Kalas yawned. "Náli fell asleep a few hours ago. I think. I'm not sure what time it is. Anyway, she still doesn't know about your…Maybe it's not a good idea for her to wake up to a wolf patrolling our camp?"

Nïmrïk curled his lips into a parody of a human grin, his canines glistening red and white in the fire- and starlight. "Probably not," he conceded.

When morning came, Kalas woke to find the others finishing breakfast and packing up their things. Abarandal handed him a bowl of lukewarm oatmeal, which he devoured in seconds while studying their lingering fire, its few remaining coals oscillating between ash gray and purple-orange. Kalas took his bowl toward the dark water, rinsed it with a splash, and was about to fill it again when the surface boiled just a few feet in front of him. Startled, he tried to stand, but the muddy bank proved too slippery, and he fell.

A huge, rough-skinned creature surged from beneath the water and snapped at him with long, many-toothed jaws: had he *not* slipped, the beast might have bitten into his arm. He didn't remember screaming, but he must have, or Abarandal must have heard the commotion, because she was there, Kalas' sword in hand. When it lunged again, she tossed his weapon to him; he caught it just in time to point it at the monster's fast-approaching maw. The beast's momentum carried it onto Kalas' outstretched blade, burying it between the fleshy folds in its mouth. The young man's arm seemed to disappear as jagged teeth scraped his flesh, but when his sword perforated the monster's skull behind and between its protuberant eyes, it twitched, then lay still.

Kalas jumped back with a shout, blood dripping from the torn skin on his arm. Abarandal ripped a corner from her tunic and wrapped it around the wound while the young man willed himself to stop trembling. Nïmrïk and Náli came running, and he realized what felt like long minutes had to have been just a few seconds. When the pair arrived, Náli gasped: "It must be twelve feet long! How did you—? Is that…is that your *sword* poking out of its head?!"

"I…yeah, I guess it is," he admitted. "I just came down here to rinse my bowl, get some water to put out the fire! If Abarandal hadn't gotten here when she did…"

"Strange," Nïmrïk said, having knelt to examine the carcass. "I wonder what it's doing so far inland. I guess this swamp is larger than I remember—I *did* tell you it's been a long time since I've been in this part of the world! You did well, lad: it takes precise aim to kill an alligator with a single blow like this!" With a knife of his own, he pried a few of the animal's larger teeth from their sockets.

"A what? So it's not some kind of dragon? Anyway, I didn't aim, I just—you know what? I don't care! I'm just glad my arm is still—Oh! That hurts!"

Kalas winced as his wounds throbbed. Abarandal insisted

he would heal without any permanent damage. As she sang, she twined her fingers through the air around his arm: maybe it was nothing more than a well-timed breeze, but cold seemed to penetrate the makeshift bandage she'd applied, followed by heat and a subtle sting. He jerked back, and she held up her hands and smiled.

Nimrïk wrenched Kalas' sword from the creature's skull, wiped it on a tuft of marsh grass, and handed it back to the young man, along with the teeth he'd pulled. He ran his fingers across the hard, spiky scutes on the deceased animal's spine and shook his head. "These teeth: you should wear them around your neck—you've earned it! The rest of it, well, it's a shame to let it go to waste…"

"You mean…you mean you wanna *eat it?!*"

"It's good meat, lad," Nimrïk defended. "Maybe a little tough, but good nonetheless. Still, we're not prepared to process it: we lack both time and proper equipment. And speaking of time, we really should get going. How's your arm?"

"It's…wow, actually, it feels pretty good! Abarandal, I don't know what you did, but thank you!"

"Could you, say, wield a sword, if you needed to?"

"I—Hmm. Let's see…"

Kalas adjusted his grip on *Sharuyandas Tshandu* and mimed a few up-and-down strikes. He nodded and extended his range of motion, tracing elaborate patterns in the air before returning it to the sheath Sifuran provided him. Náli watched, awed with his movements, and he blushed.

"If I needed to," he allowed.

Nimrïk smiled and looked around, tasting the atmosphere and peering into the shadows. "Good! Come then: time is fleeting, and Ïsriba's still a long way from here."

2.

As the fens deepened, each day seemed little more than a bleak interruption between nights, the suns-light blunted to nothing more than a drab gray respite from the dark. None of the watchers revealed themselves, but Kalas—even Náli—sensed their presence creeping ever nearer the fringes of their fires. He hoped that was a good sign. On occasion, wisps of blue light hovered among the trees: Náli insisted it was spirits; Nïmrïk insisted it was something else, something benign. The young *Serularrin* remained unconvinced. The road, recognizable as such when they started out from Dzharasa, was now a narrow trail—barely wide enough for a horse—through low branches wreathed with dangling moss.

"Is this the only road through the fens?" Kalas wondered aloud one day, about a week out from Dzharasa. "I wonder how long ago Nashmur traveled through here. Were things this bad back then?"

"We haven't passed any intersections," Nïmrïk assured him. He stopped, raised a hand, and Kalas and Abarandal reined in their mounts. "Starting from Dzharasa, it seems this route was our only choice. Perhaps the quiet people who've kept pace with us since then would be willing to offer a word of advice?"

The *egu* waited without moving for several long minutes. The thick, almost palpable silence reminded Kalas of the forest east of Lohwàlar. At last, a filthy-looking man with a mud-caked beard rose up from the mire. He stood beside the road, regarding his summoner with clear, intelligent eyes—piercing blue surrounded with dark gray.

"Well met, friend," Nïmrïk began, his voice calm and measured. "You've nothing to fear from us, as I imagine you've discovered, having had your eye on us all this time."

The man said nothing. Kalas' neck tingled, and he risked a glance toward the right, where another dirtied figure emerged from behind a tree. He thought about saying something, alerting Nïmrïk, but the *egu* pivoted the ball of his foot ever-so-slightly, and Kalas knew the newcomer's arrival hadn't gone unnoticed. From the corner of his eye, he glimpsed several other forms distill from their environment. Their "leader," the first to reveal himself, drew a chipped and battered sword. He held it in a low, nonthreatening manner as he held his ground.

"Hey! That's a *Poyïsriba* sword!" Kalas blurted when he spied specks of emerald in its falconine pommel. Its wielder shifted his attention toward the young man, and Kalas tensed. He adjusted his center of gravity and moved to draw his own sword when Nïmrïk spoke again:

"*De,* lad! That won't be necessary! Will it, friend? *Friends,* I mean?"

"Maybe you're not familiar with the lore," the mud-man said at last, his voice barely above a whisper. "The *Nimshirag Shaladme* are a dangerous place. A *hungry* place."

"You're right," Nïmrïk agreed. "We've heard about the 'spirits' that…protect this place? That's you? Your friends? I assure you: we have no quarrel with you, *shaladilmukritme:* we're simply passing through."

"This road leads to Ïsriba. Nowhere else. And you're familiar with the Falcon—the young man, at least: he knows their swords! What's your business there? What's so important that you'd brave the Greedy Fens?"

"Our friends' lives!" Kalas said. "They're in trouble—or they will be, if they get caught! Assuming they haven't *already* been caught!"

"Caught?" the leader repeated, his voice hitched with a trace of uncertainty. Several other mud-men exchanged puzzled glances.

"Look," Nïmrïk continued, "you had ample time to harm us, to rob us—even to murder us, if you wanted to, ever since we entered the fens. Once, long ago, maybe, you called Ïsriba home—I can tell from your accent. Maybe you served in Queen Ësfàyami's military, unless that sword you carry belonged—"

"*Never!*" the man spat and raised his sword.

"One of the friends I mentioned is King Rufàran!" Kalas revealed as he dismounted Daram and adopted Nïmrïk's raised-hand posture.

"Impossible!" someone else retorted. "The wolves he was hunting murdered him and all his *kindume* many Sevens ago!"

"It's true! I swear!" Kalas insisted. "He and Shosafin were on their way back to confront the queen-regent, to—"

"Shosafin?!" the leader said, shaken. "How do you know that name?!"

"It's a long story. You probably won't believe me, but we—I met him in Lohwàlar, a tiny town in the far West. He was part of an investigation: we'd been attacked by *rudzhegume*. We traveled together for a while, then he, uh, had other things to do. Anyway, we ended up in the far North, west of Melash, where we discovered—among other things—King Rufàran, trapped within what the *erume* call a 'singularity.' On our way back, we were attacked by Marugan, but—"

"Marugan?!"

"—but Shosafin managed to *unmake* him, I think. Marugan, you know, judging from your reaction: they said he died along with King Rufàran. He didn't. He's…he's a dark star, an *eku*, and he's been poisoning the queen-regent's mind. They were on their way to Ïsriba when we learned that Peradan, once a member of the Great Swath, was there. Peradan's the one who captured the king all those years ago! They don't know he's there, and they have no way to defend against his wiles: he's *ilalasdra*, after all. Please, we just need to get to Ïsriba to make sure they're safe!"

"You're saying all the right things," the fen-dwelling man admitted. "Maybe you're more cunning than you seem? If what you say about King Rufàran, Marugan—even Peradan is true, and even if you reach them before they cross paths with an *ilalasdra*, how do you hope to make a difference?"

"I have Peradan's sword—a sword forged by the *eru* and Swath member Valaran, before that *perayeku* consigned her to a singularity," Kalas informed him as he drew the weapon from its scabbard. He held it aloft, and even in the reluctant light of the muted suns, its crystalline center glowed with white-orange fire. The mud-men voiced a collective gasp, and he continued, "Shosafin drove this sword through Marugan's face: if necessary, I believe it'll cut down Peradan, too."

"If you're *really* on your way to oust the queen-regent, we can show you—"

"Danak! Enough!" the leader shouted at the young man who'd approached Kalas and the others.

"But Ësra, haven't we been waiting for this day? You've told the story many times, how you and the others *knew*, once the king was dead, once the child princess gained the throne, that she would destroy the Falcon from within. You were right about that. And the fens are all I've ever known—they're all most of us have ever known, but I remember the tales my mother told me before she died, her memories of Ïsriba under King Rufàran's rule. Ësra, if King Rufàran regains his throne—if we *help him* regain his throne…Wouldn't that be better than hiding in these swamps?"

"I'll never return to that way of life!" Ësra roared, his eyes flashing and nostrils flaring. He raised his sword. Toward Danak.

"So stay here!" someone else shouted. A woman of about three or four Sevens, Kalas guessed: it was hard to tell under all that mud. "I remember the stories, too. And I remember Vrila: if we lived in the city with all its resources, your wife would probably still be alive!"

"How *dare* you speak her name!" Ësra fumed. "Vrila would have *never—"*

"Who do you think told me those stories in the first place?!" the woman interrupted.

"Mister Ësra. Please. It's not our intention to divide your people: we just want—" Nïmrïk tried to interject, but Ësra cut him off:

"Except that's exactly what you've done! No, *none of us* will help you! And *none of us* will leave the fens! I've killed to protect my people before, and I'll do it again!" he screamed, his eyes ablaze with manic fury. He aimed his sword at Nïmrïk and charged.

"Stop!" Danak shouted as he stepped in front of Ësra's attack. Berserk, the mud-men leader didn't notice the young man until his blade pierced his abdomen and dropped him to the ground. Ësra struggled for a moment until he realized what he'd done.

"Danak? *Danak!*" he cried and reached for the young man's hand.

"I only wanted…" Danak wheezed through bloody bubbles popping on his lips.

"That's it!" one of the fen-folk shouted. "He's gone too far!" roared another. They swarmed the bewildered man.

"Enough!" thundered Nïmrïk as he exploded in a storm of black smoke and shredded flesh. Several *shaladilmukritme* fell back at the presence of such a creature. The horses reared and Náli screamed, prompting Abarandal to whisper a soothing refrain.

"Out of my way!" Kalas demanded as he pushed his way toward Danak. He grasped his free hand and said, "Look at me! *Look* at me!" The wounded man didn't seem to hear. Kalas closed his eyes and searched the Song for healing strains.

This is bad. This is really *bad,* he admitted. Ësra's sword remained embedded in Danak's body: if someone removed it, Kalas intuited, his internal bleeding would be unstoppable. *Abarandal, I need you! I can't see a way through this…*

The stargirl was beside him, her hand on his, but still the fen-dweller's injury seemed untreatable.

I don't know if we can heal this, he confessed inside her mind. She tightened her grip and whispered a few reassuring phrases. Kalas grit his teeth and willed Danak's lacerated lung, liver, and attendant blood vessels to weave themselves together. *They won't—they can't heal with that sword in the way, but if it's removed...*

Abarandal squeezed his hand, grabbed Ësra's hilt, and eased the blade from the young man's body, her song brighter. Bolder.

I'm glad you think so, Kalas thought, and furrowed his brow as he caressed Danak's veins and arteries with the Song. The young fen-dweller cried out. Several others demanded to know what was going on: Nïmrïk snarled and circled the trio, holding everyone at bay.

"Danak, I'm sorry!" Kalas said, opening his eyes and choking back tears. "The sword cut through too many things—I can *see* what I need to do, but I don't know what to do first. If I put things back together in the wrong order, I might do more harm than good!"

"I don't know what you're talking about," Danak wheezed, his breathing short and clipped. "I just know...I'm...I...Mother? Where did you...?"

He's dying! He's—Did Zhalera feel these things when she—? No! I can't think about that now! I have to focus! *C'mon, Kalas!* See *the patterns!* Ilun! Su pirathëthu—vilin yamalu!

Kalas closed his eyes again and focused on the largest vessels; he traced supernal sutures through the corner of Danak's perforated lung and rent liver, drawing the working ends taut until each separate surface returned to its rightful place. Danak's breathing seemed slower, deeper, more controlled, and Kalas thought everything would be all right—until the young man opened his eyes wide and arched his back. He screamed, and for a moment, Kalas saw Ëlbodh in his tortured frame.

"Abarandal! What—?! I don't understand!" Kalas wailed as

fresh blood spurted from Danak's wound. His breathing lost its measured cadence and his frantic eyes lost their focus. Kalas clapped his hand atop the bleeding orifice and willed white hot light from his fingers. The sweet reek of burning flesh assaulted his nostrils, but he didn't care. He thought he heard someone cry out for him to stop. Náli, maybe? One of the fen-folk? Abarandal touched his shoulders, but he wouldn't move.

"Please," Danak breathed at last, struggling to push Kalas' hand away. "Please…just…just *let me go…*"

"No! I can't! I *won't!* I have to heal you! I have to fix this! I *have* to!" he sobbed.

As he died, Danak smiled, and Kalas saw his mother in the departed man's expression.

"Why?" he mumbled. "Why didn't it work? Everything was *right!* I could *see* what I needed to do—I *did it!* It *should* have been enough, but…but it wasn't! Why?"

Abarandal draped her hands around his neck and held him close, letting sobs of her own shake her tiny frame.

"Lad, you did what you could. Sometimes The Song will not bend itself to our wills—no matter how noble we deem our intentions. We are not the Creator. We are *his instruments.* You know this. You did what you could. Let that be enough…"

Kalas let Abarandal hold him. He nodded. He knew the *egu* was right, but that didn't make it any easier to reconcile facts with his frustration.

"I'm sorry, Danak," he wept. "I'm sorry."

3.

"Ësra!" the woman accused as she rushed at him and pummeled his chest. Some of the mud caking him had dried and flaked away, and Kalas gained a better picture of just how many Sevens he'd acquired. "Ësra, you—this is unconscionable! Unforgivable! What do you—?!"

"You're right," the fen-dweller admitted, his confession naught but a choked whisper. "You're right, Pelan. Danak was right! *O shelu fie id nir!*"

"Danak deserved better than this!" someone wept.

"You're right!" Ësra cried with a hitch in his voice. "I fled— I abandoned Ïsriba to escape a selfish, authoritarian queen, and look—*look* at what I've become! I...I should have listened! I should have been less fearful! Maybe Danak..."

"Unconscionable? Maybe," Kalas said, extracting himself from Abarandal's embrace and wiping his eyes. "Unforgivable? No. I don't believe that. Maybe—"

"Well, he won't find forgiveness *here!*" Pelan huffed. Several others grunted their agreement.

"Look, I'm not saying pretend like nothing happened!" Kalas explained, "I mean—"

"No, sir, she's right. They're all right. The Greedy Fens have been my home for too many Sevens now. It's changed the way I think, the way I see people. I'm like that alligator I watched you kill: I evaluate, size up the situation, and *attack*. I deserve a sword through the roof of the mouth, too. Like he said: Danak deserved better than this..."

"You were a captain in King Rufàran's army, Ësra," someone else reminded him. "You knew your way around Ïsriba's secrets better than any of us. You wanna prove yourself? Go with them! Get them inside! Help them find their friends—the king you pledged your service to, if the boy's word is good!"

"If you choose to stay," Pelan smoldered, "you'll be an outcast, a nameless trespasser unwelcome in any of our circles."

Ësra said nothing, and an uncomfortable silence descended over the fens; at last, he nodded, sighed, and acquiesced: "You've been my family for all these Sevens. Your judgment, while harsh, is probably not harsh enough. I will do as you say. For Danak."

As the *shaladilmukritme* returned to the mud and shadows from which they'd emerged, Ësra remained kneeling on the ground, Danak's dead hand in his. Nïmrïk approached him, nudged his shoulder with his snout, and growled, "Come on, friend. What little light there is won't last forever. Help me tend to this brave young man; then, lead us toward Ïsriba."

"Our custom has been to return our dead to the fens," Ësra said, unconcerned with Nïmrïk's lupine form. "I'll show you."

"You're an *egu*," Náli stated when they resumed their journey. "Father told us about such beings, but we thought he was just telling stories. He told us *egume* were evil spirits held in the Accursèd's thrall. But he told us they had black fur and reeked of sulfur: you're silver!"

"He wasn't wrong," Nïmrïk admitted. "The rest of my kind do serve the will and whims of Ilnëshras. I did too, a long, *long* time ago. Like Ësra here, I also hope to be forgiven one day: like him, I can't return home, either.

"My wolfskin used to be black: it's only been silver for a little while. I don't know why. I thought perhaps I'd earned a measure of redemption, but someone said it wasn't because of anything I'd done. I don't know what she meant, but her words held the ring of truth."

Kalas wanted to say something, but he struggled to find the right words and grunted his frustration instead.

"You disagree?" Náli queried, catching Kalas' mood.

"I'm not an *elu*, like Nanësra, the 'someone' he's referring to, but I don't think she meant what she said the way Kadhëmba thinks she meant it. She knew him when he was an *elu*, too: *Kadhëmba* was his name back then. When she calls him by his given name, he thinks she's mocking him, reminding him of everything he's lost. When *I* call him Kadhëmba, I'm trying to remind him who he might be again someday. Like I said, I'm not an *elu*, but that's what I think Nanësra means.

"How did you cross paths with one another?" Náli asked, and Kalas told her about the Night of Angry Wolves, about Thosha and Ïsriba and Nïmrïk's selflessness within its dungeons.

"So you've been in Ïsriba's dungeons?" Ësra observed, having listened as the young man recounted his experiences.

"Last winter," Kalas affirmed. "One Commander Nashmur, Shosafin's cousin, locked us up down there. Later, he helped us escape—he's the one who sent word that Peradan had been seen in Ïsriba."

"I know the name," Ësra said. He turned and looked up at Kalas with a conflicted expression. At last, he added: "All right, I'm going to trust you. I don't know why, but what choice do I have? The fen-folk have rejected me—and rightly so. Perhaps my death between the talons of the queen-regent will redeem my name among them? No, that's not what's important…

"If you've spent any time in the dungeons, then you know how convoluted they are! There's a network of passageways under everything, hidden behind cleverly-devised façades. Ësfàyami knows about them, I'm sure, and it's possible she's blocked them off, but they are your best chance to get inside Ïsriba's walls without detection."

Abarandal performed a simple tune, and Kalas chuckled, "That's right, isn't it?" Ësra cocked his head, and the young man continued: "While trying to escape, Nashmur led us down a dead-end corridor. He seemed surprised. Maybe that was one of those façades you were talking about? Don't worry about whether such routes are blocked: just get us there—I think we'll manage."

Ësra nodded and focused on the road ahead. As he walked,

without looking back again, he asked, "You did something after I…
when Danak was pierced through. You seemed surprised when he
died anyway. The woman on the horse sang a song, but how could
mere music heal a wound like that?"

"Do you know about The Song? Creation's Prayer, they call it
in the North?"

"*Zhi Helim?* Seems I've heard about it. Something to do with
magic, right?"

"Not exactly," Kalas corrected, and explained to Ësra what he'd
learned from Falthwën. "I tried to use The Song to heal Danak.
Once, before I knew what I was doing, I helped an *eru* heal Shosafin after Marugan cut him open; another time, I stopped him
from bleeding out when Marugan cut off his arm. I used it to heal
Kadhëmba when cannibals had wounded him under Deridzhas.

"Another time, Abarandal—'the woman on the horse'—helped
me use The Song to cure my…my *grandfather* from a sickness in his
lungs and bones—but I ended up paralyzing him from the waist
down. I don't know why I—of all people—hear The Song. And I
don't know exactly how to use it. Maybe there *isn't* an *exact* way to
use it. Falthwën—Sharuyan, the *eru* I was talking about, likened
exercising the privilege to conducting an orchestra. I was *sure* I
could fix Danak's injury, but, well…"

"I'm sorry, it sounds like I'm blaming *you* for what *I* did to
him. That's not what I meant. I just…" Ësra sighed. "I just wish I'd
listened…"

Nïmrïk, still wearing his *otherform,* muttered, "I wish I *hadn't*
listened! I've had millennia to rue my weakness of spirit when the
'*usmawinadath*' entreated me to join his rebellion. Don't get me
wrong: I stopped blaming him for my decisions a long time ago;
still, the consequence remains."

"Well, it'll be another week, at least, before we're even close,"
Ësra informed them, abandoning the subject. *Or reflecting on it,*

Kalas surmised. "I know a few places where we can shelter between here and there. I know it looks dark now, but we still have a few hours before the suns *really* set. Let's make the most of what light remains. This way."

Several nights came and went, sometimes brightened with strange bouts of flickering blue-violet fire rising above the swamps. Ësra admitted the *shosakalme* were largely benign: the fen-dwellers, he said, seized every opportunity to integrate the phenomena with their efforts to dissuade travelers from spending too much time within the Greedy Fens; and, exuding a deep sense of introspection, he admitted he'd resorted to killing on those rare occasions when his ploys had been discovered. From Kalas' perspective, it seemed the aftermath of Danak's murder had forced Ësra to confront the man he'd become while living in the fens. He'd likened himself to an alligator—and not in a positive way.

The road widened between ancient conifers and rocky out-croppings as the fens and marshes disappeared. A day later, the gentle slope became an aggressive rise; the ground, wet for so long, turned hard and dry, delighting Daram and Belënshaf with its predictability.

"Turn here," Ësra instructed one morning. Kalas looked around, unsure what he meant. Abarandal and Náli seemed similarly per-plexed: even Nïmrïk cocked his head as he tasted the air for clues.

"We're still a few days out from Ïsriba, yes, but long ago, there used to be a secret path through these woods, hidden behind these rocks. I doubt it's been used in many Sevens, and it might be over-grown—I'd be surprised if it wasn't—but it's our best bet to enter the castle undetected."

It took the horses a few tries to find safe places for their hooves as they picked their way across the rocks, but after a few hours, Kalas discerned the remnants of discreetly-situated flagstones woven along the forest floor. Their pace, reasonable even through the fens, had slowed to naught but a crawl as they hacked through underbrush and low branches to clear the way.

We don't have time for this! he fumed in silence. Abarandal surprised him when she countered with a few notes inside his thoughts.

I know, he admitted: *we can't take the main road—is it still the King's Highway? The queen-regent is sure to have eyes all around.*

"Ësra," he said aloud, "Are we still in Ralothova? I mean, are we still within Queen Dàgandzhu's realm, or have we crossed into Ïsriba?"

"Depends who you ask," he replied. "By treaty, we're still in Ralothova's domain, but even in Rufàran's day, no one contested the boundary too hotly. It's mostly unusable, and the Falcon and the Whale have been allies for so long that neither pays too much attention to this place."

Before the day elapsed, Ësra brought them to a field of talus at the base of a steep bluff. Thick roots twined around heavy granite slabs, now peppered with twigs and lichen. The suns, low in the western sky—behind a distant ridge, anyway—cast peculiar shadows between the rocks as the former fen-dweller beckoned everyone to follow him into darkness. The horses whinnied, reluctant to obey, and Kalas wished Rül were with them. He dismounted and suggested Abarandal and Náli do the same. With excessive reassurance, he persuaded Daram to trust him; after that, Belënshaf fell in behind.

"Wait here. Keep quiet," Ësra instructed when everyone had joined him under the largest rock. "I'll be right back."

As the old man walked into obfuscating darkness, Kalas studied the object under which he and the others stood. At first, he assumed some natural event had lodged the irregular block of stone in its horizontal position above the mouth of the cave-like space; however, he grew less certain the longer he examined it. Indeed, when he considered the entire scene, when he pictured it without its pine-needle carpet and haphazard distribution of trees, it seemed possible someone had designed it to look the way it did.

No one would ever know…

"Okay, this way," Ësra said, reappearing without a sound. Kalas jumped. "Seems no one's been here for a long, long time. You have torches, yes? Lamps, maybe?"

The young man nodded, rifled through his pack, and handed out torches. *Falthwën's staff would be nice to have right now!* he acknowledged as he struck sparks from flint. The fen-dweller led them down an imprecise flight of stairs and stopped when he reached a heavy iron door built into the walls. Kalas played his torch across its rusted surfaces and tried to move it: he was unsurprised when it didn't budge. Daram whinnied, uncomfortable in the constrained corridor.

"I couldn't get it open, either, but between the five of us—and two horses—I think we can clear the way. This is good, though: maybe no one in the queen-regent's employ knows about these passages! Come now, let's get this door opened. If you—"

"Wait," Nïmrïk said as he backed up, dug in his hind paws, and vaulted toward the barrier. It didn't give way completely, but parts of it bent, loosing bits of rock from around its frame as the *rudzhegu* rebounded and shook his head.

"Ësra's right," Kalas winced on Nïmrïk's behalf. "I'll bet Daram can pull—"

"One more time," he insisted with a shake of his head. His silver fur rippled in the torchlight as he collected himself and lunged again. With an angry snarl and his eyes aglow, he collided with the pitted iron lattice, which sheared away from its fittings with tortured creaks and groans. The noise of clanging metal echoed down the long, dark tunnel ahead of them.

"Well, if anyone *does* know about this place, we'll cross paths real soon," Náli muttered.

Nïmrïk hesitated for a moment, shook his head again and let the tremor cascade the length of his body, then sniffed the dust-choked air.

"I don't smell anyone," he said, "but that doesn't mean we shouldn't be careful!"

"There may be more barriers like this—no, there *will* be," Ësra reminded them. "Some designed to look just like the stone walls surrounding us. I suspect they won't give way as easily as this old door—assuming we can even find them!"

"We'll find them," Kalas assured him. He drew his sword and gestured down the torchlit corridor: "Lead on."

"This way," Ësra said.

4.

Several hours later, the ground rumbled and rocked the dim passage; chips of stone and sheets of dust clouded the stale air. When questioned, neither Ësra nor Nïmrïk had an explanation. Kalas said something about the queen-regent's construction projects and wondered if her crews might have discovered—or upset—something underground: images from under Deridzhas raced across his mind's eye.

"I rarely ventured beyond Thosha in recent years, but I did hear stories," Nïmrïk replied. "It's amazing what people will talk about after a few beers! Several complained about all the *digging* the queen-regent had going on. It's been dozens—maybe hundreds of Sevens since it's done anything, but Ïsriba sits atop the remnants of an ancient volcano. I shudder to think what might happen if Ësfàyami's 'projects' disrupt the order of things under the earth…I guess we'll find out soon enough!"

"Sooner than you think," Ësra said: "we're here."

"We're where?!" Náli ran her hands along the wall. "'Here' looks just like the rest of the tunnel!"

"By design," Ësra smiled. "Follow it all the way to the end and you'll end up just outside Âivambar—assuming you know what to look for. We've passed a few such places on our way here, each hidden like this one. Let me see…"

The fen-dweller ran his hand across the mortared stonework, searching for something that proved elusive. He frowned and admitted, "These exits were designed to be accessed from *inside* the dungeons, for people seeking a way out. There are pivots inside the wall here, but the locks can only be triggered from the other side. I'm sorry: I should have remembered…"

Abarandal sang to Kalas, who nodded and stood alongside Ësra. He also examined the wall; finding thin grooves choked with years of dust and grime, he sheathed his sword and ran his knife along their edges. When he'd traced its perimeter, he called the young woman to his side and said, "Between here…and here. Probably no more than a few feet thick, but that's just a guess."

She nodded and closed her eyes. With her hand raised, she traced the outline Kalas had described; satisfied, she drew back—

"What's she—?" Náli managed before Abarandal thrust her hand toward the wall and unleashed a silver wave of power. It ripped through the stones, shearing them from their concealed pivots and rocketing them into the connecting passage. When the dust settled, when everyone stopped coughing, Kalas stepped toward the opening and swept his torch from side to side. Grinning, he invited the others to join him.

"Great work!" he said. Turning toward Ësra, he asked, "How far are we from the dungeons? Do you think anyone heard that?"

"Unlikely. We're still about a league out; still, probably a good idea to stay alert. All right, let's go. I'll remind you, though: the closer we get to the dungeons proper, the more convoluted these passages become! It's been Sevens since I've been here, and, honestly, I'll be surprised if I remember every twist and turn!"

Nïmrïk sniffed the air, sneezed, and said, "We'll manage."

"I have no idea how long we've been down here," Kalas admitted as they dismantled yet another hidden wall, the third (or fourth?) since they'd gone underground. The atmosphere turned warm, *hot,* really, and the young man wiped sweat from his brow. Even in the dark, he felt Ësra stiffen for just a moment, as though he'd inferred Kalas' statement as a slight intended against him. "I'm sure we're almost there though, right?"

"I…I'll confess I thought we'd be there by now," said the old man as he scratched his balding head. "It's possible I miscalculated. I'm sorry…"

"We *are* close," Nïmrïk asserted. "The air has a new taste to it. Reminds me of that night in the cell next to yours, lad. Your noses will pick it up soon enough, I suspect. It's not a *pleasant* taste, that's for sure! Let's keep moving!"

Maybe an hour later—Kalas wasn't sure—Nïmrïk paused, bent his face toward the ground and took a deep breath. He cocked his head and craned his neck: listening, it seemed, but for what?

"Kadhëmba?" Kalas whispered when the *egu* didn't speak, didn't move.

"Voices, lad! Faint, but voices nonetheless. We're not alone down here!"

"What do we do?" Náli wheezed. "There's nowhere to go except back the way we came, and there's nowhere to hide! We're sure to be discovered!"

"I only smell…two, maybe three people," Nïmrïk assured her. "Between all of us, I think we'll manage. Even if they're *Poyïsriba* elites, these close quarters will hamper their maneuverability.

"Náli, take the horses' reins. Keep your distance. We can't afford for them to run off should something spook them! One of us will come for you when…we've dealt with things."

"Why me? Why do *I* have to wait with the horses?!" she pouted.

"Ësra, for all his Sevens, is a *Poyïsriba* soldier; Kalas knows his way around a sword—he learned from one of the best; Abarandal is an *eru;* and me? Well, look at me!"

"Yeah, okay, when you put it like *that*…" she muttered.

Nïmrïk was right about the smell. Within fifteen, twenty minutes, the dungeons' distinct reek permeated Kalas' nostrils. He heard the voices now, too, barely audible to his human ears.

"I think they're lost, too," Ësra smiled. "That's the gist of their conversation, as best I understand it. Seems they've come from the west…from…Âivambar! Gentlemen, I am sorry! We've walked well beyond the castle!"

"We'll figure it out later," said Nïmrïk: "they've heard us, it seems! They know we're here. There's no point in postponing the inevitable: come on, let's get this over with!"

Kalas drew his sword again and followed Nïmrïk's easy lope through the tunnel; soon, he heard footsteps. It sounded like the other party was hastening toward them as well. Moments later, a dull orange smear of light bobbed into view along the passage and glinted from what the young man assumed to be swords. Nïmrïk folded back his ears and growled, his hackles raised and his bushy tail tucked between his legs. Ësra tensed, raised his sword, and shifted his weight to his back foot. Abarandal made no sound, but Kalas felt the fine hairs on his arms and neck bristle; he felt a subtle *push* as she gathered her strength for battle. He raised his own sword and braced for the attack.

That's when Nïmrïk *laughed.*

"Kadhëmba! Why are you—*Rufàran?! Shosafïn?!* What are you—? How did you—?!"

Kalas dropped his sword, rushed upon the surprised figure, and wrapped his arms around him. It took Shosafin a moment, but he patted the young man's back with his remaining arm and exclaimed, "I should ask you the same questions! No one but the king and his most trusted servants knows about these tunnels! I—how did *you* find them?!"

Before he could explain, Ësra pushed his way toward Rufàran and stared: after a beat, he let go of his sword, dropped to his knees, and cried, "It *is* you, isn't it, my liege?! The boy spoke the truth! I dared not believe it, but here you are! Whole and hale and not a day older than that black day when we learned you'd disappeared!"

The old fen-dweller held out his hands, but before the king could take them, Shosafin brushed Kalas aside and slapped Ësra with the flat of his sword: "Who dares to violate the king's person?"

"My name is Captain—"

"Ësra!" Rufàran finished. "Ësra, is it really you? You have my captain's eyes, but so much else has changed!"

"Aye, it's me, sire. Forgive my indiscretion, but the Sevens under your daughter's rule have been most unkind. I could not submit myself to her whims, and so I and several others escaped Ïsriba and hid ourselves among the fens northwest of Ralothova. I...I believed you dead. I ceased to hope for the Falcon's future. In my despair, I've done...horrible things. I am unworthy to return to Ïsriba, but it's enough to know that her king indeed lives—and that he's returned to reclaim his throne! I'll find solace in that fact. *Revehwa ihi Kàsh! Á salorosh i ëligarihath!*"

"Ësra...it is good to see another familiar face—another *loyal* face, no matter the years between! You were a hardy soldier in your day: perhaps there's one more fight in you? If even a fraction of the things I've heard about my daughter are true, I suspect we'll spill much blood before we reach her..." Rufàran shook his head, as if he hoped to shake the taste of the unpleasant truth from his lips.

"My liege, you flatter me with your words, but I am an old man now! My sword is tired, too: after many Sevens of chopping wood, protecting the fens, and…murdering an innocent young man, it's time I lay it down forever. Perhaps it's fitting that you who gave it to me should receive it again? Please, let me return to my people—to the fen-folk, I mean—and tell them what the boy said was true! I'm no longer welcome there, but they deserve to know. It might be the last good deed I have left in me."

"If that's your wish—your penance, I won't deny you," Rufàran granted after appraising his former captain and helping him to his feet. "You say you murdered an innocent man, yet I hear the remorse in your voice. Even in this dim light, I see it in your eyes. Yes, go, and with my blessing."

"Thank you, my liege," Ësra wept. He presented his hilt and placed Rufàran's hand on its worn grip, wrapped in tatters of alligator hide instead of its original green leather. The king accepted it, and as the fen-dweller turned to go, he added, "I'll tell Náli it's safe to join you. Thank you again for—"

"*Náli* is with you?!" Shosafin said, forgetting to camouflage his surprise. Rufàran laughed: "Náli? That firebrand from Serular? Somehow I'm not surprised!"

"Uh, Mister Ësra? Why don't you take Daram and Belënshaf with you? Horses are no use to us down here, and I'll bet the fen-folk could put them to work."

"Are you sure? What happens when you reach the castle? If things don't go well, won't you need—"

"If things don't go well, we'll be dead," predicted Shosafin, his face grim.

5.

"How are you two *here*?" Kalas tried to piece together while they waited for Náli to catch up. "I thought you would have reached

Ïsriba weeks ago! And Nashmur—you didn't see him on his way back from Thosha?"

"Nashmur? No, we didn't," said Shosafin with a frown. "We didn't cross paths with anyone except a few westbound riders, and we kept ourselves hidden from them! Ah, I see now: perhaps one of them was Nashmur? But why would he leave Thosha? Wouldn't he—"

"Peradan!" Kalas interrupted. "Peradan was seen at the castle! We heard he's taken Marugan's place! I'll be honest: I thought he would have discovered you by now, murdered you, probably! That's why we came east, through Ralothova—we thought it would take too long coming over land. And Ralothova! Nashmur said they were a peaceful people, but they're prepared for war. *Well*-prepared! It seemed everyone who could hold a hammer was over an anvil!"

"Peradan!" Rufàran raged. "I suppose I shouldn't be surprised!"

"We made reasonable time, but we weren't as fast as I'd hoped," Shosafin began. "The foul winds coming down from the Death-Bringing Mountain forced us south of the Highway. You remember how poorly maintained the Highway was? The roads we had to use were much worse!

"We made it to Thosha without further incident, but Ësfàyami's soldiers were everywhere. Her architects, too, devising improved fortifications, judging from what little information we could gather. I thought about getting word to Nashmur's friend Yëlisha, but I didn't want to risk it, so we kept to the shadows. Our horses were tired, near exhaustion, and so we spent about a week gathering intelligence while they healed. After that, we avoided Âivambar completely and did our best to disguise our appearances."

"We headed for these passages," the king continued. "On our way here, we did meet a wild-eyed couple fleeing from Ïsriba. They were too young to recognize me, probably too distracted to care anyway: they were desperate, and so we gave them some of our supplies in exchange for their story.

"At first, when they saw our swords, they thought we'd come to kill them: it took some doing to persuade them otherwise…They told us—and it breaks my heart to admit it, but they told us several people had tried to flee the capital after the queen closed all the gates, coerced every industry to bolster her war machine, and conscripted every able-bodied man and woman for her military. These two had started out with eight others, but they assumed they'd all been killed or captured; indeed, they fled when a soldier grabbed another young man and ran him through with his sword…"

"We told them to head west, taking pains to keep clear of the main roads, to keep clear of everyone until they reached the Áthradho. I have no idea if they'll make it, nor what kind of reception they'll receive if they do. That was two nights ago," Shosafin concluded.

"The best way to help them—to help all of Ïsriba—is to put an end to my daughter's reign of terror. We can't do that if we stay down here. Come, just a little further: there's the lava tubes up ahead, then the lowest reaches of the dungeon; after that, the castle…and the queen."

Lava tubes?! Kalas wondered to himself; Náli voiced his unspoken concern.

"The earth beneath Ïsriba has been quiet for uncounted Sevens," the king assured her. "Nothing to worry about!"

Kalas bit his lip, remembering how the Ildurgul Taruún rocked the blasted plains above the Gateway not that long ago. Falthwën said something about the mountain "waking up," and the young man hoped its recent eruption had nothing to do with Ïsriba.

"Where is everybody?" Náli asked when they reached the dungeons. With the exception of a few recent, rat-bitten corpses, the deepest levels were empty. Rufàran scowled when he saw the deceased, angered, it seemed, at his daughter's flippant disregard for human life.

"I don't know," he said, distracted and disturbed.

With every floor they gained, Kalas wondered if he'd recognize his old cell if they passed it. When they reached the uppermost blocks, Nïmrïk cautioned, "Wait! Voices!" He sniffed the rancid air and added, "Soldiers—*Poyïsriba* leather, that is. Have your swords ready!"

The party waited, but it seemed the voices' owners never moved. Nïmrïk cocked his head, sampled the air again. "Strange…" he admitted. Rufàran shifted his weight and prepared to reveal himself when Shosafin barred his progress.

"My liege, let me…"

Before the king could answer him, he flipped his sword along the length of his forearm and sidled into the thready torchlight lining the narrow corridor. A moment later, he returned, a wry expression etched within his features.

"You were right, wolf: soldiers. No, not as guards—as *prisoners.*"

"Prisoners?!" Rufàran exclaimed and stepped into the light.

"Has the queen sent you to separate our heads from our necks at last?" one younger-looking soldier huffed. Kalas could tell he wanted to sound brave, but even without Nïmrïk's supernatural sense of smell, he could almost taste the poor man's fear.

"Hold your tongue!" barked another, older soldier. "You're too young to recognize the man you're talking to, but—it's impossible, but that's King Rufàran! O King! You were dead! What—how is this possible?!"

"You wouldn't believe it. Tell me, Fóban—yes, of course I remember your name! It's only been a few—never mind! Tell me: why are you in this cell?"

"My liege, your daughter put us here when we refused to massacre innocents! When you never returned from your hunt, Ësfàyami's counselors wasted no time installing her on your throne. In mere weeks, the beautiful child who used to follow you around the castle turned cold. Hard. I can only say that now through the clarity hindsight brings: at the time, I didn't realize what was happening. Because she was your daughter, your armies obeyed her whims as best we could. Most of us: only a few, it seemed, understood what the rest of us did not.

"These last few months, soon after *Kindu* Marugan returned with his incredible tale, something happened: it seems no one knows exactly what, but she descended into a black rage unlike anything any of us had ever seen before. I don't know how to describe it, but any remaining shreds of decency she possessed disappeared. Her coldness turned to fire…And her *edicts!* A few of us resisted—too late, we now know; those she didn't slaughter she confined to these dungeons. I've been down here for…months? I don't know: I've lost track of time. Bön, the impertinent youth in the next cell, he's only been here a week or two: he says after Marugan disappeared, someone else—someone fiercer still—"

"Twice as tall as a mere man and dripping with flame!" Bön interrupted. "His stare sends fire surging through your bones, and when he speaks, countless souls scream inside his voice!"

"Sounds like someone we know," Kalas grunted. "I guess the rumors are true: Peradan *did* come to Ïsriba."

"That complicates things," Shosafin acknowledged.

"Ilbardhën?" Fóban marveled. "Shosafin, I mean! Is that—are you the one who discovered the truth about the king?! What are— your arm!"

"No, Fóban: it was this young man and woman. And a third who…is no longer with us. However, I am the one who will return his throne to him—whatever the cost," he answered, and Fóban wilted beneath his withering tone.

"Captain Shosafin, forgive me! I didn't believe you when you returned without the king! Your story was too strange, too hard to believe! I'm sorry I—"

"I don't care," he said, although Kalas guessed he *did* care. Addressing Kalas and the others, he said, "All right, let's get these men out of here: surely there's a way to open these doors?"

Before the young man said anything, Náli stepped over to Fóban's cell, jammed her knife into its lock, and twisted it back and forth a few times, demanding silence as she worked. In seconds, the internals clicked, and the body slid away from the shank.

"I told you: I used to sneak into the city. *Ade* Nàvan taught me," she defended herself as she started working on Bön's cell.

When both men were free, Rufàran ordered them to seek out any soldiers willing to confront the queen-regent and wait for them outside the throne room. Bön lamented there were too few re-maining, but Fóban said, "Unless I'm wrong, there must be several others down here! If you'll spare the girl and her magic knife, we'll free them, relieve a few guards of their weapons, then cut our way toward Ulobir's statue."

"Miss Náli?" Rufàran pleaded: "What do you say? Will you help these men free their brothers-in-arms?"

"I—you're the king, right? You're not going to, I don't know, *order* me to help them?"

"I suppose I could, but I'd rather you *choose* to help of your own volition."

"I was right before," she said, scratching her head: "you *don't* get how this whole 'king' thing works, do you?! Yes, I'll help! Lead on, Commander Fóban!"

"Don't wait too long for us," the soldier nodded: "We'll keep Náli behind us, keep her safe, but if the rest of us aren't there af-ter a reasonable amount of time, it's because we're dead. To arms, Bön—that is, as soon as we find some! For the glory of the Golden Falcon! For—"

"—for the victory of her *king!*" finished Shosafin as he set his jaw and clapped his sword across his heart.

Chapter XX

Out of the Wreck of Sundered Flesh

"How long should we wait?" Kalas whispered. He wished he had a shield; he'd retrieved someone's discarded buckler, but its straps were too large, too far apart, and so he left it behind. Instead, he held *Sharuyandas Tshandu* in one hand, his knife in the other.

The five of them had fought their way to the rotunda surrounding the green-gold statue of Ïsriba's first monarch almost fifteen minutes ago. Kalas had anticipated more robust resistance from what he assumed would be the queen-regent's best warriors. A few small pockets of well-equipped men tried to block them from getting any closer to the queen, but after a few well-placed snicks from king's and captain's blades, they—like all the others—dropped their arms and fled.

"I don't dare wait too much longer," Rufàran admitted as he traced a route toward the throne—and his daughter the queen.

"Did either of you *cut* anyone? Me neither, but it looked like some of them were bleeding. Pretty badly, too! What do you think is going on? And why did so many of them look...*thankful* that someone was coming after their queen?"

Abarandal spat a flurry of notes, but before Kalas could parse her meaning, a hulking figure thundered into view. Something in his movements, his appearance seemed *off* to Kalas. Some uncanny quirk in how his face was put together, maybe? At least a head taller than Rufàran and wielding a black-bladed glaive, he paused before guttering something with a voice like tar-soaked gravel. His sunken eyes aglow with malign energy, he aimed his weapon and charged.

"Egu!" Nïmrïk shouted as he bounded after the creature. The unsteady man swung wide: Nïmrïk jumped, landed on the flat portion of the glaive, and launched himself onto his shoulders in a frenzied parody of an embrace. The silver wolf tore at the monster's chest and face until caustic black clouds of rancid filth spurted from the wounds. Nïmrïk snapped and snarled and gnawed vast hunks of flesh from the beast until it dropped its weapon and reached for him.

Anticipating the move, Nïmrïk vaulted over its shredded shoulders and spun around, his grime-streaked muzzle curled back to reveal glistening fangs. His quarry turned, too; blind, it seemed, until it finished the work Nïmrïk had started and tore away the flesh still clinging to his skull—except it wasn't his skull: it was the matted black fur of a *zhàrudzh*. It dragged itself free from its human remains and stared at Nïmrïk.

Kalas thought Nïmrïk had been a big wolf, but this one was bigger still, maybe half again Nïmrïk's size. It *thought* hate at Kalas' friend as it crawled toward him.

"His tether wasn't secure," Nïmrïk explained, his eyes fixed on the approaching *egu*. "I'll take care of him! He's weak, not wholly here, not wholly anywhere! The rest of you: *hwer!*"

"He's right," Shosafin insisted: "The king and I will confront Ësfàyami. Our swords are ineffective against such beings: yours is not, and I've seen Abarandal…I've seen her do things I can't explain away!"

"But Peradan!" Kalas countered. "If he's with the queen—and where else would he be?—your swords won't be any use against him, either!"

"I cut Marugan through the neck: it didn't kill him, but it slowed him down. It'll slow Peradan, too. Just…just finish up here and—"

The *nathrudzh* yelped, and Shosafin and Kalas turned to see Nïmrïk wrench its lolling head from its disintegrating body. Its corpse shuddered and split into scraps of fur and flesh before dissolving into smoke. The *swënrudzh* wiped at the greasy substance smeared all over his face.

"I thought I told you to *go!*" he reprimanded them. Especially Kalas.

"I…yeah, all right, let's—"

Another figure barreled through the corridor. He hit a wall and staggered, pressing a hand against his bloodied head. When he saw the others, his eyes widened; when he realized they weren't members of the queen-regent's retinue, he threw himself at Rufàran's feet.

"Oh! Praise the Creator!" he gushed, clinging to the king's legs. "She's mad! Insane! She—no, she's something *worse!* I should have said something sooner, before…well, before all of *this!* You're here to stop her, *hish?* To put an end to this…this *madness?!*"

"We are," said Rufàran. He helped the panic-stricken man to his feet and, examining long gouges carved across his face, remarked, "You're wounded, but it looks like these have already started clotting. And you still have your sword! Come, friend: *help us!* Help us, as you said, put an end to this madness!"

"Me? Go…back?! Ha! No, you'd have to be *insane* to go in there! No! I—I can't! I—"

Kalas thought the gibbering soldier's face slackened, his eyes sinking within their sockets when he shoved the king and ran down the corridor, stumbling until he turned a corner and disappeared.

"Let him go!" Nïmrïk urged: "It's been long Sevens since *egume* have tethered themselves to men's *kelâme* without…permission, I'll say, but it seems that's what's happening. The *egu* I just tore apart, the *egu* that just took off down the hall—yes, that poor man had the stink of evil seeping from his pores! I don't know what's happening, but I don't think we've seen the last of them."

"Why now, wolf?" Shosafin said, thinking aloud, it seemed. "Why not before, when Marugan returned? Or why not a month ago, when Peradan was first recognized? Don't you think it strange these things would happen at the moment we're headed for the queen-regent?"

"I don't know," Nïmrïk confessed.

"She doesn't even know I'm here, does she?" Rufàran wondered.

Kalas suggested, "We don't know what happened to all the cultists under Glass Sword Mountain, and it's likely there were others who weren't even there—Shosafin, remember what Sifuran told us about everyone trying to board the *Lord of Winds?* Your Majesty, I said something about *privilege* when we found you. Do you remember? This privilege lets some people see things, hear things…*know* things, I guess. Maybe one of the surviving cultists is privileged: maybe he *sent* a message to Peradan? Kadhëmba, you said the cultists north of Serular were using magic: maybe that's how?"

Abarandal expressed an alternative, and Kalas admitted, "Yeah, that's possible, of course! She says maybe Peradan just went back to the ruined vault near Galámur, discovered you—all of us—were gone, and told the queen-regent himself. Anyway, to Shosafin's point, I'll bet Ësfàyami *does* know you're here. I'll bet that's why Kadhëmba senses so many *egume,* too: Marugan probably told Peradan about an *egu* who took an arrow intended for one of us; Peradan most likely told the queen."

"Yet Peradan is *eku*—not *egu*," Nïmrïk reminded him. "I told you, from a hierarchical perspective, *egume* exercise dominion over *ekume,* and—"

"Marugan had *egu*-inhabited *shagabme* with him—*obeying* him," Kalas interrupted. "East of Lohwàlar, when we first met him, and again in the dungeons. Falthwën didn't know what to make of that arrangement, either. Maybe the old order isn't what it used to be?"

"Maybe it isn't…" the silver wolf conceded.

Spattered blood and broken bodies decorated the long hallway as everyone picked his way toward the vast, gilded doors blocking access to the throne room. As Kalas and the others ascended the seven stairs—once highly polished, now dulled with dark and sticky streaks—he wondered if some of the corpses behind them belonged to the guards once stationed here. A hand wrapped weak fingers around his leg, and he cried out: someone on the cusp of death— one of the guards, he realized—held him and said, "She's…she's not who we thought she was! Who…she said she was! She seeks glory for…for some other…not the Falcon! Not…not…"

The man choked on his last words as fluid filled his lungs. Kalas winced as the shine ebbed from his horrified eyes. He shook his leg free from the dead man's grip and looked to the others. King Rufàran considered the dead man—the dead *men* scattered across the corridor, and, his eyebrows knit, vowed, "I…I didn't believe you—any of you—when you told me what my daughter had become. Even now, confronted with this evidence, I don't want to believe it: the daughter I remember could have *never* caused such carnage!"

"The daughter you remember died when you did, my liege," Shosafin posited. "Maybe even before that: you were consumed with affairs of state; her tutors raised her. Tutors with dark designs on the kingdom."

"Marugan—maybe even Peradan?—must have intended treachery against Ïsriba from before your daughter was born," Kalas observed. "It fits. I didn't know how much of what he told me was true—I didn't know if *any* of it was true, but it fits."

"Alas, my daughter," Rufàran wept. He shook his head and huffed away his tender thoughts. His jaw squared, he vowed, "This cannot stand. These men deserved better than this! The kingdom deserves better than this! Though I run my sword through my own heart, Ësfàyami must be stopped. By any—by *all* means necessary. *Zhi Ilun—fie id aswanthalu.*"

2.

The golden doors would not move despite everyone's combined efforts. Shosafin suggested they'd been barred from the other side. Rufàran agreed and recommended they try to find something to use as a battering ram.

"What about that statue?" Kalas said, pointing down the hall.

"There's no way the five of us could lift it from its pedestal, never mind carry it all the way to these doors!" rebutted the king.

"No? Right, it probably weighs tons! I guess I—Hey, let me try something…"

The young man closed his eyes and tried to view things through the Song. He tried to picture every note, every phrase as a property of the physical world. With such imagery in his mind, he tried to *adjust* the Song: he decreased some measures' tempo; he articulated other measures' dynamics; he suffused the entire movement with unbearable energy and willed it at Ulobir's booted feet.

The monument to Ïsriba's storied founder cracked and tottered; canted, it hesitated for a moment before it collapsed to the floor, sending shards of green gold and dark stone skittering across the floor. Panting, Kalas stumbled and caught himself against the slanting wall.

"I'm sorry! I thought I could…I can't. I was wrong…" he apologized.

Abarandal's silvery eyes flashed, and she stood before the doors. The others ceased their activities and watched: something in the way she moved—glided—demanded their attention. With her arms raised, she leaned forward and sang a single note, her voice pure and unwavering. The heavy, gilded slabs rattled on their hinges until the sympathetic resonance in the *eruíndas* music split them into atoms. With the doors destroyed, revealing nothing but emptiness, Abarandal fell silent and stumbled. Rufàran caught her.

"My, my, my! Aren't you a marvel!" he exclaimed. She smiled as he helped her regain her feet.

"Finally!" exulted Shosafin, and he rushed toward the black expanse.

"Shosafin! Wait!" Kalas pleaded, but he dissolved into the darkness. "If Peradan's in there…"

"It seems we've little choice," Nimrïk observed, and followed the brazen, one-armed soldier into the throne room. Rufàran followed. Kalas made sure Abarandal was all right—she still seemed weak, unsteady, but she insisted she was fine—before they hurried after the others.

Guttering torches glowed a dull, *unwilling* red at the fringes of the high-ceilinged room. The same fine thread of suns-light traced a straight course toward the elevated basalt throne. The last time Kalas was in this place, the polished floors glittered; now, red film, sometimes tacky, sometimes slippery, muted their prior brilliance. No guards waited in the shadows. None Kalas could sense, at least; even Nimrïk, tasting the air for surprises, seemed uneasy about their absence. Coming from somewhere ahead of them, wet smacks and liquid slurps echoed between the walls.

I don't like this, lad, he thought. Kalas started: he couldn't remember if he'd ever *heard* Nimrïk so clearly in his mind before. He replied: *Me neither. Something's wrong—something more than we thought…*

"*Princess* Ësfàyami!" Shosafin called. "Pretender-queen: show yourself!"

The frantic noises ceased, and someone said, "I know that voice! Shosafin-Ilfadan! You dare return to me? to the kingdom you failed to protect?"

I know that voice! Kalas noted as Ësfàyami's ice-cold words reverberated through the chamber.

The vast curtains overhead drew back—how, Kalas had no idea, revealing the queen-regent kneeling on the topmost step before the throne. Her crimson dress clung to her sculpted physique: when she stood, it dripped, and the young man realized her dress wasn't crimson after all—it was soaked in blood. She held what looked like a ragged hunk of meat in her hands, both stained red like her gown. The entire lower half of her face was smeared with blood, some of which still dripped from her once-pearlescent grin. Her coal-black irises glinted red, and Kalas wasn't sure it was because of the torchlight. He looked away from the stomach-churning spectacle and discovered the source of all the blood: her guards, splayed out and torn open as if by animals. Most were missing limbs; some their heads, but every one of them had a fist-sized hole, ringed with black, where his heart should have been.

"What are you *doing?!*" Kalas demanded, unable to restrain himself.

She laughed, her winged crown sparkling in the suns-light, and the music in her coquettish titters seemed to freeze the fluid in his spine. As if to punctuate the young man's disgust, she held his gaze and bit into the object in her hands. Someone's missing heart, he realized. When he choked back a retch, she laughed again.

"You've come to stop me, have you? Come to prevent these wars I've planned for so long?! You're too late! My machines are primed and ready, my armies are on the move, and, at last, Ïsriba is poised to dominate all the kingdoms of the earth!"

Machines?

"Queen Ësfàyami, you must know that other kingdoms have believed similar things?" Nïmrïk queried. "Why, Queen Dàgandzhu has every able-bodied blacksmith pounding out weapons for *her* military! Her fleets are faster, more maneuverable than ever, and—"

"Silence, *gidzhag!* Traitor! Peradan—an *eru* of the Great Swath, no less!—assures me the other kingdoms have no concept of the Falcon's capabilities! He—"

"Peradan's the one who captured your father all those—" Kalas began.

"*Do not interrupt me!* Your ploys are as desperate as ever, I see! No, Peradan, with his magical abilities, placed his hand on me and showed me the world through his eyes! No one—not Dàgandzhu, not Kematu—not even Mödus in the North—*no one* has any idea what's crouching at his doorstep!"

"Ësfàyami. What are you doing with that man's heart?" Rufàran asked, his voice measured as he stepped into the light.

Her expression changed: twisted revelry turned to shock as she recognized the king through long-abandoned memories.

"That voice?!" she breathed. "But no, that's impossible! My father is *dead!*"

"It's improbable, I'll confess, but nonetheless, my daughter, I am very much alive!"

"But…No! No, even if he *were* alive, he'd be older than you! I—the *kingdom's* been without him for *many* Sevens! This is all a trick! Yes, a trick! I'll—"

"By your own admission, Peradan possesses 'magical abilities,' yes? It's because of those abilities that I look the same as I did when you'd only attained your first Seven. I remember your face—cold, uncaring, and I blamed myself. I promised I would spend more time with you when I returned from the hunt. I thought—it doesn't matter what I thought. What matters is that I wasn't there when I should have been. Alas, Ësfàyami, I am sorry!"

"Father?" she wondered and took a step toward him. "Marugan said you'd been torn apart by wolves!" She took another step and seemed to discover that her gown didn't move across her body the way it used to: when she looked down, she seemed confused by all the blood; when she peeled its fabric away from her skin, the sight of her scarlet hands confused her more. She looked around the throne room and noticed—for the first time, it seemed—the rife carnage surrounding her.

"What's going on? Why are—? Did...is this *my* doing?" she gagged.

"Ësfàyami! Peradan: where is he?!" Shosafin prodded.

"My daughter, come, let's put an end to this madness! There's much to discuss, much to undo, and—"

"My liege, forgive me, but we must know where Peradan is! We have to—"

One of the murdered guards stirred, then vaulted to his feet and thrust his halberd at Shosafin. He quickly pivoted away, slicing through the dead man's leg as he prepared for more attacks.

"How is *this* possible?!" the queen-regent gasped and clutched her head. Rufàran turned to Abarandal and begged her to protect his daughter. The star girl hesitated, then took a few steps closer as the king joined the others.

"*Shosayedhume!*" Kalas shouted. Nïmrïk nodded and wrapped his jaws around another risen figure.

Shosafin and Rufàran devised a fast plan: they focused on sapping their assailants' strength with quick thrusts and arcing slashes, shredding their physical substance until there wasn't much left for anything to control; as they twitched, weakened, Kalas ran his sword through their necks until they shuddered and disintegrated into dust.

When it was over, Ësfàyami raced toward her father and wrapped her bloodied arms around him: "It *is* you!" she wept. "I don't understand how, but you move *just* like him: I still remember, even after all these Sevens!"

"But what have I done here?! What have I done to the Falcon?! I…I remember all of it—my decisions, my decrees…I've made a mess of things, Father! I only wanted to make the kingdom stronger, to protect it at all costs…"

"Your counselors," Shosafin suggested. "Marugan poisoned your thoughts through them, even before the king disappeared! You were young—too young, and Marugan designed the shape of your mind, your will, through their counsel."

Ësfàyami listened, rapt, searching his words for absolution. When he finished, she demanded to know, "Why didn't you *protect* me?! I was a little girl—you said so yourself! If you'd only—"

"I know," he soothed. "I know! I didn't know it was Marugan—not until I saw him standing in the woods last year. By the time I understood what your counselors were doing, it was too late. I tried to pierce the veil they wove around you, but…I failed…"

"Peradan is…he's like Marugan," Kalas said. "That's why we have to find him! He can move through realms most of us can't. He—you described his power yourself! Marugan is dead—for good, I think! But Peradan is worse! He—"

Electric red-orange fire flared from every torch as a dirty-citrine web of energy arced across the floor, reaching out and tickling every gold-plated surface: when the conflagration and the last forks of lightning flickered out, the *Tshaggul Kavar* remained.

"You found me," he shouted. Whispered. Bön's description of the *ekudas* voice was apt: Kalas heard the hoarse wails of unnumbered souls pouring from his mouth. Peradan surveyed the rent bodies sprawled across the throne room and smiled: "Progress! But these four? Tell me, *O Queen:* why do their hearts still beat within their chests?!"

"No! I don't—I don't know what I—That wasn't me! I mean, I don't—"

"Oho! *This* is interesting!" the towering fire marveled, and his rictus-like smile widened. "Conquered by...*love?!* An abandoned daughter's joy at her father's reappearance?! Ha! After all your imperious condescension, *this* is what destroys your power?!"

What's he talking about?

"Oh, if only Marugan were here! He, more than any, should see this! I tried to tell him—I did! Ask the boy! I tried to tell him, but of course he didn't listen! He was always like that, you know—yes, you *do* know, don't you? Of course!"

Tell Marugan? But Marugan wanted to become...

"...an *egu*," Kalas mumbled. The others looked at him, and even beneath the blood still plastered around her mouth, Ësfàyami paled. *But he's talking to the queen-regent like she's—*

"*Enough!*" she roared at last, and a wave of power knocked everyone else to the ground. Confused, the young man watched as the king's daughter seemed to writhe within her own skin. Wisps of steam—or smoke—collected around her person as she confronted Peradan.

"Ësfàyami?" Rufàran called out: "My d—"

"*Silence!*" she roared, the malice in her rage rippling like wind through his hair. "I am *not* your daughter!" She turned toward the *eku* again and repeated, "Enough! You overestimate your position, Peradan! I should have—"

"Yet you didn't!" he laughed as the space around her shimmered and she was gone. Catching Kalas' horrified stare, he added: "I'll admit it: I didn't know if that would work on her! Lately, it seems my devices lack the potency they once possessed! I mean, sure: I didn't know if I could contain the *great power* within a simple singularity, but a couple of mortals? Escape should have been impossible!

Anyway, you—where's Zhalera?"

"You know!" Kalas fumed.

"Lad, I assure you I do not, but judging from your ardor, I'll assume she's dead? Yes? She is, isn't she! That's too bad—no, I mean it! Well, I mean it's too bad I can't use her like puppet strings to control you! Anyway, as I was saying, you saved me a lot of trouble! I had no idea where to find King Rufàran! His *frequency* isn't what it used to be—and *that* I cannot explain! I can't risk losing you again, O King! Better to finish this once for all!"

The *Tshaggul Kavar* raised his enormous spear and hurled it toward the king.

It should have pierced him through, but instead, it hovered, motionless, mere inches from his chest. Rufàran stood and backed away. He glanced at Kalas, who shook his head: *Not me!* At Abarandal, who did the same.

"You will not!" Ësfàyami roared as the thin line of stained glass overhead shattered; as black stabs of *anti*-energy collected above the throne, which cracked in two; as a seared and sooty figure clad in blood-stained tatters clawed her way into existence again.

"I have destroyed my kingdom—*his* kingdom, but I will not let you destroy him!"

Peradan's flames flickered, and he shriveled until he was the size and shape of an average man. He beheld the queen-regent with uncomprehending eyes and tried to mouth his befuddlement, but no sound would come.

"Ësfàyami!" Rufàran shouted. "How—?"

"Father! Stay back!" she begged him. "I...I made a grave mistake! I—*ugh!*"

She doubled over. The king took a step toward her, but she raised a hand and coughed another warning. She dropped to one knee and wrapped her free arm around her torso and confessed, "When the boy—Kalas, you brave young man!—when he demonstrated his ability in this very room, immediately, I imagined all the ways I would command his powers! And then he was gone!"

She coughed again: louder, harder this time, but continued, "Marugan insisted he would find him—or something better!—and I believed him! He disappeared, and I never heard from him again. During that time, I…My lusts: I let them dominate me, direct my will. While I was seething with frustration, I…that's when *she* came to me!

"She was a living mirror: everything about her—her shape, her voice, her mannerisms—she was *me!* She promised me great things! Terrible things! I was so blind, I agreed. It seemed so harmless: all she wanted was—"

The queen-regent cried out and clutched the sides of her head again. The vapors rising from her body turned thick and black, and the sear marks twisting across her skin bubbled as her flesh dripped away. Her ruined gown split apart with tortured shrieks as vast, leathery wings emerged from her back. She raised the remnants of her face toward her father and made one last request—

"Aswanthalu!"

—before it cracked apart and sloughed away like the rest of her. Where Ësfàyami had fallen, a petite, well-muscled *egu* rose up on powerful hind legs. Her once-dark eyes glowed red as she flexed her glistening wings, wet with blood and filth, and stepped away from the slag of Ïsriba's departed queen.

"At last!" the beast reveled.

"Hatred's Right Hand!" Nïmrïk whined and stepped back, his tail curled between his legs.

"'Hatred's Right Hand'? I've heard that before!" Kalas remembered. "Wait! Marugan! That's who said it! But he was talking about—?! That means…that means Ësfàyami is…*Tsathrâuda!*"

3.

"She surprised me, in the end," Tsathrâuda admitted as she pumped her wings and rose a few feet above the ground—if only for a moment. "It's amazing, really, the bond between you humans! After all these Sevens, after a lifetime of resentment, that thread of love between father and daughter remained; indeed, her remorse was *almost* enough to cut the tether! *Almost.* It took me a while, but, again: *at last!* Your daughter, O King, made it worthwhile: it's been millennia since I last tethered myself to an *edhu*—sharing substance with your kind is like slogging through muck! We take on your limitations; we become *less than;* and even when we break free, the *stink* of who—of *what*—you are lingers! It's worse when our tethers just *die:* your daughter—you should be proud, I suppose! Oh! How your daughter *struggled!* She even managed to assert herself for a moment, leave you with a parting thought! All for naught, of course! 'Forgive me!'? Ha! How delicious!"

Despite her diminutive stature, Tsathrâuda possessed a *presence* that intimated tremendous force of will. She laughed as she taunted Rufàran with a voice as rough as Nïmrïk's, yet laced with sensual femininity. Peradan remained frozen in place, too afraid, it seemed, to move. His spear clattered to the ground, and, almost as an afterthought, it seemed, the *egu* made a subtle gesture and summoned black ropes from some invisible place that wrapped around the *eku*. He tried to twist himself free, but even sheets of fire and lightning proved useless against his bonds. Tsathrâuda shot him a withering glance, then turned toward the others.

"So you're the young man that has the heavens in an uproar, hmm?" she said, addressing Kalas. "One would nev—*Kadhëmba?!* Is that—?! It *is!* I almost didn't recognize you beneath that hideous silver coat! I'd heard rumors about a penitent *egu*, but I never thought it would be you! Tell me, *swënrudzh:* do your new friends know who you are? Who you *really* are?!"

"Tsathrâuda—" Nïmrïk pleaded.

"I wonder if they'd tolerate your company if they knew the truth!" she interrupted. "Tell me, Kalas: did you know that long, long ago, the world had just one sun? No, of course not! No one— no *edhu* alive knows that! Do you know why there are two suns today? It's Kadhëmba's fault!"

From her scandalized tone, Kalas understood she intended the preposterous revelation as some grand indictment against the *egu*, but he didn't understand what she meant. Growling, she elaborated: "Before the world was cracked, Tàfayan was the only sun above the world. Your kind accuse Nasrahim—the *Usmawinadath*—for the state your world is in. You call him *Ilnëshras*—the Accursèd One. He *is* chief among all created things, yes, but do you think he alone rebelled against his creator? No! He did not! And when he chose Mira above all mortal women—Indeed! Above all *elume* and *erume*, too!—do you think he executed his designs without his captains and commanders present?!"

"Mira…" Kalas mumbled as he remembered a story. "Mir…*yan*. The Beloved Sun! You mean Ilmazhasahwu!"

"Yes! Precisely! And because I know he hasn't told you *every-thing*, let me complete your education: When Nasrahim declared his independence, Kadhëmba was the first of us to rally to his side! He stood beside his new potentate, eager to do his bidding: *he* is the one who sacrificed Mira to Nasrahim's appetites!"

Kalas had no idea how to respond. He looked at Nïmrïk, who seemed smaller than himself, his tail curled around his nethers and his ears folded flat and low against his skull. Judging from the *egudas* body language, Tsathrâuda told the truth.

"Kadhëmba?" he invited, his voice a mere whisper. Nïmrïk flinched and squinted, as though Kalas' question were a blow. He tried to raise his head, to meet the young man's gaze, but he couldn't:

his yellow eyes dimmed and he turned away again. Rufàran seemed bewildered; Shosafin pursed his lips, conflicted but unsurprised, it seemed. Abarandal said nothing: her gaze remained fixed on the grinning *eguín.*

A world without two suns seemed…wrong, somehow. Unnatural. Kalas tried to imagine a singular source of daylight.

He couldn't.

Until he remembered a dream he'd had while Falthwën's ministrations scrubbed the wolf-venom from his blood: a meadow strewn with wildflowers underneath a solitary sun. In his dream, before the wolves came, everything had been beautiful and serene and *right.* Somehow he knew—*a priori*—that the sun in his dream was *not* Tàfayan. Nor Miryan. Its light was gentler than the former's, firmer than the latter's, yet it was also more than mere synthesis, more than an uninspired amalgam of the two…

Tàfayan. Nalënahwu. The Premier Sun. Did he have a different name before…? Miryan. Ilmazhasahwu. The Beloved Sun. Beloved by the first, but—? Ah! Of course!"

"All right, I believe you," Kalas said, addressing Tsathrâuda. Her cruel smile broadened, her canines dripping with saliva. "But you know what else? I also believe Kadhëmba, that he's well-aware of his sins and that he's done his utmost to atone for them. I never understood why they call Miryan *The Beloved Sun* until now. It's ironic: Marugan believed you when you told him he could become an *elu,* but even I know that's a lie. Yet a friend of mine told me a story about an *edhu* woman who became a star—a *sun,* right? He was telling me about Miryan! I thought it was just a metaphor, but it's so much more than that, isn't it!

"Kadhëmba, listen to me! I understand why you thought you couldn't tell me—tell us—the full extent of who you *used to be.* I get it. I want *you* to understand that it doesn't change anything!"

"Listen to him, Kadhëmba!" Tsathrâuda mocked with a singsong lilt. "Listen to him all you like! Pretty words from a naïve child won't change the horrors you've wrought against the world! The heavens! You're *worthless:* you know that, right? Nasrahim won't abide a twice-faithless poltroon like you, no matter how highly he esteemed you in ages past! And do you think your creator has any use for you? Do you think *he,* of all beings, would welcome you into his presence after what you've done to his handiwork?! Look at you! Your fur's all shiny and bright, but your flesh is still *zhàrudzh!* No one will *ever* trust you—no one will *ever* love you!"

Kalas felt his blood boil in his veins. Summoning courage from an unknown—yet familiar—place, he took a step toward the vicious *egu* and cried out: "Enough! You—all you know is *hate!* You've wallowed it in for so long it's tainted how you see *everything!* I don't see Kadhëmba the same way as you—nor do others! Maybe the Creator designed his world with one sun, but I've learned that even when we raise our fists against him, his sovereignty's not shaken! Maybe the world will have one sun again someday, but until then, why don't you ask Tàfayan what *he* thinks of that second sun? His *beloved?!* The Creator can—and does, I believe!—use *everything* in accordance with his purpose without regard for *our* ideas of what's good and what's not. That's the problem with your 'black god,' as someone labeled him: he thinks *his* will is best, but not even his schemes are enough to confound Ilun!"

He panted. Tsathrâuda fumed. His chest heaving, he rushed to Nïmrïk's side. The cowering figure, presuming ill-intent, drew back, but Kalas placed a hand behind his ear and petted the side of his neck. With his other, he turned his head and said, "You're my friend—with Tàran gone, with Falthwën gone, I've come to rely on your wisdom: you've been like a father to me, and even now, knowing these things about your past, that's how I see you still. You leaped in front of an arrow for me—a dark-magic arrow that would have killed me. Or worse! You've protected me many times since then. Maybe you were one of Ilnëshras' chiefs—and maybe that's how you see yourself, even today, but it's not who you are! Not anymore!

"You've spent…I have no idea how many lifetimes—as *edhume* reckon them—trying to achieve *balance*. I've tried to tell you before, but I don't think you understood what I meant: what if *you can't balance things?* What if all that's left to 'do' is *admit* it?"

"No!" Nïmrïk whimpered. "I can't! You heard her! She's right! What use does the Creator have for someone who's visited so much evil on his world? So long as I'm working to make things right, there's hope—however faint—that one day, it'll be enough! How *arrogant* would I have to be to think I could ever satisfy his just wrath against me?"

"Listen to yourself! In one breath, you talk about hope for a day when you've done 'enough'; in the next, you deny that day can ever come! Do you really think your wrongs are *so wrong* that the Creator who made you, the world, and everything in it, can't—or won't—forgive you if you ask him to?"

"But I *have* asked him! I've—"

"You've asked that your *works* prove your righteousness. That your good deeds provide some contrast against the worst you've ever done. What if it doesn't work that way? Kadhëmba, I don't think you've *trusted* him with who you are—yes, even with who you used to be! Do you possess greater power for wrong than the Creator possesses for good?"

"Oh, what a novel idea!" cackled Tsathrâuda as she pumped her wings again. Her foul wind permeated the throne room with the taint of rot. "Go ahead! 'Trust' the creator! Yes, the creator who imprisoned us in these wolf-bodies! The creator whose world you helped destroy! I'm sure he's just *dying* to welcome you into his presence! Ha!"

"What if…? Lad, what if you're wrong?" Nïmrïk whined with

a small, small voice.

"What?! You're seriously considering what this little boy is spouting?! Oh, *Kadhëmba!* How the mighty have fallen!"

"What if I'm right?"

"I…don't…I'm afraid, Kalas! I've never been *so afraid!*"

"All right, enough of this idiocy!" Tsathrâuda pouted. "There's *no forgiveness* for you! You *must* know that! You—Never mind! I'll just kill you now and—"

Kalas wasn't sure, but he thought he detected a new quality seeping into the malevolent she-wolf's speech: *fear.*

"The Creator is able to forgive you, too, Tsathrâuda!"

"*Dâethëthe,* child!" she screeched as she raised her poisoned claws and charged the young man.

Nïmrïk stood and pushed Kalas out of the way. He closed his eyes, took a breath, and whispered something unintelligible as Tsathrâuda ripped into his chest. He yowled with pain, but she wasn't interested in him: she wrenched her hands free and slashed at his sides. Nïmrïk's physical advantage seemed moot as she shoved, feinted, even climbed over him in her frenzied pursuit of the young man. Unable—

unwilling?

—to retaliate against such speed, such ferocity, Nïmrïk focused all his efforts on keeping Tsathrâuda from reaching Kalas.

After several countered attacks, she acknowledged the wounded wolf at last and roared, *"Dunà zhi kavarme gulayëthu!"* and tore away his beating heart. As she held it aloft, Nïmrïk managed to turn toward Kalas; his silver stained with scarlet, he coughed blood, *smiled,* and collapsed. The light in his eyes—already dimmed—dwindled to clouded darkness, and the grisly trophy in Tsathrâuda's hands erupted in a whoosh of black smoke.

"See?! *No forgiveness!*" she raved with renewed certainty in her voice. She crushed the cinders between her fingers and scattered them across the floor. "Once I've ripped your power from you, body and soul, I'll deliver this cracked world to Nasrahim. I've recovered a lot of ancient hardware that should make things easier! Deridzhas was a treasure trove! Ïsran, too! And—that's unimportant! Soon, I will rule this planet, seated at his right hand! Now, little child, it's time for you to come with me!"

Shosafin stepped in front of Kalas; Rufàran, too, but with a gesture, Tsathrâuda flung them from her path. Abarandal joined Kalas' side, her song a threnody, and together, they faced the ravening beast. The young man raised his sword and hoped it would be enough. The *egu* laughed again, flapped her wings, and took one step closer.

4.

"Bitëthe, tsupök!" Nanësra shouted from the center of a sudden column of white light that cracked the ceiling and spilled unbearable brightness across the throne room. "Desist, fiend! Your celebration is premature! As has always been the case with those of your persuasion! *Look!"*

The leonine *elu,* her polished armor no longer shrouded, her elegant sword drawn and ready, swept her arm across the expanse. Kalas had no idea what she wanted them to see: Peradan remained bound; Shosafin and Rufàran struggled against whatever invisible force restrained them; and Nïmrïk's shredded body remained splayed on the floor. Before Kalas could ask her what she meant, a pinprick of clean white light shot up from his discarded ashes. Others followed, and soon, brilliant silver rays carpeted the throne room. Each luminous thread twisted in the air, then rocketed toward his hollow chest and disappeared.

Nanësra held her breath. *Everyone* held his breath.

Light bloomed in Nïmrïk's once-glassy eyes. He gasped without

635

lungs as unseen hands pulled him to his feet. He screamed without vocal cords, and that same silver light surged from his throat. Beginning at the ground, white fire raced across his form and consumed his flesh, his sinews, his bones. Other than a hovering sphere of silver light, nothing remained of Nïmrïk.

The sphere exploded in a storm of inescapable radiance, hurling everyone—*everyone*—across the room. Kalas couldn't see; indeed, he couldn't hear anything except a tinny buzzing sound inside his head. He called out, but no one responded.

"Abarandal?! Nanësra?" he tried again.

No one answered.

Before the fog that obscured his vision burned away, he heard singing in his mind.

The Song. The *Song! And I know that voice!*

Abarandal must have recognized it as well; Nanësra, too: they harmonized with the new singer, and Kalas wept at the unimpeachable joy in the story their music told.

When he could see again, a lion-like figure clad in gleaming armor stood where Nïmrïk had breathed his last.

Kadhëmba! Kalas sang without question. The *fàrokelu* nodded and flexed his *feathered* wings.

Kadhëmba, lad! he sang as white fire danced within his eyes.

Welcome back, Kadhëmba! Welcome back to The Song!" Nanësra exulted.

"What sorcery is this?!" Tsathrâuda demanded. "No *egu* has ever regained his first estate! None! It's…It's impossible! *Impossible!"*

With a flourish, she produced a dark, dripping sword and lunged for the *elu:* with his own sword, he parried, and the she-wolf's blade skittered across the bloodied floor. It dissolved in a jet-colored puff of smoke.

"I thought so too, Tsathrâuda," he confessed, "but here I am: proof it *is* possible! The lad was right! *Edhu,* yes, but wise beyond his Sevens! When I finally accepted that it wasn't in *me* to—"

"Impossible!" she repeated. Her eyes darted across the room, afraid, it seemed, of everyone and everything it contained. She fixed her gaze on Kalas: he could sense her desire for him, for his *power;* instead, she loped toward Peradan. The *eku* shouted Abarandal's name, but the *egu* snarled something at him—a reprimand, and the two of them vanished in a rancid cloud.

"What just happened?!" Rufàran marveled, free at last from Tsathrâuda's grasp.

"Nïmrïk?" said Shosafin.

"Kadhëmba now," he smiled, his voice a blend of air and fire and song. He turned toward the young man and said, "Kalas, you were right! For millennia, I never dared imagine such a thing was possible: it seemed…*too easy!* It wasn't the Creator keeping me from his presence: it was me! My pride!"

Nanësra sheathed her sword, shimmered into human form, and Kadhëmba did the same. Kalas almost didn't recognize the hale figure where the lion once stood: no longer an old man, his muscled, well-defined frame suggested strength; his steel-streaked hair, lambent with unconsuming flames, fluttered in the breezes blowing down from the fractured ceiling; and his eyes—Nïmrïk's pale blue eyes—radiated nobility. She approached the *elu* and spoke with a tongue Kalas couldn't understand. Kadhëmba nodded, his expression grim, and Kalas, after watching the exchange, got an idea.

"You *remember,* don't you!" he accused. "You remember the language of the *elume!* Nanësra, that's the language that book is written in, isn't it? The book I dropped in Melash that you handed back to me? The book I *still* can't understand!"

"I…remember," Kadhëmba admitted.

"Then you can help me read it! You can teach it to me! I—"

"I…cannot…"

"Oh…" Kalas frowned, his enthusiasm blunted. After pausing to consider, he pursued a different topic: "I thought you were dead! When Tsathrâuda ripped you open, when she held up your *heart*… What happened? Can you at least tell me that?"

"Maybe it's because I betrayed the greatest trust, but your admonition seemed impossible to heed! Why should I, a traitor, dare to place my hope in the one whom I betrayed?! Yet I knew—on some level, I *knew* you were right. I was afraid Ilun would reject me the same way I once rejected him: as his creation, it would have been his right!

"And I was *tired.* I've spent—*wasted*—thousands of years trying to earn something freely given: I've searched the world over for something that has always been available! I'm embarrassed to admit how blind I was! You saw the contradiction: I knew I would never merit his forgiveness, yet all my striving centered on the same!"

Kadhëmba placed a powerful hand atop Kalas' shoulder and added, "Thank you, lad, for your…Thank you for seeing more clearly than I—than any *egu* thought possible. I believe—no, I *know* you have an incomparable destiny ahead of you. That much I *can* tell you! And I can—"

"What happened here?!" Fóban shouted as he, Bön, and several other soldiers stormed the throne room. "King Rufàran! You're safe! *Zhi Ilun tsavára nir!* We got here as fast as we could: most of the queen's men were only too happy to join us, but a significant number refused—say, where *is* the queen?"

Many older men accompanying the captain whispered their surprise at the sight of the king. Kalas heard someone smack the back of a younger man's cuirass and order him to show a little respect.

"The queen—my daughter, Ësfàyami…is no more," he said. "Despite the ignominy she wrought upon the kingdom, she died defending it against dark powers."

"And the Deathless Flame?" Bön trembled as he looked around

the abattoir the throne room had become.

"Gone," Shosafin informed him while the king's thoughts trended elsewhere.

"Then he's—?"

"No! No, he's still out there, but for now, the kingdom belongs to us! To King Rufàran! Hail! Hail Rufàran! *Revehwa ihi Nimkosra Kàsh!*" he shouted and raised his sword high.

"*Á salorosh i ikinihath!*" every warrior responded.

"Kalas?! Kalas!" Náli shouted as she pushed her way through the exultant throng. When she saw him, she ran toward him and threw her arms around his neck. "I'm so glad you're all right! I'm glad you're *all* all right! I—wait: where's Nïmrïk? And who are *these people?!*"

Náli regarded Kadhëmba—Nanësra, too—with suspicious awe. The *elume* laughed, and the young woman covered her ears: "Sounds like waterfalls!"

"I'm right here, Náli!" Kadhëmba assured her. "And this…is Nanësra, my…"

"An old friend," she finished, placing a hand on his forearm.

"What happened to you?! You're not, well, you're not *old* anymore!"

"Oh, I'm as old as I ever was! Although I suppose the Sevens weigh less heavily upon me than they used to!" he smiled.

"Are you still…you know? A wolf?"

"Kadhëmba, we have to go," Nanësra interjected. He nodded.

"Wait! What?!" said Kalas, puzzled. "Where do you have to— *why* do you have to go?!"

The *elu* knelt, gazed at the young man with crystal tears brimming in his eyes, then embraced him with such force that Kalas thought he might cease breathing. When Kadhëmba released him, he promised, "I hear The Song again! I hear my kindred, too, and in its strains I hear *my* destiny. I can't tell you more than that. I'm sorry. Nanësra is right, though: we have responsibilities, and after all this time—and as much as I'll miss you—I'm looking forward to it!

"This is not 'good-bye,' my friend! Our paths *will* intersect: even now, I'm looking forward to those reunions. Until then, resume your studies—and know that there are other *texts* than just your book. Whenever you hear The Song, listen for my voice! You'll recognize it—like you did beneath the very place we're standing now!"

He hugged Kalas one more time, grinned at Náli, then stood and stepped back. Nanësra nodded, and the *elume* shimmered into the shapes of lion-like creatures. The *Serularrin* gasped as Kadhëmba unfurled his magnificent wings. Kalas remembered the tortured look on *egu*-Nïmrïk's face when he told him how much the transformation hurt: he saw nothing like that now—only delight. With an effortless thrust, he ascended a few feet above the floor. Nanësra followed, and together, hand in hand, they hovered long enough for a parting glance before merging with a shaft of sudden light that vaulted through the ceiling, sped toward the stars, and winked out of sight.

5.

"They got away?!" Náli repeated when Kalas told her what happened.

"For now, yes, and as frustrating as that is, at least we've disrupted Tsathrâuda's plans! With King Rufàran restored, there's hope the surrounding kingdoms will follow Ïsriba's lead."

"Fine sentiments, young man, but it won't be that simple!" Fóban corrected him. "Some of us were uncomfortable with the hard lines Ësfàyami took, but others were only too happy to entertain the promise of conquest! Why would it be different for any other realm? For Sevens, the queen's been consolidating strength, concocting unbelievably ambitious projects—did you know she carved a tunnel all the way to the sea? Built a port behind the Ridësh-ilnush, too. That's the rumor, anyway: I wasn't—"

"That explains a lot," Kalas frowned.

Náli erupted: "Those ships attacked my home! They—she murdered her own people! *Her* own *people!*"

The captain inclined his head and acknowledged, "There will be a reckoning for our decisions during the king's absence, and I'll willingly accept his judgment, but that's not what this is about: I'm telling you these things because if *we* were building secret armies and secret harbors, what have the surrounding kingdoms been up to? You've flushed the seeds of evil from Ïsriba, but what about, say, Ralothova? Tsobarut?"

"Gambarad," Kalas added. "We met a soldier from there who suspected as much. You're right: Tsathrâuda—Peradan, too: they might be gone, but beings like them are still out there, wrecking everything. No, that's not fair: we *edhume* are plenty good at wrecking things all by ourselves, aren't we? I guess they're just…speeding things along. There's still a *lot* of work to do!"

"Too true, young man," Rufàran nodded, his expression grim. He looked around the throne room and sighed, "However, we're not going to get it all done tonight. Let's start by cleaning up this mess…"

"The throne!" someone said when they discovered the broken stones.

"Accurate," said the king as he hefted a fragment. "Ïsriba is broken. On the inside. We'll put it back together—and maybe, *su zhi Ilun hölidimu,* we'll build it better than it was. Come, everyone: help me carry out these men…"

Late in the morning, when rays from the rising suns filtered through the torn curtains and shattered glass above them, King

Rufàran directed a handful of soldiers to escort Kalas, Abarandal, and Náli to a suite of rooms. Even though they'd worked through the night, Kalas wanted to protest, but he knew he needed rest. Abarandal, despite her otherworldly constitution, let herself be led away, too. At first, Náli denied how tired she was, but in the end, she followed the others toward extravagant accommodations. When Kalas collapsed atop his bed, he tried to determine his next steps, but he fell asleep before ideas could come.

He woke to the sound of Abarandal's muted singing. Groggy, he sat up and listened: it took him a while to remember where he was, what had happened, but when he recognized the *eru*, he nodded.

"I'm glad *you're* still here. Seems almost everyone else is gone… in one way or another. I—what's that? *Here?* How long have I been asleep?!"

When the young man looked around, Abarandal descended upon his bed and unleashed her music at a vivace tempo: from her song, Kalas learned he'd slept for two days, that word of King Rufàran's return had reached at least as far as Âivambar, and that messengers were on their way to the neighboring kingdoms to warn them about Ilnëshras' designs. She told him most of the counselors and courtiers loyal to Ësfàyami and her intrigue had been routed from Ïsriba—or put to death. Shosafin pointed out the worst offenders, those most invested in corrupting the queen-regent, and struck them down. Lachrymose notes slowed her music as she recounted these bleaker facts: she seemed to grasp that justice was necessary, but its execution grieved her nonetheless.

"Do you think the other kingdoms will receive King Rufàran's envoys?" he wondered. "Will they believe him, or will they think it's a trick? I mean, what if…? I wonder if those men and women will ever make it home?"

"I suspect many will not," said Shosafin as he entered the room. "The majority volunteered for the job—knowing the risks—as penance, I suspect—for their roles in Ësfàyami's schemes. Should they fail to return, the king will send others. We'll defend our borders—as defined by treaty—but Ïsriba is big enough as it is, rich enough in resources. Right now, we need to lick our wounds, heal from these Sevens of deceit, and rediscover our purpose."

"*Our* purpose?" Kalas raised an eyebrow.

"As a people. Me, I have another purpose. And a promise to keep."

"When do you leave?"

"Soon. King Rufàran has statesmen aplenty: he doesn't need a one-armed soldier standing in his way! And as well-appointed as things are here, I'm not the only one ready to get back to Lohwàlar: I think Breaker misses home, too, and I suspect Thara's most concerned with *his* well-being!" he deadpanned.

"I don't…I don't think I'm going back," the young man admitted. "I lost so much when my parents died, but I thought I still had a place there. But then Zhalera died…I wish you and Thara well, Shosafin. Tell Tsharak and Vàyana—and Sàrush and Tshama—I love them, I'll miss them…you know what I mean."

"Where will you go?"

"I don't know. I have no idea, really. Before he and Nanësra left, Kadhëmba said I should keep studying. That sounds like a good idea. A place to start—or start again, at least. He knows things now, things Nanësra—maybe every *elu*—knows, but he can't tell me. She couldn't, either. It's frustrating, not knowing, but sitting around whining about everything I don't know isn't going to change things. I think I've read enough books for a while, too.

"Maybe I'll go see Rül and Pava. Maybe I'll pass through Thosha on the way, say hello to Yëlisha. I wonder if Nashmur made it back from the Gateway? I wonder if he knows what he's gonna do about Yëlisha. You know, I could see him behind the bar at Mbirin's Place. I don't know why, but just now, in my mind, that's where I pictured him—and Yëlisha, of course!

"Peradan's still out there. Tsathrâuda, too, and who knows how many other fallen monsters, bending all creation toward destruction. How am I supposed to stand against such powers?!"

"Lad, you know I don't subscribe to all that prophecy business, but I'll admit, if anyone's able to rise to such a challenge, it's you. That nobility I first noticed in Lohwàlar has never wavered, and I know there were times when it would have been easier—safer—for you to compromise your ideals. You'll figure it out."

Abarandal touched Kalas' shoulder and sang a few bars. Kalas laughed and nodded.

"You really understand what she's saying when she does that?" Shosafin wondered.

"Yeah, I do. That's right, you don't—it's all just music to you, isn't it? Well, she agrees with you. Maybe we'll see you back in Lohwàlar. Someday. I don't know when that might be. Before we go anywhere, though, we'll need to make sure Náli makes it safely back to Serular. I don't think—"

"I'm not going back to Serular!" Náli declared. "Those ships might not attack our city anymore, but the people—the *things* that sent them are still out there! Niri will be fine—that's what you were gonna say, right? I'm sure he's busy figuring out all that *Randa pïni Sifumilël* stuff, anyway. And even if you dump me there, I'll…well, you know!"

"Good morning to you, too, Náli," said Kalas as the young woman stormed into his room. "All right, all right, but know this: we won't have *erume* or *elume* or even human soldiers to protect us. It'll just be the three of us. Yes, Abarandal is the *great power*, but that doesn't mean we can just do whatever we want with it. With *her*. Begging your pardon, Abarandal, but sometimes it seems like you don't know what to do with yourself, with the powers you have.

"Náli, I'll be blunt: I have no idea what I'm doing. Where

I'm going. Tsathrâuda said something about *hardware*. And Deridzhas—a town overrun by cannibals. *Ilrâigme-edhume.* That must be the 'question' Hwanzho told us about. Hwanzho? Oh, one of Pava's people. Anyway: Tsathrâuda mentioned Ïsran, too. I'd never heard of Ïsran until we saw it on Dzholëf's chart. Maybe she found some stuff there, too. There's probably more of it out there. Maybe *lots* more. She's probably consolidating her discoveries—to what end is anyone's guess…"

"Kalas, all this *stuff,* all this technology: where did it come from?! Why is it so destructive?"

"I don't know, exactly. But not all of it is destructive: Lohwàlar would have been a wasteland Sevens of Sevens ago if someone hadn't discovered the Pump. Until recently, I don't think anyone had any idea that our Pump was based on ancient technology. Well, I suspect Falthwën probably knew, but I'm just talking about *edhume.* Anyway, turns out it *is* from before the world was cracked, as they say. We found a room filled with strange things down there. Things like nothing we'd ever seen! Tsharak thinks it's part of this *other* thing we found. Tsharak? Right, he's a friend from Lohwàlar. You know, maybe that *is* where we should begin? Maybe we should take a look at some of the *vàsume* the *erume* have yet to *unmake?* Abarandal? Náli? What do you think?"

"Anywhere but Serular," Náli shrugged. Abarandal nodded.

"I'm sure the king can spare a couple of horses," said Shosafin. "Wherever you're headed."

"All right then," Kalas sighed. "I guess I *am* going to Lohwàlar. I guess we all are."

6.

With Rufàran's blessing, a week later, they headed west. Kalas and Náli recovered from their whirlwind tour across the southern

645

horn of the continent, and, mounted on fresh horses, they reached Âivambar about a day later. Thosha a couple of days after that. At Mbirin's Place, when Kalas and the others walked inside, Yëlisha dropped the tankard she was drying, maneuvered her way through the bustling crowd, and almost smothered him with her vivacious embrace.

"It's so good to see you again! I confess, I wasn't sure you'd ever make it back this way! I'm told you've had many adventures since the last time you were here! In fact, just one moment!"

She let him go and vanished. Less than a minute later, she returned with Nashmur. The former commander was just as surprised. He hugged everyone in turn, except Náli when he recognized the *Poserular* girl. She hugged him instead and mumbled an apology. Nashmur said he was glad Rofe got his message to Lohwàlar. He said he'd been in rough shape, but the *úrukilmukritme* had been most generous to him.

"I probably should have rested longer, but I wanted to get back to the capital. By the time I realized I was still pushing myself too hard, Thosha seemed the best alternative."

He risked a glance at Yëlisha when he finished speaking, and while the woman was kind enough to maintain her discretion, she smiled—a little too broadly.

"The best alternative," Shosafin repeated. Nashmur shrugged and failed to hide a smile.

"Where's Zhalera?" he said, attempting to divert attention from himself. "I'm surprised she's not with you!"

"She's gone," Kalas said, his face burning. "Her shop caught on fire while she was inside. She never made it out."

Both the former commander and the innkeeper reeled from the revelation and offered their condolences. Kalas didn't want to dwell on the memory, so he told them about Kadhëmba. Yëlisha gasped and cried happy tears for her former patron. As they outlined their exploits, she insisted everyone sit down and eat something.

By the time they finished their tales, most of her customers had wandered off. She demanded they stay the night—she had a room, and even if they *hadn't* been exhausted, Kalas knew better than to argue with her.

"So, cousin," Shosafin began, "when do you think you'll return to Âivambar? With the queen-regent and most of her loyalists ousted, it's actually quite nice…"

"Ha! I know what you're getting at, but even with King Rufàran in power again, I have no desire to live beneath the shadow of the castle anymore. No, so long as I'm not in the way, I think I'll stay right here…"

Yëlisha snickered and swatted his backside.

"Good," nodded Shosafin, and said nothing else about it.

A few days later, having said goodbye to Yëlisha and Nashmur, they ventured west, past the Hidden River and toward the Wastes-that-Devour. The miasma Shosafin described on his and the king's journey east remained; indeed, the soldier thought it was more potent than before, if such a thing were possible. Toward the North, under the setting suns, a vast plume of red-and-silver smoke choked the otherwise unremarkable sky. Vapors from the Death-Bringing Mountain. When irregular lights flashed beyond the horizon, he suggested turning south toward the lesser roads. Kalas agreed. Minutes later, rumbles cracked the ground and hot wind blew through the feeble trees. Kalas struggled to rein in his mount. When he had things under control, he looked back to see thick darkness streaked with lightning rising into the air.

"What was that?!" Náli wondered. Kalas told her.

"Let's keep moving. The King's Highway is in rough shape, but these secondary roads are much worse. It'll take longer to cross the wastes, but we'll breathe easier."

Their detour cost them several days, but after picking their way through long thorns and grabby underbrush, they reached the plateau above the Gateway. Náli asked about Deridzhas, and Kalas told her they'd bypassed it: "And be glad we did! Nothing but misery there…"

No one waited by the gate—which was closed, Kalas noted. At least, that's how it looked, but he knew better. He waited. Náli seemed impatient, but she took her cues from Kalas and Shosafin. After a few minutes, he called out, *"Úrukilmukritme! Ib shelu tsararu! Su pirathëzhu—Kalas tsor nir, Pava tsag!"*

"Who are you talking to?!" Náli wondered.

"Just wait," he instructed.

Soon, heavy clunks inside the rocks let go, and the gates began their slow retreat. When they'd parted enough for their horses to pass, Kalas led them through the narrow opening. Several cave-dwellers armed with sparkling *tëvëtme* stood guard just inside: the young man searched their faces from someone familiar, but he didn't recognize any of these men and women. He reined in his horse and waited until a tall, chiseled-looking woman approached him and said, "This way, *Ilosar.*" He and the others dismounted and followed her underground while others tended to the horses. When Pava had first joined them, she'd been uneasy around the formidable beasts; these people however, seemed comfortable enough, and Kalas suspected Rül's influence had everything to with it.

Rül and Pava, having just finished deliberations with heads of the various houses, were elated to see everyone. They asked about the others, and Kalas told them everything. Shocked, Pava would have collapsed had Rül not caught her. Her eyes filled with red when she heard about Zhalera, but after a moment, she righted herself and wiped her tears on her sleeve. She hugged him and said, "I am so sorry, *Ilosar.* You have no idea…"

On the way to the apartment she and Rül shared, she asked

about the recent quakes. Kalas told her the Ildurgul Taruún erupted on their way west, and she nodded. She said the *iltithme* were dimmer again—not as bad as they had been, but the east winds had rimed their faceted surfaces with dust and ash. The Great Collector remained bright, she assured him as she played with the ugly ring she still wore on her right index finger.

Rive and Tsana—and Sina—joined them for the evening meal. Pava's father, it seemed, had become quite fond of his son-in-law; her mother, however, still maintained a cordial distance, and Kalas wondered if she would have come at all if Rive still had his eyes. With a wink, he introduced Náli as a mischievous girl from Serular; Shosafin he described as a former captain of Ïsriba's royal army, now headed for Lohwàlar.

After a while, Pava excused herself: some peculiar—*harmless*—illness, she said, and as the rest of them talked, Tsana revealed that the cave-dwellers kept watch over Deridzhas and the surrounding wastes. They'd killed most of the eaters-of-men, but on occasion, others seemed to spring up from nothing. Sometimes the patrols saw the *gròma* Kalas and Nïmrïk had rescued flying in low circles above the ruined mining equipment. The *úrukilmukritme* kept their distance, but even when she noticed them, she seemed disinterested in their presence. Pava's mother suspected the great beast was looking for something: *what,* she had no idea. Kalas told them about the dragon they'd evaded up North: "He wasn't there when we escaped from under the Mountain. I wonder what became of him…"

On the morning they resumed their journey toward Lohwàlar, Shosafin took Rül aside. Kalas thanked Pava—who insisted she was fine—and her family for their hospitality; Pava, still playing with her ring, nodded, but she seemed distracted. He nodded toward the gaudy piece of jewelry and asked her if everything was all right.

"What? Oh, this! No, everything's fine! It's just…well, it's *heavier* than it used to be. And it's *hotter,* too. It was always warm to the touch: I thought it's because the *erume* created it, but a month or so—maybe two now, I guess, it got so hot I had to take it off! When I picked it up again a few days later, it was cooler, but still warm.

"Anyway, you're always welcome here. Don't let Mother convince you otherwise! Honestly, as much as she distrusts *ilròumbume*, I think she loves Rül. In her own way. She just doesn't know how to show it."

Rül and Shosafin joined the others. The former farm boy checked their horses' tack and made subtle adjustments to their saddles. (*Old habits,* Kalas smiled.) He and Pava said goodbye, but before they got underway, the young *shëmiuín* grabbed his reins and whispered, "I see the weight of prophecy, heavy on your shoulders, *Ilosar,* and it seems most unfair, considering everything you've been through. When it's time to bring the light—not just to the Áthradho, but to the world—call on us! Let us bear some of what you carry, at least in some small measure. I say this as…as the *princess* of my people—and, more importantly, as your friend."

At night, as they traversed the narrow Highway, several lesser collectors redirected their output toward the road. A parting gift from the cave-dwellers that lasted until they exited the chasm and entered the wind-swept steppes. After a few days, when the early morning sun streaked the sky with fibrous pinks and purples, they reached the ancient well and replenished their water supply. On his way up from the ice-cold water, Kalas saw Nanësra's prayer still etched into the wall. Something in their edges—no, something contained within the dimensionless "non-space" *perpendicular* to their edges—glimmered; at first, he thought it was just the ripples on the water's surface: then he remembered what Abarandal helped him see in his study and looked again.

All he saw were indecipherable shapes and symbols.

'Resume your studies,' Kadhëmba said, he reminded himself.

. . .

When at last they reached Lohwàlar, Sàrush and Tshama were overjoyed to see their "grandson" again. The Chief Magistrate sent for Tsharak and Vàyana, and Shosafin waited around long enough to say hello before he disappeared: he had a promise to keep, he said.

"We have some news," Tsharak beamed as Vàyana rested her head on his shoulder. "We—"

"You're married!" he guessed, and the ancient man stared daggers at Sàrush, who laughed and insisted he'd said nothing. "You've never said much about your past, Tsharak," Kalas began, "but even though you've been alone for a long, long time, it wasn't always like that for you, was it? And Vàyana, I know your husband Këndan passed away a long time ago, too. I'm happy for both of you!"

"He'll probably outlive me—more than one hundred twenty Sevens and he doesn't look a day over nine! Ten some mornings," she winked as she nudged his elbows. "Still, I figure I have a handful of good Sevens yet to attain!"

"I'm sure you do!"

Sàrush assured Kalas that things in Lohwàlar had returned to normal. More or less. He did say there were rumors of a strange character lurking near the ashes of the blacksmith shop, but no one with whom he'd spoken had a first-hand account. When the young man expressed concern for Zhalera's broken sword, Tsharak promised him it was safe: "Find me in the morning, and I'll return it to you, if you wish!"

Kalas told them about their travels, about Serular and Náli, Ralothova and Ësra, and Ïsriba and Kadhëmba. Tsharak, to his surprise, overflowed with tears when he heard the young man's story: despite developing a tenuous trust in the old *egu*, he confessed he never imagined such a creature could ever regain what he'd lost.

"You were right, dear one," he managed at last. "You've seen things in two Sevens that I have not in nearly one hundred thirty! These are strange days! Strange days, indeed! Unprecedented things are happening—across the world and across the heavens!"

Late in the evening, long after Tsharak and Vàyana went home and Tshama prepared quarters for everyone, the stargirl knocked on Kalas' door. He hadn't been able to sleep anyway: Lohwàlar should have felt like home. It didn't. With a sigh, he invited her in.

"Can't sleep? Wait, what am I saying? You don't sleep like we do, do you?" he laughed at himself. She neither laughed nor returned his smile. "Abarandal? What's wrong?"

He offered her a chair. She sat, but her attention seemed divided. Kalas waited until at last she met his gaze, clapped a hand against her chest, and sang what was on her mind.

He couldn't believe what he was hearing.

"*That's* what you asked of Zhalera?!" he spluttered. "Is…is *that* what happened to your chest?! Why we found you at the Sanctuary?! It is, isn't it?! No wonder she was so confused! No, Abarandal, I'm not blaming you! I just…well, maybe I am! I mean, if you hadn't put such thoughts in her head, if you hadn't given her an impossible task—it *is* impossible! You know that, right?! Maybe she wouldn't have locked herself in her smithy and—What? Slow down! I can't understand!"

As Kalas unloaded on her, she turned her streaming silver eyes away and offered an apologetic requiem for the secret that might have cost Zhalera her life. Between sobs, she sang her reason for her strange request, but her notes were arrhythmic, her dynamics inconsistent. Eventually, he grasped what she'd been trying to say: when he did, he collapsed on his bed and let out a long, slow breath.

"No wonder she thought you told me something," he realized. "Look, it's not your fault: Zhalera always struggled with self-doubt.

I tried everything to reassure her, but it didn't help: I would have thought an *eru* making such a request—I don't get it, but maybe that's not important—would have inspired confidence. I'm sorry I yelled at you: I just—I miss her. *So much.* You know that. And I know you miss her, too..."

He cupped her chin and raised her downcast face, but before he could say anything else, the Song blotted out his thoughts and pressed against his mind with dizzying force. He closed his eyes and tried to contain the energy coursing through his neurons: when it abated, he opened them and saw threads of electric fire reflected in Abarandal's tears. She stood, knocking over her chair in the process, and bolted for the door. Kalas, sensing the same urgency, followed her through the house.

"Guys? What's going on?" Náli prodded, awakened by their commotion. Neither answered, but undeterred, the young girl fell in behind them and followed them into the brisk night air: "It's cold out here! Where are we going?! Kalas?"

"Dâethëthe," he shushed her with a hoarse whisper. She pursed her lips and nodded.

Minutes later, they reached the charred remains of Zhalera's shop. Many of its fire-eaten rafters had collapsed, but its cracked and canted chimneys still jutted into the star-studded sky. Even though he couldn't see anyone, he sensed a presence—an imposing presence—and he knew they were not alone. He thought about calling out, demanding the interloper reveal himself; instead, he kept quiet, too. Abarandal contented herself to observe as well, and Kalas supposed she also felt the subtleties of an uneasy energy crackling through the darkness.

Sparks snapped from the empty furnace. He turned toward the others—

Did you see that?!

—but a ball of yellow fire pulsed from its twisted walls before he could speak. Blinded, he raised his hands and chided himself for leaving his sword at Sàrush's place. When he recovered, he saw a tall, slender figure in sooty robes standing with his back to them. Neither Kalas nor either woman said anything; indeed, the three remained transfixed as the stranger raised his bowed head and looked around. After several moments, he—no, *she* addressed them all and said, "Maybe you can help me? I'm looking for a sword…"

"A…sword?" Kalas repeated. The woman chuckled and removed her hood.

Her cuffs slipped, and he noticed exquisite metal bracers clasped around her wrists. In the moon- and starlight, her gathered tresses glittered like gold atop her oval face, secured with a simple strap of well-worn leather. She brushed back an unruly lock with delicate fingers, her almond eyes flashing bronze from under thick lashes when she smiled at him.

"A sword," she echoed, her voice clear and bright—and strong, like good steel. "It *was* here. I know that! And not too long ago…"

"Not here," Kalas corrected her. "I was here when this place burned to the ground. We searched the rubble, but all we found was Zhalera's hammer and—"

"Zhalera?!" the woman arched a well-shaped eyebrow.

"You—how do you know that name? You're not from Lohwàlar, that's obvious…"

"Tell me, good sir: did Zhalera have a sword with her? Her father's sword? Her ancestor's sword?"

"How do you know about *that?!* Falthwën told us not to—"

"Falthwën?! You know, uh, Falthwën?!"

"*Knew* him. Turns out he was really Sharuyan of the Great Swath. He died—Why am I telling you this?! Lady, I don't know who you are, but look around! There's nothing here for you! Maybe it's best if you just moved on from here?"

Abarandal stepped forward and placed a hand on Kalas' forearm; with the other, she gestured for patience and answered the inquisitive newcomer in song.

"Oh! I didn't know! I've been…away…for so long! *Too long,* it seems! Good sir, I—"

"You can understand her?!" he marveled.

"Why, yes, of course! Why wouldn't I?"

"No one else can! Not even the *erume!*"

"Not even the—Really? Most peculiar," she said, almost to herself. "Most peculiar indeed…Abarandal tells me Zhalera's sword is broken?"

Kalas stared her down, his eyes narrowed and his arms crossed.

"Kalas!" Náli hissed. "Who *is* this?!"

"Kalas?! Of course! Oh! I was so focused on—Ahem! Zhalera named her sword after me: *I am Valaran.*"

The sound of her name was music in his mind, and he knew she spoke the truth. Light the color of suns-shine surrounded her and washed over them in an all-encompassing wave. She raised her hand: fire surged from the faceted planes of a tremendous hammer that hadn't been there a moment ago. Brilliant amber flames arced across her taut, supple frame as wind blew through her robe. Kalas, his burning eyes wide, stared until her incandescence abated.

"You have questions. I do, too. And maybe—just maybe—we have answers for one another, but all of that will have to wait: much work lies ahead of us, and our time, as I'm sure you know, is running short."

Blake Goulette
February 2020
Holly Springs, North Carolina

Dear Reader,

Thank you so much for reading my book! If you'd like to remain up-to-date with everything that's going on in my world, sign up for notifications at **www.blakegoulette.com**, and "like" my Facebook page at **www.facebook.com/bgoulettewrites**. That way, you can be sure you'll never miss a thing! (On rare occasions, I also post stuff to Instagram and Twitter under **@bgoulettewrites**.)

I hope you enjoyed interacting with my characters and the world in which they live. I hope you'll write a review. And I hope you'll tell your friends about the book (*and* its predecessor)! Whether you have good things, bad things, or mixed things to say about *Between the Lion & the Wolf,* I'm thankful for every review and discussion!

Warm regards,
Blake

Blake grew up in and around Guilford, Maine, delighting in its nearby woods, waterfalls, and mountains. (The ocean—just a couple of hours away—is also pretty great.) Now married, he and his lovely wife are raising their two boys in Holly Springs, North Carolina. The outdoors remains a necessary escape—whether it's working in his backyard workshop, exploring the Carolinas' breathtaking (in multiple ways) trails and wildernesses, or relaxing along the coast—because staring at a computer screen for hours on end gets old. Quickly. *Between the Lion & the Wolf,* the second volume in *The Daybringer* series, is his second novel.